Someone Special

JUDITH SAXTON

Someone
Special

St. Martin's Press
New York

ISBN 0-312-13173-9

First published in Great Britain by
William Heinemann Ltd.

First U.S. Edition: July 1995
10 9 8 7 6 5 4 3 2 1

For Tony Turner,
my Australian offspring,
who is someone special himself

Acknowledgements

Firstly, I should like to thank Marjorie Howe of Rhyl for telling me about Rhyl in the twenties and thirties and for her excellent books on local history, all of which I perused closely to get 'Pengarth' the way I wanted it to be. And thanks, too, go to Bert Mather, for telling me about Aden during the war – and about the monkeys! Then, as I pursued my characters across country the staff of the King's Lynn Folk Museum found me information about their town in the years before and during the second world war. Cassie Turner remembered the small village fairs which toured Norfolk after the first world war, and Dorothy Saxton recalled with great vividness the impact made by the abdication on a whole generation.

Research is like a detective story, however, and librarians are the Hercule Poirot of my research, particularly John Thomas of the Wrexham Branch library, who, upon hearing the word 'Fairs' uttered in despairing accents, promptly remembered a small article in a copy of a wonderful little publication – *The Fairground Mercury* – which had been lodged in the reference library by a Mr A. Plinston. I read Mr Plinston's article, then got in touch with Mr Graham Downie, the editor of the *Fairground Mercury*, who put me in touch with Chris Gibson, whose marvellous article about life on the gaff had already been of immense help. Chris sent me more copies of the magazine and Frances Brown's fascinating book, *Fairfield Folk* – many thanks to all these people, without whose unstinting and generous help I would never have managed to find out about the rich, tough life of the fairgrounds of Britain.

One

May 1926

It was raining cats and dogs and blowing a gale by the time Hester got out of the hospital, although it had been brilliantly sunny when she left home earlier that morning. She was later than she had expected to be, too, so she just tucked the baby inside her coat and scuttled. She made it to the bus station in time to join the other wet people shuffling aboard the green omnibus, most of them laden with shopping, for people mainly came into Rhyl from the outlying villages to stock up their food supplies at the larger shops.

Hester, with the baby asleep and well out of sight, climbed on to the bus, shoulder to shoulder with a fat woman in black who smelled of fish, and a pert-faced girl whose lip-salve had been applied so generously and with such nonchalance that it even covered her large front teeth. Hester had thought, seeing the crowd ahead of her, that she would never get a window-seat, but she climbed the stairs to the top deck and at the last moment a man, settled against the pane, spotted a friend and stumbled to his feet, moving up a couple of seats. Hester hurriedly slid into the place he had vacated, turned to the window and rubbed herself a viewing port in the steam. Lovely; now she would really be able to enjoy the bus ride, especially if baby Helen continued to sleep.

Someone came and sat beside her; a sideways glance confirmed that it was a middle-aged woman in black, a cloche hat pulled well down over greying hair, cracked black leather shoes on her feet. Bunions, Hester diagnosed, seeing just where the shoes bulged. There had been a teacher at her school in Liverpool, Miss Appleyard, who had bunions and several of

1

the nuns at the orphanage had suffered from them, too; Miss Appleyard's shoes had been cracked in just that fashion. The omnibus must be filling up fast, Hester concluded, since older people preferred not to have to climb the stairs, particularly if they suffered from bunions.

Rather pleased with her role as detective, Hester looked down the street towards the distant line of sea and the prom. The bus was due to depart at eleven and her glance took in the clock tower at the end of High Street and confirmed that it still lacked five minutes to the hour. She had caught this bus often enough to know that sometimes the driver started early, more often late, but this morning he was going to be on time; he sat in his seat, revving the engine impatiently now and then but remaining stationary while would-be passengers hurried across the pavement and climbed aboard.

Presently, the conductor came down the bus collecting fares and clipping tickets. Hester, being on her way home, handed over her ticket to be clipped, then shoved it back inside her coat pocket. The woman next to her paid her tuppence; she had probably come into town with someone but didn't want to wait for a ride home, Hester decided, her lively imagination endowing the woman with a rich friend who had a motor car but no patience with slow and enjoyable shopping. Just as she was about to turn cautiously in her seat to see what purchases her neighbour had made the bus jolted into motion and her attention returned to the view outside.

At first, there was little to see apart from shops and raised umbrellas, but presently they began to jog along the residential roads and Hester's attention, which had strayed back to her neighbour's shopping, returned to her peephole.

It was the beginning of May but it had been a long, cold spring and the weather was still typically April. Not so much as a leaf showed on the trees whose branches tossed wildly as the omnibus surged past them. In the gardens daffodils were finished, wallflowers were in rich, tawny flower and clumps of sweet-scented narcissus, white petalled, orange-eyed, gave their perfume to the wind. Hester, who loved flowers, noticed the pink of flowering currants, the strident yellow of forsythia,

2

and told herself that the worst of the winter was over, that soon summer, with its milder climate, longer days, would arrive. Then what flowerings there would be, what burstings of buds and ripenings of fruit, even in Hester's small, damp garden plot.

To own a garden, however poor, was wonderful to Hester. Children reared in orphanages, even such excellent ones as the Sister Servina, did not own gardens. Now her fingers itched to plant and prune, seed and sow. If she was successful . . . but she would be; she would grow rare and beautiful flowers and people would come from miles around to admire them. Perhaps one day she would own a glasshouse – she had seen such things – and would grow peaches, apricots, grapes until she was the envy of all her neighbours.

As the omnibus roared along the country roads, Hester concentrated on her peephole. She had been catching the bus into Rhyl on and off for several months, ever since she had married Matthew, but she never tired of the view. It was such a glorious change after fifteen years of Liverpool city streets, especially now that spring was so well advanced. She admired green upland meadows and stands of thin trees growing on the mountainside, clinging perilously to the almost sheer rocks. She saw a small stone cottage crouching against the side of the mountain, a stream tumbling down in a flurry of white falls, slowing when it reached the mountain's foot. Presently, as the omnibus came out into a valley, the stream ceased to hurry and began to meander around the rocks as though it had all the time in the world to reach its destination. They passed a farm, if you could call such a tiny place a farm, with scrawny hens scratching in the yard and geese paddling in the mud beside the pond. Hester saw a man carting muck, a sack around his shoulders and his cap well down over his brow, and wondered about his life; did he live in the farmhouse with a comfortable wife or was she a nag, a nuisance to him? Other people's lives were so mysterious, so fascinating, particularly to someone who had lived, at best, a sheltered life.

Soon the bus left the valley and reached another stage of its journey. To Hester's right was the plain leading down to the distant gun-metal grey of the sea, to her left the mountains,

3

hump-shouldered beneath the lowering, rain-filled clouds. She could see Pengarth Castle from a good distance away, looking so much a part of the mountain that you could have imagined it just a series of extraordinary rock formations. It was huge, too, spreading right out along the side of the cliff, in places actually built into the rock. It was grand; Hester wondered idly about the owner. He was lucky of course, because it was such a romantic building, and he must be rich, because who could afford to inhabit such a gracious ancestral home without a great deal of money? But she knew nothing else about him, because Matthew, who worked at the castle, was a man of few words.

The road wound and twisted so the castle got nearer slowly, each turn of the road revealing a little more of its face, like a shy but beautiful woman emerging from behind her veil. But they did get closer, and presently Hester could see the lodge, a bird's eye view as yet. She was trying to see whether Matthew had taken her washing in when she realised the omnibus had passed the stop she normally used. Still, the walk was probably of about equal length whether you were walking forward to the lodge or back to it.

Leaning back in her seat, resigned to the walk, Hester tried to look at her home as a stranger might; from a distance the lodge looked, if not as romantic as the castle, at least interesting. But like most things, closer scrutiny was disappointing; it was a real let-down when you saw it, as she saw it now, against the faded splendour of the distant castle. Once it might have been rather nice, built as it was of silver-grey stone and roofed with gleaming slates, but the perpetual Welsh rain had caused lichen to grow on the tiles and streaked the stone walls with green and brown so that now it was a uniform sludge colour, crouching behind the high wall with the left-hand gate partly obscuring the small bit which could be seen from the road. To Hester's critical eye it looked like a dirty-faced child squinting sourly through prison bars. A sly child, she thought, who probably picked its nose when it thought itself unobserved and wiped its harvest on someone else's furniture.

It really is an ugly house, Hester decided, turning slightly to indicate to her fellow-passenger, with a smile and a clearing of the throat, that she wished to leave her seat. Hovering there while the old woman gathered her wits, Hester acknowledged that the lodge had a thousand drawbacks – it was cold, damp, and the proximity of the front windows to the ill-kept drive meant that the panes were perpetually dirt-splattered – but it was a home, as much her own as any home could be. Though she thought wistfully that it would be fun to live in the castle, to pretend all day about Princesses and magic and giants and dragons, to have big log fires in the great hall and to order your dinner from the kitchen, something different every night. Why, if she lived there, she would never have to peel a potato, hang washing on a line or catch a bus, servants would do all the menial work, leaving the mistress to sit before a roaring fire and sew a fine seam.

As Hester half stood up, the woman sitting beside her hauled herself reluctantly to her feet. Hester slid past her, giving due thought to the bunions. The conductor, standing at the foot of the stairs, must have seen the movement in the mirror for she heard the bell tinkle commandingly and the green omnibus, which had been charging along in a cloud of spray in the very centre of the road, swerved to the left as the driver began to apply the brakes. Hester, clutching the still slumbering baby to her chest, steadying herself against a seat, saw the outposts of a tiny hamlet begin to appear outside the windows. Half-a-dozen grey cottages, slate-roofed, crouched on either side of the road, their gardens hidden by drystone walls, their inhabitants keeping indoors on such a wet and miserable day.

The omnibus stopped. Hester walked up the aisle between the two rows of seats, steadying herself with one hand. She descended the stairs, then said 'Thank you', politely to the conductor, who nodded as she got carefully down off the step. No one else was getting off. The vehicle, which had scarcely stopped at all, it seemed to Hester, roared off again, plumes of water spraying on either side of it as it went, and Hester walked a little way after it. She wanted to have a look at the hamlet – you could scarcely call it a village – where the staff from the castle must live, those who did not live in, of course.

Hester wondered what it would be like to live here, in a

small community, cheek by jowl with neighbours who must know one another intimately. For the first fifteen years of her life Hester had known nobody much apart from the staff and children of the Sister Servina Orphanage and the girls at the Convent School in Liverpool. She thought it might be rather fun but, fun or not, the cottages were not her destination so having taken a good look at them and the smithy, the solitary shop in someone's front room, she began to walk slowly back the way she had come.

The rain had been intermittent throughout the journey but now, as though it had waited for her to get off the bus, it came down hard and viciously, the drops so large that they created small explosions on the wet tarmac and bounced off Hester's unprotected head with considerable force. She tried to draw her head into her shoulders like a tortoise and gave up her leisurely gait in favour of a brisk, splashy trot. She had been walking along more or less in the middle of the right-hand carriageway, but now she dived for the shelter of the great stone wall with its jagged, raw-rock top. It gave a little shelter, though you had to offset that against the occasional shower of drops when you went under the branches of one of the trees which leaned over the wall at intervals.

It was a good walk. It must be a mile, Hester thought dolefully, as her hair began to slick to her head and raindrops sluiced down her face. She should have brought an umbrella, but it had been fine when she started out, and she could not have managed an umbrella as well as the burden beneath her coat. She sighed and tried to walk even faster; if she didn't get out of the rain soon she'd probably catch her death. For ten minutes the picture of herself on her death-bed – very pale, dignified and noble, with people coming from miles around to see the bride who had died so young – kept her occupied, but then the sheer discomfort of the heavy rain began to tell and not even the most vivid imaginings could keep her feet warm and dry or her hands from turning white and purple with the cold. Crossly she slogged along, head bent, saturated shoes sloshing indifferently in and out of the great, rain-dimpled puddles. No point in walking an additional yard or two round a puddle when you were as wet as she; might as well wade right through the middle.

So intent was she on walking as fast as possible that she did not hear the pony and cart until it drew to a halt beside her.

'Hester! You're soaked, girl! What are you doin' here? Didn't you ask the bus conductor to stop at the lodge? They will, if you asks.'

Hester looked up at the man driving the cart and gave him a grateful smile. A chance to get out of the wet a bit quicker! She put a hand on the side of the cart.

'Oh Matthew, am I glad to see you! The omnibus was past the lodge before I knew it. I'm ever so wet.'

Matthew laughed with more than a trace of indulgence. He was a dark-haired, good-looking man in his thirties, wearing a sack over his head and shoulders to keep off the rain. A skinny black-and-white border collie sat beside him in the cart, pressing close to his stained corduroy trousers, eyeing Hester doubtfully.

'You're half drowned, be the looks of it. Come on, give me your hand, I'll heave you aboard.'

He held out a square, capable hand but Hester shook her head. 'Can't take your hand, Helen's under my coat. But I can hop up.'

She hopped up unaided and sat on the wet wooden seat beside the dog. Behind them were sacks of what looked like chicken meal or fertiliser, she could not tell which; Matthew had chucked another sack or two over them to keep the worst of the rain off. As Hester settled herself the collie shifted further along, giving her an almost human look of dislike, then heaved a deep sigh. Hester patted the dog's wet head with a wet hand but received not a flicker of response. Fanny, she knew, was a one-man dog; Matthew was the only person who mattered in her life, and she rarely even acknowledged Hester's existence.

Matthew waited until she was settled, then lifted the reins and clicked his tongue. The bay mare flicked an ear back and broke into trot.

'Baby all right? You all right, too? What did they say at the 'ospital clinic?'

For the first time since she had boarded the bus, Hester turned back the edge of her coat. Slumbering in the rough sling which Matthew had fashioned for her the baby lay, tiny fists balled, mouth a crinkled rosebud, small body cuddled against Hester's ribs beneath the curve of her breast. At the sight of her child a tide of gentle love washed over Hester, bringing an involuntary smile to her lips, a tenderness to her eyes.

'She's fine; the nurse and the doctor were pleased with me and said Helen was doing just as she ought at a couple of weeks. We don't have to go back again, next time we can see the village doctor.'

Matthew nodded. 'Good. Less trouble. Cover her up again, m'dear, us don't want her taking cold.'

Hester pulled the edge of her coat across, but not before a raindrop had hit the baby full on the face, causing a pair of large blue eyes to open for a moment, squint confusedly, and then slowly close. Hester laughed and held the child even closer.

'She nearly woke up then. I was glad she slept in the bus so I could keep her tucked away from harm, under my coat. I do hate people staring and hanging over her.'

'Why? Folk think she's a pretty thing, and aren't they just right?'

'Yes, she's very pretty, but I'm afraid they might give her coughs and colds and things. I'd rather they kept their distance. She's so little, a cold or a cough might make her dreadfully ill.'

'Aye, I never thought o' that.' Matthew slowed the cart as they drew alongside the lodge. 'Wait on, I'll tie Frisk to the gatepost and get the door open for you.'

'I'm all right, I can manage,' Hester said briskly. 'Thanks for the lift, Matthew. Are you coming in for your lunch?'

'Dinner, d'you mean?'

'Sorry, yes. Dinner. Are you coming back or did you make yourself sandwiches?'

'You didn't 'ave time, I daresay, what wi' gettin' the bus?'

'Sorry, I forgot. Why didn't you remind me?'

He smiled kindly at her. Hester, climbing down from the cart, reflected guiltily that Matthew was always kind.

'It don't matter. I'll come in for dinner if it's no trouble.'

'Of course it's no trouble, silly! I'll have to feed Helen when she wakes, but I'm sure I can find something nice so you can have a hot meal. When'll you be in?'

She was standing at the lodge door, looking back at him, a hand on the latch. He glanced ahead, towards where the castle bulked pale against its dark cliff.

'Say an hour? Will that suit?'

'Of course it will, Matthew! See you in an hour, then.'

Hester hurried into the lodge and shut the door as Matthew drove off down the long muddy track towards the castle. The front door opened straight into the parlour, a room filled with heavy Victorian furniture bought by Matthew's mother and grandmother and lovingly cared for, judging by the gleam on the walnut-wood piano, with its candle sconces and shallow, yellowing keys. There were a great many knick-knacks in the parlour: artificial flowers under glass, a case of stuffed birds and quantities of cheap but pretty china from various seaside resorts, and everything was clean and gleaming. It was dim in the parlour even on a sunny day, but with the rain pouring down from a dark sky very little light filtered through the musty Nottingham lace and looped sateen curtains which half obscured the small diamond-paned window. Nevertheless it was a room to be proud of, if you could forget that it was all old Mrs Coburn's stuff and if you liked old-fashioned things, for there was almost nothing modern in the room. Even the leaded windows had intrigued her at first, with their wobbly, green-tinted glass distorting the view outside, but they were undoubtedly very old.

I still like these windows, Hester thought, they're like a gingerbread house would have, only I hate cleaning them; it takes so long. And we could do with fewer *things* around too, because they take ages to dust. One day, when I know Matthew a bit better, I may suggest we put some of the stuff away and give ourselves some space; but not yet, it's too soon to change things.

Having taken off her coat, Hester settled the still-sleeping child in the old-fashioned moses basket which stood on its stand beside the settee, and looked guiltily at the wet footprints marking old Mrs Coburn's rug. In the bedroom a great many old pictures and photographs lined the walls, so Hester knew Mrs Coburn's stern, unsmiling face very well. The older woman's ghost was often present in the parlour, looking sadly and accusingly at the daughter-in-law she had never met, suggesting that Hester could try a little harder, get up a little earlier . . . Hester seldom entered the lodge by the front door in deference to Mrs Coburn's cherished front room. But today, because of the rain . . .

Still. Matthew wouldn't mind, even if the marks hadn't dried out by the time he came in for his meal, and the Coburn ghosts were present only in Hester's imagination. After his mother's death Matthew had lived here alone until their marriage – ten years of cooking his own meals, cleaning for himself, sorting out his finances and his marketing. I think I'd go mad if I were alone here for ten days, let alone ten years, Hester thought, padding barefoot into the kitchen, her muddy shoes in one hand. It's such a dark house, so chilly and unwelcoming. Matthew probably won't mind if I change things, and I will one day, because he does want me to be happy. And because he rescued me when I needed someone, I want him to be happy too, so I won't make many changes.

The kitchen wasn't a bad room, though. The fire had been lit in the range – poor Matthew, Hester thought, conscience-stricken, to have to tackle that on top of so much else – and the kettle, though it wasn't over the heat, purred gently on the hob. She padded across the quarry tiles, slung her coat on one of the ladder-backed kitchen chairs and began to wind down the drying rack. It was old and creaky, but an absolute blessing. Each rainy morning Hester did her washing, hung it over the rack, then hauled it up to the ceiling where the clothes dried in the uprush of warm air from the range, out of sight and mind, until she brought it down the next day.

Until baby Helen had been born Hester had washed only on a Monday, but she and Matthew couldn't afford piles of towelling and muslin napkins, a dozen of each had to suffice, which meant washing every day whether she liked it or not.

So now the drying rack had come into its own, and Hester now appreciated this relic of Mrs Coburn, if no other. Fortunately I quite like washing, Hester reminded herself, draping her coat across the rack, then feeling the top of her grey jumper and the white blouse beneath it. They were both pretty wet, the rain had channelled down her neck and soaked most of her upper clothing; glancing down, she saw her navy skirt was also soaked for six inches around the hem and muddy from the dirt of the road.

Muttering crossly, Hester stripped off jumper, blouse and skirt, hung them over the rack and hauled it back to the ceiling, then glanced down at herself. Her breasts, engorged by the milk, looked huge, out of proportion on her thin body. They were far too big for the little bust-bodice she had previously worn and she had told the doctor bluntly that they could not afford a nursing bodice which she would have no further use for once Helen was weaned. As she moved, her big, rather painful breasts moved too, but more slowly, as though parodying her. They reminded her of the cows she saw swaying into the milking shed in the early mornings, their udders veined and bulging with milk. Her breasts were veined too, she could see pale blue lines on them, and her nipples had darkened and spread . . . she hated her new body, hated it.

But one consequence of her new body was baby Helen, so she must not grumble. Not even when she looked down at her flaccid belly, empty now of the child but not yet shrunk into decency. The nurse at the clinic had repeated yet again that in a couple of months, if she did the exercises the doctor had recommended, she would get her slim figure back, but at times she doubted even the nurse. Flesh wasn't elastic, how could it simply shrink back to its youthful tightness? But Sister said because she was so young that was just what would happen, and Sister had been wonderful. When Helen had been born and Hester had been in such pain and so afraid, Sister had been a tower of strength. She had been right when she had said the pain would soon be over and that she, Hester, would forget it when she held her child in her arms, so she probably knew about saggy stomachs, too.

11

Hester turned from hauling the rack back into place and glanced at the window. It was difficult to see out for the steam and the rather draggly curtains but she thought she saw a movement in the yard outside. Hastily she scurried out of the kitchen, heading for her bedroom – she did not want to be caught waltzing half-naked round the kitchen by anyone, not even Matthew. Especially Matthew, she decided, trying to cover her breasts with her arms and wincing at the pain of it. She had not yet moved back into the main bedroom with her husband, she and the baby slept in the little room; she had pleaded night-feeds and exhaustion and Matthew had agreed to wait a little, so now she ran into the small room and grabbed another blouse, a thin, much-darned jumper and her green wool skirt. She was putting them on when two things occurred to her: one was that the movement outside the kitchen window would have been the washing on the line; the other was that if she put dry clothing on before towelling her hair it wouldn't be dry clothing long.

When she had ducked under the clothes line in the back yard, she had wondered why the line was there, where it caught virtually no breeze, and not in the castle grounds. I really must rig it up somewhere else, where the washing will catch whatever sun and wind there is, she told herself, but right now I must get myself presentable again. She seized the towel which hung beside the washstand and stood before the mirror, rubbing her hair vigorously. She stared accusingly at her reflection as she did so, keeping her eyes averted from her huge, bobbing breasts. She was even paler than usual, her strong, blackish-brown hair hung in rat-tails down past her shoulders, and the thick, uncompromising black eyebrows which she always intended to pluck into fashionable arcs were drawn into a frown of disapproval. She quite liked her amber-coloured eyes framed with stubby black lashes, but they didn't seem to fit her small, triangular face with its blob of a nose. They were too big, and the expression in them wasn't sweet or meek, it was challenging, as though she were daring people to notice her plainness.

The nuns of course said plainness did not matter, especially if you were clever. They had known Hester was clever and had accordingly sent her to the paying convent school, reminding her far too often that she owed them gratitude for their generosity. She knew it, promised to do her best, make something of herself. Thank God, she thought fervently now, that she had been pupil-teaching at a school in Chester when they had realised she was pregnant and turned her out. The nuns had planned such a bright academic future for her; if they saw her now they would believe her friend Annabel had been right when she had said there was something strange about Hester.

Annabel had been a prim, conventional twelve-year-old with neatly braided blonde hair and meticulously tidy clothes, the complete opposite of brainy, impetuous Hester. But Annabel had once told her, in a moment of honesty, that Hester looked like a changeling.

'You know, the baby that appears in the cradle but never cries,' Annabel said earnestly as the two of them surveyed their images in the long mirror in the cloakroom. Annabel, conventionally pretty as well as conventionally good, smoothed her pleated tunic skirt down over her long legs in their black stockings. 'I don't suppose you cried much as a baby, Hester; you certainly never cry now. You just tighten your lips and look down and jut your chin.'

'You mean I look like an elvish brat?' Hester had said with mock indignation. 'Annabel Cranbourne, what a horrible thing to say!'

But Annabel hadn't meant to be unkind, she had just said what came into her head. And perhaps she had been right; even now, so long after Annabel's remark, Hester could see what her friend had meant. Her eyebrows tilted up at the corners and her eyes were set at a slight slant. Her chin, though small, did jut. It was a pity because she longed – what girl did not? – to be beautiful, but even prettiness had been denied her. However, pretty or not, her fate was sealed. Her lovely bright future had come to nothing because she had so wanted a bit of fun out of life, and anyway, she had Helen, didn't she? Though not yet seventeen years old, she was a married lady with a little girl of her own and it was time she started acting the part instead of driving poor Matthew into making his own lunch . . . dinner . . . and lighting his own fire.

13

Not that Matthew seemed to mind. He may not think I'm pretty, Hester thought, dragging her thick, wiry hair back with one hand and lassooing it into submission with a rubber band, but he must like me or he would never have agreed to marry me. Would he? No, of course he wouldn't. She had run back to Rhyl, not searching for him, but because she dared not return to Liverpool and thought she might get work in the seaside town. She had run into Matthew on the very first day, but had said nothing about her condition; it had not been necessary.

'Hester!' he had said. 'I thought you'd gone for good! Oh, my dear.'

He had proposed marriage and she had accepted. And you're grateful to him for that, aren't you, she asked herself severely? And for Helen, of course. Darling little Helen, who would do all the things that Hester would never do now, who would be the famous actress, the prima ballerina, the first girl ever to scale the Matterhorn or swim the Channel or ride the winner of the Grand National. Hester's dreams could still come true, though in future she would dream them for Helen rather than herself.

As she dressed, she heard the muttering cry of a child waking from sleep. Hester pushed her feet into her old slippers and padded out of the bedroom into the parlour. She plucked Helen, pink-faced and blinking, from her nest in the blankets and carried her through to the kitchen. She settled herself comfortably in the ancient rocking-chair and put the baby to her breast; as the child began to suck, Hester pushed off with one foot, rocking contentedly. She let her mind wander back to her childhood, when she had hoped for such great things: she would marry a prince, live in a castle, be someone special. Was this, then, what she had been born for, was this the real purpose of Hester Jane Coburn, née Makerfield? Was her destiny not to be someone special, but to rear and cherish someone special? It seemed likely now, with the child's dark mossy head butting Hester's thin little arm, and the baby's avid mouth tugging at her nipple, that bringing Helen up would be a full-time job.

The chair creaked, the baby sucked, the fire settled in the range. Hester was almost asleep when the baby pulled her pointed knees up hard into her small stomach, spat out the

14

nipple and began to squall.

Wind! Hester slung the scrap of humanity across her shoulder and began rubbing and patting the small, solid back.

'Poor baby, poor little one, then ... does it hurt? Never mind, mummy will make you better.'

An enormous burp rattled from the baby, making Hester laugh. She held the child gently against her face, kissing the rose-petal cheek.

'There, is that better? What a big burp that was, you nearly made mummy faint with fright!'

The baby, feeling Hester's mouth against her cheek, wove her head frantically from side to side, seeking sustenance once again. Failing to find it, she began to mutter, her fists coming up to press and push at the unresponsive flesh.

'No, sweetheart, you won't find milk there, but if you look here ...' Hester slid the child down across her bare skin, loving every touch, and pushed her against the full breast which had been dripping in sympathy ever since the baby started to feed. With the skill born of ten days of finding the nipple, Helen homed in on it and sucked. Hester's foot began to rock the chair again and her mind, freed from the necessity of dealing with her daughter, began to wander once more.

The nuns were always on about the evils of dreaming, but I never could see it, and now I'm proved right, because even if this is what my life is to be about, my dreams are still my own. I can be anyone, rich or poor, plain or pretty, clever or stupid. So I've not ruined my life, despite what the nuns may think.

But she must be practical; she began to think about Matthew's meal, because that was her next task when the child was fed, changed and put back in her basketwork cradle. There was a bit of meat pie, and a heel of cheese ... was there still bread? If not, she really should bake, but she made awful bread. If the rain stopped and she took Helen out in her sling, she could buy a loaf in the larger village a couple of miles from the lodge. It was a good walk, but perfectly possible in an afternoon. The baker was friendly too. He spoke Welsh, of course, but he changed to English when he saw she had entered his shop. Different from the butcher, a big fat man with mean little eyes who addressed Hester in Welsh though he knew she hadn't so much as a word of the language.

I really ought to learn Welsh, Hester told herself, rocking gently, smoothing her free hand around Helen's face. But it's so hard when no one else speaks it – Matthew didn't, he'd lived in Sussex until his employer had inherited Pengarth Castle from a profligate uncle, and of course his employer, Geraint Clifton, didn't speak Welsh either, since he too had come from Sussex. Matthew had worked for the Cliftons on their dairy farm, with its neat little house and eighty well-kept acres, before Mr Geraint had inherited the vast, rambling castle in the wild hills of Wales, as well as the mountain of debt which accompanied it.

It was a pity in a way, Hester mused, that the old man, as Matthew called Mr Geraint, had taken to Pengarth Castle like a duck to water. If he'd had any sense, he would have looked at the state of it, and the size of the debts, and got back into his motor and returned to Sussex. But he had fallen in love with the castle, Matthew told her, dreaming of the day when it was mended and made good, when it was the sort of home he wanted and could be proud of. He was a worker, the old man. He'd worked with his own hands inside and out, making good wherever he could. Matthew and he had laboured side by side to make a couple of rooms habitable and he had recently sold a farm which had been more or less derelict when he arrived and had made good money out of the deal. He had parted with his Sussex home years ago, of course, and ploughed the money into Pengarth.

Hester had never been in the castle or met her husband's employer, but Matthew had told her about them both. The old man with his passion for the place, his stubborn refusal to give up, and the great hall with the roof so riddled with holes that pigeons and jackdaws flew in and out without let or hindrance. The long gallery, empty of the family portraits which had once graced its walls – the old man had sold many of them to pay for re-roofing the kitchen – and the bedrooms in the towers, the windows broken, the floors unsafe. But it seemed to Hester a place of infinite romance and infinite possibilities. She could not blame the old man for loving it, wanting to restore it, even though a sensible, down-to-earth part of her mind knew that there was a difference between dreams and reality, knew that if the place was as bad as Matthew said, restoring it would be impossible unless you were a millionaire several times over.

What millionaire would want to live here, she thought looking discontentedly at the rain-smeared pane, hearing the wind getting up and tugging at the little house as though it wanted to raze it to the ground. There wasn't much doing, though if you had a motor – and the old man had a lovely one – you could get to Rhyl in the summer, see a bit of life. Indeed, it was because the old man had gone to meet some friends in Rhyl that she had met Matthew.

That summer! So warm, so wonderful . . . her first little taste of freedom. A summer job at a hotel so that she could earn some money and see a bit of life before plunging into her first real job as a pupil-teacher at the convent school in Chester.

She had so enjoyed her summer of freedom. The hotel work had been hard, but she hadn't minded because she always had mornings or evenings free. And once she got to know Matthew they spent a lot of time together one way and another. He had wanted to marry her then, but she'd said no. She wanted to earn her own living, see something of life. She had had no idea, of course, that the growing intimacy with Matthew was the way you grew a baby; no one had told her anything about babies until the horrible old mathematics teacher at the convent school had forced her to see a doctor. He had confirmed what the teacher had so cruelly suspected – that Hester was pregnant.

She had been close to despair that winter day in Rhyl. She was six months gone and was beginning to show and she guessed that even if she got work, before long someone would realise her condition and throw her out. Meeting Matthew again had been like a wonderful dream after the nightmare of the past few weeks. And Matthew had been so good; he had asked her once more to marry him and she had accepted without hesitation. Even if marriage wasn't exactly freedom it could be made into a lovely thing. There was her garden . . . she would walk into the village for the bread, and while she was there she would see if anyone was selling seeds or little plants. She would ask Matthew which would be best; he knew most things about gardening and growing. He was too busy up at the castle to bother much with their own plot but when his mother had been alive she had planted the garden at all seasons, providing them with fresh vegetables; Matthew had told her so and, flushed with enthusiasm, she had vowed to do the same.

Hester glanced down at the child in her arms; baby Helen was sucking very slowly now, her eyelids drooping. Hester, warm in her dry clothes, close to the range, found her own eyelids drooping, too. It wouldn't matter if she just had forty winks, provided . . .

The pair were sleeping soundly when the back door opened. The noise of it, for it grated against the quarry tiles and creaked protestingly, would have woken the dead. Mother and child woke simultaneously, the child to murmur a protest, the mother to cover her bare breasts.

Matthew, who had been enjoying the sight of his wife's newly developed body, felt like one of the dirty old men who hang around bathing beaches trying to catch a glimpse of girls changing their clothing. He looked away, his face growing hot, and stepped forward softly on stockinged feet, having shed his rubber boots outside the back door.

'It's only me, Hester. Don't stop, if she's still 'ungry.'

Hester tugged the child free of her nipple and clasped her to her breast. Matthew could see that she was using Helen as a shield. She turned a pink, guilty face towards her husband.

'Oh, Matthew, I'm so sorry, I must have fallen asleep . . . just let me put Helen down and I'll get you some dinner, only it'll have to be bread and cheese . . . oh, there isn't any bread, is there? Well, there's some cold pie . . .'

He crossed the room in a couple of strides and took the baby from her, then he turned away from her, looking down into the small face, the eyes already half-closed, the mouth working only reminiscently, as though tasting again the pleasures of her recent meal. He did not look around, knowing that she was hastily buttoning up, embarrassed by the thought of his seeing her big, swollen breasts. He wanted to turn and take her in his arms, to caress her, to tell her how beautiful were the breasts which she strove to hide, but he knew that would be fatal. She was shy as a wren and sometimes looked at him as a wren would look at a cat, her round amber eyes full of fear and confusion. So he would go gently, win her confidence. She was such a child, with no more knowledge of men and women than the wren he had called her. But time would mend her fear, she would trust him, given time.

'I'll put her down for you. You make us a cuppa. Cold pie's jest fine, if that's all we've got handy. A man with a child expects up'eaval, so don't go blamin' yourself.'

She sighed tremulously and he heard the rocking chair creak as she stood up, then a pair of thin little arms wrapped themselves round his shoulders and she stood on tiptoe to kiss the back of his neck, a featherlight touch.

'Matthew, I don't deserve you, you're the kindest man in the world and I'm probably the worst wife. But I do try . . . lie her on her back, won't you? I'm afraid she'll suffocate if she's on her front.'

For a moment he stood very still, more affected by the spontaneous caress than she could ever know. If only she knew how I feel, he thought, if only I could tell her . . . if only she could love me back! But she will; the old man says love comes late to many a marriage, she'll love me one day and not spend all her time being grateful because I'm kind. . . . Kind! When I want her so badly to feel as I do when our bodies join in love. She's so sweet, so young, so rare. I'd give my eyes to please her. But it'll come, it'll come. I must be patient, and I've always been a patient man.

Aloud he said, 'I'll put her on her back. Blessed lamb, she's all but asleep already. Is that kettle boilin'? A nice, hot cuppa would go down a fair treat.'

It was a very smart nursing home, right in the centre of the city of Norwich. Constance Radwell lay in her private room which overlooked the bustle of Thorpe Road and the railway station just across the way, and received the homage of friends and

19

relatives, the ministrations of the nurses, and the attentions of the handsome obstetrician who had delivered her daughter ten days ago. She had been allowed up the previous day, to walk as far as the bathroom – and hadn't the bath been a treat, after sponge-downs for so long? They'd taken her to the nursery too, where she had seen baby Anna in her beautiful, hygienic pink cot; before that the baby had been brought to her at regular intervals for feeding, though the nursing staff had advised her to wean the child on to a bottle as soon as she could.

'Better for your figure, Mrs Radwell,' the senior staff nurse assured her. 'It gives you more freedom, too. You're having a live-in nanny, of course?'

Constance said wearily that they had engaged a very experienced woman and the senior staff nurse nodded.

'Best to leave the early training to an expert,' she said. 'Well, Mrs Radwell, you've made an excellent recovery. You'll probably be able to go home in a week or so.'

It was an expensive nursing home and they took very good care of their patients. The food was equalled only by first-class hotels, and the staff waited on one hand and foot, but Constance couldn't wait to get away from it, to go home. Not that it was the sort of thing you admitted – the nurses would think she was insane or sex-mad or something if she said she was missing her husband, and even though she and JJ had only been married a year she knew it was not the sort of thing you told JJ either, not unless you wanted trouble.

She adored him! That was her Achilles heel, the dark secret which she had managed to hide from him during their courtship, engagement and early married life. Because JJ was used to women adoring him and would never have proposed marriage had he realised that she was like all the others. He could have had his pick of women, that was understood. Blondes, brunettes, redheads, all swooned at a glance from him. So tall, so dark, so sultry, so incredibly handsome. Constance thought he had finally proposed to her because she had held aloof, but his mother had not agreed.

'He won't get control of his money until he marries or is forty years old, which his grandfather thought a responsible age,' she had explained, her small, bright eyes fixed on Constance's face as though hoping for tears, protests, perhaps even a threat to break off the engagement. 'I'm not saying he doesn't want to marry you, Connie, I'm sure he does, but I do think you should be told about the inheritance.'

'I did know, actually,' Constance lied, sounding fashionably bored. 'He'll have Goldenstone, too, won't he?'

Goldenstone was the old house out in the country, surrounded by trees and with a small round lake on which swans sailed serenely, paddling to and fro among the ducks and the leaves which fell on its mirror surface. Constance had seen Goldenstone for the first time the previous autumn and could not forget the white of the swans, the blue of the water, the gold of the floating chestnut leaves.

'Upon his marriage, yes,' Mrs Radwell confirmed. The hopeful look had disappeared, to be replaced by a sort of calculation. 'You liked Goldenstone, I understand? James John said you did.'

'He was right,' Constance had said, coolly, unemotionally. 'So perhaps I'm marrying JJ to get my hands on Goldenstone, just as you seem to think he may be marrying me to get his hands on his money.'

And mine. The words, unsaid, floated in the air between them, for Constance, an only child, would inherit a great deal of money one day.

Mrs Radwell made a vague sound which might have been agreement or protest. 'Darling Connie, how you tease! So when's the wedding to be?'

Constance had smiled. They were sitting in the pretty drawing-room of Mrs Radwell's town house on Chapel Field, which overlooked the gardens. These were in their early spring finery, with snowdrops and crocuses massed beneath the trees and the first of the daffodil spears showing in the damp winter grass.

'JJ says soon,' she drawled. 'A month? Perhaps two? I rather fancy April, myself; such a pretty month.'

'Very wise.' Mrs Radwell picked up her teacup and poured a second cup of tea. 'It wouldn't do to wait, would it? I would never call James John fickle, it's the last thing I'd call him, but he does have so many girlies hanging on his every word . . . yes, April would be a nice month for a wedding.'

Mrs Radwell senior, wrong in so many things, had been right about April 1925. It was a glorious month for a wedding and they had a perfect day, all gentle sunshine and warm breezes. They honeymooned in the south of France, in a borrowed villa with a staff of three, so Constance didn't have to raise a finger, and a private beach where she and JJ swam naked and made love on the sand – or rather on a blanket on the sand, since JJ, who knew about these things, said that sand under the foreskin was something he preferred not to contemplate, let alone experience.

It was perfection. There were tall pine trees, masses of purple bouganvillea, and a stunning scarlet sports car in which JJ drove her along the coast to the casino to eat roast chicken and strawberries and drink champagne and gamble a little, but not too much, before driving home in the starlight. There was sunshine by day and starshine by night, balmy breezes and gentle music; looking back, Constance realised that first love and the sheer romance of being with JJ had coloured every moment.

He could have married anyone but he chose me, Constance thought on and off, all through the first glorious fortnight. She looked at herself in the mirrored walls of the bathroom and saw half-a-dozen pretty little Constances, all with fashionably bobbed silver-blonde hair, long, golden-brown legs and small, pink-tipped breasts, and she knew JJ had made a good choice. She loved it when he came to her in here, caressing down her back, titillating, teasing her into an ecstasy of wanting him, and watching her all the time in the mirrors. She thought him the perfect lover, having no comparison, and pitied girls who were married to other, ordinary men.

Then the second fortnight came, just as hot, just as sunny, just as pine-scented and beautiful. But during the second fortnight the serpent entered Eden: a serpent with long red hair, a husky voice, and a very unfashionable figure, all curves, Constance thought scornfully. She, with her small breasts and slender hips, could wear the modern fashions – short skirts, dropped waists, fringes and beads – and look just right. In her sports slacks and shirt she looked like an adorable boy – JJ remarked on it whilst clutching the one part of her where such a resemblance was most lacking.

Yet he liked the redheaded Cynthia. Some sixth sense told Constance that JJ liked the other woman even before she had proof. Another sixth sense, the one which had helped her to get JJ to propose, told her to pretend like fun that she didn't know, that it wasn't happening. Because how could it be? They were on their honeymoon, JJ couldn't keep his hands off her, and Cynthia was with a man called Malcolm Short, a large, coarse character who wore a gold necklace under his shirt and gold bracelets on each wrist. He smoked a big cigar and wore the loudest suits ever to appear on the Riviera; even his swimsuit was loud, striped in navy and puce. So was it possible that in this case, at least, her sixth sense was wrong?

It was during the second fortnight that a crowd of people they knew went out to dinner together, to the casino, and afterwards the men went to the tables and the women clustered in groups on the terrace, drinking and talking. Constance was with Betty, who came from Hampshire, and a French girl, Lise. The other two were brunettes and Constance was congratulating herself on finding two friends she genuinely liked who could not possibly compete in the 'who's the blondest?' contest she always held in her head when she met another fair girl, when she happened to notice that Cynthia, who had been talking to Rosie and Maud only seconds earlier, had disappeared.

'Where's Cynthia?'

She hadn't asked the question, that was Betty's chirruping little voice.

'Gone back to the tables,' someone said. 'She's a real gambler, not like the fellows. They play at it; with Cynthia, it's for real.'

'Is that how she got Malcolm?' someone else asked. 'What a prize!'

'He's filthy rich,' Rosie volunteered when the burst of laughter had died down. 'Owns half of Birmingham.'

'So?'

That was Constance's one contribution: 'So?' Little enough, but perhaps it spoke volumes. At any rate, Rosie shot her a quick, rather apprehensive glance.

'Cynthia doesn't have a bean, old dear,' she explained. 'She needs someone who'll let her gamble with his money. Malcolm's ideal; she won't want anything else from him and all he gets from her is the status of having a beautiful woman in tow.'

'Is she beautiful, though?' someone asked cattily. 'She's certainly got heaps of sex appeal, and the most enormous breasts, but as for beauty . . .'

'She has a certain appeal,' another girl drawled. 'Ah, there's a waiter; anyone want another little drinkie?'

The waiter came on to the terrace and the girls crowded round him and his tray. Someone began to dispense champagne cocktails and Constance turned and left the terrace, sliding unobtrusively back into the building, though she had no idea what she intended to do. She thought about going over to the tables, checking the whereabouts of JJ . . . she would not lower herself to checking on Cynthia . . . and suggesting that they go home, have an early night. After all, they were on their honeymoon.

She went into the casino. JJ wasn't at any of the tables, but perhaps he'd gone outside for a smoke. Smoking was not encouraged around the tables. She already knew he was not on the terrace.

She finally ran him to earth on the beach. It was quite a small beach. Despite the darkness she could see him easily enough, his active bare buttocks gleaming in the moonlight. He was naked, but he wasn't lying on the sand, risking his foreskin. He was lying on Cynthia.

Constance went back to the casino and was sick in the primrose-coloured handbasin in the ladies' toilet. Then, with shaking hands and a dreadful pallor, she went back to the gaming tables and bought some chips. She slung them down on number fifteen and won. When JJ finally showed up, she was brisk, pink, laughing, with half-a-dozen men trying to drink champagne from her slipper and with notes bulging out of her little evening bag.

She never told him what she had seen on the beach, by the light of that large golden Riviera moon, but it taught her a dreadful lesson. Never trust a man and never let him know it. If there had been the sort of scene she yearnd to make she would have made him look a fool and probably lost him. But because he thought her ignorant of his *affaire* he took her to bed and made love to her – how *could* he, she mourned, letting him, murmuring that she was tired, he mustn't mind – and then he rolled over and slept deeply, his dark hair rumpled, his mouth slack in repose, with a cruelty she had never noticed before in the line of his lips.

She was sick several times in the next few months, and when she told him she was expecting a baby he was delighted, genuinely pleased and proud.

'It'll be a boy ... the way my confounded grandfather left his property it's got to be a boy,' he said, hugging her exuberantly. 'Give me a kiss, my little golden angel-girl.'

She knew, though, that as her figure burgeoned and billowed, he would be unfaithful again. She cared, but there was little she could do. She did say she wanted to live at Goldenstone, to move out of their flat in the city and into the country when the baby was born. He wasn't in favour, but he said if that was what she wanted he supposed it would be all right. And though she knew he thought it a temporary thing, just while the baby was small, she was determined to keep him out at Goldenstone. His infidelity was bearable only if she did not have to see it, and besides, country living would be better for the child and for their marriage.

He wasn't present at the birth but she was deeply disappointed when he did not come and visit her in the hours following Anna's arrival. She supposed, tearfully, that he was angry because Anna wasn't a boy, but even so ...

He came the next morning, carrying drooping red roses. He was still drunk from his excesses of the night before, his eyes bloodshot, his hands trembling. For the first time he was not beautiful and she was quiet with him, not pretending to be overjoyed to see him, though she was, she was!

'Pity it wasn't a boy this time,' he said thickly, hugging her, shoving the roses, thorns and all, into her arms. 'But who cares, eh? Who cares a jolly old bean, so long as you're safe an' well an' the kid's got all its fingers and toes. Better luck next time, eh, old girl?'

A small frosty voice Constance didn't recognise as her own observed that there would not be a next time. She had not enjoyed giving birth, her pelvis was narrow so it had taken thirty-six hours of protracted bearing down to get the baby born and she was still sore and torn. JJ bent over her, then winced as the movement hurt his head.

'No next time? Nonsense, nonsense, you'll want a big family, especially if we live at Goldenstone, the way you say you want.'

'I do want,' Constance said. 'But I think one baby is quite enough.'

He shrugged. 'You'll change your mind, or I'll change it for you. Darling, when will they let you come home? I'm lonely.'

She smiled at him. He missed having a woman about the place, someone to order the meals, to laugh at his jokes, to answer the telephone. A woman in his bed was another matter; she supposed, miserably, that he had already remedied that particular defect.

'I'll come as soon as they think I'm fit enough. Have you seen the baby? Isn't she the most perfect thing? And fair, like me.'

'And perfect, like you,' he murmured, taking her hand and planting an impassioned kiss in the palm. 'Sweetest Constance, you'd be astonished how much I miss you!'

She wasn't, that was the odd thing. She accepted the fact that he could miss her despite the fact that it gave him freedom to pursue other women, while simultaneously worrying that he might discover life without a wife was more fun than life with one. But she wouldn't leave the nursing home a day before they wanted her to do so, because with that first glance at her baby she had known the child would be the main weapon in her armoury against losing JJ. No one, she was convinced, could fail to fall for that sweet, pink and white, blonde-topped scrap.

So Constance continued to lie in bed most of the day, to

take gentle exercise when the nurses said she might, and to contain her fear and impatience over what JJ might do in her absence. She took pleasure in her little daughter, wrote letters, read books, listened to the wireless, and reminded herself ten or twenty times every day that he was missing her, that it would do him good to realise that she was not always at his beck and call.

Her mother, a languid willowy woman, still determinedly blonde in her mid-fifties, came quite often and baby-worshipped, though she made no bones about telling Constance that she must not spoil the child, must hand her over to the nanny as soon as she got home, the nanny who had experience and would understand what to do in all circumstances.

'My pet, JJ is the sort of man who needs a woman's whole attention,' she said earnestly. 'Darling, he's far too handsome ... be thankful you're such a pretty thing and remember a woman can only hold a man by working at it. If you start neglecting your looks or spending all your time with the baby your marriage will suffer.'

Constance remembered her honeymoon; it hadn't taken either self-neglect or a baby to make JJ unfaithful then, it seemed to come naturally to him. But she would take her mother's advice and do her very best to bind JJ to her with ribbons of velvet. The dear little baby would have to take second place – it was only right and proper, after all. One's husband must come first.

'Did you know that the Duchess of York, what's her name, yes, Elizabeth, had a baby the same day as me? She's going to call the child Elizabeth Alexandra Mary.'

Constance indicated the announcement in her newspaper and looked curiously across at JJ's larger and more imposing broadsheet. She had been home for ten days now and little Anna was all but weaned from breast to bottle. In her ignorance she had thought that this would be an easy matter, but it had proved quite otherwise. The baby didn't care for the bottle and Constance's breasts did not wish to find themselves bursting with milk. Binding had proved painful, and being forbidden more than a couple of sips of drink each day had been a real deprivation now that the finer weather had come. JJ's attitude – that he rather liked her big breasts and that they should be allowed to remain – had caused Constance not only annoyance but also some doubts about the wisdom of bottle-feeding.

But she had to keep her figure; JJ would soon get tired of large breasts if they began to sag, which everyone said was what happened when you breast-fed for too long. And while she fed the baby she was tied to the house; JJ doubtless rather enjoyed that, she thought bitterly, but he would have to realise that this state of affairs could not continue. The baby had a good nanny, so once breast-feeding was finished Constance would be free to go everywhere with JJ again, and if it spoiled some of his plans, hard luck!

'What did you say?'

JJ lowered his paper and looked at her rather ill-temperedly across its top. Last night, during the two o'clock feed, Nanny had been forced to come and fetch Constance because her charge had cried so hard and refused the bottle so emphatically that the noise had woken JJ.

'I don't advise putting baby to the breast again,' Nanny had hissed as the two of them stood in the corridor discussing the situation, Constance white with tiredness and sleep interrupted. 'But if you'd just hold her, Mrs Radwell . . .' Constance had held the baby and given her the bottle and after a sniffle and a mutter or two, Anna had taken the lot. Nanny, gratified, had promised that it wouldn't happen again, it was just that baby still hadn't quite accepted . . .

Constance went back to bed. She was sleeping alone, JJ was in the dressing-room since he hated being disturbed and some disturbance was inevitable while the baby was being weaned. But apparently her voice and Nanny's had woken him and he was cross and bleary-eyed at the breakfast table as a result.

'I said that the Duke and Duchess of York had a little girl on the twenty-first of April, the same day our baby was born,' Constance repeated patiently now. 'They're going to call her . . .'

'I know. It's in here.' JJ raised his paper again. From behind it Constance could hear him crunching toast. 'I expect lots of people did.'

'Did what?'

Really, he made things very difficult sometimes; why couldn't they have a normal breakfast-time conversation like other people?

'Oh, Constance, honestly! I expect a lot of people had babies on the twenty-first of April. Babies get born all the time, you know.'

'Well, yes, but the Duke of York's the king's son so baby Elizabeth is the king's granddaughter. That makes her a bit special, doesn't it? And it's always nice to share a birthday with someone special.'

'Our kid's someone special on her own account,' JJ said, flinging his paper down on the table and apparently discarding his ill-humour with it, for he gave Constance one of his most blinding smiles. 'Poor darling, was I cross? But I hate disturbed nights and, dearly though I love the baby, her caterwauling did wake me, and then you two hissing away like the witches in Macbeth right outside my room completed the job and I lay there for hours trying to nod off again. I'll come back from the office early, I think, and have a nap after luncheon, then I'll be my usual cheerful self. Because I've got a rather important dinner date tonight, I shall need to be at my best.'

'I'm awfully sorry, darling, but she's nearly weaned,' Constance observed, trying not to sound abject. The trouble was she did hate being in JJ's bad books. 'Soon we can move out to Goldenstone; it's such a marvellous house, so big and roomy, and the baby will be up on the nursery floor, where we shan't hear her if she howls all night. Not that she will, because Nanny Galbraith's a marvellous woman, she'll soon settle down. And what's this about a dinner date? I don't remember anything.'

'No, well, it's a club function, darling, so women aren't allowed, I'm afraid. Why not ask a friend round to dine if you think you'll be lonely, or you could ask your mother. That's the only objection I've got to moving out to Goldenstone;

29

you're bound to be lonely when I'm not able to spend the whole evening with you.'

Constance folded her paper, laid it by her plate and stood up.

'Oh, if you're out I'll go round to Felicity's this evening, then,' she said with totally false cheerfulness. 'She's always nagging me to do so. And now I'll just pop up to the nursery and have a word with nanny. See you at luncheon, then, darling.'

Mrs Day leaned over the crib and pulled the covers right up to the occupant's small, rounded chin. The baby stirred, then settled again. She was a love, this latest nursling, Mrs Day decided, forgetting that she had said this of every single one of her babies. Elizabeth, the Duchess of York as she had become on her marriage, was a natural mother. All my babies – the girl-babies – are natural mothers, Mrs Day thought, using the muslin napkin which hung from her wrist to wipe a dribble of milk from the baby's pillow. One of my successes was Elizabeth Bowes-Lyon, a thoroughly sweet-tempered child, a charming woman and now the sort of wife most men can only dream of.

Mrs Day had never been married, her title being a courtesy one only, but that didn't mean she was ignorant about marriage, because she was an expert. The onlooker sees most of the game, Mrs Day told herself, crossing the spacious nursery to tidy away the baby's day-wear, the talcum powder and soap, the big white bath-towel, all the paraphernalia of feeding, bathing and bedding one small girl-child, the one who now slumbered sweetly in the crib. Oh yes, when Elizabeth turned him down, I thought she was running mad – such a dear boy, so polite and sensible, with such love in his eyes when he looked at my dear Lady Elizabeth – but she wanted to be sure, she's always wanted to be sure. She didn't want or need high position, the Family (Mrs Day always gave them a capital F in her mind) was an old and honoured one. But Bertie hadn't let a refusal put him off; he had continued to court her, sweetly but with determination, until Elizabeth had realised she loved him, and said she would marry him after all.

I knew they were right for each other, Mrs Day thought now,

contentedly tidying. They made a lovely couple even when they were courting, but as bride and groom . . . well, I never did see a couple better matched. You don't often see perfect love but she'd seen it the day her dear Lady Elizabeth had said 'yes' to Bertie Windsor, the Duke of York. Now, as their nanny, she was privileged to see that same expression on the faces of the young parents when they looked at their little daughter.

The nanny finished tidying and adjusted the curtain across the window, so that the sun, already low in the sky, would not fall across the baby's face and wake her. Little Elizabeth would sleep in here until after the ten o'clock feed, when she would be transferred into the night nursery next door, but experience told Mrs Day that a child, even a sleeping child, is soothed by the soft and careful movements of someone it loves in the same room. Accordingly, having screened the cradle, she took her place in a chair beside the fireplace and picked up her knitting. My babies never wail because I'm never far, she was wont to say. You can't give a baby too much love, but you can make it unhappy and confused by blowing hot and cold and not being reliable. Babies need love, reliability and firmness, in that order. And that's what a good nanny gives: love, reliability and firmness.

Thinking of the firmness part of it made her remember weaning baby Elizabeth from breast to bottle at around five weeks. The changeover had been accomplished without any untoward fuss due at least in part to Mrs Day's expertise, because Mrs Day had been nannying for twenty-five years. But it had been eased first by the baby's sweet-natured acceptance of the change and next by the Duchess. She had shed tears, had the Duchess, because as she told Mrs Day she so enjoyed the closeness which breast-feeding engendered, but she knew her duty; she had to help her husband in his various royal tasks and could scarcely be a proper helpmeet while she was tied to four-hourly feeds.

Mrs Day had wondered, in this latest job, if she would have any interference from royalty, because her dear Lady Elizabeth marrying King George's second son meant that Mrs Day was nearer the royals than she had ever thought to be, and folk said that royalty could be difficult, but it had proved to be quite otherwise. Royalty were used to their children being nannied, and respected the dedication of the nannying profession, knew they needn't interfere.

And Elizabeth – the Duchess of York, Mrs Day reminded herself hastily – was too much Mrs Day's nursling to kick against the pricks. She knew her duty and would abide by it, though sometimes handing your baby over to another woman, no matter that you loved that other woman as much as you loved your own mother, must be hard. But as the wife of a young man who was in line for the throne of England, not that Bertie would ever come near it of course with a handsome older brother who won all hearts, the Duchess had not only to be dutiful but be seen to be dutiful. She would always have to take her share of public appearances and so on, though once the Prince of Wales married the Yorks would be able to move thankfully out of the limelight, and let the prince's wife do the lion's share.

Mrs Day, knitting a shell-pink jacket for 'her' baby, remembered the wedding, how proud she had felt, how she had wept a little weep as the young couple exchanged vows. And wasn't it only natural that she should feel strongly at such a moment? Had she not nannied for the bride and for her brothers and sisters? Even allowing for the fact that she was delighted with Prince Albert, who, royal or not, was a real gentleman, she still realised that Lady Elizabeth Bowes-Lyon was taking an inevitable step away from her loving care. Unless you could say she was less losing the child than gaining the young man? Ever so polite was Prince Albert, the sort of young man who never let his eyes skim over you just because you weren't important. No, he'd chat with anyone, would the Duke of York, especially anyone of whom his young wife was fond.

Mrs Day knitted away as the light faded from the sky, but before it grew quite dark she got up, drew the curtains across, shutting out the quiet, refined life of the other inhabitants of Bruton Street and pottered over to the small kitchen. She poured milk from a jug into a pan, added some water, put the pan on the stove, lit the gas beneath it and watched the milk begin to warm. Presently she poured it carefully into a bottle, then stood the bottle in a larger pan of cold water, now and again testing the milk for warmth against her wrist. Presently the bottle was ready, wrapped in a nappy to keep it at blood-heat. Mrs Day stood it in the hearth and went quietly back into the nursery.

Baby Elizabeth was waking up; her head moved on the pillow, her mouth worked a little. Mrs Day, smiling, picked her up and carried her across to the chair by the dying fire. She sat down, waited for the baby to wake up properly and then offered the bottle of warm milk. The baby began to suck at once, her small hands balled into fists, her eyelids beginning to droop with drowsy contentment.

Mrs Day was bringing up the tiny Princess's wind when the door opened. The child sat solemnly on her lap while Mrs Day massaged the small back, taking no notice of the opening door, nor of the merry, pink-cheeked face which appeared.

'How is she, Ellen?' The Duchess kept her voice low but the baby's eyes opened and the wind which had rumbled so uncomfortably round her small frame left her in a loud belch. Mrs Day and the Duchess smiled at each other.

'She's doing very well, m'lady. She likes her food but she's not greedy, like some, and she's as sweet-tempered as you were yourself. Do you want to take her while I turn back the covers?'

'Oh yes, Ellen.' The girl took the child and cradled her to her breast, her face warm with love as she looked down into her baby's face. 'Hello, little one! Oh, isn't that a lovely smile? Well, what a clever girl to smile for her mama.' The Duchess continued to murmur lovingly to her daughter while Mrs Day prepared the cot and came back into the room. She smiled affectionately at the picture presented by mother and child, but tapped the Duchess on the arm.

'Time she was in bed, my dear, and time you followed suit. I'll just change her before I put her down . . .'

'Shall I do that? I'm not terribly tired and . . .'

'No, indeed! It's my job, m'lady, and besides it takes but a few minutes. You come back tomorrow and see the Princess when she's all bright and lively. Goodnight, m'lady.'

'Oh, goodnight, Ellen.' The young woman bent over the child

and kissed the round, rosy cheeks, then the brow, then the tip of the small nose. 'Goodnight, baby Elizabeth; your mama will see you in the morning.

Mrs Day watched the Duchess out of the room, then turned her full attention to the child once more.

'You're a very lucky little lady,' she said, beginning to unpin the baby's towelling nappy. 'Your Mama dotes on you almost as much as I do!'

Two

'But Hester, it were always understood, see? I'm not sayin' you don't have a point – you do, with the baby an' all – but it's . . . it's *expected*, like. I'll keep an eye on Helen, just for an hour or two, if you go up there this evening.'

Hester, up to her elbows in dough, tightened her lips and shook her head. She pummelled the dough as though it were a personal enemy while sweat ran down the sides of her face and anger and obstinacy blazed in her cheeks and brightened her eyes.

'It wasn't understood by *me*, Matthew, can't you see that? I know I'm your wife, but even so, that doesn't mean the old man should be able to take it for granted that I'll work for him, too.'

Matthew sighed. He stood there in his worn corduroys and sweatstained shirt, running brown, calloused fingers through his thick black hair, looking miserable and helpless.

'It won't be hard work,' he muttered. 'Just some cleaning an' that. Come on, Hes, say you'll do it. That's rare awkward for me, else. Besides, we could do wi' the extra money. He'll pay you, of course.'

Hester made the dough into a big, smooth ball and then divided it into smaller pieces. She had her loaf-tins greased and ready so she put a piece of dough into each tin and then set them down by the oven to prove. Outside, the June sun blazed down on the parched countryside, for it had been hot for a couple of weeks, and Helen slumbered in the broken-down old pram which Matthew had found in the cart-shed weeks before. Hester knew without looking that the child would be lying on her back, one arm above her head, her small thumb wedged into her mouth.

'I don't want . . .' a sense of fair play cut the words short. Matthew worked all the hours God sent and still they had a struggle to manage the extras which the baby needed; one day she would need much more, and unless her mother worked how would they pay their way then? But she hadn't considered working up at the castle; she had always assumed she'd find work either in the village or the town, had even dreamed, vaguely, of getting a job in Rhyl when the little one went to school.

'I know you work hard now,' Matthew said, looking down at his feet. 'You do your best, love, but I mean it's not as if you'd got a couple o' kids, or another job . . .'

Honesty forced Hester to answer. 'I don't work hard, not really,' she said grudgingly. 'I do my best, but I do have time to spare. You do so much for me, Matthew.'

He grinned, suddenly. He was very attractive when he grinned, showing off his white teeth and the amusement crease in one cheek.

'Well, I can't go up to the castle and scrub floors for you, or peel spuds or whatever. I would if I could, but it 'ud give rise to talk.'

Hester laughed, as he meant her to, but that didn't mean she intended to give in.

'Look, suppose I get myself a job, down in the village, perhaps. Would that mean I wouldn't have to go up to the castle?'

His smile faded; he looked miserable again. Boring, too, Hester thought nastily, carrying her cooking things over to the sink and slamming them in with such force that she was lucky not to chip the stoneware. Why couldn't he always look handsome and amusing, like he had that day in Rhyl? But that had been before he fell in love. Once that happened, he'd gone soft on her. He was so eager to please her that he let her ride roughshod over him, and though she did her best not to be selfish she knew she often despised him, even for his kindness and generosity.

'Hester? I don't want to throw my weight about, but you aren't leavin' me much choice.'

She bristled up at once, turning sharply to scowl at him. She might tell herself she liked him to be masterful, but she wanted her own way more.

'What does that mean? Do you intend to order me to go up to the castle?'

He loved her and was by nature easy-going, but she could see his complacency cracking at the seams. He crossed the room in a couple of strides and caught hold of her shoulders and there was nothing lover-like in his touch. Uneasily, Hester wondered if she had gone too far; she realised suddenly that she didn't really know Matthew at all – suppose he became violent, hit her? He had shown no signs of such behaviour over the past months of their marriage, but then she had never defied him before. They had rubbed along, she realised now, without so much as a harsh word.

'Hester, are you goin' to do as I say?'

He actually shook her and Hester, unprepared, bit her tongue. It hurt and she gave a little whimper, then tried to struggle free. Matthew didn't seem aware that she had so much as moved, he was still scowling down at her, his eyes narrowed, his big hands clamped on her shoulders as though he would continue to hold her there, if necessary, for all eternity.

'Well?'

'I don't want to work up at the castle,' Hester said sulkily. 'But I suppose, if you're so set on it . . .'

He released her at once, the smile back in his eyes.

'That's good. I'll tell the old man you'll go up this evening, and whatever they want it'll have to be arranged around the baby. He won't mind, so long as the work gets done. You could do a bit this evening, come to think. I'll give an eye to Helen.'

'Who'll tell me what to do?' Hester said, still crossly, returning to the sink. It occurred to her, belatedly, that it would be quite fun to work up at the castle really. She would be a part of things instead of always on the outside. Why had she not thought of that before? To be accepted, a part of a community, had always been a dream. Orphans, even clever ones, are always outsiders.

And besides, she was very curious about the castle and its occupants, had been curious ever since she had come back here with Matthew over five months ago. But having tried to get out of it she could scarcely just capitulate now, admit it wasn't such a bad idea after all.

'Who'll give me my orders?' she repeated, wiping round her mixing bowl and heaving it out on to the draining board. 'A man won't understand about cleaning and cooking.'

'A man? No, you're right there, the old feller wouldn't know how to start, you probably won't even see him. Mrs Cledwen will tell you.'

Hester, humping the big black kettle over from the top of the range, tipped it laboriously up so that the contents splashed, boiling hot, all over her cooking things and then turned an enquiring face up to her husband's.

'Mrs Cledwen? Who's she?'

'She lives up at the castle, sees to things,' Matthew said after a moment's thought. 'Been with him a year or two, now. She'll tell you what needs doing.'

'All right, I'll go up this evening, then,' Hester said, still sounding a little sulky but unable to keep the interest entirely out of her voice. 'Why didn't you mention Mrs Cledwen before?'

'You never asked and I never thought,' Matthew said equably. He picked up a tea-towel and began to dry up as Hester washed. 'You must have knowed someone had to do the housework, didn't you? We've talked about Willi and Dewi because you see 'em going past . . . Haven't you ever seen Mrs Cledwen? Mind, she probably does out t'other gates; nearer town, see? Now you go there right after we've had our tea and when you come back I'll have a surprise for you, perhaps.'

Matthew rarely talked at such length, which might mean that the surprise was a nice one. But surprises, in Hester's experience, were a two-edged sword. Her life before Matthew had not been exactly crammed with pleasant surprises and the unpleasant ones, well, she had no wish to repeat a single one of them.

'What sort of surprise?' she said, therefore, immediately suspicious.

He shrugged, putting a dried plate carefully on the table. 'Wait an' see, eh?'

Tea was rather a quiet meal. Homebaked bread, cheese, the pickled onions which Hester had bought from the village shop. Then a piece of apple pie each with thin custard poured over it. And tea in the big brown pot, of course. And all the while they ate Hester wondered about the castle; she had quite made up her mind that she would never get to go up there, and this had disappointed her in a way, because of a perfectly natural curiosity, but somehow she had never seen herself working there. Scrubbing floors, peeling spuds – she had quite enough of that at home, thank you, she could well manage without any more.

But Matthew said she would be paid, which would help. And there was this woman, Mrs Cledwen . . . she had wished often enough that there was another woman near, someone with whom she could discuss the difficulties which arose from time to time. Why had Matthew never mentioned her? Was she an unpleasant sort of woman? With a name like that she might speak nothing but Welsh, and she would be old, that went without saying, and probably cross, and if she was Mrs Cledwen where was Mr Cledwen? Matthew had never mentioned him either. But there was no point in cross-questioning Matthew; she would find out for herself soon enough.

'I'll have to feed Helen before I go,' Hester said, when the food was finished. 'I'll take her through.'

Helen could smile now, and frequently did. Lying in her pram, she smiled at the dance of the bright new leaves on the branches above her head; lying in her mother's arms, she smiled at the familiar face so near her own. Hester, walking across the kitchen, felt her own smile start; she did love her pretty little daughter. Happiness was holding Helen, kissing the baby's petal-soft cheek, playing with her until that big, innocent, take-it-all smile broke out on the small trusting face.

She and Helen still slept in the small room and she fed Helen there when Matthew was home. She opened the back door and bent over the big old-fashioned perambulator. Helen was just waking, two fists waving idly as she stared sleepily up at the blue sky above her. Hester picked the baby up and turned back indoors. Matthew was at the sink, clattering dishes. He was good, she acknowledged that; he usually cleared away the tea things while she fed the baby. She went to go past him but he shot out a large, capable hand and caught her arm.

'Hes? Why not feed the little'un in here? Then we can talk.'

Hester wavered, then hardened her heart. Look what had happened over her working up at the castle; the moment she gave Matthew an inch he would undoubtedly take a mile, and for some reason which she had never tried to analyse she dreaded the resumption of 'all that mauling', which had stopped with the baby's birth.

'All the baby things are in the little room,' she said now. She shook his hand off and continued across the kitchen. 'It's easier to do her in there. I shan't be long.'

In the small room, comfortable and familiar to them both, mother and child went through the nightly ritual together. Hester fed Helen, washed her, changed her into her night-gown and then laid her on the mat to kick and coo whilst she considered what she should wear to visit this Mrs Cledwen. She was going cleaning, so her oldest clothes seemed called for, but since she was also going to meet a strange woman, and she was visiting the home of her husband's employer, surely that meant that she should wear a decent dress and her most respectable shoes?

In the end, she compromised. She washed thoroughly, brushed her hair hard and put on a clean blue cotton dress. Since her footwear consisted of the shoes she had got married in, some wellington boots and a pair of ancient sandals her choice in this line was limited, and it shrank further when she thought of the length of the neglected gravel drive which led from the lodge to the castle. Trudging up there in her best shoes would be hell, and it wouldn't do the shoes much good either. She would sweat like a pig in her wellingtons, so the sandals it would be.

Having made up her mind about her clothing she then tried her hair loose, tied back, and pinned to the crown of her head with a couple of tortoiseshell combs which had once belonged to old Mrs Coburn. She looked really elegant in the tortoiseshell combs, but practicality told her that she wouldn't look elegant long, not scrubbing floors she wouldn't. So she tied her hair back with a clean piece of string, checked her appearance again, and went through to the kitchen with Helen tucked under her arm.

It was clean, cleared, tidy; of Matthew there was no sign. She found him in the front room, reading a newspaper, sitting beside the empty cradle. He looked up and smiled as she laid the already sleepy child among its blankets.

'You look very smart,' he said approvingly. 'Are you off then?'

'Yes,' Hester said shortly. 'Shan't be long.'

'It's all right, I can manage.'

'Not when she begins to squall for her ten o'clock feed you can't,' Hester reminded him. 'But I'll be back long before then.'

Matthew, realising that she was still cross, grunted and returned to his paper, so Hester went back and patted his shoulder, then bolted out of the front door before he could grab her hand and start any silly nonsense. That was the trouble, she thought half-guiltily, she had quite enough to do with the house and Helen, without starting any of *that* up again, so she couldn't let him think . . . Of course the present arrangement was only temporary, but . . . Her thoughts broke down in confusion and she turned them determinedly away from her marriage and Matthew and fixed her eyes on the castle.

In the golden evening light, for the sun was sinking over a cobalt sea behind her, it looked more romantic than ever. The trees were in full leaf now, the creeper which decorated the walls was luxuriant, the ornamental trees, planted long ago by a richer owner than the present one, were in flower. As she got nearer, Hester guessed, the flaws would begin to show but from here it was a fairytale castle, beautiful, impregnable.

The drive was a long one, though unimpressive. Because of the lie of the land — and the wind from the sea, Hester guessed — there were no trees until you got into the shelter of the cliff, so the drive passed across flat pastureland, grazed by sheep and a few cattle, with scarcely a bush to vary the monotony. If you had driven up it, in a carriage and four or

41

a common-or-garden motor car, you might not have found it a particularly trying ride, but to Hester, slogging along on foot, it seemed a boring journey. It would be easier to go into the village, Hester thought crossly, willing the castle to get closer more quickly. It would be nearer to walk into the little town. Why shouldn't I get a job somewhere else? Why shouldn't I catch a bus into Rhyl each day and have some fun? Imagine walking all this way in the rain or the snow! And at the end of the walk an icy old ruin, whereas if I went into Rhyl I could work in a nice warm hotel, or a shop, or even at the pier theatre, or a dance-hall. I'll have to talk to Matthew about it. After all, it's me that's doing the work, not him – or the old man!

But no walk lasts for ever and at length Hester found herself going in under a perfectly enormous arch and entering the courtyard. At such close quarters, she could see that the castle was as dilapidated as Matthew had led her to suppose. Above her head, the creeper which looked so romantic from afar was entering the slit windows, straggling across some, twining its way into others which had no glass in them. Birds had nested in the eaves, judging by the mess on the great paving slabs nearest the building, and from the range of stabling to her right a gaggle of geese suddenly erupted, hissing and flapping at the stranger in their midst, big orange beaks gaping, tiny eyes sparkling with cold fury.

'Get away,' Hester said feebly. It had never occurred to her that geese could be threatening, but these creatures were positively terrifying to a city girl. 'Go away, go on!'

The geese ignored her strictures, so Hester traversed the courtyard a good deal faster than she intended, fairly flying across the paving stones and up the steps to the front door. The geese looked as though they might mount the steps in pursuit so she rattled desperately on the door, shyness and diffidence forgotten in her fear of the enemy.

No one answered her frantic knock so she grabbed the iron ring and twisted it and was relieved when the door creaked open, showing a dark and gloomy space behind. Hester glanced back. The largest of the geese was stretching its neck at her, horrible thing, so she shot inside and pushed the heavy door to behind her.

She was still leaning against the door, panting, when another door opened and someone came out of a room to her left. It was a man, she could tell by the shape of the silhouette, but other than that she could not have said whether he was fair or dark, young or old. He must have heard the slam of the front door, though, because he glanced in her direction, then addressed her.

'You! What d'you want?'

'I–I want to s-see Mrs Cledwen,' Hester quavered, all her natural self-confidence having disappeared with the arrival of the geese. 'M-my husband sent me.'

The man made a disbelieving, grumbling sort of noise.

'Why d'you come to the front door? What's wrong with the kitchen entrance?'

'The g-geese,' poor Hester said in a small voice. 'They chased me, and I don't know where the kitchen entrance is.'

'You go round the back, ignore the arch . . . oh, hold on.'

He sounded horribly cross still, but at least, Hester realised, he was not about to eject her into the goose-ridden courtyard once more. He crossed the hallway, still just a tall dark figure to her, and opened a door. He shouted something through it, then returned.

'Wait,' he said curtly, and disappeared, shutting the door firmly behind him.

Having little alternative, Hester waited, and presently, from the doorway through which he had shouted, another figure emerged. A woman's silhouette this time, a woman in a black dress, with a pale face framed in masses of dark hair. She peered across at Hester through the gloom.

'Mrs Coburn? Is that you? Didn't Matthew tell you to come to the back door?'

'He just said to come up and see you,' Hester said. 'The geese chased me. I'm very sorry . . .'

The woman laughed. 'Those bloody birds! All right, follow me.'

43

She had sworn! She had the voice of a lady but the vocabulary of a docker, Hester thought, thoroughly confused. And no matter how dark it was, she was sure that Mrs Cledwen was neither old nor ugly; there was youth in that tall figure, that mass of dark hair, and judging from the way she moved and spoke she had plenty of that unthinking self-confidence which rarely accompanies ugliness.

Hester followed the other woman down a long, dark corridor, through another doorway and into a large, warm room which proved to be the kitchen. It was not dissimilar to Hester's own kitchen, though it was roughly four times the size. There was an old-fashioned kitchen range, two enormous, scrubbed wooden tables, two sinks, both at knee-level, and an open fire, with bake-ovens set into the wall on either side. In every available space there were floor-to-ceiling glass-fronted cupboards, and two long, low windows looked out on to a stableyard. Hester stared all round the room, then at last let her gaze rest on her companion, who was surveying her thoughtfully.

Mrs Cledwen was not just beautiful, she was striking. She was tall and slender, with a rich mass of coal-black hair, very white skin and blue eyes, and she had scarlet lips which parted as she smiled at Hester to reveal perfect, pearly little teeth. Hester, dazzled, thought she had never seen a woman so beautiful.

'So you are Matthew's little bride! No wonder he's kept you hidden away – you're very pretty. Now I wonder just what you saw in our worthy Matthew?'

Hester, who had sometimes wondered the same thing, found she was bristling at the implied criticism, but before she could speak Mrs Cledwen shook her head at herself, with a grimace so comical that Hester could not help but smile.

'Listen to me! What a perfectly beastly thing to say, especially as Matthew is not only worthy, he's one of the handsomest men I know. But he is shy with women, even with me, and he's known me for a number of years, so I can't help wondering how he brought himself to propose marriage.'

'He is shy,' Hester allowed, 'but once we got to know each other we got on very well and perhaps my being not very old made it easier for him.'

'Were you still at school last summer? You do seem very young, my dear.'

'I'd left school,' Hester said quickly. 'The summer in Rhyl was a – a holiday before I started work.'

'I see. And how long have you been married now?'

'Not terribly long,' Hester said stiffly, telling herself that it was a nasty, nosy sort of question for anyone to ask. Despite Mrs Cledwen's prettiness and charm she was beginning to dislike the other woman's inquisition – if she had been here, as she said, for years, she must know very well when Matthew brought his bride back to the lodge. 'Can you tell what you want me to do?'

'To do? Oh, the housework.' Mrs Cledwen plunged a hand into the pocket of her full black skirt and produced a small watch on a length of gold chain. She consulted its face. 'Just cleaning, my dear, and I should prefer that you start earlier, tomorrow. At about ten in the morning, I think. You may bring the child. You have a perambulator?'

'It's very old; but I daresay it'll survive being pushed up the drive,' Hester said. 'Suppose the baby cries, though?'

'You know best how to hush her,' Mrs Cledwen said briskly. 'Tomorrow morning, at ten, you may start in here. You can clean right through, and I'll keep an eye on you so that no mistakes get made. If you work hard you'll be free by lunchtime. I'll pay you weekly; you should earn about two shillings and sixpence a week, which isn't bad for a dozen or so hours.'

Hester thought of the girls she had met who were waitressing in Rhyl; they got five shillings a week, but then they worked a ten- or twelve-hour day, and there were tips too. Probably half a crown was fair, especially since she would have to take time off to see to Helen.

'All right, I'll be here by ten,' she said equably. 'What else will I be required to do, apart from cleaning in here?'

'You'll do the rough work,' Mrs Cledwen told her. 'Scrubbing, carting coal, laying and lighting the fires in the winter.'

'Ten o'clock's too late for fires,' Hester pointed out. 'It

takes an hour for a room to warm up. Fires are usually lit before breakfast.'

Mrs Cledwen gave her a glance in which annoyance and a grudging respect were mingled. 'Yes, of course, I was forgetting. Very well then, you had best come earlier, in winter.'

Hester shook her head. 'I can't, Mrs Cledwen. Don't you have a housemaid to do things like that? I have to do my own work before I come, I have to see to the baby and Matthew. Ten o'clock is the earliest I can manage.'

Mrs Cledwen chewed her lip, a faint frown marring her perfect brow.

'I see. Well, the fire in the range stays in all the time, but I shall have to light the other fires myself, until we get a house-maid. Your job will be to keep the scuttles and wood-boxes full, the floors clean and the paintwork and furniture polished. You must be flexible, so that if I tell you to do something different you can learn to do it, whatever it may be. And you'll start at ten o'clock tomorrow morning; is that all right?'

'Yes m'm,' Hester said, hoping that she now sounded suffi-ciently like a scrubbing woman. She guessed that Mrs Cledwen would keep an eye on her to start with, but after that she would be able to explore. After all, she had yearned to know what the castle was like; what better way to find out than to work here? It would not be fun, of course, in the way working in Rhyl would have been fun, but it was convenient in other ways. And she had always known in her heart that Helen would make it impossible for her to apply for the more interesting jobs. 'What'll I do now, Mrs Cledwen?'

'Now? Oh well, since you're here you'd best come with me into the scullery. I'll show you where the cleaning things are kept.'

Leaving the castle, by the back way this time, Hester reviewed her visit. Mrs Cledwen was a strange person, friendly one min-ute, nosy the next, frosty the next. She's very beautiful but I don't think she's very nice, Hester decided. She's the sort to take advantage – I bet I slave for that half a crown!

Despite her attempts to find out, she still didn't know precisely what job Mrs Cledwen held at the castle. Housekeeper? But a self-respecting housekeeper wouldn't light the fires, she would insist that the old man got a housemaid, probably two or three. A poor relative, perhaps? But poor relations who were as young and beautiful as Mrs Cledwen didn't stay poor relations long. If I hadn't known I might have thought her the old man's daughter; could she be a niece, perhaps, or some other relative? Not a poor relation but a rich or eccentric one, someone who chose to live at the castle because she wanted to do so, not because she had nowhere else to go.

However, asking herself unanswerable questions did not help much and since she was to start work in the morning she would have countless opportunities to satisfy her curiosity. The extra money would be nice, of course, but the more Hester thought about it the more sure she became that working at the castle might yet prove a doubtful pleasure. The cleaning things, kept in a tall cupboard in the smelly, chilly little scullery, consisted of a bass broom, some torn-up shirts, a couple of buckets and a very large, very new scrubbing brush. Mrs Cledwen bought the brush when the old man told her I was going to work for her, Hester thought, aggrieved, but Mrs Cledwen didn't know enough about scrubbing floors to buy soap as well. She had pointed out the lack and received a chilly glance from those magnificent blue eyes, but Mrs Cledwen had seen her point.

'I'll buy soap tomorrow,' she had said. 'Oh, put a pan of water on the range when you arrive or you won't have any hot water to scrub with. I daresay hot is needed?'

'Yes,' Hester said baldly. 'Cold just spreads the dirt around.' She hesitated a moment, then decided that if she didn't ask she would never know. 'Who was your last scrubbing woman, Mrs Cledwen?'

'We had a – a girl from farther up the coast.' A shadow crossed the older woman's face, but whether it was of sadness or annoyance Hester could not have said. 'Mr Geraint dismissed her; she was an idle creature and none too bright. I hope and trust you'll be very different from Katie, Mrs Coburn . . . no, I shall start as I mean to go on and call you Hester.'

47

'Very well, Mrs Cledwen. Shall you be here tomorrow morning at ten?'

'Yes, I'll be here, though perhaps not every morning. And come in the back way, if you please. Mr Geraint would not be amused to find you in his front hall every day.'

'I'm not walking by those geese,' Hester said firmly. 'If I have to get bitten to death to get here I'll give the job the go-by.'

Mrs Cledwen smiled. She looked quite different when she smiled; she ought to do it more often, Hester thought, smiling back.

'No, it's all right, the geese live in the main courtyard. If you turn to your left, ignoring the big arch, you'll find another, smaller arch. Go under that and . . . but you may as well leave by the back door now, then you'll see the back way for yourself.'

She let Hester out into a courtyard with what she assumed were coalsheds and woodsheds to one side. Across the cobbles Hester went and under a small arch, to find herself in the wild gardens which she had noticed as she approached the castle, though seen at close quarters their resemblance to gardens was not striking. It's downright dangerous, Hester thought, pushing painfully through rampant rose bushes and stopping to kick viciously at a clump of nettles threatening her bare legs. Poor old Prince Charming, if he had to tackle this lot to reach the sleeping beauty then he really needed that damned great sword.

She had been longer in the castle than she had thought, though; the sun had set and night was approaching fast. In the dim half-light it was hard to see where the path had once led, and soon Hester realised that she was lost. No, not lost precisely, she corrected herself, glancing behind her at the dark bulk of the castle; she just couldn't find her way out of the maze of the wild garden. Now that almost all the light had gone, the paths, hard to see in daylight, merged with all the rest. If she went straight ahead she would get bogged down in the beds and clawed to pieces by the straggly roses and the great mass of brambles which flourished where flowers had once massed in the borders. The only way out was back – she would find the castle wall, make her way along it until she reached the big arch, and then dive for the driveway below, hoping that the geese were roosting, or snoozing, or whatever it was geese did after dark. Just so long as they weren't prowling after trespassers, preparing to spring out on the unwary . . .

Hester found the castle wall and clung to the grey stone, feeling the most complete fool and praying that no one would come out and find her in this most embarrassing of predicaments. To lose oneself within feet of the house one has just visited, how could she admit to such a thing? But she began inching her way along, one hand on the wall, now and then having to move away for a moment when a shrub or a particularly large bramble patch barred her path but returning to the wall at once, as one returns to one's mother when lost and alone. It was slow work but at least she was making progress, though she burned from nettle stings and could feel a thousand scratches where brambles and rose thorns had snatched at her undefended flesh.

She rounded a buttress and it was then that she noticed the lighted window. It was quite high up, and it threw a golden glow right across the wild garden, illumining – oh, thank God, Hester thought exultantly – a small, meandering path. If she could reach that path it would surely lead her on to the driveway once more. She fixed her eyes on the path and began to hurry, which was her undoing; she walked into something solid, clutched at what felt like someone's arm, let it go with a squeak of fright and realised it was a statue just as she began to fall, totally unable to help herself.

Hester and the statue hit the deck together in a welter of arms and legs, Hester landing in what felt like a gorse bush. She disentangled herself and scrambled painfully to her feet, her fear and misery giving way to a much healthier emotion: anger. What a stupid place to put a statue, halfway across a path! The thing had virtually attacked her; if she hadn't bumped into it she would have been well out of here by now, on her way home. What was that word Mrs Cledwen had used with such force? Yes, bloody! It was a *bloody* statue, a beastly stupid statue, and she just hoped it was as injured by the encounter as she was.

She was cursing the statue in the worst words at her

command – and they turned out not to be nearly bad enough – when someone spoke to her. A deep, low voice came from above her head.

'What the devil . . . just who do you think you are, crashing about down there?'

She looked up. A dark figure was leaning out of the golden window; silhouetted against the light she could not make out any features, but the voice had been a man's.

'I'm . . . I'm sorry,' Hester stammered. It must be the old man, that would be just her luck, and what would he think of a scrubbing woman who got lost on her first visit to the castle, crashed through his garden wreaking havoc and – she glanced down at her enemy, supine at her feet – breaking a valuable statue into three distinct and separate pieces? 'I was lost. I'm going home now.'

'Wait.' It was the voice which had shouted at her across the hall, she was sure of it. 'Don't try to move, wait.'

The golden light streamed out again; the figure in the window had disappeared. Hester drew a sobbing breath and looked wildly round her. If she ran like anything she might still get away, he couldn't have got a very good look at her, he was in light, she in darkness. If she could only escape before he appeared . . . But she had gazed up at the window too long; her night-sight had temporarily deserted her. She could not pick out the path, all she could see were brambles, roses and more statues, or they might even be wicked fairies for all she knew, waiting to finish her off. No path, gleaming in the lamplight, no way of escape for a bruised and battered scrubbing woman.

She stood still while her night-sight returned and starlight illumined the wild garden once more. But before she could take advantage of it a dark figure emerged from under the big arch. He came towards her, clearly knowing the paths like the back of his hand. He reached her, and caught her arm just above the elbow in a firm grip.

'Come along; I'll set you on the right road,' he said, his voice sounding half annoyed, half amused. 'You can tell me who you are and what you're doing in my garden as we go.'

'I came about a job,' Hester said breathlessly, thanking

God he hadn't appeared to notice the dismembered statue. 'Mrs Cledwen said I was to leave by the back way, but it was nearly dark and I came in through the front door so I didn't know where I was. I must have strayed off the path.'

He had been leading her forward, rather like a prison warder leading a prisoner, but as she spoke he stopped and peered at her. Then he gave a muttered exclamation and pulled her into the beam of golden light falling from the window of the room he had just left.

'My God! What are *you* doing here?'

The light which fell on her face hid her questioner, but Hester frowned up at him. The voice was familiar, it sounded . . . She pulled away from him and moved sideways so that the light fell on his profile.

'You! I thought I recognised that voice. I might ask you the same question, John. Do you work at the castle too?'

He was still staring down at her, so she had ample opportunity to stare back. He had a harsh face, all planes and no curves, a hooked nose, thick black hair streaked with grey. His mouth gave nothing away, it was just a line, his chin jutted, clean-shaven usually but now blue with the day's growth.

'Work at the . . . ? Oh, I see. Yes, I do. And what job did you come after?'

'Scrubbing woman,' Hester said. 'Are you the gardener? Matthew never mentioned there was a gardener.'

'Matthew?' The man frowned, his firm grip on her upper arm beginning to make Hester's muscle ache. She tried to pull away but he held on.

'You must know him; Matthew Coburn. He lives at the lodge,' Hester said. Suddenly she did not want to tell John she was married to Matthew. Let him guess, she thought, staring up into his grim face. He never told me he worked here when we met in Rhyl. 'I thought you said you were going to put me on the right path?'

'Yes, but I didn't know it was you, then,' the man said. 'What happened to you? You disappeared.'

'So did you,' Hester pointed out. 'Look, I must go, and you've left that window hanging open. If the wind gets up it'll probably swing and break. Show me the path home, please. I'm late already.'

'You live locally; right on my doorstep and I never guessed,' the man murmured. 'Hester, I . . .'

'John . . .'

He drew her into his arms and Hester found herself clinging, raising her face to his as she had raised it once before, only then there had been bright summer stars above them, and the lights on the promenade had twinkled and shone, then the sounds of the funfair had drifted to them on the breeze and presently the sand had been cold and soft beneath her shoulders, his body warm between her and the dark night sky. And she had clung to him as she was clinging now, her lips parting for his kiss, her body tingling to his touch.

On that enchanted night last summer he had made her forget everything but his arms, his touch; now it was the same and she only came to her senses when she felt her shoulders against the castle wall and the warm weight of him leaning on her, trapping her against the stones. Abruptly she realised that anyone could look out, anyone could see, as he had seen, out of that lighted window. And it was different now, she was a married woman, she could not, must not, should not . . .

'John, no! Don't, I mustn't . . . think if anyone else looked out of the window. Let me go.'

Rather to her surprise he sighed and pulled her away from the wall, to rest against the breadth of his chest.

'Foolish little Hester! There's no one up there, I was alone. Will you come with me, into the castle, up to my room? We can be comfortable there, you can tell me how you came to be here.'

'I can't do that,' Hester said. 'I can't just go with you, I'm not, I'm not . . .'

'You've changed,' John said. He stroked gently down the swell of her breasts, making her heart skip a beat, then double its pace. 'You were a sweet, wild child. Now you're a woman.'

It was useless to deny it once he had noticed the change in her; indeed it would be very wrong to deny her marriage, her motherhood.

'Yes. I'm married now. I have a child.'

He nodded, eyes still steady on her face. 'I should have guessed; is that why you went?'

In her turn, Hester nodded. It was too complicated to tell him the whole story.

'Yes. And why I must go now, if you please.'

He took her shoulders and swung her round, to face away from the castle and the golden light from the window.

'Of course, if that's what you want. See the drive? I'll walk down to it with you, then we must both return to our own places.'

They walked in silence to the drive. Reaching it, he stopped and turned to face her.

'Who did you marry?'

'Matthew Coburn; at the lodge.'

To her surprise, he grinned. She saw the flash of his teeth in the starlight, the laughter crease in his cheek deepened.

'Really? We're neighbours, then. Did you say you'd got a job up at the castle?'

'Yes. I'm going to work there.'

He touched her cheek with the backs of his fingers, then lowered his voice, the tone of it as intimate, suddenly, as the most tender of caresses.

'Then we'll see each other again. I'm glad. Take care, little Hester. There's your road.'

She half expected him to kiss her, at least to squeeze her hand, but he simply turned away, walking with the long stride she remembered, and disappeared under the great arch without once looking back.

'Well? It weren't so terrible, were it? Did Mrs Cledwen tell you when to start an' that?'

Matthew had come to the back door as soon as he heard her hand on the latch and now he smiled down at her in the hazy lamplight, his pleasure at her presence warm and comforting. Hester came right into the room and closed the door behind her. She smiled at Matthew and took his hand in hers. Suddenly, all the things that had happened this evening

53

shrunk into perspective; the strange Mrs Cledwen with her bad language and lady's voice, then Hester getting lost in the wild garden and being found by the man she had met last summer – they were all unimportant beside Matthew and his gentle, loving smile.

'Is Helen all right? I got the job, I start tomorrow at ten. Mrs Cledwen says I can take the baby with me, in her pram. Is she a sort of housekeeper, Matthew, or a poor relation or what? She's obviously the boss, but she talked so strangely, it confused me. Still, the job seems all right – I'll get half a crown a week.'

'That's very little,' Matthew said. 'How long d'you work, for that?'

'Two or three hours a day. From ten until lunchtime Mrs Cledwen said. I'm not sure when she counts lunchtime, but she didn't say I'd get a meal, she said I'd have to get back to you, so I expect it's just the two hours.'

'Once you're into the job we can ask 'em for a bit more,' Matthew said now. 'Baby's been fine; asleep all evening. I made you a cheese sandwich and I boiled the kettle; want some tea?'

'Oh yes please, that would be . . .' Hester stopped short. 'Oh Matt, look at my skirt!'

It was the first time she had ever shortened his name but in her distress she scarcely noticed. Glancing down, she had seen her blue cotton dress snagged and torn, and below the hem of the skirt her legs were stung and scratched, the sandals stained. She put a hand to her hair; it was like a bush. What a mess she must have looked, even in the faint light from that upper window – what a mess she looked now!

'Whatever have you been doin', my love?' Matthew was back beside her in a couple of strides, his concern heart-warming. 'My, you've got in a pickle; your poor little arms! What happened, did you miss your way?'

'Yes, I got lost in that so-called garden. Then I bumped into a statue – it was awfully dark, Matt – and fell over. The brambles scratched me and the nettles stung me and I'd probably still be there, only the gardener came out and showed me the way to the drive.'

Matthew ran a hand down her cheek, then stopped, an arrested look on his face.

'Gardener? There ain't no gardener.'

'Yes, he said he was the gardener. John, his name is. He was rather nice to me. A tall, dark man, not very young.'

'That's the old man,' Matthew said positively. 'You met him? I didn't mean for you to meet him like that . . . he can be difficult.'

'He was all right, but he said he was the gardener, or something very like that,' Hester insisted. 'Who's called John, then?'

'There ain't no John up there, nor no gardener, and there ain't no visitors neither,' Matthew insisted. 'It were Mr Geraint up to his games, I'll swear it were. As for Mrs Cledwen, she's a relative, so I believe, yet she's a sort of housekeeper too, as you can see. I don't understand it too well meself, but she's been up there three year, now, and the old man hasn't married her nor turned her out. Ne'er mind them, Hester love, come and have your tea. We can sort it out later.'

Hester did not know quite what he meant by sort it out, but she obediently sat down by the fire and drank her tea, glad of the warmth but gradually aware that she ached all over, that she had skinned her knee on the garden path and that her stings were throbbing. She could not believe that her John was Matthew's Mr Geraint, but what did it matter, after all? She would find out in the fullness of time and right now the cheese sandwich was tasty and it was good to relax by the fire after her adventurous evening. Now and then she glanced at Matthew, uneasily aware that he was feeling rather pleased with himself, though she could not think why this should be.

'Matthew? Why do you think it was Mr Geraint I saw? I've been thinking and maybe it was me who said he was the gardener, but he never said I was wrong and he definitely said his name was John.'

'There isn't a gardener and there's no one up there named John,' Matthew said patiently. 'That'll be the old man, playin'

55

silly beggars. Finished wi' your cup? Want me to bring Helen through?'

Hester sat very still; something was definitely up, Matthew looked so pleased with himself, yet a little apprehensive with it.

'What have you been up to, Matt?' she said suspiciously. 'I'll go through to the small bedroom and do Helen there.'

Matthew cleared his throat.

'I moved your stuff through; the bed's stripped down and the cradle's on the bedstead,' he said. 'You're comin' back in wi' me tonight, Hester love.'

Hester got to her feet. She went through to the small room and picked the baby out of the cradle. A glance confirmed what Matthew had said; the room was just the baby's room, now. All her personal possessions, even the cracked swing mirror on the oak stand, had disappeared. She carried the child, rosy with sleep and reluctant to wake, back into the kitchen and sat down in her chair. Matthew was washing up their teacups and her sandwich plate. He clattered dishes as she fed the baby, washed her and changed her, puffing talcum on to her pink bottom, swaddling it in a nappy. Without a word Matthew worked around her, preparing for the night, making up the fire, getting out the breakfast dishes, never glancing across at her once, behaving as though she was not there. She contemplated telling Matthew that she intended to sleep in the small room a little while longer, but she was too tired to start remaking the single bed, far too tired for an argument. Besides, she had always known she would have to move back some day, so why not now?

She tucked Helen up, then sighed and went through into the main bedroom. Matthew was washing, his broad back, which tapered so surprisingly to such narrow hips, turned towards her, soap suds frilled around the base of his neck. He continued to wash while she changed and got into bed, her cotton nightie rucking around her knees and being hastily pulled down to her ankles again.

Matthew finished washing. He took his trousers off; she could tell what he was doing though she was steadfastly regarding the wall, and pulled his nightshirt over his head. Then he climbed into bed. Presently he turned over and put an arm across her.

'Hester?'

'Yes, Matthew?'

'It's nice to 'ave you back beside me. You all right? Tired?'

She was tempted to answer the unspoken question rather than the spoken one with a sharp, 'No I don't feel like any of that old messing about, so leave me alone, I'm here to sleep,' but she thought of John with his thick, grey-streaked hair, the way he had held her, caressed her. She had not refused him, not pulled back as quickly as she ought, so she should not refuse this man who had given her his name, who had fathered her darling Helen.

'I'm fine, Matt,' she whispered. 'It's nice to be back beside you too.'

He rolled over and took her in his arms. She could feel his mounting desire, knew he would harness it if she so wished. Instead, she moved her body against his and put her mouth to the base of his throat, licking the little hollow there, kissing up until she reached the lobe of his ear, taking it between her teeth, giving it little mock-fierce bites.

He groaned deep in his throat and rolled her on to her back, then began to caress her. He tried to take her nightdress off gently, then lost patience with it and tugged it free, nearly removing both her ears in the process. She squeaked and complained, then laughed and grabbed his ears, only somehow the horseplay turned into loveplay and suddenly, before she really knew what had happened, they were making love, their movements at once sweet and fiery, their mouths melting as limbs tangled, hearts pounded, and the rush of their mutual desire mounted and peaked into ecstasy.

'Hester, Hester, I love you more'n anything in the world,' Matthew muttered as they lay quiet at last. 'I'd die for you, Hester.'

Hester sat up and patted his cheek, then struggled into her nightgown and lay down again, curling round him.

'Don't be daft,' she said drowsily. 'I don't want anyone to

die for me. And I don't want to die for anyone else either. Let's go to sleep now; Helen will be shouting at six.'

Matthew chuckled. 'Eh, I'm a lucky chap. G'night, Hester love.'

'Goodnight, Matthew.'

His breathing steadied and deepened. Hester lay awake for a little longer, puzzling over her day, but soon enough it no longer seemed to matter. Whether she loved Matthew truly, or just loved being a married lady, whether she could have resisted John's blandishments had they continued, whether she was a good girl or a bad; none of those things mattered, not really. She was comfortable, her body warmed by lovemaking, her mind relaxed by it. Soon she slept, a hand pillowed beneath her cheek.

Rather to her own surprise, Hester enjoyed working at the castle. And the half-crown, though she had been prepared to despise it, made a considerable difference to their finances. It enabled her to buy meat more than once a week, and to splash out, now and then, on fruit, or a vegetable other than cabbage or carrots. What was more, Mrs Cledwen welcomed Hester's company and before long she and Hester were, if not friends, at least on moderately friendly terms.

Hester, scrubbing her way across the kitchen, the hallway, up the big stairs and around the gallery, did not discover precisely what Mrs Cledwen's relationship was with their employer, nor did she find out whether her John and Matthew's Mr Geraint were one and the same, since for the first month she worked at the castle Mr Geraint was in London, attending to business. But since no John appeared when she went to the back door and called the men in for elevenses she began to conclude, reluctantly, that John was Mr Geraint and that he had deliberately deceived her.

'If that fellow – who told me his name was John, that one – really is Mr Geraint, then why do you call him the old man?' she asked Matthew crossly one day as the two of them sat at the kitchen table, eating cauliflower cheese and frizzled-up bacon pieces. 'Because he's not old really, is he?'

Matthew chuckled and crunched bacon. A thread of fat ran down his chin and Hester leaned over and wiped it off as though he were no older than Helen, tutting at him.

'He *is* old, love. He's pushin' fifty.'

'Well, he doesn't look it,' she said obstinately.

Nor act it, she thought, eating cauliflower cheese, but she kept such thoughts to herself. It was a lot easier to forget how she had felt in John's arms when he wasn't there, but she had always known, of course, that such expert and practised lovemaking denoted a misspent past at least. He was a rake, a seducer of little girls, but he had roused feelings in her which she had never known she possessed, filled her with desires which it seemed only he could satisfy. Matthew's lovemaking, his solid, dependable affection, paled into insignificance beside the inferno of feeling which his master had aroused. Indeed, though she never allowed herself to acknowledge it, deep inside her she knew that when Matthew made love to her it was of John that she thought, it was his body she responded to when she and Matthew lay together.

She was not sorry that she and Mr Geraint had not encountered each other since that first evening at the castle because she had not, as yet, decided what attitude she should take when next they met. She would be cold, that went without saying, but should she show that she knew? Or should she pretend she still thought him a gardener, an employee of the big house like herself? And then there was Mrs Cledwen; how would she feel if Mr Geraint behaved affectionately towards his scrubbing woman while she, who appeared to have a much closer relationship with their employer, stood by? All in all, keeping well clear of Mr Geraint seemed the safest thing to do. In the meantime, life had to be lived, so Hester went off to work each day at ten, and earned her half-crown. She worked hard and uncomplainingly, partly because she needed the money and more, perhaps, because a huge curiosity about the castle and those who lived there drove her. But for that first month she found out nothing new, though she did get to know the castle quite well.

The big kitchen was the heart of the house for her, for

Matthew on the rare occasions when he entered the premises, and for Willi and Dewi Evans, who worked with Matthew on the land. Mrs Cledwen was very much the boss so far as Hester and the men were concerned and this, it appeared, was quite usual.

'The old man comes out from time to time, tells us what he wants done,' Matthew confirmed, 'but the little, everyday things he tells Mrs Cled and she passes them on to we.'

Once a week, after she had finished in the big kitchen and the drawing-room, Hester had to scrub her way across the black and white tiles of the hall, up the graciously curved staircase and along the upper gallery. She had been told by Matthew that the bedrooms were in a bad state of repair but since she never saw a door open, she was unable to agree or disagree with that statement. And despite her hopes, Mrs Cledwen kept a close eye on her when she was upstairs, so she didn't get the chance of a quiet snoop.

Downstairs, however, was a different matter. One afternoon, when she had worked past her usual time to oblige Mrs Cledwen, Hester asked if she might see the great hall and was told, abruptly, that she might please herself. Interpreting this as permission, Hester went through the small, heavy oak door and saw for herself the vanished splendour, the roof open to the sky, the birds swooping and quarrelling in the rafters, the pigeon-droppings underfoot. She smelt the smell of damp and decay and mourned the passing of what must once have been a magnificent sight, for even though the wood was riddled with worm and dry rot the carvings remained, still complete in places, the serene faces of saints and the mild countenances of animals gazing out across the ruin of a once-beautiful room.

There were other ruins too. Rooms open to the four winds, their rafters rotting, plaster crumbling, floorboards a danger to any but the lightest of footsteps. The old man had managed to rescue a dairy, a shippon, a couple of cowsheds and some stabling, but with only Willi, Dewi and Matthew to see to it all, it was a constant fight against the elements, the proverbial bad luck of the farming fraternity and the fickleness of supply and demand, just to keep the place going and pay the wages.

And that was the farming side of things; the house, with only Hester to scrub and Mrs Cledwen to manage, was clearly in a parlous state.

'Cursed it is, see, girl,' Willi told her, when they were chatting over a cup of tea, Mrs Cledwen having gone off with Matthew to town to buy provisions. 'Long ago a nun was ravished by the lord of Pengarth here, and with her dying breath she cursed the castle and them that live 'ere. That's why they can't get no girls from the village to housemaid up at Pengarth. They won't live in, see, and it's too far to walk each day.'

'Nonsense, Willi. I walk, don't I? And you and your brother walk,' Hester said bracingly. 'Besides, if the nun was ravished how could she curse the castle?'

Willi looked shifty; Hester concluded that she had caught him out and stopped believing a word he said, even when she discovered that being ravished wasn't quite the same as having a sword thrust through your heart.

'Though to a nun, it might be worse, I suppose,' Mrs Cledwen said, having enlightened Hester as to ravishment in general and the ravishing of a nun in particular. 'They're brides of Christ, so possibly . . . but there, it's just a foolish tale told by foolish and ignorant people. The reason we've no live-in servants is because Mr Geraint would sooner spend money on his land than on his home.'

'I've never seen Mr Geraint,' Hester observed. She was cleaning the cutlery with a saucerful of pink powder and water and enjoying the chance to sit down, though she had done her scrubbing work first and, strictly speaking, should have been on her way back to get Matthew's dinner. But Mrs Cled was fair and always paid her extra when she worked late, and besides, if she was still working at one o'clock she would get fed here, which was a rare treat, for Mrs Cled could make a delicious meal out of almost anything. 'He's away a lot, isn't he?'

'Even when he's home you won't see much of him; he's writing a book,' Mrs Cledwen said. 'He spends a lot of time in the little room over the arch – the gatehouse room. But he doesn't usually leave the old place much; this past month he's been in London. He has money invested and solicitors, men of business, to visit. He likes to keep an eye on them.'

'What's the book about?' Hester asked. She had soon discovered that Mrs Cledwen liked talking cosily, in the kitchen; she must be as lonely as I am, Hester concluded. It did not occur to her that, with Matthew and the baby, she could scarcely count herself as lonely. 'Is it a story-book . . . fiction, I mean?'

Mrs Cledwen laughed. 'Since it's about Mr Geraint's family it's probably both – a story-book and fiction, I mean,' she said. 'I told him that what he doesn't know he shouldn't make up, but he got annoyed, so I left it. You may not see much of him even when he comes back from London, but when you do you'll discover he's a strange man, full of wild ideas.'

'I've got a few wild ideas myself,' Hester said comfortably, rubbing hard at the bowl of a huge silver spoon. 'It's all you can have, once you're married, with your own baby.'

'Yes, I suppose . . . you've never told me much about yourself, Hester. I know you were at a convent school in Liverpool, but I don't know anything else and you never talk about a family, brothers or sisters. Here, you'll rub right through that spoon in a minute, the bowl's thin enough as it is. Have a couple of forks.'

She passed them over and Hester finished the big spoon and laid it reverently back in the long, baize-lined box.

'There isn't much to tell,' Hester said, starting on the forks. There was no reason, however, to confess to her deplorably pitiful past since Mrs Cledwen was only asking out of idle curiosity, so Hester squared her shoulders and put her fertile imagination to work. 'I was an only child, my mother died when I was very small, my father was a soldier, so my paternal grandmother brought me up. Well, I say that, but really the nuns brought me up, because grandmama, though she adored me, was crippled with rheumatism and confined to a wheelchair. Of course grandmama was awfully kind to me, she read me stories and sent me off to the zoo with her servant, or to the pantomime in the winter, but in the summer I usually spent the long holiday in Rhyl with my other gran.'

'And was she a kind woman? Did you enjoy your time with her?' Mrs Cled asked. 'It sounds a very varied sort of childhood, Hester.'

'Yes, I suppose it was. But it was quite fun, really,' Hester said, polishing forks and blessing the inventive streak which had so often got her into trouble in the past. She might have known it would be useful some day despite the unkind things the nuns had said about little liars. 'Grandmother Sybil – my Rhyl grandmama – used to cook me marvellous meals and gave me a great deal of freedom. She didn't mind me playing out most of the day and scarcely ever made me come home by a set time, though she liked me indoors before dark. But the evenings are long in the summer time, and anyway, when I was older I used to go to my room, then climb out through the window and slide down the kitchen roof and escape. I went to the dances, the cinema, the pier-shows; that was how I met Matthew. But when I was younger I loved the sea, the sand, and freedom to be with other kids. I spent my pocket money on cream ices and donkey rides, and I went on the funfair till my money ran out and then hung about down by the railway station, carrying luggage for a penny. In Rhyl I was far freer and happier than in Liverpool – I liked being with Grandmother Sybil much better than with grandmama, though they were both good to me in their way.'

'It sounds wonderful,' Mrs Cledwen said. She was embroidering a large tablecloth and delicately stitching at a golden butterfly. She bit off her silk and held the needle up to the light to rethread it with a different shade. 'How often do you visit your Rhyl grandma now that you live so close to the town?'

There was a moment's silence; Hester's fingers stopped their work for a second or so, then she resumed her polishing with redoubled vigour.

'Oh, didn't I say? Sadly, she passed on just before Matthew and I were married.'

'And your Liverpool grandma? Have you taken her greatgrandchild visiting yet?'

'My Liverpool grandmama didn't approve of my marriage,' Hester said sadly, laying the clean fork back among its fellows. 'She said if I married Matthew I need never darken her doors again; so I haven't, of course. But perhaps one day, when Helen's a bit older, we might go back. Mrs Cled, do you have brothers and sisters?'

'I've sisters, two of them, both married,' Mrs Cledwen said. 'I go and visit them a couple of times a year, but they've grown very staid, with successful husbands and a clutch of children. They consider me, well, shall we say rather unconventional?'

'Why?' Hester asked baldly.

'Well, it's a little unusual for a woman of my age to reside in a bachelor household,' Mrs Cledwen said, dimpling at Hester. 'My sisters would be happier if I was to marry, settle down. But what would Mr Geraint do without me? He wasn't cut out to make meals or darn socks.'

'I supposed he could get another housekeeper,' Hester observed. 'Or he could marry, perhaps.'

Mrs Cledwen had been smiling; the smile cut out as though someone had switched it off. She bent her head so that her face was hidden and Hester could see only the crown of her dark head. Without looking up, she spoke. 'No. He's not the marrying kind. And now, if you've finished those forks I'll give them a wash in warm soapy water before returning them to their drawer.'

Feeling unaccountably chastened, Hester gathered up the forks and laid them on the draining board, tipped the rest of her saucerful of pink plate polish down the sink and rinsed her hands under the tap. Then she turned to the older woman once more.

'All right if I go now, Mrs Cled? Matthew's awfully good, but he does like his dinner by one o'clock.'

Mrs Cledwen had tidied away her silks and was folding her tablecloth. She smiled pleasantly at Hester.

'Yes dear, you run off now. I'll see you at ten o'clock tomorrow.'

Making her way down the drive with Helen sitting up and staring around her, Hester thought that perhaps she should not have mentioned those grandmothers; too easy to check. Still, Mrs Cled shouldn't have been so nosy – but then I shouldn't have upset her. Yet what had she said? Only that if Mrs Cledwen was to leave him, Mr Geraint could marry or get another housekeeper. Perhaps it had been a bit tactless, but not unkind surely?

'Dadadada,' Helen burbled, reaching for the woolly bobble which Hester had painstakingly made and hung on the front of the pram. 'Dadadada!'

'Oh, you!' Hester said, leaning forward across the handle of the pram and kissing Hester's small button nose. 'You don't care for anything or anyone, do you? You'll never invent a couple of grandmothers and a whole interesting childhood, not if it were ever so. But then you won't need to, my honey-pot darling.'

And Helen, beaming and chattering in baby-talk, seemed to agree that she most certainly would not.

Three

It was a beautiful spring day with a breeze coming off the distant sea and golden sunshine pouring down on the lodge and its struggling garden while the birds sang their hearts out and flirted and courted around Hester's cherished vegetable patch. It was the sort of day when seaside holidays and other excitements come to mind and though Hester, fastening Helen into her pram, was only going to work, she felt a glow of vicarious pleasure because today Mrs Cledwen was going off to stay with her family for a week or so, leaving Hester, if not in charge, at least to her own devices so far as cleaning went.

'No pram, no pram,' Helen shouted as her mother lifted her up. She wriggled impatiently. 'Nell walk!'

'No, love, it's too far. Just sit in the pram for a bit, then when we reach the lamb field you may walk.'

'Wanna walk,' Helen whined as Hester tied her securely into the pram. 'Nell wanna walk.'

Helen had been too much of a mouthful for a small child so the baby had christened herself Nell and although Hester had been sad, at first, to lose the name she had chosen so carefully, Nell was a lot easier to shout – and now that the baby was toddling Hester found herself shouting a good deal.

'Well, you shall walk, sweetheart. When we get to the lamb field.'

'Nell wanna walk now,' Helen insisted, trying to wriggle out of the piece of washing line which Hester had secured under her arms. 'I's big girl . . . wanna *walk*!'

'We'll pick some dandelion leaves for the lambs,' Hester said, beginning to push the heavy old pram round the side of the lodge and out on to the drive. Experience had taught her that arguing with Helen, young though she was, seldom resulted in victory and usually meant frayed tempers all round. I don't know where she gets her pig-headedness from but it isn't me, and I don't really think it comes from Matthew either, Hester thought as Helen continued to try to escape from her bonds. I suppose it's from way back. Perhaps my father was obstinate and my mother weak-willed, and the strain was mixed in me but came through truer in Helen. Or perhaps old Mr Coburn was a tartar, or Mrs Coburn . . .

'Feed lambs?'

Helen, who had earlier seemed to brush aside her mother's remark, now repeated it thoughtfully, a smile spreading across her small triangular face. She was not a pretty child in the accepted sense of the word, but she was a fascinating little creature. At her age, most children had baby hair, soft and fluffy, but Helen's black and silky crop had grown until Hester had been forced to cut it into a fringe. This made the child look like a Dutch doll, especially so today because she was wearing a white cotton bonnet which she had tugged rakishly over one eye. Hester straightened it and kissed her daughter's small nose.

I don't know where she got those eyebrows from either, Hester thought, pushing the pram into the drive. They were strongly marked for a baby, winging above the slanting, amber-coloured eyes which were the only feature, Hester concluded wryly, that she had passed on to her daughter.

'Mummy, Nell feed lambs?'

The shrill little voice showed no signs of developing temper now; she could be distracted by guile, and she adored animals. She was at that age when she was closer to her father's skinny border collie and Mrs Cledwen's ginger tom-cat than she was to anyone else.

'Yes, you shall feed the lambs. I'll pick some dandelion leaves when we reach the drive and you may hand them over. Only we mustn't be long or Mrs Cled will be cross with me, because she's off on her holidays today and won't thank me if I make her late.'

Helen chuckled and pointed over the side of the pram at

a clump of primroses growing at the foot of the wall which surrounded the lodge.

'Feed lambs?'

'Yes, but not with primroses; lambs don't like primroses. When we reach the dandelions I'll tell you, pet.'

A short way up the drive she saw the dandelions, flowerless but growing strongly in the short wiry grass. She put the brake on the pram and bent to pick. Behind her, Helen squeaked and struggled.

'My pick, my pick,' she shouted urgently. 'Nell . . . get . . . out!'

'Not yet, sweetheart . . .' Hester was beginning when she heard a loud thump. Heart in mouth, she turned. The pram was upside down on the gravel and from beneath it there came no sound.

Matthew had driven Mr Geraint into St Asaph in the Lagonda early that morning to take a look at the sheep on sale in the market. The flock on offer had not been particularly impressive, but Mr Geraint had also wanted breeding sows and had fallen for the charms of a couple of in-pig gilts, Tamworths with bristly ginger bodies and the tiny, squinty eyes of their kind. Having bought them on sight, they loaded the young sows into the trailer and decided to go straight back to the castle to settle them into their new home. Normally, they would have stayed in St Asaph, having a pint at The Plough at lunchtime, maybe even a round or two of their speciality, raw beef sandwiches, but the pigs were good ones and Mr Geraint was obviously itching to see them in his newly restored sties.

'Everything's ready for 'em,' he remarked to Matthew as they removed the ramp and closed the gate across the end of the trailer. 'No point in hanging around here. You can have a meal with Willi and Dewi up at the castle if your wife's not prepared anything.'

Matthew stiffened a little.

'Hester always does a dinner,' he said. 'If she's workin' over I'll get it a mite late, mebbe, but it'll be there.'

Mr Geraint shot him an amused look, one eyebrow hiked up.

Matthew knew just what expression would be on his employer's face even though he had not taken his eyes from the road ahead. Mr Geraint hardly ever mentioned Hester, but when he did he often looked . . . oh, mocking, as though he doubted the girl's ability, not just as a housewife but in other spheres too.

Matthew frowned at the ignoble thought. They had the child, surely Helen was proof enough that he and Hester enjoyed an active married life? But it was Mr Geraint's way to mock; he should take it in his stride, ignore it. It was only because his Hester was so young that he felt he must defend her, even against a criticism which was covert, never put into words.

'Why should she cook a midday meal on market day, when she doesn't expect you home until late afternoon?' Mr Geraint asked equably. 'I don't doubt she has something hot for you each evening.'

The words were innocent enough but the tone was not; Matthew actually took his eyes off the road to shoot a fulminating look at his employer. What was he up to now? Why couldn't he save his breath to cool his porridge?

'She's a good girl,' he heard himself saying, his tone almost defensive. 'We do right well, me an' Hester.'

'My dear chap, who am I to suggest otherwise? I believe Mrs Cledwen is very pleased with her work, so I'm sure I've no possible grounds for complaint. No, what worries me at the moment is whether we should put both gilts in one pen or whether they would be better apart?'

'Ask Dewi,' Matthew said grumpily, though he would not have put a couple of in-pig gilts in the same pen himself for fear of fights and rollings-on when the sows farrowed. 'He's your pig-man; tes all one to me.'

'You're good with stock, better than Dewi. I thought you might give me the benefit of your experience.'

It was mildly said, and Matthew knew that the glance which accompanied the words would be rueful, almost apologetic. The old man was a card all right, he'd needle you and needle you to get a sharp response and then, when he did, he'd be sorry, couldn't wait to set all straight again. Mrs Cled said it was because he didn't have sufficient employment, that his brain was so quick it sought any means of amusement, but he, Matthew, didn't know about that. All he knew was that Mr Geraint could be a real bugger at times.

'Matt?'

'Keep 'em apart, then,' Matthew said gruffly. 'Next sty, so's they can see each other, touch through the bars, even. But apart, so there's no fighting.'

'Good man; that was my own thought but I'm still a beginner with pigs. Now you've bred pigs, so what do you think of the Tamworth as a breed?'

It was a question after Matthew's own heart and he answered it seriously, happy to mull over the advantages of Large Whites, Gloucester Spots, Tamworths and Landrace whilst Mr Geraint listened, argued and became absorbed. They were still deep in discussion as they swung into the drive, Matthew slowing automatically as they passed the lodge. He glanced into the front room as he always did, but could see nothing, no movement, no duster being rubbed over the panes or broom-wielding figure attacking the carpet. Of course Hester might be in the kitchen, but likelier she was either on her way to the castle or there already.

As he rounded the bend in the drive Matthew changed down, noticing that there was an obstruction on the road ahead, something oddly boat-shaped. He saw Hester bending over it, saw her reach down – and recognised the inverted pram. He slammed on the brakes and the heavy car screeched to a halt a foot or two away from the accident. Beside him, Mr Geraint looked over his shoulder.

'Damn you, Matthew, think of the ladies in the trailer! They're in a delicate condition, remember, if you . . .'

'It's Nell. Hester love . . . I'm coming!'

Matthew was out of the car and running whilst Mr Geraint was still speaking. He had guessed what must have happened in that first shocked glance. The pram had obviously overturned and his wife was tugging frantically at it the way a woman would instead of lifting it carefully away from – from whatever lay beneath.

70

He picked Hester up as though she weighed no more than the baby, stood her to one side, then bent over the pram.

'She'll be all right, love, just stand back, soon have it . . . ah!'

He righted the pram, great, heavy thing that it was, and there lay Helen, her woollen coat dirty, her bonnet askew. Hester snatched the baby up, clutching her to her heart, murmuring endearments while tears of fear and shock ran down her pale cheeks, and as though Helen had been waiting for a signal she hiccuped, snatched some breath and began to wail. She was alive! And unhurt it seemed, save for a bruise on her forehead. Relief weakened Matthew's knees; he sagged, had to grab hold of the Lagonda's long bonnet as support.

'Oh Matt, you're so wonderful, you're always there when I need you. She turned the pram over, trying to get out to pick dandelions for the lambs . . . Oh Matt, she didn't cry or anything, I thought, I thought . . .'

Matt pushed himself away from the Lagonda and gathered his weeping wife and wailing daughter in a close embrace. He forgot Mr Geraint, the pigs in the trailer, everything. Hester's hair was against his face; it smelt sweet, and her body in his arms was sweeter still, warm and familiar. The baby, hiccuping, reached up and patted his cheek.

'Daddy, Nell walk, no pram, Nell walk!'

'No no, Nell must not walk, Nell shall ride,' a deep, amused voice said. 'Come along, little lady, you shall sit on my knee and ride up to the castle like a queen. Your mother shall push the pram while your father drives us in style.'

'She's only just two – today,' Hester said, sniffing and knuckling her wet eyes with the backs of her hands. 'She won't understand a word you've been saying, she doesn't even know what a queen is!'

She sounded resentful, Matthew thought, almost rude. But Mr Geraint had meant well, he just knew nothing about children.

'She'll soon get the idea,' Mr Geraint said cheerfully. Without asking, he took the baby neatly from Hester's arms and walked back to the car. Matthew could hear him talking to Helen as though she were an adult, telling her that there were pigs in

71

the trailer at the back so they would have to travel slowly, but even so they would reach the castle well ahead of her mother, pushing the pram.

Helen, who could be a little devil as Matthew well knew, sat placidly in Mr Geraint's arms, watching his face. When he got into the car and sat her on his knee she bounced twice, then sat still, staring curiously at the dashboard, piping up with questions now and then, which Mr Geraint's deep burr answered.

Matthew tried to give Hester another hug, but she was in one of her sudden, strange moods and pushed him away. 'Go on with you,' she said crossly and rather too loudly for Matthew's peace of mind. 'If Mr awfully-important Geraint walks off with my daughter and leaves me to push this damned pram, what can you do about it? Now don't you let him cart her off indoors, you wait for me up at the castle, the pair of you.'

'He won't want much of her company, she don't sit still for long enough,' Matthew said uncertainly, and watched Hester walk off, straight-backed, pushing the heavy pram. You could have knocked me down with a feather, he thought, seizing the starting handle and beginning to crank the engine again, when the old man took the kid from Hester – it weren't his style, not his style at all. Though Helen was a fetching little thing and the old man wasn't getting any younger; perhaps he'd begun to wish he had sprogs of his own, you could never tell, though so far as Matthew could recall Mr Geraint had never shown the slightest interest in children.

The engine coughed, spluttered, purred into life. Matthew ran for the driver's seat and Helen shouted, 'Daddy! Brrr-brrr-brrr!' Mr Geraint laughed, Matthew put the car into gear and they trundled up the drive, passing a pink-faced Hester who would not wave, though she did give Matthew a quick, almost furtive smile.

In the stableyard, Matthew tried to take the baby from his employer, but Mr Geraint was back in his needling mood and refused to relinquish the child.

'You go about your business, Matthew,' he said crisply. 'I'll just have a word with Mrs Cled before she goes. Get Dewi to give you a hand with the pigs, I want them unloaded and fed; that'll quieten them down after the journey.'

'I can tek the baby ...' Matthew began, but he was talking to empty air. Mr Geraint and his burden had disappeared into the castle.

Hester seethed all the way along the drive, across the courtyard and into the kitchen.

The cheek of the man, commandeering her baby and leaving her to walk up the drive alone. Not that she would have dared to let Helen walk, not with that great blue bruise on her forehead, and to put her back in the pram after her experience seemed rather unkind. It occurred to Hester that Helen might be concussed, though she had seemed cheery enough, prattling away and bouncing up and down on Mr Geraint's knee as though she had known him all her life.

Which she most certainly had not done, since Hester had scarcely seen Mr Geraint in the two years she had worked at the castle. Oh, he came through the hall sometimes when she was on hands and knees, scrubbing the tiles, or into the kitchen when she was up to her elbows in dirty dishes, or carting the heated iron off the stove to replace the one Mrs Cled was laying aside. And he took absolutely no notice of her; ignored her completely. She might have been a piece of furniture for all the notice he took.

Not that I want his notice, Hester reminded herself quickly. He lied to me that night in Rhyl, then again in the wild garden. Why, his name wasn't even John! He used me in Rhyl, just used me, and now perhaps he's ashamed and wants to forget – well, that's all right with me.

So they steered clear of each other and behaved like, well, like the lord of the manor and his scrubbing woman, I suppose, Hester told herself now, guiding the pram round a chunk of rock and letting it crunch sideways into an empty puddle, almost turning it over once more. If I never speak to him again, it'll be too soon. Matthew is loving, kind, a wonderful father to Nell. I don't need Mr Geraint, or his castle, though his half-crown does come in useful each Friday.

73

She and Mrs Cled never discussed Mr Geraint, though Mrs Cled sometimes made remarks which seemed to indicate that she was getting fed-up with her position at the castle. Just what that was, Hester still didn't know. Sometimes she suspected . . . but she had no proof, no proof at all. Mrs Cled was a wonderful housekeeper and manager and if she and her employer spent their evenings together in the drawing-room, why not? The tiny housekeeper's room next to the big old kitchen was not inviting, and most of its meagre space was taken up with the bedstead, a wardrobe and an old-fashioned treadle sewing machine.

Did they share more than the drawing-room, though? Did they share a bedroom − a bed? If so, it's none of my business, Hester told herself stoutly, turning to go into the back yard and then hesitating. The Lagonda was in the front yard, pulled up beside the front steps, but she had grown no fonder of the geese over the past two years and they would come running as soon as she appeared. Perhaps she would go in the back way, after all.

She turned the pram on to the narrow path, suddenly remembering vividly that first night when she had been lost and rescued by Mr Geraint. He had not only rescued her, he had clutched her. He had no right, Hester reminded herself angrily, trying to ignore the fact that even thinking about it made her stomach knot in a strange way, he had no right at all to lay hands on me. If I'd told Matthew . . .

But she hadn't, of course. It would have been pointless, especially when you considered that for two years now she had worked in Mr Geraint's house, lived a mere stone's throw away and had only exchanged the most casual of greetings with him. 'Good morning, Mr Geraint.' 'Morning, Hester.' 'Good afternoon, Mr Geraint.' 'Hello, Hester; nice afternoon.'

Sometimes I wonder if I imagined that night in Rhyl, Hester told herself crossly, clattering the pram across the paving slabs and stopping outside the back door. Or perhaps it really was a fellow called John and not Mr Geraint at all; certainly he hasn't shown the slightest interest in me since. Not that I want him to, of course; it's better that we treat each other like strangers, far better.

She had parked the pram and was approaching the back door

when it opened. Mrs Cledwen stood there in a smart, violet-coloured coat with fur round the collar and hem. She wore an elegant hat with a narrow brim and a small feather in the crown, and in one hand she carried a gladstone bag. Hester saw that her face had been carefully made up with powder, pink lip salve and a touch of rouge. She looked excited and a trifle impatient.

'Good morning Hester, you're a little late. I'm just off. I've left a list of instructions for you and a letter for Mrs Bellis, who will arrive later this morning, I believe. I don't think there should be any problems, but if there are have a word with Mr Geraint. Where's Nell? Not actually sleeping, surely?'

Hester laughed. Helen had now given up her morning nap and spent the time between ten and one in a play-pen which Mrs Cledwen had found, frequently throwing toys on to the hearth-rug and demanding their return at the top of her healthy lungs. She was well on the way to being spoilt, but school would change that; in the meantime, Hester enjoyed watching her as she became dexterous, began to talk, experimented with every-thing she touched.

'No, she isn't asleep. There was a bit of an accident, that's why I'm late. The baby wanted to climb down and managed to turn the pram over, so Matthew stopped the car and righted it for me and Mr Geraint gave her a lift. I expect she's in the drawing-room.'

'Is she all right? Little monkey, whatever will she think of next? I'll miss her while I'm away — and you, my dear — but I really must be off or I shan't catch my bus. If I'd known Mr Geraint was coming back so early from the market I'd have begged a lift from Matthew, but as it is I'd better hurry.'

'When are you coming back?' Hester said, picking up the gladstone bag. 'This is quite heavy, Mrs Cled; Matthew's parked round the front, why not get him to take you at least as far as the bus stop? Or I could wheel your bag in the pram if you'd rather. Only I'll have to fetch Nell first, of course.'

'Coming back? Oh, in a week or so,' Mrs Cledwen said vaguely. 'Let's see how Matthew is situated, then. If he's very busy I'll manage my bag somehow, but if he's got a moment I would appreciate a lift.'

The two women walked across the back yard, out under the arch, and along the winding path through the wild gardens. It was a sweet, sunny morning and a heavy dew still bowed the heads of the narcissus, the patches of bluebells, the tall, purple irises which throve in the beds despite the choking brambles and the insidious march of nettles and dock.

'I keep meaning to do some tidying out here,' Mrs Cledwen murmured. 'I believe it was very lovely once. You're fond of gardening, aren't you, Hester; perhaps we might tackle it together when the longer evenings arrive.'

'It'll need double-digging,' Hester observed. In two short years she had discovered that there was nothing romantic about growing things. It meant hard work – digging, manuring, planting out, constant weeding – and then you reaped only half of what you had sown, what with rabbits, slugs and other pests. 'Still, I wouldn't mind having a go, Mrs Cled.'

'I'll have a word with Mr Geraint when I come back,' Mrs Cled observed. 'Ah, Matthew!'

They had rounded the corner and were entering the front courtyard under the big arch and there was Matthew, just coming down the front steps. He grinned at Hester and made a vague salute-type gesture in Mrs Cledwen's general direction.

'Mornin', Mrs Cled. Mr Geraint said if you hadn't left I might as well give you a lift, 'cos he wants me to pick up a Mrs Bellis at the station. She's the lady what'll be looking after us till you return, I reckon.'

'Where's Nell?' Hester said before Mrs Cledwen could reply. 'Have you put her in her play-pen or is she tied into her high-chair? Because you know what a one she is now for getting about, she'll . . .'

'She's in the drawing-room wi' Mr Geraint,' Matthew said reassuringly. 'He's reading to her from a book of fairytales. You can fetch her out if you want, but she's rare happy, Hester.'

'Oh, all right,' Hester said lamely. 'I'll get her presently. Why were you back so soon from the market, Matthew? You don't usually get home until after our dinnertime.'

'The sheep weren't up to much, but we bought some pigs. Here, give us that bag, it looks 'eavy. Hop into the car, Mrs

Cledwen, and I'll run you to the station. If you're early for your train, at least you can leave your bag and get yourself a cup of tea and a cake whiles you wait.'

'Thanks, Matthew,' Mrs Cledwen said. 'Goodbye, Hester. Take good care of yourself and keep an eye on Mrs Bellis.'

They both waved and Mrs Cledwen cranked her window down and leaned out. 'Give Nell a kiss for me,' she commanded. 'I'll miss you both, dear.'

'Oh, a week or so will soon go,' Hester said cheerfully. 'Have a lovely holiday, Mrs Cledwen! Goodbye, goodbye!'

She was still gazing after the car when the geese came hissing and wheezing round the corner of the arch, so with one last wave, and a menacing gesture towards the geese, Hester trotted back through the wild garden, across the yard and into the kitchen.

Her list was on the table, weighted down by the salt cellar and side by side with a letter in a large white envelope addressed, in Mrs Cled's flourishing hand, to Mrs Ena Bellis. Hester glanced at the list, then went across to fill the kettle and put it on the range. It was a huge blackened thing which took its time to reach the boil, but by the time it did so Matthew would be back with Mrs Bellis and everyone would be glad of a cup of tea.

Hester's last job the previous day had been to fill the six buckets at the pump; she glanced at them and five were still full, so that was one job which could wait until later. Now, she tipped one of the buckets into the kettle, then stood another on the top of the range, as near the heat as she could get it. If Mrs Cled had seen her there would have been a row, but Hester needed hot water for cleaning and boiling up a bucket was a quick way of getting it, even if it did weaken the bucket as the housekeeper claimed. While the cat's away, Hester concluded, pushing the kettle over so that the bucket got a bit more heat and then heading for the kitchen door. Not that Mrs Cledwen was in the least catlike; as employers went she was a good one. We get on well, Hester reminded herself with a hand on the latch, but now I'd best get Helen off Mr Geraint before he gets cross with me for leaving her so long.

She was familiar with the drawing-room, of course. She often cleaned out the grate, laid a new fire and then lit it, taking the ashes through to throw on the paths of the wild garden, one of her more sensible attempts to make sure her way out was not completely overgrown. But as she reached the door, she hesitated. She had never entered the room when Mr Geraint was in it; she supposed she should knock. She remembered the nuns' insistence on the children in their charge knocking at doors, speaking only when spoken to, giving a little bob of a curtsey before uttering a word and prefacing every remark with 'Please, m'm', or 'Please, sir'.

Was that how she should behave? But in her memory was that night on the sands in Rhyl and her subsequent encounter with Mr Geraint in the wild gardens. She had not behaved the way an orphan should behave on either of those occasions, so she had best act naturally now and say she had come to take Helen back to the kitchen. However, when she approached the door her courage failed her; good manners, after all, were not something which should be dispensed with just because she had met Mr Geraint on previous occasions. So she tapped on the door, waited a second, then entered.

Mr Geraint sat on the couch with Helen on his knee, an open story book before them. Helen lolled against his chest, patting his arm absently with one hand; the other, true to form, was jammed against her mouth. Thumbsucking usually preceded sleep, but Helen's round amber eyes were fixed on the book, and you could see she was following every word Geraint read.

'So then the handsome Prince leaned down out of his saddle and gave his hand to the beautiful Princess. And she leaped up, on to his noble white steed, and they rode off into the sunset. The End.'

Mr Geraint closed the book and glanced quizzically across the room at Hester. 'Have you come for the child? She's been very good.'

Helen reached for the book while Hester was saying how kind of Mr Geraint to bother but she would take Helen back to the kitchen now. While she was speaking Helen was opening the book at random and shoving it back into Mr Geraint's hands.

'More,' she announced, and leaned back again, with the air of one who expects entertainment. Hester smiled, she couldn't help herself. Trust Helen to take compliance for granted.

'No more, Nell. Your Mama has come to take you away,' Mr Geraint said. He closed the book a second time. Hester saw, with some dismay, a frown etch itself between her baby's soft brows. She tried to take the book again, but Mr Geraint placed it out of reach and stood her down on the floor. 'Off you go, littl'un,' he said firmly, 'I'm busy now.'

Previous experience had taught Hester the impossibility of reasoning with Helen when she wanted something, but to her surprise the little girl seemed to accept Mr Geraint's words as final. She set off across the floor towards her mother, holding up her arms.

'Feed lambs?' she said. 'Nell feed lambs?'

'Later, sweetheart,' Hester said diplomatically. 'Mummy has some work to do first.' She picked Helen up and sat her on her hip, then kissed the top of the child's silky head. 'Thank you for looking after her, Mr Geraint. Say goodbye, darling.'

'Bye, man,' Helen said briefly. 'Nell feed lambs *now*, Mummy.'

Carrying her out of the room, doing her best to explain again that work had to come first, Hester heard Mr Geraint's quiet laughter behind her. It sounded mocking.

'Say "Mummy", darling. Come on, say "Mummy", and Mummy will make you a daisy-chain so splendid that you'll look like a little queen! Come on, sweetheart, upsadaisy!'

Constance and her sister-in-law, Ella, were sitting on the bank of the river Yare a couple of miles from Goldenstone, with their small daughters playing on a rug at their feet. Over their heads arched the blue Norfolk sky and standing beside them were two push-chairs. Constance bent, plucked Anna from the grass and buried her face in the child's sweet-smelling neck, blowing a raspberry against the soft skin. Anna gave a bubbling trill of laughter and clutched a handful of her mother's golden hair, then laughed again as it slid through her fingers.

'Ma-ma-ma,' she crooned. 'Ba-ba-ba . . .'

Ella bent over and grabbed Nancy, who was about to set

off, fat-legged, pink-cheeked, to find fresh amusement.

'No you don't, young lady! Come and persuade your little cousin to say "Mummy", darling. Nancy can say "Mummy" beautifully, can't you, my sweet?'

'Nancy's three,' Constance pointed out, cuddling Anna for a moment longer and then setting her back on the rug. 'When Anna's three she'll probably talk just as nicely as Nancy. But she does seem rather slow; she's only just got all her front teeth and a couple of back ones. How old was Nancy when she started to talk, Ella?'

'She was talking at about eighteen months, but she had the boys, remember. Older children teach the younger ones more than you know. Why, William said almost nothing until he was two and a half, and he wasn't dry until well after his third birthday. You just can't generalise with kids.'

Nancy, small, dark and active, got to her feet and grabbed at the handful of daisies Constance had been building into a chain of mammoth proportions. She held them up and let them swing over the younger child's head.

'Here you are, baby Anna,' she said, bending over to smile straight into her cousin's face. 'Nancy's giving you a pretty present. Take it, little Anna.'

Anna made her cooing noise again and chubby hands, star-fished, reached for the flowers. Nancy drew them back a little.

'Say "Mummy",' she commanded coaxingly. 'Say "Mummy" for Nancy.'

'Ma-ma-ma,' Anna said cheerfully. 'Ba-ba-ba . . .'

'She's just a baby,' Nancy said, letting her small cousin grasp the daisy-chain and plonking down beside her. 'Give Nancy a kiss, then!'

She leaned forward, offering a rosy cheek, and Anna obligingly leaned forward too and made contact. Nancy squealed and drew back.

'She kisses *wet*,' she said forcefully, rubbing her cheek with the back of her hand. 'Only babies kiss wet. Can I have a bicky?'

Constance giggled.

'It isn't only babies, unfortunately,' she said to her sister-in-law, reaching into the basket which contained their picnic tea.

She found the nursery biscuits with the picture of a cow on one side and a sheaf of wheat on the other and handed one to her niece. 'Have you ever been kissed by Sammy Firth-Askew?'

Ella, who was ten years Constance's senior, smiled but shook her head.

'No, indeed! He's one of JJ's repellent little friends, isn't he? I don't think he had come on the scene before I left to marry Philip.'

'Well, take it from me, he kisses wet,' Constance said. She leaned over and ruffled Anna's mop of dark gold curls. 'Anna's kisses are damp and sweet, but Sammy's are wet and smothering and – and forceful.' She looked plaintively across at her sister-in-law. 'He traps me, you know. He lurks when he comes over to see JJ and he lurks when we go over to see his parents.' She shuddered. 'Odious young man!'

'Funny you should say that,' Ella said thoughtfully. She took a bottle of milk out of the basket and poured some into a mug, which she handed to her small daughter. 'Don't spill it, darling,' she said. 'Would Anna like some milk, now?'

Anna reached out both hands and made cooing noises so her aunt filled a beaker and handed it to her.

'Carefully, sweetness,' Constance said. 'Oh, quick, a bib – that pink dress is a fiend to iron, Nanny says.' A bib was produced and tied around Anna's chubby neck. The two young women waited until their offspring were deep in milk and biscuits, Anna scattering both freely, then Ella resumed her interrupted conversation.

'As I was saying, it's funny you should mention Sammy, because to be honest my dear, there has been some talk. Mother mentioned in confidence that she came out of our drawing-room a few weeks back and there were you and Sammy . . . she said you sprang apart!'

'Mother shouldn't say horrid things about me,' Constance said. She could feel the heat rising in her cheeks, and guessed her eyes were shiny with embarrassment. 'Who else has she told? Why on earth didn't she ask me? I'd have told her Sammy was a pest.'

'I'm sure she's only told me,' Ella said hastily. She took the flask of tea out of the hamper and stood it on the bank beside her, then fished out the red bakelite picnic cups. 'She said she did try to say something, but you cut her off short.'

'She asked me if I liked Sammy, and I didn't cut her off short at all, I just said, rather sharply, that he was a friend of JJ's and thus a friend of mine,' Constance said. 'Ella, what else could I say? It's awfully awkward because he and JJ are very thick.'

'Perhaps you should tell JJ,' Ella said slowly. 'He could warn Sammy off better than anyone else could.'

'Yes, but he mightn't believe me. He might think I was getting back at him for . . . for things,' Constance said vaguely. 'You must know your brother well enough to guess that he's no angel himself. If I said anything about Sammy – well, it would look like a dig, don't you think?'

'Connie, what on earth do you mean? You're not trying to say that JJ still squeezes kitchen maids?'

'I mean he does much more than squeeze, and not just kitchen maids, either. But what's the point in talking about it? I knew when we got married that he had a roving eye, I just didn't realise that three years and a child later he would still – well, you know.'

'But mother said he was a changed person, so attentive, absolutely adored the baby . . .'

'Yes, and your mother said I was having an affair with Sammy,' Constance said reproachfully. 'So I think we can discount what she says in this context at any rate. Ella, be a dear. Tell her she's mistaken and see whether you can think of anything to keep Sammy at bay.'

Ella was preparing to answer when someone hailed them. Both girls turned to the gate to the lane and there was JJ, swinging towards them in a white open-necked shirt and flannels, with a broad smile on his handsome face.

'My four favourite women,' he called. 'Hello, darling, who's come to find his golden girl, then?'

Constance felt the colour rise in her cheeks. One hand flew to her throat and she leaned forward, addressing her sister-in-law in a low whisper.

'Ella, not a word! I adore JJ, he's my life, I'll work something out. So long as I'm the most important person in his life I can put up with . . .'

The words died in her throat. JJ was dropping on his knees at the edge of the rug. He gave Constance a quick, perfunctory smile, then held out his arms.

'Who's my precious, then? Who's Daddy's golden girl?'

Anna dropped her beaker but clutched her biscuit and scrambled to her feet. She toddled across the rug and into her father's arms, cooing, laughing.

'Daddy, Daddy, Daddy,' she shouted, 'Daddy ha' bicky!'

JJ pretended to nibble the biscuit, picked his daughter up and hugged her, smiling at his wife over the top of the child's dark gold head.

'Hear that? She said "Daddy" clear as clear,' he announced. 'Come on, beautiful, let's go and paddle in the river and see if we can find some fishes.' He held out a hand to Nancy, who was staring adoringly up at him. 'You coming too, sprat?'

When they had gone Constance began to put the picnic things away. She felt slow and heavy, and the afternoon was dark suddenly, the breeze which had delighted her earlier cold and unwelcome.

JJ had everything now, even Anna. The baby would say 'Daddy', though she did not seem able to get her tongue round 'Mummy'. She remembered when she had been her husband's golden girl; now, without a thought, he walked past her and bestowed the name on her small daughter.

So why shouldn't I let Sammy pin me in corners and put his tongue in my mouth and squeeze my breasts and fumble with my directoire knickers? Constance asked herself defiantly. It's only his way of saying he admires me – thank God someone does! I just hope I put old Ella off the scent. Not that I *want* Sammy, he's a bore; it's JJ I want, but if I can't have him, oh, to hell with them all.

Mrs Bellis arrived at the castle when Hester, Dewi and Willi were sat round the kitchen table having their mid-mornings: tea in a big brown pot and slices of Mrs Cledwen's homemade currant loaf, spread thinly with margarine. On a rag rug inside her play-pen, Helen lay asleep with her toys scattered around her, worn out by her unusually active morning.

The door opened and the three at the table looked round, chewing momentarily suspended.

Mrs Bellis was a plain woman of indeterminate age, with thin grey hair scraped back from a long purplish face, a bulging body shapeless as a cottage loaf, and very large feet. She waddled into the room, told Matthew, following with her case, to 'put it in the 'ousekeeper's room, wherever that may be', and subsided into Mrs Cledwen's chair at the table without being asked.

'I'm Mrs Bellis, the actin' 'ousekeeper; cut me some cake,' she said without preamble, nodding at Hester. 'And pour me a cuppa; I'm gaspin' for a cuppa.'

'Milk, Mrs Bellis? Sugar?' Hester asked. She watched out of the corner of her eye as Mrs Bellis removed her shoes and examined her feet. Even through the flesh-coloured cotton stockings she could see the other woman's gnarled, misshapen toes and throbbing bunions. I wonder what causes bunions, Hester mused, putting both milk and sugar into Mrs Bellis's cup as commanded. I hope I don't get them when I'm old, they look painful as well as ugly.

Mrs Bellis had started to eat; she dunked the cake in the tea, an action which would have had the nuns' palms itching to slap her head had she been a child of the Sister Servina Convent. But Mrs Bellis sucked at the soggy cake and ignored the crumbs floating in the cup, though they made her choke when she began to drink her tea. Gasping, she fought to control herself as tea ran down her chin and marked the already stained collar of her blouse. It had clearly been worn for a while and had sopped up several spilt drinks already. All Hester could do was look away and try not to catch anyone's eye – what on earth had Mrs Cledwen been thinking of, to get this woman in to replace her during her absence?

'Well, miss?' Mrs Bellis had finished the cake and drunk the tea; now she turned to Hester. 'And who might you be? And these gentlemen?'

'These gentlemen are Dewi and Willi Evans, they work on the land with Matthew, he's the one who fetched you from the station. And I'm Hester Coburn, I'm the charwoman.'

Mrs Bellis leaned her elbows on the table and stared hard at Hester. She had very small pale eyes in her narrow face and Hester could not help wondering, when Mrs Bellis smiled, whether her false teeth had been originally made for a larger woman. They filled her mouth, making her look like an overcrowded graveyard.

'Hester, eh? You're a bit young for a char, ain't you?'

'I'm almost eighteen. I don't think age matters when you're scrubbing floors and lighting fires, do you?'

'No, I wouldn't say it mattered,' Mrs Bellis agreed after a moment's thought. 'I'll be glad of your young legs, I dessay. Many stairs, is there?'

'The usual number,' Hester said solemnly. 'But your room's on the ground floor.'

'Aye, so I were led to believe. But what about cleanin', eh? Will they 'spec' me to climb them stairs?'

'Only to make Mr Geraint's bed I imagine,' Hester said. Willi and Dewi were staring stolidly before them, but God alone knew what they were thinking. 'I don't think Mrs Cledwen uses the stairs much – oh, I quite forgot, there's a letter for you here.'

She handed the letter over. Mrs Bellis slit the envelope, squinted at the page for a moment, then gave a martyred sigh and handed it to Hester.

'I can't see a word without me glasses; read it out, there's a good girl. What's that Matthew doin' wi' me traps, be the way? He's bin gone a longish while.'

Hester, who had been thinking the same thing herself, was about to embark on a mythical explanation when the kitchen door opened and Matthew came into the room.

'Pour me a cup, love,' he said, sitting down in the chair by Mrs Bellis and addressing his wife. 'Mr Geraint popped out of the drawing-room as I was crossing the hall; wanted a word. It held me up.'

'Wanted to know what I was like, I dessay,' Mrs Bellis said knowledgeably, reaching across and tapping the side of the teapot with the back of her fingers. 'Is there another cup in there? I'm fair parched. Well, he'll see soon enough . . . am

I to go through?'

'He didn't say,' Matthew said uneasily. 'Better not. He'll be up in the gate-'ouse soon enough, working. Leave it till later, Mrs Bellis, when you take him his dinner.' He turned to the two men, stolidly sitting. 'Better get back to work fellers, or we won't get finished be dinnertime.'

The brothers finished their tea, pushed back their chairs and left the kitchen while Mrs Bellis poured herself another cup and then, after a moment's thought, cut a second slice of fruit loaf as well, and addressed Matthew through a full mouth.

'So you think I should meet this Mr Geraint later, eh? Well, per'aps you know best . . . wait on, the girl hasn't read me letter, yet. Come on, whatsyername, read it out.'

Hester, blushing, read the letter. It consisted mainly of menus, meal times and suggestions for shopping. Mrs Cledwen had said that she, Hester, knew her job as did the men, so Mrs Bellis would mainly have to look after Mr Geraint and see that his washing and ironing were done and his meals prepared and served on time.

'I'm a plain cook and I can't do no laundry,' Mrs Bellis announced defiantly when Hester's voice trailed into silence. 'I told that uppity woman when we met at the agency . . . a plain cook, that's me. She said it'ud do, now I'm beginnin' to wonder.'

Hester cast an anguished look at Matthew; she knew he was grinning inside. His face looked solemn enough, but Hester hadn't been married to him for two years without being able to recognise a well-buried grin.

'Matt? What should Mrs Bellis do?'

'See the old man at dinnertime, I reckon,' Matthew said. His voice was serious but the grin was still there, underneath. 'You could probably manage the laundry for a week or so, Hester, but not all the rest of the work.' He turned to Mrs Bellis. 'Mrs Cledwen does most things about the house you see, apart from the heavy scrubbing.'

'You mean his shirts and that?' Hester asked, horrified. That meant using starch, getting the iron heated just right, all the things which Mrs Cled took for granted, things Hester had never had to think about. 'Matt, I'm not sure I could. Does Mrs Cledwen make his bed, do his room? Because I've never been in there, and I don't know that I can manage that as well as all the scrubbing and the fires . . . but if Mrs Bellis can't climb the stairs . . .'

'I'll peel me own spuds and bring in the water,' Mrs Bellis offered. 'An' I'll see to cleanin' in the kitchen an' the scullery. I'll keep an eye on the kid whiles you go upstairs, too. Only me knees won't take stairs.' She eyed Hester with a mixture of pleading and calculation. 'I'll put you in for overtime. She said I were to count up the hours and let 'im know at the end of each week who'd worked what time, like. She said there wouldn't be no argy-bargy about it.'

'We'll manage,' Hester said. She felt suddenly sorry for Mrs Bellis, who had undoubtedly been chosen as the person most unlikely to catch Mr Geraint's eye, and she felt cross with Mrs Cledwen, who had given her the job with no thought for the difficulties she would make for others, such as Hester. 'Tell you what, Mrs Bellis, if Matthew's agreeable I'll come up at eight tomorrow, see how things are going for you.'

'Would you? That's kind,' Mrs Bellis said. 'She didn't oughter 'ave told me it were just plain cookin', I'd not 'ave come if I'd known. Still, if we all works together . . .'

Helen, snoozing in one corner of the play-pen, suddenly woke up and began to heave herself to her feet by grabbing the bars.

'Feed lambs,' she said, her voice still heavy with sleep. 'Nell feed lambs, Mummy!'

Hester sighed and plucked her daughter from the play-pen, cuddling her comfortingly against her breast.

'Nell go back to sleep,' she said soothingly. 'Cuddle down, sweetheart; we'll feed the lambs on our way home – remember me telling you?'

Helen, her eyelids drooping once more, stuck her thumb back in her mouth. Hester lowered her back on to the rag rug and shooed Matthew out of the back door. She tiptoed into the hall and beckoned Mrs Bellis to follow her.

'She'll probably sleep until dinnertime,' she whispered. 'So until she wakes I'll get on with my work, but first I'll take you along to the housekeeper's room.'

'It ain't much,' Mrs Bellis remarked when she stood in the small, bare room, with the unwelcoming single bed, the treadle sewing machine and the gaping wardrobe, empty now of Mrs Cledwen's possessions, if it had ever contained them, of course. 'What do she do, of an evening?'

Hester shrugged. It was scarcely her place to tell Mrs Bellis that Mr Geraint and his housekeeper had been on sufficiently good terms to share the drawing-room.

'That bed looks damp,' Mrs Bellis continued. 'She did sleep in it, I suppose? I mean, where's 'er stuff, 'er personal things?'

Hester had often wondered about Mrs Cledwen, and now she realised that Mrs Bellis had put her finger on it. If Mrs Cled had really lived and worked in this little room, where were all her personal possessions, for they could scarcely have been crammed into one small gladstone bag. She did not intend to say any of this to her companion.

'Put away to give you room, I suppose,' she said. 'If that's all, Mrs Bellis, I'd better get on. It's my day for the hall and stairs and if I've got to do the washing as well . . .'

'I don't understand it, Matthew,' Hester said that evening, as they sat over a beef stew with the fluffy dumplings Mrs Cled had taught Hester to make. 'Mrs Bellis was right, that room's practically empty. I mean Mrs Cled couldn't live there like that, she must have things, everyone's got *things*, even I had bits and pieces, but that room's empty.'

'So you said,' Matthew agreed. 'Perhaps Mrs Cled's the sort o' woman who doesn't need things.'

'Yes, but what about clothes? Everyone's got clothes and Mrs Cled's got more than most; she can't have crammed them all into that little bag, she just can't have.'

Matthew glanced at her, then quickly down at his stew. He cut a dumpling in half and put it in his mouth. He looked awkward, and it wasn't just because his cheek was bulging with dumpling.

'None of our business, love,' he said thickly, through his mouthful. 'Mrs Cled will be back soon enough.'

'Yes, I know, but it made me think, and I couldn't help wondering . . .'

'Don't wonder,' Matthew said, his voice almost sharp. 'It's none of our business, love. What Mrs Cled does shouldn't concern us.'

'Then she . . .' A withering glare from Matthew killed the words in her throat. Sighing, Hester finished her stew and picked up the empty plate. 'All right, all right, I can take a hint! There's an apple duff for afters; want some?'

Next morning was a rush. Hester set the alarm for six, got up, made breakfast, woke the baby half an hour later and fed, washed and dressed her. By eight she was pushing the big old pram in under the small archway, parking it by the back door and untying Helen, who was cross at this change in her routine. With the child on her hip, she went into the kitchen to find the doors of the range shut and the fire still damped down, last night's dishes piled in the sink and an air of neglect much in evidence.

Tutting to herself, Hester put the baby into the play-pen and began tidying up. She riddled the fire through, filled the buckets at the pump, enjoying the vigorous exercise in the bright early morning, then pulled the kettle over the flame and got out the heavy black frying-pan. She got eggs and bacon from the pantry and set them out on the scrubbed wooden table ready for Mrs Bellis, sliced the loaf, fetched the butter off the cold slab, found a jar of marmalade and another of honey, and all the while she sang softly under her breath because she was happy, and busy, and because it was nice to be doing something different.

At twenty past eight, when Mrs Bellis still hadn't appeared, she wondered whether she ought to go along and wake the older woman, but hesitated until twenty to nine, when she was beginning to get seriously worried. Mrs Bellis was old, she might have had a heart-attack or a stroke or something, it would be downright wicked not at least to go along to her room and tap on the door, make sure she was all right.

Halfway across the kitchen, it occurred to her that she could take Mrs Bellis a cup of tea; that would be a nice gesture. She turned back and suddenly realised she had no idea at what hour Mr Geraint breakfasted, or where for that matter. He might eat in his study, his bedroom or in the room over the arch, the only thing she was sure of was that he didn't eat breakfast in the dining-room since it was miles away from the kitchen and was used only when he had guests. So she ought to have a word with Mrs Bellis anyway, otherwise they would all be in trouble.

She made the tea and poured it into a large white china cup. In the play-pen Helen sat foursquare on the rug, feeding pieces of a large wooden jigsaw through the bars on to the floor, then reclaiming them. She looked as though she would play happily for a while yet, so Hester carried the cup out into the corridor, and along to the housekeeper's room.

She knocked on the door. Silence answered her. Timidly, she tried the handle, wondering what on earth she would do if the door was locked, but it opened beneath her hand and she peered into the small, musty-smelling room. Mrs Bellis was a big lump beneath the covers; she was also snoring, faintly but definitely. So she's not dead, Hester thought, she's just a lazy old woman who doesn't like getting up in the mornings. She stood the cup of tea on the bedside table, clattered across the floor and swished back the curtains, letting in the sunlight.

'Morning, Mrs Bellis,' she said loudly. 'You've overslept; breakfast's all ready for you to cook. You'd best hurry; Mr Geraint will be down any time.'

The bed heaved like an erupting volcano and Mrs Bellis appeared. She was wearing what looked like a trawlerman's net on her head and her cheeks and mouth seemed to have sunk, giving her the look of an incredibly ancient and ill-treated monkey.

'Whassa time?' she lisped, reaching towards the bedside table not for the cup of tea, as Hester expected, but for a round pink bakelite mug which stood by the tea. 'Issit late, 'en?' As she spoke she removed her large, pink and white dentures from the mug and scrunched them horribly into her sagging jaws, which became full and self-confident again.

'It's getting on for nine,' Hester confirmed. 'Did you see

Mr Geraint yesterday? What time does he want breakfast?'

'Oh my Gawd, at a quarter to the hour. Get back to the kitchen an' start cookin',' the woman in the bed quavered, clutching the tea and bearing it carefully to her mouth. 'Tell 'im I'm not well – travel sickness, me monthlies, tell 'im anything; I'll get up now, keep 'im outa the way, I'll be as quick as I can.'

'I'll do my best,' Hester said doubtfully, moving towards the door. 'But I can't cope with everything, you know.'

She hurried back down the corridor and burst into the kitchen, her heart hammering. She was no cook; after many early disasters she had taught herself to make reasonably decent meals for Matthew and herself but she had no confidence in her cooking abilities. Mrs Cled cooked lovely food for the men, and had taught Hester how to make good pastry and a respectable dinner, but though she felt able to fry bacon and eggs, she did not intend to start doing Mrs Bellis's job as well as her own. The lazy old devil would just have to learn to get up earlier. Having made up her mind to tell Mrs Bellis that so far as cooking went she was on her own, Hester hurried over to the range, threw a knob of dripping into the frying-pan and pulled it over the heat. Today was an emergency, she would make breakfast today, but tomorrow . . .

She had the bacon spitting and the eggs ready for the pan when she realised she had forgotten to ask Mrs Bellis where Mr Geraint ate his breakfast. Was she supposed to take it to his room on a tray? What on earth would she do if she'd cooked the meal before Mrs Bellis put in an appearance?

Her dilemma was solved, just as the second egg slid into the hot fat, by the kitchen door opening.

'Thank goodness you're here,' Hester said in heartfelt tones, scooping hot fat over the golden yolk and turning to look over her shoulder at the doorway. 'Did Mrs Cled tell you . . . ?'

He smiled at her. He was in shirtsleeves and stockinged feet and a red china mug swung negligently from one finger.

'Good morning, Hester, how pink you look, all flushed from the fire. Is my porridge ready?'

'Oh! I thought you were Mrs Bellis. I d-didn't know you

had porridge, but there's eggs and bacon,' Hester gabbled, totally taken aback. 'Where do you eat it? In the study?'

'In here; where else?' He put his mug down on the wooden draining-board, then sat down at the table and turned expectantly towards her. 'Well? I can't see my coffee pot.'

'You can't see your cook, either,' Hester snapped, then could have bitten her tongue out. This was her employer, Matthew's employer, she must not be rude to him no matter how badly he treated her. 'I'm sorry, Mr Geraint, but this isn't my job so I don't know where things are. Mrs Bellis isn't well.'

He raised a dark eyebrow, looking sceptical. 'Not well? Do you mean drunk?'

Hester frowned, sliding the bacon and eggs on to a warmed plate, arranging them nicely, carrying the plate over to the kitchen table. She set it down before her employer and then turned to the stove once more.

'Drunk? I don't know what you mean, she isn't well. Can you have tea this morning instead of coffee? I've never made coffee.'

'Then you'll have to learn,' Mr Geraint said, reaching for a slice of bread. 'Suppose Mrs Cledwen had been taken ill? Would you have expected me to make my own breakfast?'

'Matthew made his own breakfast when I had Helen, in fact he made all his own meals after his mother died,' Hester observed. 'So I suppose you would have done the same. I'm not usually here until ten you see, so I couldn't have made it. Only Mrs Bellis was in such a state yesterday that I said I'd come in early for once.'

Mr Geraint took a big mouthful of bacon and eggs, then spoke thickly through it. 'Well, you'd better come in early every day. That woman can go; I'm not having a drunk in my kitchen.'

'She's a woman; women don't drink,' Hester said uncertainly. She knew men got drunk but it had never occurred to her that women drank at all, far less to excess. Walking in a demure crocodile along the Liverpool streets, the children had sometimes seen men lying in the gutter, drunk and incapable, the nuns told them, but on the rare occasions when they saw a woman in a similar position, the nuns always said the poor creature was unwell.

Mr Geraint stopped eating to stare at her. 'Women don't . . . good God, girl, where were you brought up?'

'In Liverpool. By the nuns at the convent school of Sister Servina.'

'Oh, well, that explains a lot.' Mr Geraint started to eat again, chewed, swallowed, then turned to face her once more. 'If you can't make coffee, tea will have to do. I'll have a mug, not a cup, no sugar and not too much milk.'

'All right,' Hester muttered. 'But what you said about Mrs Bellis, sir . . . you didn't mean she'd have to go, did you?'

'Indeed I did. But I'll have a word with her later. Have you made any toast?'

'No, but there's plenty of bread cut,' Hester said. Didn't he know that people had toast spread with dripping at teatime on a Sunday, not at breakfast? She felt like telling him a thing or two – just what did he think she was? Cook, scrubbing woman, toast-maker, what next, for God's sake? Aloud, she said, 'There's butter and stuff on the table. No, it's on the dresser – can you get it? I'm trying to make you fresh tea.'

He got up and fetched the butter and marmalade, then began to spread it on a round of bread. When the tea had brewed, she poured him out a big mugful and took it to the table. He must have brought the newspaper with him for he laid it down beside him and began reading it, ignoring her. Hester put the mug down rather too firmly for politeness and turned away from the table. As she did so, Helen gave a squeak; she was trying to retrieve a piece of jigsaw which she had thrown just too far from the bars and annoyance and frustration were turning her cheeks pink and making her lower lip wobble ominously.

'It's all right, darling, I'll get it,' Hester said quickly, knowing how rapidly Helen's patience would give out once she realised her task was impossible. A screaming child was really more than she could bear on top of everything else. 'Here it is, darling. Say thank you.'

'Ta,' Helen cooed, taking the piece of jigsaw and promptly beginning to suck it. 'Ta, ta, ta, ta . . .'

'Good Lord, I hadn't realised she was down there,' Mr Geraint observed, putting his paper aside. 'Good morning, young lady, and how is Miss Nell this morning?'

'Book,' Helen said at once, clearly remembering their previous encounter and staggering to her feet to clutch the bars of her play-pen in grubby fists. 'Book man, book!'

'It isn't a book, it's a newspaper . . . here, come and have a read.'

And without so much as a by-your-leave he lifted the baby out of the playpen, sat her on his knee and spread the newspaper out, while Hester could only watch and seethe.

'Here we are; today's news. Once upon a time . . .'

I ought to be pleased that he's paying Helen so much attention, Hester thought, starting the washing up. Why aren't I, I wonder? Why do I resent it? After all, she's my darling baby, I should be complimented that he seems to like her. But she was not; she was annoyed over his presumption that he might do as he liked with her child.

Worse was to come. When he finished breakfast Hester went to take Helen away from him and put her back in the play-pen, but Mr Geraint made no attempt to hand her over.

'She can come with me; I'll be working in the room over the great arch,' he said easily. 'She'll come to no harm there, and you'll be able to get on with your work unimpeded. Send Mrs Bellis up to me when she finally appears, will you?'

Hester started to say that the baby would do very well in the play-pen, but found herself talking to an empty room. Mr Geraint had walked out, closing the kitchen door firmly behind him.

Mrs Bellis arrived in the kitchen around ten o'clock, looking dreadful. When Hester told her that Mr Geraint wanted to see her, she gave a little moan and began gabbling that it was too bad, she had been brought here under false pretences, did not intend to stay, would charge Mr Geraint for her fares, for the work she had done, for the meal she had cooked him the previous evening.

'But Matthew fetched you from the station,' Hester pointed out. 'And I remember Mrs Cledwen saying she'd sent money for your train fare. Anyway, if you explain you weren't drunk I'm sure Mr Geraint will understand.'

'Wasn't *what*? I'm sure I don't know what you mean, Miss, and if you'll take a word of advice –' Mrs Bellis had gone all dignified suddenly, Hester was alarmed to notice, '– if you'll take advice, you'll watch that nasty tongue of yours before you perjure people and get give a slap in the eye.'

'It wasn't me that said you were drunk, I said you weren't,' Hester exclaimed, outraged at this unfair and nasty remark. 'But perhaps I was wrong, perhaps you were drunk – at least, you're being awfully rude for someone who's supposed to be ill.'

Mrs Bellis snorted, then swayed out of the kitchen and into the back yard. Soon she swayed back in to say she'd be much obliged if Miss would accompany her to the room above the arch since she didn't seem able to find it for trying, and what was them big white birds, a-hissin' and a-carryin' on in the next yard?

Hester explained that they were geese and took the older woman round to the narrow stairway which led up to the room above the arch, but Mrs Bellis took one look at the steep stone steps and said firmly that she hadn't the slightest intention of going up them since she'd either get stuck halfway or never get down again. Hester thought about getting behind and pushing her, then decided against it; if Mrs Bellis fell on anyone it most certainly wasn't going to be on Hester Coburn, who had a dependent child and a husband to think about.

'I'll ask Mr Geraint to come down,' she said wearily. 'You wait here.'

She ran quickly up the narrow stone stairway and found herself facing a low, arched door at the top. She knocked sharply and went straight in, too incensed for once to worry about the rights and wrongs of her behaviour. It was nearly eleven o'clock and she'd hardly started on her morning's work thanks to Mrs Bellis and their employer.

The room was attractive, far nicer than she would have

guessed from the outside. It was about ten feet long and six feet across, the walls were whitewashed and covered in paintings, mostly bright, modern-looking water-colours of the local countryside, and sunshine simply flooded in through the three arched windows which overlooked the wild garden and the drive.

Mr Geraint sat behind a big desk with his back to the window so that the light fell on the page before him. The floor was carpeted and cushions were scattered across it, and Nell lay on her tummy on the carpet with a fat red crayon in her hand, scribbling on a piece of rich-looking, cream-coloured paper. She looked up when her mother came in, smiled and made a contented little purring sound, then returned to her work. Hester saw that the cushions had been put all round Nell so that she could not fall and hurt herself and, angry though she was with Mr Geraint for taking her child away and for involving her with Mrs Bellis, she was grateful for his forethought.

Mr Geraint looked up as she came in and frowned at her. He seemed impatient and abstracted, but Hester was in no mood to apologise for her presence.

'Yes?'

'Mrs Bellis is in the courtyard, sir; she can't climb the stairs so I said I'd come up and ask you to come down.'

Mr Geraint sighed and pinched the bridge of his nose with his thumb and forefinger. 'Can't you just tell her ... no, I suppose I'd better go down. You stay here, keep an eye on the child.'

Hester stared at him, open-mouthed. Did he think she would dream of leaving Helen alone here, even surrounded by cushions? Besides, she might as well take her down with her now, back to the kitchen. Yet when Mr Geraint passed her and left the room, closing the door none too gently behind him, she did not immediately pick the baby up and follow him. Instead, she walked round the desk and peered out of the big middle window directly behind the chair in which Mr Geraint had been sitting.

There it was below her, the wild garden. The paths were

96

clearer from up here than from down below. It was thus that he had seen her, nearly two years ago, lost in the wilderness, trying to make her way home. She remembered the statue; it had been taken away by Matthew in the wheelbarrow, because it blocked the path and also because Hester told him she felt like a murderer every time she came across it. It no longer lay there, a mute reproach, but their encounter on that long-ago night had probably been noisy enough to bring Mr Geraint to the window. She disliked the thought, even in retrospect, that he might have watched her struggling through the brambles and briars, cursing as she went. Because if he had seen her his face would have worn that mocking, amused look . . . She was glad it had probably been her falling out with the statue which had caught his attention, made him look down.

Abandoning the window, she sat on the wide windowseat and looked around. She really liked it; it was much nicer than the drawing-room, which was very grand and formal and not terribly comfortable. Here there was a big couch against the wall to her right – it must have been piled with the brightly patterned cushions which now walled Helen in – and a footstool, comfortably upholstered in worn blue velvet. Against another wall was a sturdy table made of interesting wood – a deep shade of gold with satisfying, swirly patterns all over it – and in a small wall alcove above the table stood an elegant green china vase which held a breathtaking display of flowers. They were nothing special, just flowers which flourished at this time of year in the wild garden, but they had been gathered with care and arranged in the same manner, and to Hester's eyes they looked prettier than any hothouse blooms.

Hester turned her attention to Mr Geraint's desk. It was covered with pages and pages of cream manuscript paper and the paper was covered with writing. Rather nice writing, done with a broad-nibbed pen so that the downstrokes were thicker than the upstrokes, which gave the writing the look, almost, of a Chinese painting. It was, however, awfully untidy. Hester's fingers itched to set it straight, but instead she glanced at the shelves to her left, and thought she had seldom seen so many books, or such large ones. Musty, dusty books, not the sort you longed to open and read but the sort you gazed at with awe in museums and libraries, scared even to open them for fear they might either fall to pieces or prove to be Latin or Greek or some other foreign tongue.

Not all the books were big or old. There was a small, very fat little book bound in red leather lying next to her, on the cushioned windowseat. Hester picked it up and opened it. More of the beautiful writing met her eyes and without even thinking twice she began to read.

14 August 1925: Got home before dinner and walked into an atmosphere; Beth not at her happiest last night; actually accused me of being unfaithful; said she'd heard I'd picked up some little piece while I was visiting the O'Maras. Told her she was a fool, no cause to be jealous etc etc., but suggested I'd never even think of other women if she could bring herself to be a bit easier before me, for example instead of coming to bed in the most voluminous white cotton nightgown I've ever had the misfortune to get entangled with if she came in her own beautiful, creamy skin. Slapped my face, but laughed, too. Quarrel – if you can call it that – ended happily in bed. I gave it three stars, she said more like ten. I asked if she'd missed me and and she proved she had. Must warn her not to listen to gossip, though. She's a fine woman.

Hester put the book down. Her palms were sweating and her heart hammered in her breast as though she had suddenly found herself in Bluebeard's tower room, waiting for him to return and murder her. The red leather book was a diary and she had read it. The implications, even the date, passed her by for the moment at least; the nuns would be horrified that their teaching had not penetrated her thick skull: no one, ever, read another person's diary . . . Mr Geraint had trusted her, had left her alone in his room with the diary actually unlocked on the windowseat. It had never crossed his mind that she would read someone else's personal day-book.

Impatient footsteps mounting the stone stairs brought Hester flying away from the windowseat, her hand to her mouth. He would catch her, guess what she had been reading, dismiss her, dismiss Matthew, throw them out of the lodge. She realised suddenly what this place meant to her and to her husband. It was security, a home of their own, food on the table and a fire in winter. It was the difference between a good life and the sort of life she had seen people living in the Liverpool slums. She knew which she preferred.

Mr Geraint came into the room and began speaking at once, as though the last thing on his mind was diaries and the sort of person who would read another's secrets.

'That's that,' he said grimly. 'She'll be out of here by lunch-time, Matthew's driving her down to the station. I've arranged with him that you'll move in here just until Mrs Cledwen gets back and he's arranging for a girl from the village to do the rough work.'

'Oh dear,' Hester quavered. 'What about Helen . . . I don't think . . .'

'It's all arranged,' Mr Geraint said impatiently. 'You'd better start getting luncheon now; can you serve it at one o'clock?'

'Ye-es, I suppose, though I don't . . .'

'I'll come down today, you may serve mine in the study,' he said, breaking through Hester's wild ramblings, for on the spur of the moment she could not think of a good reason for saying she had to go home, she could not remain here. 'But tomorrow, well, tomorrow can wait. No, leave the child here; she's easy to amuse and it will keep her out of the way while you're cooking.'

'All right,' Hester said, too confused to object. She went to the door. 'One o'clock; I'll try to get a meal for one o'clock. Bye-bye, Nell; be a good girl.'

Mr Geraint sat down and pulled the half-written page towards him. He read, one hand reaching out for the pen without taking his eyes off the sheet of paper. On the floor, Helen selected another crayon and began overing the red scribbles with blue.

Hester made her way down the stone stairs, across the courtyard and back to the kitchen, still in a daze. Matthew had said she would move into the castle while Mrs Cled was away? Could it be true? If so, whatever was Matthew thinking of? She would have to have baby Helen with her, she would

99

not dream of letting the baby stay with Matthew at the lodge, good though he was with her. And would she sleep in the housekeeper's room, in that cold, musty, damp little place, in that unwelcoming single bed? And would she have to put up with all this upheaval, all this unhappiness, because she had been silly enough to read a page of Mr Geraint's diary and therefore dared not object to his plans for her? But it wasn't just that; it was their dependence on him, Matthew's love of his home and his job. They could not risk losing their place here.

With a heavy heart Hester began to peel potatoes and onions and to prepare a meal. Come back soon, Mrs Cled, she beseeched, onion-tears mingling with real ones. Come back soon and let us all go back to normal again!

Four

Nell knew very well that a ghost lived in the Long Gallery, so she usually ran very fast past the door, unless she was carrying something, in which case she tiptoed, but she felt happier running. Today, with the rain sluicing down the window panes as though it intended to bring about a second Flood, she just walked fast. And she didn't close her eyes either, but looked challengingly around her, daring the ghost to put in an appearance, almost wanting to see it so that she could tell Dan just what she thought of ghosts in general and the Pengarth ghost in particular.

Dan had been at the castle for just over a year, and he was Nell's greatest friend, the person who mattered most to her after mummy, daddy and Mr Geraint. He had the advantage of being closest to her in age, too, though he was three years her senior. It was unfortunate that mummy didn't seem to care for him much.

Or perhaps it was Mrs Clifton she didn't like. Mrs Clifton had been married to a younger brother of Mr Geraint's, who had been killed in a motor accident, leaving her and her little son in straitened circumstances. Mrs Clifton was a poor relation, or that was what mummy had said, softly, to daddy after Dan and his mother had been living at the castle for six months or so.

'I don't want to wait on *her* the way I have to wait on the old man and his friends,' her mother had complained to Matthew as the three of them sat in the lodge kitchen that evening, Hester having served and cleared up dinner at the castle. 'I know she's awfully pretty and very charming, but she's only a poor relation. It's true I could do with someone to give me a hand, but can you see that one raising a beautifully manicured finger? I can't.'

Matthew chuckled. 'I know what you mean, but the old man did say she'd pull her weight if he had her an' the boy to live. If you ask me though, Hes, she's settin' her cap at him. I wish her luck; a wife'ud be cheaper than a poor relation and a deal more useful, too.'

'How can she marry him? She's his sister-in-law; I thought you couldn't marry your brother's wife.' Hester clattered plates, then turned and addressed her husband triumphantly. 'I may be unworldly, but I do know the bible; the nuns saw to that! And has it ever struck you how similar Dan is to the old man? In looks, I mean. Were the brothers alike?'

Matthew was taking his chauffeur's boots off, using a yellow duster so that he didn't leave fingermarks. Nell loved those boots, she thought they were beautiful, or tophole as the boys at school would have said. They were made of beautiful leather, and sometimes Matthew let her polish them, using beeswax and spit and a great deal of rubbing. Well, Nell called it rubbing but Matthew called it elbow-grease. He usually wore the leather boots with his best breeches and Nell thought – and said – that he looked like a king when he was driving the Lagonda, but Matthew complained that though comfortable on, they were hell to remove. So now he was sitting on the edge of the ladder-backed chair which always stood by the kitchen door, going puce in the face and breathing heavily whilst trying to heave the first boot off.

At his wife's words, however, he stopped tugging for a moment to consider her questions, frowning thoughtfully.

'Mr Geraint and Mr Paul were different to look at; chalk and cheese you might say. But in their ways – well, they were both headstrong, self-willed, living life at a gallop, whereas I live it at a trot, like Mr Samuel did. Mr Sam's the youngest brother; got a nice little place over in Kent. As for marriage 'tween brother and sister-in-law, that's legal all right, it's just coveting while they're both alive that you can't do. But if they were to marry, well, do you 'member Mrs Cledwen? She did all the cooking, his laundry, the marketing; you'd find yourself on easy street if he took young Rosie Clifton to wife, love.'

'But Mrs Cled wasn't married to the old man. Matthew, you've never said and I never asked again, but was Mrs Cled his you-know-what? Come on, it's five years since she went, you can tell me now, can't you?'

Nell, practising her writing at the kitchen table, kept her head bent and her hand moving, but she was all ears. What did Mummy mean? What on earth was *his you-know-what* and who was Mrs Cled? The name stirred the faintest of faint recollections, but nothing more.

'I don't suppose it's any of my business. It were a long time ago, but I always reckoned she was,' Matthew said, starting to tug at his boot once more. 'I could ha' been wrong, mind. I can't think why else she stayed, an' worked so hard, because I don't reckon he paid her much.'

'And you think marriage would bring with it certain obligations,' Hester said thoughtfully. 'I wonder if it would? Young Mrs Clifton's a lazy cat, but I suppose he could insist. Oh, and then I could spend more time here, I might even get to work in my garden again. Why, before Mrs Cled left I was only up at the castle for two or three hours each morning; it was a different life. Nell hardly knows her own home!'

Matthew shot a warning look at his wife but Nell continued copying – and listening – and after a short pause Hester continued, though she lowered her tone a trifle.

'No, but it's true. The child spends more time up at the castle than she does here. Even in schooltime she has to go there after her classes and hang about until I've finished his dinner and done all the washing up and clearing away. It's no life for a child, Matt!'

Nell, sensing danger, longed to put her oar in, to glance up from the book and say that she adored the castle, couldn't be happier, found her life totally satisfying, but you didn't do that when you were seven years and three months old, you kept quiet, listened and said a lot of secret prayers, after the real ones were finished, to influence God and persuade Him to do His best for you.

Matthew got the first boot off and used his boot-removing duster to mop his brow; Hester didn't notice so he didn't get told off, to Nell's relief. She hated it when her mother was sharp and her father apologetic; it wasn't fair, she thought confusedly, when this happened. A man as lovely, as kind, as her father shouldn't have to sound humble and sorry when he'd done nothing wrong.

'She's better off than most,' Matthew said now. 'Think on, love; the improvements the old man's made over the past few years mean at least the main rooms are dry and the furniture isn't going mouldy or rotting away any more. There's kids in the village 'ud give their eye-teeth for a chance to play in a great old barn of a place like Pengarth. And we gets to eat pretty well an' all.'

Hester had sighed and come over to where Matthew sat. She had bent over and kissed the top of his head, and then knelt in front of him.

'You're right and I know it,' she said, taking the boot duster from him and rolling it carefully round her hands. 'When I think of the way I was brought up . . . oh Matt, you're right, we don't do badly. There's kids in town who don't eat every day, let alone eat meat. I shouldn't grumble, only I did like having my home to myself. Now I'm going to get this old boot off your foot in one pull, so hang on to the chair!'

There had followed one of those times when families come closest, Nell remembered, slowing her pace to an amble as the Long Gallery fell behind her. Mummy had heaved on the boot, Daddy had clung to the chair, and then the boot had come off, Daddy had tipped forward as Mummy fell backwards and they had all ended up on the floor in a laughing, kissing heap.

But it hadn't solved the problem of Mrs Clifton and Dan, because though Nell was bright enough to realise that daddy thought Mr Geraint might marry Mrs Clifton, she was sure that nothing of the sort would happen. Mr Geraint was kind to Mrs Clifton and patient enough with Dan, but Nell couldn't imagine the old man marrying anyone, let alone a fluffy little giggler like Dan's mother. And Hester really didn't like poor Mrs Clifton and was sharp with Dan as a result. As though Dan could help who his mother was! Mum even seemed to blame him for looking a bit like Mr Geraint, which now that Hester had mentioned it, Nell could actually see for herself. Was that why mum sometimes snapped at Dan? But it didn't seem to make sense to Nell.

Not that Dan minded. Probably he didn't even notice, and he was really fond of Matthew, trailing round after him in a fashion very similar, Nell supposed, to the way she trailed round after Dan. And for the time being, at any rate, life went on as usual. Mrs Clifton behaved like a guest, Dan behaved like a guest's son, and Hester did all the work.

Nell reached the head of the stairs and stood on the top step, looking down into the hall. The banister was a long, glorious swoop of dark, highly polished wood, but if mum or Mr Geraint came into the hall and caught her halfway down there would be trouble. She'd been told and told . . . Hester was afraid she'd lose her balance and fall off and kill herself on the hall tiles, Mr Geraint, much more practically, was afraid she'd catch a foot in the barley-sugar twists which held the banister in position, break a leg and ruin his staircase. Or that was what he said; Nell thought he knew very well she was safe as houses really, but agreed with her mother for the sake of peace.

The hall, however, remained empty. Nell knew where Mr Geraint would be at this time of day: in the room over the arch, writing. His huge work on the history of his family was still unfinished, but he had discovered he had an ability to write what he contemptuously called 'pot-boilers'. Nell had never read one, of course, but Hester had and said, albeit grudgingly, that they weren't half bad. Which meant she enjoyed them and admired Mr Geraint's ability, Nell knew.

'They're sort of spooky adventure stories,' she had said when Nell asked. 'About big old castles, and ghosts and treasure and secret passages. They're fun to read, anyway. You'll enjoy them when you're older.'

So Mr Geraint would be in his room, boiling pots. And Hester? Nell glanced down the stairs again. The Cliftons made a lot of extra work, which was why she had been upstairs at this time of day. Mum had said she wouldn't make their beds any more, she had enough to do without that. She said Mrs Clifton was quite clever enough to pull sheets and blankets into place and plump up pillows, but she had told Nell to go to the Cliftons' rooms and empty the chamber pots, a task which, it seemed, she believed might be beyond Mrs Clifton. Nell, not liking the job, had done it the easy way, by sliding up the sash windows and emptying the blue chamber pot with the gold edging and the smaller green and red one into the wild garden below. No one had been out there, though she had thought it might be rather fun if Mrs Clifton were cutting roses or wandering along the overgrown paths. It wasn't that she particularly disliked Mrs Clifton – as Dan's mother she had at least one use – but Nell foresaw a good few menial tasks coming her way if Mrs Clifton stayed on and on and didn't marry anyone. She knew she should have carried the pots downstairs and emptied them properly, rinsed and returned them, but she had not. She agreed with Hester that guests should either empty their own chamber pots or go downstairs and use the earth closet close to the side door. Mr Geraint always did, but perhaps the rules were different for owners and guests.

Nell finally decided that her mother would be in the kitchen making the midday meal, and that she was, to all intents and purposes, alone in the hallway. She flung a leg over the banister, wriggled herself into a good position and pushed off briskly with both hands. It was wonderful, the next best thing to flying, an activity which Nell had only experienced in dreams. The rushing air lifted her dark hair, her short skirt flew up, her knees gripped the rail, controlling her speed. It was glorious, glorious, she wished she dared shout and scream!

Unfortunately she hadn't paid enough attention to the curve. When she felt it coming she should have braked hard with hands and knees, but she was enjoying the illegal swoop so much that she forgot, shot off the end of the banister at speed, and thumped straight into something – or rather someone – who uttered a deep, barking grunt as her weight landed amidships. For an awful second she thought it was Mr Geraint, then, as she struggled to get to her feet, fighting clear of someone's legs and elbows, she realised it was Dan. Flattened, winded, looking as though he would tell her a thing or two when he got his breath back, he rolled around clasping his stomach and casting black looks at her as she stood apologetically over him.

'Oh Dan, I'm awfully sorry, I didn't see you . . .'

'Aaargh, eeeeze, eeeze . . .'

'You're winded; I hate that,' Nell said cordially. 'I expect you feel you aren't ever going to breathe again, but you will, honest.'

'Ki-ki-kill . . .' Dan wheezed, rolling over on his front and beginning to kneel up. 'Aaargh . . .'

'You aren't killed,' Nell said bracingly. She tried to heave him to his feet but he lunged out at her and she stepped diplomatically out of range. 'Didn't you see me coming down the banister? I always come down that way, don't you? It's tophole!'

'Didn't say I was killed,' Dan wheezed at last, scowling at her from all fours. 'Said I'd kill *you*, you stupid kid! And when I get my bloody breath back I will!'

'Oh Dan, don't be cross,' Nell said anxiously. 'I didn't mean it, it wasn't really my fault, I was coming so fast my eyelashes got into my eyes, I couldn't possibly have seen you. Come on, let's go into the kitchen; there might be oatmeal biscuits!'

But Dan, usually partial to Hester's oatmeal biscuits spread with butter and honey, shook his head until his black, silky hair flopped over his eyes, and made a grab for Nell.

'You aren't getting out of it that easy, you stupid little ninny; how d'you like that?'

As he spoke he caught her wrist between his fists and began to turn the flesh, his left hand pulling to the left, his right to the right, in an extremely painful Chinese burn. Nell, taken aback, simply stood for a moment. Boys didn't hurt girls, did they? She frowned up at Dan, whose expression was not pleasant; he was waiting for her to cry, she could tell. Well, he might wait; she certainly didn't intend to start sobbing for mercy. Instead she turned in his grip and brought her fist round; it hit his nose with a satisfying crunch. Dan let her go; one hand flew to his face, the other proceeded to punch her as hard as he could.

'Little bitch! You're a pest, that's what you are, you and your bloody mother, trying to get rid of us, trying to bloody kill me. I'll teach you a lesson you won't forget in a hurry, Nell Coburn!'

Even love will only stand a certain amount. As Dan's other fist abandoned his nose and joined its brother, Nell forgot that she adored him, forgot she was a young lady, forgot everything except that Dan was hurting her on purpose, and therefore must be hurt back. She was a small, skinny seven, Dan a husky ten-year-old, and he should have been able to beat her to a pulp with one hand tied behind him, but perhaps he held back a bit or perhaps Nell's outrage gave her additional strength. At any rate she launched herself at him, scratching, kicking, punching, and in seconds the two of them were rolling on the marble tiles, locked in a deadly embrace, Dan using language Nell had never heard before. When his hand slammed into her face, intent it seemed on gouging out her eyes, she bit his finger as hard as she could and held on, clenching her teeth like a small bulldog. Dan swore and shouted, kicked and punched, but was unable to free himself of her unwelcome attentions.

'Daniel! Helen! What on earth do you think you're doing?'

Mr Geraint's voice was like a douche of cold water on a couple of warring mongrels. Nell was so surprised and horrified to find Mr Geraint looking down on them that her mouth dropped open and Dan's finger slithered thankfully out. Dan, probably already remembering his years and superior strength, struggled to his feet and held out his hand to her.

'Get up, Nell,' he said rather shakily. 'Are you better?'

Nell stared. Better? did he think she was ill?

'What's going on?' Mr Geraint said sharply. Nell saw with surprise and dismay that his face was not only angry but shocked. 'Fighting like a pair of street arabs . . . Dan, what have you to say for yourself, boy?'

'Sorry, sir. I was trying to – to – catch her. I tripped, we collided. I didn't mean are you better just now, I meant are you all right?' He turned to Nell and gave her a strained and imploring glance. '*Are* you all right, Nell?'

'Yes, I'm all right,' Nell said quickly. 'I'm sorry about your finger; are you all right, Dan?'

Mr Geraint looked from one to the other. His mouth twitched, Nell saw it.

'Just a – a collision, was it? Not a fight at all, then?'

'She's three years younger than me,' Dan pointed out so self-righteously that Nell had hard work not to gasp.

'And a girl,' Mr Geraint reminded him.

'Yes, and a girl, of course.' Dan had the grace to look a little red around the gills, Nell saw with satisfaction. 'Can we go now, sir?'

'Shake and make up?'

'We can't,' Nell said quickly. 'Because you only do that if you've quarrelled and we haven't, have we, Dan?'

'No, we haven't,' Dan said equally quickly. 'We were just going through to the kitchen, sir, to see if Mrs Coburn had made the oat biscuits yet. Can we go now, sir?'

Nell, glancing from face to face, blinked. She had never heard Mr Geraint called sir quite so often before, nor quite so fervently. Dan plainly wanted his good opinion – as indeed, she did. But Mr Geraint was looking amused again and not cross, which was a relief.

'Yes, you may go,' he said. 'And if you can convince your mothers that you've not been fighting you're cleverer than I thought you. Off with you!'

They left, making for the kitchen, until Mr Geraint had turned on his heel and headed for the study. Then with one accord they headed for the side door.

'That was a narrow squeak,' Dan said in amicable tones as they left the castle behind them and headed for the woods. 'I'm sorry for starting the fight. But you got me right in the bread-basket, you know – it really hurt.'

'That's all right; how's your finger?' Nell asked solicitously. 'I don't think I drew blood, did I?'

Dan examined his finger. 'It's dented,' he announced. 'You broke the skin; remember your dad telling us how beavers kill trees by ring-barking them? Well, if I were a tree . . .'

They grinned at each other.

'I'm glad you're not a tree,' Nell said shyly. 'Dan, did I ever tell you about the ghost in the Long Gallery? Well, this morning, when I was walking past . . .'

Miss Huntley was hiding behind a handsome rhododendron bush, with the railings of Hamilton Gardens at the back of her and the sooty bush providing cover. It was hide-and-seek, and the Princesses were the hunters.

Standing very still, she watched through the branches as the two little girls searched, Princess Elizabeth with determination and thoroughness, Princess Margaret Rose, who was only three, in more desultory fashion. She wandered along, glancing idly from right to left, her fat little legs going slower and slower. Then she realised that her big sister was almost out of sight and set up her familiar cry: 'Lilibet, wait! Wait for me!'

Around the perimeter of the garden, faces were pressed close to the railings, watching. It was interest and affection which drew them, Miss Huntley knew, but she found herself resenting it as much for the children as for herself. They were royal, to be sure, but why couldn't they be allowed to grow up in peace, like other children? Neither Elizabeth nor Margaret Rose ever commented on the silent audience, but Miss Huntley knew they noticed.

'It will take a great burden from them when the Prince of Wales marries and has a family of his own,' the Duchess had confided once, when Miss Huntley had remarked on the public's fascination with her young charges. 'It isn't as if either of our little girls was in line for the throne, so it's hard that they should be followed around. Between you and me, Huntie, it's another reason why I dress them simply, in sensible print dresses and stout shoes and tweed coats and hats. It makes them blend in better. But I suppose people love to see them because they're the first grandchildren of the king, and there isn't much we can do about it. However, when the Prince marries . . .'

But as yet, only rumours of affairs and 'unsuitable gels' were discussed. Dear David, as the family called him, had not yet met the woman for him, so Miss Huntley had to ignore the watching faces, as her young pupils did. It was a shame, because in many ways the older Princess at least would rather have been outside the railings than in. On a trip to the theatre to see a pantomime the previous Christmas Elizabeth, in the royal box, with one of the complimentary chocolates bulging in one pink cheek, had hung so far out to look down at the audience that her father had been frightened and hauled her back so suddenly that her blue sash came unstitched.

'I'm sorry, Papa, but I was quite safe really,' she had said. 'Oh, but I wish we could sit down there, with the other children! It would be such fun, wouldn't it Margaret?'

Miss Huntley had seen the Duke's rueful grimace, and the way he had squeezed his little daughter before letting her go and hang once more over the edge of the box. He and the Duchess did their very best to make life at 145 Piccadilly as natural and easy as possible for their children, but there was a limit to how far they were able to go. Even a simple shopping expedition or a trip to the park meant detectives hovering and the inevitable little group of followers.

'Got you, Huntie!'

Miss Huntley jumped and squealed; she had been so immersed in her thoughts that Elizabeth's gleeful grab had taken her completely by surprise. Margaret, trundling round the bush in her sister's wake, also pounced.

'Got you!' she echoed. 'Got you, Huntie! Now we'll hide and you can search.'

Miss Huntley glanced at her wristwatch and Margaret did the same, shooting out her wrist to reveal the toy watch just beneath the blue and white cardigan she wore.

'Yes, it's time for luncheon,' she said in her clear, piping voice. 'Lilibet, it's time for luncheon – shall you have yours with me today?'

Elizabeth was sometimes allowed to lunch with her parents, a great treat, though she always had a milk pudding instead of the more sophisticated dessert enjoyed by the Duke and Duchess. Now, however, she towed her governess out of the rhododendron thicket and consulted her own watch, a real one.

'No, Margaret, I'm lunching with Mama and Papa today,' she said importantly. 'But you may come in at coffee time. Goodness, Huntie, we had better hurry, we're both rather dirty and need a good wash. It would never do to let Papa see us all hot and bothered, would it?'

'No indeed,' Miss Huntley agreed. 'And when luncheon is over, if you're very good, we'll have a little treat.'

'Oh, Huntie, we'll be ever so good! What sort of treat? The naughty sort?'

Lately, Miss Huntley had begun to take the children over to Hamilton Gardens and then to slip quietly through the gate into Hyde Park before the gatherers had realised they were out. In their sensible coats, hats and shoes no one took the slightest notice and they were able to stroll along the sandy paths, watch the yachts on the Serpentine, and the best (and naughtiest) treat of all, watch other children at play.

Once, a skinny girl with a kite which kept getting away from her had asked Elizabeth if she would like to have a go; Miss Huntley had smiled and nodded, and the Princess, cheeks scarlet, eyes bright, had raced up and down the path with the kite, whilst Margaret jumped up and down, cheered her on, and declared that Lilibet was better even than Trudy, the kite-owner, at flying it. But later that evening, when she mentioned the incident to the Duchess, Miss Huntley was told that such casual friendships should never be encouraged.

'It's this business about security,' the Duchess told her. 'Poor darlings, they're fascinated by other children and one of these days they'll be able to mix as everyone else does, but now, in the heart of London, it really won't do. I trust you, Huntie, to see that it doesn't occur again.'

The Princesses grieved when Miss Huntley told them that they must be onlookers and not participants in future, but they were very good about it. Elizabeth was almost too good; she sighed and that expressive mouth drooped, but that was the extent of her complaint. Miss Huntley, to ease their disappointment, took them for a ride on top of a London bus, and their delight and fascination with this bird's eye view of ordinary people made up for the death of their friendship with Trudy and her kite.

'You can see into people's gardens; you can see their swings and their washing, and sometimes even into their nurseries and bedrooms,' Elizabeth said, pressing her nose against the glass. 'This is the most wonderful thing we've ever done, Huntie – I wish we might travel by bus every day!'

But soon it became clear even to Miss Huntley that London could be a dangerous place for two little girls with royal connections. The Irish Republican Army began to put bombs into letter-boxes and to commit a good many other crimes which put a firm stop to their trips outside. In Balmoral or Sandringham they could have more freedom, but not in London, and that was where the little girls spent most of their lives.

'Never mind,' Elizabeth sighed when Miss Huntley broke the news to her charges that their outings, in future, would stop at Hamilton Gardens. 'Uncle David's bound to have a family one day; then things will be easier – Mama says so!'

Hester was in bed after a long and exhausting day at the castle and on the very edge of the sleep which she craved, when she realised that the big pan of beetroot she had been boiling on the range at the castle had not been pulled off the heat. The pan would boil dry, catch fire, the flames would shoot ceiling-high, the castle would ignite, and Mr Geraint would be burned in his bed. It would all be the fault of a silly little Hester Coburn who was so tired at the end of her fourteen-hour working day that she'd forgotten to finish off her cooking.

She sat up. Beside her, Matthew gave a small, choking snore. For a moment Hester contemplated waking him, then she remembered that, hard though she worked, today at least Matthew had worked harder. They were harvesting barley and he had been unable to rest even when he came home because he'd cut his hand badly when bailing and the wound had to be cleaned, disinfected and bound up. And though Matthew never complained, Hester hadn't liked the look of the inflamed skin around the jagged cut and he admitted that it was aching badly. No, she could not possibly disturb his slumber, it would be a wicked thing to do. So, since she could not contemplate allowing the old man to burn alive in his bed, she had best do something about it.

Hester slid cautiously out of bed. It was a warm night but she put her macintosh round her shoulders, shoved her feet into her old sandals, and flapped quietly out of the lodge. She was relieved to see, when she reached the drive, that the

113

castle looked calm and benign in the moonlight with no trace of smoke floating on the summery air, but having got up and semi-dressed, she had no intention of returning to bed to lie worrying for the rest of the night. She would have to make sure.

It was odd walking quietly up the long drive by moonlight, but rather nice. Romantic, exciting even. The sheep were silvery blobs, the cattle larger, darker ones, and when she reached the wild garden the scent of the roses and lavender was so sweet and strong that she stopped for a moment just to drink it in. She passed the big courtyard where silence reigned. Whatever geese did at night they did it quietly, Hester told herself, glad that they hadn't come out honking and hissing at her. As good as watchdogs, Matthew always said – funny old watchdogs which slept when someone crept through the wild garden only feet away from their front door. Still, it was a blessing; it wouldn't do to wake the old man, particularly if she was up here on a fool's errand. She was beginning to believe that she must have pulled the pan off the heat; the castle seemed so quiet and peaceful, dreaming in the moonlight.

She reached the small courtyard and slipped in under the arch, padded across the paving stones, put a hand on the back door. The door was old and creaked, she remembered, turning the handle cautiously. It occurred to her that if the old man had remembered to lock up she would be in Queer Street, but he rarely did so, and tonight it was unlocked. Hester threw the door open and hurried into the room and there, just as she had known it would be, was the big, black saucepan full of beetroot, boiling away on top of the range. Breathlessly, she heaved it off the heat and carried it across to the sink. She tipped the blackish red water away, then put the plug in and emptied half a bucket of water over the gleaming spheres of beet.

Phew! The pan wasn't burnt, the beet were cooked, the situation had been saved. Good thing I remembered, though, Hester said to herself, moving soft-footed around the room, otherwise the story could have had a different ending. She didn't bother to light the lamp; the moonlight flooding through the window illuminated the room sufficiently for most purposes. She knew the beet would be easiest to skin hot so she dealt with them as soon as they were cool enough to handle, then fetched a deep earthenware bowl out of the cupboard, sliced the beet and sprinkled them with a little vinegar, not much but enough to keep them moist. She damped down the fire, closed the doors, pulled the hob cover over and glanced round the room again, just to make sure she had left nothing undone. All looked peaceful and normal so she let herself out, shut the door quietly and padded across the yard, under the small arch and out into the wild garden.

She was level with the big arch when someone called her name, very softly, in a husky whisper.

'Hester? Wait.'

She turned, a hand flying to her heart. The dark figure which emerged from the shadows beneath the big arch could only be Mr Geraint – what on earth was he doing out here in the middle of the night? He came up to her, smiling, his face gentle in the moonlight. He took her hands in his.

'Not sleepwalking, my little love? Not searching for me?'

It was strange how immediately she knew that the man holding her hands so tenderly was John again, the John who had loved her, but at the same time she acknowledged that he was still Mr Geraint, trying to get round her. She shook her head at him, unable to stop herself from smiling indulgently even though she recognised what he was doing and deplored it.

'Mr Geraint, I'm not your ... your anything. I'm Hester Coburn, who works for you.'

'I'm not Mr Geraint; didn't you realise? Sometimes, when I'm free to do as I choose, I'm just John.'

Hester shook her head but did not pull her hands away. 'No. No one can be two people inside one body, Mr Geraint. It isn't fair, do you see? You can only be yourself.'

'And my self loves Hester Coburn and wants to be loved by her. Is that so wrong? My darling, I've missed you!'

'You saw me five hours ago and told me your greens weren't cooked through,' Hester said grimly. Or as grimly as she could, with her heart beating hard in her throat and a painful flame of desire stirring in her stomach. 'And then you turned to Mrs

Clifton and asked her if she'd had any hard cabbage, what's more.'

'Oh, that! That's how I have to be when I'm not John. Why, you're shivering . . . come up to my room, the fire hasn't died down yet, I can give it a poke and we'll soon have a blaze going.'

'No,' Hester said, but the denial lacked conviction.

'I'll make a hot drink,' Mr Geraint said. Somehow, he had managed to get his arm around her shoulders and now he was leading her, unresisting, under the big arch and across to the narrow stone stair which led to his room. 'Why did you say you'd come up to the house? Well, it can't be important, what's important is getting you warm and comfortable again.'

'I came to take a pan of beetroot off the fire,' Hester said. 'And now I'm going home again,' but she did not resist as she was propelled gently but firmly up the stairs and in through the low door. 'The castle could have burned down, that's why I came. I dared not leave it until morning.'

He nodded, closing the door behind them and, taking her hand, he led her to the couch. It had been pulled away from the wall and stood on the richly coloured rug in front of the dying fire.

'Sit down, sweetheart. I'll just mend the fire – it's colder now, wouldn't you say? I always find moonlight cold.'

He stirred the fire with the poker until it glowed red, then he threw a log on and watched, apparently absorbed, as tiny blue and gold flames began to lick and curl about the wood. Hester had not sat down but stood against the couch; now she glanced at the door. If she ran quickly and quietly across the carpet she could be out of the room and down the stone stair before Mr Geraint had so much as looked over his shoulder. In ten minutes she could be in her own bed, cuddling against Matthew's broad back. If she went now, tomorrow she could take up her life where she had left off, and Mr Geraint's polite indifference could be accepted more easily because she had been cool and sensible, had refused to play his games, refused to be drawn back into their long-ago liaison.

Mr Geraint stood very still, staring at the flames, which

were licking the log with increased appetite. Hester did not move a muscle. Belatedly, she realised that she did not want to move. She had waited for this moment for more than seven years, now it had come. Her heart was beating fiercely, her mouth was dry and her body was trembling with anticipation. Of course it would be sensible to leave, but when had she ever been sensible? Oh John, John, I love you despite knowing you aren't for me, and I've wanted you so badly – much worse than you've wanted me, or you'd have engineered this moment years ago, you wouldn't have waited until fate threw us together.

He moved at last. As though in a dream he turned to her, smiling; Hester read his expression and went to him, straight into his arms as a child goes to its mother. She rested her head against his chest and sighed deeply; and with the sigh all the waiting and frustration, all the longing and bitterness which his neglect had brought disappeared. She was where she yearned to be; she would enjoy this moment.

His hands caressed her back, then slowly he pulled her tightly against him. Hester felt giddy with delight and anticipation. She had been a feckless young girl with no worries or responsibilities when this had happened so long ago – had that made their lovemaking special? Were her memories of that moment so rich and sweet because he had been the first man to touch her? She no longer cared, and when he picked her up and laid her on the couch she had no thought of the unwisdom of it, no thought beyond the pleasure to come. He undressed her tenderly, caressed her, murmured love-words, kissed her whenever she tried to speak, told her that her milky skin, painted rose and gold by the firelight, was the most beautiful thing he had ever seen, told her she tasted of honey and smelled as sweet as a bed of tiny pink rosebuds.

'Who am I?' he asked at last against her mouth, their bodies still for a moment. 'Tell me who I am, little Hester.'

'You're John, my John,' Hester murmured. Her mouth travelled across the base of his throat, over his collar bone, up the line of his jaw, the beard already prickling against the softness of her lips. 'Oh John, I love you, I love you!'

He ran a hand the length of her quivering body.

117

'And do you want me, sweetheart?'

She could not speak but her eyes said what her mouth could not utter. He laughed softly as she turned towards him.

'Sweet little Hester, my only love! One day we'll be together for ever, one day you'll be mine and I'll be yours, because I can't live without you. God knows I've tried, you belong to Matthew now, but I know we're meant to be together. Kiss me, my darling child!'

She stole down the stairs and across the yard as dawn was greying the sky. Stars still pricked the dark blue above and a little breeze stirred the branches of the leggy roses in the wild garden. She was consumed with guilt, and fear stalked beside her. Suppose Matthew had woken, missed her warmth? What on earth would she say to explain her absence, not only from her bed but from her house, for half the night?

She reached the lodge at last, and slid in through the back door. The kitchen was warm, the familiarity of it comforting. She could say she had sat down before the fire and dropped off, but suppose he'd been searching for her and knew she wasn't around an hour, two hours, ago? She could say . . .

It was needless. Worn out by the harvesting, Matthew slumbered still. She stood by the bed for a moment, looking down at him. Poor Matthew, he worked so hard, so uncomplainingly, and she had done him a great wrong. She was afraid of what would happen if he found out and ashamed of her behaviour, though she knew she would not undo it, would not wish it had not happened. But getting back into bed, chilled from her walk, would be asking for trouble. She padded softly out of the room again and went into the kitchen, stirred up the fire, made herself a drink. Twenty minutes later she returned. Matthew had turned over, but he slept still. She slipped carefully between the sheets, keeping her feet clear of his sleep-warmed body, and pulled the covers over her head.

Two minutes later she slept.

Nell and Dan were slicing beans. It wasn't a bad job if you had a sharp knife and at least they were left alone to get on with it. Furthermore, on a nice day they could slice beans outside, in the courtyard, with the sun on their heads and the promise of play when the beans were finished much more real, somehow, than when they were incarcerated indoors. More and more now, Hester was getting Nell to give a hand with small jobs which were within her capabilities, and Nell was wheedling Dan into helping her. After all, it was Dan's mother who caused a good deal of the extra work and there was no sign that she ever intended to do anything more physical than cutting a few roses for the big vase in the hall, or podding peas on the rare occasions when she found herself in the vicinity of the kitchen and Hester asked her to do something.

Nell felt sorry for her mother, but sorrier for herself, because if Mummy did manage to get rid of Mrs Clifton Dan would leave as well and that would be unbearable. Lately she had relied heavily on Dan for companionship because Mummy was always busy and Daddy was harvesting, working harder than ever because Dewi had broken a leg falling out of the hayloft. Not knowing how to get all the work done had made Matthew moody and quick to anger, and he had always been the quiet, patient one, who deflected Hester's bursts of ill-temper from their small daughter and kept life in the lodge on an even keel.

There was something wrong besides Daddy's work though, Nell knew, but she couldn't put her finger on what it was. Perhaps it was because Daddy had refused to try to get another job, away from here. She had been so glad and happy, but she could tell that Mummy had been glad in one way but cross in another.

'Remember I asked you, Matt,' she said with ominous quiet when Matthew had finally said, sullenly, that he was happy enough where he was and why on earth couldn't she be happy, too? 'Remember I wanted us to go away from here.'

'You dunna, not really,' Matthew had growled. 'But sayin' you do meks you feel better.'

Interpreting the startled look in her mother's dark eyes, Nell thought that daddy was right and Mummy knew it, so why say she wanted to move? The strangeness of adults was beyond belief, certainly beyond the understanding of a seven-year-old, so Nell decided to put it out of her mind and get on with her own life, which had all the usual children's excitements and dangers, even if at least half of them were imaginary.

Slicing beans for the winter, which was only just around the corner, or so Hester said, ignoring the late August sunshine, was not an exciting pastime however. So when the kitchen door opened both children turned to see who had come in, hoping for a diversion. It was Mr Geraint, holding a sheaf of papers. He nodded to them, then addressed Hester.

'Busy, Mrs Coburn? I've popped in to tell you that I intend to take the children off your hands tomorrow. I've got a parcel to send off to London and Dan's been here a while and not visited the shore yet, so I thought I'd ask you to make us a picnic lunch – something fairly substantial – and to pack a couple of towels and a flask of coffee. If Nell has a swimming suit then pack it, too. We'll leave early in the morning, deliver my parcel to the post office and then Matthew can drive us to a good stretch of beach and abandon us for a few hours. It will do us all good.'

Hester turned from the sink and began to dry her hands on a small piece of towelling. She looked confused, almost as though Mr Geraint had been unpleasant to her, whereas he had been at his most friendly.

'A picnic? I see. And is Mrs Clifton to accompany you?'

Mr Geraint smiled. 'No, I don't think Mrs Clifton would care for such an expedition, but I'm sure the children will enjoy it, and it will give you some time to yourself. Would you ask Matthew to pick us up in the Lagonda no later than ten, please?'

He left the room. The children, bright-eyed, began to talk about the seaside, the strange creatures to be found on the shore, the birds, the fish, the seaweed which flourished on the rocks. They were still talking when Matthew and the others came in for their midday meal.

Hester, serving piles of potatoes, fish cakes and cabbage, told Matthew rather stiffly that she wanted a word when the meal was finished, so after Willi had left Matthew helped Nell to clear and stood for a moment by the back door.

'What is it, Hes?' he asked. 'Mustn't linger too long, the weather's too good to waste; besides, I wouldn't be surprised if it broke, later in the week. That's the way of it, in high summer.'

'It's the old man; he wants to take the kids to the seaside tomorrow and I'm none too keen, he's never taken them anywhere before,' Hester said. 'Why does he suddenly want to take our Nell on the spree? He never did anything without a good reason, you've said it yourself, Matt. I'm going to tell him she can't go.'

It had been a brilliantly hot day with almost no breeze, the sort of day farmers long for and then grumble about because it makes the workers tire quickly and slow down in their work. Matthew stood in the doorway to catch what breeze there was and looked impatiently at his wife, working at the sink.

'What's wrong wi' a trip to the beach, if the weather 'olds?' he asked reasonably. 'The kids will 'ave fun and likely the old man will 'ave fun, too. I'm to take 'em down, am I? Well, I'll see our Nell don't come to no harm.'

'Well, in that case,' Hester said grudgingly, 'there isn't much I can say. Only it seems strange to me, this sudden interest.'

Matthew left and Nell was given a basket of fruit to peel. Dan, who had his midday meal with his mother and Mr Geraint, came through to ask if Nell might go berrying with him.

'Mr Geraint said if we did you might make blackberry and apple jam, and some pies,' he said craftily, joining Nell in her task of peeling tiny, bright red crab apples which Hester would make into jelly. 'We're going to give the men a hand with stripping the orchard as the fruit ripens, aren't we, Nell?'

Hester approved of apple-picking and usually of blackberry-picking too, but now she went to the door and looked out at the brilliant blue sky as though she expected it to shower them with snow at any moment.

'It's too hot for berrying; besides, I need Nell to take tea down to the harvest field,' she said. 'I suppose you were going out through the woods and up to the moor? Well, why not pick in the lane this afternoon? Then you'll be able to get back to carry the tea-jugs down.'

'There are better berries up on the moor. I thought you could come, too,' Dan said hopefully. 'Couldn't Matthew come back for the tea-jugs? We could take our teas with us. We're having a picnic with Uncle Geraint tomorrow, so why not have one with you today, Mrs Coburn?'

Hester laughed but shook her head. Her hands went behind her and untied the big apron she wore for kitchen work.

'You're not getting round me like that, young Dan,' she said. 'Get some berries in the lane, then come back in time for tea. I'm just going to have a word with Mr Geraint about this trip to the seaside. It's not that I want to spoil your fun, I just want to know why, after weeks and weeks of ignoring the pair of you, he's suddenly decided to treat you to a day out.'

'Uncle's working. I thought no one was supposed to disturb him when he's working,' Dan said.

Because of the heat, he and Nell had sat themselves down on the back door step to peel the tiny, fiddling fruit, and they had to move to one side to let Hester squeeze past. 'You'll catch it if you go up there, Mrs Coburn!'

Hester snorted. 'Working, is he? Well, he'll have to stop for a moment,' she said grimly. 'I want to know what all this is about!'

'Let's go and listen outside the door,' Dan suggested, when the crab apples had been peeled and floated in a bucket of water. 'Or we could go berrying; your mother said we could if we went in the lane, and we could easily wander too far by accident and find ourselves up on the moors. It's not fair that we should have to cart jugs of tea about, we're only kids.'

'You may only be a kid; I have to help,' Nell said loftily. She picked up the bucket of apples and carried it over to the sink, then put the bucket down with a thump. She glanced at the kitchen clock above the dresser. 'We'd better wait, hadn't we? It'll be teatime in an hour and Mummy's been gone ages already. I suppose we ought to start getting things ready if she doesn't come back soon. Or we could go down the lane, like she said.'

'I'd love to know what your mum's saying to my uncle,' Dan said longingly. 'He can be horrible when he likes; he's probably being horrible to her right this minute.'

Nell could tell that Dan would have enjoyed hearing Hester taken down a peg; Hester was fond of saying, in Dan's hearing, that she could not understand a boy of ten being satisfied with the company of a girl three years younger, and of course this made Dan feel that perhaps he ought to find a friend nearer his own age. However, Nell could imagine what would happen to them if they sneaked up the stone stair and were caught at the top: heads would ring and punishments would be handed out wholesale, for eavesdropping was a serious offence. They wouldn't get a sniff of the seaside if they were found listening at doors.

'No, don't let's. We'll get caught,' she said. 'Let's raid the biscuit tin and go berrying.'

Dan agreed, though he made it plain he thought her a little ninny. They crunched Hester's new-baked oaties with naughty delight, then dashed into the little lane which led up into the hills, intending to pick some berries. The trouble was that Willi came along, leading Bess the Clydesdale mare and reminded them sharply that harvesting was thirsty work. Conscience-stricken, Nell insisted on returning to the kitchen where, in Hester's absence, she boiled the two huge blackened kettles, made tea in the blue and white enamel jugs and buttered a number of her mother's scones. Dan helped, but they had their work cut out to get everything up to the harvest field, though Matthew and the other men were full of praise when they did arrive.

Dan started to say that they'd not only delivered the tea, they'd made it as well, but Nell managed to shut him up and the two of them hurried back to the kitchen to make afternoon tea for the family.

'Matthew wouldn't have minded if I'd said we'd made the tea,' Dan observed as they put the kettle on a second time. 'He often says your mum works far too hard.'

'Ye-es, only I don't think he'd like her arguing with Mr Geraint,' Nell explained. 'He's the boss. The lodge is his house.

Anyway, I thought it better not.'

'I think it's time your mother came back and did her work,' Dan said severely, getting out the tea service with the rosebuds and beginning to set the cups and saucers out on the walnut-wood trolley. 'I'm not a housemaid.'

Nell giggled. 'Nor am I, but I don't mind helping out. I just hope Mr Geraint isn't being as horrible to Mummy as you said. Can you pass me the tea-caddy, please?'

Nell made tea in the Georgian silver teapot, cut some rather hefty cucumber sandwiches, buttered the oat-cakes and waited for Hester to return and praise their forethought. Above the children's heads the clock ticked out its message that four o'clock teatime was long past and Nell began to fear for the welfare of the jug of milk in the hot kitchen, but still Hester did not return.

'We'd better take the trolley through; but don't blame me if my Mum says something,' Dan said at ten to five. 'She won't think much of me being turned into a housemaid either, you know.'

Nell giggled again, but she did wonder why her mother was so long and, having a good share of her mother's vivid imagination, remarked as they wheeled the trolley down the long corridor and across the hall, that she hoped Mr Geraint hadn't throttled Hester and thrown her down the old well, which was situated handily for the room over the arch.

'He's likelier to throttle my mother if he throttles anyone,' Dan observed, guiding the trolley over a patch of missing tile. 'When she wants him to do something she puts on a silly little voice. He gets mad, I know he does, though he never says so. And she's got some woman to tea today, she sounds even sillier than my mother does when she talks to Uncle Geraint.'

'I hope mother isn't persuading Mr Geraint not to take us to the seaside,' Nell said fervently. 'I do want to go, Dan! Other kids go to the beach often and when we're older we'll be able to go on our own, but now we have to wait for a grown-up to take us!'

'When we're older? When I'm older I shan't be here, I don't suppose,' Dan said, not sounding too sad about it. 'Anyway, it's back to school in a week and once I get there . . .'

They reached the drawing-room door and their conversation was suspended as they steered the trolley unskilfully across the threshold. Mrs Clifton and her friend, a goggle-eyed blonde wearing an elaborate tea-gown in pale peach with tassels in coffee-brown silk, were bent over a book, opened out on the occasional table.

Mrs Clifton turned at the sound of the door opening and gave them her practised, lash-fluttering smile.

'Tea? So soon?' Mrs Clifton consulted the small gold watch on a fine gold chain at her waist. 'Oh, it isn't so soon, I see, it's quite late. Where's Hester?'

'She's busy,' Nell said shortly. Every instinct told her that to admit her mother had gone to see Mr Geraint and not yet returned would make trouble for everyone. She checked that everything on the trolley was as it should be, then left the room, closing the door thankfully behind her. 'Let's go out the front door and see if Mum's still in the room over the arch,' she whispered. 'There's no harm in *looking*. They might be arguing, though I don't think Mummy likes to argue – not with Mr Geraint, at any rate,' she added, remembering occasions when Hester had seemed only too keen to argue with Matthew.

'I'm game,' Dan said promptly. 'Come on!'

But no sooner had they set foot on the paving than the geese arrived, waddling and hissing, and by the time they had kicked and shoved their way through the flock Hester was coming down the narrow stone staircase, not looking as though she had been arguing with anyone, Nell noted. Her mother looked flushed and happy, not at all like someone who had failed to get tea twice over.

'We took the tea through,' Nell called as her mother pushed through the cackling geese. 'We took the jugs out to the men in the harvest field and then we did afternoon tea for the drawing-room. We made the sandwiches and everything!'

'Good girl,' Hester said, mopping her brow. 'It's very hot still, isn't it? Thanks very much for helping her, Dan. I really am grateful to you both. And now how about getting those blackberries? I'll start dinner now, and clear tea later. You have some fun.'

She sounded breathless, happy, quite different from the grim-faced woman who had stormed up to Mr Geraint's room two hours earlier.

'We'll have our tea first, then,' Dan said. 'I'm parched, I am.'

Hester laughed. 'Fair enough. I'll make you pancakes with sugar and lemon, and you can have some of that lemon barley I made instead of tea.'

'What did Mr Geraint say when you asked him about the seaside?' Nell ventured, when they were safely ensconced in the kitchen once more, watching Hester make the pancakes in the big black frying-pan. 'We aren't to go, I suppose?'

Hester twirled a pancake merrily in the air, fielded it neatly, slid it on to a warmed plate, then put the pan down and gave her daughter a hug.

'What a spoilsport you must think I am,' she said lightly. 'And you're wrong, for indeed you are to go. I shall make a splendid picnic and daddy will drive you down. You'll have a marvellous time. Here, Dan, the first pancake is for you.'

'I wish you could come too,' Nell said in a small voice, reaching up to kiss her mother's pointed chin. 'You don't have much fun, Mummy.'

Hester looked down at her. Her cheeks were pink and her eyes were very bright, almost shiny.

'I do have fun,' she said, and there was a teasing sort of laugh in her voice. 'Indeed I do have fun, Nell.'

The children had a glorious day at the seaside. Mr Geraint had provided them with an elderly shrimping net and a galvanised bucket and he rolled up his trouser-legs and waded into the pools with them, examining, identifying, marvelling. Nell lifted the great, gleaming curtains of weed around the base of the big rocks and exclaimed over the crabs, the quick, flickering fish, the elegant painted shells which were revealed. Dan caught a really big crab, but Mr Geraint advised that it be put back since it was not suitable, he said, to eat. Dan fancied taking it triumphantly home to Hester and his mother, and was disappointed at first, but then he found a sea-urchin's shell and Mr Geraint said he would show Dan how to mount it over a candle so that the delicate colours showed to their best advantage. Dan decided a crab would have been pretty commonplace after all. A sea-urchin lamp would be a much more acceptable gift.

'Hello, Dad, we've had a topping time, I wish we could go to the beach every day,' Nell said as she and Dan piled into the back of the car. 'We did have fun, didn't we? And the picnic was lovely, but I'm hungry again now.'

Matthew turned in his seat to smile at them.

'You've caught the sun,' he observed. 'As for being hungry, your Mum's made you a big tea, I can tell you.'

Mr Geraint climbed into the front passenger seat and turned to smile at them as well.

'So you're hungry? Well, I'm exhausted. I never thought the seaside could be so tiring. I hope Mrs Coburn's got a big dinner for me as well as a big tea for you.'

'Uncle, why do you call Matthew, Matthew, when you call Hester, Mrs Coburn?' Dan said suddenly. 'Even my mother calls her Hester.'

'It's a courtesy because she's a married woman,' Mr Geraint said. 'I call your mother's friends Mrs Woodley and Miss Blackburn, don't I?'

'Ye-es, but you don't know them very well.'

'You could say I didn't know Mrs Coburn very well, old man. Sometimes we don't see each other for days on end.'

'Yes, but other times you see her three or four times a day. And Mrs Woodley and Miss Blackburn don't have a joke with you, do they? Sometimes you and Mrs Coburn have a laugh, and you . . .'

Nell saw Mr Geraint's shoulders stiffen slightly. He was tired of being questioned, she guessed. She cut in quickly, 'You've known my dad for ages, haven't you, Mr Geraint? Right from when he was a little boy?'

'That's right.'

To Nell's relief, Mr Geraint sounded amused rather than annoyed. 'Who picked up the bucket? Are the seashells safe?'

The difficult moment passed. Matthew and Mr Geraint began to talk, and in the back of the big car Nell and Dan argued amicably over the shells and wondered whether tea would include an apple and blackberry pudding, made from their spoils of the previous day.

'Let's hear you have a bit of a sing-song,' Matthew said suddenly, when Mr Geraint seemed inclined to snooze. 'Not too loud, but loud enough. What songs do you know, Dan?'

'Lots of war songs,' Dan said with relish. 'Can we have "Pack up your troubles"?'

They did. And before they reached the castle Mr Geraint had woken up and was joining in with a will.

'Can I go with you to the station, Dad? Do let me . . . Mum, can I go with him? It's the last time I'll see Dan for ages and ages and I'm going to miss him so much . . . I won't blub, I'll be good, and I'll wave and wave. Oh, please say I can!'

September had arrived, the days still blue and gold, the heat still intense at midday, but September meant school and that Nell and Dan would have to part.

'I'll be back before Christmas,' Dan had said gruffly the previous evening, shaking hands all round in the kitchen after dinner. 'The time will soon go. Uncle says when I come back he'll take us all over the place – to the market in St Asaph, for one. Christmas markets are topping.'

Now, with Mrs Clifton already sitting in the front passenger seat and Dan, pale and stiff in a grey suit and large striped cap, sitting in the back with his luggage in the boot, Matthew looked doubtfully from the vehicle to his small daughter, hopping with impatience on the back doorstep.

'You won't embarrass the lad, Nell? No tears or fuss?'

'I promise – cut my throat and hope to die,' Nell said, drawing her finger across her throat with some relish. She loved all Dan's expressions and used them whenever she could. 'Ten weeks is years and years!'

Matthew laughed but gestured her into the car.

Nell hopped in. Dan scowled.

'What are you doing in here? Well, don't you go letting

me down before the chaps. There's a couple of fellows who live near Rhyl, they'll be at the station. Are you going to write to me?'

It was threateningly said; Nell nodded hard, gripping her hands tightly in her lap.

'A letter every week?'

Nell nodded again, swallowing a sudden lump in her throat.

'Every week, on my honour. Two if you like.'

'One will do. I'll write back, of course.'

Nell stared out the window. The trees and meadows shimmered strangely, as though under water. She did not turn from the window until the shimmering had steadied and gone.

The train disappeared down the track and Nell's bursting tears were allowed free rein. They ran down her face; she rubbed at them with grubby fists and clung to Matthew, shaken with distress. Ten weeks was a lifetime, how would she live without her favourite – her only – playmate? But there was school, and she would help Mum up at the castle, and Mr Geraint, who was a very understanding man, had told her she might have a treat next week: he was going to take her to the Pleasure Beach in Rhyl.

'Are you all right now, old lady?' At her watery nod Matthew tucked her small paw in the crook of his arm. 'Right; then off we go, marching like a couple o' soldiers . . . left right, left right, left, left, left . . .'

Five

After Dan's departure, life seemed quiet and strangely featureless to Nell. School was quite fun; her best friend Bron had joined a troop of Brownies and suggested that Nell might join too, and Hester seemed to have quietened down, to be less annoyed over Mrs Clifton's presence and various demands.

Mr Geraint kept his promise and took Nell on the Pleasure Beach where she enjoyed the rides, threw hoops over various obstacles and ate a gloriously pink and sticky concoction known as candy floss. It dyed her lips an improbable shade of scarlet and Mr Geraint told her to keep her hands to herself when she clutched him as they climbed into one of the cars.

And then there was the strange affair of the painting.

Years before, Hester told her daughter, the paintings had hung in the Long Gallery, which was where the ghost lived – one very good reason why Nell hadn't realised that some of the paintings now hung there again. She might never have done so had she not been running with heedless speed (and firmly shut eyes) past the door to the Long Gallery, her arms full of clean sheets and pillowcases for Mrs Clifton's room, when she distinctly heard the creak of a door opening. Her eyes shot open in time to see a sinister black shadow slide across the unpolished wooden floor in front of her feet.

A ghost or a demon or both? Well, the shadow of one anyway. A confused conviction that if you stepped on a shadow the owner promptly took a share in your soul made Nell skid to a stop. Unfortunately the tottering pile of bed linen, not familiar with superstitions regarding shadows, continued on its way to land in a heap on the dusty corridor floor. Nell gave a shriek which would have done credit to a steam train at a crossing, tripped over the linen and landed in the shadow-maker's arms.

'Hey, what's the matter?' Mr Geraint said, catching Nell neatly and standing her upright before bending over the sheets and pillowcases. 'Did I startle you? I'm sorry.'

'You frightened me ever so,' Nell said resentfully, rubbing an elbow which had come into sharp contact with the wall. 'No one ever comes out of that room . . . and there's the ghost . . . I thought you were the ghost.'

Mr Geraint picked up the sheets and piled them in Nell's out-stretched arms.

'Ghost? What ghost?'

'The one in a long white gown, with her head tucked under her arm,' Nell said with relish. 'She's horrible; her eyes roll when she looks at you and her hair-ends are all bloody.'

'You morbid little beast,' Mr Geraint said roundly. 'And when did you see the lady last?'

'Well, I caught a glimpse of her white gown once,' Nell said. 'But I usually run past the door with my eyes shut. I only opened them today because I heard the door creak.'

'You're a danger to man and beast, running along with your eyes shut,' Mr Geraint pointed out. 'And you've not done the clean linen much good, either. Whose bed are you making?'

'Mrs Clifton's,' Nell said gloomily.

'Hmm. Well, go and dump the stuff on her bed and then come straight back here. There's something I've been meaning to show you, but we'd better quash this ghost story once and for all. There isn't a ghost in the Long Gallery, you little duffer, the only ghost stories about the castle centre on the Great Hall and the turret in the West Wing, and no one goes there any more. It's falling to bits. So who filled your head with non-sense, eh?'

'It might have been me,' Nell admitted. 'You see I saw the white gown and I thought it didn't have a head on it, and there was something under the arm which might have been a head. So there really isn't a ghost in the Long Gallery then?'

'Sorry to disappoint you, but I've been in and out of there for days and I've seen neither hide nor hair of a headless haunt.' Mr Geraint had fallen into step beside her and now they turned into Mrs Clifton's room. He looked round rather disparagingly, Nell

131

thought. 'Put the stuff on the bed, then come with me.'

'I'm supposed to make the bed,' Nell pointed out. '*And*
I have to empty her chamber pot.'

'She can do both, she's not helpless,' Mr Geraint said firmly.
'Come on, follow me.'

'What's my Mum going to say?' Nell said uneasily. 'She
said to make the bed and tidy the room, and to empty the . . .'

'Your Mum, if I know her, will probably say it won't hurt
Rosalie to do her own dirty work for once,' Mr Geraint said.
'Come on, stop chattering.'

Nell shrugged inwardly and followed. Mr Geraint was the
boss, after all, it was scarcely her place to argue with him. So
she skipped along beside him, asking questions about ghosts,
until they neared the Long Gallery, whereupon she fell silent,
glancing uneasily up the long shadowy corridor.

'What's the matter? Cat got your tongue?' Mr Geraint said
bracingly, opening the door, which creaked, and ushering her
into the room. 'Now does this room look at all ghostly to
you?'

Nell clutched Mr Geraint's sleeve and looked carefully about
her. Sunshine flooded through the long windows, a soft breeze
carried the scents of the autumn garden to her, and the room,
which had once been leaky and damp, smelled of whitewash,
sunshine and late roses.

'It doesn't look ghostly,' she admitted slowly, releasing her
hold on her companion. 'What have you done in here? Oh,
haven't you made it into a pretty room, Mr Geraint!'

Now that she was more relaxed, she saw that the entire
wall facing the windows was hung with pictures and portraits,
mostly portraits. Beneath them were set out small gilded chairs
with spindly legs and round or heart-shaped seats upholstered
in glowing velvets and silks. The chairs were clustered in little groups around tiny, well-polished tables, some half-moon
shaped, some round, some hexagonal, but not one conventionally square. Looking again, she realised that the scent of
roses was not only from the garden; several of the tables had
vases filled with blooms on them, as well as small piles of what
looked like printed leaflets.

'Nice, isn't it? I got what's left of the picture collection out of the attics and cleaned them up. I'm planning to open some of the house to members of the public but that's for later, when I've more rooms respectable. This is just for the North Wales Water-Colourists. They're coming, forty of them, to paint, explore the countryside and have lectures from well-known painters.'

'Golly! Will they pay you lots of money?' Nell asked guilelessly. She knew from listening to her parents that Mr Geraint had to make money from all his schemes and ventures. 'Where will they sleep, though?'

'In the village, this time. But if it goes well then I'm going to get your mother some help and we'll open up the bedrooms to them, fit them out as dormitories, perhaps. Now take a look at these portraits; most of them are my ancestors. Tell me what you think.'

Rather to Nell's surprise he sounded as if he actually wanted to know, so she followed him obediently, scrutinising the faces until he drew her to a halt before a picture of the prettiest of all the ladies. She had the most beautiful blue eyes, set wide apart with the whites like snow and the blue part a very dark, almost violet shade. Her skin was white and her ringlets, threaded through with a piece of white ribbon, were dark and glossy as a blackbird's wing.

'That's my great-grandmother. Her name was Emily Susan Geraint-Hughes and she lived here when Pengarth was in its heyday. What do you think of her?'

'She's very pretty,' Nell said. 'I like her dress, but you can see through it, can't you? I wonder if she knew that?'

Mr Geraint gave a short bark of laughter.

'I daresay she did, the minx,' he observed. 'But does she remind you of anyone?'

'I don't know many ladies apart from the teachers at school ...' Nell was beginning, when the door opened and her mother stood framed in the doorway, frowning at them both.

'Nell, I've just been in to Mrs Clifton's room and ... oh, I'm sorry, Mr Geraint, I didn't realise she was with you. But she does have her tasks to do and Mrs Clifton won't thank me if she goes up to bed tonight and finds it unmade and the room still in disarray. Nell, if I've told you once . . .'

'Don't nag, Mrs Coburn. I told the child to leave the bed. Mrs Clifton is quite capable of making it herself, and of emptying – of tidying her own room. I wanted to get Nell's opinion of the work we've done in here.'

Hester glanced around her and Nell could see her mother's eyes widen.

'Goodness, Mr Geraint, what an improvement,' she said. 'What's it all in aid of?'

'Forty water-colourists,' Nell said before her companion could reply. 'And Mr Geraint says this lady might remind me of someone . . .'

She pointed to the portrait. Hester walked towards them, glancing up at the paintings as she came. She stopped once, to examine a water-colour of a seascape, then, reaching them, she glanced casually up at the portrait on the wall. She froze into a momentary stillness so complete that Nell wondered whether a giant spider hovered over the picture, or whether the lady had come alive and was about to step down and join them.

But there was nothing. Only the ringleted, dark-haired beauty, her long, white fingers toying with the stem of a red rose, her face smiling enigmatically.

'Well?'

Mr Geraint's voice cut across the silence like a whip-crack. Hester relaxed; unfroze, as it were.

'Well what, Mr Geraint?'

'Well, who does my great-grandmother remind you of, Mrs Coburn?'

'No one, Mr Geraint,' Hester said sweetly but positively. 'No one at all. And now, if you don't mind, I think Nell and I had best make our way back to the kitchen, where we both belong.'

Was there a slight emphasis on the word *both*? Nell saw Mr Geraint's lips tighten for a moment, but then he walked casually away from them, to hold the door open for them. Puzzled, Nell followed her mother out of the gallery, along the corridor and down the stairs. Back in the kitchen, she flung her arms round Hester's waist and squeezed. Hester did not squeeze back, or laugh, but remained stiff in her daughter's embrace.

'Mum, I'm sorry I didn't do the bed, but it truly wasn't my fault. After all, the old man is the boss, isn't he?'

She had heard her parents throw the remark at each other's heads when it suited them, and now it made her mother laugh, took the stiffness out of her slim, strong body.

'Oh, you! Yes, he's the boss, but he's ... he's nothing else. Nothing to either of us. And now let's prepare them a cold supper, then we can get back to the lodge early for once.'

The next day was Sunday. On a Sunday they all went to church for the eleven o'clock service, Matthew driving everyone, but the Coburns would slip out before the sermon to go home and start getting Sunday dinner. Supper was a cold meal, a buffet set out in advance so that they could go to evening service if they wished, but the morning was always given up to church first and then to preparing the Sunday roast.

Lately, Mr Geraint had said he thought Nell should stay for the whole service with him and Mrs Clifton but Hester had disagreed. She had said briskly that Nell got quite enough religion with most of the morning service and all of the evening one, and that cooking the hot Sunday dinner was a task beyond her powers if she was given no assistance. Mr Geraint, who was sometimes flush and generous but usually broke and tight, had sighed but not pursued the point, so today Nell and her mother were driven back to the castle by Matthew in the Lagonda, and began to cook the vegetables, to turn the joint, to baste, to lay the table, to prepare.

It was hot in the kitchen, even hotter than outside, which was saying something. An Indian summer had descended on the land and the heat seemed sultry and unseasonal in mid-September. Nell, laying the table in the dining-room with many trips to and fro and her best dress a size too small and scratchy round the neck, longed for the time when they would all have eaten and would be able to please themselves for the rest of the afternoon.

She intended to go berrying up on the mountain above the

135

castle, to take some apples for a picnic and to eat them at the very top of the mountain, on a big boulder with a magnificent view of the sea, where she and Daniel had often sat before his return to school. It was a good place, up there on the mountain. You walked along the lane, which wound higher and higher into the hills, until you came to open, rocky country dotted with gorse, furze and bramble, and then you climbed farther until it was just rocks. She and Dan had gone there less than a month ago, playing high cockalorum on the rocks, pushing each other off the biggest boulder of them all, then sitting back to back and gazing across the misty plain below, dreaming of the day when they were old enough to walk to that distant line of blue which was the sea.

'Nell, is that table ready yet? Good girl, well, push the trolley through, would you? I've done the vegetables, they're in the tureens, so if you take them in, the old man will be back by the time you deliver the pork.'

Trundling the laden trolley, Nell could smell the pork, crispy in its crackling jacket, the roast potatoes, golden-brown without and softly white within; the gravy bubbled with golden fat in the gravy boat. For pudding there were apple dumplings and custard . . . I'm going to eat everything on my plate and then take my picnic and when I'm right at the top of the mountain I'll write to Dan, she decided, decanting the tureens on to the gleaming dining table. From the hallway she heard the scuffle and murmur of voices which meant that the church party had returned. Today it was Mrs Clifton, the old man, Miss Carruthers and the vicar and his wife. No wonder the weight of vegetables in the tureens had almost caused the trolley to founder, Nell thought, hurrying back to the kitchen. Vicars were usually especially hungry, and cleared their plates just as she meant to clear hers.

The rest of the meal was rush, rush, rush, just as it always was when the old man had guests. Hester served, Matthew carried, Nell pushed the laden trolley. The old man called for wine. Hester had a bottle of red breathing and a bottle of white dangling down the well in a string bag, keeping cool. Matthew fetched tall crystal glasses, Nell carried through last year's walnuts, a glass jar of celery, some cheese on a round blue dish and Hester's oat-cakes. The guests cracked walnuts with their fingers or with the elegant silver nutcrackers, laughed, ate. Nell helped to make the coffee and then poured it into a tall silver jug, heated the milk on the fire, poured that into a squat silver jug, wheeled everything through on the trolley, smiled, hurried back to help with the washing up . . .

By three o'clock they had finished and Nell was so hot and tired that she considered giving up on her berrying and walking down to the stream instead, to paddle her hot feet, fish for tiddlers and possibly have a snooze. But she did want to write to Dan and she couldn't keep telling him that she had done nothing interesting. Anyway, it was breathlessly hot, the air was full of those little black flies which often mean thunder and she thought how nice it would be high on the mountain, where the air would be cool and the wind fresh.

Hester put the last clean dish away and flopped into a chair, her legs stretched out before her, her face pale with heat and exhaustion.

'I am totally worn out,' she said. 'Next time his lordship wants to host a lunch party he can choose a cooler day. And where are you off to, dear?'

'Up the hills, berrying,' Nell said briefly. 'Can I take some left-over coffee?'

'No, the milk will turn in this weather,' Hester murmured. She had shut her eyes and looked half asleep already. 'Why don't you pick the blackberries in the lane, though? It's a long walk up into the hills on a day like today. Come to that, if you pick in the wild garden you'd be even nearer home. You could duck back into the house if it rains; that seems more sensible.'

'Ye-es, I suppose I could,' Nell said unwillingly. 'Or I could go on a ghost hunt, that would be indoors. But could I take a picnic, Mum? It would make it more fun.'

'I don't see why not. In fact I made you some jam sandwiches, they're on the dresser, wrapped in greaseproof. And there's a bottle of lemon barley-water keeping cool under the sink.'

'Thanks, Mum,' Nell said, fetching the deep, stained basket they always used for berrying. She put the sandwiches into the pocket of her dress and the drink into the basket. She saw no point in saying that she had already made up her mind to go into the hills. Grown-ups were so strange, they could forbid you to do something you most urgently wanted to do for no real reason. She patted her mother's hand, lying loosely on the chair-arm. 'You have a nice rest now.'

'Mm-hmm, I will,' Hester droned. 'Don't be late, love. Supper's easy today; just salad, cold pork and a junket. I'll make bramble jelly tomorrow, if you get enough berries.'

'All right,' Nell whispered, stealing across the kitchen and slipping out of the back door. She did not want her mother to realise that time was getting on and they should be preparing supper in less than an hour. I'm sick of making meals and serving them and washing up, she thought rebelliously. I wish Mum had another job, a different sort of job, where I didn't have to help so much. It isn't fair, other kids don't work as hard as me!

But the work would be forgotten once she had left the castle behind, she knew that. It's Mum I ought to feel sorry for, Nell told herself, slogging along the lane and longing for the moment when the high banks began to dwindle and she could feel a breath of breeze. Poor Mum, working from crack of dawn until ten at night, and she isn't even very old. She's much younger than Dad, but he's free from six o'clock most nights – earlier, in winter. Mum just keeps on and on . . . golly, shan't I be glad to reach the top!

However, even when she was quite high up where the brambles were thickest and began lethargically picking berries, she could feel no breeze. The sky was an ugly metallic colour yet the sun blazed down relentlessly and the myriad tiny insects still whirred and buzzed in the listless air. Perspiration trickled down Nell's face, soaked into the collar of her old shirt and gathered in the small of her back. Still, she was out of doors and doing something she enjoyed; anything was better than dancing attendance on Mrs Clifton.

She had promised Hester a good picking of berries, so she had best get on with the job. As she worked, the very act of picking the berries became soothing, and she ate a good few, letting the slightly bitter taste ease her increasing thirst. I ought to leave the lemon barley water for later, when I've done all the picking, she told herself righteously, moving higher up the mountain. I'll have a drink when the basket's half-full. As she filled the basket a breeze got up at last, quite a cooling breeze, so Nell took a quick swig at the barley water. With renewed vigour, she began picking again, going up through a great thicket of furze and on to the very top of the mountain, where the big boulders were and even the brilliant green and gold gorse did not prosper.

She filled her basket completely with the enormous blackberries on those brambles which had gained a foothold in the thin soil. She was just about to call it a day and have her tea, for the basket was brimming, when she heard the first distant rumble of thunder.

'Figgins,' Nell muttered. She didn't much like storms. 'Perhaps it won't be much, though. Perhaps it'll stop soon.'

Even as she said the words there was the most enormous crack, seemingly right overhead, and a lightning fork arrowed to earth in the valley below. Nell jumped and dropped the basket which, by a great piece of good fortune, landed stolidly on its bottom without the loss of as much as one berry. 'Oh! Oh, that was hateful!' she muttered, picking the basket up once more and looking wildly round her. She would get soaked, and wasn't there something about lightning liking wet things? Things which stood out on a bare mountainside? What should she do? Where should she run? She dared not stay here, she must be the clearest target for miles around!

She was still wondering how quickly she could run downhill without breaking her neck when the storm was on her in earnest. The thunder roared and reverberated around the hills, the lightning flickered and stabbed at the earth, the air seemed one moment stifling, the next so alive with electricity that she was sure her hair was standing on end.

Panic-stricken, Nell ran up the hill to where the biggest boulder stood. She and Dan had been here together – would that he were here now! She crouched by the boulder and watched, terrified, as the lightning seemed to pursue her, actually striking one of the pines only twenty or thirty feet below.

The pine tottered, smoked, then flared into vivid blue and yellow flames which roared into the dazzling air.

Then, without warning, the wind came. A gale which tore at the trees, gripped the gorse and flung it about madly, tipped the bottle of lemon barley water on its side and sent it bouncing wildly over the rocky scree, snatched at Nell's plume of hair and her brief brown gingham skirt. For a moment it was almost exciting, then the wind seemed to realise its own power and howled round the mountain top with such strength that Nell was forced to throw herself flat on the ground and cling to the boulder like a limpet so as not to be bowled down the hill after the barley water.

Lying there, she realised that she was in real danger; this wasn't an adventure, it was something which could cause her death. And she didn't want to die, not at all, not one tiny bit. But her choices were narrowing: if she stood up she was sure she would be knocked off the edge of the mountain; if she stayed put she might be struck by the lightning which was now playing round the mountain top with such frequency that its livid, unnatural light flickered around her constantly. Where to go, where to be safe?

Nell opened her wind-torn eyelids and peered around her. If she got to the further side of the boulder, where it rested against the side of the rocky mountain, might she not be safe? Protected from the rage of the storm, she could lie quiet until it passed over. And storms always did pass over, she knew that much. She crawled painfully towards the rock-face, and found, to her infinite relief, that there was a small gap between the boulder and the side of the cliff against which it rested. If she could get down flat she could slither into the crack, curl up and be safe. She squeezed behind the boulder, and found that there was more room than she had imagined; the ground fell away so that she slid downwards into a small shallow cave. There was a sandy floor and the rocky roof, though too low to allow her to stand up, was high enough for her to sit rather than lie.

It was cooler in here too, and quiet. She could still hear the storm raging outside, but the peace seemed to envelop her, calming her fears, slowing her thudding heart. Even when she heard the loudest, most terrible crack of all, followed by a splintering roar, she was not really afraid. Another pine tree had been struck, she supposed drowsily, resting her head against the rocky wall. From her small refuge the storm was muted, tamed; she could not see the livid flashes of lightning and the noise of the thunder was no longer so terrifying. Besides, though dim in the cave, it wasn't totally dark by any means, even with the great boulder excluding most of the light, and with the coming of the storm an early dusk had fallen, so Nell did not worry when she realised that it seemed to be getting darker still.

She must have fallen asleep, for presently she woke with a start, feeling stiff and hungry. She rubbed her chilly arms, then rooted in the pocket of her old skirt and found the packet of sandwiches. The lemon barley water was long gone, a casualty of the storm, and she had dropped the basket and the berries some time earlier but now she unwrapped the greaseproof paper and bit into the first sandwich. It was delicious. She ate it very fast, looked longingly at the others but rewrapped them; she might need those later, if she was stuck here for long. Only then did Nell notice the silence which had fallen; she could not even hear the wind and the thunder had grumbled off into the distance some time ago. Pushing the packet of sandwiches back into her pocket she crawled to the entrance to have a closer look at the weather; by the sound of it the storm was over and she could go home safely.

She pushed her head out of the crack, then drew it back, puzzled. She couldn't get out there, not even a rabbit could get through that narrow gap. There must be another entrance, she must have become confused by the darkness and tried the wrong one. She shuffled down and back until she reached the middle of the small cave, then peered around her. The only light came from the slit she had just proved was too small to let her through. That was her way out, it had to be.

Nell crawled back to the opening and took a careful look around, then she sat back on her heels and began to whimper. The crash she had heard must have been the boulder shifting; it had blocked her only exit. Unless someone came to her rescue, she would be stuck here all night! She did not allow herself to think further than that as she stared dully at the crack. Then she told herself that sitting there wasn't going to do her much good and went through her pockets again. There was the packet of squashed and sticky jam sandwiches, one crumpled piece of paper, one stub of pencil; she had been going to write to Dan. Now if she could catch a mouse or a rabbit and tie a note to its leg, telling of her predicament, perhaps the creature would bring help.

She toyed with the idea for a few minutes, then began to shout. Very soon she began to cry, letting the tears run down her filthy face and drip off the end of her chin. Later still she ate a couple of sandwiches. Then, worn out and unhappier than she had ever been in her life, she curled up on the sand and went sadly to sleep.

Hester was still asleep in the chair in the kitchen when the thunder began to roll. She woke slowly, stretched, yawned, then blinked around the room, looking for Nell. There was no sign of her, but Hester sat up, glanced at the clock and went over to the sink. If the cold supper was to be on the table in good time, she really should start on it now. She had made the junket before church but there was lettuce to clean, cucumber and tomatoes to slice, and the rest of the cold pork to carve. Mr Geraint liked the meat carved on Sunday evening so he could help himself, eat and go off. It wouldn't do at all, Hester thought sarcastically now, tipping half a bucket of water over the lettuce lying in the old stone sink, if the boss had to hang about waiting to carve for someone else.

She was beginning to clean the lettuce, wrinkling her nose with disgust at the number of insects trapped – or lurking – in its multitudinous folds, when the thunder rumbled again and the yard broom, propped against the toolshed, fell over with a clatter. Hester sighed and peered out through the glass; it wasn't raining, not yet, but the wind had got up with a vengeance and was lashing the great beech tree which grew just outside the courtyard.

It was very hot, still. Hester went to the butler's pantry and fetched a beautiful cut-glass bowl. She stood it on the draining board, then began to pile the cleaned lettuce in it. When it was full she got a bowl of tomatoes from the larder and a cucumber and began to slice them both over the lettuce. Willi had pulled her a bunch of spring onions, earthy still but smelling strongly enough to remind Hester of their presence. She was bending down and fishing out the spring onions from under the sink to clean them in the lettuce water when the thunder rolled again, much louder; the noise was cymbals and drums, the wind rose and the light began to fade as the great black and purple clouds raced across the sky. Hester leaned over the sink to look out again into the yard. Where was Nell? Her daughter wasn't keen on storms, and this looked like being a storm and a half. If Nell was in the lane she could run in, but suppose she decided to shelter under a tree? A great white spear of lightning forked to earth, making Hester jump and blink. Gracious, it was downright dangerous to be out there in such a storm, she had better just check . . .

She ran into the yard and out of the small arch. The wind snatched her pinafore, then whipped her hair loose from its band and lashed it across her watering eyes. Hester retreated into the comparative shelter of the courtyard just as the thunder crashed and the lightning flashed right overhead. She should go into the lane and get Nell back . . . she had a vague recollection of the child saying she might do something else, but what it had been she could not recall. She set off across the yard once more and, with lowered head, was charging under the arch when someone caught her shoulders. She opened her eyes, hoping it was Nell, but it was Matthew, hurrying in from the fields. He held her back from him, his eyes on her face.

'What are you doin' out here, woman? There's a tree been struck at the top of the hill, you want to keep indoors in weather like this.'

'Yes, but Nell's out. She went berrying in the lane, I know she's sensible, but . . .'

Matthew pushed her before him into the kitchen, then stopped in the doorway. Sweat was trickling down the sides of his face and his shirt was sticking to him.

'Nell, out in this? She must've taken shelter. I came up

the lane and I didn't see hide nor hair of her.'

'Well, she's not in the house,' Hester said. 'Or if she is, she went in some other door.'

There was another enormous clap of thunder; the plates rattled on the sideboard and the lamp hanging from the ceiling swayed so violently that Hester ducked.

Matthew turned and made for the back door.

'Something's been struck,' he observed. 'Oh dear God!'

'What? What is it?' Hester cried, hurrying across the room. 'Is it the castle? the lodge?'

'It's the tall tower at the end of the west wing,' Matthew said. 'Well, that'll put an end to the old man's ghost; he thought it would attract visitors so he was keen on finding out about it, but . . .'

Ghosts! Hadn't Nell said something about ghosts? And if she had been berrying in the wild garden when the storm started but didn't want to come back to the kitchen and be set to work, what better place for her to take shelter than the tower at the end of the west wing?

'Matt, Nell could be there! She could, she said something about hunting for ghosts. I suggested she might pick the berries in the wild garden . . . oh Matt, I'm frightened!'

'Our Nell, in there?' Matthew leapt for the doorway. He was across the courtyard in a few long strides with Hester on his heels. They bypassed the main courtyard and ran through the garden, heedless of scratches, stings, uneven ground. Even from here they could see the tower, leaning drunkenly and half the height it had been ten minutes earlier. It looked extremely dangerous, and even as they ran towards it there was another crash and a pile of masonry came tumbling into the wild garden.

A figure stood watching; Mr Geraint, in shirt-sleeves and corduroys, a pen still in his hand and his horn-rimmed glasses well down on his nose. He must have run out as soon as the first crash sounded and now he turned and gestured them back.

'Keep away – it's dangerous. Nothing we can do, anyway.'

'I must . . . ,' Matt gasped, trying to push past his employer. 'Nell's in there.'

'Matt, there's nothing of any value, nothing worth risking

your life . . . *what* did you say?'

'Nell's in there!'

Hester was past them, heading for the sideways tilting door at the foot of the tower. She was shrieking as she ran. 'Nell, Nell my darling, come to me, come to me!'

Someone grabbed her from behind, pushing past so violently that she fell to the ground. Mr Geraint shouted, 'I'll go. Stay with her, Matt, don't let her . . .'

He disappeared through the narrow doorway.

Matthew followed him and Hester trailed behind. She was very frightened. The tower's tilt was against nature and the darkness within looked sinister, but still she followed. She saw Mr Geraint halfway up the stair which curved round the tower, climbing steadily. He saw her and called down to her. 'Get out, it's bloody dangerous, Hester! I'll just check the top . . .'

Matthew was following him up the stair.

'If you take the top, Mr Geraint, I'll check the tower room,' he shouted. His voice echoed hollowly around the edifice and Hester cringed, fearing that the sound would bring the whole tottering building down around their ears. 'Get out of it, Hes – now!'

She was doing no good where she was, so Hester left the building, suddenly sure that Nell wasn't in there anyway. If she had been in the round room she would have come out and run down the stairs as soon as the lightning struck; if she had been on top of the tower her body would have been flung down with the masonry now smoking at Hester's feet.

The lane? Not the lane. What else had she said? Something about hunting ghosts? No, that wasn't it, she'd said right at the start that she wanted to go up into the hills and Hester had said it was silly on such a hot day and had suggested berrying in the lane. Yes, that was it, the little madam would have gone up into the hills. She would be a lot safer there than down here, with the bloody castle tumbling about their ears. Thank God, thank *God*, she should be perfectly all right up there. Hester stared at the hill directly above them and froze; the tallest pine, almost at the summit, had been struck and flamed still. Smoke, black as the clouds overhead, poured from its fallen trunk. As the men came out of the foot of the tower she began to run, pointing, yelling over her shoulder at them.

'She's gone up the mountain, where the biggest berries grow. Oh dear God, and the lightning . . . a tree's been struck.'

Mr Geraint overtook her. He was running fast, with determination, his face set and grim. Behind her, she could hear Matthew's laboured steps. It occurred to her to marvel that Mr Geraint, who was older and less used to violent physical activity, should be able to out-run Matthew, and on a hill at that, but then she began to draw ahead herself, youth and anxiety lending her wings. Elbow to elbow, she and Mr Geraint slogged up the increasingly steep slope. The thunder still rolled, the electric tingle in the air made her gasp for breath – why didn't it rain, for goodness' sake? The summit was in sight now; they were on the verge of the trees. Ahead there were brambles, gorse, wild, wind-whipped grass, and above that, just the sheerness of the cliff and the great boulders which, long ago, must have tumbled down from the peak.

'All right, Hester?'

That was Mr Geraint, only now she realised that it was also John, the man she loved rather than the man for whom she worked.

'I'm all right,' she said breathlessly. 'Can you see . . . oh, John!'

She pointed ahead of them. There lay the basket, tipped on its side, its burden of berries all over the rocky scree. Relieved of the weight of the blackberries the basket was being blown around and was showing signs of strain, the stained wickerwork coming apart. The bottle which had contained lemon barley water was shattered, its fragments scattered across the scree.

'Where the devil is she?' John shouted above the noise of the wind and thunder, beginning to climb the steepest stretch. Hester found herself slipping behind until, with an impatient exclamation, he reached back a long arm, caught her by the hand, and pulled her up beside him. 'There's nowhere to hide a cat, let alone a healthy seven-year-old! She's not here; should we go down? I'll shout to Matthew . . .'

'She's here; she wouldn't have dropped the basket and

gone, she must be here!' Hester said, her voice rising to conquer the howl of the wind. She continued to climb and saw without surprise that John was climbing steadily beside her. 'It's so noisy, but when the thunder eases off we'll shout. She could be behind any one of these boulders.'

'Yes, you're right. Come on!'

He set a punishing pace, but Hester kept up with him. Once she glanced back and saw Matthew, a hand to his side, hanging on to a tree at the edge of the wood, far below. Then she forgot him and concentrated on searching for Nell.

In her tiny slit of a cave something woke Nell, some sound other than the crash of thunder and the howl of wind. She stirred, then sat up. Recollection of her whereabouts was instant and unpleasant. Her mouth felt dry and her throat ached but she crawled up to the crack of daylight, glad that she hadn't slept for long. She could imagine the horror of waking when it was dark outside, to see no light whatsoever.

Again, she squeezed as close to the crack as she could and was sure she could hear the murmur of voices. It must be Mum and Dad, come to find her; her heart lifted and began to pound with excitement. She must make them hear her, she dared not face the terror of hearing those voices growing fainter and fainter! She put her face as far into the crack as it could go and shrieked with all her might.

'Mum, Dad, it's Nell, I'm behind the big rock, I'm stuck.'

'What was that?'

It was Nell . . . oh thank God, thank God!

Hester crouched on the ground and peered behind the big boulder leaning against the cliff. But there was not enough room for a kitten to get through there; her poor baby must be behind some other boulder, or in a cave somewhere, and the sound of her voice must be travelling to this spot. There wasn't room for the tiniest child behind this enormous chunk of rock.

But John knew better. He looked at the rock, at the cliff behind it, and then he took Hester's face between his hands and spoke very clearly so that there could be no misunderstanding.

'The boulder's been struck, Hester . . . look at the top of it, look at the ground to the side. It's half toppled over, that's why she's caught. We'll have to shift it, somehow.'

Hester looked fearfully at the boulder, then at her companion. 'But we can't,' she whispered. 'It's too big, no one could move that.'

'We've got to,' John said. She couldn't think of him as Mr Geraint, not with that white line around his mouth, that desperate urgency in his eyes. 'We don't know how deep the crack is, but it won't be a proper cave. Come round the other side and we'll start shoving.'

They were pushing fruitlessly when Matthew came over the ridge. His face was scarlet with effort, his hair was slicked to his forehead with sweat. He glared at them both. 'Where's my girl?'

Mr Geraint stopped pushing and straightened.

'Ah, Matthew, good man,' he said briskly. 'Go down the hill and fetch a crowbar, if you please, and fetch Willi and Dewi at the same time. We've got to shift this thing, the kid's somewhere behind it. She must have crept into a crack in the cliff when the storm was at its height and then the boulder was struck and it's trapped her. Hurry!'

'You go,' Matthew said. He spoke very loudly and glared at Mr Geraint as though at his deadliest foe. 'You go; I'll try to get at the littl'un. I reckon if I were to dig under it one end, unbalance it like . . .'

'Matthew, get that crowbar!'

Matthew dropped his gaze, half turned, then turned back.

'What right—' he began furiously. 'That's my little girl . . . oh, very well.' He began to lumber downhill a good deal faster than he had lumbered up. Hester, who had taken no notice of the short altercation, knelt on the ground and pushed her head as far as she could between the cliff-face and the boulder.

'Nell? Nell, darling, are you here? Dad's gone to get a crowbar to shift the big rock and Mr Geraint and I are going to try to undermine it so it tumbles back and lets you out. It may take a little while, but you won't mind that, will you?'

There was a short silence, during which Hester realised that her heartbeat was so loud she doubted she would hear if Nell spoke, but then Nell did speak, and she heard each word.

'Mummy! Oh, Mummy, I've been so frightened, but it's all right now you're here. I am glad you found me before it got really dark.'

Hester was about to answer when she found herself pulled backwards and Mr Geraint, without a word of apology, knelt down and inserted his own head into the gap between cliff and boulder.

'Nell, it's me, Mr Geraint. Are you hurt, sweetheart?'

Hester could not hear Nell's reply, but imagined that she had said she was not hurt.

'Good. You're in a little cave, aren't you?'

Again, Hester could not make out her daughter's words but guessed that the answer was in the affirmative.

'Good again. Stay there and keep well back, because the boulder may rock a bit once we get it moving. Is that clear? Stay well back.'

Hester waited until he had backed out and was standing up and wiping his face on his shirt-sleeve, then she touched his arm timidly.

'We *are* going to get her out?'

He nodded, glancing measuringly at the boulder. 'Oh yes, we'll get her out all right, but it may take time and she's too young to relish being stuck down there for very long. Ah, here comes the rain. It may help.'

Hester followed his gaze. Sweeping across the green and gold plain which separated the hills from the sea came a curtain of rain, billowing from the heavens. The thunder's crash was receding, it was muttering off into the distance when the rain reached them.

In seconds, she and Mr Geraint were soaked to the skin, but he gave a grunt of satisfaction and ran lightly and nimbly down the hill a short way, to where the giant pine still smouldered. He broke off a big branch, then returned to the hilltop and began to push the branch into the softening earth at the foot of the boulder. Seeing his intention, Hester also ran down the hill, rescued a branch for her own use, and joined him. In five minutes, between them, they had dug a narrow trench along one side of the boulder and when Mr Geraint leaned against it, it moved. Not much, but a definite movement.

'It's going!' Hester said. She knelt the better to dig with her branch, indifferent to the long streaks of yellow mud which caked her arms and legs. 'We're going to do it!'

'I never doubted it,' Mr Geraint grunted. 'Ah, here comes Matthew with the crowbar . . . shove it here please, Matthew.'

Without a word Matthew complied. This time the great boulder seemed to sigh as it settled. With renewed vigour, Hester and Mr Geraint dug and scratched with their branches and Matthew wielded his crowbar until the great boulder made a horrible sucking noise and settled several inches. Matthew stood up and mopped his brow, not that it made much difference with the rain sluicing down like a waterfall.

'This'll take a week,' he said gruffly. 'Stand back, both of you. I'm goin' to wedge the crowbar behind the boulder, see if I can win a few inches that way. Seems to me a few inches would do it – she'm a little thing, our Nell.'

But it was not to be so easy. Matthew and Mr Geraint both strained on the crowbar until their muscles cracked, but the boulder would not budge.

'It'll have to be an undermining job,' Mr Geraint concluded, leaning against the cliff to get his breath back after the last effort. 'Hester, run down and fetch more help, we need manpower, the more the merrier. Matthew and I will keep digging here.'

'I don't want to go . . . she's my baby. Can't one of you go?' It was an illogical and stupid reaction because she was not as physically strong as either of the men, but she was not thinking logically or sensibly. 'I can dig, I've been digging.'

'You'll have to go into the village; Dewi and Willi went off when the storm started,' Matthew said. He looked challengingly at Hester, his dark eyes suddenly cold. 'You'd better hurry, girl.'

Hester nodded, then crawled around the rock once more. 'Nell? Are you all right, darling?'

There was a pause during which, Hester supposed, Nell

made her way to the front of the cave.

'Mummy, will it be soon? I'm awfully cold and I'm sitting in a sort of river. I – I don't like it much.'

A river! Hester's blood ran cold. The rain beat on her head, as insistent as Chinese water torture, as threatening as the Flood. If it continued to rain and the rain continued to build up in the tiny cave, what would happen to Nell? She could tell by the sound of the child's voice that the cave must be lower than the crack . . . oh God, what if Nell were to drown within a few feet of help? But it was useless thinking like that.

'It won't be long, darling,' she called back. 'I'm just going to fetch the men to give us a hand. Chin up, Nell!'

She backed out and Mr Geraint took her place. 'Keep right to the back, there's a good girl,' he called. 'Won't be long once Willi and Dewi get here.'

As he backed out, Hester caught his arm.

'John, she's sitting in water,' she said urgently. 'The cave's lower than we are – she could drown if the rain doesn't stop.'

'Off with you; we'll get her out long before the rain gets to that depth,' Mr Geraint said bracingly. 'Hurry, Hester, but go carefully.'

Hester nodded, smiled blindly at both men, then set off down the hillside.

The rain poured on, forming big puddles in the clay soil of the cliff top. Matthew was steaming; he glanced sideways. The old man was steaming too, his greying curls flattened, his glasses cast aside, his shirt transparent with wet. His face was all bones, Matthew thought contemptuously, bashing his crowbar into the solid rock at the foot of the boulder, nibbling away at it inch by inch. The old man's stronger than I credited though, he got up that mountainside like a bloody goat . . . he is a bloody goat, a bloody old goat. I saw them, I heard them, when they thought I was too far behind to notice. All those years of calling her Mrs Coburn, now it's Hester this and Hester that. What's the old goat playing at, eh? Answer me that! If he's got an eye on her then he'll have me to answer to; not that she'd stand for anything, not my Hester.

'Come over here, Matthew. Have a crack at that.'

The old man had unearthed another patch of rock. Matthew was inclined to tell him to do it himself; what was the point of continually bashing away at different spots? He'd got down a couple of inches with that last blow, it would probably pay him to keep on undermining just there. But old habits die hard. Sighing, he moved, to thud the crowbar into the new challenge, though his shoulders felt as though someone were sticking red-hot daggers into them and the ache in his lower back had to be felt to be believed. He had been harvesting in the thundery heat since six that morning; he wasn't fresh from a nice, sit-down job in the study, like Mr Geraint.

'Well done, Matthew. Now let's have another go at moving her. Put some beef behind it this time.'

Mr Geraint grinned encouragingly and put his shoulder to the rock. Matthew scowled, then bent to his crowbar. If they could just shift it four, six inches . . .

It rolled! Sluggishly, with a horrible squelching sound. Then it settled, and Matthew felt his heart contract with horror. It was settling nearer the cliff, not farther from it, they'd never get her out at this rate.

'That's no good,' he shouted roughly, heaving the crowbar free. 'That'll make it worse, Mr Geraint, she's movin' nearer the cliff, not farther off. We'll have to try something else.'

'It's all right,' Mr Geraint panted. His cheekbones were showing dull patches of red, his mouth hung open, but his eyes were very bright. This was an adventure to him, Matthew told himself, just an excitement. But to Matthew it was his child's life or death. 'It's all right, Matthew, we've got to lose some to gain some . . . can't you *see*?'

For two pins Matthew would have brought the crowbar down on the old man's head, using that patient, sarcastic tone with him! And he could not see what good it did to crowd the boulder closer to the cliff face; they were trying to release Nell, not pen her up for good.

'Come on, man, don't just stand there,' Mr Geraint's voice was sharp, impatient. 'I want to get this done before dark falls.'

That was the final straw. Matthew flung the crowbar down

and jumped forward, seizing Mr Geraint by his shirt-front.

'You want this, you want that! Whose little girl is trapped behind there, eh, old feller? It's just a bleedin' game to you, isn't it, just a bleedin' game! But that's my daughter behind there, wi' the water creepin' higher with every drop of rain that falls. You don't give a toss, all you care about . . .'

Mr Geraint turned and looked at him. Really looked, as though he was seeing Matthew for the first time, seeing him as another man, not as a servant.

'I don't give a toss, don't I? It's a game, is it? Well, you're wrong, Matthew, quite wrong.' Mr Geraint's voice was full of scorn and mockery, the tone Matthew particularly hated. 'That's *my* little girl behind that boulder and I'm going to get her out whole and well with or without your co-operation. Now hand me that crowbar!'

Matthew shook his head and charged, like a bull. All the pent-up frustrations of years, all the fears for Nell, all his love for Hester, his uncertainty whether she truly returned his love, boiled to the surface. Within thirty seconds the two men were rolling to and fro in the yellow mud, fighting, gouging, swearing, their goal forgotten.

Hester had gone only as far as the castle; as she was running past the main courtyard a car had come cautiously out from under the arch with its windscreen wipers going and the driver leaning forward to see better. Fortunately, the driver's window was open and through it Hester could see Mr Seddon, with his wife beside him. Hester guessed they had come up for afternoon tea with Mrs Clifton and were about to depart. Realising that this could save her time, she ran forward and leapt for the running board, catching hold of Mr Seddon's shoulder through the window and giving it an imperious shake. She saw her hand on that immaculate dark suit, the fingers bleeding where she had grazed her knuckles on the rock and the skin yellow with clay. Mr Seddon jammed on the brakes, bringing the car to an abrupt halt.

'Mrs . . . er, er. . . is something wrong? You seem in some – some distress.'

'Oh Mr Seddon, my little girl's trapped in a cave at the top of the mountain; there's been a rock-fall. Matthew and Mr Geraint are trying to dig her out but they need help. Could you possibly . . .'

Mr Seddon caught on quickly. 'A rock-fall, by heaven! I'll drive into the village, get a car full of men. Tell Geraint I'll be with him as soon as possible. Whereabouts on the mountain?'

'At the top, above the tree-line,' Hester gabbled. 'I'm going back but I'll come down again when I see you in the lane and guide you to the right spot.'

Mrs Seddon leaned across. 'My dear, can I help? I could make a flask of tea, bring it up the mountain.'

'That would be very good, but I must go,' Hester said. She jumped off the running-board and the engine coughed, then steadied into a purr as Mr Seddon drove off. Hester was already hurrying back the way she had come, her breath short in her throat, the nagging pain of a stitch in her left side beginning to make itself felt. At this moment Nell might be struggling out of her prison, or she might be gasping for breath as the water rose . . .

Hester's lumbering run turned into an agonising race as she tackled the steepness of the mountain.

She came out of the trees, a hand to her side, her breathing so harsh that she could hear nothing else. She looked up constantly as she plodded through the soaking furze, but the rain made an effective curtain; she could not make out the boulder through the downpour.

As she neared the summit she saw the top of the great rock, looking exactly as it had looked when she had left some twenty minutes earlier; of the men there was no sign. They must be getting Nell out, she thought excitedly. But why should they need to do such a thing? Why could the child not wriggle out unaided? Oh, dear God, has the water . . . ?

Forgetting her exhaustion, Hester broke into a shambling run once more.

*

154

Geraint, gaining the upper hand for a moment, saw a movement out of the corner of his eye and thought that it had to be Hester returning. The child was still trapped and here he was acting like a fool, fighting young Matthew as though they were two schoolboys instead of grown men.

He pushed Matthew away, trying to say this was mad, that a child's life was at stake, but the man came at him with such force that they both fell heavily to the ground. Matthew's face was suffused with rage, the look in his eye reminded Geraint of a cornered wildcat he had once shot. He realised that Matthew had no intention of stopping the fight, that he would continue to battle on until one or other of them confessed to being beaten, or, he thought suddenly, one or other of us is dead.

Well, it's not going to be me, you murdering bastard, Geraint said to himself; he moved back a little, startling Matthew, then lunged forward, grappled Matthew by the ears, and brought his head down on the rocky ground with a sickening thud. It was enough. Matthew, covered in mud from head to foot, lay on his back, looking like a huge felled ox. Geraint struggled to his feet just as Hester panted over the ridge.

'John, what's happened, where's Nell? Good God, has poor Matt collapsed? Help's coming . . . I'll look after Matt, you keep digging!'

Geraint grinned muddily; that's my girl, he thought, turning obediently back to the task on hand. Singleminded, that was Hester; she always concentrated on the job in hand, whether it was being seduced on a beach, making a hot dinner, marrying the wrong man or rescuing her daughter.

He wedged the crowbar under the tipping end of the rock and heaved again, muscles cracking with effort. And this time it began the slight, almost rhythmic movement he had hoped for. Now it was possible! Now, if he could keep up the rhythm, the boulder would work with him and would topple by its own momentum as much as by his puny efforts.

The rain poured down, sweat stung his eyes, his body gasped for a rest, but the slight, rocking motion continued relentlessly, and the gap between boulder and cliff face grew, fraction by fraction, until it was an inch, two, three . . . six.

'Mummy, the water's too cold. Can I come out yet?'

The small, weary voice went to his heart, filling him with a novel feeling; a need to protect someone other than himself, a desire to cherish, to give instead of take. He wedged the crowbar, then dropped to his knees.

'Nell, my dear, can you come to the opening now? I think it might be wide enough for you to wriggle though.'

He put his head behind the boulder and after a moment's unnerving silence, he saw a small white hand, closely followed by another. She was holding on to the lip of rock at the front of her little cave. She turned her head and saw him; her smile was wide though tears had carved twin paths down her filthy face.

'Hello, Mr Geraint! Can I come out now?'

'Do you think you can get through? If not, my dear, I'll start levering again and we'll have you out in no time.'

'I think I'd better try,' Nell said diffidently. 'My legs are so cold I keep sliding down, and my hands won't hold on for much longer, I don't think. The water's really deep at the back.'

He had never admired anyone more; his heart swelled with pride though he knew what she was saying. It was now or never, get through the tiny gap or . . . but no sense in thinking of that.

'Right. See if you can reach my hand.'

He grunted, pushed his hand as far into the crack as he could reach, bringing his head out to do so. But no small fingers clutched his, no human warmth reached him. He shoved and strained until he could feel the blood trickling down his shoulders and the side of his neck, but still could not reach her.

Hester had propped Matthew up against a rock. She was crouching by the boulder, staring. When she saw what he was trying to do, she came closer.

'John, come out of there. I'm a lot thinner than you, let me try.'

'But you don't have the strength; you'll need to heave her out physically. You can't do it, Hester, you mustn't try.'

'I must. I will. You must let me.'

156

He knew she was right. He withdrew, then put his head back into the crack for a moment.

'Mummy's going to see if she can reach you, Nell. Her shoulders aren't as broad as mine, she'll have a better chance.'

He changed places with Hester, who reached into the crack; her entire shoulder vanished and he could tell by her expression that she was feeling without success for the child's hands. She came out, then went in again, head first this time. He could hear a muffled conversation, then Hester began to ram herself into the crack. He poked her none too gently in the back.

'Be careful! If you get stuck we're lost.'

She must have turned her head, because he could hear her clearly. 'She's sliding back. I'll have to go further in. Give me a push!'

'It's madness! Hester, my own darling, if you get stuck . . .'

'I shan't, but it's our last chance! Push, damn you!'

She had never spoken to him in that tone of voice before and he could understand her desperation. So he seized her by the curve of her hips and pushed hard, glad of the slippery clay, of the constant downpour, glad of anything which would help her to slide further into the narrow crack. She was right, it was the only way.

'Got her!'

It was muffled by the rock, but clear enough. Geraint sat back on his heels and rubbed his eyes, not ashamed of the tears brimming in them but anxious to be calm as the most difficult part of the operation started: getting them both out safely.

'Are you sure? Has she got you, as well? I won't start to pull you out until you've got a good grip.'

'She's hanging on like a limpet,' Hester's voice said, faint but joyful. 'Aren't you, my pet?' She turned her head and her voice came strong and clear to Geraint's listening ears. 'Start to pull ever so slowly and carefully, John. I can't move at all without letting go of her.'

The next few minutes were a nightmare. Geraint pulled, slowly and carefully, gripping Hester round the knees, but even so she screamed once, a cry of real agony, and once she told him to stop before he tore her clean in two. But they were winning. He heard a muffled thud and a squeak, then Hester spoke again.

'She's out! She's lying on her tummy, the whole of her top half is out. Keep pulling!'

Suddenly, like a cork from a bottle, Hester shot out of the crack, arms at full stretch. Grinning gleefully out of a mask of mud, Nell followed.

Safe! The three of them hugged, then turned with one accord towards Matthew.

'Matt! Good lord, I'd forgotten, is he still unconscious? What happened, John?'

'We put too much weight on the crowbar and he slipped on the wet clay and landed on a ledge of rock, knocking himself cold,' Geraint said untruthfully. 'He's concussed, we'd better get him down the hill fast; he'll need medical attention, and you two could probably . . . ah, thank God!'

The rescue party came swiftly over the ridge, faces anxious, Willi and Dewi well in the lead with the Seddons close behind. They were armed with blankets, a flask of brandy, a door for a stretcher.

'We're all right,' Hester said when the men wanted to put her and Nell on the stretcher and carry them down in triumph. 'But poor Matthew's had a nasty fall. John . . . Mr Geraint thinks he's concussed. Can you take him?'

They all stumbled down the mountain, though Nell was carried. Geraint put his arm around Hester; no one would wonder at it, after what they had been through. Matthew remained ominously still, the colour drained from his face, his eyes closed. Nell patted his hand, stroked his cheek, but Matthew knew nothing.

'I've sent for the doctor,' Mr Seddon said as they trailed into the castle. 'He'll take a look at all of you, but I think Matthew ought to be taken straight to hospital. He's been out for a good half-hour, possibly longer.'

They put him in the car, all muddy on the back seat, and Mr Seddon dropped the female Coburns at the lodge to wait for the doctor. Mr Geraint stayed in the car; he would see

Matthew safely in to the Alexandra Hospital and then return. The doctor arrived minutes after the car had left. He heard the story, examined Nell briefly and Hester perfunctorily, then patted Nell's head and Hester's shoulder and advised them to get into a hot bath as soon as possible.

'You've had a pretty frightening experience,' he said, including both of them. 'Got any soup? Good. Put it on the stove to warm while you bath; get into the tub together, then go straight to bed. You're both young and strong, you'll be right as rain in the morning. And Matthew's a tough fellow with a head like a bullet. He'll be fine too, they'll probably send him home tomorrow.'

Hester couldn't be bothered to heat up kettles and pans of water for a hot bath so she and Nell had a thorough all-over wash, including their hair, then sat at the table in their night things and drank hot soup. Nell's eyes were drooping when Hester tucked her up, but she was still awake enough to ask her mother, drowsily, whether concussion was dangerous.

'No, love, it's just another name for a bang on the head,' Hester said cheerfully. 'Your poor Dad will be so cross that he wasn't able to help get you out, but he did most of the heavy work before he had the fall.'

'Mr Geraint was kind, wasn't he?' Nell mumbled, eyes already closing. 'But it was you who reached me, Mum. I'd still be there if you hadn't got into that crack. Your poor soldiers!'

'Shoulders, love,' Hester corrected automatically. 'And my shoulders will mend. Now go to sleep like the doctor said; we'll have plenty of time to talk in the morning.'

Six

Hester had no sooner tucked Nell in and left her, however, than the back door opened and Mr Geraint came into the kitchen. He smiled at her but did not apologise for not knocking.

'Is she all right? Matthew was beginning to come round before I left, but he was still groggy. He vomited as we got him out of the car.'

'Nell's fine; tucked up and probably asleep by now,' Hester said. She had been sitting in the chair near the range, for the thunder had taken the unseasonal warmth with it and it was quite chilly. She was uneasily conscious of her attire, for she was clad in her long white nightgown, with an old blue cardigan over it which had once belonged to Matthew's mother. 'I'll go to see Matthew first thing in the morning.'

'I'll take you in the morning; the child can come with us. No harm in that.'

'Thank you,' Hester murmured. 'Will you visit him too?'

Mr Geraint hesitated, then crossed the kitchen and dropped into the chair opposite Hester's.

'On the whole, I think I'd better not. Hester, you and I need to talk.'

'What about?' Hester said, genuinely surprised at the suggestion. Nell was safe, she herself had bruised and bleeding shoulders and she ached in every limb, but what could Mr Geraint have to say to her? And why did he look so worried? 'What about?' she repeated.

'About Nell. You know she could be my child, don't you, Hester?'

160

'*Your* child? She's Matthew's daughter, John. That was why we got married.'

'You got married because you were expecting a baby. My baby, not Matthew's. And, after today, I want to acknowledge her.'

'*Acknowledge* her? Tell people she's yours, d'you mean? You can't. It wouldn't be fair on any of us, particularly Matthew.'

'No, no, I don't need other people's approval or otherwise of my actions,' Mr Geraint said impatiently. He glanced towards her, then turned his gaze on the leaping flames of the fire. 'But between ourselves. I want her to go to a better school than the village one, mix with a better class of child. I'll pay the fees, of course. When the time is ripe, I want her to go abroad, learn foreign languages, live a fuller life than is possible here. And I want her to spend more time with me, at the castle. Surely we can arrange these things between us?'

'Without people talking? Without Matthew becoming suspicious? John, you must have taken leave of your senses,' Hester said impatiently. 'As for the school, I think she has a good chance of winning a scholarship to a better school when she's a little older. And besides, you can't *know* Nell's yours, it isn't possible.'

'Isn't it?' John said grimly. He got up from his seat and went over to Hester, taking both her hands and pulling her to her feet. 'Darling Hester, why do you think I showed you that picture in the Long Gallery? My great-grandmother is the spitting image of Nell, or rather Nell's the spitting image of her.'

'They are a little alike, but that's just coincidence,' Hester said stoutly, while her heart lurched uncomfortably. Could Mr Geraint use the likeness against her in some way? She knew that he loved her but that he would use her for his own ends if he had to. And he wanted Nell; she could see it in his eyes as he smiled down at her. 'I don't want any trouble, Mr Geraint. Now that Nell's safe, we just want to get on with our lives.'

'If you work with me, let me share her, you won't have any trouble, my dear. But if you defy me, try to keep the child from me and deny that she's mine, I'll have the law on my side, and sufficient money to make it relatively easy for me to become her guardian, if nothing closer.'

Hester tried to wrench her hands away but he hung on. He grinned down at her, looking suddenly devilish in the firelight. He would do it, she was sure, he would take Nell. She would have to agree, have to find some way of making Matthew agree; she could not bear to lose her baby, the only person bonded to her by unselfish, uncomplicated love.

'I'll do what I can,' she said sullenly, looking at the floor. 'But I won't have her sent away to boarding school, I tell you straight.'

'If I can find a decent school in the area she may go daily, but if necessary she will board,' Mr Geraint said. 'I want the best for her and you should, too.'

Hester tugged herself free and walked away from him, picking up the blackened old kettle as she passed it, filling it at the bucket, returning to stand it over the fire. These small actions gave her time to think, to decide how best to tackle the situation. She turned away from the kettle and sat down again, then looked up at him. He looked mocking, triumphant, yet there was uncertainty behind his smile. This really mattered to him, or it mattered now. By tomorrow, or this time next week . . .

'Very well, since we both want the best for her I suppose I must agree,' she said, unsmiling. 'You're blackmailing me, Mr Geraint, and doing it very successfully, but things don't always work out the way one expects. I am one thing, Matthew quite another.'

The uncertain look fled. His smile was gentle, but triumphant.

'Good girl! Leave Matthew to me. I'll call for you early tomorrow morning to take you both down into Rhyl to the hospital.'

After he had gone, Hester went into the child's tiny room and looked into that much-loved, sleeping face. Once only with Mr Geraint, and in her mind there had always been an uneasy suspicion that the baby could have been the older man's. But Matthew had accepted that Nell was his, had welcomed her, adored her. She had simply grown accustomed to thinking of

Matthew as Nell's father, and thinking of Mr Geraint simply as . . . well, an experienced lover who occasionally desired – and took – his servant's wife.

Was there a law which allowed a father to claim his child, to take her away from her mother? She knew nothing of the law, but Mr Geraint had seemed certain. She could not imagine Matthew allowing Mr Geraint to give the orders so far as Nell was concerned, not even if he were paying the bills. Matthew would say Nell was happy at the village school and doing well and there she would stay; he would say he wasn't having anyone, not even the old man, interfering between them and their daughter.

That was the rub; their daughter. What if Matthew suspected . . . ? what if Mr Geraint, in order to get his own way, told Matthew about that night on Rhyl beach, before she and Matthew had met?

Hester turned slowly from her sleeping daughter and went into her own room. In a daze of unhappiness and uncertainty she took off her cardigan and climbed into bed. What she really needed was a night's rest to set her straight; perhaps in the clear light of day she would see a way out.

It had been a long day and a tiring one. Hester cuddled down in bed and was soon asleep.

She awoke because she heard a noise. Someone was thumping hard on the back door. Startled and scared, Hester sat up in the big bed, trying to make out from the amount of light coming through the curtains what time it was. Had she overslept? Was it Mr Geraint coming to fetch her for the hospital trip? But the old alarm clock was ticking solemnly, and in the faint light she thought it only showed seven o'clock.

Someone thumped on the door again. The clock must have stopped, Hester decided. Oh, dear heaven, she was in trouble already and she had only just woken up. She left the bed with a flying leap, grabbed her old coat off the back of the door, and slung it around her shoulders. She ran across the room, her bare feet slapping first on the linoleum and then on the tiled kitchen floor. She unbolted the back door top and bottom, then flung it open.

It was a damp, misty morning, and very early. The sky was grey and a heavy dew hung on the grass, drops spangled the creeper by the back door and Hester's breath puffed out into the autumn air in little white clouds. The man who stood on the doorstep muttered something and lurched forward. Hester fell back a step.

'Matthew! Whatever are you doing here? You should be in hospital. How did you get here? Here, let me give you my arm.'

She tried to take hold of him but was roughly pushed aside. Matthew shambled past her, then turned and grabbed her by the shoulders. His hair, rough and uncombed, fell across his forehead and his eyes were blazing with fury.

'Matt, what's happened? Why are you so angry? Nell was saved, it's all right, she's safe in her bed.'

'Nell?' His voice was hoarse. 'What do I care about your wretched brat? What are you doing in my house?'

He still held her shoulders; his face was so close she could see the little red veins in the whites of his eyes, the strong growth of his black beard, the line of spittle running down from the right-hand corner of his mouth. He looked old and ill – and as dangerous, she realised, as a mad bull.

'Your house? Matt, it's me, your wife . . . don't you recognise me? And Nell's your daughter, your child . . .'

He shook her again and pushed her from him. 'You? My wife? I want none of ye,' he shouted, his voice thick, slurred. 'Get out of my sight, and stay out!'

Hester gasped as he pushed her away from him with such force that she collapsed into the easy chair. 'You're ill, Matt, you must go back to hospital!'

'Ill? I'm not ill, but you will be if you stay. If you're my wife, I can beat you to a pulp and chuck you in the river. I could stone you to death – in the bible they stoned adulteresses.' He loomed over her, strong, square hands clawed. 'I could tear you in pieces and feed you to the ravens . . . and I will, if you're not out of my sight in five minutes.'

'But Matt, there's Nell . . .'

The name was like a red rag to a bull. He seemed to swell with rage and Hester, who had been frightened before, was almost paralysed with terror. If he wanted to, he could kill her and the child. He was insane, but that would not help her. She would run to Mr Geraint, he would take her in.

'Don't move!' He had seen her involuntary glance at the door. 'Stay there. I'm going up to the big 'ouse. I want you gone by the time I get back, you and your child, or . . .'

He drew a finger significantly across his throat.

'What are you going to do up at the big house?' Hester asked fearfully. 'Who are you going to see?'

He was halfway to the back door, weaving, uncertain. He paused, turning towards her a frowning face on which she saw not only rage but unhappiness.

'See? That's none o' your business. Just you get out!'

She waited in the chair until he had gone, then jumped to her feet. He knew! He knew about Mr Geraint, perhaps about that evening on the beach, though because of the accident he couldn't remember exactly what he did know. But he knew himself wrongèd and would probably kill both her and the child if they stayed.

Where can I go? What should I do? The thoughts scurried around her mind, confusing her more than ever. If I decide to brazen it out and stay, Mr Geraint will try to take Nell . . . if Matthew doesn't kill us both first. She ran into her bedroom and began dressing. Matthew was mad . . . Mr Geraint was bad, between them she was helpless. If Matt turned her out, then Mr Geraint would take Nell. He wouldn't want Hester, she was just a woman, it was his own flesh and blood he wanted.

But Nell was her baby, the most important thing in her life. She could manage very well without Matthew, had done so for the first sixteen years of her existence. She could also manage without Mr Geraint; she had lived cheek by jowl with him for seven years and most of that time he had simply ignored her. But she could not imagine a life without Nell.

Dressed, she shoved a few things into a bag, then ran through to Nell's room. The child was sleeping deeply, but Hester, after only the smallest of hesitations, shook her awake.

'Get up, darling, and get dressed. We have to leave here in rather a hurry. Come along, don't bother with washing ... hurry, Nell darling, do hurry! If you hurry we can catch the first bus.'

She snatched some of Nell's clothing and shoved it into the bag with her own, then ran into the kitchen and got her small savings out of the teapot at the back of the deep pantry. Nell came through and began to make breakfast, but Hester stopped her.

'No time, my dear, we've a bus to catch! Come along, I'll explain as we go.'

As they left the lodge, the rain was just starting: a fine, misty rain which hid the castle from view and veiled the plain leading down to the sea. Hester took one last look at the lodge, then glanced towards the castle. All she could see was the broken tower at the end of the west wing, bleak and black above the mist.

'Are we going to the hospital to see Dad?' Nell asked as they almost ran, hand in hand, towards the bus stop. 'Didn't Mr Geraint say he'd take us?'

'Yes, but things have changed. I'll tell you all about it when we get there.'

The bus came after what seemed years to Hester, and they climbed aboard and took their places on the top deck. As they passed the lodge she looked down and saw, with real horror and fear, Matthew coming out of it. Even at a distance she could see his anger, as though it could not help but show itself even in his gait. He came out of the gates and she saw that there were tears running down his face. He looked miserable, uncertain, but then he caught sight of her and the sadness went. He gave a bellow which she could not hear for the bus's engine, she just saw his mouth gape, saw his chest swell with the intake of breath, then he set off in pursuit, stumbling and waving his arms. Hester's heart began to gallop, but no one noticed Matthew and the bus drew inexorably ahead, leaving him, at last, clinging to a tree, his head sunk on his chest, the picture of despair.

The blow on the head has affected his mind, Hester told herself. Matthew was always gentle, always good. Perhaps I

166

should have stayed? But she knew it would never have worked, not once Mr Geraint had decided that Nell was his. He must have deliberately told Matthew, turned the poor man's brain, then the fall had finished the job.

'What were you looking at, Mum? Was it Mr Geraint, come to take us to Rhyl? He won't be pleased that we've gone on the bus, you know.'

Hester jumped. She had almost forgotten Nell was there, sitting quietly beside her. 'Oh, I was just looking back. Now as soon as we reach Rhyl, dear, we'll get on another bus . . . We shan't go to the hospital today.'

To her horror tears threatened to close to her throat. She made a little choking sound and fell silent, struggling with herself. She must remain calm for Nell's sake.

Nell took Hester's hand timidly. Her small fingers tightened until the knuckles gleamed white.

'Mummy, is Daddy dead? Is that why we're running away?'

Hester clutched at the straw her daughter unwittingly offered. 'Oh darling, I'm afraid he is. We have to go away, we can't stay at the lodge without him. Just for a little while, until things are settled, we'll live somewhere else.'

Nell quietly detached her hand from Hester's and bent her head. Her hair hung forward so that it was impossible for Hester to see her face, but she could see the big, hot tears falling on to the small, clenched hands.

Matthew had woken in the early hours, when it seemed that all the other patients in the hospital slumbered. His clothes were in a rough, string-fastened parcel on a chair at the foot of his bed, so it was a simple matter to pick it up and take it along the corridor until he came to the lavatories. With considerable difficulty, he dressed himself. He was still stupid with sleep and could not remember how he came to be in hospital, though he supposed vaguely that he must have been ill. The only thing he could remember was that his wife was an unfaithful slut and an adulteress and that the child he had adored was the woman's bastard and nothing to him.

He walked to the lodge. At first the dawn air was cool and

167

misty, but it began to rain long before he arrived. By the time the lodge came into view he was beginning to feel the heat of anger and disappointment stirring in his belly once more. There was some man . . . he couldn't remember who he was or why they had fought – had they fought? The man had told him about his wife, about the child, and he had known it was true. Now all he wanted was to confront her and get rid of her, 'see her off', he said to himself.

She came to the door. She looked so clean and white-faced, so innocent somehow. But he knew her now, he could see the black heart which she tried to deny with her soft smile, the dark passion which she hid beneath a pretence of obedience. He pushed past her; she tried to take his arm. He avoided her until he was in the kitchen, then grabbed her, told her what he thought of her, shook her, saw the fear blossom in her gaze, saw her lips tremble, her eyes fill.

She was tearing him in two! Half of him wanted to crush her underfoot, to see her dead for dishonouring him. The other half wanted to take her in his arms, kiss her, tell her it was all a mistake, that he knew her too well, she was no man-hungry siren.

But that was the fool's way, the coward's way. The cuckold's way. Yes, that was it, she had cuckolded him and now she was looking at him with her big, innocent eyes, as though she didn't understand why he was incoherent with rage.

Even so, he had been tempted to give in, to shrug, to say it was a mistake, and take his place in the easy chair, tell her to put the kettle on, to make him a cup of tea. But there was that man, whoever he was. He would enjoy thinking that Matthew Coburn was content to be cuckolded, to be deceived. And there was the child, the cuckoo in his nest. How he had loved her, admired her! He had been so proud. She had the look of the Coburns, he had told himself a hundred times, and she had her mother's bright, enquiring mind and quick intelligence. She would go far.

And so she would. Far from him. So he had frightened the woman with threats and ordered her to go, then he had left the small, damp house and headed up the drive towards the castle.

Only he realised halfway up the drive that he had no idea why he was hurrying in this direction, or whom he intended to confront when he got there. He felt ill, confused, and soon his footsteps slowed and he leaned against a gate, the better to think. Had the man really said Hester was unfaithful? His Hester? The pretty wife of whom he had been so proud? Surely no man would say such a thing, and why should the man be at the castle? Someone lived at the castle, he knew *that*, and he worked for the fellow. He couldn't remember the name but it would come to him in a minute. In the meantime, he turned and hurried down the long drive. He should never have told Hester to go, not when he was ill and confused. Who would nurse him if she left?

He reached the lodge again and burst through the kitchen door. A part of his mind acknowledged that it was not locked and knew it to be a bad sign, but he searched each room anyway, calling her name, calling for the child. They couldn't go far; they had nowhere to go. Hester was an orphan-child, the lodge was her first real home, Matthew her only relative. She would go to the village, to some woman or other, but she would listen, would come back to him.

He left the lodge, but the world was beginning to behave very oddly indeed; trees tried to strike him with their branches, he had to duck to avoid their attack, and the lodge gates began to swing open and closed as he approached. Using considerable cunning, he ran between them when they weren't watching, and on to the road. He saw the bus approaching and stayed where he was; the road was slipping and sliding like a pulled ribbon, no sense in stepping under the vehicle's wheels.

The bus drew level, and something pulled his gaze up to the small faces in the window on the upper deck. And she was there, watching him, her eyes big and black in her pale face, fear in every line. He ran at the bus. He screamed her name to the four winds, 'Hester, Hester, don't leave me, don't go, I didn't mean . . .'

The bus trundled on. He followed, though his heart felt it would burst with effort and his breath burned in his chest. It got farther and farther ahead and he knew there would be no catching it, no second chance for him. The bus rounded the corner and disappeared and Matthew made one last enormous effort. He slogged on and on, no longer knowing why he was running, simply running, slower and slower, the breath in his throat harsher and harsher. He bit his lip until blood came, then his legs gave way and he felt the wet tarmac come up and smite his hands, his knees. Uncaring, he let go, almost welcoming the darkness which rushed up and dragged him into its chilly depths.

Mr Geraint arrived at the lodge early, to take Hester and the child down to the hospital. He was feeling pleased with himself. For seven years he had shilly-shallied, not sure whether Nell was his daughter, unsure whether to claim her as such. Then he had found the picture in the Long Gallery and had been intrigued by a likeness which had struck him at once. Surely this meant she was his child? He had always suspected it, but there had been no need to rock the boat, no need to say anything.

Then Nell had got herself trapped in the cave, and all at once he had known he loved her. The feeling he had for Hester, he told himself, was not love, simply an unusually strong physical attraction. The fact that in all his promiscuous life he had never felt it about a woman for longer than a few hours – in fact, never after he had possessed her – was something he ignored because it did not suit him to acknowledge it. But his feeling for Nell was different; purer, simpler. She was the child he had wanted. She was clever, brave, affectionate. She needed him and he needed her; who was Hester to stand in the way? Or Matthew, for that matter?

So he made his plans; bribe Hester and Matthew with promises of good schooling, money, advancement. Threaten if necessary; and then step in.

He drew the car to a halt outside the lodge, putting the brake on gingerly, for he rarely drove when Matthew was available. He got out, looking hopefully up at the sky. It was clearing – good. It might be possible to put the hood down on the way home, give them all a good blow. The car ran with condensation on a wet day and it took a good deal of the pleasure out of a motor trip.

He approached the front door and tried to open it, but it wouldn't budge. Locked. Well, of course it would be, cottagers never used their front doors. Hester and the child would probably be in the kitchen, getting ready. He strode round to the back yard and pushed open the door. He entered the room breezily, as of right, but it was empty. He frowned; the fire wasn't lit, last night's supper things were still on the table. If he hadn't known better, he would have thought the house deserted.

He searched it, of course. No thought of an employee's right to privacy entered his mind. It was his house, they were his servants, the child was his child, he had every right to find them when he wanted them. But he didn't find them because they weren't in the house. Little spitfire, she had probably taken umbrage at his remarks last night and caught the early bus to visit Matthew. He was annoyed, of course, but couldn't help an appreciative grin. How typical of Hester, his wild-child, to make a fool of him, teach him the unwisdom of trying to dominate her. He would dominate her, of course, and he had every intension of carrying out both his threats and his promises. Nell was too good to be wasted on a country yokel; he loved her; he had every right . . .

He went through the house again, but idly this time, out of curiosity. He sat on Nell's hard little bed and examined her possessions, an ill-made reed basket with some badly blown birds' eggs in it and some old, grimy children's books. He peered behind the hanging curtain and frowned; she had very few clothes, even fewer than he would have thought. I'll buy her more, he thought complacently; I'll take Hester with me and we'll choose some really pretty things. She would look lovely in primrose cotton, or a clear, pure pink. That wonderfully shiny black hair needs pastel shades to set it off.

He went into the room Hester and Matthew shared. There was a rickety table on Hester's side of the bed with a couple of drawers and a shelf. The shelf contained more books, equally thumbed. Old romances, several volumes of Dickens, a set of Shakespeare which, he realised with a wry grin, she had almost certainly filched from the library up at the castle. And in the first drawer he found a pressed wild-flower collection, carefully arranged in a small, cheap exercise book with her name on the outside: *Hester Coburn. Wild flowers of Pengarth.* Close by it, small tins. They had once contained shoe polish, Glaxo, Pears soap; now they held a collection of dry moss, some unusual stones, a few birds' eggs and some fossils – a fern, sea-shells, a curly ammonite, all labelled and stuck on small pieces of card.

For some reason it touched him, brought unexpected tears to his eyes. She was only a child herself, Hester! She had missed out on a normal country childhood, shut up in her Liverpool orphanage, and she had been making up for it. He imagined her, by night a woman whether she liked it or not in Matthew's bed, by day an eager child, searching the lanes for wild flowers, for birds' eggs, for strange objects for her collection. She had not had time for such things since she took over at the castle, of course. He knew that, acknowledged now that he had worked her too hard, been unfair. But he would change, be different. He would see to it that she had help, that she took time for herself. He remembered the day she had come storming up to the room over the arch, wanting to know why he was suddenly interested in Nell, suddenly taking her to the seaside. He had laughed and made love to her and she had forgotten her anger and her questions, but now he felt faint stirrings of guilt. Now he realised she would have loved to accompany them, paddle in the pools, push a shrimping net under the heavy swags of seaweed in search of miniature monsters of the deep. He could imagine how it would have thrilled her to find a sea-urchin's shell, to see the green, scuttling crablets, to gloat over a silver and brown flatfish, undulating across the bucketful of seawater in which she would keep her temporary treasures.

But this was doing no good; he closed the last box, replaced it in the drawer, closed the drawer and looked around him. What a dull room! A chest of drawers with a small piece of mirror on top, a curtained-off corner where her clothes hung, Matthew's too, probably; one wobbly kitchen chair beside the bed and linoleum on the floor. Not exactly a love-nest, but then Matthew wasn't exactly a lover – a husband perhaps, but not a lover!

Geraint left the room, closing the door firmly behind him. He would buy her some pretty things. Why had he not thought of it before? She would resent his interference far less if she had a pretty room with a few nice knick-knacks around.

Outside, he cranked the starter, thinking ruefully that it had been a good few years since he'd started and driven his own car, then drove slowly down to the gates. If he turned left he would reach the village, but there was no point in doing that; he would turn right and drive into Rhyl, pick the pair of them up when they left the hospital and take them somewhere nice for luncheon – why not? They deserved a treat after the ordeal they had all suffered the previous day. And later, if the weather improved, they might even go on the beach. He turned right and had driven perhaps a mile when he saw, sprawled on the tarmac ahead of him, what looked like a man. It was probably a drunk from the village, though it was a funny time to find a drunk, at nine in the morning, unless he was ill or worse.

Geraint applied his brakes and steered the car into the verge. He climbed out, but left the engine running. He walked over to the recumbent figure. It was Matthew! Geraint bent over him and rolled Matthew on to his back. The fellow was soaked, his face was bruised, he looked terrible. He was breathing though, and a hand slipped under his jacket proved that his heart was beating, though it seemed to Geraint a faint, jerky beat. Well, the man should have been in hospital and Hester and the child would be distraught when they got there to find him gone, so he had best be taken back before he caught pneumonia lying on the wet road.

Geraint heaved Matthew on to the back seat of his car and drove off, still puzzled by the whole business. He was sure that Matthew had run away from hospital for some reason, though he could not imagine what that reason could be, and had collapsed before he reached his home. Why no passing driver had noticed him, assuming he had been there for a while, was a mystery. Still, no point in fruitless conjecture; the thing to do was return him to the ward at once, where he could get the treatment he so plainly needed.

It took twenty minutes to reach the hospital and by then

173

Geraint, glancing over his shoulder to the back seat every now and then, thought Matthew's colour was a little better. But the invalid did not regain consciousness until he was being carried to the ward on a stretcher, and then he didn't make much sense.

'She's gone, then,' he said as the ward nurse scolded him and began gently undressing him. 'She wouldn't wait for me, wouldn't let me explain. She just upped and went.'

'Who did, Matthew? Who are you talking about?' Geraint asked gently, but Matthew just frowned and sighed and repeated what he had said.

'He's still concussed, sir,' the ward nurse said, leading Geraint away from the bed. 'He isn't in his right mind yet. 'Twill take a while, I daresay, before he comes to himself.'

'But he'd walked all the way to Pensarn,' Geraint objected. 'Surely he couldn't have done that in a state of concussion?'

'I've known men, and women too for that matter, who've walked miles and miles, even ridden bicycles, and all without knowing it, because they were asleep,' the nurse observed. 'The mind's a strange thing, sir. Now you come back in twenty-four hours and he'll likely know you and be able to have a proper chat. Right now he isn't making sense.'

Taking the nurse's words as a dismissal, Geraint accompanied her down the long corridor towards the entrance hall, but as he was about to leave something else struck him. 'Oh, nurse, what did you tell his wife?'

'His wife?'

'Yes; Coburn's wife and daughter must have come to visit him earlier.'

'Ah, I wasn't on the ward then, sir. I was on Morrison until forty minutes ago.'

Geraint nodded and left. It was pointless questioning the hospital staff as to the whereabouts of the Coburn females. Hester and the child must have come into town on the bus and doubtless they intended to return by the same route. He would walk into town and have a look at the timetable, see what time the next bus left for Pensarn. Then he would take a look in the cafés, see if he could spot them, and reassure them that Matthew was back in his hospital bed.

174

He searched diligently, but saw neither hide nor hair of them all that long, wet morning.

When Hester and Nell climbed off the bus, Hester had no idea what to do next, but scarcely had they set foot on the pavement before another bus, which had drawn up beside them, began to show signs of departure.

Hester was wondering whether to get aboard or whether to find out first where it was going when she saw, out of the corner of her eye, the familiar shape of Mr Geraint's dark blue Lagonda. Without giving herself time to think she jumped aboard, pulling Nell with her.

'Only just made it, my love,' the bus conductor said, helping them on to the vehicle. 'Put your bags in here, there's two seats up the front.'

Presently he came along the bus, calling 'Tickets, please,' and whirring the handle on the little machine which produced the tickets. Hester waited until he was directly behind her, then listened intently.

'Tickets, please.'

'Return to the Beast Market at Wrexham, please.'

'Right; change at Ruthin, love.'

The money changed hands, the conductor moved along to stand beside Hester and Nell. 'Tickets, please.'

'One single and one half to Wrexham Beast Market please.'

'Change at Ruthin,' the conductor said automatically. 'Goin' to take the littl'un on the fair? I wouldn't mind a go on the gallopers meself!'

Hester muttered something noncommittal and tucked her change into her old black leather purse. Nell, who had been uncharacteristically quiet all morning, gave a small bounce in her seat.

'A fair, Mum? Can we go? Can we?'

Hester, who was simply acting on the impulse to put as much ground as possible between her and Matthew, nodded quickly. 'Yes; why not? I wouldn't mind going round the fair. It's ages since I've been on a roundabout or a cakewalk.'

It had stopped raining by the time they got to Wrexham.

175

They got off the bus and stood uncertainly in a wide street, with shops either side and a big inn at one end. Seeing them staring, a fellow-passenger, a plump woman with a tiny boy attached to one hand, stopped for a moment.

'Fair's down there, dear, on Eagles' Meadow. See? I daresay the little girl would like to buy a fairing, have a go on the rides.'

'I would, I really would,' Nell said. 'Come on, Mum, let's go and have a look.'

They descended the long, green slope of the meadow to where the fair, all bright awnings and loud music, was enticingly spread out before them, and Nell tugged at her mother's hand again.

'Mum? Are you very sad? Would you rather not go on the fair?'

'I am sad, but it's no use being sad, darling. You and I have got to make our own way in the world now. And if it would make you happy to go on the fair, then that's just what we'll do. Only I will have to get a job of some sort, and you'll have to go to school one day.'

'Can't we go back? Not ever?'

Hester took refuge in adult vagueness. 'Perhaps one day, love. But Mr Geraint will want the lodge for someone else, you see. I can't drive a motor car or work on the land.'

'But you can cook and clean and run the castle,' Nell pointed out. 'And if Daddy's dead, all the furniture and things are yours, so why are we running away?'

Hester looked at her with mingled annoyance and admiration. The acuteness of her! She was only seven, but she could put two and two together in a very practical fashion.

'Darling, I'm sorry I told you a fib, Daddy isn't dead. But do you remember I once talked about a lady called Mrs Cledwen, who lived up at the castle once?'

'Ye-es. When I was really small.'

Hester nodded, holding the small hand warmly in her own.

'That's right. Well, she went away. I think Mr Geraint didn't like her any more. And that's how it is with Daddy and me. He – he doesn't like me any more and wants me to go. I can't tell you any more than that, but we can't go back, either of us.'

She looked down at her daughter. Nell's small, heart-shaped face was solemn, intent. Hester could see her daughter was doing her best to understand.

'Doesn't he like me any more either, Mum? Was it because I got caught in that cave and he and Mr Geraint had that fight?'

'Oh, I don't think they had a fight, love,' Hester said gently. 'Gentlemen like Mr Geraint don't fight with their servants. If you heard their voices raised it was probably because they were arguing over how best to get you out.'

The black shining bell of hair swung from left to right in a slow, determined negative. 'No, Mummy, they had a fight, really they did. Daddy said it was his little girl trapped and that Mr Geraint didn't give a toss, and then Mr Geraint said, in a really horrid voice, that I was *his* little girl. And then they hit each other; I heard them.'

Hester was bereft of the power of speech. She stared at the child as though Nell were not a child at all but a witch. Then she recovered herself and gave Nell a hug. Her little girl was truthful and intelligent; she was simply reporting what had happened while Hester had been fetching help.

'Do you know, Nell, I think you're right, they must have had a fight. I don't know what was said, but I knew in my heart that someone had said something. Nell, darling, that's why Daddy doesn't want us to live with him any more. Because you aren't really his little girl.'

'Then whose little girl am I?' Nell asked plaintively. 'I love Daddy, I don't mind if he isn't my real Daddy, so I don't see why he should hate me just because I'm not his real little girl.'

'He doesn't hate *you*,' Hester said quickly. 'He hates me, because I let him believe that you were his little girl.'

'Then whose girl am I?' Nell said again, her voice quivering. 'I must be someone's girl, mustn't I?'

'Yes darling, of course you are. You're my little girl, my very own little Nell. And now let's go and see if we can have a ride on that roundabout, and we'll buy ourselves a cake and some ginger beer, shall we? I'm awfully hungry!'

'Oh, if I'm still yours, then it's all right,' Nell said, giving a little skip as they walked down the long green hill. 'I'm hungry too, Mummy. Can we get some chips?'

Geraint fetched Matthew from hospital after three days. Riding back in the Lagonda, with Geraint driving and Matthew sitting in the passenger seat, they were very quiet. Apart from generalities, Matthew did not say a word until the car drew to a halt outside the lodge. Only then did he turn and look directly at his employer.

'She's gone, hasn't she?' he said bluntly. 'She's taken my Nell, too. I shouted at her, you see, called her names. I weren't in my right mind, of course, but she didn't know that.'

Geraint shot a cautious glance at the other man. For three days he had kept off the subject of Hester and the child, hoping to find them in the meantime, but he had no idea where they'd gone. He had travelled to Liverpool, visited the orphanage where Hester had been brought up, the convent school where she had been educated, all to no avail. She had not been back, they had had no word. And in all that time he had not managed to discover just how much, if anything, Matthew remembered. And since he had no wish to lose his chauffeur, handyman and farm manager all in one, as well as the best housekeeper he had ever possessed, it behoved him to tread carefully.

'Yes, they've gone,' he said. 'Did Mrs Coburn come to visit you in hospital, Matthew? Is that what you're trying to say?'

Matthew shook his shaggy head. His hair needed a trim and he had cut his chin twice, presumably while shaving; tufts of cottonwool clung to his unhealthy looking skin, looking like some mould growth.

'No. I went home to the lodge. Or I think I did. They told me off at the hospital for runnin' away, so I must have, mustn't I?'

He sounded miserably uncertain, but Geraint thanked his lucky stars. The concussion had fogged Matthew's mind; perhaps they would get through this whole business without Matthew remembering precisely what it was that had happened to put him in hospital. And Hester was bound to come back, bringing the child. She would find Matthew complacent once again, Geraint more thoughtful and much less demanding. They would all pick up their lives and jog along comfortably again, he was sure of it.

But Matthew was waiting for an answer, so he pretended to think deeply, then nodded. 'Yes, you may have reached the lodge. I found you lying in a puddle on the side of the road; if I'd not found you, well, least said soonest mended, eh?'

Matthew cleared his throat. 'You saved my life, Mr Geraint, they told me so at the 'ospital. And I'm grateful, very grateful. Only, without my Hester and little Nell, I can't think my life will ever be much.'

'Good God, man, they'll come back!' Geraint exclaimed, turning to stare at his passenger. 'This is just a whim, a temporary thing. Hester wouldn't leave us!'

Matthew shook his head again.

'No, she won't come back,' he said with unhappy certainty. 'I called her a whore; I said I'd kill her if she stayed.'

'You . . . *what*?'

'And I don't even know why I said those wicked things,' Matthew confessed miserably. 'I never had no cause, she was the best was Hester. They said in the hospital my mind weren't my own, 'cos of the concussion. Couldn't we put a message in the newspapers, Mr Geraint, saying as how I'm terrible sorry but I'm in my right mind now, and want 'em back?'

'You said you'd kill them?'

It was worse than Geraint had feared, far worse. No wonder the poor kid had fled, taking her beloved daughter with her. For the first time for days Geraint remembered his own threats: blackmail, she had called them. No wonder she had gone. Matthew was right, she would never come back.

'I did, Mr Geraint. But I never would've . . . I wouldn't hurt a fly, I wouldn't, let alone them I love.'

All this time they had been sitting in the car outside the lodge with the engine running. Now Geraint turned off the engine and got out, going around to open the front door for Matthew.

'I know you wouldn't hurt her, Matt, but she must have believed different and this does put a different complexion on things. We'll do our best to get a message to her, but it's not going to be easy. You'll have to resign yourself to a long wait.'

Matthew nodded dully and shuffled in through the front door. Geraint thought the man had aged twenty years in the last three days and told himself vengefully that if he ever got hold of Hester he'd give her a good spanking. Life without her was going to be bad enough, without having Matthew stumbling round in a daze, doing his work at a snail's pace, getting things wrong, making mistakes.

As he was going inside, Matthew turned round. 'I'll put up wi' a wait, so long as she does come back,' he said wistfully. 'She's the apple of my eye, is Hester, and Nell's another. I don't reckon I'll ever amount to much without 'em.'

'I'll draft an advertisement tonight,' Geraint promised. 'Will you be fit for work tomorrow, Matthew? Only there's a deal been left undone these past few days.'

He wondered whether Matthew would remind him that he had only just risen from his hospital bed but the man's eyes brightened and he straightened his shoulders slightly.

'Oh ah, the fellers don't go along too well without someone to tell 'em yea or nay,' he observed. 'I'll be back on the job first thing in the morning, Mr Geraint. I'll soon get them sorted!'

Seven

The doctor's waiting room was crowded. Nell, sitting numbly at Hester's side with a piece of towel wrapped around her crushed fingers, had long stopped crying and was dozing uneasily, her head on her mother's arm.

Hester looked down at her with a heavy heart, seeing as if for the first time the dirt-streaked face, the tumbled hair, the faded, too-small cotton dress. What had she done to her little girl? In the six months since she had run away from Matthew she had been too busy just trying to keep them fed to take a long, cold look at their circumstances. But because she had to remain in this stuffy little room until the doctor was free, she had, at last, time to look back over those months. On top of everything else today was the twenty-first of April, Nell's eighth birthday, and with the best will in the world Hester had been unable to do much to celebrate the occasion. She had no money, no prospects, and after what she had said to Mr Hicksome, she would certainly have no job. Indeed, she told herself, with a momentary resurgence of her old spirit, she did not want a job with that wicked old skinflint. Not that she had always regarded Mr Hicksome as a wicked old skinflint. Indeed, eight weeks ago he had seemed more like a saviour.

Hester and Nell had not remained in Wrexham, it was too near Rhyl, a mere thirty miles inland, so after they had visited the fair she had made her way to the railway station and taken tickets to the only other place in Britain that she felt she knew: the city of Liverpool. She was well aware that she could not go back to the Sister Servina Convent. She had disgraced herself with the good nuns by getting in the family way, but she was grimly determined that nothing would part her from her child. Still, she did have some knowledge of the city and was able to find a job of sorts, and a roof over her head. She worked for a greengrocer and slept in a dreadful lodging house, but at least the greengrocer had been glad of Nell to fetch and carry for him and had allowed them to stay together.

Then there had been the notice in the paper. Not that she had seen it, she had only heard about it from a customer. 'Ever so romantic it is,' the old woman had said when telling Mr Ransome, the greengrocer, about the advertisement in the *Echo*. 'A feller advertising for his wife an' kiddie to come home.' She had beamed toothlessly across the counter at Hester. 'Same name as you, chuck, though not the kiddie, the kiddie's name was Helen, not Nell.'

As soon as the shop closed, Hester had seized Nell and hurried her back to the lodging house. She shared a filthy slip of a room with another woman and her two children but she had only stayed long enough to tell Jess that she was leaving.

'I've gorra better job,' she gabbled breathlessly, clutching her skimpy bedroll. 'See you some day, Jess.'

Back she had hurried to Lime Street Station with a bewildered Nell at her side. More travelling, until the money ran out, then another brief job followed by another flit. Hester was convinced that Matthew, or Geraint, or both must have guessed she would make for Liverpool, why else should they advertise in the *Echo*? So it stood to reason that she must be far, far from the city or they would find her. Matthew meant to kill her, Geraint to take Nell from her. Neither Matthew's murderous desires nor Geraint's cupidity could be risked.

They travelled indiscriminately for a while, sometimes on foot, sometimes by bus or train. But at last they reached a place where Hester felt safe, a sizeable town on the very edge of Norfolk, where Hester had once more obtained work, this time as a housekeeper to an elderly widower, Mr Hicksome. She was travel-stained and weary, not at all the sort of person most people would employ as a cook-housekeeper, and had been almost tearfully grateful to Mr Hicksome for giving her a chance.

And in King's Lynn, for the first time, Hester began to relax a little. She and Nell shared a tiny, stuffy attic room with a ceiling so low neither could stand upright, and a round window which did not open. The house was damp and difficult to keep clean for it was hard up against the railway line and smoke from the trains smuttied the house day and night. Hester was beginning to believe it got to her lungs as well, for she began to show alarming signs of illness – she, who had never ailed in her life. What was more, though Mr Hicksome had offered her a low wage, he had made no objection to Nell's presence, so when he began to dock her money each week, taking off a penny here for food, tuppence there for fuel and lighting, Hester did not have the will to complain. She needed the job so desperately and was so drained of energy and hope that she did not even consider contesting the deductions. She had a hacking cough which wouldn't go away and her back ached and ached all the time so that even in bed at night the pain would wake her. She got through her housework somehow, cooked meals as nourishing as she could manage on the money Mr Hicksome allowed, and simply stumbled through the days in a nightmare of weakness and misery, tumbling into bed at midnight only to wake again in an hour or two with worries whirring in her head.

She had longed for spring, thinking that her cough would go away with the finer weather and her general health improve, but this had not been the case. Instead, she got worse, dragging herself wearily through the days until even Mr Hicksome, who moved with the speed and agility of a very old tortoise, commented on what he termed her lazy, slovenly ways.

Nell did her best to help in any way she could, but she was always hungry and, although Hester had only just realised it, she had another preoccupation: avoiding Mr Hicksome. The dreadful old man, it transpired, had probably only employed Hester because he had a wicked weakness for little girls, and had been trying to get his hands on Nell for all of the eight weeks they had lived in his house.

'I didn't want to worry you,' Nell had said in a small, exhausted voice as the two of them had fled the house and made for the doctor's surgery. 'I kept out of his way, or ran to you. Only tonight he trapped me as I was coming into the kitchen and when I tried to push him away he grabbed the poker and . . .'

Nell had shuddered, indicating the crushed fingers.

'I'll have the law on him,' Hester had muttered. 'But not until the doctor's done what he can for your fingers, love. Just you be brave and he'll have you right in a brace of shakes. *Then* we'll tackle the disgusting old monster.'

For that moment she had felt strong and brave, capable of tackling anyone: Mr Hicksome, Mr Geraint, even Matthew, whom she had grievously wronged. But by the time they had explained to the doctor's wife why they were here and had entered the crowded little waiting room, most of her courage had evaporated.

What will we do? she thought listlessly, even the arm that cradled the child aching now. Where can we go, how can we live? No one will believe a child of eight if it came to court and anyway I suppose it isn't a hanging offence for a dirty old man to put his hand in a child's knickers; better just keep our mouths shut and move on. Again.

But she was so tired! Because she was sitting down the ache was easier, but soon they would have to find themselves a bed for the night – oh, how could she do it? How could she keep on when all she wanted was to lie down and die?

'Next!' The doctor's door had opened and a woman, fat and red-faced, came out. The man closest to the door got up and went in, closing the door behind him. Everyone moved up a seat, shuffling themselves along one nearer. Nell was actually sleeping though and Hester was wondering how on earth she could move the child without waking her when the problem was taken out of her hands.

'You sit still, gal, you look fair wore out. I'll give the tiddler a lift.' The speaker was a young woman, probably about Hester's age. She had thick, streaky brown-blonde hair, rosy cheeks, almost black eyes and a wide, friendly smile. She was also strong; she lifted Nell and her chair to one side, pulled the empty chair out of its place, shifted everything along and replaced Nell again, all in one swift, practised movement.

'Thank you ever so much,' Hester whispered. 'She's crushed her fingers, I don't want to wake her until I must.'

'Oh, so the kid's the patient, is she?' The girl looked hard at Hester. 'You look poorly yourself, gal.'

'I'm just tired,' Hester said. 'And I've got a cough. But Nell's fingers are badly crushed.'

'Kids mend good,' the girl said. 'When you see the doc you want to mention that cough, gal. No point wastin' a bob. I doubt he'll charge you more for two than he would for one; he's a good feller, Dr Burroughes.'

'I might mention it,' Hester conceded, as her new friend settled herself once more. 'I'm not usually this tired. I ache, and . . . but why are you here? You look very well, if you don't mind my saying so.'

The girl smiled again and stuck out a square, sun-tanned hand, the wrist covered in rather grubby bandage.

'I am well, except for my wrist. I did it in a week back,' she said cheerfully. 'We'd better interduce ourselves if we're going to sit here chattin'. My name's Barbie Grace Allingham; what do they call you and the littl'un?'

'I'm Hester Makerfield,' Hester said. She had reverted to her maiden name, feeling that she had no right now to call herself Coburn. Besides, it would make her harder to trace. 'And this is my daughter, Nell.'

'Nice to meet you,' Barbie said. 'In fact . . .' she lowered her voice, though no one in the waiting room seemed to be taking the slightest notice, '. . . In fact, between ourselves, I'm not the only patient I'm tekin to the doc's. See my bag?'

Hester had noticed the gladstone bag at her new friend's feet. She nodded, looking curious.

'Well, that ain't luggage, nor yet shopping. It's my livin', you might say.' Barbie looked hard at Hester. 'Scared of animals, are you?'

'I thought I saw it move a bit just now,' Hester said. 'No, I'm not scared, I like 'em. What is it? A dog? cat?'

'I'll show you,' Barbie said. 'The old feller's not too brave, he've got a bit of eye trouble. Doc'll give me some ointment

185

when he checks my wrist, he's real good like that. Got more sense than most vets, I tell you straight.'

As she spoke she was unfastening the bag, giving Hester a look loaded with mischief as she did so. Hester, leaning forward, saw what looked rather like a couple of fat and bulgy bicycle tyres piled in into a pyramid and then, on top of the pyramid, she saw a small, spade-shaped head and a pair of bright, reptilian eyes.

'It's a *snake*,' Hester whispered, choking on the first laugh she had had for months. 'You've got a big snake in that bag!'

Barbie nodded, grinning. 'That's it, that's Phillips. Want to give him a stroke? Some folk can't bear 'em, mind; I know that. In fact my feller, John, he've got a thing about snakes. Won't let 'em near nor by. Which, as you can imagine, makes life awkward for me right now. Go on, stroke him.'

Hester leaned forward and put her hand cautiously into the bag. The snake's skin felt smooth yet she could also feel the slight roughness of scales. And it was warm, not cold. She remembered a grass snake which Nell had brought in once; that had not repelled her either, she had thought it both beautiful and strange, neither slimy nor frightening. But Matthew had not liked the snake at all. He had shouted at them for bringing it in and his face had gone quite white when Nell had picked it up and walked past him to the back door.

'Gosh,' she murmured, 'he's big, isn't he? He must be a weight.'

'Aye, he's eight foot long and he weighs getting on for a stone, I guess,' Barbie confirmed, closing the bag and fastening it down again. 'I'm with the fair on the Tuesday market place – I'm Barbie the Barbarian, the snake woman. I wrestle with old Phillips here twice nightly, mat'nees at weekends. Only not with a broken wrist, I don't.'

'Gosh,' Hester said again. She eyed her companion with considerable interest. 'Who's wrestling with him now then?'

'No one. That's a strange old thing, but most folk seem scared to touch Phillips, let alone wrestle. Still, we've movin' on in a few days, going farther into Norfolk. Perhaps I'll get someone to take my place there.'

'We're moving on, too,' Hester said, all her tiredness flooding back. 'Not that I really want to, but . . .'

Suddenly the whole story came tumbling out; leaving her home because of the men's threats, getting work, losing it, feeling pursued, arriving in Lynn and now having to leave because of Mr Hicksome's behaviour. Every now and again someone emerged from the surgery and they all moved up a seat but Hester scarcely noticed. It was so good to share her troubles with someone her own age, so good to talk openly of her fears and doubts. She found she was feeling better just for the experience and when Barbie nudged her at last and said, 'Your turn now, gal,' she was almost disappointed.

'Come on Nell, darling,' she said, gently shaking her daughter awake. 'We're going to see the doctor now, he'll make your poor fingers well again.' She turned to Barbie. 'Thank you for your company,' she said formally. 'You've been ever such a help.'

The doctor proved as helpful and sympathetic as Barbie had implied. He was middle-aged, grey-haired, weary, but he unwrapped the filthy piece of towelling with surprising gentleness, then put his head out of the door and called his wife in.

'Can you dress the young lady's fingers while I have a word with her mother, my dear?' he said. 'I won't keep her long, but she's got a nasty cough.'

Nell went out happily with the doctor's wife, perhaps because Mrs Burroughes was a sweet-faced, motherly woman but more likely because she had promised Nell a piece of fudge when the ordeal was over. Hester, sitting on the chair opposite the big desk with Dr Burroughes behind it, fumbled in her purse, but the doctor stayed her with a wag of the head.

'Don't worry about payment yet,' he advised her. 'How long have you had that cough?'

'All winter,' Hester said. 'I don't seem able to throw it off, doctor. And I'm most awfully tired.'

'Just slip your coat off and jump on to my couch,' the doctor said, taking off his glasses and pinching the bridge of his nose for a moment as though they hurt him. 'I'll take a look at you while you're here. No harm in giving you a check-up.'

Hester took off her coat and climbed on to the examination couch, which was covered in prickly horsehair. She looked anxiously at the doctor as he loomed over her.

'Nell's fingers – are they very bad? Will they heal?'

'There are no bones broken, it's just bruising and abrasions. They're very swollen, but they'll go down as the bruising fades. Now take a deep breath, Mrs Makerfield, and hold it while I listen to your chest.'

Thirty minutes later Hester came limply out of the surgery and Barbie stood up.

'Don't you go runnin' off, gal,' she said fiercely. 'Just you sit there and wait for me. I've got an idea.'

'He wants me to go to hospital,' Hester muttered. 'I don't know what to do . . . He says if I don't I'll get worse and worse. I've got to get Nell, I can't . . .'

'I'll have a word with the doc, explain you're in a bit of a pickle, but you're to *wait*,' Barbie said, giving Hester's arm a shake. 'Say you'll still be here when I come out, do I won't go in!'

'I'll wait,' Hester said with a watery smile. 'I've got to get Nell, though; she's with Mrs Burroughes.'

Nell was perched on a stool eating toast and honey and chattering to the doctor's wife. Her fingers were swathed in clean white bandages and someone had washed her face and brushed her hair. She looked almost respectable, almost happy.

Mrs Burroughes looked up as Hester came into the room. 'Ah, here's your mother,' she said. 'A slice of toast, Mrs Makerfield?'

Worried though she was, Hester's watering mouth had said 'Yes, please', before she remembered that she had been threatened with hospital, that she should be running. And once she was eating it, and drinking the cup of strong tea which Mrs Burroughes pushed into her hand, sitting in the comfortable kitchen chair before the stove . . . well, it seemed easier to tell Mrs Burroughes that the doctor had given her a note for the hospital, but that she simply did not know what to do.

'I was working as cook-housekeeper for a Mr Hicksome, who

lives in Old Market Street,' she explained. 'But we've left there and now we don't even have a roof over our heads, so how I could go into hospital and leave Nell I can't imagine.'

'I think that can be arranged,' Mrs Burroughes said comfortably. 'Now what operation did the doctor recommend, my dear?'

'He said it was nothing much, just a couple of stitches. I've got a – a prolapse,' Hester said. 'He thinks, after Helen was born, that things didn't go quite right and it's got steadily worse. It's why my back aches all the time, he says, and why I'm so tired.'

'Well then, you've got to go into hospital for a day or so,' Mrs Burroughes said practically. 'We have a spare room with a comfortable bed in it; Nell is welcome to stay with me while you are in hospital, and you are welcome to come here for a few days until you are fully recovered. Would that solve your problem?'

'It would be so wonderful, but how can I trespass on your kindness to the extent of leaving Nell with you?' Hester stammered, very confused. How kind some people could be, as good as others could be bad. She turned to her daughter, now drinking milk and only lifting her face from the mug to beam at her mother. 'What do you say, darling? Would you like to stay with Mrs Burroughes for a day or two?'

'While you're in hospital being made better again?' Nell said. There are no flies on my daughter, Hester thought with affectionate pride, she's been listening to every word even when she was up to her eyes in honey and seemed engrossed in her own thoughts. 'I'd like to stay in this house with you,' she ended, turning towards her hostess.

'She's a big help,' Hester ventured. 'And once I've had the operation I'm sure I could manage. If you could keep her though, while I'm in hospital, it would make all the difference.'

'Then that's settled; you'll take the note in tomorrow morning, early, and probably be out the next day. Ah, here comes the doctor; I think you were one of his last patients.'

'Yes, the girl next to us was last,' Hester was beginning, when the kitchen door opened.

Barbie stood there, her bag in her arms.

'Good gal; you waited,' she announced. 'Evenin', Mrs Burroughes, the doc won't be a minute. He's give me ointment for Phillips's eye and a telling off like you wouldn't believe. But we had a laugh together.'

'What mischief are you up to this time, Barbie?' Mrs Burroughes said. She turned to Hester. 'Barbie's family always over-winter in Lynn. Did she tell you she came from the fair?'

'Yes, she did. And you told me what was in your bag, didn't you, Barbie?' Hester said. 'Mrs Burroughes is going to keep an eye on Nell and have her stay here while I have a small operation. After that . . .'

'After that, if you like, you can come wi' us,' Barbie said decidedly. 'Look, someone's got to mind Phillips for me while my wrist's queer. I'll teach you all the business and fair folk is friendly folk. And you in't scared of snakes, for a miracle. I reckon you could do what I do as easy as easy.'

'The fair!' Nell exclaimed before Hester could answer. 'Oh, Mummy, if only we could!'

'I don't see why you shouldn't have a go,' Dr Burroughes said. He had followed on Barbie's heels and stood listening in the doorway. 'You're going to feel a different woman after the repair.'

'Repair! That make her sound like an old traction engine,' Barbie objected. 'Never mind, eh? You'll be well again, Hester, and that's what count.'

'You're all so kind to us,' Hester said, with trembling lip. 'I'll never be able to repay you. We've been nearly desperate at times, Nell and me.'

'Don't worry about it; we were put on this earth to help one another,' Mrs Burroughes said briskly. 'And now, if everything's settled, I think it's time we had a meal and then made for our beds. Tomorrow will be a full day, one way and another.'

Matthew sat in the lodge kitchen, preparing the vegetables for a beef stew. He had not come to terms with losing Hester, but about a month previously he had looked at his situation and decided that something must be done. Here we are, two grown men, letting the lack of Hester drive us, in our separate ways, to perdition, he had told himself. Mr Geraint's taken to drink, he's half-seas over by eight most evenings. He kicked Mrs Clifton out because she taunted him with mucking up his life and then he dismissed the girl he had brought in to manage the castle while Hester was away. Now he sits up there, hunched over his whisky bottle, and damns the eyes of anyone who tries to interfere. Even me, and he's always listened to me in the past. Besides, in a way we're in the same boat, though I've got a real reason for missing Hester. All Mr Geraint misses is his well-managed house, his comfortable existence.

Not that I can criticise him, Matthew's thoughts continued. Not while I continue to let the house go to rack and ruin, and don't eat properly, or enjoy my life. All I do is get through each day's work and then spend the evenings moping. What I ought to do is take heart, use my head. She'll come back; Mr Geraint says so when he's sober, and what will there be for her here if I don't pull myself together? Nothing, that's what there'll be. So I've got to eat right, sleep right, keep the place decent and learn a bit of patience. If I do that she'll come back, and come back to something worthwhile, what's more.

He missed his wife and daughter horribly. Couldn't seem to come to terms with loneliness the way he had before, now that he'd had them to share his life. But Mr Geraint was behaving so badly that it made him see he must reform or go under.

He finished the swede, carrots and onions and tossed them into the pan in which the meat already simmered. It wouldn't be like one of Hester's beef stews – he winced – but it would be comforting after so many scrap meals, and he needed whatever comfort he could find.

He was setting the table when a knock sounded on the back door, which immediately opened to let his employer into the kitchen. Mr Geraint, Matthew was pleased to see, was looking almost respectable, almost himself. He was unshaven to be sure, and his hair was hanging over his collar, but he seemed in command of himself. He glanced around the kitchen, sniffed appreciatively, then sat down in the chair which Matthew had drawn up beside the table.

'Matt – I've news.'

'Oh?'

There must have been hope in his tone, for Mr Geraint shook his head, his eyes softening. 'No, not that news. Sorry. It's Uncle Leo. He's dead.'

'Sorry to hear that,' Matthew said conventionally.

He had known Leo Clifton of course, though not particularly well. An old rip, Matthew's father had called him, but indulgently. Folk liked Leo, for all his bad habits, and the place he had farmed – Sagebush Farm – had done well for him. He was reckoned to be a good employer too, though with the family weakness for a pretty face.

'Don't be sorry. It could be the making of us. He's left me Sagebush Farm; I'm thinking of shifting.'

'Reckon you're right,' Matthew said after a few moments' thought. 'You've lost interest in Pengarth, haven't you?'

'Aye. But what about you? Want to come or stay here? I'd leave you in charge, of course, you could do as you pleased. But it's up to you. You've got as good a reason as I for wanting to leave – better.'

Matthew did not have to think. He shook his head and reached for the salt. He added some to the stew, then turned to face his companion. 'I'll stay here. You think they'll come back, don't you?'

'I did. But it's near on a year. Still, you must please yourself. There's no one I'd rather leave in charge, you must know that.'

Matthew nodded. 'Aye. I'll not cheat you. When will you leave then?'

He could see that the mere prospect of moving on had brightened the older man's eye, given him back some of his optimism. Typical, Matthew thought indulgently. Cliftons could take things to heart, but only for so long, then their appetite for life and excitement would begin to come back and they would charge at the nearest obstacle and forget the temporary setback.

'Oh, there's no desperate hurry, not now that I've somewhere to go. I'll be able to write there. Can't do it here any more, don't really know why.'

Because you miss my little girl and my young wife, Matthew

thought without anger, with compassion even. They were never yours, but you'd come to think of them as a part of Pengarth. Yes, you'll be better away from here.

Aloud, he said: 'Let me know and I'll drive you down. I can come back by train.'

He knew Geraint would not leave the car but then he would not need it either. But the older man was shaking his head. 'No, I'll drive myself. In a week, two perhaps. What's in the pan?'

Matthew grinned. He knew what was coming.

'Beef stew. Care to share it, Mr Geraint?'

'Good of you, Matt. Got any beer in the house?'

'Aye, in the cupboard under the sink; it keeps cool down there.'

The older man began to rummage under the sink, then stood up with a couple of bottles swinging from one hand. He walked to the sideboard and got down a couple of pint mugs, then poured the beer into them.

'Then you'll definitely stay? Be my foreman, manager, whatever? You won't be lonely?'

Matthew shrugged. 'I'm used to it,' he said gruffly. 'Twon't be no worse with you down in Kent.'

'I'll come back a couple of times a year, see how you're making out. You'll probably do better than I've done. You always were steadier, more single-minded.'

'I'll do my best,' Matthew said stolidly. 'Here, get some plates down and I'll dish up.'

Hot August sunshine burned down on Nell's head as she swung on the gate watching Wally, Annie Gate-leg and Tod play hopscotch with a piece of slate and squares scratched in the dust. The gaff had been set up, the gallopers, the dodgems, the swingboats and the joints were all ready, sitting patiently in the sunshine waiting for customers. Already, though it was only eight o'clock in the morning, the flattie kids were gathering. Nell had trailed around after the others, putting up the posters in the village last night and they had spoken to several kids then, reminding them that the fair was in Gaffer Thorne's long meadow for three days, so they had best make the most of it.

193

The trailers were parked in the shade of a stand of beech trees and Nell could see the thread of blue smoke from her mother's cooking fire – or, rather, the Allinghams'. The Allingham family was a large one but they closed ranks against strangers. Hester had been grudgingly accepted because she was useful, but Nell was still very much an outsider so far as the fairground kids were concerned.

Which was probably what always happened, Nell supposed, looking wistfully at the other children. Annie and Tod were Nell's age: Annie redheaded, freckled, sharp; Tod plump, dark-haired, slower. Wally was Annie's little brother, a redhead like his sister but lacking her quick wits and repartee. Nell had seen how the children closed ranks against outsiders but she always tried to hang about near them, hoping – so far in vain – for an invitation to join them.

The older people were all right with her and with Hester, thanks to Barbie. Barbie had liked her Mum and when she liked someone she was prepared to put herself out. And then there had been the broken-wrist-that-wasn't because, although Nell hadn't realised, Barbie's bandage covered a perfectly healthy arm.

'But I wanted an excuse to train someone else up wi' Phillips,' she told Hester, just before she left. 'Tis only me that's ever handled him for I never thought, you see, that I'd fall head over heels for a flattie, but that's just what I went and done. My John can't abide snakes, as I said, nor he don't want me handlin' 'em, he want us to get married and work his farm. But no one else wouldn't take Phillips on, so I had to think o' something. I was going to advertise, till I met you at Doc Burroughes. That seemed like a miracle, when you put your hand in the bag and stroked Phillips, a bloomin' miracle. So I set about recruitin' you, acourse.'

'And wasn't I happy to be recruited?' Hester had replied, giving her friend a hug. 'You and Phillips between you are just about the best thing that ever happened to Nell and me. And I knew about the wrist from the moment you picked Nell up, chair and all, and moved her along in the doctor's waiting room. No one with a damaged wrist could have done that.'

'Oh well, one little mistake ain't much,' Barbie said, returning the hug. 'Doc Burroughes he give me a rare rollickin', but he laughed afterwards. He know John, you see.'

'Lucky John. We're all going to miss you badly,' Hester told her friend. 'But your Mum says Nell and I can share your bed in the trailer when winter comes, which is a worry off my mind, and Nell will go to school in Lynn when we're fixed there.'

'She read right well now,' Barbie had pointed out. 'What else do she want school for?'

Swinging on the gate, with the glorious smell of crushed grass and woodsmoke in her nostrils, Nell quite agreed with Barbie; who needed school once they could read? She certainly hadn't missed formal lessons, though each night before they got into their bedrolls in the tiny tent which Barbie had taught them to pitch, Hester insisted on Nell doing sums, geography and history, with quite a lot of practical work as well. Nell would have liked to carry her pencil and the oddments of paper outside, away from the stuffy little tent, but Hester would never let her.

'You wouldn't work the same,' she insisted. 'You'd be distracted. And I do want you to keep up with other children your age, love. Try to put up with it – you'll have real school again when winter comes.'

It did not help, though, that she did lessons while the other kids played. They thought her stuck-up, conceited, they even called her flattie Nell, a real insult. They wouldn't let her join in, though she didn't tell her mother, who would have been distressed and who might have tried to insist on acceptance. One day they'll need me, Nell dreamed now, swinging on the gate. One day they'll see I'm not a flattie any more, I'm fairfolk, like them.

'Flattie Nell, ain't you a dream, then? Your ma's shouted you twice, now she's a-wavin' like a windmill. Breakfast's ready, I guess.'

Nell climbed over the gate and dropped into the long, whitening grass with the other kids close on her heels. If her breakfast was ready the chances were that they too were about to be called. The four of them raced across the grass and threw themselves on to the ground by the fire. The illusion of friend-ship brightened Nell's cheeks for a moment, then the other three moved away from her. Not too obviously, but definitely enough for Nell to notice.

Never mind, she told herself. The delicious smell of sausages cooking had brought the mongrel dogs around, eyes bright, tails wagging with anticipation. Nell adored the dogs, told herself their companionship made up for the other children's scorn. Now, she fussed them, knowing they might not get the sausages, definitely would not get them, but they would probably have slices of bread dipped in the fat when the pan was empty. Hester too loved the conglomeration of dogs which slept under the trailers at night and gave the fair folk warning of intruders. They never went short when she was cooking.

'Good girl, Nell, you came very quickly. Pour the tea, will you?'

Enamelled mugs were set out on the trailer step and the big, blackened enamel tea-pot stood beside them, steam rising gently from its spout. Nell hefted the pot – not without difficulty, for it was heavy – and filled the mugs, then looked around for milk. She had seen a couple of the older boys going off with jugs earlier so she knew it would be somewhere close at hand, keeping cool. It was under the step. Nell picked it up, sloshed some into each mug, then went back to her mother who was wrapping sausages in thick slices of bread and handing them round.

'Thanks, Mum,' she said, her mouth watering as her fingers closed round the untidy, delectable sandwich. 'Is your show all set up?'

There wasn't much to setting up, not in this weather. A fine array of pampas grass and dried bulrushes plus any plants or other foliage which could be cadged or borrowed, wreaths of ivy pulled from the trees and wrapped round the tent-pole and the rail of the enclosure in which Hester and Phillips 'wrestled' at every performance, and sand on the ground simulated what Mr Allingham imagined were jungle conditions. Nell was occasionally roped in, to be covered in Cherry Blossom boot polish and dressed in a raffia skirt. She took the money, turned the handle of the gramophone which blared out what Fred Allingham thought of as suitably foreign music, and made chattering noises when she thought of it, which wasn't often.

'The tent's up and the sand's down, but I could do with a hand, dinnertime,' her mother admitted. She gestured to where her tent stood with the sign outside proclaiming, 'See the Snake Woman Wrestle with Venom, the Poisonous Python, Hear the Tale of how She Saved His Life and Tamed Him to her Touch!'

'The red lettering is fading in the sun and needs touching up; and I don't want to put the jungle in until the last minute; the plants flag in this heat.'

'I bet you and Phillips will flag a bit, too,' Nell observed, speaking thickly through a mouthful of bread and sausage liberally laced with crispy fried onion. 'Shall I paint up? Only the boot polish runs in the heat.'

Hester gave a snort of laughter. It occurred to Nell, not for the first time, that her mother was looking fitter and happier than she had done for ages and ages. The repair operation had been a great success and, there was no doubt about it, Mum loved working with Phillips, cooking for the Allinghams when it was her turn, sleeping out under the stars when the little tent got too stuffy to be borne. It wasn't an ordinary job, not like keeping house had been, and though it involved quite a lot of hard physical work, Nell thought of it as one long holiday. She voiced the thought aloud to her mother and Hester nodded immediately.

'I know what you mean, pet, but it isn't a holiday, it's a way of life, and a way of life we both enjoy. It won't always be sunny meadows and pleasant folk though. When winter comes it'll be tough, believe me.'

'I don't think I mind toughness, so long as we're all together,' Nell said. 'Barbie seems like your sister, and Mr and Mrs Allingham are as nice to us as if they were family, aren't they?'

Hester smiled again, more broadly this time. 'I wish she was my sister, but I do know what you mean, pet. And the kids are all right with you, I can see that. As for you painting up, there isn't much point for a little village like this. But when we're nearer the coast, doing the little villages by the sea, then we'll paint you up. The next gaff isn't far from Norwich, so we may take a morning off, go and look at the sights. It's the city where they hold the Christmas fair with the gaff on the cattle market. Now that'll be worth taking a look at, or so they say.'

'There's a castle in Norwich, up above the cattle market,' Nell observed, ignoring the remark about the other children and shoving the mugs along so that she could sit on the trailer step. 'It's got a museum in it with butterflies and birds' eggs and a Red Indian in a canoe and ancient Egyptians . . . all sorts. It's free, too.'

'And there's dungeons and torture instruments,' Annie volunteered ghoulishly, panting up beside them and accepting the sandwich Hester was holding out. 'Ma and the rest'll be over in half a mo; ta, Hester, that smell wonderful.'

'Even if she didn't manage ole Phillips like a nat'ral, we'd keep ole Hester anyway, for her cookin',' Mr Allingham observed, coming down the steps of the trailer with one hand extended to take his sandwich. 'Why, if young John had tasted your rabbit pie afore he laid eyes on our Barbie, she wouldn't ha' stood a chance!'

Everyone laughed and Hester, pink-cheeked, scooped fried onions from the blackened pan and heaped them on top of the sausage balanced on the next round of bread.

'You're a lucky gel, Nellie, to have a Mum what can cook like that,' remarked one of the chaps who helped to erect the joints, as the side-shows were called, 'Cor, them dumplings we 'ad last week was better'n my old ma make 'em!'

Nell, basking in the compliments, added her own. 'Everyone says Mum's a good cook; even Mr Geraint,' she remarked. 'When we lived in Wales . . .'

Her words petered out as Hester tipped the pan sideways and flames shot head-high as the smoking fat hit the red-hot heart of the fire.

All fair folk are anxious about fire; too many of them have suffered from it. A cast-down cigarette and a small fortune in canvas can be destroyed, to say nothing of lives put at risk and important equipment ruined. There was a concerted roar, then separate voices made themselves heard as the flames died as quickly as they had sprung up.

'Only a bit o' fat – 'twon't do any 'arm.'

'That'll larn you, my woman – never take your eye off a fry-pan, do you'll see your breakfas' go up in flames.'

'Calm down, everyone, no harm done. Any more sausages, Hester m'dear?'

That last was Mrs Allingham, Mizallie to the fair folk. No one stood on ceremony here and Mr Allingham was called Al by everyone, though Hester tried to get Nell to be more respectful. Now, Mizallie stood at the top of the trailer steps smiling guilelessly, but Nell, gazing up at her, had a shrewd suspicion that Mizallie knew that Hester's 'accident' had been just about as much of an accident as Barbie's broken wrist.

I should've kept my mouth shut about Wales, Nell thought guiltily. Mum never mentions anything about it – not Wales, nor Daddy, nor Mr Geraint.

'Plenty of sausages,' Hester said as though nothing had happened, turning to smile at Mizallie. 'I put a pile on that plate . . . oh damn, that was the jukels' grub I just shot into the fire. Still, there's plenty of dripping, I'll warm some more through. Fetch the yellow bowl over here, there's a good girl, Nell.'

Hester hardly ever used fairground slang, but she'd called the dogs jukels without a thought. Nell, who stored up every precious new word because she wanted to talk just like her friends and her new adopted family, smiled to herself as she ran across to the trailer. Out of the corner of her eye she saw Kipsy, her favourite jukel, loping across the gaff towards them. He had been injured as a pup and now ran three-legged, but despite this disadvantage he usually managed to get to the food in time to receive his fair share. Nell hurried up the steps and into the trailer, snatched the yellow enamel bowl full of hard white fat, and ran back to where the fire was burning evenly once more and Hester waited with the stale loaf sliced and ready.

'Here you are, mMm,' she said cheerfully. 'Can I give Kipsy his grub? He needs more than most 'cos he's only got three legs to hunt with.'

'They all get the same,' Hester reminded her daughter, cutting a wedge of dripping and dropping it into the empty frying-pan. 'You can feed them all if you like, and then you can go into the village and see if you can get a couple of rabbits or a chicken for Phillips. Only don't be long, because I'll need a hand with the jungle, after. Can't expect the chaps to do everything.'

The 'chaps' covered all those casual workers who helped with the heavy manual work on the gaff: putting up the rides and side-shows and then pulling them down, leaping on and off the dodgem cars to take fares, evicting drunks and laying 'roads' in the wet over which the customers might walk. They were classed neither as fair folk nor flatties, but as something in between. Some of them were 'steadies', who stayed with the fair while it was travelling, then went home for over-wintering, returning to the gaff in time for the first fair of the season. Others were simply extra muscle, brought in each time the fair arrived at a gaff and paid off when they left. They ate with the showmen though, and some of the steady chaps were as near family as could be. Ruddy Fred and Black Fred, for example; both in their mid- to late-forties, wiry, tanned men who spoke little but ate and worked prodigiously, they were usually known as Ruddy and Black and were trusted members of the team. Ruddy had got his nickname from his high colour, but Nell had been mystified by Black until he told her his hair had been the same colour as hers when he'd been young.

'That must have been a long time ago,' Nell had said artlessly and Black had grinned and said aye, it were a good few years and wasn't she a silver-tongued rakli, then?

'What's rakli?' Nell asked eagerly, trying to help Black to set up the Wheel-em-in joint so that she could have a go at rolling the penny she would earn before the flatties came in. No one minded her helping the chaps, not even the other kids. It saved them having to do so.

'What d'you think? What are you? It's a silly young gel, acourse.'

'Oh, I see. And what's silver-tongued?'

But Black would only laugh and adjure her to hold her

silver tongue for once while he concentrated on getting the canvas straight.

Right now, Nell took the fat-soaked bread and began to hand it out to the eager dogs. They stood around her, taking their turn, not snatching or trying to get the biggest pieces. Al said his dogs were the best mannered in the business and he was right, for all that Sinda, a huge alsatian crossbred, had heaved a man out from under the gallopers a week last Saturday by one ankle, doing the ankle no good in the process. But that was why the fair kept them, to keep the flatties in their place, so no one dreamed of blaming Sinda.

'More tea, anyone? Do that Nell, would you?'

Nell trotted around collecting the empty enamel mugs for refills, feeling the hot sun caressing her shoulders through her cotton frock, aware, from the top of her shining black head to the tip of her toes, that life was good and would be better if she could think of a way to become part of the children's lives.

The morning's sightseeing in Norwich had been a big success, but Hester and Nell had to hurry back because they were in the village of Blofield which was quite seven miles out of the city and had to set the show up betimes.

It was another hot day. They were on a recreation field with the church and its tree-shaded churchyard to their right, a wood at the bottom and someone's orchard on their left. The pub was handy, just across the turnpike road which led to Great Yarmouth, and there were two village shops not more than three minutes' walk away. Blofield was quite a sizeable village so they should have a good audience. Annie, Wally and Tod had been here often and had said, in front of Nell, that the local kids were fairgoers to a child.

'There are kids at the big house too,' Annie Gate-leg told little Tod, who was hanging on to her cotton skirt and demanding answers to a thousand questions. 'Last year the boy let us fish for tiddlers in their pond. He brung us out 'ot scones an' lemonade. It's awright, round here.'

Nell knew better than to comment, because if she did the kids would all take off, leaving her alone. But she had confided

201

in Hester at last, though not the real size of the problem, just saying that the kids weren't all that keen on her.

'Keep working hard and when school starts in the winter, they'll be pleased enough to have your help with their lessons,' Hester said shrewdly. 'Until then, don't worry about it or push it; you'll be accepted in time.'

Right now Nell helped to set up the jungle, carting the plants across to the tent from the shelter of the ditch which surrounded the wood, where Hester had put them to keep cool, the pots in the trickle of water at the bottom. The sand was already scattered, the rails set up. Now, she wound the long strands of ivy carefully along them, then up the tent-pole. Hester was always full of bright ideas to keep the ivy and the tent-pole together, but they never quite worked out. The fair on the move was well organised by necessity and Al would have had small patience with anyone trotting around holding a huge pot of ivy beside one particular tent-pole.

'I'm nearly ready, you can let them in when you've finished the ivy,' Hester called from behind her screen. It was a small screen, but sufficient to change behind. Nell knew her mother would be taking off her faded cotton dress and her sandals and applying oil to give her skin a sheen; in winter she would have to use the bottle of wet-white which Barbie had left behind, but at this time of year Hester's natural tan was considered sufficient, together with her loosened hair falling in waves down her back. Indeed, the first time the Allinghams had seen her in costume they told her delightedly that she looked just right.

'Foreign an' a trifle sultry,' Al said, after a long, serious look, while his wife chimed in with, 'But classy, my dear, very classy.'

The costume was not so much classy, as rude, Nell thought. It had been Barbie's snake-wrestling costume, and consisted of an abbreviated Indian sari in brilliant colours which tied just above Hester's breasts and fell to the top of her thighs, with a starry cloak to put over it before and after each performance. When Hester and the snake wrestled you could see Hester's silk knickers, but Nell never said anything; she just held the cloak when Hester shed it, and handed it to her quickly as the music ground to a halt. Her mother, Nell realised, was unaware that the flatties could see her knickers; better let it stay that way.

'Is there a crowd out there, yet? Phillips is still a bit sleepy. It's the heat, but I won't wake him until they're in.'

Hester's voice, hissing out from behind the screen, brought Nell back to the present with a jolt. It was her job, now that the jungle was in place, to tip the wink that they were ready to whoever was drumming up. She scuttled across the small stuffy enclosure to the door-flap and pulled it back. Outside, Ruddy was banging the flat of his hand on an upturned half beer barrel.

'Walk up, walk up, ladies and gents! This way for 'Ester the marvellous jungle gal who tamed the great poisonous snake, Venom, and brought 'im back to England for your pleasure! See 'ow she charms 'im with music, wrestles 'im for amoosement. Walk up, walk up!'

'Ready, Ruddy,' Nell hissed, then giggled and ran back into the yellow light of the tent, her grass skirt swishing round her knees. Her own knickers could occasionally be seen if she leaned over the rail but she took good care as a rule. Besides, no one looked at a little girl when Hester and Phillips were wrestling.

Behind her, the people began shuffling in, exclaiming at the heat, then at the jungle, or Nell thought that was what they were exclaiming over since there wasn't much else until Mum and Phillips emerged from behind the screen. There was a record on the gramophone, however, so she wound vigorously, set the needle on the black disc, and stood back.

Music flowed into the air just as Hester, right on cue, came out from behind the screen. She was wrapped in her starry cloak with her hair floating free and she held Phillips above her head, or at least she held his neck, the rest of him was looped carelessly across her shoulders, his tail fell down to her knees. The audience gasped, and someone said, 'Ugh, 'ow can she touch the slimy thing? I'm gonna chuck me dinner all over this 'ere sand in a minute.' It was a girl; Nell watched as she snuggled against her young man, giving huge theatrical shudders.

Stupid rakli, Nell thought scornfully, Phillips wasn't slimy. Hester untied her cloak with one hand and held it out and Nell, skirt swishing, took it from her and stood to one side. Behind the rail, Hester made a fuss of Phillips, stroking him in the way he loved. He writhed pleasurably and the audience gasped again. All the women pretended to hate it and the men gaped – not always at the snake, Nell had noticed more than once. Then Hester began the pretend wrestle, which Phillips seemed to enjoy as much as having his throat stroked, or at least he joined in with what looked like enthusiasm.

He was a big snake, more than eight feet long, and it was eight feet of heavy muscle. Hester sweated when she lifted him above her head, little drops of water ran down the sides of her face, and Phillips would suddenly turn in her grip and push his face close to her, rubbing against the oiled surface of her skin, looking dangerous to anyone who hadn't watched the act a hundred times.

The music began to fade and Nell went to the machine. She took the record off and turned it over. As the music swelled Hester held up her arms, and showed how, in wrestling, she had somehow managed to wind Phillips round her body, only she always took care not to let him anchor himself with his tail because, she told Nell, that was how a boa constrictor killed his prey in the wild: he squeezed it to death. And even Phillips's fun squeezes could make you gasp louder than the audience.

'And now, ladies and gentlemen, the Snake Girl will charm Venom into a deep sleep . . .'

That was Ruddy, whose rendering of the story of Hester and Venom was enough to send Nell to sleep, for he was not a gifted narrator. Usually Al did the job, but this was only a small village and Al was busy getting the fair into shape before they descended on the coast in a few days. They had been having trouble with the engine of the biggest lorry, so Ruddy Fred, who was no good with lorries, had taken over barking for Hester.

'Sing 'im a lullaby, folks, for he's gone up the wooden stair to Bedfordshire,' Ruddy said facetiously. 'Ain't that a pretty sight?'

On cue, Nell stepped forward and flung the starry cloak over Hester and the snake. Hester bowed deeply, blew kisses to her enthusiastic audience, and disappeared behind the screen. The men and their girls waited for a moment, murmuring to one another, then began to file out of the tent; another performance successfully concluded.

Now, Nell thought gleefully, we'll go back to the trailer and have that gorgeous plum duff Mum made earlier.

'There's a fair on in the village. Daniel Clifton went last year, he said it was prime. Do take us down there Daddy, please, please!'

'Can't, sweetheart. But I'm sure Mummy will take you tomorrow. After tea, probably. Fairs are always best in the evenings. Tell you what, why don't you invite Daniel? He could take care of you while Jamie looks after Mummy.'

JJ was sitting at the dining table with Anna perched on his knee, nibbling the cheese and biscuits he had left and occasionally stroking his cheek. JJ had dined alone because his wife had gone into the city to see her own mother, which meant Anna had an opportunity to get round him without her mother putting a spoke in her wheel. But it didn't look as though it was going to work; Daddy had been delighted to see her, had kissed her, let her sit on his knee, offered her cheese and biscuits and a sip of his strong, horrible black coffee, but he didn't seem about to be wheedled into taking her to the fair. His suggestion that Mummy might take them could be treated with scorn; Anna was very sure that Mummy would not go to anything so vulgar as a fair, particularly a small one. But it was a *good* fair, Daniel and the servants said so; there was a merry-go-round, dodgem cars, side-shows. Anna felt that the marvellous start to the summer holidays, weatherwise, would not be complete unless they went to the fair.

'But Daddy, Mummy hates things like that. Why can't you take us? Oh do, do,' Anna coaxed. 'We'd be ever so good, Jamie and me.'

Jamie was usually good. He was an angelic-looking little boy of four with tiny pearly teeth, big blue eyes and an affectionate disposition. Anna loved him because he was her little brother, though sometimes she thought it unfair that he should be so pretty when she was undoubtedly rather plain. But such feelings never lasted. There was no point in feeling jealous of Jamie's blond curls and pink-and-white complexion and anyway he would grow up one day and change from a dear little boy into a tough, or so Daddy told her sometimes.

'Darling, I can't; don't you listen? I'm going out in about ten minutes and tomorrow evening I'm attending a dinner in Bury St Edmunds.' He lifted her up by her elbows and stood her down beside him. 'Ask Mummy when she comes home, or better still, get Jamie to ask Mummy.'

The two exchanged conspiratorial grins; little girls weren't supposed to know their mothers had favourites, and Daddies, even if they knew, weren't supposed to acknowledge the fact. But my Daddy is different, Anna decided. Besides, I'm his favourite, which makes it fair. And Jamie was rather a darling so you could scarcely blame Mummy.

'All right, I'll get Jamie to ask then,' Anna said. As her father stood up she skipped ahead of him to the door. 'And I'll mention it to Daniel, just in case.'

'Do. Tell Mummy I suggested it. I'm sure she'll play along.' JJ looked at his watch. 'Heavens, look at the time – I must fly! Cheerio, old thing.'

They walked along the village street, the four of them in two pairs: Mummy and Jamie went first, Anna and Daniel followed. The fair was in full swing: *Last night here*, screamed the posters. *Moving down to the coast tomorrow.*

They were to be allowed a couple of rides, the merry-go-round, the dodgems or the swingboats. Jamie loved the horses with their wide nostrils outlined in red and their vivid saddles. He clambered aboard the chestnut stallion – at least that was what Jamie pretended it was – and Mummy climbed on to the horse next to him, a black one with fiercely open eyes and an emerald green saddle. Jamie, at almost four, was scarcely old enough to ride his mettlesome steed unattended.

'Come on, Anna, don't be a scaredy-cat,' her mother called, but Anna, though offended, pretended not to hear.

'I don't want to go on the round-about, it's for babies,' she said to Daniel. 'Daddy said any two rides we liked and if we go on the horses Mummy will only let us have one more go, I know she will. What do you want to do, Danny?'

'Dodgems,' Daniel said so promptly that Anna guessed he'd been longing to be asked. 'Come on, they can't do much, the ride's beginning to turn.'

Anna, hugging herself, ran across the flattened grass. The dodgems was the biggest ride easily, with pictures of racing cars all around the roof part and three wooden steps up; the electric light bulbs gleamed scarlet, purple, white.

Anna grabbed Daniel's arm as he stepped out on to the shiny, dusty surface of the dodgems track. 'Can I go in the same car as you? We can have two goes like that. I wonder where they get the 'lectricity from? The church hasn't got it, nor the hall.'

'Generators; they make their own, that's why there's always such a row,' Daniel said briefly. He shoved her into the passenger seat of a scarlet car with silver bumpers and slid behind the wheel. All around them others were getting into cars as well. Anna recognised Bert, their garden boy, and Ruth, the kitchen maid, as well as villagers whose names were unknown to her. 'Come on, let's see if we can hit Bert, or Georgie over there.'

The cars began to move. Daniel, who obviously knew how to go about things, held up a hand with some money in it. A tall skinny young man, filthy dirty and with fingers blackened through constantly handling money, leaped on to their bumper and took Daniel's proffered largesse. The car jerked, then zoomed off. Daniel's fingers tightened around the steering wheel, his knuckles whitening as he gripped. Anna, taken by surprise, shrieked. Daniel glanced at her. 'That's right, the girls always scream, you yell as loud as ever you can,' he advised. There was a bone-jarring crash as the scarlet car bashed into Bert's maroon vehicle. Ruth out-screamed Anna, hand over mouth, eyes laughing at them.

'Two can play at that game, Master Daniel,' Bert shouted. 'Watch yourselves, the pair on you!'

Anna shrieked again as Daniel, manoeuvring to get their car out of Bert's path, was rammed in the rear by Peg from the post office. Peg was driving and her young man, who worked for Farmer Hissop, encouraged her to ram vehicle after vehicle, which she did merrily, laughing and shouting rude remarks at the top of her voice.

'I hope Mummy stays away from here,' Anna said rather nervously. 'Did Peg say a swear then, Danny?'

'I'll say she bloody did,' Daniel replied breathlessly. 'Old Dave caught her a right smart one – must have made her arse tingle.'

'*Danny!*' Anna was genuinely shocked. It was bad enough for Peg, a woman, to swear, but for Daniel to do so was a lot worse. Even Daddy would have been shocked, she thought, then Bert careered sideways into them, locked bumpers and carried them round with him and she, too, fell into the prevailing mood.

'Oh, bloody gosh,' she shouted at Daniel. 'That made *my* . . .' she flinched from using the word in cold blood, however. 'That made me tingle all over,' she finished.

The cars were slowing down though, slowing right to a stop. Some people jumped out and made their way across the floor, but Daniel sat fast and when Anna would have climbed out, caught hold of her skirt and tugged her back down again.

'We've got three more goes left; I reckon there isn't much else on the fair as good as this,' he said. 'You can drive next time if you like.'

Making their way tiredly home, having dropped Daniel off at his house in the village, Jamie asked Anna the question she was waiting for.

'What did you do else, Anna, as well as the dodgy-cars?'

'Well, nothing, except walk round and eat some candy-floss and watch people having goes on the penny-rolls and the darts and things,' Anna admitted. 'But the dodgems are fun. Really exciting. I liked them best of everything.

Mummy, wandering along holding a hand of each, said

nothing; she seemed to be in a world of her own.

'How d'you know you liked them best, when you didn't try nothin' else?' Jamie asked reasonably. 'The roundy were nice, so it were, and so too were the snake lady.'

'Oh, did you go into the snake lady?' Anna said, wishing, just for a moment, that she had done the same. 'That must have been fun; tell me about it.'

'Well, there were a man with a drum-drum, and inside came him, and there was a little girl with a grass skirt who held the snake lady's sparkly mackytosh . . .'

'Sparkly cloak, dear,' Mummy murmured, so she was listening, or half-listening at any rate.

'Uh-huh, sparkly coat,' Jamie said obediently. 'And the little girl played music on a gammy, and the snake lady fighted the snake, and Mummy said she were goin' to faint, only she didn't, she just stood there with a sickish sorta face and then comed out wi' me,' he ended disappointedly.

'Was it good, Mummy?' Anna said. 'I'd have liked to see the big snake. Still, the dodgems are the best, honest.'

'It wasn't bad; the girl with the snake was . . . quite clever,' her mother said. She had a dreamy little smile on her lips. 'But you'll never guess, Anna, I saw an old friend in there. While your brother was squeaking that he wanted to touch Venom – only he said Vermin – we arranged to meet for a drink later. So I'll have to hurry you home now, and let you put yourselves to bed.'

'I always put myself to bed,' Anna said rather indignantly. 'Is Nanny out? I'll give Jamie a hand then, if you like.'

'Thank you, dear, that would be a real help. Nearly home now, Jamie, so step out, there's a good lad!'

Eight

Anna knelt on the windowseat in the nursery, peering down through the white-painted bars at the big side lawn and the cedar tree; in two days' time she would be ten years old and she would be having the biggest birthday party ever. On the twenty-first of April 1936 you're into double figures, so we shall have to celebrate in a special way, Daddy had said, coming into the nursery to read them a story after tea, though she could easily have read the book he had chosen. But Jamie, who was not quite six, enjoyed the stories and Daddy liked reading them, so Anna never said anything. Besides, it was a treat to get him to themselves for a little while, so the after-tea read was their favourite time of day.

After a great deal of solemn discussion, the form the party was to take had been decided. They were to have a conjurer, with a magic hat and a white rabbit, a Punch and Judy Show, and tea – with ice-cream – on the lawn under the cedar tree, which was a bit brave in April, only Daddy said he would hire a marquee if it looked like rain.

Jamie, sitting on the dumpy while Nanny ran his bath, had got very excited, bouncing up and down and clapping, even though it wasn't his party. But Mummy, when she heard about it, hadn't been nearly as enthusiastic. She had come up to the nursery for a word with nanny the evening Daddy had announced the special party, and immediately her expression, which had been all smiles, had changed to a look which Anna rather dreaded. Not because it was a cross look; Mummy was rarely cross with either of them and never cross with Daddy so far as Anna knew. It was an anxious sort of look, the sort of look grown-ups wore when they had lost a very important letter or missed the last bus home.

'Oh, but what about Jamie? He's awfully young for a big party, a conjurer will go right over his head and he'll be tired out well before bedtime,' Mummy said. She had plumped herself down on the windowseat, the very one on which Anna now knelt, and then put her head on one side, and looked across at Daddy, pulling a pretty, rueful face. 'I'll be the one who'll end up doing all the work, JJ; you'll have lost interest in parties by the time the great day arrives. Besides, won't Anna want a special party before she goes off to boarding school? And Jamie really is too young for all that excitement.'

Jamie was Mummy's favourite. Still an angelic-looking little boy with blond curls and big blue eyes, he had yet to go through any of the 'ugly' stages which Anna had suffered mainly due to horrible things called teeth. She had lost her baby pearls and had hated her bare pink gums, knowing toothlessness did not help her appearance. Then her grown-up teeth had arrived, much too big for her mouth and making her feel like a walrus. The family dentist, a lovely man when he gave you pink drink and rides in the chair, an ogre when he jabbed at your sensitive mouth with his prodder, decreed she must wear a horrible metal brace to make sure they grew straight. And as if this wasn't uglification enough, her hair had become darker, so that she was no longer truly Daddy's golden girl. Yet here was Jamie, with curly golden hair and tiny white teeth, everyone's favourite – even Anna's.

Not Daddy's, though. Daddy said if they didn't watch out Jamie would be a cissy, a real little nancy-boy. He wanted Mummy to cut Jamie's hair and not dress him in frilly shirts and pastel-coloured shorts, but although Mummy agreed that Jamie would have to have his hair shorter when he started junior school, no one had done anything about it. Mummy said Jamie was still just a baby and Daddy had to allow him to grow up naturally. Daddy muttered a bit but left it at that.

However, at Mummy's suggestion that the party should be put off Daddy went very still for a moment. Then he said quietly but firmly that since Anna would not be going to boarding school until she was thirteen, and perhaps not even then, a party to celebrate double figures did not seem unreasonable.

Ten friends from the high school were coming, all girls of course, and two boys from the grammar school who happened to catch the same bus as Anna in the mornings. Several cousins were coming, some children from the village and, best of all, Anna's friend Daniel Clifton. Dan was older than she, but they had got on well from the first time Mrs Lucas had brought Daniel round and told Mummy that he was going to live with her now since his mother had remarried and moved abroad.

'Although she's my daughter, Mrs Radwell, and I shouldn't really say this, I've been very disappointed in Rosalie,' Mrs Lucas told Constance in tones meant to be hushed and confidential but which were easily audible to the two youngsters playing on the terrace outside the drawing-room. 'She's treated her son in a very cavalier fashion, and now she's simply left him with me without an apology. She went merrily off with her Italian count – he's most certainly Italian, though I can't say whether he's a count – without giving a thought to the boy's future, though she does pay his school fees and so on. Her first husband died in a car crash. She was heartbroken at the time, and her loss seemed to make her determined to enjoy her own life, if necessary at the expense of others. However, Daniel is a good boy and he's in boarding school most of the year, so I can just about manage. But as I get older . . .'

'She's my gran,' Dan said later, when Anna asked why his name wasn't the same as Mrs Lucas's. 'My Mum's mother. She's all right, gran.'

But right now, kneeling on the nursery windowseat and contemplating the cedar tree, Anna wasn't really worrying about Dan, or Mrs Lucas, or any of her other guests. She was worrying about the weather. If it was fine she would have a wonderful time, but suppose it rained? Goldenstone was a big house but although Mummy had promised tea in the conservatory if it rained, this would not compare with tea under the cedar. And what about games? Games out of doors could be much rowdier and more fun than games in the house.

And suppose the rain held off until tea was laid? Then it would be too late for Daddy to do magic things with a marquee and they would have wet sandwiches and soggy potato crisps, to say nothing of melting puddles of ice-cream, and everyone would say it served the Radwells right for showing off.

Anna had already heard nanny say it was a bit ostensomething-or-other to have such a party when times were so difficult. The depression had just put nanny's brother Bill out of work and heaven knew, nanny said gloomily, what would become of him, his wife Betty and their five small children.

'But it won't help Bill if I don't have a tenth birthday party,' Anna had pointed out, ever practical. 'I wish I *could* help him, nanny, but I can't.'

Nanny sighed and gave Anna a hug. 'You're right, but that don't make it any easier,' she said. 'That in't as if farm work was well-paid, but when you lose even that . . .'

'Couldn't Bill help in the garden?' Anna suggested brightly. 'If he's done farm work he'll know all about growing things and Daddy was saying we could do with more help.'

'That's a long way to come, my woman. It 'ud be a good walk, then a bus ride, then another walk. Bill, he live in Acle, just up the road from where I was brought up,' nanny said. 'But you're a good girl to try to help, I won't forget that.'

'Anna, whacher doin'? I wants my tea I does. Where's nan gone, eh?'

Anna glanced around and smiled; Jamie, back from his ride in the motor car with Mummy, beamed back at her, his yellow-chick curls on end, his cheeks reddened from sun and wind.

'Nanny's down in the kitchen, with cook. She's making us a pancake each, Jamie, only don't let on I told you, it's a surprise.'

Jamie, a most satisfactory person in many ways, uttered a crow of delight, then clapped a grubby hand over his mouth. 'I won't say nothin',' he promised through his fingers. 'Them's my favourite things, Anna, pancakes is.'

JJ deplored his son's use of English, but Anna secretly agreed with Mummy that Jamie's own special way of talking was rather fun and would be missed when he began to put words in their proper order and to their proper use.

213

'Yes, I love pancakes, too. Hey, don't throw your coat on the floor, someone's only got to pick it up you know.'

'Ye-es, only I can't reach the 'ook,' Jamie said amiably, picking his coat off the floor and hurling it in Anna's general direction. 'Can you 'ang it on the 'ook for Jamie?'

'For who?'

'Sorry, Anna; can you 'ang it on the 'ook for me?'

Anna, giggling, got off the windowseat and hung the coat on the lowest hook behind the door. There was a stool kept specially so that Jamie could hang up his coat but somehow it was always tipped over, carted off to Jamie's bedroom for some purpose, or upside down and playing the part of a submarine or a tank; at any rate, it was rarely available at coat-hanging times. What'll happen to him when he gets to school, though, Anna thought, turning to unlace Jamie's shoes and find his slippers. He won't have a big sister to wait on him there. She said as much, and her small brother cast her a roguish glance out of his big blue eyes.

'No, not a sister; but teacher will put me boots on,' he announced cheerfully. 'Or anuvver kid, a bigger one.'

'Little beast,' Anna observed. 'Come on, you can help me lay the table for tea.'

'Tea and lovely pan . . . oh, sorry, Anna. Not a word,' Jamie said, remembering. 'Where's spoons put?'

The day of Anna's tenth birthday party dawned fair; as the children ate their breakfast they noted the light breeze and the sunshine, and a shower of rain at eleven o'clock just seemed to freshen the grass, add a gloss to the flowering shrubs and the primulas and rock roses starring the garden beds.

Although Bill lived in Acle, he had indeed approached the Radwells about a job and had been taken on to help in the garden. Despite the distance, he arrived each morning by half past eight and did not set off again until five-thirty; in between he was everywhere and doing everything, or so it seemed. He cleaned shoes, carted coal and chopped wood. He dug, weeded, planted. He barrowed logs into the woodshed from the very edge of the estate and sometimes he drove JJ into Norwich, dropped him off at Norwich Thorpe in time for the London train and picked him up again at six o'clock, even though it made him late home. But he only drove if Constance was too busy; in the main she preferred to chauffeur JJ herself.

As Anna was brushing her hair before putting on her party dress of peach-coloured voile, she saw Bill and Roddy, the garden boy, staggering a bit as they carried out the long table from the kitchen, setting it down under the cedar tree. They produced chairs next, folding wood and canvas affairs which had been hired, she believed. Then Cook came out with a very big white cloth. It was too early for wasps and bees, thank goodness, but Anna hoped they wouldn't put the food out too soon or the birds which twittered and sang in the cedar tree might decide to make their mark on things.

Next was a screen for the conjurer; the Punch and Judy man would bring his own puppet theatre later on, to entertain them after tea. So it had been decided that they wouldn't need a marquee, then. Anna was half glad, half sorry. She had never been to a party in a marquee, unless you could count the marquee they had hired for Aunt Audrey's wedding. It had been a lovely wedding; eight bridesmaids, all dressed in what Aunt Audrey had called 'rose shades'. Anna had liked the swimming lemony light inside the marquee, the scent of crushed grass and scent, the soft sound of the rain pattering on the canvas, and the sheer unreality of it all. Outside, you knew the rain-soaked daffodils hung their heads, the beech tree's bare branches moved restlessly, scattering drops as the wind caught them. There was the chill of the gusting rain and a nippy Norfolk wind straight off the North Sea, while inside it was all summer, all light dresses, sandals, and the smells that go with cricket matches, hot sunshine, cream teas.

But that had been more than a year ago; now it's my turn, Anna thought, staring at the preparations. It would have been fun to have a marquee, but having the sunny garden would be even better. Very soon now she would be dressed and brushed and allowed to use a little tiny speck of her mother's nicest scent. She would go downstairs to greet her guests, girls and boys so subdued by parental presence and best clothing that they would look quite different, peep at her shyly, mumble their greetings. They would carry interestingly wrapped parcels for her, she would unfasten the string, open the paper, exclaim, and then they would troop out into the garden, a game would be suggested, they would start to play . . .

'Anna darling, are you nearly ready? The cousins will be here in half an hour, they are to arrive early, to help with the games.'

Mummy's voice echoed round the room; she was calling up the stairs, Anna realised with relief, so she didn't know that her daughter was still mooning around clad in nothing more than her white liberty bodice and pink cotton knickers.

'Nearly ready, Mummy,' Anna shrilled. She dropped her hairbrush, grabbed her party dress and began to struggle into it. Next door, she heard Jamie shouting at Nanny for pulling his hair; he must be further on with getting ready than she was; Nanny always combed Jamie's curls last because it was the worst part.

'Don't tug so hard, it don't matter if there's tanglies, nan,' Jamie said. 'Oh not them shoes, them shoes pinches me toes!'

Rumble rumble went Nanny's reassuring answer. Anna couldn't hear what she was saying but she knew the gist of it. *Don't wriggle, young James, or you'll feel this hairbrush on your b.t.m. and them shoes was bought specially to go with your sailor suit and well you know it, young man!*

In self-defence, dreamers have to learn to move rapidly. Anna was into her dress and white sandals, with her hair pulled back and her peach silk ribbon ready in one hand, when her mother pushed open the door.

'Good girl, you do look nice! Now will you wear your hair in a tail or shall I tie the ribbon round your head and fasten it beneath your hair, like an Alice band? You could have it loose, but when you play games it's probably easier if it's tied back.'

'Daddy likes it with a bow on the front bit,' Anna said. She sighed as her mother's face was momentarily darkened by a frown. 'But it doesn't matter – whatever you want.'

'A bow on the front bit is rather common, darling,' Constance said gently. 'I think it's best tied back.' She brushed briskly, then

216

tied Anna's heavy fall of dark gold, silky hair back into a pony-tail. She fastened the ribbon so tightly that Anna's eyebrows and eyes rose and became elongated and slitlike; Chinese, in fact, Anna thought, examining her reflection in the mirror on her dressing table.

'There you are, darling; very neat,' Constance said briskly.

'How do I look? Suitable for your party?'

She looked beautiful, of course. The gleaming cap of white-gold hair was always in perfect trim, her slender, boyish figure looked wonderful in a navy and white dress with a pleated skirt and dropped waist. She wore silk stockings and her shoes were navy and white too, like the dress. Anna, who had thought her peach voile the height of fashion, sighed.

'You look lovely, Mummy. I wish I could look even a little bit like you do.'

'Oh don't worry, darling,' her mother said. Her voice was slightly frosty, though Anna could not think why. 'Daddy will think you're a dream of loveliness in that colour, even though it clashes with your hair. As for me, he's so used to me he scarcely sees me any more.'

'He does! He thinks you're the most beautiful person in the world, he *dotes* on you,' Anna said loyally. 'And it's true, Mummy. If I grow up to be half as pretty as you I'll be terribly lucky. Nanny says so, and gran, and Uncle Luke . . . oh, was that the bell?'

'It's the cousins!' Constance cried at once, a hand going automatically to tidy her immaculate hair. 'Come along, Anna, we'll welcome them together!'

They ran down the stairs hand in hand, Anna conscious that she must look heavy and ungraceful beside her willowy, golden mother.

It was a marvellous party; it would have been a marvellous day but for one small incident.

They had played games, watched the conjurer, had tea, played more games. And then the Punch and Judy man arrived. Everyone came out to watch that, even some parents who had arrived early to pick up their young. The Punch and

Judy man was at his best; Dog Toby was the smallest, sweetest dog in the world – the birthday girl got to shake Dog Toby's paw – and the crocodile, the policeman, all the other characters were just right, frightening enough to be exciting but not enough for nightmares.

Then it was time for everyone to troop indoors, flushed and chattering, to receive the small presents (penknives for the boys, manicure sets for the girls) which nanny had toiled over. Anna, running across the hall, was nabbed by Mummy, standing talking to her friend.

'Anna darling, Daddy's going to take the cousins home; he told me to tell you to put your outdoor things on and go with him, for the ride.'

'Where's my coat?'

'In the cloakroom, silly. Wash your face and hands and comb your hair while you're in there.'

Mummy shushed her off into the small side cloakroom and sure enough there was Anna's navy school coat, her brown lace-ups, and the beret Mummy had bought her. She was washing her hands and face sketchily when she heard her mother starting to talk to Aunt Beryl; they must have been just the other side of the door, for their voices came to her as clear as a bell.

'She was a pretty little thing until about a year or eighteen months ago,' her mother was saying chattily. 'It so often happens though, don't you find? Now she's plain as a pikestaff; how I'm going to get her married off I don't know and you know JJ; he adores pretty women but plain ones leave him cold. How he'll feel when he realises he's produced an ugly duckling I shudder to think.'

'Oh, she'll probably change again,' Aunt Beryl said in her light, amused voice. 'Diet works wonders too, Connie. Kids these days eat too many sweets, that's why they get spots and are so often overweight.'

Anna began to dry her hands on the towel which hung beside the basin; they were talking about her and it was all true, she knew it! She was fat and even if she didn't have spots yet, she probably soon would have. Her face grew hot as the blood rushed to her cheeks and she turned away from the basin and took her coat off the hook. She began to struggle into it, her fingers on the buttons all thumbs.

'A diet, for a child of ours? JJ wouldn't hear of it, but he'll blame me if we find ourselves landed with a great lump one of these days,' her mother remarked. 'Isn't it sad though? Jamie's such a handsome child, and looks aren't nearly as important for a man. I'm afraid Anna is going to find life very difficult as she gets older. Plain girls have a hard time of it.'

Anna crouched on the cloakroom floor, trying to do up her laces as she fought tears. Her face burned with humiliation. She had been pretty once but she was plain now, she knew it was true, but she didn't think it was her fault. She ate her crusts, but her hair wasn't nearly as curly as Jamie's and he chucked his crusts on the fire. She brushed her hair a hundred times a night, but still it got darker. She cleaned her teeth, wore the brace . . . she was worse than plain, she was a fat, scarlet-faced toad, ugly and unwanted, a child no one could possibly love.

She could not shut out the conversation, no matter how hard she tried.

'How do you know plain girls have a hard time?' Aunt Beryl's voice was mocking now. 'You've always been the prettiest girl around, and you've always known it. But there are plain girls who have enormous sex appeal, or haven't you noticed?'

'Oh, *sex* appeal,' Anna's mother said, as though Beryl had mentioned drains or bowels. 'Anyone can have sex appeal, but you're either pretty or plain.'

'Rubbish,' Aunt Beryl said briskly. 'Look at Andrea Hopkins! You can't call her pretty, but men buzz round her like bees round a honeypot.'

'She won't get a good man, though,' Anna's mother said. 'she's just not marriageable, all she's got is this sex appeal you keep on about.'

Beryl laughed. 'I don't keep on about it, and the only reason Andrea hasn't married is because she's too busy playing the field. Do you know, Connie, some of your remarks sound most awfully like jealousy. It does you no credit, my dear.'

'Me? Jealous? Of Andrea Hopkins? I should have thought, Beryl . . .'

Beryl cut across her words, her voice ice-clear. 'No, not necessarily of Andrea, of anyone who gets between you and JJ, Connie dear, even if that someone is only a child!'

But it had all been too much for Anna. Listeners always hear ill of themselves, but Mummy had *known* she was in the cloakroom, she might have gone somewhere else to say such horrible things – unless she wanted Anna to hear, of course. Unless she was trying to warn her daughter that she must get pretty for her own sake. But it was no use telling herself to be sensible; Anna had wept until she was as soggy as a sponge and now, to her horror, the cloakroom door began to open. Someone would see her blubbing in here, and on her birthday too!

She left the cloakroom at an inglorious run. She bumped into the person who was trying to get into the room and recognised Phyllis, the elder sister of one of her guests. The girl went sprawling, but Anna took no notice. She charged at the stairs and thundered up them, red-faced, tearful. Well, if she was ugly she might as well act ugly; no point in trying to be nice when people must hate looking at a child so hideous.

'Anna, come down at once. You knocked Phyllis clean off her feet . . . my dear child, you must apologise . . .'

Anna ignored her mother's voice; she rounded the last bend in the stairs and began to hurl herself at the straight. She was not going back, all red-faced and blubbery, to be laughed at, not she! That Phyllis was pretty – she would be all right, she would marry and have babies and be happy. She would never be a great lump, the despair of her parents! But as she ran across the upper landing heading for the nursery stairs, a door opened and someone caught her arm.

'Hey, what's up? I thought you were coming with me to take the cousins home?'

It was Daddy, of course, smiling gently down at her, but even as Anna flung her arms around him she saw out of the corner of her eye her friend Mabel's mother emerging from one of the bedrooms. Mabel's mother was tidying her hair, brushing the shoulders of her cream blouse, smiling to herself.

'Oh Daddy, I forgot . . . you weren't down there. Are you *sure* you wouldn't rather take Jamie?' Her father returned her hug, then turned her so that they could walk down the stairs side by side. He did not look at Mabel's mother and she hung back, not wanting to interfere between father and daughter. What a nice lady she was, Mrs Platt, as nice as Mabel, who was Anna's best friend.

'Why should I take a baby boy in the car when I can take my beautiful daughter?' Daddy asked, squeezing her. 'Now then, what's upset you? I can always tell when things haven't gone right for my girl.'

But she would not, could not, say. To admit that she had listened while Mummy said how plain and ugly Anna was growing, how she would never get a husband, would make the worries even more real, more important. As yet, Daddy hadn't noticed her new plainness, so instead of answering, she took his hand in both of hers and dropped a kiss on the back of it.

'Nothing's wrong really, I was being silly. Daddy, what happens to girls who don't marry?'

'They stay at home and look after their old, old fathers,' Daddy said promptly. 'But you'll marry all right, darling . . . if you want to, that is. The handsomest, most eligible man in Norwich, I shouldn't wonder. Look, sweetheart, if Mummy's been on about marrying you off one of these days, don't you worry your head about it. The trouble is, Granny Peyton-Grant thinks all girls must marry well, and it's made Mummy . . . well, a bit silly about things like that. So forget it, eh?' They had reached the hall, which was emptying as children were called for, and Daddy pulled her to a halt and smiled into her eyes. 'No more worrying, eh? Promise me?'

'I promise,' Anna said weakly. 'Oh Daddy, I do love you!'

'Feeling's mutual, darling. Now we must round up the cousins or we'll be late for dinner.'

He took her hand. Mummy was standing in the doorway, saying goodbye to a group of guests. As they passed, Mummy gave Anna a big, bright smile and reached out and smoothed a hand over her hair.

'The birthday girl! Had a nice day, poppet?'

Anna nodded and smiled back and would have gone on, but Daddy lingered for a moment.

'Someone had been having a go at her, Con – I hope it wasn't you? It's her birthday, her special day, no time to find fault.'

To Anna's horror, bright colour suffused her mother's cheeks and she was almost sure she could see tears shimmering, unshed, in her eyes.

'Me? Darling, of *course* not! Poor baby, who was nasty to you? Who made you unhappy?'

Anna, head down, mumbled something, but her mind was whirling. Mummy *knew*! She knew very well that Anna had overheard that conversation, she had read the knowledge in her mother's eyes. What was it about grown-ups that they could be so strange? Now Mummy's eyes implored her not to tell – as if she would! But it was very confusing. Children must not lie, but grown-ups, it seemed, could do so whenever they liked. And then turn round and, with a look, ask a child not to split on them.

Daddy took her hand, leading her out of the front door and down the steps to the motor car. 'Oh dear, pet, we're late, the cousins are already in the back. Never mind, we'll show them how a Humber eats up the miles!'

Anna was squeezed happily in the front seat with her cousin Lionel when Mabel and her mother came out of the house. Daddy leaned across her and called out through the open window.

'Would you two like a lift? It's a bit of a squash, but I can get another couple in!'

Rather to Anna's dismay they accepted, so she and Lionel, being nicely brought up, had to get into the back with the others while Mrs Platt and Mabel sat in front. But it was fun in the back with the cousins, all squeezed up together giggling and kicking, reciting rude rhymes under their breath and now and then breaking into song. And when they reached Unthank

Road and dropped the cousins off, they continued on to Judge's Walk and Mabel came in the back with her while the grown-ups talked in the front.

'You like Dan, don't you?' Mabel asked as they drove along. 'He's going back to boarding school in a couple of days; wasn't it lucky your birthday wasn't after term started?'

'Very lucky,' Anna said. 'Who's Amanda?'

She had just heard the name on her father's lips.

'That's my mother, silly,' Mabel told her. 'Only I suppose you think of her as Mrs Platt.'

'Yes, I do. I thought Daddy did too.'

Mabel shrugged and produced the bag of jelly babies she had won in Pass the Parcel.

'Oh, I don't know, they must have known each other for years, ever since we were small. Want a jelly baby? I like the green ones best.'

Forewarned, Anna selected a red one. The two of them sat in the back ignoring the quiet conversation taking place in the front, chewing jelly babies and gossiping. It was, Anna decided that night as she climbed into bed, the perfect end to an almost perfect day.

Almost. Who cares if I'm not pretty, Anna told herself with drowsy defiance as she was hovering on the verge of sleep. At least I can have sex appeal, then I can play the field.

And without the slightest idea of what this meant, she fell happily asleep.

'But he said he'd come! He should keep his promises. I'm supposed to keep mine, and Margaret Rose is supposed to keep hers though she's not even six yet. Hunty, why didn't he come?'

'He didn't come because he's the king now, and he's most dreadfully busy, and important though your birthday is, my dear, the business of the kingdom is more important still.'

The garden at Royal Lodge was in glorious blossom and the princesses had enjoyed a birthday tea under the apple trees with a score of small friends and relatives, but now Elizabeth was upset because Uncle David had promised and not performed. It was so difficult, with a child as well brought up as Elizabeth, to explain that an uncle who had been charmingly attentive had found an alternative attraction so strong that a promise to a niece could become a straw in the wind.

'It's that woman, isn't it? That Mrs Simpson?'

Miss Huntley, startled, could not immediately think of a reasonably honest reply. Instead, she took the coward's way out and asked a question of her own.

'Why that tone, Elizabeth? You scarcely know your uncle's ... I mean you've only met Mrs Simpson once, when they popped in for a cup of tea.'

'Uncle David came to show my Daddy his new car, and I didn't like her and she didn't like us,' the princess said calmly. 'Mummy didn't like her either, nor did Daddy, nor did you, did you, Margaret Rose?'

'No,' squeaked the small princess. 'I did *not* like her; she said there was cake crumbs on my cheek.'

'There were,' Elizabeth said sternly, then smiled at the small girl beside her. 'But she shouldn't have said so; it was rude. And Uncle David shouldn't do as she says. He's the king, he should do what he wants.'

'Kings can't always do what they want, but perhaps he'll come tomorrow,' Miss Huntley said diplomatically. 'And he did send you a present, didn't he? A very handsome present.'

Elizabeth's eyes, which were a surprisingly dark blue, brightened and the familiar, three-cornered smile broke out.

'Yes; a pony, a real beauty. I'm going to call her Beauty as well.' Her face darkened again. 'But I wanted to thank him properly, not just with a letter, and I wanted to show him which stall she'll have and which bridle she'll wear. Uncle David's let me down, Hunty.'

He's let a lot of people down, Miss Huntley thought to herself, and if you ask me, he'll do worse than that. But you couldn't say that sort of thing to a child, especially a princess. Elizabeth met the great and the good and conversed with them on equal terms; you had to watch every word you uttered in front of her because all children are a bit like parrots.

'It's time the two of you were in bed,' she said instead.

'Come along, you've had your baths, you've had your hot drinks, you mustn't try to make even the best of days last for ever, you know. Off with you both!'

'Margaret Rose is supposed to go to bed earlier than me,' Elizabeth objected. 'You let her stay up, Hunty, because it was my birthday. Now shouldn't I stay up as well?'

Miss Huntley laughed with genuine amusement. Children were children, no matter how royal!

'Very well dear, just for half an hour. You may sit in the chair by the fire and read one of your new books. I expect it will be about ponies, or dogs, or budgerigars.'

The princess, selecting a book from the shelf which ran the length of the nursery, shook her head. 'It won't, not tonight. I want that book about the wicked stepmother and how the little girl got the better of her. I can't remember the title, but it's a blue book with gold writing. Hunty, can you find it for me?'

'Ye-es,' Miss Huntley said, half-laughing. 'And why do you want to read that book, pray?'

Elizabeth looked down at her feet, then up at her companion through her thick, curly lashes.

'Just in case Uncle David gets his way and Margaret Rose and I find ourselves with a wicked step-aunt. I want to be prepared!'

It was raining in the resigned, steady way it does in December, which usually means that there won't be a change in the weather for some time. Nell shivered and wrapped her arms round herself because she was cold despite the hissing naphtha flares lighting the hoopla stall where she stood; she hadn't bothered to put on her coat and her much-darned jumper and draggly skirt were small protection against the cold. Still, once this job was over she would be able to get back in the warmth of the trailer, eat a meal and read a book before the evening opening.

Hester and Nell were still working with Phillips but they were no longer with the Allingham fair. They had continued very happily with the Allinghams right up to June the previous year, but Mizallie had died of a heart attack and things had begun to be difficult for Hester. Al had speedily found consolation with

Bet, Mizallie's handsome, self-willed cousin, who had come to 'help out' when Mizallie was first took bad, and who stayed on to woo the boss. She was a jealous woman, however. She soon had Hester and Nell out of the trailer – said it wasn't proper for an elderly widower to share his home with a young widow – and began to push in other ways too.

Hester and Nell had soldiered on for a bit, sleeping in their little tent during the heat of the summer and doing their best to placate Bet. But when autumn came Al had decided to make Bet his new wife. He missed Mizallie so bad, he told everyone, that he could no longer sleep at night nor eat his victuals, but Mizallie had come to him in a dream and suggested that Bet would be a good replacement, if replacement were possible.

Bet now began to make life impossible for the younger woman. She bullied Hester, told lies about her to Al and denied her the use of the communal cooking fire at mealtimes.

Hester did not much mind. She knew Al understood that the lies were just that and she took to lighting her own fire in front of the worn little tent, but she worried, Nell knew she did. The winters were hard, even with the trailer to come home to. What would life be like in the tent during the snow and ice? The jungle in her show-tent did not much like the oil-stove necessary for Phillips's good health, and Hester seemed to spend a great deal of time and money remedying this fault. But Bet, seeing how the chaps clustered around Hester's fire in preference to her own – Bet was elderly and sour and her cooking lacked imagination – decided that the fair would be a happier place without the Makerfields.

So she began to get at Nell, seeing that Hester was impervious to her nastiness. She set the child difficult tasks, demanded her presence when she should have been helping her mother with the act, refused to let the two females take shelter in the trailer and insisted that, instead of squeezing into the cab of the big lorry which pulled the trailer from gaff to gaff, Hester should travel with the dodgems, the galloper, and assorted chaps.

At the backend of the year, they moved to a small village just outside a sizeable town they hadn't visited before and found another fair only a couple of miles from their gaff, right in the centre of the town. Gullivers, the other fair, was bigger than Allinghams, but not enormous, and because of a natural curiosity plus a certain idea stirring in her head, Hester took Nell to one side and asked her to stay around the gaff and not to talk to anyone much.

'Sweetie, I'm going over to Gullivers but I don't want anyone to know, so if someone asks where I am, just say I'm shopping. Be good, now.'

It was a drizzly day and Hester hurried along, the hood of her light macintosh thrown over her hair, trying to decide whether she was being sensible in talking to the Gullivers. But her options were shrinking and she and Nell had already had a good look at the other fair and had liked what they saw. The larger fair had no snake charmer or snake wrestler, so to approach them seemed the obvious thing to do. By now, Hester thought it must be as plain to Al as it was to her that there was no place for her and Bet on the same tober. And this fair, being larger, was surely richer? Perhaps, if she approached the boss – Mr Gulliver, presumably – he might make the Allinghams an offer for Phillips, and since she was the only person who knew the snake, surely Mr Gulliver would want her to work for him as she had worked for the Allinghams? The least she could do was suggest it.

And that was what she did. She approached the biggest trailer of all and knocked timidly on the door.

A round, fat woman answered her knock. She stared very hard at Hester. 'Yes?'

'I'd like to see the boss, Mr Gulliver,' Hester said quickly, before her courage drained away. Suddenly it occurred to her that what she was doing might seem disloyal to someone who did not know the circumstances. 'Is he in the trailer or out on the gaff?'

The woman turned and shouted into the van. 'Jack, there's a woman wanting a word wi' the boss, but Big Tom's gone into town. Can you spare a moment?'

Jack came to the door and Hester had to stifle a gasp. He was a huge man, well over six feet tall and broad with it, and he had a craggy face with a broken nose and a scar running across his left cheek. Like the woman, he stared at her hard for a moment, then his face was split by an enormous grin and he stood back, gesturing her inside.

'Afternoon; now what's your business with Gullivers, Miss Hester?'

Hester was so surprised that her mouth fell open. She stood with one foot on the step and gawped at him, while her mind raced round in circles, totally confused.

'I don't . . . I'm only here . . .' she stammered at last. 'Who are *you*?'

'I'm Ugly Jack. I run the dodgems for my Dad, Big Tom. You're the gal who works the snake for Allinghams, ain't you? I heard talk while I was in town so I went over to your gaff a couple o' days back, took a shufti, liked what I saw. Now you turn up on me doorstep, cool as you please. What can I do for you?'

Just like that! Making things so easy that Hester too was blunt.

'Buy me and Phillips, that's the snake,' she said breathlessly. 'We can't stay with Allinghams once Al has married Bet, she wouldn't stand for it. She'll want Al all to herself, and I can't blame her. But no one works Phillips like I do, so I thought, if you could afford it . . . I'm sure Al wouldn't strike too hard a bargain, he'll see reason. And if he doesn't, Bet will make him.'

Ugly Jack grinned again, then sat down on one of the upholstered seats in the dining section of the trailer and pointed to the opposite bench.

'Take the weight off your feet,' he advised. 'This is business; it may take a while.'

After that, it had been easy. Ugly Jack had made an offer for Phillips and Al had been quick to accept it, but he had mumbled an apology to Hester and Nell in a quiet moment.

''Tis difficult, wi' a new woman,' he had said diffidently. 'You don't mind shiftin', Hes?'

'Glad to go, Al,' Hester had replied truthfully. 'It's better all round. Besides, I like the Gullivers and they like me, and Nell will soon make new friends.'

But there, at least, she had been wrong. Nell had done her best in every way: a fair is a family business and the fair children have to do their share, so Nell helped out on the joints, continued to work with Phillips and her mother, took money on the rides, nannied smaller kids, minded the hoopla or darts joints whilst the owners had a cuppa, rode the junior scenic to make sure no small flatties got hurt, even peeled mounds of potatoes for chips or helped the chaps to empty the peep-show machines at the end of a good day.

But though adults were decent enough to her, it had not made her acceptable to the fairground kids, any more than it had with Allinghams. In fact poor Nell was just beginning to be accepted, more or less, when Hester decreed they move on. So all Nell could do was wait and see how things panned out.

For the first few weeks, it had been worse than Allinghams, because the girls took, it seemed, a dislike to Nell and set the boys on her, as they would have set them on any girl trying to horn in on their territory. Worse, the jukels did not take to her the way Allinghams' jukels had.

Then, the previous winter, help had arrived, in the unlikely person of Snip Morris.

Snip was three years older than Nell and as tough as they came. He was strong and able, could handle most of the rides as well as the chaps could, and because he was fearless and completely without nerves he was quite a leader among the fairground kids. It seemed that he took one look at Nell and decided, in his own words, that she was 'a nice kid, a bit of awright'. The other kids realised that it was either accept the newcomer or lose Snip's friendship – and Snip was a force to be reckoned with.

It was odd that the kids accepted Snip as someone to follow, because Snip's father, Abel Morris, bullied his son and underfed him. But Nell, becoming one of the gang, positively hero-worshipped Snip and began to enjoy Gullivers even more than she had enjoyed Allinghams.

Today, after a morning of driving rain, Chicken Joe had been glad to hand over his hoopla to Nell and have a break, though usually at this time there would have been lads and lasses wandering around in their dinner-hour and Chicken Joe would have been shouting his wares: 'Have a go with Chicken

Joe . . . your Sunday dinner for the lucky winner . . . come on, gal, see if your feller can win you a nice 'un . . .' Chicken Joe's hoopla was hung with dressed chickens and other tempting groceries and his prizes usually had people eager to have a go but, either because the fair was moving on tomorrow or just due to the weather, customers were thin on the ground. Despite Nell's hopes, for Joe would increase her payment from the tuppence promised to as much as sixpence if she did good business, no one had lingered by the hoopla joint. There were one or two flatties about but they were cutting through the fairground to the bus station or checking on the times of the evening opening. At any rate they weren't interested in trying to win a dressed chicken. This was the fair's last stop before the big fair on Norwich cattle-market, where they would most likely meet up with Allinghams, because it was too big an occasion for just one fair, even a biggish one like Gullivers, to manage alone. Then it would be close-down, when they went into winter quarters at King's Lynn and the kids went to school, which Nell missed during the spring and summer, though no one else appeared to do so, Snip especially disliking winter quarters.

'Hi there, young Nell! I'm a-goin' into town to see a mat'nee; want to come? There ain't no customers so you won't be missed, Joe'll probably close when he get back from his dinner, anyroad. And it's a cowboy fillum, one of them gunslinger things. You'll like it, honest.'

Nell screwed up her eyes and peered through the curtain of falling rain around the hoopla joint, though she knew very well whose voice had hailed her. Sure enough, leaning against the junior scenic with its blazing lights and throbbing music was the sturdy, unkempt figure of Snip Morris, his dark curls flattened to his head by the rain, his dark eyes fixed on her face.

'Well? You coming or what?'

'I can't, Snip. You know I would if I could, but Chicken Joe's giving me tuppence if I stay. Anyway, where have you got money for the flicks all of a sudden? And what are you minding?'

'The junior scenic, only there aren't going to be no kids out in this, not if they've got a home to go to, anyroad. 'Sides, our Pete can manage without me on a quiet afternoon. Aw, come on, Nell, you'll freeze, else.'

'I wish I could, but I need the tuppence,' Nell said obstinately. It went against the grain to deny Snip, but she was very short of money and she wanted to get Hester something really good for Christmas. Also, she planned to send Dan a Christmas card and that meant money for a stamp, too. 'Christmas is coming, Snip, I'm saving up.'

'There's plenty of time before Christmas, another . . .' Snip came forward into the circle of light from Nell's joint, his face screwed up with concentration '. . . another fourteen days for earnin' money, just about. You'll have all the cash you need by then, without Joe's tuppence. 'Sides, he'll be back quick enough if folk start to arrive, he won't leave you in charge then, you might snabble some of his cash. Come on, let's have three pennorth o' dark!'

'Snip, you know I can't,' Nell said patiently. Snip might be her hero and her saviour, but boys could be awfully stupid when it suited them. 'Any more than you could leave the junior scenic if you were minding it alone. I suppose you can get your leg loose if Pete lets you, but there's no one here apart from me. Besides, you never have any money and if you did have, you wouldn't spend it on the flicks. So what's your game?'

'There's a side door to the place. I found out yesterday how to lift the bar and slip in when the doors part for a minute; it's easy,' Snip said sulkily. It was plain he did not like to have his generosity questioned and then thrown back in his face. 'Aw, come on, Nell, we'll get some chips when we get back an' all. Sara's cooked a lot, she'll be handing 'em out later.'

That bit was definitely true, Nell thought longingly, sniffing the rich smell of fried potato drifting across from the chuck wagon, where Sara stood whenever the fair was open, dispensing chips, fat, split-sided sausages and cheese and onion pies which she made herself. The only good thing about a wet and chilly day was that Sara's chips wouldn't get sold and by ten at night she was happy to hand them out to the fairground kids. But even so, Nell had no intention of leaving her post until Chicken Joe reappeared.

Snip glanced behind him at the junior scenic; Nell, following his glance, saw Snip's older cousin, Pete, lying in the whale-car, with a motorcycle paper in his hands. Pete wanted to be a Wall of Death rider one day but so far a push-bike was all he could run to. Still, he was saving up . . .

'Pete don't mind,' Snip said. 'Come on, Nell, or we'll miss the beginning.'

'I'll come as soon as Joe gets back,' Nell said. 'I love a cowboy film, but I can't let Joe down. He's been gone an hour already, he'll be back any minute I shouldn't wonder. Tell you what, if we go to this matinee, why don't you come back to our trailer afterwards? My Mum will make us supper and we can play cards when we've eaten, if they don't need us here.'

She felt grand, giving an invitation like that. All the grander, probably, because until quite recently she and Hester had lived once again in their little tent and worried about the coming winter. In previous years the three coldest months of the year had been miserable and Nell had felt very much the poor relation among the fair kids. Despite her resolve to take life as it came, she could not help remembering, with real wistfulness, how different life had once been. The lodge, the castle, the wonderful countryside, all hers! A roof over her head, a fire, warm clothes; her own Daddy, permanent friends, school. But it had all ended after she had been rescued from the cave, and since then she had done her best to accept it and stand by Hester through thick and thin. She was doing her best to forget that part of her life before the fair. She tried to behave as if the first seven years of her life had been wiped out and, faced with a clean slate, she meant to follow her mother's example and make a new life for herself. The move had not helped because at ten or so, you need a home, friends, family almost more than you need anything else.

But she did what she could. When Hester was being the Snake Woman, wearing a new costume now, though she still had her sparkly cloak, Nell was there to help. She stopped the kids from climbing the barrier, took the money, blacked up for big gaffs, wore her raffia skirt and a raffia frill round her flat little chest, and trekked into town once a week with some of the takings to buy butcher's offal for Phillips.

There were a lot of Gullivers; Ugly Jack had four brothers

and a sister and they all worked somewhere on the fair. Tom Gulliver didn't pay Hester much for battling with Phillips, any more than the Allinghams had, but he fed Hester and Nell morning and evening and at first he had let them sleep in his trailer. Only Mrs Gulliver had got nasty one night and had made what Hester afterwards described as 'wild accusations', and someone had found the Makerfields another little tent and they had taken up temporary residence in its smelly folds.

'Why don't you get another job, the sort of job you had before?' Nell had asked Hester when they had first taken up with the Allingham fair. She had hated the tent, the flies which buzzed under its canvas roof in summer, and had feared the terrible chill of winter. 'I could go to school and things, then.'

'Oh sweetheart, don't! I have to keep moving, I'm so afraid of . . . of someone finding out where I am and trying to take you away from me, so the fair's ideal. Folk don't even know our names, we're just Hester and Nell – Snake Woman is for the flatties. Do you mind this sort of life very much?'

Nell had been scarcely more than eight then, but she had thought seriously about their wandering, unsettled lives. She wanted somewhere she could call her own, but night after night for the first few months of their exile she had lain in her makeshift bed listening as Hester sobbed herself to sleep, and by day had seen the pain and worry increase in her mother's eyes. If she said she did mind, which was the truth, Hester would not feel able to continue her life as the Snake Woman. She would have to move on, they would be caught . . . Nell could not imagine a worse fate than being torn from her mother's loving arms.

'No, I don't mind very much,' Nell had said. 'I like the fair all right, but I miss my old school friends. It would be nice to go to school and have a house again.'

'One day we'll have a trailer of our own,' Hester had promised recklessly. 'I'm doing my very best, darling, and I've got some money saved. One day we'll have a trailer just like everyone else. That's as good as a house, isn't it?'

'Better,' the young Nell had said stoutly. 'Much better, Mum.' But her conventional soul had longed for bricks and mortar, regular schooling, a life in one place. After that, of course, she had settled in, as Hester had, and become happy and satisfied, but with the move to the new fair – and the loss of her friends and status – dreary unhappiness had set in again. She had disliked the fair and all its works until, in the winter before her tenth birthday, she met Snip.

Snip's father, Abel Morris, was a hard man; he'd married and buried two wives before the present Mrs Morris, an anaemic, yellow-haired girl who flinched whenever he spoke and couldn't cope with the clutch of kids her predecessors had produced. Abel had little time for women, children or anyone weaker than himself. But he was a showman through and through. His junior scenic was always freshly painted, the engines worked without trouble, his lorry was one of the few which didn't break down now and then. And the Gullivers wanted a big fair, so they needed Abel Morris and his clutch of kids, especially the older ones, Sunny Ray and Blinky. Snip, who was thirteen, was a ragamuffin, but promised to become as useful as his elder brothers. So they were accepted immediately on to the gaff and the kids crowded round the Morris junior scenic, the Morris swingboats and the Morris penny joints, envying the owner of such riches.

Gullivers travelled the east of England, which might not have suited the Morrises, who had always worked the Midlands, but something had happened to Abel in their last gaff and he was eager to work with someone else instead of alone.

'Reckon he've killed a man,' Mrs Gulliver opined darkly, but Fat Tom said he was a first-rate showman and the matter was allowed to drop. Nell, fond of asking questions, hung around by the junior scenic when the Morrises were taking it down one day and actually had the cheek to address Mr Morris, asking him why he wanted to travel into the eastern counties.

'There's good money in East Anglia, better weather, bigger audiences,' Abel said, reefing the tilt with practised ease. 'Eastern fair folk stick together, so they say. Me an' the missus could do wi' a change from all them tightfisted Midlanders.'

Nell hadn't really believed him, but she said nothing, because by then she was already fond of Snip, not just because he had forced the others to accept her, but for himself. He was older but he had time for her. Snip was dark-haired and dark-skinned,

234

usually dirty, muscular and tough; gypsy-looking, Hester said disapprovingly. But he was clever enough to keep ahead of the pack and made sure that Nell was included in their doings. In return, Nell helped him with his schoolwork and tried to make sure that the flatties – the teachers and kids – at their winter school looked beneath the dirt and toughness to the warm-hearted, humorous person who was Snip Morris.

Flatties were foreigners to fair folk. You might like some of them and dislike others, but by and large they simply didn't count. Before Snip came along, Nell had not dared to mix with flatties or become friendly with them in school, because it would have meant automatic exclusion. Until Snip came into her life, that was; once he made it clear that Nell was under his protection and could be friendly with anyone she pleased, everything became much more fun. When school was over for another year, she could say goodbye to her flattie friends, secure in the knowledge that the fairground girls would talk to her, include her in their games, link arms with her and walk around the summer meadows, heads together, just as though she had been born on the gaff.

The boys teased her, took her side in arguments sometimes, shared the fairground grub with her. In Snip's company Nell tasted a great many things of which Hester disapproved: candy floss, stick-jaw, salted peanuts, the harsh gingerbeer which burned the back of your throat, the fizzy lemonade in bottles with a marble in the neck instead of a cork.

So since Snip, Nell's life had been good and had recently got better. In the summer, Cissie Barnweather's feller had run off, leaving Cissie and her daughter, Fleur, to manage as best they could on their own. Cissie was Ugly Jack Gulliver's cousin and she and her husband, Alf, had run a small cake-walk between them. Alf had taken the cake-walk when he left, which meant Cissie had to help with other rides, having none of her own. What was more, she had to give an eye to Fleur, who suffered from bad colds in winter and wheezes in summer and was generally thought to be delicate, so she couldn't work all hours and was finding it difficult to make the money go round. Then it occurred to her that she had one asset which her feller hadn't been able to pinch from her: the trailer. Now that Hester and the kid looked like a permanency, who better to share her trailer? Both young women had a daughter, though Nell was ten and Fleur only six, Nell was a sensible kid, and Hester seemed to have little or no interest in men. Cissie thought she would never trust a man again, but a young woman her own age, who could help in the trailer and contribute something for rent . . . it seemed the ideal arrangement.

'I'll charge you for livin' in and we'll muck in for meals and that,' she told Hester. 'I don't see why we shouldn't get along great.' Hester had agreed at once, and she and Nell had moved in that same day.

It wasn't a huge trailer. Fleur and Nell shared a narrow bed, Hester and Cissie a rather larger one, but it seemed wonderful to the Makerfields after three years of hand-to-mouthing it the length and breadth of Great Britain. They had somewhere to keep their clothes, a cupboard for food, a table to eat on and comfortable padded benches where they could sit while Hester knitted and Nell read anything she could lay hands on. They could cook on the small paraffin stove when it was too dark or too inclement for a fire outside and, best of all, they feared neither rain nor wind. To Nell it was permanency, a place to call her own, not quite as good as a house perhaps, but getting that way.

'Come to supper in your trailer?' Snip said now, a wide grin spread across his face. 'Will it be all right wi' your Mum and Cissie though? Didn't you oughter ask 'em first?'

'It'll be fine with them, they'll be happy to feed us both,' Nell said at once. She knew it was true; her mother would never deny a child food. 'Hey-up, Snip, someone's coming!'

A man, thickset and dark-haired, strolled into the circle of light around the hoopla. He jingled his money in his pocket, staring around him, whistling tunelessly between his teeth. Snip saw him and moved back a bit, out of the circle of light. Flatties didn't appreciate being crowded when they were deciding whether to honour a joint with their custom.

'Have a go, sir? Wouldn't you like to win your wife a chicken for Sunday dinner? There's no competition tonight, you may as

236

well have a go,' Nell wheedled. If she could interest this feller, you never knew, more might follow; it was a well-known fact that one customer drew others. 'Come on, sir, you've got a lucky face!' But he of the lucky face, having tried and failed to win a chicken, wandered off without anyone else so much as strolling by. Nell slid the pennies into the box Joe had given her and leaned across between the tall wooden stands over which the hoops could just about fit to continue her chat with Snip.

'Well, Snip, what do you say? Want to come to supper wi' me and my Mum?'

'And Cissie Barnweather, and Fleur,' Snip reminded her, unnecessarily, for another good thing about the trailer was having a built-in baby sister. Nell loved Fleur dearly. 'How d'you know they'll want me?'

Nell smiled at him. 'Everyone wants you, Snip,' she said. 'Everyone likes you.'

She might have added, 'everyone but your pa, that is', because it was common knowledge that Abel Morris often hit his unfortunate son. This was unusual, because most showmen appreciated their kids and wanted the best for them, but Abel seemed to dislike Snip for no obvious reason, and the boy generally kept out of his father's way. But right now, Snip was looking gratified. He leaned over the stall and lowered his voice, but not too much, because of the thrum and crash of the music coming from the organ which played for the galloper, just behind the junior scenic.

'Well, if you're sure. Tell you what, come to the flicks when Chicken Joe comes back, jest for an hour, say. Your Mum needn't know; she's on with Phillips tonight, ain't she?'

Nell shook her head. 'No, they aren't opening up the side-shows; Mrs Gulliver says when you're moving on there's no point setting up. Not when it's raining, anyway. My Mum's giving an eye to your Dad's galloper for an hour, just like me and this place.'

A couple, entwined beneath an umbrella, strolled past. The girl was grumbling that her shoes were sinking into the mud, that the noise hurt her head. She'd rather go up the King's Arms for a small gin and orange . . . her querulous voice faded into the distance just as Chicken Joe arrived back at the hoopla. He grinned at Nell and feinted a cuff at Snip's untidy head; he was a tall, yellow-haired young man whose bright idea to give dressed chickens as prizes had earned him his nickname. On a good day you could hear his battle-cry a mile off: 'Have a Go with Chicken Joe – the bird you win will make you grin!'

Now he thanked Nell, handed over two pennies, and began to close up the joint.

'Too wet, luv,' he said when Nell asked him why he was closing so early. 'It'll be a tough day tomorrow, pulling down in this weather. I'm going to get me some kip.'

'We're going to the flicks,' Nell said. 'Will we reach King's Lynn tomorrow, Joe? I want to earn some money to buy my Mum a Christmas present.'

'It'll be late when we arrive,' Joe said. 'You walkin' into town in this rain? Oh well, it takes all sorts. Enjoy!'

It was still raining when the two youngsters reached the small town. There was a damp, dispirited queue outside the picture house.

'The big fillum will be finishin' any minute, an' they'll all be mekin' their way out,' Snip remarked, having given the queue a judicious look. 'Let's git round the back.'

'Yes, all right,' Nell agreed, then stopped short, pointing. 'Snip! D'you see that?'

'Fly sheets,' Snip said laconically. 'What's strange about that?'

'It's what's on 'em! Have you got a penny? We'd best buy a paper.'

'Us, buy a paper? I'd nick one, only the feller's still awake,' Snip said. 'I can't hardly read that flysheet, the rain's washed the writin' out, almost . . . what d'you reckon it says?'

'King Edward ab- abdic- abdicates,' Nell read. 'I've got tuppence. I'm going to get one.'

The two children huddled in a nearby doorway, perusing their purchase. 'We're going to have a new king,' Snip said at last, having digested the huge banner headlines and most of what lay beneath them. 'It's that married feller, ain't it? The one with two little gels?'

'Yes, that's right,' Nell said slowly. 'One of 'em, Princess Elizabeth, was born the same day as me; we're both ten. Does this mean she'll be queen one day?'

'Nah,' Snip said condescendingly. 'Women can't be queen unless they marry a king. Cor, what a go, eh? Now let's get into the picture house before they closes the exit doors.'

But Nell shook her head. 'No, Snip, let's go back to the gaff and tell everyone the king's gone and stood down or whatever they call it. No one else knows and it may be important.'

'Important? For us? There was goin' to be a coronation anyroad, now all it means is they'll put the crown on the 'ead of a different feller,' Snip pointed out. 'Still an' all, you bought that paper; I reckon if it's what you want . . .'

'We ought,' Nell insisted. 'My Mum will want to know; she's been talking about the coronation for ages. We can go to a matinee another day, when we get to King's Lynn, if you like.'

'All right, then,' Snip said. The two of them set out the way they had come, splashing briskly through the puddles and the still-falling rain. 'Tell you what, this new one, this Prince Albert, if he's a-goin' to be king he'll be at Sandringham over Christmas. It ain't far from King's Lynn and we'll be there after Norwich, over-winterin'. Mebbe you an' me could get a ride out there, see the royals an' them two little princesses.'

'That would be prime,' Nell said at once. She handed Snip the already damp newspaper. 'Put it under your coat before all the writing's washed off, and then we'll run.'

It's always good to be first with the news, but Snip and Nell had not dreamed of the furore their breathless information would bring about. They waved the paper at Chicken Joe, taking down his hoopla with a good deal of bad language, and he forgot what he was doing and who he was cursing and snatched the paper from them, reading it carefully before abandoning his work and accompanying them to Cissie's trailer.

'The king's abdicated; long live the king,' he shouted, and Nell saw her mother's mouth drop open, Cissie's eyes widen, as Chicken Joe told them what it said in the paper.

'It can't be true, though,' Hester kept saying. 'Why does he want to marry that woman so badly? She's really ugly and he could have anyone he liked. He could have had the Duchess of York, I expect.'

'She wouldn't have wanted him,' Cissie said decisively. She was a keen royal-watcher and knew everything there was to know about the royal family, or so she said. 'Ooh, the Duchess is ever so lovely, much too nice for anyone but Prince Albert. And he had to work hard to win her, I can tell you. Won't they make a lovely king and queen, though?'

'What's all this?' Mr Gulliver, dripping water, stood in the doorway. He had a shiny yellow cape around his shoulders and a rain-darkened cap on his head. Close behind him were at least two members of the Morris family and even as Cissie moved forward to invite them in, a couple of children pushed through, soaking wet, hair in rat-tails.

'Oh come along in and catch up wi' the news,' Cissie called. She had already spread old newspapers on the floor to sop up the rainwater. 'Here, Hester, put the kettle on for a nice cuppa. 'Tisn't every day we gets ourselves a new king. And pass that paper round so we all know what's happenin' and why!'

Nine

Anna sat in the back of the car with Nanny and Jamie, trying very hard to keep cool and calm; Daddy drove and Mummy sat beside him in the passenger seat. They had started their journey very early indeed, when dawn was just lightening the sky and the birds were shouting their heads off to welcome the new day.

Anna was going to be very good indeed, because for the first time in her life she was visiting London, and more importantly, she was going to see Princess Elizabeth, who had been born on the very same day as Anna, and who might one day, be queen of England. Anna was not sure why the Princess might now become a queen but felt the reflected glory strongly and ever since Daddy had mentioned the coincidence, had eagerly devoured all news of the older Princess. Princess Elizabeth would be right in the thick of the coronation, and Anna was to see her great moment.

There was a lot of fuss and bother of course, as Mummy kept stressing it wasn't a light task, to take an eleven-year-old and a six-year-old to London to see a coronation. At last the luggage was wedged into the big boot, the picnic basket, the little primus stove and the kettle were stowed away under the feet of the backseat passengers and they were off, driving into the cool grey of early morning with the hood down, despite Mummy's warnings that it would almost certainly rain.

So far, all had been well. The car sped silently along the empty road, Nanny snoozed, Mummy and Daddy talked in low voices. Jamie jabbered for a bit, then fell abruptly asleep the way he sometimes did, his curly head resting on Nanny's shoulder and his thumb creeping towards his mouth.

241

They stopped, as Daddy had promised, on Thetford Heath. Jamie went on sleeping but Nanny and Mummy got out of the car and, just as the sun came up, they spread a waterproof sheet on the bright new grass and covered it with the red and white checked tablecloth. Daddy lit the primus and Nanny emptied two big bottles of water into the kettle and made tea. Mummy unwrapped delicious-looking sandwiches – honey, marmalade, egg and cress – and Daddy took his binoculars in one hand and Anna's small paw in the other and walked across the springy turf until they reached a stand of pine trees.

'See the birds? There are a pair of chaffinches . . . a great tit . . . a tree-creeper,' Daddy said. 'See the squirrel? Watch him through the binoculars, you'll see how clever he is and how quick.'

Jamie woke up; they heard him shout as he ran clumsily across the heath towards them. 'It's ready,' he shouted. 'Mummy says to say the kettle's boilin' an' the sangwidges is gettin' cold.'

Daddy laughed. He was in a good mood, the best sort of mood, when he teased Mummy without upsetting her, talked to Anna as though they were equals, and didn't keep correcting Jamie's speech.

'Thanks, old son, we're coming,' he called back. 'Tell Mummy I want my sandwiches piping hot and my tea ice-cold.'

They all laughed and Anna ran ahead, suddenly starving, eager for the wonders of her first open-air picnic breakfast.

'Tea or milk, Anna darling?' Mummy asked as soon as they were close enough, another proof that all was well. Mummy didn't call her *Anna darling* every day of the week. Today was special; she was almost an adult, Daddy had let her use his binoculars.

Anna, who enjoyed milk and did not much care for tea, answered without hesitation. 'Tea please, Mummy.' She panted up to the picnic group and collapsed on to the grass. It all looked wonderful, the sandwiches on red and blue celluloid plates, the cups from the picnic set being filled with tea, a blue bowl with ten rosy apples piled up in it – two each – holding down the cloth. 'Can I have an egg sandwich, please?

And may I have it in my hand so I can look round while I eat it?'

You could tell what a special day it was; Mummy agreed without hesitation, poured Jamie a mug of milk and handed him a honey sandwich.

'You wander off too, Jamie,' she said. 'It's such a wonderful morning, it will do you good to stretch your legs.'

Daddy had a cup of tea and took four sandwiches. Then he sat down and put his arm round Mummy's waist. She went pink with pleasure, but then she reached for her own cup of tea and Daddy released her and began to eat. Anna and Jamie wandered over to the pines and Anna tried to show Jamie the birds which Daddy had showed her, but he wasn't interested. He asked if this was where Winnie the Pooh lived and began to scout around for signs. All too soon the picnic was packed away, the grown-ups returned to the car, and Anna and Jamie found themselves tucked up in the back seat once more. Nanny, who had been packing, she said, for the best part of a week, tried desperately hard not to fall asleep and to keep them both amused.

As they got nearer London, of course, the roads became busier, the pavements more crowded. Mummy turned in her seat to explain that people were beginning to congregate for the coronation early to get good places.

'We have places, in Aunt Ella's window,' she said, laughing at their excited faces. 'But even so we'll need time to settle in, so Daddy thought it was wisest to arrive the day before rather than fight our way through the crowds on the day itself.'

This meant that they would be spending two nights away: a great treat, because though they had enjoyed trips to London pantomimes and other entertainments they had never spent a night, far less two, in London. They had never seen the Plunketts' flat before either; it would be fun to sleep in someone else's house, to sit down to a meal with them, to bathe in their baths, sit on their lavatory seats and see how the cousins ordered their lives when at home and not having country holidays at Goldenstone.

The journey had been fun, Anna decided, but London was too crowded. The car crept along, passing cyclists, horses, carts, people, hemmed in by other vehicles, going slower and slower, then stopping for long periods while drivers got out of their seats and craned their necks to see what was holding them up.

There was one delay which seemed as though it would never end. 'Traffic jam,' Daddy muttered and Jamie said 'Where?' and everyone laughed, even Jamie, when it was explained that a lot of cars all stopped at once was called a traffic jam. 'I thinked you meaned jam-jam,' Jamie said, and Mummy gave a little squeak and got out the sandwiches again and they had another little meal sitting in the car.

'Motornic, not picnic,' Jamie said sagely, and just as Daddy began to get cross the traffic started moving again and they were near now; this was the West End. Mummy began to tell Anna about the buildings they were passing. She told them the great spidery constructions they could see were stands from which people could watch the coronation and Anna listened and tried to give the sort of responses Mummy wanted, only she was cramped and hot and it was difficult to hear because of the noise of traffic.

At last they reached their destination: a big block of red-brick flats reared ahead of them. Mummy gestured. 'Look up, darlings! Auntie Ella lives on the sixth floor, we'll get an excellent view from there!'

Daddy drove round to the back of the flats, where there was a courtyard, a block of garages, a plane tree. He parked the car and he and Nanny began to struggle with the luggage, then a man in uniform came out of the flats and helped them and Mummy ushered the children into a large, stuffy lift which whisked them up to the sixth floor. At least, Anna supposed it was the sixth floor since when the lift door opened there was Auntie Ella, beaming at them.

'Darlings, how beautifully early you are, just in time for a hot cup of coffee and a rest before we start our programme of events. After lunch we thought we should go out and take a look at the abbey, the palace, that sort of thing. Come along in, all of you . . . where's JJ?'

'He's bringin' up the boskes and bagses,' Jamie said, squeezing past Mummy and entering the flat first. 'Nanny's helpin' 'im; vey won't be long.'

Auntie Ella was nice; she was Daddy's sister, and she had three children, two boys, Ben and William, and a girl, Nancy. Ben was sixteen, William fourteen and Nancy just a bit older than Anna, which was nice for them, or so their parents seemed to think. In fact Anna thought Nancy found her boring and automatically became so in her company, and she thought Nancy smart and clever, which made her worse.

'Boxes and bags too! Well, I expect the porter's helping them,' Aunt Ella said, ushering them into a large room with french windows leading to an equally large balcony. Their boy cousins lounged on a big, fat sofa, Ben reading a book, William writing, and Nancy, who was little and dark and intense, could be seen on the balcony, draping a huge Union Jack carefully across the brick and wrought-iron balustrade. 'I would send Ben and William down to help, but you're only staying for a couple of nights so I don't suppose you've got much luggage despite all the boxes and bags.' She smiled brightly at them, then raised her voice, addressing her own children. 'Here are your cousins, kids — find them some orange squash or something, and there are biscuits in the tin over the fridge.'

Nancy came in from the balcony and grinned at Anna. 'Hello there! Come into the kitchen and we'll see if cooky's got any of those scrummy chocolate bar things. Looking forward to seeing the procession?'

'Very much,' Anna said rather breathlessly. Even in the lift she had been conscious of all those stairs. 'I'd like to be on the ground though, because all we'll see from up here will be heads!'

Nancy frowned and Anna realised, too late, that her first remark had been a critical one.

'Just heads? My dear kid, all you'd see if you were down below would be heads all right, the backs of heads! You'll get a good view from here, and then later we can go down, perhaps.'

'Of course; I forgot all the other people,' Anna muttered. Jamie, with his usual sang-froid, had darted ahead of them and was ingratiating himself with Auntie Ella's cook. 'I want to see the Princess Elizabeth very much. We were born on the same day, you know.'

'Really? Lucky old you,' Nancy said. 'I wonder if she'll ever get to be queen? I suppose she might, only the Duchess of York's bound to have a son, don't you think? Queens usually do.'

'Daddy said she might be queen one day, but I thought it all depended on who she marries,' Anna observed. 'I thought you had to marry a king to be queen.'

'What do they teach you, little country mouse?' Nancy said, getting a bottle of squash out of a tall cupboard and pouring it carefully into a big green jug standing ready on a tray. 'I've got a royalty chart in my room . . . we'll go and look at it when we've had our drinks. Daddy's gone for his morning constitutional – he goes twice around Kensington Gardens every morning, it's a huge park, he must walk *miles* – but when he gets back I'll get him to explain about the crown and the accession. Here, choose a biscuit!'

'Oh, thanks,' Anna said distractedly, picking a biscuit quite at random, a thing she rarely did since Mummy was always on at her not to eat too many sweet things because men didn't like fat girls, or girls with spots. Quite without meaning to, she had wished a lecture from Uncle Phil down on her head, and she was scared of Uncle Phil. He was tall and handsome and had a hooty kind of voice and made fun of children who didn't immediately take his meaning. Anna did her best to appear worldly-wise in his company but she was sure he was not fooled for an instant and knew her for the duffer she was. 'But don't let's trouble Uncle Phil, Nancy, let's go and look at your chart instead.'

'Okey-dokey,' Nancy said. Anna thought she was very brave to use slang so near to parental ears. Even Ben and William watched what they said when their father was home, and Auntie Ella was quite capable of giving any slang-user a telling off. It was strange, really, because all grown-ups used slang themselves – but not old grown-ups – and, what was more, Anna's Daddy swore when he wasn't supposed to, Anna often caught a whispered curse or even quite a loud one, but if she so much as said 'Darn!' someone would jump on her for sure.

'Let's take our drinks on to the balcony shall we? Jamie's happy enough, buttering up cook.'

Jamie was happy. He was sitting on a tall stool, staring owl-eyed at the cake the cook was decorating, and now and again he would ask a question in his own strange way, and listen very solemnly to the answer.

'What means royal icing, Cooky? Do it be just for kings and queens? Ain't it just *stiff*, then? And sweet, lovely and sweet! How d'you make it pink? What if you wanted it yeller to be?'

It was lovely on the balcony, only Anna didn't like heights and had no desire to hang over the balustrade and exchange remarks with Nancy about the people gathering below. But she guessed that if she let on she would be thought a little ninny, so she took quick peeps, crunched her biscuit as slowly as she dared, sipped at her squash and enjoyed the warm air spiralling up from the ground and lifting her fringe from her hot forehead every time she took a look below. When the drink and the biscuit were finished, she was taken to Nancy's room, which was smaller than hers and a good deal fancier, with pink and white wallpaper, lots of frills on everything and very educational looking pictures on the walls. Many of them, Nancy explained loftily, were reproductions from the big London galleries. Nancy also explained that the spare bed was for Anna and Anna, who had never shared a room until now, was both pleased and dismayed that she and Nancy would, as Nancy put it, be able to talk till ever so late. I bet I fall asleep and then Nancy will think I'm a baby as well as a country mouse, she thought dismally.

Nancy got out her scrap-book and the two children pored over the pages.

'I'm collecting royalty, especially Queen Elizabeth,' Nancy said proudly. 'Not only photographs from the papers but any little bits about her. I started at Christmas, and look how many I've got already! It's much more fun than racing cars and aeroplanes – they're what the boys collect. Do you have a scrap-book?'

'Yes,' Anna said truthfully. 'But it isn't very full yet.'

'What do you collect? Or is it who?'

Thus challenged, Anna made a lightning decision. 'Oh, the

Princesses, particularly Elizabeth,' she said airily and completely untruthfully. 'I haven't got a lot yet, but I'm sure I'll get heaps soon.'

'The Princesses!' Nancy looked almost chagrined, Anna saw. 'Now that's a good idea. We must help each other, Anna; I'll send you the Princess ones I get and you can send me Queen Elizabeth.'

'What a good idea,' Anna said and found, to her surprise, that she meant it. It would be fun to exchange cuttings with her cousin and to have a collection. 'Lots of the photographs have the Queen and the Princesses on, though. Perhaps we could cut them apart?'

Nancy thought this would not be necessary; you could always get another copy of the newspaper or magazine, she explained. And then she produced the chart, which proved to be a chart on one side and a wonderful panorama of the 1911 coronation on the other. They had a fine time poring over it while Nancy explained who was who and what was what and Anna said she understood everything now, even the abdication. And indeed she did understand the abdication because it had been almost the sole subject of conversation among the servants, everyone at school and all her mother's friends for the past six months; one would have had to be deaf and an idiot not to know that King Edward had refused to take the crown unless Mrs Simpson could share it, and that some mysterious person, probably Mr Baldwin, had said that since Mrs Simpson was a divorcée having her as queen was impossible. So now Prince Albert, who had been Duke of York, was to become King George VI, and the dear Duchess would be Queen Elizabeth.

But Nancy was still explaining about the monarchy.

'You understand then, that a woman can be queen in her own right? It's called . . .'

Nancy went on and on and Anna nodded now and then and let her mind wander off into dreams; she would go downstairs to watch the procession and Princess Elizabeth would see her and they would smile, each divining that the other was some-one special. And Princess Elizabeth would invite her to hop up into her golden coach and of course Anna would do so and they would have a long talk and the Princess would quite understand about Anna's weight problem, why Jamie didn't talk properly yet, like other boys who were his age, and how very precious and wonderful was Anna's dear Daddy. And she would nod understandingly and say she was just the same when Anna told her how troubling sums were and how she wanted to be pretty for Daddy's sake, and when Anna explained about Jamie talking badly she would nod again and say that Jamie was only young and would talk just like everyone else when he was ready.

'So you see?' Nancy ended triumphantly. 'It's all quite easy really; if the Duchess of York – the queen now of course – doesn't have a baby boy then Princess Elizabeth will be queen one day. When Prince Alb – I mean King George dies, of course.'

'What about the one who's queen now?' Anna ventured as the two of them left the bedroom and headed back to the balcony room. 'Won't she be Queen still?'

Nancy thought, a frown marring her clever little face.

'She'll be so old when the king dies that she'll be advised to abdicate,' she pronounced finally. 'Really, Anna, you ought to be able to work things like that out for yourself – you're eleven, aren't you?'

'Just eleven,' Anna said humbly. 'Sorry, Nancy.'

'When you're old, really old, chick, there are certain things you'll remember. The first is the abdication – you'll remember what you were doing on that day when you've forgotten your best friend's name – and the second is the coronation. And it's nicer for you because you and Princess Elizabeth are exactly the same age, you even share the same birthday, so make the great day memorable for yourself; take everything in.' Hester, doing their washing in an old enamel bath, twisted around to smile at Nell, who was putting the linen through the mangle while little Fleur strained to turn the handle. 'And you, Fleur, you'll remember the coronation when you're old and grey!'

The fair was in London, in a grimy suburb, set up on the green so that the revellers could patronise it when they tired of watching processions and cheering. The Gullivers had never got nearer to London than Essex before, but this was different. London was the hub, and they wanted to be there. And despite the fact that the coronation was not until the following day, Tom's feeling that they should make the effort had been right; the fair had been buzzing ever since it opened.

The previous evening Hester and Cissie had walked along the route the royal procession would take, or a part of it rather, with their children, Hester doing her best to explain what would take place.

'Look at the height of the stands – people pay good money, a great deal of it, to climb up there and watch,' she had explained. 'And see those big office windows overlooking the route? You can hire a whole window if you've got enough money.'

'How much money?' Fleur had asked hopefully. She clung to Nell's hand, looking around her with wide eyes. More'n we've got?'

'Much more. Probably hundreds of pounds,' Hester admitted. 'Only the really rich can afford to hire windows, you've got to be pretty well-to-do even to have a stand-seat, I believe. But there'll be no flatties around the fair till evening, so we'll go up west then and I daresay we'll see as much as most.'

Nell had only recently learned that she and the Princess shared the same birthday and she was much more interested in the coronation as a result. How strange but wonderful it must be to have the king of England for your father and the queen for your mother! Not that I'd swop, she told herself resolutely, heaving a sheet out of the rinsing water. I really like being myself and living in a trailer and having Fleur for my little sister. Princess Elizabeth has a little sister, too, the Princess Margaret Rose – and I'm to see them both tomorrow!

'Mum, if we're really to remember the coronation when we're old, couldn't we drive up in one of the lorries?' Nell said craftily, feeding a folded sheet into the rollers and giving Fleur a hand with the difficult part, the first six inches or so. 'Wouldn't it be a grand thing, to be right above the crowds, seeing every mortal thing with our own eyes? Or we could pretend we'd paid and squiggle through to the front of one of those windows – that would be all right, too.'

Hester laughed and scooped the last sheet out of the suds. She began to wring it, the soap bubbles running down her arms and soaking the old grey shirt she wore. She was paid for her washing and ironing and deserved every penny, Nell thought, because she did a thorough job even in winter when the water got cold so quickly and it rained on her lines of wet linen.

'You and Fleur may wriggle and squiggle through the crowds and end up right at the front; the beautiful queen will wave specially to you and the little Princesses will blow you kisses and the guardsmen in their grand uniforms will wink at you. But I'm too big, I'll be stuck at the back, seeing nothing but heads and the backs of necks.'

'You could ask Ugly Jack to sit you on his shoulder,' Fleur remarked. 'He wouldn't mind – he'd like it, I 'spect. He'll come with us, won't he?'

Nell was watching her mother and saw the rose-pink tide wash up over Hester's pale face. Hester heaved at the sheet, wrung it as hard as though she were wringing a neck and not a sheet at all, then threw it into the cold-water tub, pushing her wet hands into her thick, springy hair as though to dry them off that way.

'Jack? Oh, I don't know, probably he'll be too busy to take time off,' she said with a studied casualness which did not fool either child, Nell thought, seeing Fleur's thoughtful expression. 'But we'll go anyway, shall we? I'm sure Cissie will want to come; it's not every day we get the chance to see a king crowned.'

'And we'll make it a day to remember, like you said,' Nell remarked, picking up another sheet and beginning to fold it for the mangle. 'You'll remember it too, Mummy, when you're old.'

Hester, rinsing in the cold water tub, shot her daughter a quick glance, then smiled at her.

'I'm old already,' she said cheerfully. 'I'll be twenty-eight in August. But you're right, chick, I do want tomorrow to be a memorable day for us all. We'll leave at the crack of dawn and maybe we'll manage to get a decent place if we steer clear of the area nearest the palace and the abbey. We'll

251

take sandwiches and a drink, and we'll have a lovely day I'm sure.'

It rained, of course. Probably every major event in British history had been accompanied by squalls of rain, Hester thought, but with Ugly Jack lifting her up to see over the heads of the crowd while the little girls, true to their promise, wriggled and squiggled their way to the front, she had never enjoyed herself more.

The pageantry of it! The colour, the excitement, the goodwill of the crowd! It was like nothing she had ever experienced, and she laughed and cried, drank cold tea and ate soggy sandwiches, stood on tiptoe until her calf muscles screamed and then collapsed back against Jack, just so happy, so thrilled with every tiny glimpse that she could scarcely put her feelings into words.

'I'll never forget it, never, never!' she vowed, smiling up into Jack's craggy, sun-browned face. It was a long way up, for Jack was six feet six inches and built like a prize-fighter, with a strength that he used carefully, as though aware that he could easily cause an injury by mistake.

'I doubt anyone who's here today will forget a moment of it,' Jack assured her. They had been standing at the side of the road but now they were being carried along by the crush of people, all following the procession to Buckingham Palace. 'I know I shan't. We'll be at the palace quite soon at this rate and no doubt the royals will come out on to the balcony and wave, but after that we might just fight our way out. So what would you like to do next?'

'I want chips,' Fleur said. 'Where's me mam?'

'Your mother's safe enough,' Hester said guardedly. When last seen, Cissie had been wrapped in the embrace of an upstanding young clerk, and responding to the commandment to love thy neighbour with considerable enthusiasm. When Hester remembered the bitter things Cissie had said about her missing husband and about men in general, it seemed strange, but today was a day for kissing and hugging, for joy and exuberance. Hester had been comprehensively kissed by Jack, and had not tried to push him away.

'Hang on to my skirt though, love – and you, Nell darling.'

They surged across Piccadilly Circus, Hester glancing affectionately up at Eros as they circled him. A boy had scrambled over the great board fence which surrounded the statue and was clinging to Eros's foot. He must have had just about the best view of the procession possible and Hester was about to comment that kids could do anything when Nell jerked at her skirt.

'Mummy . . . that's Snip on the statue's foot! Can I go up to him?'

'So it is and no you can't,' Hester panted. 'How on earth did that little monkey get up there? We're moving again. Keep up with me, there's a good girl.'

'Sni-ip!' shrieked Nell. 'Snip, we're down here!'

'No use, love,' Ugly Jack said, smiling down at her. 'He can't hear you, the band's makin' too much row. Come along, we're gettin' near the palace!'

The crowd pressed onwards, carrying the little party with it, and soon they passed the Queen Victoria Memorial and into the open space before the palace. They were just in time to see the state coach disappearing between the huge wrought-iron gates and even as it did, the heavens opened. Rain poured down as though it had waited until the new king reached home but could wait no longer. Umbrellas went up, heads snuggled into collars, but Hester just leaned against Ugly Jack and occasionally wiped at the rain which ran down her face and watched and cheered with the rest.

Late that night, with the children sleeping soundly, Hester and Cissie sat on their double bed and brushed their hair and talked about their wonderful day.

'You said it would be unforgettable, gel, an' I reckon you was right,' Cissie remarked, inserting a curling rag into a strand of limp brown hair and tying it tightly to her scalp. 'I met a soldier on the gondolas . . . he's comin' back tomorrer to take me out on the spree. But it ain't that, it was, oh, the feel of everything, the jolly way everyone acted. That's what I'll remember when I'm old and grey, the way you said.' She looked curiously across at Hester, placidly brushing. 'What'll you remember, Hes?'

'Same as you, I reckon,' Hester said. She threw back the covers and climbed into bed. 'Dear God, I'm tired! Goodnight, Cissie.'

'Goodnight,' Cissie mumbled. She sounded rather surprised, but Hester did not intend to talk, not tonight. Today had been too important, too special. She wanted to go over it all again in her mind, to ensure that some of the brilliance and pageantry would remain with her always, as she had told the children it would. But she rather thought, as she drifted on the edge of sleep, that the Coronation Day of King George VI would live in her memory longest because it was the day Ugly Jack had asked her to marry him. Which meant it was also the day she had regretfully refused.

She was very fond of Jack, that was the sad part. But she was already married to Matthew and her heart, she thought rather grimly, belonged to Mr Geraint. Or did it? She longed for him, thought about him, even dreamed about him, but he had been cruel to her, had threatened to take Nell away from her, so how could she possibly love him? She did not know, perhaps she did not even want to know. But she could not ruin Jack's life by agreeing to a bigamous marriage which could not even be a true love-match. So she had said 'no', as nicely as possible, and Jack had said humbly that if she ever changed her mind he would be the happiest man on earth. And Hester had made an excuse and gone off to spend a penny in one of the temporary lavatories which had been erected in the park, and had cried bitterly for ten whole minutes.

Because Hester knew that, even had things been different, she could not possibly make a man happy. Not after the way she had been punished after she had left Matthew. The first months after she had joined the Allinghams' fair had been hard beyond her worst nightmares and it had been bad too when they had lived in the Gullivers' trailer. Fat Tom was all right really, but he liked to fondle young women and she had fought off the old man's advances on more than one occasion. This had given her a genuine distaste for being touched which had lasted for many, many months. She bore Mrs Gulliver no grudge for evicting them, was even rather grateful, but it had been no joke trying to live through the winter in the flimsy little tent. Nell had sometimes been so cold she had cried with the pain of chilblained fingers and toes and Hester had suffered not only from the cold but had been filled with black despair and with the fear that she would not make a go of it, that she would wake up one day and find the trailers gone and the fair with them, leaving the two of them alone and destitute.

Destitution was her worst fear; that and freezing to death in winter. This year, before Cissie's offer, she had been saving every penny she could so that she and Nell might live in lodgings when the weather was at its worst and the fair was over-wintering, but she could always have been caught out by a snowstorm in March, or a sudden frost in November. And what, in God's name, could she do then? There was the workhouse, but she would never go there, not while she had breath in her body to resist. They separated you from your child, shut you up with the sick and the old and the useless. She would have killed herself rather than end up in a workhouse, dependent on others to the end of her days.

Inevitably, her pleasure in the physical joining of a man and a woman disappeared during those dreadful days. Cissie sometimes talked wistfully about finding the right man; for Hester, such a thing had ceased to matter. Mr Geraint had been her lover, Matthew her husband, and they had brought her misery and bad luck. Jack was a good man, she was sure he would take care of her, cherish her, but it would mean all that bare-skin stuff, as she put it to herself, all that bouncing and grunting and sweating. And afterwards, all that pain, for lovemaking, to Hester, had become almost inseparable from the pain of loss and the agony of guilt. She had loved well but not wisely and look how they had all suffered for it: Geraint had lost his housekeeper and the little girl he loved, Matthew had lost his wife and the little girl he had believed to be his own. And she? Ah, she had lost hope, and that was the hardest loss of all.

She had never considered, even in her darkest hour, that she might go back to Matthew. She did not regret leaving him, for he had frightened her so badly on that awful day that she had no doubt he would have killed her had she stayed. She was, as he had said, an adulteress; she accepted the truth of that. She had been unable to refuse Geraint's loving, she had been weak and sinful and the bible said that adulteresses had little chance of anything but eventual damnation, so that put heaven out of the question, except that Hester, raised by nuns, knew that God forgave repentant sinners. She was repentant all right, and now that it was too late she wished she had been a good girl, had refused that first wild loving on Rhyl beach with Geraint so long ago, and his subsequent advances. She could still remember the moment when she had looked into her little daughter's face for the first time and seen the innocence in those limpid eyes, the sweetness of the baby's mouth, and she thought it quite likely God had forgiven her for making love with Mr Geraint. Probably He had decided to let her off from his planned punishment for wickedness as soon as she married Matthew and became a respectable wife. The punishment had come only after her adultery.

She adored her daughter. Nell was hers, her very own, in a way nothing else had ever been or would ever be. She had made Nell out of nothing, within her own body, and though she knew that she could not have become pregnant without the man's seed, she could not convince herself that he had had anything to do with her little girl. Hester had not loved him that first, exciting night, she had known nothing about love, she had just wanted to be cuddled and kissed, and when he had demanded more it had seemed polite to give in to him. Besides, she had enjoyed it – such a wonderful sensation, better than anything before. She had happily lain with Matthew when Geraint had disappeared from her life, for the pleasure it gave her. She had married him, not as Geraint seemed to think because she was pregnant, but because Matthew had wanted her to marry him and she had wanted to go on making love with someone, almost anyone would have done. She had had no desire to go back to being a dull little girl working in a shop or a factory or even an office, and watching life, hot and exciting, pass her by.

Her sins might not have found her out but for Geraint wanting her all over again and using his experience of her desires to persuade her. I did try to be good, she told herself desperately, every time she remembered it; I tried and tried, but he knew me too well, he knew I couldn't resist. Yet she could not blame him entirely, nice though it would have been to pile the guilt on his shoulders. Now that the dangers and miseries of living in a tent and never having a penny to spare had receded, she had felt a couple of times that surging heat of desire and knew she could easily go to the bad again, if she let herself.

There was a Hester who desired Ugly Jack, who thought that since no one knew she was already married perhaps she could get away with it, and perhaps the bare-skin part was what mattered to men, really. Perhaps Ugly Jack could be content with half a wife. . . was half a wife better than no loaf, she thought confusedly as sleep thickened in her tired brain?

But Matthew might find her; worse, Geraint might find her. And she would have to run again, to abandon the fair and Ugly Jack, because they would try to take Nell away from her and that must never happen. She was doing a good job with Nell despite everything and she wanted desperately to finish it, to see Nell a well-rounded grown-up. When that had happened, perhaps she might find time for herself again, but until then it was Nell who mattered most.

Nell was happy in the trailer with Fleur, regarding her as a little sister, and with Cissie, a fond adopted aunt. If I married Ugly Jack, Hester told herself, Nell would lose Fleur, and Nell might remember I was married before, which would start all sorts of awkward questions. Better to be content with what she'd got. She would still see Jack each day, work next to him on the rifle range or the scenic railway. That she would probably, one day, dance at his wedding to someone else was possible, but she did not consider that. She had tried marriage once and found it did not suit her; she preferred Ugly Jack as a friend rather than a lover, and she had proved herself capable of bringing Nell up without any help from anyone and would go on doing so.

But there was no doubt that Ugly Jack's proposal and her

rejection of him would colour her memories of Coronation Day for many years to come.

Nurserymaids have always got up betimes, but Coronation Day saw Peggy out of bed at an unnaturally early hour, woken by what she described to herself as all the 'fuss and botheration' of the troops, the police and various other officials getting into position outside the palace.

The children were to go to the abbey of course, with their grandmother, the Dowager Queen Mary. Peggy, moving quietly around the room, glanced now and then at the child's sleeping face and hoped devoutly that the dear Duchess . . . no, Queen Elizabeth, might soon give birth to a boy. Elizabeth was a good child, a sweet-natured child, but too serious already. And now she was heir presumptive. She'll be queen one day if we don't watch out, Peggy thought, smoothing a wing of golden-brown hair away from the child's eyes. She would make a very good queen, but what she likes is her dogs and her ponies and her books, she wouldn't want all that State stuff, no young girl would.

Elizabeth stirred; Peggy watched the thick lashes slowly lift, the dark blue eyes turn towards her.

'Peggy, it's the *day*, isn't it? What's happening outside?' Without waiting for a reply, Elizabeth jumped out of bed and padded to the window, leaning on the sill and staring out at the grey and misty morning. 'Oh, it's been raining – all the poor people!'

'It fairly pelted down last night,' Peggy told her charge. 'Now you put your slippers on, my girl, and you'd best wrap the eiderdown round your shoulders, it's a lot chillier than you'd expect for May. Do you know what time it is?'

Elizabeth glanced towards the bedside table where her wrist-watch had ticked away the long night hours.

'No-oo, but it feels awfully early. What time is it, Peggy?'

'It's half past five. Shall I make us a cup of tea, since we're up betimes and you've got a long day ahead?'

'Tea would be lovely; milky tea,' Elizabeth said. She was sitting on the windowseat, resting her forehead on the glass and staring at the bustle beyond the walls and railings. 'There are people on the stands already – children, too – I wonder what they'd say if they knew I was watching them?'

'They'd say "Good morning, Princess",' Peggy said promptly, to be rewarded by her charge's rich, gurgling laugh. 'Are you sure you wouldn't rather get back into bed, love? It really is chilly.'

The Princess sighed and shook her head impatiently. 'No, Peggy, really, I'm toastie-warm in this eiderdown and I can see all sorts . . . oh, there are more soldiers . . . I hope none of them faint. Did you know that the guards on duty at the gate faint sometimes? Uncle Kent told me.'

'Standing for too long, I daresay,' Peggy said. 'Poor fellers. I shan't be long, just you wait there.'

Buckingham Palace was a rambling, ill-planned place, however, and it was a good twenty minutes before she returned with a tray of tea and some biscuits, to find Elizabeth standing by the dressing-room door, looking through the doorway at her state robes swaying slightly in the draught from an ill-fitting window.

'Tea, Elizabeth, and just you shut that door now; it's colder in there than it is in here, and that's saying something. It's far too early for you to dress, but when you've drunk your tea perhaps you ought to go along to the bathroom. I've brought some of your favourite biscuits, so if you hop back into bed and cuddle down I'll put your undies to warm by the fire.'

The fire was a small electric one which gave out quite a good heat. Peggy arranged the white vest and knickers, liberty-bodice and short white ankle socks on the fireguard, then got the Princess's dressing gown from its hook behind the door and put that on the fireguard too.

'There you are! When your tea and biscuits are finished then go along to the bathroom and have a quick bath. The room will be nice and warm by then so you can dress and go up to the nursery as soon as you're ready and get your breakfast.'

'Should I wear my robes for breakfast?' Elizabeth said, staring solemnly at Peggy over the top of her teacup. 'I wouldn't like to get egg on them, it would be dreadful!'

'It would indeed,' Peggy agreed fervently. The Dowager

queen would probably have me beheaded, she thought, sipping her own tea, if I sent her granddaughter out on the most important state occasion for years with egg down her chest. 'I've been told to dress you and Margaret Rose in your state robes after breakfast, not before. A skirt and blouse and a warm cardy will do until then.'

'All right, Pegs,' Elizabeth said placidly. She drained her teacup, crunched down the last biscuit, and hopped out of bed. 'Isn't it exciting, though? I wonder how darling papa feels? And Mummy, of course.'

'A bit nervous, but excited too, I expect,' Peggy said. 'Now run along, dear, we've a lot to do today!'

'Oh, look at all the children! Does someone put them in the front or do they just wriggle through the big people's legs?'

Queen Mary smiled affectionately down at Princess Margaret Rose; she was exceedingly fond of both her granddaughters but sometimes thought the elder a little too serious. Margaret Rose was far more happy-go-lucky. She was sitting on two cushions so that she might see and be seen and waving spasmodically as the glass coach swayed through the streets. On Queen Mary's right-hand side, Elizabeth, who had been staring out just as interestedly and waving automatically as she did so, leaned forward to smile at her sister.

'I expect they wriggle,' she said. 'Aren't there a lot of them, Margaret Rose? Children, I mean. I wish we could get down and talk to them, I expect they could tell us all sorts of interesting things, don't you?'

The small Princess looked doubtful. 'I wouldn't know what to say,' she said. 'But they have very exciting things to eat, don't they? And some have balloons and little flags as well as lollipops and sticky buns.'

'We had nice food in the abbey,' her sister pointed out. 'It was a real picnic, wasn't it? You had two glasses of lemonade.'

'Yes, and it made me honk,' the smaller Princess said regretfully. 'I honked twice, didn't I, Grandmother? But I didn't *mean* to, so that was all right.'

Queen Mary hid a smile. 'You didn't honk, dear, you hiccuped,' she said. 'And ladies don't discuss their bodily functions, as I've told you more than once. Look, more soldiers, and what lovely uniforms!'

'The soldiers are brown,' Princess Margaret Rose said. 'I wish I was brown. I wish I had a lovely scarlet coat and a tall fur hat instead of these horrid robes.'

The Dowager Queen recognised the weariness behind the words and was about to make some soothing comment when Elizabeth remembered a sore point.

'I *said* you were too little for such a lot of dressing up; I *said* you'd get tired of that great long train,' she announced, shooting a triumphant glance at her grandmother. 'But would they listen to me? No! *You are always dressed the same, the Coronation will be no exception,*' she mimicked.

Queen Mary smiled and shook her head reprovingly.

'Little girls are little girls, my dear. I think both of you have managed the whole day beautifully, despite the robes.' The queen mother leaned forward to peer through the window. Ah, we're crossing Piccadilly Circus, then it's Trafalgar Square, the Mall and then home. When we get back to the palace you'll both be able to have some tea and a rest.'

'I don't need a rest,' Elizabeth said primly. 'I don't get tired, I shall see if there's anything I can do to help papa . . . oh look, Margaret Rose, look at Eros!'

'What? Where?' the little Princess almost fell off her cushions in her efforts to see what her sister, protocol forgotten, was pointing at. 'Is it a monkey?'

'No, it's a naughty boy! He's climbed over all that scaffolding and then he's climbed the statue and he's right at the top! Oh, grandmother, Margaret Rose, he's waving to *us*!'

'But Anna darling, why did you fight with Nancy? She's your dearest cousin, such a delightful girl, and besides you're a year younger than she is, so if she was being bossy . . . JJ, have you talked to her?'

The Radwells were heading for home, and Anna was in disgrace. She and Nancy had got along fine all through the coronation, they had leaned over the balustrade together, exclaimed over the procession, cheered and clapped, gone down with their fathers when they were allowed and walked all the way to the palace, sharing a large black umbrella without so much as a cross word. They had even had an adventure, for they had been separated from their fathers and had wandered alone through the crowds for some time, discussing the brilliant climbing abilities of boys versus girls.

This had been raised when they had seen a boy perched on the statue of Eros.

'What a view he's getting!' Anna had exclaimed. 'Oh look, Nancy, he's waving to the little Princesses – and they're waving back!'

'I wish I was up there,' Nancy had said longingly, standing with her head tipped back, momentarily indifferent to royalty and the grand occasion. 'Boys have all the luck.'

'And they are better climbers,' Anna had reminded her cousin fairly, only to be told briskly that, given the opportunity, Nancy fancied she could climb as well as any boy.

But then the crowd had surged after the royal coach and the girls had perforce followed and had ended up with a group of youngsters who had been sleeping on the pavement for two nights. They were given sandwiches and good advice and had eventually been found by a policeman, who took them in charge and saw them home to the flat where two very sheepish men were about to admit that they had inadvertently lost their off-spring.

It had all been lovely, absolutely lovely, and Anna had been totally happy. Even sleeping in the same room as Nancy had been fun, talking half the night had been grown-up and exciting, and she had scarcely thought about her bulges which Nancy told her kindly were only puppy-fat and would go when she reached her teens.

'No, I haven't said anything to her, Constance, because you've done enough nagging for two. A couple of kids having a scrap isn't the end of the world. How d'you feel about Nancy now, darling?' JJ flung over his shoulder to Anna, sitting beside Jamie on the back seat and looking morosely out of the window as London fled by.

'I'm sorry I punched her nose . . . no, I'm not sorry, but I wish she hadn't made me,' Anna said stiffly. 'I don't mean to sneak or tell tales, but you'd have punched her, Dad, if you'd been me. Probably harder. Probably in the teeth,' she finished.

JJ gave a shout of laughter.

'There you are, Con, she was provoked beyond endurance,' he said cheerfully. 'I only punch people when I'm provoked and my daughter's the same. End of story.'

'It can't be the end of the story when we don't know what Nancy said or did – if anything,' Constance said bitterly. 'Poor Ella was dreadfully upset and Nancy's nose *bled*. That a child of mine could resort to violence with her own cousin . . . I'm *ashamed*, Anna, truly ashamed. I must insist that you tell me why you punched poor Nancy.'

In the back of the car, Jamie snoozed and nanny slumbered. Anna looked carefully at them both. They looked asleep, but suppose they weren't? Suppose they woke up and heard?

'That's enough, darling,' JJ said abruptly. Before anyone realised what he was going to do, he pulled the car to a halt at the kerb. 'Anna, come with me. Constance, stay with the car.'

'It's about time she got a good talking-to,' Constance said, as Anna climbed carefully out of the back seat and stood on the pavement, head drooping. 'You spoil her hopelessly, JJ.'

JJ said nothing, but took Anna's hand and tucked it into the crook of his arm. Then he walked her along the pavement towards one of those square gardens which are so attractive and usually unattainable since residents of the square are the only people with a key. But this garden was open to the public. There were rose-beds, grass dotted with daisies and several wrought-iron seats. JJ headed for one of these and sat down, pulling Anna round to stand in front of him. He smiled lovingly at her.

'Well, old girl? Going to tell Daddy?'

'All right. Nancy said when were we going to do something about Jamie. And, and I said what should we do, he seemed very happy to me, and, and Nancy said . . .' Anna heaved a big sigh and put on a voice like Nancy's – sharp, clipped, incisive. '*Anyone can see he's a penny short of the shilling . . . he's not all*

263

there, is he? He should be at a special school or in an institution or something.'

JJ stared at her. His handsome face was tanned to a clear, golden brown and his eyes were blue as summer skies. Now a flush burned up into his cheeks and his eyes went cold, like ice.

'She said that? The little bitch! Darling, you were quite right to hit her, I'd like to tan her backside until she couldn't sit down. Why, if Aunt Ella ever finds out what she said she'll lock her in her room and put her on bread and water for a month. And you deserve a bloody great medal . . . oh Anna, darling, don't cry!'

'I c-can't help it,' Anna sobbed, throwing herself into her father's arms. 'It's b-been so horrid, being b-blamed all the time. Nancy did say it was partly her fault, but her nose was so swollen no one heard her properly, I don't think. And I do love Ben, and he said I d-deserved to be h-horsewhipped!'

'The bigoted little bastard,' JJ said. He gritted his teeth, Anna could hear it through the ear pressed against the side of her father's neck. 'I'll ring Ella as soon as we get back and tell her . . .'

'No, don't,' Anna begged, releasing her stranglehold on him for a moment to wipe her nose on her sleeve. 'Nancy's terribly honourable, I expect she's already told. And I don't want any more fuss, honestly Dad. If you could just stop Mummy from talking about it. I really don't want Jamie to know.'

'I'll explain to Mummy,' JJ said gently. 'Now dry your eyes, darling, and we'll walk slowly back to the car. No, I've a better idea. We'll sit here quietly for a few minutes because unless I'm much mistaken the old lady in black is about to feed the pigeons. You'll like that.'

They sat, side by side, on a wrought-iron seat which left bar-marks on Anna's behind, and they watched in perfect harmony as the old lady scattered crumbs and crusts for the birds. When Anna's eyes were no longer swollen and her breathing had steadied, they made their way back to the car, where Mummy waited impatiently and Nanny and Jamie told each other stories about their London visit.

'I'm going to collect pictures of the Princesses and stick

them in my scrap book,' Anna said, as the car sped through the suburbs with their neat red-brick houses and tiny front gardens. 'Nancy collects the queen, so we shall swop sometimes. She says we should cut out little stories about them too. If any of your photographs come out, Daddy, can I have the Princess ones for my book?'

'Of course you can, darling,' JJ said at once. 'And you can send the ones of the queen to Nancy, of course.'

'Thanks,' Anna said contentedly, sinking back in her seat. How nice it was to have a Daddy who understood. But her mother turned round in her seat and smiled at her very kindly.

'Anna, I'm sorry I was so cross,' she said. 'Sitting in the car waiting for you and Daddy to come back I remembered that kitten you brought back from the village. I misjudged you then, thinking you were telling stories to keep the kitten, but I was wrong, those boys really had tried to drown it in the duckpond. So I thought, if my little girl told the truth then, why should I doubt her now? I do wish you hadn't hit Nancy, but I'm sure she must have been horrid or you wouldn't have done it. So come here and let me give you a big kiss to say I'm sorry.'

'Oh, Mummy,' Anna said, flinging her arms around her mother's neck. 'It will be all right, truly!'

'I'm sure it will,' Constance said comfortably. 'Where are we stopping for lunch, JJ?'

'At Newmarket,' JJ replied. He leaned over and pecked her cheek, then squeezed her knee. 'You aren't such a bad old stick,' he said affectionately. 'Your Mummy's all right, isn't she, kids?'

'I do love her a big lots,' Jamie said, bouncing up and down in his seat. 'When's Mewmarmy, Daddy?'

Ten

'Well, darling, we're really at war.' JJ put his arms around Constance as she sat at her dressing table, carefully painting her lips with deep pink lip-rouge. 'Now you've got to admit I was right to join up early because I was able to choose the service I wanted. And the uniform does suit me, you said so yourself.'

'Air Force blue would have suited you just as well,' Constance said. She spoke stiffly because she was holding her lips stretched and because her inside fluttered with alarm whenever she thought about war and JJ leaving her. At first, she had thought it rather fun going up to London, ordering his uniform from Gieves in Piccadilly, and staying at the Dorchester so that he could go for fittings, then dancing in his arms half the night and going back to the hotel to make the sort of passionate love they hadn't shared since their honeymoon.

It had been wonderfully romantic before war had actually been declared. Of course there had been the inevitable worry: what if there really *is* a war, and he's taken away from me for months on end, but that had been forgotten as the weeks passed and JJ came home each weekend, full of enthusiasm and love.

Still, there had been moments when she saw her father's worried face, understood that he was remembering the last time with dread that it might be repeated. But now we have leaders who care, he had said once, in her hearing. We have men of honour at the helm who won't send our young men away to certain death. It will be a very different war, this time. It will be, not it might be. But even then she had not believed until that Sunday morning when she had listened in fear and trembling to that old fool, Chamberlain, telling the country

266

they were at war with Germany. With the words, all her peace of mind had vanished. She felt terror that she might truly lose him and had been unable to face it, so had turned instead to a sort of brittle disbelief – he was too old for active service, someone would see he got a shore job, she would persuade him to change his mind, hand in his beautiful uniform and return to his nice, safe bank.

But now JJ was speaking, indulgently, as to a child.

'The Air Force wouldn't have done at all; I don't like heights and the only time I took a flip in an aeroplane I was sick. But I've sailed small boats since I was knee-high to a grasshopper, and bigger ones for a good few years now. Besides, Norfolk men have the sea in their blood. And the Navy's the senior service.'

'So you keep saying, but it's all so horribly dangerous,' Constance said, looking at him through the mirror, her eyes pleading for reassurance. 'If you'd gone into the Army, at least you'd have had both feet on the ground. And they would probably have given you a commission just as quickly.'

JJ had joined the Wavy Navy in April, before Anna's thirteenth birthday, and had speedily gone through basic training. His acknowledged expertise with small boats had stood him in good stead and now he was on frigates as a first officer. His skipper just happened to be an old school friend, a man with a very similar background, so he and Simon Crewe got along excellently and understood each other almost without putting their thoughts into words. Indeed, had JJ been offered his own command, he would not have liked leaving the *Moonraker*.

'The *Army*?' JJ said now, his disgust palpable. 'My dearest girl, I'm not cut out to be a Tommy Atkins. No, I've always been happy at sea and even though a frigate must be the most uncomfortable craft going, old Simon and I manage to keep the crew happy and enjoy ourselves. What's even more important, I feel I'm doing something, Con, something worthwhile. Besides, they're conscripting all sorts of chaps in non-essential jobs now, and if I hadn't already found my niche I'd have been sent off to one or other of the services without having any say in what or where.'

'They won't conscript men of your age, surely?' Constance

saw his lips tighten and could have bitten her tongue out. What a dam' fool thing to have said, especially when she was trying to say what he wanted to hear. But why should she not speak the truth? JJ was thirty-eight, hardly a youngster. He should have a shore job – would have had one had her father behaved the way a father should. She had *asked* him to use his influence to keep JJ on land, and he had simply said that since JJ was an experienced seaman he would probably prefer to be afloat and would be of more use to his country at sea.

'You make thirty-seven sound like Methuselah,' JJ grumbled, automatically cutting a year off his age, Constance noticed. 'I'm pretty damned fit, I can tell you that, a lot fitter than some chaps in their twenties. Do you know, some of our fellows can't swim? It's true, there are men in the ranks who've been in the Navy for years and they've never bothered to learn.'

'I hope none of you will have to swim,' Constance said hollowly. 'I just wish you'd request a transfer, to the Admiralty or somewhere.'

'That would be in London, and London's going to be pretty unsafe once the Jerries start bombing,' JJ said, almost with relish. 'I'd sooner have a deck beneath my feet than a building crashing down on my head. Now what you've got to do, sweetheart, is to keep cheerful, take care of the kids, and generally keep the home fires burning, as they said in the last little lot.' He gave her a squeeze, then stepped back. 'Come on, darling; your face is perfect, as always, so let's go down and have some lunch before it gets cold.'

'They're going to evacuate city children,' Constance remarked as she got up from her seat, giving one last look in the mirror to check that her seams were straight, her cream and green georgette dress not caught on anything, and her shoulders clear of stray hairs. She had taken the remark about her perfect face with a pinch of salt. She did her best, but she was conscious that, at thirty-two, she was no longer a girl, although she had kept her figure and her complexion was still as smooth as silk. 'I'm supposed to take several kids, so I suppose I'll have to, but God knows what they'll do to the place, little ruffians. They're coming down from London, you know,' she added as they walked across the bedroom.

'Yes, you said earlier. Well, they'll be company for Anna and Jamie I suppose. Actually, I did wonder whether they might move you out so that they could requisition Goldenstone, as they did last time. Only then they took the horses too, and I don't suppose they'll want Miss Muffet or Tandy.'

'They're welcome to them, if they're going to call up all the servants,' Constance said sourly. She had already suffered with a gardener joining the Royal Norfolks, two maids announcing their intention to go into Norwich to make munitions or aeroplanes, and the scrubbing woman who came from the village demanding a rise since she was, she said, being asked to do more. The thought of having to look after the ponies as well as the house was too much. 'They can have Libby and Growser too, if they like.'

Libby and Growser were JJ's labradors. As they began to descend the stairs, JJ turned to her and caught hold of her arm, pulling her to a halt. There was a frown etched on his brow and his eyes had grown cold. He adored his dogs, Constance knew it, and she was almost as jealous of them as she sometimes was of Anna. She smiled quickly, patting the hand which held her arm, speaking before he could say a word.

'Just joking, darling. I wouldn't hurt a hair of their heads, you know that. I'm fond of them too, even though they trek dirt in and jump up at me when I'm wearing my cream linen skirt! Do you really think the Army might requisition Goldenstone, though? I shouldn't have thought it was big enough.'

'It's awfully convenient, that's the trouble. It's out of the city, but not too far,' JJ said rather gloomily. He loved his home and could remember the mess the Army had left behind last time, when they handed it back to the Radwells in 1920. 'Oh well, if you fill it full of evacuees they won't have a leg to stand on, so look on the bright side, my old darling. Every curly-headed little ruffian you take in keeps Goldenstone safer from the British Army. Now let's forget the war for a bit and concentrate on luncheon.'

Anna was in the hall, about to hit the gong a resounding blow when her parents came down the stairs. She smiled at them, then gave the round brass gong the slightest of slight strokes; there wasn't much need for a gong really, since Jamie was in the kitchen helping Mrs Pound to make gravy and they didn't have any visitors. Daddy was on leave because something was being done to his ship and he had said he would rather have a couple of days with his wife and children than parties and social engagements.

'Thanks, darling.'

Constance smiled at Anna as she passed her and Anna smiled back. How strange it was to be as tall as her mother, but then she was thirteen and a half now, her school tunic had had to be let down, for decency's sake Mummy said, and her hair, though normally confined in two long plaits, reached her waist when it was loose. The despised chubbiness, which she had hated so much, had disappeared as she got taller, as though she had been stretched from short fat into long thin.

'Where's Jamie, dear?'

'He's helping Mrs Pound, but he'll be through in good time. Jamie's always hungry these days.'

'Good.' The three of them went into the dining-room and sat down at the table. 'I must say I wonder how we'll manage when food is really rationed, what with Jamie's appetite and the dogs and everything.'

'We'll eat lots of vegetables,' Anna said as Jamie and Mrs Pound came into the room, pushing the trolley between them. Mrs Pound was a wonderful cook; she was also sixty-six, so how long she would stay when the evacuees arrived was anyone's guess.

'Ah, luncheon,' JJ said heartily. 'Thanks, Mrs Pound. Come along, James, sit up to the table, there's a good lad.'

'Okay, Daddy,' Jamie said equably. His speech had improved as everyone had said it would and although he usually came twenty-fourth out of a class of twenty-four, he went to a per-fectly ordinary school and was, the headmaster said, probably a late developer. Constance had been worried that JJ would want him sent to a prep school next year and to public school when he was thirteen, but now the war had started that probably wouldn't happen. Anna was glad for Jamie's sake; he was happy at the village school, talked merrily of going on to one of the Norwich schools, but never mentioned the twin bugbears of Going Away and Boarding School. Anna, who knew him better than most, agreed with her mother that Jamie would never stick it. He wouldn't whine or complain, he would just run away, and that would make things difficult all round. So in one way, at least, the war was a blessing.

'Well, Anna?' JJ said as soon as Mrs Pound had waddled away, wheezing, and the soup had been served. 'Been riding?'

'No, not today. But I'm going sailing with Dan tomorrow; he asked me to crew for him and Mummy said I might so long as I go to church first. Which is fine, since Dan's going to church first, too.'

'Dan? Why isn't he at school?'

'He is. But his mother had to take him away from boarding school because it cost so much so now he's in the city, at the Grammar. It's nice to have someone to muck about with, and we often catch the bus together in the mornings.'

'I like Dan,' JJ said, spooning cream of chicken soup into his mouth with great speed and accuracy. 'Not too keen on his mother, but he's a decent enough lad. Tell me, Anna, have you written to Nancy lately?'

'Not for a week, but she telephoned me two nights ago. They've been doing dummy runs to the air raid shelter, she says it's great fun. And William's joined the Wavy Navy like you, Dad, because he was a sea cadet at school; did you know? And Ben's going to join the Air Force just as soon as they'll have him. He wants to fly . . . oh heck, I forget the name of the plane, but it's a fighter, Nancy says.'

'So William's in our little lot, is he? It'll be a couple of years before Ben has his chance though, and by then, with luck, it'll all be over. I say, Connie, has it ever occurred to you that if they're evacuating kids out of the London slums, other kids might be evacuated from London too? Why can't you put in for Nancy and Ben? I mean they are our relatives and if Ella came with them . . .'

'She won't,' Constance said briefly. She finished her soup

271

and put her spoon down neatly. 'Jamie darling, try not to splash your soup – look at the cloth!'

'Why won't she? Surely she understands the danger they're . . .'

'Auntie Ella's got war work,' Anna put in, realising that her mother had no wish to answer the question. 'She's doing something with the WVS, catering or something, some sort of neighbourhood thing, Nancy said.'

'Oh! Good for old Ella,' her brother said. He glanced across at Constance, pointedly collecting the soup dishes. 'Are you going to do something like that, darling?'

'If I'm asked,' Constance said coolly. 'But we don't live in a city, villages are different.' She brightened. 'I could volunteer as a driver or something . . . I wish I could join one of the women's services, they have such glamorous uniforms, but I don't suppose they'd want a married woman.'

'What about us, Mummy?' Jamie said plaintively into the small silence which followed his mother's words. 'What would we do if you went away?'

'It's all right, old man, I won't really go,' Constance said quickly. 'You and Anna are my war work – and those wretched slum children, of course.'

Anna was up early on Sunday morning, to see what the weather was like. She intended to crew for Dan wet or fine of course, but acknowledged that she would have a battle with her mother if it was wet, and probably another battle with Dad, who knew far better than Mummy how dangerous wet boats could be. But I can swim, Anna thought rebelliously, sitting up in bed and swinging her feet to the floor, so what would it matter if I slid on the deck and ended up in Oulton Broad?

However, as she swished back her curtains, she realised the question was academic. Pale September sunshine flooded the lawn and the cedar tree and deluged the field of barley with its gold. Anna let her glance stray upwards; small white puffs of cloud were moving steadily across the blue arc of the sky. That was good, too; sailing in a flat calm was no fun, Dan would say it was a waste.

272

So that was all right, then. She would get dressed and go downstairs right away – her wrist watch told her it was only half past seven – and get a breakfast tray ready for Mummy and Dad. After all, Dad was going back to his ship tomorrow or the day after and breakfast in bed was beyond Mrs Pound, who couldn't manage the stairs. Besides, she and Jamie had been told that, with fewer servants, their mother needed all the help she could get. They were still at the stage of enjoying the novelty of housework and Anna, washing perfunctorily in the bathroom at the end of the corridor, was looking forward to trying her hand at orange juice and coffee, eggs and bacon, crisp brown toast.

Anna cleaned her teeth, brushed her hair and tied it up on top with a piece of green ribbon. Then she examined herself in the mirror. *Why* wouldn't Mummy let her wear a brassiere? She admitted – but only to herself – that she didn't have much to put in it, but a brassiere would make her look so much more grown-up, so sophisticated. Besides, if she had one she was sure breasts would obligingly grow whereas a liberty bodice was not only no incentive, it was a positive discouragement. Mind you, Anna's friend Sandra, whose Mum kept the village post office, had recently started being unwell every month and said it was rotten, really horrible.

'It's messy and smelly and *vile*,' she had confided roundly. 'What's more, gal Anna, I get belly-ache somethin' turble. My Mum, she says I can have babies now, but I don't see that as no advantage, do you?'

Thinking it over, Anna decided that Sandy was right; having babies and being unwell once a month were a big price to pay for under-arm foliage and something to put into a brassiere. Besides, it would all happen one day, so she might as well wait patiently.

Back in her room, she surveyed her wardrobe doubtfully. She didn't have any really suitable clothes, not the sort of things other girls wore when they went sailing on the broads. She didn't have a sailor top or daringly cut slacks . . . boring old baggy trousers and a striped navy and white blouse would have to do.

The trouble was that she was madly in love with Dan and

knew that he thought of her as just a friend. He was always nice to her, sat next to her on the bus when his friends got off, bicycled around the countryside with her when he had nothing better to do, but he simply didn't consider her as – well, as a girl. If I had a brassiere, or really smart clothes, perhaps he'd see I'm growing up, Anna thought yearningly, heaving on her old trousers and slipping her feet into sandals. But at least he did notice her; he had commented on her slimness at the beginning of the summer holidays.

'Stopped eating?' he had asked quizzically. 'My God, you're a regular beanpole, young Anna. Here, have an aniseed ball. If you get any thinner, I shan't be able to see you at all when you stand sideways on.'

She had laughed because she knew he meant it as a joke, but it did warm her heart to realise that she really must be a lot thinner, because a boy wouldn't have noticed, far less commented, had she lost only a few pounds. Mummy, who had nagged her unrelentingly when she was fat, had hardly commented on her new long shape, except to say that she was outgrowing her strength and really should try to stop before she reached six foot.

'Tall women have the most awful job to find husbands,' she had lamented, eyeing her daughter. 'You're as tall as me already, Anna, and you're only thirteen.'

'It doesn't matter because there are lots of girls taller than me in my class,' Anna had said defiantly. What did her mother want – perfection? 'And at least I don't have pimples. Lots of girls my age have spots and things. It's all right, Mummy, honestly.'

But Constance had pounced on this information as yet another source of discontent. 'You'll get spots in another month or two if you go on eating the way you have been,' she said grimly. 'I didn't get spots until I was fifteen, though they didn't last long because I took care of myself. Just remember, Anna darling, that men . . .'

'Don't like fat girls, tall girls or girls with spots,' Anna finished for her. 'As if I could forget, Mummy, when you tell me so often!'

'You may laugh, but it's true. And I'm only telling you . . .'

'For your own good,' Anna chimed in. 'Anyway, who wants to get married? I'm sure I don't!'

This remark had left her mother open-mouthed with horror but mercifully bereft of words, so Anna had made some excuse to leave the room, heartily and healthily annoyed with the marriage obsession which made her relationship with her mother so difficult. Oddly enough, Constance had kept off the subject ever since, though when Anna was enjoying a meal she sometimes felt her mother's accusing eyes on her, and would put her knife and fork down and refuse a second helping.

Now, Anna tightened the belt she wore to keep her trousers up – they were a relic from fatter days – and went down to the kitchen. She expected to be alone there, but Mrs Pound had the kettle on and was setting ingredients out on the big wooden table.

'Mornin', my woman,' she said, beaming comfortably at Anna. 'Hungry, are you? You're quite an early bird today!'

'I thought I'd get Mummy and Dad breakfast in bed,' Anna said. 'Ooh, Mrs Pound, you've made golden pennies!'

Jamie had always referred to sliced fried potatoes as golden pennies and the nickname had stuck. Mrs Pound laughed. 'I ha'nt made 'em yet, my woman, but I'll put 'em in the pan in a trice. You can make the tea if you've a mind to be helpful – and then take the tray up.'

Anna made the tea, stood the hot toast in the silver toast rack and then, despite Mrs Pound's laments that the food would get cold, nipped out to the big rose bush by the stable and picked a couple of sweetly scented, half-open buds for the tray. She filled a wine-glass with water, stood the roses in it, and carried the laden tray carefully up to her parents' room. She knocked on the door, as she had been taught, opening it when a faint 'Come in!' sounded.

'Mrs Pound did the cooking, but I helped,' she announced as she entered the cool, dark room. The curtains were closed, but the window must have been open for Anna saw her father hunch himself under the covers as the breeze caused by the opening door swirled around him. Anna noticed, though, that her mother was sitting up and seemed to be searching for something, she could not imagine what, down beside the bed.

'Ah, Anna, put the tray down on the dressing table, dear, and then you can trot off,' Constance said in an artificially bright voice. 'No need to pull the curtains back, I'll do that myself.'

'All right, Mummy,' Anna said dutifully. She put the tray down carefully and set off across the darkened bedroom, heading for the door, but as she passed the bed she caught her foot in something and nearly measured her length. 'Oh crumbs, whatever was that?'

'It's all right, it's . . . it's my bed-jacket,' Constance said, leaning even further out of bed to pick up the flimsy garment now wound around Anna's ankles. 'It's a bit chilly to sit up in bed with nothing round my shoulders. Don't trample on it, darling . . . just let me . . .'

Anna, bending to unravel herself, realised two things. One was that her mother was naked, at least as far as her waist, and the other was that the bed-jacket was a transparent black nightdress.

'I don't think it's . . .' Anna began, taking the nightdress from round her ankles and putting it on the bed, but then some sixth sense made her cut the words short and change the sentence. '. . . Umm, if you want more toast, give me a shout,' she muttered. 'Only I'll be leaving in half an hour, it's a sunny day so Dan is bound to be taking the boat out.'

'Lovely, darling. Don't be late for lunch,' her mother said automatically. 'And thanks again for our breakfast.'

'It's all right,' Anna said, going quickly out the door. She felt awkward, as though she had put her foot in something even more delicate than a transparent black nightdress. 'But I won't be in for lunch, we're taking a picnic.'

'That's fine,' Constance said. 'Enjoy your day.'

Anna escaped on to the landing and closed the door behind her. Then she let out her breath in a long, silent whistle. Pheeew! Something odd had been happening – she did not understand it, did not want to understand it, but she was glad she'd delayed carrying up the breakfast tray to put those sweetbriar roses in the little glass.

'Everything hunky-dory?' Mrs Pound enquired as she re-entered the kitchen. 'You all right, my woman? You look a bit on the 'ot side.'

'Everything was fine,' Anna said hurriedly. 'Mrs Pound, I'm going sailing with Dan Raymond, can I take some sandwiches? We'll be out until teatime if the weather stays fine.'

'So I picked it up off the floor and it was Mum's best nightdress, the one she bought in Paris when Daddy took her there last year,' Anna concluded later, when she and Dan were sitting on the bank beneath a willow tree, the boat moored to a convenient post while they ate their sandwiches and drank cold tea from the flask provided by Mrs Pound. 'I can't imagine what it was doing down there.'

'Not wanted on voyage, I imagine,' Dan said briefly. 'Pass me a ham sandwich, would you?'

'Not wanted on . . . does that make sense? I mean what voyage?'

Dan clicked his fingers impatiently and Anna hastily handed over the ham sandwiches and watched as he selected one, bit into it and spoke rather thickly through his mouthful. Was he going to enlighten her?

'My dear Anna, it was a hot night, wasn't it?'

'Was it?'

'Yes, it was. I was hot, I threw most of my bedclothes off in the early hours.'

'Oh, d'you think Mummy was too hot then?'

Dan, chewing, nodded. 'Uh-uh, she was hot. But mothers don't like their kids seeing them with nothing much on, do they? So she tried to pick it up before you noticed.'

'Oh, I *see*,' Anna said, her brow clearing. 'Well, aren't I silly, to feel so . . . no, Dan, it can't be that.'

'Why not? Chuck us a tomato.'

'You've eaten them all,' Anna said, examining the brown paper bag which had held the small, sweet tomatoes. 'Want an apple? There are still quite a few left.'

'An apple will do. I wouldn't mind another swig of tea either.'

'There's plenty of tea, have all you like,' Anna said hospitably, handing over the flask. 'Only, Dan, Mummy said she wanted her bed-jacket because her shoulders were chilly, and the wind was blowing straight in . . . it was quite cold.'

'That was *then*,' Dan said impatiently. 'It was hot at about two or three in the morning; that'll be when your mother shed her nightdress.'

'Oh,' Anna said thoughtfully. 'Oh, I *see*. Yes, that'll be it, of course. I'm glad you explained, because I felt a bit uncomfortable, as though . . . oh, I don't know. Just uncomfortable.'

'Well there was no need,' Dan said bracingly. 'I've got some iced buns somewhere, I'll see if I can find them.'

For a while they munched in companionable silence, but a frown settled on Anna's brow once more.

'It is odd though, Dan, because I throw off my covers like you do, I don't take off my nightdress.'

Dan stared at her, but then shook his head. Chidingly, as though he thought she was being deliberately stupid.

'You and I sleep in single beds, by ourselves, right?'

'Right. I suppose you mean we're cooler, but . . .'

'Just listen and stop interrupting! Your mother and father can't throw off their covers. The other one would feel cold, wouldn't they?'

'Oh, I *see*,' Anna said for the third time, having given the matter some thought. 'Well, that's all right, then! Don't iced buns make you thirsty? Chuck the flask back so I can have a drink!'

Dan stood up and came over to hand it to her. Then, as though he had changed his mind, he stood it down on the bottom-boards and squatted in front of her, staring into her face. Close to, like this, Anna could see how handsome he was, his eyes such a dark blue that at first glance they seemed black. His hair really was black, with a gloss on it like Daddy's uniform shoes, and a dimple came and went beside his mouth as he looked at her. But she did rather wish he would stop staring – did she have a smut on her nose, or a piece of lettuce stuck in her front teeth?

She asked him straight out in the end, having stared her fill at him. 'Dan, what's up? Is there food on my face?'

He laughed softly and put a hand on either shoulder, then

swayed slowly towards her.

'Silly little Anna, no of course there isn't. It's just that you look very pretty and . . . well, and I felt I wanted to . . .'

He leaned forward, until she could feel his breath warm on her face. Half of Anna wanted to pull away, to get back her space again, but the other half was breathlessly anticipating whatever it was Dan was about to do and would not spoil things by an unwary move.

He kissed her. Very gently his mouth touched the soft skin to the side of her mouth. She didn't move at all, surprise and delight – because it must mean he liked her – keeping her totally still. He made a small purring sound and his mouth moved until she could feel his lips very, very lightly, touching hers. He kissed her again, with exquisite care and gentleness. Then he put his arms round her and pulled her close and kissed her again, a tiny bit more firmly. He let her go and sat back on his heels.

'Darling Anna, how refreshing you are – you really don't know a thing, do you?' he said puzzlingly. 'I bet you've never been kissed before, have you?'

'Of course I have; Mummy and Daddy kiss me, and Jamie kisses me on my birthday,' Anna said. Her voice was wobbly from tension and excitement. 'Or did you mean . . . boys?'

'I meant . . . boys,' Dan copied her hesitation with a laugh in his voice. 'Well, now you've been kissed, albeit rather unexcitingly.' He picked up the flask. 'Here, let me pour you a drink.'

'Thanks. And it wasn't unexciting,' Anna said in a rush, feeling the blood rise to her cheeks at her temerity. 'It was v-very exciting and I – I liked it a lot.'

'Well, don't go expecting chaps to keep kissing you, because you're far too young really, only just out of the egg,' Dan said disappointingly, pouring the coffee with a steady hand. Kissing her had not affected him the way it had affected her, Anna saw. Dan looked as though he could have poured boiling oil if necessary, whereas Anna's hands were still shaking so much that she was afraid to take the cup. 'You'll grow up one day though, then I'll kiss you again, and more excitingly.'

'Thank you,' Anna said humbly. 'That would be very nice.'

She was not offended when Dan put down the cup and roared with laughter. So far as she was concerned he could do anything, provided he went on liking her.

Despite constant reminders that time was passing and the chauffeur would be getting chilly waiting, the short winter's day was fading into dusk by the time the children had spent their hoarded pocket money to good effect.

'Come along, my dears,' the governess urged, while Peggy, shepherding them around the tempting shelves, remarked that war or no war, Woolworth's still had plenty to offer.

'Why should war make a difference to Woolworth's, Peggy?' the older Princess asked their nursemaid seriously; the younger, hands in pockets, leaned against the nearest wooden counter, at eye level with some fascinating wooden soldiers. 'The Germans don't want toys or sweets, do they? No, of course they don't,' she added, answering her own question. 'But the people who make them will want to join the services, so they won't be able to make toys or sweets any more. Is that why?'

'Pretty much,' Peggy said. 'We've all got our identity cards and our ration books, so the government is looking to when things aren't so easy to get hold of, once the war effort really gets into its swing.'

She looked at Miss Huntley, and the governess smiled and patted her elder charge's shoulder in its neat tweed coat with the brown velvet collar. The three women who were closest to the Princesses had agreed that it was idle to try to hide the facts of war from their charges; Elizabeth read the newspapers and even Margaret Rose could quote the headlines, since she was a good reader and always struggling to keep up with her big sister.

'People are leaving shops and offices not only to join the services but to do war work,' Miss Huntley pointed out. 'So factories which used to make dolls will be making uniforms, equipment, radios, all sorts. But, as you've noticed, shortages aren't too bad yet.'

'They shall turn their swords into ploughshares,' Elizabeth said. 'Only in reverse. My cousin Philip's in the navy, fighting the Jerries at sea. I wrote him a long letter yesterday, but there isn't much to write about, stuck away from it all up here. I do hope Papa will send for us soon, so that . . . When do you think the shortages will start, Huntie? Soon?'

'Soon enough,' the governess replied quietly. 'I know nothing much has happened yet – they're calling it the phoney war down in London – but the Germans won't just sit back and do nothing, they'll take their time and then strike when they feel they can do most damage. Now let's get back to Angus and the car before it's dark.'

'I like Aberdeen very much,' Princess Margaret Rose said solemnly as they left the shop and began to hurry through the grey, nose-nipping chill of late afternoon. 'But we aren't usually here in the winter and it's nicest in the summer, wouldn't you say?'

Her sister looked around the governess, who held a hand of each, to grin her monkey-grin at the smaller girl.

'Well of course we like summers best, because Papa takes us and the cousins to the sea, all piled up in the car singing happy songs, and watches us swim, and helps with sandcastles. Anyone would like it best.'

'And I like Sandringham at Christmas,' Margaret Rose continued a bit wistfully. 'The dogs will miss us . . . it said in the paper the other day that some people were having their dogs put to sleep because they won't be allowed in air raid shelters. Can't they leave them in their own homes, Huntie?'

'Newspapers often get things wrong,' Miss Huntley said tactfully. She was very aware of how much their pets meant to her charges. 'I'm sure most people are keeping their dogs and cats despite the restrictions.'

'Will they ration dog-biscuits?' Elizabeth said as they reached the long black saloon car parked at the end of the street. 'I wouldn't like to think of our dogs going short . . . well, we wouldn't let them, would we, Peggy? They might have some of our rations, and welcome.'

'They won't do that,' the small Princess said protestingly. They reached the car and Margaret Rose opened the front passenger door to speak to the chauffeur. 'Hello, Angus, weren't we a long time? But we've got the last of our Christmas presents. And tonight when Mummy rings up, she'll tell us where we are to spend Christmas! They might come to Balmoral, but I'd much, much rather we went to them, wouldn't you, Lilibet?'

'Just so long as we're all together,' her sister said wistfully.

The phone, ringing at the appointed hour, had no chance to get going. Elizabeth darted across the hall and took the call, with Margaret Rose at her side, face bright with anticipation. And her hopes were not disappointed. The children rushed back to their nursery to report to Peggy that their parents' minds were made up; everyone would spend Christmas at Sandringham.

'With presents, and all the people we love, and our dogs and ponies,' Elizabeth said, throwing herself into the armchair to the right of the nursery fire. 'We'll act a play for them, we'll go to church, we'll ride every day unless there's a hard frost of course . . . oh, Margaret Rose, it will be so nice to see Mama and Papa again! And I wouldn't be surprised if Philip comes – if he's home by then, of course.'

'Ooh, I would like Philip to come very much; and Grandmother,' Margaret Rose reminded her. 'And the dear dogs!'

It was a wickedly cold winter. The fair, in winter quarters once more, was licking its wounds. Quite a number of the younger men had joined up, though the ban on all entertainments, which a panic-stricken government had enforced the previous September, had been lifted at Christmas. But there were enormous problems: movement orders, fuel rationing, the blackout had all meant travelling fairs could not hope to compete with more static entertainment, such as picture theatres.

'Look, Hester, I'm not asking you to marry me. Not again, I know it ain't possible. Nell told me your old man's not dead, you just ran off . . . I'm not goin' to ask you why because I trust you, but I can't bear the thought of you livin' in that tent again. Move in wi' me, at least until you've something else in view!'

Hester and Ugly Jack were sitting on the bottom step of his galloper, which had been set up for the King's Lynn Valentine fair on the Tuesday market place. Tom was talking about moving from Lynn next winter, finding somewhere for the trailers nearer a big city, Norwich for instance, but nothing definite had been done so Lynn would, as always, have the first fair of the season.

'It's good of you, Jack, but what'll people say?' Hester asked. Cissie Barnweather and the regular soldier she had met at the Coronation had married at last and she and her trailer had moved to a permanent site down in Dorset, near her Sidney's parents' home. Hester patted Jack's enormous hand, then took it between her own and looked into his face, seeing his eyes anxious, his mouth gentle. 'Besides, one of these days you'll want to marry and it wouldn't do for folk to say you were fickle.'

'I don't give a toss what people say and there's only one gal I'll ever want to marry,' Jack said flatly. 'But marryin' in't that important, not to me. It's bein' together. Knowin' you're safe, you and Nell. They won't have me in the forces because of my knee, but that do mean I can keep the fair running, keep the family together. It mean you won't be let down by me goin' off, Hes.'

'Suppose I were to fall in love with someone else?' Hester suggested after a pause. 'I don't think I will, but you never know.'

'Up to you. Leave, stay . . . but just move in until you find something better,' Jack urged. 'You've had two nights in the tent – in't that enough to remind you it's tough goin', especially for the kid?'

Hester sighed. It was true, she and Nell had been miserably cold in the tent despite the little oil-heater which had burned all night. And she suspected that Phillips had been cold too, though his hay-filled box was swathed in blankets and pulled closer to the oil-stove than seemed really safe. She was worried that if he began to feel chilly he might hibernate too deeply, so that he would not want to do the show for the Valentine fair, but even that would be nothing to the disaster if he froze to death. Over the years – and it was years, she realised, astonished at how the time had passed – she had grown very fond of Phillips and wished him nothing but good. He was no longer just her livelihood, he was a fairly intelligent and interesting pet, almost a personality. No, she must not risk Phillips.

'But what about Phillips? Can he come too?'

Jack nodded, and there was something about the way he looked at her which told Hester that Jack would have agreed to a nest of vipers sharing the trailer, provided she shared it too.

'And you won't . . . I mean Nell and I will share a bed, like we did with Cissie? You won't feel I'm cheating on you? Letting you down? If I just share the trailer as a friend, I mean.'

'I swear it,' Jack said solemnly. Then he got to his feet and pulled her to hers. 'C'mon, let's get your gear over.'

'And Phillips,' Hester said anxiously, following him as he headed for the tent, discreetly parked against the hedge but with a frosting of snow on it already.

'And the snake,' Jack said jubilantly. 'Let 'em all come, so long as you and the kid's in the warm.'

'I'll cook for you,' Hester persisted, diving into the tent and coming out backwards, her arms laden. 'I'd cook whatever you fancy, so long as I've got the ingredients, that is. Rationing isn't going to make cooking easier.'

'That's a rare old promise, but tonight I'm gettin' us fish an' chips, seeing as how the van's coming round,' Jack said, taking the tent down with incredible speed and neatness. He folded the filthy, stiffened canvas and trimmed the oil-stove, then picked Phillips's box up with ease, though he gave it a slightly anxious look when it hissed and rustled. 'Where d'you want the snake?'

'Somewhere warm,' Hester said. She staggered up the steps to Jack's trailer, then dumped their bedding in a heap on the floor and turned to go back for the rest. 'He's going to be a precious commodity in wartime, is old Phillips. No chance of replacing him if something awful happened.'

'No I can't see the government agreeing to send a troop carrier off to Africa to fetch Phillips number two,' Jack agreed, chuckling. 'So we'll keep him warm. Tell you what, I'll set up your stuff for tomorrow and the oil-stove can burn in there all night. Warm the atmosphere.'

'Good idea,' Hester said thankfully, dumping the two large suitcases which contained all the Makerfields' clothing beside the small room with the two bunks in it which Jack had said she and Nell might use. 'I'd like to say he needn't work until spring, but it can't be done. We need the dosh.'

Jack laughed and looked around. The trailer was empty save for themselves and though the door was still wide open, no one stirred outside in the grey afternoon. He turned to Hester. 'We'll make a real showman of you yet! Oh Hes, I'll do my best to see you're happy.'

Hester saw it coming and braced herself, but she did not attempt to push Jack away. Gently, his arms enfolded her. Gently, his mouth came down on hers. Gently, as they kissed, he swayed her from side to side, surrounding her, or so it seemed, with his love and care.

When he broke the embrace he was flushed, his eyes shining like stars. 'Sorry, that weren't part of the bargain, eh? But you know how I feel, Hester . . . all I want is to see you right, all I want is that you'll let me look after you.'

'You're a good man, the best I've known,' Hester murmured. She told herself she hadn't enjoyed the embrace and knew she lied. 'We'll rub along very well, dear Jack!'

'The children won't leave without me, I won't leave without the King, and the King will never leave.'

The Queen had said it and Peggy had applauded it, along with Miss Huntley and Mrs Day, because they had no desire to see the Princesses facing the dangers of an Atlantic crossing, neither did they want such a fate themselves.

On the other hand, Peggy thought now, watching her charges as they built a fire in the orchard, there were dangers other than bombs. That young Charlie was joking around with Elizabeth as if she was just an ordinary fourteen-year-old, with no notion that she might one day be Queen of England. The King and Queen, bless them, would probably applaud the fact that the evacuees who had been quartered on almost every-one living on the Windsor estate never dreamed of treating the Princesses with unusual respect. They behaved as though Elizabeth and Margaret were just two more children, coaxed them into their games, argued with them, occasionally pushed or shoved, frequently contradicted, and left them their share, if not more, of any dirty work going.

Like now; someone should have been helping Margaret Rose, who was only ten, after all, to build the wigwam of sticks which Lilibet brought her, but, apart from Charlie, who hung around offering at frequent intervals to 'do the bit wiv the matches', the other children had rushed off to help bring out the picnic tea. Peggy had been told by Miss Huntley to stay out of sight and just keep an eye on her charges, but on no account to interfere, so she didn't step forward with an offer of help as she longed to do. Margaret Rose continued doggedly to pile up the sticks and soon Elizabeth came over, gave an exasperated sigh, and rearranged the wigwam, telling her sister in her bell-like voice that she really should remember to leave enough room at the base for the air to be sucked through once the fire caught.

'Leave it, Lilibet!' the younger girl commanded crossly. She seized the twigs Elizabeth had rearranged and put them back in their original positions. 'Just leave it alone, Bossy!'

'You do as you're told, Margaret Rose, you're only little, someone's got to tell you how to do things and since I'm the oldest . . .'

'You ain't, Lil, I am,' Charlie interrupted. 'My burfday's in March an' yours ain't till April, so I can give you a flippin' month.'

Elizabeth gave him one of her famous looks. It would have crushed some, but not Charlie. 'Don't glare, gel,' he said cheerfully. 'Let the kid alone, why don't you?'

Peggy waited for either an outburst of temper – Elizabeth could really shout when she was angry – or a chilly set-down. Neither happened.

'But Charlie, the fire won't catch,' she said plaintively. 'It's no use letting her do it wrong, is it? She's got to be taught.'

'But not by you,' Margaret Rose growled, standing foursquare in front of her wigwam and wagging a finger at her sister. 'Don't you dare interfere, Lilibet, or I'll *lambast* you!'

'Just let me . . . ouch, you little cat!'

The royal teeth of Margaret had sunk into the royal arm of Elizabeth, and now the royal hand of Elizabeth was slapping at the royal legs of Margaret. Peggy's lips twitched, but she sat quiet in the long grass under the old Blenheim orange tree, determined to stick to her brief.

'Stop it, you beast. You said I was little, you shouldn't slap little girls ... get *off*, Charlie, or I'll bite you as well, I'll bite you to the *bone*!'

The well-meaning Charlie, trying to get between the sisters, was slapped by one and bitten by the other, but he had not, Peggy saw, spent most of his life in the East End without learning a thing or two. He grabbed Margaret Rose and spun her round, then gave her a push, at the same time putting out a foot. Margaret crashed to the grass where she lay still for a moment, no doubt winded. Then she rolled over and grinned at Charlie, who now had both Elizabeth's wrists trapped in one grimy paw.

'No use to wriggle, Liz, I'm stronger than you,' he said breathlessly, because Elizabeth, scorning to struggle, had landed him a forceful kick on the ankle. 'You'd better kiss and make up, the pair of you, else there'll be a grown-up along.'

'Well, I am sorry,' Margaret Rose said, getting to her feet, her dress grass-marked, her hair a positive bird's nest. 'Can I get on with my fire now, without anyone showing me anything?'

'Yes, you can,' Charlie said grandly. 'Me an' Liz won't take a bit of notice; in fact, we're goin' in to 'elp get the picnic, ain't we, Liz?'

Elizabeth rubbed her wrists thoughtfully, then smiled at him. 'Yes, all right. Have you got the matches, Margaret?'

Margaret's eyes and mouth rounded; she had never been allowed to handle matches before, Peggy knew. But then she gave the delightful, three-cornered smile which meant extreme joy and nodded vigorously, a hand delving into the pocket of her pink gingham dress.

'Yes, here they are! Can I try to light it right away?'

'Of course,' Charlie said grandly. 'See you later, kid! Come on, Liz.'

They turned to leave the orchard and Margaret, tongue protruding from the corner of her mouth, knelt reverently before the twigs, the box of matches like a votive offering in one hand.

Peggy watched the two children making for the gate which led out of the orchard and into the formal gardens. She saw that, though stringy, Charlie was several inches taller than Elizabeth, and she noticed, for the first time, that the elder Princess was beginning to get a figure, her waist was formed, you could see the woman's shape beginning to emerge from the child's straight, strong little body.

She was still watching when Elizabeth turned to Charlie and said something which made him stop, laugh, and put both hands on her shoulders. She turned towards him, looking up, laughing back . . . and he kissed her.

It was a quick, light movement, but there could be no doubt in Peggy's mind that that young scallywag had kissed the heir to the throne of England, then chucked her under the chin, taken her hand, and wandered out of the orchard and across the formal gardens towards the castle.

The cheek of it! The astonishing sauce of the young devil! I'll have him banned, I'll see him sent back to London tomorrow, invasion or no invasion, Peggy told herself, a flush of annoyance making her feel as if the temperature had soared into the hundreds. Good lord, if she let him remain here at Windsor, heaven knew what liberties he might take next!

But it was July, and the first bombs had dropped on England, though London, so far, had proved to be too much for the German planes to tackle. British Expeditionary Force had been evacuated from Dunkirk and even Mr Churchill had not stopped talking about the possibility of invasion. *We shall fight on the beaches, we shall fight in the fields and in the streets, we shall fight in the hills; we shall never surrender.* That was what Mr Chuchill had said the previous month, so if she, Peggy, got young Charlie sent home and there really was an invasion . . .

Well, I guess I'd rather have Charlie here, on our side, than penned up in London, Peggy told herself, preparing to stroll over to Margaret Rose to see how she – and the matches – were getting on. Anyway, what's a kiss between two youngsters, even if one of them is the future Queen of England?

It was a hot and breathless afternoon. Nell had been pea-picking in the fields with an ancient straw hat on her head to protect her from the searing rays of the August sun. Now, the field stripped at last, she had wandered away from the Gullivers into the cool green depths of a little wood.

She was missing Snip terribly, but was coming to terms with being left behind. Snip had joined the Navy and was at a training school in Scotland; he talked of being a submariner, which made her shudder, but he wrote lovely long, if ill-spelt, letters and came back to whichever gaff they were on whenever he got leave.

He had not been back for several weeks though, so Nell wandered into the wood alone. It was nice in here; outside, flies buzzed, midges bit, and sweat channelled down the sides of her face whenever she moved. In the shelter of the trees there was a little stream, not much more than a ditch really, tinkling along on a sandy bed. No doubt the sound of moving water was what made the wood seem cooler, as well as the dappling sunshine and shadow which fell through the leaves; whatever the reason, it was a haven of peace after the harsh heat of the harvest field.

And it wasn't just the heat Nell was escaping from either; she was giving her mother the chance to be alone with Ugly Jack for an hour or so and, on a more personal note, she was escaping from one of the chaps, her friend Riggy.

Riggy Evans was a Welshman, small and sly, with a lively sense of humour and a habit of talking without moving his lips which Ugly Jack once said had most probably been learned in prison. He had dark, curly hair, a broken nose, almost black eyes, and enormous muscles; he was taciturn with the other chaps but he told Nell he had worked in the coal mines and that was the reason for the little blue scars all over his body. When your pick hit the wall tiny chips of coal flew out and embedded themselves in your flesh, he explained. You could always tell a miner by the scars.

No one knew what he was doing on the eastern side of the country, working the fairs, but Nell took to him at once because of his Welshness; it reminded her of the village, of Pengarth Castle, of all the good things from her dimly remembered early life. Riggy had been remote at first, but then she had addressed him in stumbling, half-remembered Welsh and they had become good friends, with Riggy returning her childish admiration in a pleasant and uncomplicated fashion. He had stolen books for her – well, he might have bought them, she supposed doubtfully, but Riggy was known to be light-fingered – and because he was illiterate she had taken to reading to him on quiet afternoons, out of the local paper usually, but occasionally from a story-book. Then he had brought her chocolates or sweets, a pretty piece of ribbon, a few early strawberries, and approved when she shared them with Snip. She had been a child, after all, and children like nice things. Besides, Riggy could be amusing; the stories he told were often improbable but usually funny, and Hester sometimes asked him in for a meal and would talk, guardedly, about Rhyl and the inland villages, though she never told anyone directly about Pengarth or their lives in Wales.

Riggy was one of those chaps who went off in the winter, so they didn't see him from December until around April. This year, when spring came round, he hadn't turned up with the other chaps to start the season. Nell always had great difficulty with the age of anyone over fifteen, so she thought him probably youngish – did he not have dark hair without any white in it? – but not as young as the soldiers, sailors and airmen who thronged to the fair whenever they could. She imagined, therefore, that Riggy had gone into making munitions or working on the land, and when he tapped on the trailer door and walked in on a drizzly day in June she was just glad to see him, she didn't wonder at all.

But Hester wondered. 'Hello, Riggy, nice to see you,' she had greeted him. 'Where've you been?'

'Dunkirk,' came the laconic response. 'Need a hand?'

'Dunkirk? I say, were you one of the soldiers taken off the beaches? If so, how long have you got before they want you back in the army?'

'Yeah, they got me but I'm not goin' back; they've 'ad enough of me, see? Like to look at me war wound?'

He heaved up a trouser leg; the knee-cap was criss-crossed

with fresh scar tissue, you could even see the stitch marks.
Hester gasped, a hand flying to her mouth.

'Oh, Riggy, whatever did that?'

'Landmine. Trod on it, bloody near. Lucky to be alive,'
Riggy said, lowering his trouser leg. 'But I can work; need
another chap?'

'Well, you can try,' Hester said doubtfully. 'See Jack, when
he comes in presently. In the meantime, take a seat, I'll make
you a cuppa.'

'I'll make it,' Nell had said, jumping to her feet. She had
read all about Dunkirk and the BEF in the papers; now they
had a Dunkirk hero in their trailer. What stories Riggy would
be able to tell, what tales of heroism and tragedy!

It was then that the trouble started, if you could call it trouble.

'Ello, young Nell,' Riggy began, then stopped abruptly. As
Nell unfolded herself from the bench he took in, in one startled
glance, all the changes that had happened to Nell in his absence.
She felt his eyes roam over her budding breasts, the little waist,
the curve of her hips, and for the first time she became aware
of her own body, of the changes which were turning her from
child to woman.

Nell didn't like it. Riggy, her friend, had become like one of
the flatties, staring, assessing. Snip accepted her as she was, he
never made her feel uncomfortable even when he remarked
on some change in her, but Riggy did. She had recently told
Hester that she would no longer wear the raffia skirt and the
frill, or paint up with Cherry Blossom boot polish. She was
too old, she said, feeling her cheeks go hot at the thought of
those staring, knowing flatties, sizing her up, thinking things.
But even when Hester, after a shrewd glance, had agreed that
she was too old for the raffia skirt, she had not known exactly
why she felt the way she did.

Until now; until she saw Riggy, her old friend, look at
her with a sort of hunger. But that had been two months
ago, and she had grown accustomed to the looks and the fact
that flatties who would normally have ignored her and ogled
Hester, now tried to get into conversation with her, suggested
she might like to go to the flicks or take a walk after the show.

291

She refused them all, of course, turned them down flat. Even the soldiers, sailors and airmen in their fascinating uniforms with their tired eyes and nervous movements. In a way they needed her companionship, she sensed it, but she still turned them down, turned away. She was Nell Makerfield, she was her own person, she didn't want all the giggling, nudging nonsense the older girls indulged in whenever someone caught their fancy, whenever a brawny soldier whacked the peg with the mallet and sent the striker soaring up to the high bell. The triumphant *ting* sent them into some sort of silly ecstasy, Nell thought scornfully, so that they competed for the attention of the man whose strength had rung the bell without pausing to consider whether he had a brain in his head or was kind to animals, both attributes of considerable importance to Nell.

But now, in the cool greenness of the little wood, Nell felt at peace with the world. Her mother and Ugly Jack seemed to have entered a new phase in their relationship recently; she acknowledged the fact without understanding why this was, and she was happy for them both. When their hands touched, a wave of colour would rise to Hester's forehead and Ugly Jack would grit his teeth so tightly that a muscle jumped in his cheek. They exchanged glances, not the sickly ones of the fair girls but quick, loving looks in which tenderness and something else mingled. Nell thought they liked to be alone sometimes, too, so she tried to be out of the trailer for a good bit of the day and was happy enough, at this time of year, not to return to the trailer until the evening was well advanced.

'Have you ever caught them at it?' her friend Babe Ellis asked, when Nell had tried to explain why she stayed out of the trailer so much. 'Does they kiss an' cuddle much?'

'Kiss and cuddle? No, of course not, they aren't a couple of youngsters,' Nell had said indignantly. 'It's just, oh I dunno.'

'They must *do* it, livin' in the same trailer and bein' so friendly together,' Babe said thoughtfully. 'Us could sneak back one evenin', tek a look through the winder at 'em.'

'Look through the window and see them doing what?' Nell asked suspiciously. 'You don't mean what the jukels do, do you – what made Prick-ears have those puppies?'

'That's it, gel,' Babe agreed. She was fifteen months older than Nell. 'Only if they does it, they won't 'ave puppies, exac'ly.'

'I know that, stupid,' Nell said, nevertheless relieved to hear it. She knew very little about the workings of people or animals, only knew about the jukels because she had been woken as day dawned one dewy June morning by Sinda and Prick-ears thumping into the trailer as they bounced, untidily attached, round and round the van. She had roused Hester and told her that the jukels had somehow got welded to each other.

'Oh, they're dog-locked,' Hester said sleepily, peering through the side of the curtain at the two dogs, circling unhappily, seemingly as worried over their sudden attachment as Nell had been. 'It's all right, sweetheart, it happens to dogs when they . . . when they make puppies. In a while they'll come unstuck.'

She had giggled, given Nell a quick embarrassed glance, and curled down under the covers again. Later, she had got a book out of the village library and tried to explain things, but Nell had blocked her ears and run out, crying that she didn't care, she didn't want to know. Jack told Hester the kid was too young for all that stuff, and advised her to leave the book around for a week or two so that Nell could read what she wanted for herself. Nell had been strongly inclined to give the book a wide berth, but curiosity won and she and Babe spent a frustrating afternoon in the hayfield, looking at diagrams – at least one upside down – and puzzling over the wordy but inconclusive text. The book had explained that only married people indulged in these strange acts – they had not been specific about jukels – so obviously Hester and Ugly Jack did not, which was a relief. It seemed, from what she had read, to be a strange, athletic sort of exercise and one she could not imagine any of the married people she knew undertaking.

No, Nell had decided, putting the book back in a prominent position on the window-shelf, there must be another way to procreate, and fair people, who lived in trailers and were short of space, must have discovered it. The thought gave her a good deal of quiet satisfaction.

She was thinking about Hester and Jack and trying to

decide whether Hester would like her help in preparing tea or if it would be better to stay out a little longer when she heard a twig crack. Someone else was in the wood then – Babe? Or Hester, come to call her in to give a hand?

She looked behind her, then stepped quietly into a small hazel copse, out of the main part of the wood. What if it were Riggy? She felt instinctively that it was not wise to be alone with him though he had reverted, almost, to his old casual friendship with her. Almost, but not quite; perhaps it wasn't possible for them to share that carefree relationship again. It was a pity, but if it was Riggy walking along under the trees she would prefer he did not know she was there.

It was a man, anyway. Dark-haired. Probably Riggy. He looked as though he was searching for someone, peering to right and left as he walked. She could see the silhouette of a turning head against the bright patches of sunlight though she still could not see who it was. Best be off, then, Nell decided. Quietly, taking care, she slid out of the shelter of the hazel copse and made for the farther side of the wood. Suddenly the wood seemed too dark, too cool. She would be happier under the brilliant blue of the sky.

She made very little noise and gained the edge of the wood without being conscious of pursuit, but as she emerged from the trees the flies found her. She stepped into the waist-high bracken and they attacked her, buzzing in a column a foot above her head, touching, settling, horrible. Still, she was in the sunshine, out of the dubious shelter of the wood. She might as well go back to the trailer now, she could help Hester with the tea. There were peas; what could be nicer than a big pan of fresh peas, and there had been talk of a piece of boiling bacon . . .

She turned towards the gaff and saw the man break out of the wood, hesitate, look around. It was not Riggy or any one else from the fair; it was a flattie. When he saw her, he grinned, showing very white, pointed teeth. He had a narrow face, slicked-back black hair, and round, protruding eyes which seemed to glisten when he saw her. He reminded her of the ferrets the village boys carried round, showing them off to the girls to make them jump and squeak. Ferrets were dangerous, they could kill a rabbit twice their size, and she found she did not want the man anywhere near her, anywhere at all.

The trouble was, the stranger was between her and the fairground and even as she hesitated he began to push his way through the bracken towards her. Immediately she turned in the opposite direction and began to run, panic lending her wings. The flies buzzed around, following her relentlessly; as relentlessly as the man, for he was definitely following her, coming fast, she could hear the rustle of his progress far too well. She looked back and saw that he was no more than five yards behind and he, too, had a buzzing column of flies over his head. Her heart bumping unpleasantly hard and sweat trickling down between her breasts, Nell tried to run faster, realising that though she was leaving the gaff behind she was approaching the village, albeit indirectly. It crossed her mind that she might be making too much of it, perhaps if she stopped the man would stop too, pass the time of day, go ahead of her, disappear. But instinct knew more than Nell knew herself, and it was telling her to keep running, to escape from her pursuer; she obeyed, though her chest was aching and the heat prickling all over her body as fresh runnels of perspiration began to trickle across her skin.

She saw a ragged hedge looming and ducked beneath the long hawthorn branches, getting a moment's respite before she entered its nettles, gorse and brambles. In a few moments she was burning from nettle stings and bleeding from the thorns, but she ran faster; he was coming on through the wuzzy as though he were impervious to stings and clutching brambles, with that horrid leer fixed on his thin lips and his hungry, wet-looking eyes raking her body.

Her breath was sobbing in her throat and her hair had come undone from the plait which had kept it off her face in the harvest field. She wished Snip were here, why had he gone and joined the Navy? Her right foot hurt but she scarcely heeded the pain because she had to run until she dropped – and dropping, she realised, was not unthinkable because it was still a good way to the village. She knew she was running more slowly but a glance behind proved she was not the only one. The man was no nearer than he had been, but no farther off either.

Another hedge loomed, a thicker, better-kept hedge. Nell looked for a gap, could not find one, ran desperately one way, then the other. Behind her, the man laughed, breathless, triumphant. He would gain on her if she wasted any more time, no use looking for a gap that would not take him, he was about her build; if she could get through it, she would follow. Nell dropped to her knees and squeezed through a gap at the bottom of the hedge, then rolled forward, straight into a ditch. It was boggy and black at the bottom, with only a trickle of water, but it felt cool on her burning skin and for a second she revelled in that coolness. Then she saw that he was coming through farther up, pushing and shoving, his shoulders, it seemed, finding it hard to get between the stout, thorny branches.

Nell scrambled to her feet, slid, stumbled, emerged. She realised that she was on the dusty lane which led to the village. Fresh hope coursed through her but another quick look back showed her pursuer free from hedge and ditch, seemingly about to reach out and grab at her clothing, which was torn and trailing. She gulped and forced herself to run, though she was almost at the end of her strength. She staggered, collected herself, and reached a bend in the lane just as a hand grabbed at her hair, jerking her to a halt.

She screamed, a sound as shrill and terrified as the scream a hare gives when it feels the teeth of a hound on its neck. She tried to jerk her hair free, then turned and faced her attacker, muddy hands pushing feebly at him, mouth open to scream again, all but finished. He seemed to be jeering at her, his lips drawn back from those pointed teeth, his hands holding her shoulders now, digging into the soft, slippery flesh. He was pulling her nearer, his expression changing, then she saw his eyes widen and fix on something behind her. His hands gripped tighter for a moment, then he let go, almost pushed her away. Nell heard running feet scuffling in the dust, and a voice spoke breathlessly.

'What the hell goes on? Is that man . . . hey you, come back here! It's all right, he's gone, he won't hurt you . . .'

She turned. The tall, black-haired young man in a blue shirt and flannels running towards her must have seen what was happening as he came round the corner and dashed to her aid. Her attacker had vanished.

'Oh, thank you,' Nell gasped. She swayed where she stood and the young man put a protective arm around her shoulders. 'He's chased me for . . . for miles, I was so f-frightened.'

She looked up into the young man's face. A pair of eyes so dark a blue that at first glance they appeared black looked back at her. Familiar eyes, set in a familiar face.

'Dan!' Nell gasped. 'Dan Clifton!'

The young man frowned and stared into her face. He saw, Nell knew, mud, tangled locks, scratches and stings. Would he – could he possibly – recognise her?

'Well I'm damned! It's little Nell Coburn, isn't it? You used to live at the lodge with your parents. There was some mystery . . . you used to write me letters at boarding school but then I left, and . . . well, I'm damned, if it isn't little Nell Coburn!'

'Yes, it's me,' Nell said. Her breathing was slowing, the sweat was cooling on her, but she wished with all her heart that she didn't look such a mess. Still, he had recognised her, which showed he couldn't have forgotten her. 'What are you doing, Dan, walking down a lane in the middle of nowhere?'

'Rescuing you from a very unpleasant character, by the look of it,' Dan said seriously. 'I'm staying with a friend. I walked into the village to buy some stamps and now I'm walking back. Look, you'll want to clean up and calm yourself, have a cup of tea or something, but then we must talk. Did you know your father had been searching for you and your mother everywhere? Where are you living? Where is Hester? I'll come home with you and you can tidy, then we'll talk.'

How she wanted to talk, to confide, to take him back to the trailer and tell Hester that Dan had rescued her! But she couldn't. For years Hester had made it plain that to make any sort of connection between themselves and that other life was dangerous. She could not let Hester down by taking Dan to the gaff. But that did not mean she had to leave him immediately, they could surely exchange a few words first?

'I can't take you home, I'm only staying here too,' she said slowly. 'The lady that I'm staying with wouldn't be too pleased. But there's a stream across that field . . .' she gestured ahead, '. . . so I can clean up there and we can talk. Would that do?'

'A stream? No, it won't do. Nell, have you looked at yourself? You've been evacuated, I take it?'

Nell nodded guiltily. The lies she was telling!

'Right, then I understand you can't take me back, but there's nothing to stop you coming back with me to the Tillet's place if you can get that far. It's not much more than a mile. What about your feet?'

Nell looked down; she was wearing one sandal and the other foot was bare, cut and bruised. Her skirt was torn to ribbons and so was her short-sleeved shirt. Earth, grass stains, hedge clippings, brambles – she was coated in them. She felt tears come to her eyes and rubbed them defensively with filthy fists.

'I didn't notice losing the sandal,' she muttered. 'I can't come home with you looking like this, what'll your friends think? And what'll I tell . . . the lady?'

'It's all right, I'll take you straight to the downstairs cloak-room and clean you up; as for clothes, I'm staying with cousins, two boys and a girl. Daisy will lend you something,' Dan said reassuringly. 'In fact I expect she'll give you a skirt and blouse or a cotton dress, God knows she's got enough of them. She's about your size, too, only a bit fatter, so if the things are too big you can borrow a couple of safety pins, make them fit. Come on, you'd better take the other sandal off and walk barefoot. Who was chasing you, by the way? I didn't ask.'

'I don't know him. He's horrible, one of those horrible men,' Nell said, padding along beside Dan and hearing her voice begin to shake without being able to do a thing to stop it. 'If only I'd had the jukels . . . I'll never go out without them again.'

'What's a jukel, a good luck charm, or a friend, or what?' Dan asked curiously. 'You certainly shouldn't wander in the woods and fields alone at your age, Nell dear.'

'The jukels? Oh . . . they're a family I'm friendly with,' Nell

298

said, hating the lies but seeing the necessity of keeping Dan in ignorance of her new life. 'You're right, Dan, I'll never go out alone again.'

'Good girl. See that white house over there, against the wood? That's the Tillet's place. Not far now, eh? Best foot forward!'

Nell got back to the gaff in time for a late tea and, rather to her own surprise, said nothing about meeting Dan. It would involve too many questions, too much explanation. She and her mother almost never mentioned Pengarth, far less discussed their life there. It had become taboo. But she did tell her mother about the terrifying chase through the wood, describing the flattie as accurately as she could.

Hester was horrified, but Ugly Jack was more practical.

'Sounds like Geoff Brewer to me; it's high time the Brewers were told their son ought to be kept closer,' he said. 'I'll go over there tonight, have a word. I'd noticed him hangin' about starin' at the girls on the gondolas and cakewalk. He'll do someone a mischief one of these days despite them sayin' he's just a bit soft in the head.'

'Is that the man they were talking about the other evening? The one Edie said was a poor lack-wit, only your Mum said it was in-breeding, and the fellow was a danger to young girls?'

'Aye, that's the one,' Jack said grimly. 'I'll have a word.'

He left the living waggon and Nell turned immediately to Hester.

'What does that mean, Mum? In-breeding?'

'It's what happens sometimes in small village communities. Cousins marry cousins generation after generation, then a widowed uncle takes his pretty niece behind a haystack and the child doesn't know who he or she is and marries someone who might be a half-brother or sister. That way you get village idiots, men with peculiar appetites, fellows like Geoff, who can't understand what is theirs and what isn't,' Hester said grimly. 'If you ask me, love, you had a very lucky escape. Another time, take the jukels, or Riggy, or someone else from the fair, who knows you.'

299

'When Snip was here I went everywhere with him; I wish he hadn't left,' Nell said forlornly. 'And Riggy ... Mum, he likes me.' She had not previously mentioned her change of feeling over her old friend, but thought this was the moment. 'I feel embarrassed at the way he looks at me sometimes.'

Hester was ironing. She put her iron down and went over to Nell, sitting down beside her on the long windowseat. She put her arms around her daughter and gave her a squeeze.

'Darling, I know what you mean, but Riggy would never do you harm. He is really fond of you and astounded to find how grown-up you are, but he would never, never take a liberty. However, you're right, of course, that a pretty young woman shouldn't be alone in quiet places with a man. You'd be safe enough with Snip, I daresay, you've been pals for so long, but I think you should look on this as a frightening lesson and be more careful in future. Take a couple of jukels with you when you go walking; jukels are good friends, they'd not let harm come to you.'

So was Dan a good friend, Nell thought. How nice it would be if we were settled near his home so we could see more of each other. But she said nothing.

Eleven

'He's there, Lilibet – right in the front row!'

'Where? I can see Aunt Kent. Is he to the left or right of her?'

Peggy, who had helped to dress the two principals in the royal pantomime at Windsor Castle, watched as they tried to see through the gap in the red velvet curtains without being seen; Margaret Rose already in costume, her sister lacking the wig and jacket which she would presently don.

'To the right, silly . . . oh, you must be able to see him – he looks so handsome! Huntie thinks he looks like a Viking plunderer, and his hair really is almost yellow, isn't it? Will it make you nervouser than ever though, knowing he's watching?'

'Will it make me more nervous, not nervouser, goose,' Elizabeth corrected automatically. 'Yes . . . no . . . I'm not sure. Ah, yes, I can see him. Oh help, he's looking this way! We'd better finish dressing, Margaret, or they'll call us and we won't be ready.'

She moved back from the curtain, the pink deepening in her cheeks. Margaret Rose pushed her sister gently back again. 'There's plenty of time,' she said robustly. 'You 'ave a gander, me old dear.'

'Don't, Margaret, you shouldn't talk cockney in case people think you're poking fun,' Elizabeth said, moving back from the curtain. She turned away and saw Peggy standing patiently waiting, the jacket in her hands. 'Oh, we've kept Peggy hanging about! How long before we're called, Pegs?'

'Seven minutes,' Peggy said. 'And you without your wig, Lilibet! Now come along both of you and stop hanging about peering at your audience. This is serious, remember, the people

301

out there have paid good money to see the pantomime and even though it's for charity they should get good value.'

Elizabeth nodded at once, her face serious, though her cheeks were still pink and her dark blue eyes shone like stars.

'Yes, I know, Peggy. And Margaret knows too, don't you, Margaret Rose? It's the only good thing about the war – we can help to raise money and do something we enjoy at the same time. Is Papa sitting down yet, or is he still talking to the guards officers backstage?'

'He's just come through to sit down,' Peggy said, crossing her fingers behind her back. 'He had a word with Prince Philip earlier, and welcomed one or two others. Now he's waiting to be entertained, so go through, there's good girls, and finish getting ready.'

'Papa's watched so many rehearsals, he must know the words as well as we do,' Margaret muttered as Peggy followed them towards their makeshift dressingroom. 'Still, Philip hasn't, has he?'

Elizabeth nudged her sister hard in the ribs. 'Hush, don't go on,' she hissed. 'You don't want to make me nervous, do you?'

The train was late and crowded, and the small Devonshire railway station, when they reached it, was completely blacked out.

Anna hefted her kitbag on one shoulder and climbed down on to the platform, looking around her. Another figure, also clad in the grey-blue skirt and jacket and peaked cap of the Women's Auxiliary Air Force, saw her and moved tentatively closer. They stood there awkwardly, almost shoulder-to-shoulder, while other passengers jostled and pushed their way out of the station or on to the train the two girls had abandoned.

'Hello! My orders said transport would meet me at the station – are you going to RAF Colport, too?'

'Hello.' Anna smiled at the other girl. 'Yes, I am as a matter of fact. My orders said I'd be met. D'you think we ought to leave the platform and go to the station forecourt, to see if there's a lorry or something out there? Oh, I'm Anna Radwell, by the way. I've been in the service six weeks.'

The other girl stuck out a hand. She was an attractive redhead with a great many freckles, a cheeky grin and a broken tooth which did not detract from her prettiness in the least.

'Rita Brownlow. I was a shorthand-typist in civvy street six weeks ago, so I expected to be turned into a cook or a pilot, but they tell me I'll be a shorthand-typist in the WAAF, too. So much for square pegs in round holes. What did you do?'

'In civvy street?' Anna smiled to herself at how readily the expression came to their tongues – you could scarcely call them old hands at service life, not after six weeks. 'I was secretary to a bank manager, so I was a shorthand-typist as well. But I got sick of it and applied for the WAAF. I'm going to be a driver so they've been teaching me engine maintenance, which is quite interesting. Now I'm having on-the-job training, which should be even more interesting since Colport's an operational station. And of course it means I've left home at last.'

'Me too. Mother's apron-strings were getting a stranglehold, I couldn't have stuck it much longer. How old are you, then? You don't look terribly ancient from where I'm sitting . . . standing, rather.'

'I was eighteen three weeks ago. You?'

'I'll be nineteen in a couple of months. Well, Aircraftwoman Radwell – that sounds good, doesn't it? – perhaps you're right and we'd better head for the forecourt. It's plain no one's going to claim us here.'

Anna looked around her. Whilst they had been talking the station had cleared completely and now there were just the two of them on the darkened platform, while the train chugged into the distance. There wasn't another soul in sight. They couldn't have been forgotten, could they?

'I agree; someone's bound to be waiting out there. Quick march then, Brownlow.'

The two of them, hefting their new white kitbags – What a target for the Luftwaffe, I wonder they don't make us roll them in cocoa when we're out at nights, Rita said – went out on to the forecourt. A few people were still there, queueing for a taxi, but there was no sign of an RAF vehicle. Anna plonked her kitbag on the ground – that would help to sully its whiteness – and sat on it.

'Well, we're obviously in for a wait,' she said with as much cheerfulness as she could muster. It was a cold night and the sea breeze, although excitingly salty, was not going to help them keep warm. 'What time is it? Was our train so late that they just haven't waited?' She peered at her wristwatch but could not make out anything but the round whiteness of its face in the dark.

'It's two a.m.,' her new friend said gloomily. 'It *is* May, isn't it? We haven't made some ghastly mistake and turned up in the wrong month? Because it feels more like December.'

Anna chuckled. 'I think it's just the time . . . always coldest before dawn. Look, you can read your watch, so let's give them fifteen minutes and if they still haven't arrived we'll go and find a waiting room and wait there. Anyone searching for a couple of WAAFs is bound to look in the waiting room, aren't they?'

'The average AC Plonk probably doesn't know what a waiting room is,' Rita said. 'Is it far to Colport, d'you know? Ought we to try to walk it? Was there a porter or someone we could have asked? Oh help, there's a person still queueing for a taxi, we could ask him.'

Anna stood up. 'That's an Air Force uniform, I'm almost sure; if he's going to Colport, he might let us share his taxi. I'll have a word.'

'Hang on, suppose he's awfully important? Suppose he's a wingco or even higher, whatever that may be? Do be careful, Anna. Oh, and don't say where we're going because of spies . . . how do you know he's really an Air Force officer, it would be quite easy . . .'

Anna ignored her new friend's panic-stricken hissing and walked across to where the officer stood. She saluted rather awkwardly, spoke to him for a few moments and then returned to Rita, now agitatedly gnawing her fingernails.

'He's coming home on leave so he can't take us all the way to the station, but he says it's only a short way outside the town so we can get in the taxi with him and he'll put us on the right road. Shall we go?'

'But suppose the transport turns up in five minutes and finds us gone? You said yourself we ought to give them a quarter of an hour,' Rita objected. 'We could be in awful trouble. Have you noticed how easy it is to get into trouble in the Air Force? There are so many rules and half of them you don't know even exist until you've broken them.'

'I know, but two young and beautiful girls like us oughtn't to have to wait on a station platform all night. Come on, by the time his taxi arrives the fifteen minutes will probably be up. And he's awfully nice, really, not a bit frightening. I think he's a pilot officer, so salute. I did.'

The young officer bundled them first into his taxi when it came, reassuring them that the authorities at Colport would be glad the two girls had used their initiative to get back when the transport arrangements had let them down. The taxi-driver, however, was not so pleasant.

'I'm not taking you on to RAF Colport when I've dropped this gentleman,' he growled, turning round to give them a fulminating glance. 'Bin on dooty since eight o'clock yesterday morning, I have, so I'm goin' home to get some kip.'

'Is it very far?' Anna asked apprehensively. 'We don't want to arrive there dead on our feet.'

'It's probably three miles on foot, but it's more like nine by road, because you can only cross the river by the roadbridge, whereas if you go the way I'll send you, you can cross by the footbridge,' the pilot officer explained. 'Don't worry, I wouldn't put you in a bind on your first day.'

'It's their fault; they should have sent a transport,' Anna said calmly. 'If anyone says we're in trouble I'll tell them where they get off.'

'That's the spirit. And if I ever make an emergency landing at Colport I'll be sure to ask for you both. Ah, here we are!'

'I was almost asleep,' Rita grumbled, getting out of the taxi. 'Wasn't the driver cross?' she added as the cabby did a three-point turn and roared back the way they had come. 'I don't see why he wouldn't take us out to Colport – we would have paid him, after all.'

'What with?' Anna asked tartly. She was tired.

'Promises,' Rita said equally tartly. 'That's all I've got – I'm totally skint. I bought a cup of tea and a wad on some tiny station and that was the last of my cash. I *say*, isn't it dark?'

'As pitch,' the young officer agreed, making Anna jump. She had forgotten he was still there. 'Now come with me down to that stile – can you see it?'

They could, just. They followed him down and saw, in the faint light, a thin but definite path wending its way across a field of corn.

'See that little path? Follow it across three fields, it goes pretty straight, and then over another stile and into a lane. Turn right along the lane . . .'

The instructions seemed to go on for a long time but they were plain enough and the officer made both girls repeat them until he was satisfied they knew when and where to change direction. Then he helped them over the stile and stood and waved them off.

'He was nice; quite young to be an officer, wouldn't you say?' Rita remarked as they plodded across the field, carefully sticking to the narrow path. 'I wonder what he does in the Air Force?'

'Flies, or at least goes up in an aircraft; didn't you notice the wings on his tunic?' Anna said. 'They all seem rather young, the aircrew I've met so far. I suppose it's because they lost so many of the more experienced ones during the Battle of Britain.'

'Probably. I say, are those cows? I don't mind cows I don't think, but I don't fancy meeting a bull.'

'I don't suppose there's a bull, not roaming across a public footpath,' Anna said reassuringly. 'If there is, he won't mind us. Just keep walking.' She had seen a bull, unmistakable even in the semi-dark, but thought it best not to mention the fact.

'Oh. All right,' Rita agreed. 'Tell me, Anna, do you have brothers and sisters?';

'One brother, Jamie. He's fourteen, or will be in August.'

'And were you happy at home?'

'Yes, happy enough,' Anna said shortly. She remembered

the day she had signed on for the WAAF, how Constance had shouted and she herself had wept.

'You don't understand!' Constance had shrieked across the bedroom at her stunned, scarlet-faced daughter. 'You're only a child. For nineteen years I've known that JJ was unfaithful to me and I've put up with it and told myself it was just his way and gone on loving him and being faithful. But to start on Cressie, when his leave only lasted a week, and she was no more than a child herself . . .'

'I really don't understand,' Anna had said coldly. 'What on earth are you talking about, Mummy? I come in and find you . . . the way I found you, with an American soldier, and all you can do is try to blame Daddy!'

'Because he's been making love to *Cressie*,' Constance had shouted, indifferent who heard her. 'Your father, the man you think is so wonderful, your dearest Daddy, was found by me, *fornicating* in the back bedroom with a fifteen-year-old evacuee who is in my care. Do you get it, Anna? Do you understand now?'

'And you took Chaz Palmer into your bedroom and let him make love to you because Daddy did it with Cressie? And you think that I shouldn't mind? Mummy, really!'

Anna tried to sound sophisticated, unshockable, but her voice trembled and her hands kept clasping and unclasping.

Constance shook her silky, white-blonde hair off her face and sat down on the bed. She rummaged in the bedside locker for a packet of cigarettes, got one out, lit it and took a quick, nervous puff, then blew smoke at the ceiling. She was wearing an apricot silk dressing gown and she was naked underneath it, as Anna knew only too well. Colour Sergeant Chaz Palmer was in the bathroom next door, no doubt getting dressed very hastily and feeling more of a fool than even Anna felt.

'Anna, darling,' Constance said gently. 'I'm not a wicked woman, but I am human. Daddy isn't cruel to me, but in a way indifference is cruelty, if not the worst kind. When a man gets a week's leave and comes home and . . . and spends it carrying on with a fifteen-year-old child and ignoring his wife, that comes as near cruelty as dammit. And I can't stand it because I need love and attention. People do. I realise I can't justify what you saw, but it was so good, you see, to be the centre of attraction for one man, even if JJ couldn't care less about me. I've tried so hard, but I'll never make you understand, will I? Just don't say anything to anyone, please. I'm not proud of what I've done, and I'd hate anyone to be hurt by it, particularly Jamie.'

She sounded beaten, almost pathetic. Anna's initial disgust and horror at finding her mother heaving and grunting beneath the large black American soldier had already begun to fade, and she felt a sudden surge of sympathy and even a degree of understanding. Her mother had been unfair to her often, sometimes even unkind, but she had never lied. Now she was saying that Daddy . . . JJ, her very own father, had been carrying on with that loose-mouthed, big-breasted Cressie Carruthers, who might be only fifteen years old, but who was a Methuselah in experience, or so the other evacuees said, and Anna knew that her mother was speaking no more than the truth.

Looking back at her father's last leave, standing there in the bedroom as Constance blew smoke from her nostrils and stared at her neat, pink-enamelled toenails, Anna began to remember. She remembered how envious she had felt because he took so much notice of Cressie and had made it plain to his adoring daughter that he did not want her along on expeditions with the younger girl. She had not realised that there was an ulterior motive, had actually accepted that he needed time alone with someone not too demanding . . . what a fool she had been not to realise that JJ was up to something. Long ago there had been maids, a friend of her mother's, a teacher at school . . . Oh Daddy, Daddy, Anna mourned, how could you do it to us, when we loved you so?

It was far worse for her mother, of course. To find the man she worshipped in such a degrading position, humping and heaving over the eager body of an over-sexed little girl who would tell everyone – everyone but Anna and Constance. No wonder Constance had done what she had done.

'Mummy?'

Anna's voice was tentative. She put a gentle hand on her mother's silk-clad knee. 'I'm sorry. I didn't know. But now you've said, I think perhaps I did have an inkling; Daddy didn't take any notice of me either, and I was hurt by it. I would have loved being taken out in a boat on the river, or for long walks, but he took Cressie. I'm sorry I said what I did, and I'll try to understand, only . . .'

'Thank you, darling. Only what?'

'Only you won't do it again, will you? Jamie might have come in, and he'd be most awfully upset.'

'I'll be good as gold,' her mother said, 'I wouldn't upset Jamie, you know that.'

But something in the way her eyes met her daughter's and immediately slid away told Anna that Constance wasn't speaking the truth. Her mother would like to be good, but looked as though she doubted her own ability now that she had experienced someone else's lovemaking. Constance might be unable to deny herself such pleasure and reassurance if it was offered a second time. But Anna could scarcely say that, she must pretend to take her mother's words at their face value.

'I know you wouldn't upset anyone if you could help it.' Anna leaned over and kissed her mother on the forehead, thinking as she did so how smooth and white her mother's skin had looked, against the richly shining blackness of the American's brawny body. 'I'm going into the city. I'll tell you why when I get back.'

She had always intended to join the WRNS on her eighteenth birthday because JJ was in the Navy, but suddenly she found the thought of the Senior Service repelled her. How could he do it, deny his own wife and ignore his own daughter, and start an affair with horrid Cressie, whose only claim to anything was her insatiable appetite for men. So she'd gone into the recruiting office and asked to join the WAAF, asked that she might go quickly, boasted about her abilities as a secretary, her ARP experience, her work with the Women's Voluntary Service and that she could drive and had driven a good deal.

'I can read maps and I hardly ever get lost,' she said hopefully. 'I drove an ambulance in Norwich for a bit, too.'

'A driver who knows how to navigate around the country might be very useful,' the clerk behind the counter said. 'Especially now.'

309

He had explained no further, but a week later her papers had come, and a month later she was on her way to Harrogate for initial training. Which brought her here, to the dark countryside, the pretty girl at her side, grumbling as they got mired down in a gateway.

'I bet that was cow-muck,' Rita said as Anna closed the gate behind them. 'So what made you join up? I'm an only child, see? My Mum's great on housework and worrying and now my Dad's not at home – he's in India with the Army – she was driving me round the bend. But from the sound of it things weren't so desperate for you that you had to do something this rash.'

They were crossing a lush meadow, the long, wet grass brushing the hems of their skirts. Anna laughed.

'This isn't rash, but I know what you mean. I joined the WAAF because . . . oh, hell, I found my mother in bed with someone who wasn't my father. I can't condemn her, I do understand in lots of ways, but it's hard for us to act naturally now. As you can probably imagine.'

'Cripes,' Rita said. 'It wasn't your boyfriend, was it?'

Anna laughed. 'Don't make it any worse than it is – no, it was *not* my boyfriend. The chap was a GI, or whatever they call themselves. And it wasn't her fault, not really. She was provoked.'

'Oh,' Rita said uncertainly. 'How d'you provoke someone to get into bed with someone else?'

'I see what you mean; wrong word. Not provoked, but sort of pushed into it. By my father, who spent his last leave making love to a stupid girl two years younger than me and ignoring my mother.'

'Cripes,' Rita said again. 'Happy families, eh?'

The two of them stopped walking and laughed and laughed, until they were hanging on to each other and tears were running down Anna's face. They were the first tears she had shed since she had discovered Constance in bed with Chaz and she didn't really know whether they were tears of laughter or of sadness for lost innocence. Her own innocence.

*

310

The alarm clock, shrilling in her ear, had Nell sitting up in bed and fumbling for her clothes before she remembered that it was Dot's tι rn to milk and not hers. She lay down again, but there wasn't ιch point in it, not once she'd woken up. The small attic room the two girls shared was bathed in bright light and Dot's bed, now that she looked at it, was empty.

Not for the first time since Paul had come to the American Air Force base not a mile from Withies Farm. Dot had been dreamy, a bit half-soaked, but a reasonable work-mate. Now she was just in love and thought, talked and dreamed Paul. On the wall above her bed there was a huge poster which she and Paul had stolen from a hoarding in Norwich: DANGEROUS TALK COSTS LIVES. Beneath it Dot had pinned all the photographs of Paul she could get hold of. Film was in short supply of course – what was not? – so Dot had got him to send to his mother for photographs and there he was, from the age of five until now, twenty-five, in every possible pose, with a baseball bat, with a pair of motorcycle goggles, holding a kitten, pulling a face . . . The annoying thing was that Dot could only see the pictures properly by sitting on Nell's bed, but Nell could see almost nothing else; Paul's entire history danced before her eyes. He was a nice enough fellow, but she did wish Dot would keep her obsession somewhere more private.

Nell had joined the Land Army as soon as she was allowed, and she knew it had been a great relief to Hester. The fair folk did their best but what with the blackout and fuel rationing life was not simple and the various ways they had kept body and soul together during the dead winter months were, by and large, no longer available to them. Before, they had used the winter months to repaint, repair, and generally to tidy up their shows for the new season. If money ran low, the men had earned more by chopping firewood and carting goods in their lorries while the women sold their lace tablecloths, homemade toys and wooden clothes pegs door to door. Now, even if they had been able to obtain the raw materials, make do and mend would have beaten them. Every housewife in the country was painfully learning to do for herself all those things the fairground folk had done for them. About the only thing they didn't do was to whittle pegs, and there is a limit to the number of pegs a house-wife will buy.

So times were really hard, especially as women who would have gone into factories or shops in the winter and moved on as soon as the fair season started again, found themselves supplanted by others who would remain in employment for the duration of the war, however long that was. In extremis, the women could sell their clothing coupons, but that was about the extent of their winter income.

When the weather and petrol rationing allowed, the Gullivers took their fair up and down the country, to any gaff they could reach, because chartered fairs could only continue provided a showman or two erected his stuff on the gaff when the charter allowed, and plied for trade among the townspeople. But it did not always mean money in their pockets, not with so few attractions. Sometimes Hester oversaw the galloper when she wasn't showing Phillips; Nell stood in the wooden O of the hoopla stall or shouted the shooting gallery – more popular than ever with caricatures of Hitler, Goering and Ribbentrop to fire at – and Ugly Jack and a casual chap or two manned the dodgems. They had customers all right and did earn some money, but when their charter period was up they had to move on to any gaff they could find, and do any business they could. So between shows and in the depths of winter, Ugly Jack worked like a navvy at any task which needed strength, Hester sewed, worked in the fields and did the rough work at the big houses. They managed to keep Phillips fed and warm enough, but it was easier to feed three than four and when Nell had announced that she was going to be a 'girl in green', Hester and Jack had looked as relieved as they undoubtedly felt.

'At least you'll be fed, darling,' Hester had said. 'And safer than we are, when we take the stuff to a town gaff.'

Nell had agreed, promised to write weekly and to return whenever she got leave, but she could not help wondering how much of Hester's pride in her daughter's smart uniform and increasingly knowledgeable conversation on matters agricultural was laced with the feeling that Nell's job meant Hester and Ugly Jack might have their living wagon to themselves.

Still . . . lying in her bed, Nell made a long arm and opened the lid of the little box which held all her secret possessions. She felt around, and drew out her special photograph. Dan looked back at her; incredibly handsome, smiling, her Dan, the man she was fighting this war for. Well, perhaps that was a slight exaggeration, but she would never have joined the Land Army had it not been for Dan. Once she was settled at the farm she had sent Dan her proper address and now they could exchange letters, visits even. He was in the Air Force, stationed in Lincoln, not a million miles away. Furthermore, his home was in Norfolk now – in the small village of Blofield – so he would be coming back in this direction at any time. It didn't do any harm giving him this address because when the war ended she would leave and Matthew Coburn would not be able to find them, even if he found out from Dan where they were and came hunting for them.

That was the main reason she had become a landgirl: an address of her own, a place where Dan could visit her without upsetting Hester.

When Snip came back on leave though, he had not approved of her chosen career; he thought she was being very silly. 'You can earn a deal o' chink makin' munitions, or aeroplane parts, or bits for wireless sets,' he had urged. 'Why be a bloody landgirl and work your fingers to the bone jest so's you can feed people? It's plain daft!'

Snip had been as good as his word and was now in submarines. He didn't like it, Nell knew, but he stuck it because of some crazy idea he had. He had told her on his last leave that the bloody U-boats had sunk his pal Griff, so he, Snip, would not rest until he had sunk every U-boat in the seven seas. Which wasn't much of a reason for risking your life in the worst conditions, but that was Snip for you.

Nell wrote to Snip too, of course; he was still her best friend and she was fond of him. At twenty-two, he was taller and broader, but no more beautiful. He had a broken nose which had healed crooked – Abel Morris had been responsible for that – a face which was square and pugnacious and small, rather heavy lidded eyes. He had a twisted knee – how he had ever got into the forces, let alone into submarines, was anyone's guess – and being a submariner had affected his breathing so that he wheezed when he ran or exerted himself. Despite all these things, he was doing rather well; he had risen to the rank of artificer, whatever that might mean, and although he had mentioned idly to Nell that submariners did not, as a rule, live long, he seemed not to worry overmuch.

He was very fond of Nell, called her his girl, and teased her that she must wait for him. Snip wasn't serious of course; Nell knew he wasn't because she had told him it was Dan who mattered, Dan was her serious boyfriend. Dan had rescued her from that awful man, he was a hero, someone who would be special to her for the rest of her life. Snip was someone with whom she'd shared many laughs. You didn't marry those men, you married the ones whose presence made you breathe short and fast, whose kisses melted your bones, whose slightest whim must be satisfied.

The door opening cut Nell's thoughts short and at the sight of Dot's pale, weary face and dark eyes she remembered that the alarm had gone off and someone – Dot for choice – ought to be down in the kitchen putting the kettle on and hurrying out to get the cows in for milking.

'Nell, I suppose you couldn't possibly do my stint this morning? Only I've been with Paul and I'm dog-tired and I'll only fall asleep on Cowslip's flank and get wrong with Earny. He can be very unkind, considering we're related,' Dot said with some bitterness. Mrs Earnshaw was Dot's mother's sister, but Mr Earnshaw did not think this a good reason for allowing Dot to get away with murder and treated her as he did the other landgirls – kindly but firmly, he would have said.

'Oh all right, but you'll have to make your own excuses if Earny says anything, because I'm not telling lies for you or anyone,' Nell said, getting out of bed and slipping Dan's photograph back into the tin box. She had a picture of Snip, too, in his naval uniform, but she didn't bother to look at that, she knew every detail of it by heart; it was only Dan's picture she felt she had to examine at regular intervals. 'Go on then, get into bed. I'll tell Mrs Earny you're still up here and she'll probably pop her head round the door later.'

'You wouldn't like to tell Earny it's one of my poorly days, would you? He's so embarrassed by women's complaints that it would shut him up for good and all,' Dot said hopefully, flinging off her jersey and overalls and climbing into bed in her underwear. 'He's not a bad bloke, really.'

Nell, chucking her clothes on, shook her head. 'No. I told you, I won't lie for you. What you tell your aunt, of course, is up to you. When's Paul flying again?'

'Not for two more days. Thanks, Nell, I'm asleep already.'

Dot disappeared under the covers and Nell sped down the stairs in her stockinged feet. Their boots were shed each night outside the back door and donned each morning, which was a help to Mrs Earnshaw's floors, though hard on their long green stockings. She burst into the kitchen, panting, to find Mrs Earnshaw down before her, making cups of tea.

Mrs Earnshaw looked nothing like a farmer's wife. She was a thin, active woman in her late forties with a thin, handsome face. Her dark hair was bobbed, 'for ease', she said, and she was somewhere near the top of the WVS hierarchy, which was probably why she never seemed to stay still for more than a few moments.

'Mornin', Nell,' Mrs Earnshaw said now, pouring boiling water from the kettle into the teapot. 'What's your 'urry? You in't on today, that I do know; today that's the gal Dot.'

'She's still in bed; I said I'd do her stint this morning,' Nell said, reaching for a cup of tea. 'Where's Joyce?'

Joyce lived out but came in early in the mornings and did yeoman service with everything. A farmer's daughter, she found herself at a loose end when her elder brother married and brought a wife back to deal with the farm chores, so she had come to work for the Earnshaws and mucked in with most of the landgirls' tasks.

'Taken a cup out to the old feller,' Mrs Earnshaw said placidly. 'I'll tek a cup up to Dot; that'll ease her if she's got her monthlies.'

'She's very tired, she might be better left for now,' Nell said tactfully. 'She'll probably be glad of a cup when we have our elevenses.'

'Hmm.' Mrs Earnshaw shot Nell a shrewd glance. 'That Paul with her last night?'

'Umm . . .'

'No names, no pack-drill,' Mrs Earnshaw said rather obscurely. 'Well, two more days, luv, and you're off 'ome for the week. Where's they got to now, eh?'

Nell's background fascinated everyone and Mrs Earnshaw, in particular, took a keen interest in the whereabouts of the fair and how they were managing. She was particularly interested in Phillips, getting her husband to shoot a rabbit for him whenever Nell went home for a few days and sending in addition a clean meal sack bulging with food for Hester and Ugly Jack, who were extremely grateful. If the fair was in the country it wasn't too bad, they could find something to supplement their supplies, but city tobers meant nothing over and above the meagre rations. Hester found it difficult to fill Ugly Jack with his pathetically small allowance of meat, and he scarcely tasted his butter ration even when she added her own to it. So Mrs Earnshaw's homemade cheeses, pots of honey and joints of pork were welcomed with open arms.

'They're down on the coast for a week or two,' Nell said. 'They're on the village green in a small village, but it's an enormous green which means plenty of room for the stuff on the gaff. I'm looking forward to seeing everyone, and I did think, since I'm off all week, that I might meet up with Dan as well.'

Everyone knew about Dan because Nell had to keep using his name. She brought him into every available conversation and sometimes saw the other girls exchanging indulgent glances; isn't it sweet how she loves him, their glances said. Don't you wish you were in love?

'Oh, has he got leave too? I'll send your Mum a few little extras, then,' Mrs Earnshaw said, as though it was a totally new idea which had just occurred to her. 'That'll be nice for you, love, to share your leave with your young man.'

Nell murmured agreement but as a matter of fact she was doing nothing of the sort. As far as she knew, Dan didn't have

316

leave, but she intended to tell her mother a whopper and say she only had four days off. Then she would bid the family farewell and set off for Lincoln. Once there, she would see Dan, if only for half an hour, and then make her way back to the Withies. She had not told Dan she was going to try to see him, let alone that she would be in Lincoln for two days. She intended to explain when she arrived and leave to him the decision as to whether or not she should stay. The thought that he might suggest she stayed *with* him made her heart beat faster, but she was not expecting it. Men weren't like women, they didn't fall in love when they were seven years old and stay that way until they were fully grown and beyond. She would have to win Dan all over again, she knew that.

Nell was not a conceited girl, but after a year of living away from home and being courted by several eager young men, she knew herself to be reasonably attractive to the opposite sex. She did not count Snip, but there were others: farmers' sons home on leave, sailors back while their ships went for refits, and the ever-present Air Force. Dan was, of course, handsomer, nicer and more desirable than any of these; he had liked her once, who could say that he did not still, in a corner of his heart, have a soft spot for her?

So Nell, walking briskly up the muddy lane with Earny's sheepdog, Patch, at her heels, could see no reason why her break in Lincolnshire should not be a success.

'It isn't fair, Huntie, it really is most *un*fair. She has all the fun! She doesn't do lessons any more, she waltzes off to Aldershot each day to play with cars and engines . . . she comes home filthy quite often, absolutely filthy . . . and what happens to me?' Margaret paused dramatically, posing, conscious of the part she was playing even in her temper, for it was definitely temper, Miss Huntley thought, which had brightened her eyes and tightened her lips this morning. 'Why, *nothing* happens to me, because I'm the youngest! And now she's driving that beautiful big Red Cross van, and I'm supposed to sit in the schoolroom and study French verbs.'

'Yes, that's right, just like every other child of fourteen,'

Miss Huntley said cheerfully. 'So sit down and get on with it, Margaret. You'll do all the things that Elizabeth does when you're her age.'

The schoolroom at Windsor had been abandoned because it was a beautiful day, so Miss Huntley and the younger Princess were sitting out on the side lawn, Margaret with her verbs to learn, Miss Huntley with some knitting. Margaret pushed her book to one side and lay down full length on the grass, then rolled over on her back and eyed her governess thoughtfully.

'Huntie, what's going to happen to Elizabeth?'

'What do you mean, happen? All the usual things. She'll go to dances, and open fêtes and help Mummy and Papa – that is, she will when the war ends. Until then she'll learn engine maintenance and drive Army vehicles and do all the other things that ordinary girls of her age . . .'

'Oh, I know all that, especially the bit about girls of her age. No, I meant what will happen with Philip, Huntie, with Philip. She's in love with him, you know, and he's in love with her. They want to get married, and I want to be bridesmaid – now that would be fun, wouldn't it? I'd really enjoy that.'

'You shouldn't talk like that, dear; Elizabeth isn't just an ordinary girl who can please herself over such matters. One day she's going to be Queen and . . .'

'Oh, one day, one day! Besides, just now you said she was an ordinary girl. Look, Lilibet and Philip write every day and they spent a lot of time together when he was last home on leave. She thinks he's ever so lovely – he is, isn't he, Huntie? – and he's a proper Prince, even if he is a bit Greek. And anyway, how can he be Greek when his surname's Mountbatten, the same as Uncle Dickie's?'

'I think he took the name Mountbatten. Anyway, none of this has anything to do with you or with me, Margaret Rose. Let's talk about something else, shall we? How soon do you think the war will end? Things seem to be going rather well for us, if it weren't for those beastly V-1 rockets I think we could claim to be almost home and dry, wouldn't you?'

The V-1s were the only things, Huntie thought, which actually frightened her two charges. It was nerve-racking, watching them buzzing ahead and feeling the rush of terror that the engine might cut out and that the creature – it seemed too horribly capable of making its own decisions to think of it as just a bomb – might land right where you were. But neither Elizabeth nor her younger sister ever showed the fear Huntie knew they felt.

Margaret smiled and sat up. 'Yes, I'm sure you're right. We all hate those buzz bombs; Lilibet said they're calling them doodlebugs at Aldershot. Huntie, is it time for luncheon yet? I always seem to be hungry these days.'

'That's because you're a growing girl,' Miss Huntley said sententiously. 'I believe it's time we went indoors. Bring your verb book, dear.' It was not until they had entered the castle and were making their way to the schoolroom and lunch that it occurred to Miss Huntley that, one way and another, Margaret had not done a single verb that morning.

The little monkey – she had made up her mind not to work and she had held Miss Huntley's attention very neatly. Now, running ahead of the governess, Margaret looked back, mouth curved into her sweet smile, eyes sparkling.

'Did I do it, Huntie? Is that what you're thinking?'

Miss Huntley, following at a sedate pace, had to laugh.

Anna got leave early in August, but she didn't feel much inclined to go home to Goldenstone and Constance. They spoke on the telephone, they exchanged polite and interesting letters, but Anna did not want to get home and begin to realise that her mother, entertaining the troops, was doing for them what she should be doing only for JJ.

JJ was at sea and Anna had talked to other men who were in the Navy. She knew that JJ's life afloat would be both hard and dangerous, and she pitied him, despite herself, because her mother was unlikely to be faithful to him now. Of course, the fact that he could not commit adultery while at sea did not mean that he would not start an affair the moment he set foot on dry land, but for the moment he was concentrating on winning the war and not on persuading someone to sleep with him. And though Anna knew she was being unfair, she could not accept her mother's infidelity while her father was, perforce, being whiter than white. And in her heart, a man's carryings-on, though reprehensible, were not as bad as a woman's. It's because a woman could have a baby, my mother could have a baby, Anna told herself. And could not help giggling at the thought of Constance, not at all maternal, having to explain a little black baby to her friends.

All in all, it seemed better to take herself off to Lincolnshire, to spend a few days with a fellow-WAAF who had recently been moved up to RAF Waddington as a wireless operator. And to see Dan. She had telephoned him. He wasn't at Waddington but at Scampton, which was quite near, and when she said she would be staying in Lincoln, at a friend's house, and visiting other friends at Waddington, he had said at once that they must meet.

'Good of you to phone, Anna,' he had said. 'Phone me again as soon as you arrive, then we can make a date.'

A date with Dan! It would be heaven to see him again, Anna decided, absolute heaven. And if he took her out for a meal, or to the cinema . . . she gave a delicious shudder at the thought. Dan liked her, she knew he did. He had been very attentive since that time when he had kissed her beneath the willow tree. Perhaps attentive was the wrong word, but he had been kind and had sometimes sought her out.

He had not kissed her again though. Which was a pity, because she had expected him to, had waited hopefully for the moment when he would take her in his arms. They had met less than a year ago at a party, bumping into each other by accident in the corridor, and Anna had smiled up at him, sure that this time . . . But he had not kissed her. He had stopped to talk, had congratulated her on what he called 'growing up so prettily', and had moved on, going back into the main room to rejoin his friends. But she had been little more than a child then, it would be different now, wouldn't it? They were both grown-up, she was an aircraftwoman first class, she drove important RAF officials around, she navigated all over the country and had driven through London at the height of the rush hour (not that it compared, of course, with pre-war rush hours, but still) and she would shortly be promoted; her wing

320

officer had told her so, had said, furthermore, that she deserved it.

Dan flew Hurricanes, which was a responsible, grown-up kind of thing to do. She wished he flew Spitfires because they were the best, Jamie said, but to be any sort of pilot was important. He was a flight lieutenant, which meant he'd moved up a bit in his squadron, but she would have loved him had he been a driver or a mechanic, she would have loved him had he cleaned latrines or cooked spuds in the cookhouse; her love wasn't dependent on externals. She loved Dan the boy as well as Dan the man. All that was necessary for her complete happiness was that he should love her too.

After all her anticipation, Nell didn't see Dan during her leave. Or rather, she saw him but he didn't see her.

She was in Lincoln, having decided to have a look around the city before ringing Scampton to speak to Dan. To tell the truth, now that the moment had arrived she found she was very nervous and any excuse to put off the evil moment was reason enough. So she wandered up the road which led from the railway station to the city, eyeing the shops, the busy people, the ancient buildings. She was intrigued to find a river, tamed to be sure but still a river, running right through the streets, so that you were always conscious of it. She found a sort of inland harbour and quay where there was shipping, bustle, people. And boats. She saw that you could hire a rowing boat, and thought wistfully that it would be fun to hire a boat if Dan were with her. It would be wizard to sit in the stern while Dan rowed, and smile and talk and watch him watching her, waiting for the moment when they might tie up somewhere quiet and . . . and get to know each other better.

She had walked most of the way round the inland harbour, and discovered that it was called Brayford Pool and that you could indeed hire a rowing boat for a small sum from the bent and wizened little man sitting on an empty fish barrel in the sunshine, smoking a pipe which looked – and smelt – even older than he was. But the clock confirmed that she had best get back into the city and find a telephone

321

and somewhere to spend the night. She walked through the streets and climbed a bridge where she half-remembered seeing a telephone box. At the crest of the bridge she looked down and a rowing boat was coming along, a young man in Air Force blue rowing, a girl, also in Air Force blue, reclining in the stern.

One look was enough; it was Dan. Now and then he rested on his oars and leaned forward and spoke earnestly to the young woman whose smooth, blonde head was all Nell could see of her. Just as they were about to pass out of sight, two things happened: the girl spoke, leaning forward; Dan leaned forward too, putting out a hand to stroke the side of her face, speaking . . .

The intensity of Nell's stare, she thought afterwards, was probably what made Dan look up, but she turned away from the bridge so quickly that she hoped he had not seen her. She ran, then, back towards the station; she had come up here on a fool's errand. Dan clearly had a girlfriend, a beautiful girl with wonderful golden hair, a girl who was in the same service as he was, who could understand his hopes and fears. And anyway, why on earth would Dan want her? She was such an ordinary person when all was said and done. Oh, she was a landgirl now, but that was only until the war ended. When peace broke out she'd just be a fairground girl again, shouting the hoopla or the shooting gallery, helping her mother with Phillips, whittling pegs in the winter or crocheting lace. She was a traveller, a gipsy, as good as, though God help you if a showman heard you call him that! She had nothing that could appeal to Dan, nothing whatever.

She returned to the station and caught the first train out of Lincoln. She cried at first, but then she ran out of tears and simply sat, small and silent, in the corner of the carriage and told herself that it didn't matter, she'd had a crush on Dan, that was all. She would pull herself together and try to make something of her life, instead of just living from day to day.

Perhaps I ought to settle for Snip, she thought drearily as the train chugged through the increasing darkness. He does like me; oh, but liking isn't enough, it isn't, it isn't! Love is so special, and I do so want it for myself!

Hot August sunshine and the smell of the river. Swans, sailing like great dignified barges and ducks bustling, babbling, upending themselves in the clear waters of the river. The banks gliding past, Dan bending to his oars, talking, explaining, laughing.

I am so happy, Anna told herself dramatically, that if I died right now, this very instant, I'd not complain. Most people don't have any happiness as intense as this, ever – I've been happy for the whole of a sunny afternoon.

'We'll have a meal at the Saracen's Head, in the city,' Dan was saying as he rowed past buildings, among streets. 'Then we'll walk up to the cathedral, it's a beautiful building, everyone who comes to Lincoln has to see the cathedral and the Lincoln Imp, of course. It's most awfully steep, but you won't mind that. Where did you say you were staying?'

'I booked a room in a boarding house in Lindum Hill,' Anna said. 'It's quite a small house, but clean, and the landlady seemed very nice. But I could always cancel it, if you wanted me to.'

'Cancel it? Why on earth? Oh, you mean because I'm flying tomorrow night? But we can still meet tomorrow morning, have a walk around. In fact, if you're going to Waddington I might come with you. I've several friends there. Or did you have something else in mind?'

Anna let her eyes rest on his face for a moment. He looked both understanding and amused, as though the possibility of Anna making the suggestion she had been making was laughable. But having said so much, she would have to go through with it.

'No, that wasn't why I thought you might want me to cancel it exactly,' Anna muttered. She felt the hot colour rising up her neck, flooding her cheeks. She twisted in her seat to hide her embarrassment from Dan's amused eyes. Ahead of them and above, a girl was leaning over the little grey stone bridge. She wore a bright blue blouse or dress, Anna couldn't see which, and her hair hung down, a blue-black bell, on either side of a small, oval face.

'Why did you think I might want you to cancel your boarding house?' Dan asked. His voice was warm, but the amusement was still there. 'Darling Anna, is there something I should know?'

'Umm . . . my r-room's only got a s-s-single bed in it,' Anna stammered, scarlet, she was sure, from top to toe. She fixed her eyes on the bottom-boards of the boat and on her black uniform shoes. 'I thought y-you might . . .'

Dan put an end to her misery. He brought his oars inboard, leaned forward and tilted her chin so that she had to look up at him, then he stroked her cheek. His eyes were very gentle, and the amusement had vanished.

'A single bed is very comfortable for a single girl,' he said. 'Anna, what you're suggesting . . . my *God*!'

He let go of her chin and stood up so abruptly that the little boat rocked and nearly capsized. One oar, which had still been in the rowlock, clattered on to the bottom-board, the other would have gone overboard had Anna not grabbed for it.

'What's the matter? What happened?' Anna asked wildly, trying to turn round in her seat to see why Dan had leapt to his feet like that. 'Are we going to sink?'

Dan sat down again, slowly, and reached for the oars. 'Sink? I doubt it. I thought I saw someone I knew, but she's gone. My God, I hope she didn't. . . look, Anna, we'll have to go ashore. Our time's nearly up anyway.'

'Yes, all right,' Anna muttered. She had really done it this time; her suggestion had been so unwelcome that Dan had invented a convenient friend to get them both out of the boat and to take her mind off her indecent proposal. Still, at least she hadn't asked him outright to take her to bed, if that was any comfort.

She was very quiet while Dan tied up the boat, helped her on to the quayside and settled with the boat-hire man. She was very quiet when he ran up to the road ahead of her, looking right and left and quiet still when he came despondently back and said that his friend had gone. Would Anna mind very much if he walked her back to her boarding house now and left her?

The friend, he explained, might ring Scampton and he would kick himself if he missed her.

'Anyone I know?' Anna asked listlessly. It was a sensible question, since they came from the same small village and had a large acquaintance in common, or so she thought.

'No, you don't know her. I met her long ago, in Wales, when I was ten, then I met her again in Suffolk when I was staying with cousins, oh, three or four years ago it must have been. She'd been evacuated to a house nearby . . . we've written a few times. I wonder if it really was her . . . anyway, I must get back, in case. She – she's an old friend, you see.'

'Is she a close friend?' Anna asked as they walked along Silver Street. 'But I suppose she can't be, if you've not seen her for three or four years.'

'She's someone special,' Dan admitted. 'I don't think I could forget her, even if I wanted to. I'd really like to see her again.'

'Does she have black hair and a white face?' Anna said, visited by inspiration. 'I looked around when we were getting near the bridge and saw a girl in a blue blouse leaning over, looking down at us. Was that her?'

'I think so,' Dan said soberly. 'Look, can you ring me at ten in the morning? We can talk then. For a start, I'll know whether it was her, because if it was she's bound to ring me, wouldn't you say?'

Just for a moment, Anna hated Dan, hated the pleading note in his voice. How dared he ask for reassurance about another woman from her, who loved him so helplessly. But she remembered the aircrew on her own station, the sort of lives they led, and she didn't voice the tart response which had been on the tip of her tongue.

'Yes, if it was her she's bound to ring,' she said gently. 'Look, you go off now, no need to take me any farther, I can see Lindum Hill from here.'

'Well, if you're sure . . .'

She gave him a little push and he was gone, loping rapidly down the hill, turning to give her a quick wave before he disappeared.

*

325

They stood in the garden: the small, straight-backed girl wearing a faded pink dress, the tall, yellow-haired young man in his naval uniform. They were talking earnestly, heads close, hands touching.

They make a lovely couple, Peggy thought sentimentally, standing in the nursery window shamelessly watching, for they would know they were observed, realise that their friendship was the source of a great many rumours. I wonder if they'll be allowed to follow their hearts, those two? With Elizabeth heir to the throne it could not simply be a matter of personal choice, and he was foreign, though he neither looked nor acted it.

'Peggy, don't look!' Margaret Rose stood at the maid's side, tugging her elbow. 'It isn't fair to stare. She's asked Papa, you know, if they might exchange rings before he sails again, but Papa thinks it's too soon, he says she knows so few young men. Well, unless you count a brigade of guards officers as a few, I suppose he's right, only what about the evacuees, and the people who come down to the castle to talk to Papa and his ministers? We see them, me and Lilibet, and most of them are nice and fun to be with, so if she says she loves Philip and he loves her, why can't they at least get engaged?'

'Your sister is only eighteen, dear,' Peggy said gently. 'I know it seems old to you, but it's awfully young for a big commitment like marriage.'

'Queen Victoria was queen when she wasn't much older than Lilibet,' the Princess said promptly. 'And no one said she was too young. A while ago, when . . . when it was necessary, Lilibet signed things for Papa. I don't think she's too young to say who she wants to marry.'

'No, nor do I,' Peggy said. 'But I'm not the king of England.'

'You aren't even the queen,' Margaret Rose said, giggling. 'Ah, he's leaving and Lilibet's coming indoors. But mark my words, Peggy, no matter what Mummy and Daddy do or say, she'll marry him. My sister's a very good girl, but she does know what she wants. She always has.'

Twelve

'I wish we were out there, oh how I wish we were just two ordinary girls, throwing fireworks, shouting, kissing and hugging, instead of having to wave and wave until your hand aches and then come indoors and listen to a lot of pompous old men telling one another how they won the war.'

Princess Margaret Rose flounced away from the long windows and addressed her sister in a piercing whisper. 'I'm as glad as anyone that it's over – gladder, probably – but don't I just wish we were down there with them!'

Miss Huntley smiled her sympathy at her young charge and Elizabeth nodded and sighed wistfully.

'Margaret's right – if only we could go down! It's so nice to feel that those horrible doodlebugs aren't going to come over ever again, and it's wonderful to see the streets lit up and the buses and cars using proper headlamps. Everyone down there is so *happy*, you can almost feel their happiness coming up to us over the balcony. I'm sure they wouldn't notice us if we went down for half an hour.'

'They most certainly would, Princess,' Miss Huntley said in her most repressive tone. 'You'd probably be mobbed and you wouldn't like that one bit. Now settle down, both of you, and we'll send Peggy down to the kitchen to get hot cocoa and biscuits.'

'I'm hot already, hot with excitement,' the younger princess said defiantly. 'I'm going to find Mama and Papa, they can't have gone far, I want to ask them . . .'

She was tugging the door when someone came through it. The King smiled at his younger child. 'Feeling a little flat after all the excitement, darling? Well, Mummy and I have arranged a small treat for you both. I've spoken to some of your friends in the Guards, and they've agreed to take very great care of you and take you down into the crowd. You'll be good and stick close to the fellows won't you, my dears?'

Elizabeth came over to where her father stood and touched his arm. 'Oh, Papa,' she said, her eyes shining. 'That is exactly what Margaret Rose and I were most wanting to do. You are so good to us!'

The younger princess said nothing; she launched herself into her father's arms and kissed him with a violence which said more than any words.

The convoys had to keep going, of course, particularly those heading for Russia.

When the frigate *Moonraker* was hit, they were in the Barents Sea with the ragged coastline of Sweden giving way to that of Russia; they could have been only a mile or two from their projected landfall at Murmansk. Lieutenant commander JJ Radwell was in his cabin, snatching a much needed nap, when the torpedo struck. He woke when the explosion rocked the bunk where he lay and staggered, half asleep, to the door, to find it apparently blocked. He threw himself at it two or three times before it gave and as he burst into the short corridor beyond he knew why it had proved so obdurate. Water, swirling knee-high, rushed at him, turning his legs numb with cold within seconds. Poor old *Moonraker* had been holed, or worse. He had to get up to the bridge without delay.

The water got worse, though, and at the foot of the companion-way he changed his mind; no point in heading for the bridge, he would never make it, the ship was listing badly already and would be down in seconds rather than minutes by the look of it; anyway the water roaring down the stairs towards him did not augur well for escape.

He managed to make the deck. It was night, but summer nights were never truly dark up here. The coastline was in sight and JJ could see the men struggling to launch the boats, a few poor devils already in the water. They would not last long out there, not in water as cold as that of the Barents Sea.

They were getting the last men into the last boat when the next torpedo struck. The little boat was never launched, it simply tipped into the heaving sea, but by the grace of God it remained the right way up. Someone screamed an obscenity and JJ echoed it in his mind, though aloud he only said, 'Steady, chaps, don't move more than you have to . . . has someone got the oars?'

Next to him the coxswain said, 'There ain't no bloody oars, sir, someone must 'ave nicked 'em. Bloody 'ell, there's some lunatic in that bloody U-boat what doesn't know the war's over! Unless it's a bloody Jap, of course.'

The other boat had been launched ten minutes before theirs and JJ watched enviously as it drew steadily away. He could have gone in the first boat, but had chosen to stay with his men until everyone who could make the deck was aboard. It was no use repining; they simply sat in their cockleshell craft and watched as the poor old *Moonraker*, which had been a good little ship, took its final plunge beneath the waves.

JJ looked around. The convoy was nowhere in sight but the coastline was near; he had to cling to that thought and not envy the men in the first boat as they rowed steadily away. Someone shouted to them, another voice joined in, but it was impossible to get their attention with a big sea running and the distance between them steadily increasing.

JJ sighed and was about to see if there was a bailer or anything that could be used to propel them forward when something terrible and monolithic rose from the deep. It was huge and black, and it surfaced ahead of them and right below the other boat. It actually carried the boat and its crew of rescued seamen several feet up in the air before their frail craft tipped. One moment the water was full of screaming men and oil and bits of their boat, the next the sea-monster had dived again, carrying the human flotsam and jetsam with it. Total silence reigned for the space of ten seconds. Then the men in the boat began cursing and shrieking, calling down the wrath of heaven on the submarine.

'Was that . . . that *thing* a U-boat?' JJ hissed to the man sitting next to him. The man nodded, face red with rage.

'Aye, and them buggers did it on purpose, they wanted to do more than finish off poor old *Moonraker* and 'alf me mess-mates, they wanted to kill the rest of us. Eh, I'd like to get that feller, that capting, with 'is bleedin' pants down for five minutes. He'd never mek another woman I'm tellin' you, sir.'

'They couldn't 'ave done it on purpose,' someone else said quietly. 'I don't reckon a sub knows what's above it, not if it's a small thing like a boat. Eh, but I reckon I'll never forget that; never.'

'Nor me,' another man put in, his voice subdued. 'Nor me.'

JJ knelt up and addressed them. 'It was a terrible thing and we'll none of us forget it, but right now, take a look around you; can anyone see any wreckage we might use as oars to get us ashore?'

'Ye-es, but it's too cold to go overboard . . . Hey, there, port bow – grab it, young Sandy, if you want to taste 'ot tea agin!'

Someone grabbed young Sandy and he leaned over the side, white-faced but determined. After minutes of hard effort the crew had a pair of oars and were beginning to make use of them. The oarsmen were probably, JJ mused as he got steadily colder, the only people on board whose blood wasn't almost frozen in their veins. They were farther from the shore than he had thought, or perhaps the tide was carrying them out to sea. Everyone would have to take a turn with the oars.

Time passed. Someone handed round some very hard ships' biscuits and everyone had a mouthful of stale-tasting water. JJ took a turn at the oars and found it harder going than he expected because he could not grasp the wood with his numb fingers. He wished fervently he had managed to grab his duffel coat before he left the cabin. He wished he wasn't wet to the waist. He wished he dared go to sleep.

Snip and the HMS *Hesperides* heard about VE-Day when they docked at Trincomalee; the crew were desperate for fresh air, fresh food and showers after a long sea patrol and apart from the relief they felt over the safety of loved ones, they took little notice of the news. Japan was fighting on and their orders were to remain in tropical seas until that country, too, had surrendered.

'Three days ashore at least, probably longer,' the skipper said. 'But see about the prickly heat before you start painting the town red. There must be something which at least will ease it.'

'I want to see someone about some spares,' Snip said. He was now engine officer on the *Hesperides* and was fanatical over the maintenance of his engines. 'The piston rings are worn; it means we're not steerin' accurately, and we've smelt exhaust gases a couple of times when we was submerged for too long. Can't go to sea again till that's put right.'

'She needs a refit,' agreed Lieutenant Collis. 'They'll do what they can here, but I've no idea how they're fixed for spares.'

'I'll see to it,' Snip said. 'But not until after I've had a beer and a shower; where are we staying?'

Collis was a good sort, and Snip had served under several commanding officers by now. Some of them didn't give a damn what happened to their men in port as long as they were comfortable themselves, but the lieutenant wasn't like that. He had them billeted in a decent hotel where the staff looked after them, awed by the state of their skin and the stories of weeks with a minimum ration of drinking water and no washing allowance at all. Snip, who was used to being dirty on the gaff when the weather was bad and heavy machinery had to be shifted through thick mud, had never known anything like it. You cleaned down an engine, then you cleaned down yourself. But not in HMS *Hesperides*. You remained filthy for six weeks, sometimes more, until you docked. No other ship had this problem, and the German U-boats and American subs all had reasonable facilities so their submariners did not suffer from skin disease, near-starvation when food and water ran short, extreme frustration when they had to surface every twenty-four hours to recharge their batteries – and near-death when they had to stay under because the hunting pack were out and it would have been certain death to surface.

Still, submariners' pay was good – if you lived long enough to spend it – and the war in Europe was over, so he would no longer have quite the same worry over Nell. Nell was Snip's girl and, not only that, she was his reason for going on – he would have said his reason for living, except that it sounded so silly. The crew's quarters were very cramped but on the bulkhead above his bunk he had a wobbly photograph of her in a faded print dress with her hair pulled back and a rifle in one hand. She had been in charge of the shooting gallery at the time, he remembered. There was another photograph, a better one, but somehow he didn't look at that quite so often, or with quite such nostalgia. The second photograph showed Nell in her landgirl uniform, complete with the squashed cowboy hat which they wore occasionally. It was a nice photograph, Nell was smiling lovingly at the camera, but Snip had a bad feeling about the picture; he felt that Nell had had it taken for someone else.

Still, she wrote long, loving letters to him; she had let him take her to the flicks just before his ship sailed for the tropics, and although she had never allowed him any liberties – an arm around her shoulders in the one and nines and a kiss on parting was about as far as she was prepared to go – he comforted himself with the thought that Nell would be the same with everyone; kisses would be strictly rationed.

There had been no letter from her since, but he had spent too long waiting for letters, only to find six or eight awaiting him at the next port. He did not worry now; after all, the big worry should be over. Those blasted doodlebugs; now they *had* worried him. The awful feeling of wanting them to drone on, praying they would fall elsewhere, had worried him deeply: it had overtones of banging tin trays to drive the locusts on to the next village. But Nell was so precious to him! He did not need the photographs to conjure up her image – the dark blue eyes which could express such warmth, such love, the gentle line of rose-pink lips, the trick she had of dimpling and then smoothing the dimple out with one finger. She was the best thing that had ever happened to him and he did not intend to let her slip through his fingers as so many other things had eluded him. Family love, brotherly love, any parental warmth had all disappeared, unregretted, when he had finally made up his mind to get out of the Morris set-up; when the war had come and his father had taken his shows on the road with just the family, Snip had decided to quit.

He had got a job in a garage, mending cars, and then he had joined the Navy, being put almost straight into submarines, though only as a stoker at first. From there had begun the slow climb to his present lofty position as engine officer, which he enjoyed as much as anyone can enjoy anything in a submarine. But he was saving his money; not for him the relief at being alive which caused the rest of the crew to blue every penny they earned on wine, women and song – or more accurately, booze, bed and cheapjackery. He was saving for afterwards, when he would be able to stand before Nell with his head held high and tell her about the future they would share.

A little farm up in the hills somewhere, he dreamed mostly, with airy rooms; never again the airless prickling heat of a submarine in tropical waters or the frowsty, cheesy atmosphere of a living wagon full of too many possessions, too many kids. There would be a stream, willow trees along the bank, the hills purple and gold with heather and gorse and a clean wind lifting his hair from his forehead. The farmhouse would have its windows open to let in the air and he and Nell would lie, naked, on the big, soft feather bed and . . .

His mind broke off, shocked. How could he think such things, as though Nell were a sixpenny whore on the docks. Nell was a little lady, far above that sort of thing; she would welcome him home on the doorstep, smiling at him, wearing a clean pink dress and with her hair shining from vigorous brushing. He would pick her up and carry her up the creaking wooden stairs to the bedroom under the eaves and . . .

I'll marry her first, he told his outraged conscience defensively. I mean to do right by her because I've loved her all my life and I love her still. Ah, we'll be so happy, Nell and me!

They were in port two days before Snip felt properly clean and decent again. He had spent most of the first day in the bath in the little hotel, getting every inch of filth and grime out of his pores. Then he and one of the other chaps went to a Turkish bath and sweated out anything that was left, enjoying the sensation of being truly clean once more.

Then he went to visit *Hesperides* in her dock and make sure she was getting the treatment he wanted for her. He and the engineer in charge talked long and intently about the intricacies of a submarine's engine, and the engineer produced the gleaming new piston rings which had begun to seem the be-all and end-all of existence to Snip and promised that they would be in place before *Hesperides* sailed.

Only then did Snip begin to relax. He bought a gaudy post-card and sent it to Nell, a rude one went to Ugly Jack and a pretty, scenic one to Hester. He had hoped for post to arrive while the sub underwent its refit but there was none, so he settled down and wrote Nell a long letter. With the war in Europe over, he hoped she might receive it within the next three or four weeks, but you never knew. Things were probably still pretty tough at home, though his only means of finding out were newspapers several weeks old and what the Air Force told them.

The refit was completed at last, Snip did some sea-trials with the rest of the crew, then it was their last night ashore. Everyone had a few drinks, but not too many. Snip wrote to Nell again, and sent her another card. Then at dawn the following day the submarine *Hesperides* nosed out from Trincomalee Harbour into the Bay of Bengal. Sealed orders might mean a battle or an attack on an enemy harbour, but from the way they were headed Snip guessed they were making for the South China Sea. What mischief had been planned for them there they had no way, as yet, of knowing.

So they proceeded on the surface at night, dived during the day, and waited for what would come next.

By great good fortune, Nell was on leave from Withies Farm when VE-Day was announced, so the family abandoned the fair and went off to enjoy the celebrations. Nell, Ugly Jack, Hester and Fleur went into Norwich to see the firework display in the market place. Fleur had joined up with the Gullivers again the previous autumn and Nell and Fleur had already regained some of their old intimacy.

The age-gap between sixteen and nineteen seemed less than the gulf between seven and ten, and the two girls found they had a good deal in common as well as from the vanished 'sisterhood' which had once meant so much to Nell. Fleur worked on the fair now, so whenever Nell came home there she was, ready to take her old place in her friend's affections. At sixteen Fleur was beginning to revel in her newly discovered charms, Nell thought. She was short and inclined to be stocky, with sultry bedroom eyes and full lips; boys clustered around her like bees around a honeypot. It did not seem to matter that Fleur bleached her hair an unlikely shade of yellow, nor that she wore skirts so tight she could only hobble and heels so high she looked like Clown Joey on stilts. The young men who chased after her were indifferent to her apparel, what they liked was the promise they read in her sultry glances and the way she used her body to say she was a good-time girl searching for a good time.

But appearances are deceptive. Fleur was searching for a good time all right, but not the sort the eager boys imagined. She wanted someone to pay for her seat in the cinema, for a meal afterwards, for games on the slot machines and a trip to the seaside or to London to see the sights. In return she would give them, Nell knew, sweet smiles, her enchanting gurgle of laughter, a quick kiss on the chin – and nothing else. 'I'm not into heavy petting,' Fleur would say dismissively at the first sign of a boy wanting to put his arm around her. 'If you want that sort of thing you'd best go with Daffy Elgin or Sue Anstruther.'

'A bit of a hug in the back row isn't heavy petting,' Nell said on one occasion, a trifle worried by Fleur's naiveté or puritanism, she wasn't sure which. 'Even I let boys hug me in the back row, Fleur, and I've got a steady.'

Fleur shot her a sparkling look. 'When I meet someone I really like he'll be welcome to hug me in the back row or anywhere else for that matter,' she said. 'But right now, all I want from them is a bit of fun, Nellie love.'

Hester said that Fleur's come hither glances were nothing but a tease, a come-on-go-back, but she laughed as she said it and told Nell and Ugly Jack privately that the kid was on to a winner and who could blame her if she rode her winner the full distance.

'Ye-es, but she could land in trouble,' Ugly Jack said, giving Hester a doubtful glance. They were having tea the day following VE-Day, boiled eggs and bread and margarine with a few stewed apples to follow. 'Some men can get real nasty if they think a gal's goin' to give 'em what they want and then she don't. I'd rather see Fleur behave like our Nell does; like a little lady.'

Nell took the top off her egg and ate it slowly, savouring every mouthful. One egg a month was the ration . . . well, she was luckier than that and so was Mum, because the farm kept bantams and very delicious their little eggs were when they were laying well.

'I shouldn't worry, Jack,' Hester said, through her mouthful. 'Fleur can't help looking as though she's easy; she really doesn't act it – well, not on purpose, anyway.' She turned to Nell. 'Does this mean that Snip will be coming home, darling? I suppose it must, they surely won't keep him any longer? It's such a dreadful, dangerous life in a submarine.'

'Oh, he's way off on the other side of the world,' Nell said rather uneasily. 'Anyway, Snip isn't exactly . . . I mean we're good friends, but . . .'

'But you told Fleur you had a steady; I was sure you meant Snip,' Hester said reproachfully. 'Who else could you have meant?'

'Well, there is someone else, in a way,' Nell muttered. She had never mentioned Dan to her mother because it seemed pointless, besides bringing back their time at Pengarth which Hester so patently wanted to forget. 'Look, I'm going to start the washing up, then I can give you a hand this evening. Do you want me to shout for Phillips or help on the dodgems or the galloper?'

A brisk discussion ensued and Nell clattered plates at the basin, relieved to have got out of that questioning session so lightly. Dan was continually in her thoughts. Indeed, beside his well-remembered crooked grin and the look in those dark blue eyes, other men faded into insignificance. With her hands in the greasy hot water, Nell let her mind wander to the last time she had seen him.

After the fiasco of her visit to Lincoln the previous August, she had gone glumly back to Withies Farm, convinced that she had seen Dan with the love of his life and that her hopes in that direction were dashed. For forty-eight hours she had nursed a mixture of sorrow and resentment – sorrow for her loss, resentment that she had been supplanted. And then, on the Wednesday evening after her return, when they had been rained off the harvest fields early and were trying to dry themselves out before an unseasonally large fire, someone had knocked at the kitchen door.

Visitors who knocked at the back door were few and far between; most people just walked in. Mrs Earnshaw put down her knitting and looked at Dot and Nell over the top of her glasses.

'Either one of you expecting a visitor?' she asked. 'Where's Patty?'

Patty was the Earnshaw's thirty-year-old daughter. She had lived in the city with her two small sons – her husband was in Aden – but the family had been staying at Withies Farm ever since a bomb had destroyed their neat little semi on Ipswich Road earlier in the year.

'She's up with the children, reading them a story,' Nell said, putting down her knitting and getting to her feet. 'I'll go, Mrs Earnshaw.'

But Dot was quicker. With Paul constantly on her mind, she flew out of her chair and across the room, pulling open the big back door.

A tall figure, muffled in a Royal Air Force raincape, stood in the downpour. It was not particularly cold, but it had rained for most of the day and seemed to have decided to keep it up all night. At least it looked like that, Nell thought, peering past the figure and seeing what looked like a stormy sea between the kitchen step and the shippon.

'Paul? Come in,' Dot said uncertainly. 'I thought you were duty officer to . . . oh, gawd!'

The tall young man had taken off his cap and pushed back his cape. It was now Nell's turn to fly out of her chair.

'Dan!'

He stood almost sheepishly, dripping on to the quarry tiles, grinning as though half in doubt of his welcome.

'Nell, I'm sorry to spring this visit on you, but I felt we had to talk. I was on the river last week with a girl from my village when I . . . well, I thought I saw you! I spppose it was just imagination but I've thought of nothing else since. I chased all over the city trying to catch up with you . . . you weren't really there, were you?'

Nell, her face as hot as though it had been roasted over the fire, nodded dumbly. She was staring up at his face as though she could never see enough. Dan was here – her Dan!

'Well, why didn't you give me a tinkle? Come out to Scampton? I searched for you, then I went back to the station and waited for a call. Since then . . . well . . .' his voice died. He glanced apologetically at Mrs Earnshaw knitting and watching, at Dot, simply watching, at the other landgirl, Brenda, staring at him open-mouthed.

Mrs Earnshaw, quick to take the point, laughed and got to her feet. 'Take that wet cape off, lad, do you'll catch your death,' she said briskly. 'Dot, put the kettle on, make us all a nice cup of tea. Nell, take your guest through to the livin'-room. Brenda, find up some of them ginger biscuits I made last week.' She turned from giving orders to her troops back to Dan, who was struggling out of his wet things. 'Boots an' all, lad. I don't want my carpet ruined, do I?'

'Umm, no, I'm sure you don't,' Dan mumbled. In seconds he was standing before them in his stockinged feet and blue shirt and trousers. Nell, coming to her senses, had taken his cape and cap through to the scullery where she hung them on the big clothes airer. She came bustling back, bright-eyed.

'Anything else, Mrs Earny? Then I'll take Dan through to the living-room. Can you carry your cup, Dan?'

'Just you put them cups down,' Mrs Earnshaw said immediately. 'I'll bring the tea and the biscuits through all properly, on a tray. Want the fire lit?'

'It's quite all right . . .' Dan began, but Mrs Earnshaw had followed them into the empty drawing-room and plumped to her knees before the fire.

'You're damp, if not soaked,' she pronounced severely. 'Don't want you laid up here for a week, wi' an infection o' the lungs.'

The fire crackled and Dan and Nell, exchanging sly glances, took their places on either side of the hearth. They talked stiltedly until the tray of tea and biscuits had been delivered – with two slices of rich plum cake, a rare treat which had Dan's eyes glistening appreciatively – and then, with the door safely shut, Dan stood up, walked across to Nell's side of the fireplace and sat down on the arm of her chair.

'Nell, it was you, wasn't it? Where did you go? Why didn't you tell me you were in Lincoln?'

'It was going to be a surprise; I had a couple of days' leave,' Nell mumbled, staring at her feet in their darned green socks and elderly carpet slippers. 'And then, when I saw you with that girl . . .'

'Good God, you can't have been silly enough to think that little Anna meant anything to me? I've known her for years, she's just a neighbour. Nell, I thought you and I had something going for us.'

'You leaned forward and stroked her cheek,' Nell said, her voice even lower. 'She – she was so pretty, I wouldn't have blamed you . . . we've only met once since I was seven.'

'But we've written a great many letters,' Dan said softly. 'I meant what I said in those letters, Nell. There has never been a girl like you for me. Never.'

'We've never even kissed each other,' Nell protested, abruptly removing her gaze from her slippers and transferring it to his face. 'So it's just silly, Dan, to pretend. Why, you could have come and visited me any time, all you had to do was write and make arrangements.'

'You kept moving about,' Dan pointed out. 'It's hard enough to get leave anyway, without having to get it and then find where someone is.'

'I've been at the Withies for more than a year, sitting right

339

here,' Nell said with spirit. 'That sounds awfully like an excuse, Dan.'

'It isn't an excuse, honestly. But I didn't want to make a move and risk losing you,' Dan said ruefully. 'You were always quite an elusive kid, Nell, and when you and your mother upped and left Pengarth I didn't know what to think.'

'You left too.'

'Yes, because Geraint didn't want my mother and me staying at the castle any more. He said we made too much work and he'd have to go down on his bended knee to some woman – Cledwen I think he called her – to get her to come back. My mother left in a rage, you can imagine, and said she'd never go back. I just didn't have a choice.'

He sounded wistful. Nell remembered how she had felt when she was deprived of Pengarth and timidly squeezed his hand. He bent and kissed the smooth crown of her head.

'Poor little Nell, it wasn't your fault. My mother was always an exacting woman, I suppose poor old Geraint just got fed up with doing her bidding – or rather, getting your mother to do her bidding. So anyway, I was afraid of getting too close to you in case you just disappeared again. But when I saw you leaning over the bridge, looking down at me, I just sort of knew. I've had lots of girls, and I'm sure you've had a heap of boyfriends, but there's only one girl who will ever mean anything to me, and that's Nell Coburn.'

'Makerfield,' Nell mumbled. 'We changed our name.'

Dan stood up and took his cup of tea from the tray, balancing a couple of large ginger biscuits in the saucer. Then he sat in his own chair, put the teacup on a small side table and moved over so that a sliver of cushion was vacant. He patted this encouragingly.

'You changed your *name*? For goodness sake, why? You'd done nothing wrong, committed no crime, so why run away? Come and sit on this spare bit of chair and we can really sort out what's been happening since we both left Pengarth.' He smiled his old beguiling smile, a long amusement crease beside his mouth. 'Come on, I won't bite you.'

Nell stood up and shuffled over. She squeezed into the big

old chair with him, warm thigh crushed against warm thigh, and leaned back against the comfort of his arm.

'You start,' she said. 'Where did you go?'

'To relatives, again. In a small village about six miles outside Norwich. I stayed at Wellington for a bit, then Mama ran out of money, or said she had, and I transferred to the Norwich Grammar School. When war broke out, I volunteered for the Air Force and started my training then and there. I've never been back to Wales, let alone Pengarth. It's funny, but it would have seemed, well, disloyal in a way. Because I knew Mama wanted desperately to go back but felt she couldn't.'

'Poor Dan; did you miss Wellington dreadfully?'

Dan considered, staring into the flames. 'No-o, not dreadfully, not after a bit. And my old friends were very good. I was staying with a cousin who was still at Wellington the day you and I bumped, quite literally, into each other. I was very cut-up when I realised I'd let you get away without you giving me your address, but then you sent me that post office one, and I wrote to you . . . and the rest, as they say, is history. Now you.'

'We had a bad time at first. Oh, but I've not told you what happened, not really, to send us off. Sorry.

'It's quite a long story and I only know a little bit of it, but I'll try to make it as clear and short as I can. It seems that Mr Geraint told my father that I was his little girl, not Matthew's. Matthew came home in a terrible rage and told Mum that if she didn't clear out and take me with her, he'd kill us both. Mum believed him and we ran.'

'Where did you run to? What did you do for a living?'

'Oh, we went all over the place, but we started off in Liverpool,' Nell said airily. 'Mum worked at keeping house for people, cleaning, anything. We moved about a lot because she was afraid of Da . . . Matthew, I mean, for absolutely ages. She really thought he would come after us and either steal me away or kill us. No, I think it was Mr Geraint who was supposed to steal me away . . . oh Dan, I'm sorry, it's very complicated and for a bit I think Mum wasn't sure what she was frightened of. But then she met Ug . . . she met Jack and they're settled down together and everything seems fine.'

341

'Ug Jack did you say?'

Nell laughed. 'His nickname is Ugly Jack but really he's Jack Gulliver. He's the best and kindest man, he even puts up with Phillips –' she broke off, looking self-conscious. 'So anyway, that was that until I was old enough to leave home and I joined the Land Army and here I am!'

'Here we both are,' Dan said. He squeezed her, then rested his chin on the top of her head. 'How would you like to marry me when this little lot's over?'

'Oh, Dan, but we don't know each other very well,' Nell said feebly. 'You don't marry someone you've only met a couple of times.'

'I do,' Dan said at once. 'Why not? Don't you believe in love at first sight?'

'Love? Oh, Dan, but we haven't even . . .'

'Kissed? We can soon remedy that.'

The new fire crackled, pale flames shooting chimneywards. The ginger biscuits remained uneaten, the tea cooled in the cups. Curled up in the big chair, Dan and Nell experienced the giddying glory of first love.

'Come on, dreamy, whatever's got into you? The war's over bar the shouting, and there you stand with your hands in cold, greasy water, mooning away. Are you going to bark for me and Phillips or not?'

Hester's warm and teasing voice broke into Nell's thoughts, bringing her abruptly back to the present, to the last night of her leave and to the realities of her mother's job.

'I'll bark for you,' she said readily. 'And afterwards, when the show's over, can we have fish and chips? I know we had a good tea, but I'll be back on the farm tomorrow.'

'Course you can, gal,' Ugly Jack said at once. 'No harm in a few chips once in a while. Phillips gets 'is rabbit tonight, what's more, so we'll all feed well.'

Phillips, uncoiled by Hester once they got to the show-tent so that he wouldn't be sluggish or bad-tempered when the flatties arrived, had grown a good deal since Nell had last laid eyes on him. 'He really is huge, Mum,' she said uneasily as she raked

342

the sand smooth and wound the ivy around the tent-pole. 'He could crush you easy as easy, I should think. You are careful, aren't you?'

'Well, I am, but old Phillips wouldn't hurt me, love,' Hester said reassuringly. She was brushing out her long hair, smoothing oil into her skin, struggling into the small garment she wore for her act. 'He's soft as a brush really, though he is getting rather heavy. I keep warning him he'll have to go on a diet, but he takes no notice, of course, and guzzles away once a week as though he knew there was a war on and he was lucky to have a job and a full belly. Besides, the bigger he gets the more he amazes the flatties.'

'Well, so long as you're sure,' Nell said, still uneasy. She had realised that Phillips wasn't just a family pet, the way she had once thought of him, but a rather wild and quite possibly dangerous reptile. You might work up some rapport with a lion or an elephant, but a cold-blooded snake? If Phillips got really hungry and his food was not immediately forthcoming, who could say that he would not simply decide to squeeze Hester down to swallowable proportions? But when she voiced the thought to Hester she was laughed out of court and, indeed, Phillips behaved like a perfect gentleman throughout the performance, although Hester nearly dropped him twice.

'And now, ladies and gentlemen, you will see Jungle Woman wrestle the snake for a piece of silk, rare silk from China's distant shores. See how Venom lashes his head, see him consider his next move, while Jungle Woman, who has known him since he was no longer than a skipping rope, works her will on him, charming him into submission.'

The familiar words rolled out, Nell pitching her voice above the constant rumble from the audience.

'Funny sorta cobra that – thought they 'ad 'oods, like, round their little 'eads?'

'Aw, you don't know nothin', you don't! I just see the p'ison drip from its fangs – ooh, in't it an 'orrible great thing, though?'

'Mum, I want to wee-wee, can I wee-wee in the grass?'

'If that little begger piddles on my best boots he'll get wrong wi' me, I tell you straight, nephew or no nephew.'

Hester and Phillips came to their conclusion and Nell dropped thankfully out of character – her throat was sore – and threw her mother the starry cloak. Phillips was folded hastily into his hay-box behind the screen and the audience, still mumbling over the wonders they had seen, filed out.

'Chips now,' Nell said brightly as the two of them left the hut behind Ugly Jack, who carried the python, box and all, beneath one arm. 'We don't often get chips on the farm, being stuck miles out in the country. Does the budget run to fish as well? All that crispy, oozing batter!'

'We'll have both,' Hester said, linking her arm in her daughter's. 'While we hot the plates, dear old Jack will nip down to the pub on the corner and bring us back a jug of ale as well as the fish and chips. And while he's gone, we can have a nice, cosy, mother-and-daughter chat.'

'Lovely,' Nell agreed. She supposed she really ought to tell Hester about Dan now. After all, she and Hester had always been close, they had never had any secrets from each other. Furthermore, she could reassure Hester with proof that their secret was safe with Dan – had he not known where they were for almost six years and never breathed a word? Besides, he and his mother had fled from Pengarth just as she and Hester had; they should be brought closer by their mutual rift with Mr Geraint, not pushed further apart.

There is nothing more painful, anyway, than not being told something important by someone you love. I've got to tell, so it might as well be now, Nell thought as they reached the steps of the trailer and climbed into the living wagon. Ugly Jack deposited the snake and went out again, only to reappear seconds later with two rabbits, still in their fur but otherwise very dead.

'Don't you skin them?' Nell asked, torn between fascination and horror as her mother dropped the first of the rabbits into Phillips's haybox. 'Surely all that fur can't be good for him?'

'It is though; he needs roughage and rabbit skin supplies it,' Hester said at once. 'I never watch him eat, it's not a pretty sight, but Jack does and he says Phillips really relishes a bird with all its feathers or a rabbit with its fur and that. He's been very fit ever since we've taken to giving him his food as it comes instead of going to the trouble to pluck hens and skin rabbits.'

'Oh. Well, so long as he's happy. You're happy too, aren't you, Mum?'

Hester smiled gently. 'Very happy, dear. Of course I'd be even happier if you came home to live. Are you going to, now that the war's over?'

'It isn't all over, not yet,' Nell temporised. 'Anyway, I can't leave the Land Army until I'm allowed. But then . . . I'm not sure. I – I might get married.'

'Not to Snip?'

'Well, he hasn't asked me, but no, not to Snip. To another fellow.'

'One you like, but haven't brought home. Darling, are you ashamed of us, Jack and me? Or are you ashamed of him – the boyfriend?'

'Neither, honestly Mum. I've never told him we're with the fair . . . you'll understand why in a moment, but he's in the Air Force, stationed up in Lincolnshire, so our friendship has been a bit difficult and we've neither of us met the other's people. That is, well, you have met him, in a way, though it was a long time ago.'

'What's his name?' Hester's voice was light; she was getting plates down from the dresser, arranging them in front of the fire to warm. 'What's his rank?'

'Flight lieutenant. His name's Dan.'

'Dan. Now that's a nice name . . . d'you remember when you were small, dear, you had a little friend called Dan?'

Hester sounded relaxed, easy, as though the recollection gave her pleasure. Now or never, Nell resolved, and took a deep breath.

'It's the same Dan, Mum. Dan Clifton. We've been writing to each other for years, but about twelve months ago we met again, and we've been meeting on and off ever since. He asked me to marry him just after my leave last summer and I said I probably would. I'm longing to introduce him to you all over again, but he's hardly changed at all. He's still absolutely

345

gorgeous . . . and he thinks I'm pretty nice, too.' Nell smiled at her mother, then the smile slowly faded; never had she seen such an expression on Hester's face. 'What's the matter, Mum? Don't you remember Dan Clifton?'

'Yes, I . . . remember him. How strange, the two of you meeting up after all this while. Darling, there's something, I don't know how to say this, but . . .'

'Mum, do you know something about Dan that I don't? He was a little beast when we were young, I expect, but . . .'

Hester looked deathly white and her eyes would not meet Nell's. She played with the edge of the tablecloth, she re-arranged the knives and forks, she picked up the salt cellar and put it down again. Then she took a deep breath.

'Darling, do you really mean to marry?'

'Yes, we do,' Nell said baldly. Her mother's reaction had shaken her, but that didn't mean she had changed her mind. She loved Dan and he loved her, so surely marriage was the happy ending they both wanted?

'If I tell you it just isn't possible . . . can we leave it at that?'

'Don't be so silly . . . *just isn't possible*! As though the king was about to forbid it, or the archbishop of Canterbury! Mum, I'm beginning to wonder if you're all right in the head, or if it's me that isn't.'

Unexpectedly, Nell felt large tears form in her eyes and trickle down her cheeks. She had expected her mother to be surprised, then pleased for her, but this!

Hester's cheeks went slowly from white to scarlet. She stared straight at Nell, her eyes suddenly hard. She looks as if she hates me, Nell thought wildly; what have I done? All I've done is to tell her I'm in love with Dan Clifton and she's acting as if I'd told her I'd murdered someone.

'Nell . . . I have every reason to believe that – that Dan Clifton is your half-brother.'

Nell laughed. She had never heard anything so absurd; what was her mother going on about this time? She obviously didn't like Dan so she had thought up this monstrosity to put them off the whole idea of marriage. Half-brother indeed!

'Sorry to laugh, Mum, but that's ridiculous. I mean, well,

it just is. How could such a thing be true?'

'Matthew Coburn, my husband, threw me out of the house because he said he wasn't your father. Do you remember?'

Nell frowned, unease beginning to prickle along her spine. 'Ye-es, I remember something like that. So?'

'Mr Geraint told Matthew that he was your father. And it could have been true, love. I – I think it probably was true. I did have an affair with Geraint before I met your father. Just before. And it was common knowledge that there was always something between Mr Geraint and Mrs Clifton. And, well, I don't know if you remember the portrait of the lady in the Long Gallery? She was awfully like you.'

'It can't be true,' Nell said slowly, but even to herself her voice lacked conviction. 'It just can't be true. Anyway, why should Mrs Clifton have made love with Mr Geraint? She was a real lady.'

Hester hung her head and Nell jumped up from her chair and ran to her mother, hugging her, petting her, smoothing the thick, springy hair from her broad, pale brow.

'I deserved that,' Hester muttered. 'But I was very young, darling, younger than you are now. I was just sixteen and I'd been cooped up in the Sister Servina Home for as long as I could remember. I desperately wanted love, any sort of love, and . . .'

'Don't, Mum. I spoke without thinking, honestly I did. You're the best mother and the nicest person. Whatever happened it wasn't your fault! Why, Matthew was years older than you and that Mr Geraint older still. They had no right to try to rule your life because of a mistake when you were even younger than me. Besides, half-brother and sister isn't the real thing, is it? I don't see why we shouldn't marry, Dan and me. We love each other, and . . .'

'Darling, it's not only forbidden in the bible, it's forbidden by the law of the land. I don't understand it, I just know you can't marry Dan. It's all my fault, but perhaps the way you feel for each other is really the natural love of a brother and sister. Could it be that?'

Nell collapsed into a chair. She was remembering the things they had done, the way they had clung, that night at the farm.

The wonderful, arousing intimacy of it had been a sin . . . it could have resulted in something terrible, like that man who had chased her in the wood that time, who had been strange because his parents had been related to each other. But at the time she hadn't known, she had had no more idea than Dan had that they were even distantly related. Sitting there, she felt her stomach turning over, bitter bile rising in her mouth. She stood up, heaving, and made for the door. She hadn't meant to do wrong, she hadn't known . . .

She was halfway across the room when Ugly Jack, laden with newspaper parcels, came into the living wagon.

'Hello, Nell, can't wait for your fish and chips, eh?' he said cheerfully, plonking the jug on the side and the newspaper parcels on the tablecloth. 'Come along, let's get these ate whilst they're . . . what's wrong?'

'I – I've got to go back right now,' Nell gabbled. 'I can't stay for the chips. Mum, I'll write to you.'

And on those words she plunged out of the trailer and into the night.

Thirteen

They had fired the torpedoes and scored two direct hits before the hunters homed in on them. So close inshore, in such a narrow channel, they must have felt themselves safe, and now they were no such thing; a shark had entered their waters. The problem now, for the shark, was how the hell to get out without being spotted.

The trouble was, Snip thought, squatting by his silent engines and trying not to count the clanging roars as depth charges exploded around them – now near, now far – the trouble was that the hunters had moved so fast. Of course it was theoretically possible for a sub to make its escape after firing its 'fish', but the enemy must now have a shrewd idea that they were trapped. Which meant, God help us, absolute silence for as long as it took . . . and it would take, Snip reckoned, as long as the air lasted.

Everything is turned off when the hunter becomes the hunted. The Asdic, sweeping its listening ear in ceaseless circles, cannot help you now. You are too low to use the periscope; indeed, you can't use anything, or nothing which makes a noise. Up above the hunters circle, trying to see through the limpid water; thank God that here in the narrow channel the current swirls the sandy bottom so continuously that eye contact is virtually impossible. They use their listening devices constantly, hoping for some desperate seaman to use the heads, or touch a spanner against metal. In the end you are afraid even to breathe, especially when the air is stale and has every man aboard panting like a dog.

It's going to be a tricky one this time, Snip mused as

the depth charges clanged around them. We're in shallow waters with strong currents running; they know we're here, and they'll be very angry, very keen to get us. The old man is pretty sure we got the Jap U-boat and a troop-carrier but checking was impossible. Whether they had hit or not, a lot of people would have been scared and would now be very angry; a lot of little yellow men up there would be intent on revenge whatever the cost. Snip reflected that you could scarcely blame them. It had been an audacious attack – now they must pay for it.

The air in the engine room grew clammier as the temperature rose. One of the officers came around with a chemical spray designed to absorb the noxious gases which made what air there was foul, but despite the assurances of the scientists who had worked on it, the stuff made the men cough and clutch their chests. Snip, who already suffered from asthma, began to retch and waved the man away hurriedly. When it was safe to move – if it ever was – his engines would need him.

Presently Snip's chest began to ache ominously. It was as though his ribs were telling him his lungs were on their way out and didn't he intend to do something about it? But there was nothing he could do except to lie on the floor and pray that the pursuers would give up, go back into harbour, let them off the hook.

Near at hand, a man gave a strangled moan and began to be sick. The smell, acidic and strong, had an inevitable effect on someone else, who followed suit. Snip lay still and tried to remember what it was like to wake at dawn and go out of your tent, take a deep breath of clean mountain air, amble down to the river for a quick dip . . .

Sickeningly, he returned to the present, to the humidity, the airlessness, the stench. The skipper would have to take a decision pretty soon or they'd all be dead. A little tin coffin for thirty or so men, rocking on the currents at the bottom of the ocean. No one would know that they had died of carbon-dioxide poisoning, perhaps no one would care very much. It would be just another case of submarine overdue, the resigned shrug of comrades in the service, an hour or so of conjecture, then it would be forgotten, pushed under the carpet. Another preventable tragedy which had not been prevented.

Nell would care. They would have got married if he'd made it back to Blighty. He'd not asked her, but he knew how it would have been. He had loved her since they were kids . . . she loved him too, it stood to reason. What would she do if he didn't get back, then? Marry someone else, he supposed dully, that fellow she had talked about. He couldn't blame her, all he could do was hope she found happiness. She was a good kid, was Nell.

He tried to lie very still, to conserve what strength he had left. Waves of blackness kept swamping him; he lost consciousness, then came round again, sick and giddy, for just long enough to register that they were still on the bottom, that the depth charges were still sounding, though fainter and farther off, or was that the effect of lack of oxygen? He didn't know, hardly cared.

Then, suddenly, he found he wanted to look at his photograph. He had a picture of Nell which he kept somewhere on his person at all times; if he still had the strength he could fish it out and at least die with her steady gaze on him. He rooted feebly in his shirt pocket; his fingers found the photograph. It seemed huge and heavy, big as a church bible, but he got it out after a terrible struggle which nearly finished him and looked down at it through the red mist coming and going before his eyes. He saw his sweat drip down and mark the picture but it didn't matter, not now. No one would ever see the picture again . . .

He had time to smile at Nell before he tipped forward into the blackness. He had lost consciousness before his face hit the deck.

He came to gradually when someone started to shake him. A voice reverberated around his head; was he imagining it or had he really heard those wonderful words?

'Start engines, Snip; they've give up, we're goin' to surface!'

It was a life-saver – just the knowledge that it was over, that they would soon be able to breathe again. He hauled himself to his knees, then to his feet, the blood pounding in his ears like a regiment of foot soldiers. His fingers knew what to do even when his oxygen-starved brain was forgetting everything it had ever known; the engines hummed softly into life and *Hesperides* began to creep along the bottom with her nose lifting, like an old hound which smells meat.

'A bit more speed please, Morris. We'll surface as far away from here as we can manage.'

Snip increased the speed; with the engine's hum, life returned to the ship. What air there was moved sluggishly, but at least it moved. Electric fans sprang into life, the sweat stung as it dried on the little red spots of prickly heat.

'Up periscope!'

Marvellous words; and presently they were wallowing out on to the surface of the Bay of Bengal with fresh air rushing in and the men beginning to grin stiffly, to compare notes.

Far overhead, they could see a plane, a silver dot against the blue of the sky. On either side the ocean stretched, calm and placid beneath the sun. A radio message came through and a sub-lieutenant hurried to the bridge with it. Good news or bad? A recall, or orders to return to enemy waters?

The sub-lieutenant came down into the engine room. He was smiling. 'We've been recalled to Trincomalee,' he said cheerfully. 'And the radio says we got the U-boat and the troop-carrier, so that's all right. We've done our bit, now the Yanks are going to take over. This means a long leave; it might even mean Blighty!'

There was some cheering then, though it was subdued. No one had quite got over their recent experience and, besides, they were on the surface, a sitting duck if they were caught by an aircraft or an enemy vessel. Snip, having done all that he should, was about to go to his bunk when he noticed something lying on the floor at his feet. He had been standing on it – a bit of paper, oily, dirty. He bent and picked it up. It was his photograph of Nell. He grinned ruefully at it and her steady gaze seemed to hold his own.

'You're in a bit of a mess, old lady,' Snip told her, trying to wipe the oil and grime off the picture with only limited success. 'But it doesn't matter, because I'll be seein' the real thing after all. Well, there's a turn up for the books. Nell Makerfield, you and me is goin' to get married!'

Nell went through the days in a daze of unhappiness so deep that not even the VJ-Day celebrations in August meant much to her. National events such as Labour winning the election blared across the headlines, but she was not yet a voter and, apart from feeling sorry for Winnie who everyone knew had won the war, she did not worry overmuch about politics.

She did not worry about the new bomb which had caused the Japs to surrender, even though she thought the name – atomic bomb – quite catchy. All these things were happening in a world outside her own capsule of misery and self-disgust. She often thought about the poor idiot who had chased her across the woods and meadows on the day when she had met Dan again. Hester had explained that the man was touched in the head because of in-breeding, close relatives marrying. If she and Dan had gone ahead, unknowing, they might have produced a human misfit like that.

So when she got leave Nell did not return to the Gulliver gaff, though she wrote a couple of times to Hester – stiff, difficult letters. None of it was Hester's fault, she knew, yet she could not help wishing that her mother had been a nicer sort of girl who had simply made love with and then married the man she loved, the way Nell had meant to do. If only Hester had been sensible, hadn't been wooed by a sophisticated lover and the moonlight shining on the face of the waters and lighting up the silvery sand . . . if only! Her daughter could have loved the man of her choice, married him, had children by him. Indeed, if Hester had said nothing, Nell and Dan might have gone ahead in all innocence; ah, but the consequences of such innocence could have been so hideous that Nell could not bear to contemplate them. The recollection of the idiot's snatching hand and greedy, animal-like face still had the power to send a shudder through her.

So when she got a couple of days' leave she went to visit Fleur at her mother's in Ipswich. Cissie's husband, Ronnie Chelsworth, had left the Army when he and Cissie married.

353

He had used his gratuity to buy property and the pair of them settled down to farming it. Nell had gone over by bus from the Withies; she really needed a change, but she fretted for her old friends.

'Snip will be coming home soon I suppose,' Fleur said when the two of them met outside the cinema. 'It'll be fun to see Snip again, won't it?'

'Yes,' Nell said dully. It was not being able to tell anyone which was hardest, she thought. And not being able to tell Dan was worst of all. But what was the point of telling him? Why should she expose him to the sense of sick shame which had flooded over her when she understood that she and Dan might be half-brother and sister? The sensible, practical side of her mind knew that it was no one's fault, that it was just a horrible accident of birth, so she told herself to forget it, put it out of her mind. Telling Dan would simply make things worse; all Dan needed to know was that she had made a mistake and wouldn't be getting in touch again.

There was no point, though, in telling Dan while she was still at the farm; it would be too easy for him to come and see her. When she left the Withies, she would not leave a forwarding address, which suited her fine. So she was working out her time, knowing she would not be needed once the troops came home, and helped by the fact that Dan wrote miserably, saying he had been posted to Aden and would not be able to see her before he left.

'But never mind, sweetheart, we'll meet just as soon as I get back and I can't be away for longer than twelve months because that's the length of the Aden tour,' his letter said. 'Keep your pecker up and think of me each day as I'll think of you. And at least neither of us will have to worry about the other being bombed, because we're out there to help with getting the chaps home, we're not fighting anyone. Tons of love, little Nell, your Dan.'

'You must be worried about Snip, though. Is he anywhere near Japan, where that awful atomic bomb went off? Not that they'd have exploded it with any of our people in the area, I don't suppose. Lots of our troops are still out east, so they'd have to be careful, wouldn't they?'

'Dunno; in his last letter from Trinco-whatsit, Snip said the Americans seemed to want to see the back of the Brits, so he rather thought his next lot of orders, after the refit, would be for Blighty. But that was three or four weeks ago, I've not heard since.'

'Well, I hope he hasn't been blown up,' Fleur said reproachfully. She clearly felt that Nell should have been more interested in the fate of her old friend. 'By the way, what happened to that chap you talked about . . . Danny, was it? I really thought the two of you might meet up when the war finished.'

The two girls were queueing for the cinema, waiting impatiently to have their withers wrung by yet another Great Romance. This time it was *Now Voyager*, with Bette Davis and Paul Henreid, last time it had been *Random Harvest* with Greer Garson and Ronald Colman, two stars who were great favourites with both girls.

'His name's Dan, not Danny. He's in Aden now and I've just written to him to say I'm sorry but it's all off,' Nell said briefly, unable to resist telling someone that the deed had been done, though she would not have dreamed of giving reasons. 'There's no point in going on when you know you've made a mistake. Dan wasn't for me.'

'No,' Fleur agreed. She shot a quick look at Nell out of the corner of an eye whose size was almost doubled by the enthusiastic, if inexpert, use of mascara. 'No, if you've made a mistake you should always own up. Only I thought . . . is that why you've been so quiet, Nell?'

'No. Why should it be?' Nell snapped. 'How could I be anything but quiet with you chattering away? Anyhow, I told Dan it's over and asked him not to write again. He won't be home for a year, his tour lasts that long. By then I'll be miles away from Withies.'

'Yes, you'll be back with Gullivers by then, I daresay,' Fleur said brightly.

'I shan't, or if I do join a fair, it won't be Gullivers,' Nell said. She surprised herself by her words but realised she was speaking no more than the truth. She would not live with her

355

mother and Ugly Jack again, not because she disliked either of them but because she had outgrown them. 'I couldn't go back to being a daughter again, you see. I've been independent for too long.'

'Yes, and your Mum's had Jack to herself for too long; I know they say they'd love you home, but sometimes it must seem a sort of backward step,' Fleur said, with surprising shrewdness. 'But now the war's over we'll be able to do all sorts of things. No one will make us work in factories or shops if we don't want to, we'll have a choice.'

The queue edged forward, the two girls with it. Nell examined Fleur's last remark and found it flawed. 'We shan't be able to choose at all,' she said scornfully. 'You are a little silly, Fleur! With the fellers coming home us girls won't have a chance of a decent job, just you wait and see.'

The return of HMS *Hesperides* to Trincomalee had been in the nature of a triumph. As they slid into harbour, with the seamen standing at ease on deck, a great cheer rose from the many hundreds of sailors lining the decks of other shipping. Having received confirmation of what they had done, the little *Hesperides* was flying her Jolly Roger with two red bars, one with a U in the middle, to indicate their 'kills', and the rest of the Navy was giving them a cheer for their exploits. It was a good moment, and it was followed by an excellent few days' leave while necessary repairs were done in dry dock. Then, of course, it was back to work as usual.

The submarine was many days out of port and riding on the surface of the Java Sea when Snip's own personal disaster struck. They were on their way home, having been ordered back to England, and were instructed to travel on the surface; with the war now officially over, there should be no need to dive. But *Hesperides* was not the bright young thing she had been four years earlier, when Snip had joined her. She was tired and creaking, and her engines needed constant nursing, constant small adjustments. Consequently, when a bearing was found to be defective Snip, with the skill born of long practice in many similar situations, set to at once. He was working when

356

he should have been resting, the sweat dripping off him into the machinery, his mind for once more on his next meal than on the job in hand. A screw toppled and dropped, Snip reached for it . . . and there was a horrible choking, screaming sound. His right hand had been seized by the machinery and all but ripped off.

The agony was unbelievable; appalling. The screams worried him, too, because he had no idea they were his own. Passing out, which he did when the stokers tried to move him, was the only relief he was to get for three long days. He remembered almost nothing of the rest of the voyage, coming round and passing out in constant pain, seeing dimly remembered faces coming and going, hearing boots on the deck, clattering down the companionways, having nightmares which were almost better than wakefulness. Finally, he came round to find himself being rocked like a baby in a big cradle. Perhaps I am a baby, he thought hopefully; perhaps it was all a nightmare and I'm just a soft, cuddly baby rocking in my cot.

The thought gave him pleasure, but then he opened his eyes and looked around him. There it was – machinery, men's feet in heavy boots, the thrum and clatter of engines. He moved and pains shot up his arm, though not with the vivid, scarlet agony he had come to expect. This pain was fainter, duller. He turned his head a little to look around him. A face swam into his vision.

'All right, mate?'

'Where . . . ?'

The face grinned understandingly. 'You're in a flying-boat, cobber. On the Sulu Sea. We're taking you back to Sydney, where the doc will clean up for you. Guess it'll be amputation, but that'll be better than gangrene, eh? I've given you a shot of morphine which should dull the pain for a bit.'

Snip thought he had imagined what the man was saying, because who had heard of a boat which flew? There were boats that dived and boats that didn't, but a boat that *flew*? It seemed preposterous.

'Sure, sure,' he said sleepily. 'Pigs have wings, eh?'

The man snorted a laugh. 'Pommy bastard,' he said, not unkindly. 'You go to sleep now.'

For once, Snip was happy to follow instructions.

The next time he came round he was being carried. The sensation, once again, was that of a child, very young and defenceless, being pushed in a pram by an adult.

Snip opened an eye. He could see a dusty pavement, more feet – good God, was he going mad? That last set of feet had worn high-heeled sandals and a narrow gold chain had circled one slender ankle. Snip's other eye opened and he stared wildly around him. He was in a street, being carried along a pavement on a stretcher. Even as he looked, the street disappeared and he was in a large, clean-smelling building. He saw girls in white aprons, and the familiar smell of disinfectant caused his stomach to clench with apprehension. This was a hospital, he hadn't dreamed any of it; somehow he had been whipped from a submarine thousands of miles from land to this modern hospital, where they were going to clean up his hand.

'He's awake. He's probably pretty confused, but he took a couple of looks around just now,' a woman's voice said. 'Straight to theatre, sir?'

A confirmatory rumble. Snip was past wondering now; he was just letting it happen. He was transferred to a wheeled trolley which whizzed along a great many corridors and, eventually, into a small antiseptic-smelling room. Someone lifted his good hand and took his pulse; the fingers on his wrist were slim and cool. He didn't open his eyes; better not. If this was a dream, he might as well stay in it. He had no desire to return to the nightmarish agony of the engine room on the *Hesperides*.

Suddenly, just as someone rolled up the sleeve on his good arm, a horrible thought entered his head. Suppose they had got it wrong? Suppose they thought it was his good arm which needed 'cleaning up' and then amputating? His eyes shot open as a needle was plunged into the muscle. Another smiling face looked down at him.

'Relax, soldier, you'll be asleep before you can count to twenty and back on the ward and demanding a drink in no time. You're in good hands, couldn't be better.'

'It's my right,' Snip said, slurring the words horribly as

the stuff began to circulate in his veins. 'It's my right . . .'

'That's it, soldier, every man has the right to a good surgeon in times of need and this feller . . .'

Snip felt the icy tingle spread through his body, felt his fingers and toes lose power and feeling, and shuddered down into darkness.

'Mummy, he's in Aden! Isn't that the foulest luck? To be sent abroad just when it's all over, when even Daddy's home! Oh, I could scream.'

Anna was sitting on the edge of the kitchen table reading the latest letter from Dan while her mother cleaned lettuce, radishes and potatoes for their evening meal. Anna had managed to arrange a 'forty-eight', only three weeks after her father's homecoming and had been in a celebratory mood until she had opened Dan's letter. The fact that he had been posted was bad enough, but he would be in Aden for a whole year. It seemed intensely unfair.

'Never mind, love. You said yourself that you're probably in for a further twelve months,' Constance said comfortingly. 'And Anna, darling, I've been meaning to tell you . . . Daddy seems different.'

'Different? How d'you mean? He looks pretty good, all things considered.'

It was a fine September evening. The sun's long rays lit the kitchen at Goldenstone, while outside in the garden JJ dug a trench for the asparagus crowns he intended to plant. Anna laid her letter down and peered out at him. Naval shirtsleeves rolled up, thinning hair hanging over his face, he was digging with what looked like great enthusiasm.

'He *is* pretty good. But that spell in hospital after his ship went down seems to have sobered him up. He was quite ill, you know, he couldn't even write a letter for six weeks. But I've taken him to see the family, we've been to a couple of parties . . . and, darling, he hardly looks at other women! He's been sweet to me, absolutely sweet. So I do think it's all going to work out.'

'That's marvellous,' Anna said sincerely. 'Poor Mummy, you

deserve a break from all that worry. It's good to know I can think of you two as Darby and Joan.'

Constance turned from the sink to pull a face. 'Darby and Joan! Oh well, I suppose I'll have to settle for that and forget being a bright young thing. Daddy is over forty, but I'm not exactly in my dotage, you know.'

'I didn't mean . . . I just meant a happily married couple,' Anna said, confused. 'Anyway, so long as you won't . . .'

'Perish the thought!' Constance said quickly. 'Darling, would it be asking too much if I said would you please forget all that – that other business? I trod the straight and narrow from that moment on, well, almost, and I certainly don't intend to . . . Daddy's my *life*, you know that.'

'Yes, of course I do. Daddy and Jamie,' Anna said. 'How is my baby brother, by the way?'

'He's gone camping with the scouts, which worries me to death, but I'll just have to get used to it, I suppose. He's never going to get to university or anything of that nature, but then I'm not at all academic myself. He's making his way in the world very nicely apart from that.'

'Daddy isn't academic either,' Anna said thoughtfully. 'But actually, Mummy, you're going to have to face up to the fact that I need a career. I've been happy in the WAAF, but I don't want to stay once they say I can be demobbed. So – so I've applied for a place at university, to read economics.'

'*You?* Darling, how awfully brave of you, but why economics? Why not something a bit more feminine, like . . . like . . .'

'You can't get a degree in ballroom dancing or embroidery,' Anna said, trying to keep a straight face and failing dismally. She crossed the room and gave her mother a quick hug. 'Mummy, you never change! Remember, if I want to marry, I shall – I shan't be short of offers. And I think I will, but in my own time and to the right man. So don't worry about me, because I don't intend to be a bluestocking who puts men off by being cleverer than they are. I did all right at school, you know, so there's no reason I shouldn't do all right at university.'

'I'm sure you'll do very well,' Constance said loyally. There was a short pause. 'Have you told Daddy yet?'

'I haven't told him yet. I thought I'd rather you knew first,' Anna said, and understood why her mother gave a muffled little sob and flung her arms around her daughter's neck, giving her the most fervent embrace the two had ever exchanged.

'Thank you,' Constance whispered. 'You're a lovely daughter, Anna!'

Dan read Nell's painful, tear-blotched epistle with disbelief and flung it down with a short laugh. She didn't mean a word of it, that was for sure, she was just peeved because he'd been sent abroad. As if he could help it!

Aden was a pretty grim spot and Dan couldn't help wondering whether he could swing a transfer if he showed the letter to the right people. Weren't there special postings for men whose women kicked over the traces, or was that just talk? But a little thought, and a good deal of poring over the now sweat-blotched pages, convinced Dan that his best hope was to write back, lovingly and understandingly, and tell her that he hoped she would not cut him out of her life but would continue to write as a friend. Cunningly keeping the channel of communication open, he would bide his time, wait until he was back in Blighty and then find out what it was all about.

She had said something about having a talk with her mother; he wondered whether Hester had put the boot in and, if so, why? He guessed his Uncle Geraint had been carrying on with Hester because it was Uncle Geraint's way; his mother had said so and she should have known. His mother, he knew, had been close to Uncle Geraint and it had gone further than mere friendship, whatever she might pretend. As a boy of ten he had been sick in the middle of the night shortly after their arrival at Pengarth and had gone seeking his mother, tearfully, uncomfortable in his vomit-streaked pyjamas. He had gone to her room and it had been empty. He had trailed, hiccuping and miserable, down the wide staircase, into the moonlit hall. The drawing-room was empty, the little study, the sewing-room. Upstairs again, he had looked around him uneasily, wondering what had happened. Had all the grown-ups fled the country? What was he to do? Then he remembered Uncle Geraint and the room over the gatehouse. He had set off, still in his sticky pyjamas, across the yard and up the outside stair.

A line of light showed under the door and he tapped gently. Too gently as it turned out, since there was no answer to his knock. He knocked again, louder, and heard scuffling sounds behind the wood.

He was a polite little boy. He had waited, shivering, and the door had opened.

Uncle Geraint stood there. He looked hot and bothered, and his hair, that thick greying hair, stood on end.

'It's the boy,' he said over his shoulder. 'What's the matter, Daniel?'

'I've been sick,' Dan croaked. 'I feel ever so bad, Uncle. And I c-can't find Mummy.'

'Oh, she's gone . . . look, old boy, go back to your room and I'll fetch her. She'll be with you in five minutes, I promise.'

Dan had trotted obediently back to his room, but he had not been fooled. Mummy had been in there, with Uncle Geraint; he had smelt the faint perfume of roses she always wore. He felt that bad things had been happening, but when Mummy came to him, flustered and pink-cheeked, she said she'd been in the kitchen making herself a cup of cocoa to help her to sleep, and, poor darling, he must get into her bed for the rest of the night since his sheets were stained. She had helped him to change his pyjamas, popped him, cleanly clad, into her own bed, and then settled on the couch with a blanket over her so that if he woke again she would be near at hand.

'They were Doing It,' Dan had concluded in later years, when he was more knowing. Fancy my pretty little mother playing about with that old horror! But it hadn't bothered him really. He liked Uncle Geraint and perhaps he'd had hopes of the two of them marrying so that he and Mummy could stay at Pengarth for ever. But it had all ended and they had moved on.

He remembered now, with real gratitude, those ill-penned but lively letters which had plopped down on the breakfast table at school from the little girl called Nell whose mother had taken her far from Pengarth. He had been unable to reply because she had never given him an address, but the letters had been like a strong rope, linking him to all the things he liked most, and he had clung to it for years, until his mother had taken him away from school and the rope had been broken.

Perhaps she went on writing the letters, but if she had, the school hadn't forwarded them. A shame really, and too bad, but it hadn't mattered because they'd met again.

Now she was trying to break the relationship; well, she wouldn't do it. He loved her, wanted her, would marry her no matter what anyone said. Immediately, before she could do anything foolish, he would write and tell her that she must not act precipitately, and that however she felt, he would always be her true friend. He would tell her how much her letters had meant to him at boarding school all those years ago, and beg her not to desert him now, when he was stuck in this hell-hole, with prickly heat, malaria and dysentery threatening.

Dan reached for the pad of blue writing paper which his mother had given him in the hope that it would encourage him to write to her often. The tip of his tongue poked out in concentration and a lock of jet-black, gleaming hair fell forward over his brow.

Above the young man's head the little brown monkeys which infested the RAF camp dived amongst the rafters, squeaking, chasing one another, occasionally dropping down and seizing anything which wasn't nailed down. They were famous thieves and gave the men hours of amusement; in their turn, the monkeys got hours of amusement from the tanned, shorts-clad young men, who behaved very oddly, not at all as the Arabs behaved.

The monkeys saw the man stop scratching on the blue paper with his piece of stick and fold the paper. And then he dropped his head on his arms, and his shoulders shook. There was wetness on his brown hands and some of the drops fell on the blue paper and made dark, wrinkly spots.

Nell had spent the day hunting for frogspawn, because her landlady's daughter, a real little townie, had said the previous day, over high tea, that she had never seen a tadpole, let alone a frog.

363

'Good God, you must have,' Nell had protested, shocked that any child could be so deprived. She remembered expeditions at Pengarth when she, her mother and Matthew – she no longer thought of him as her father – had gone down to the flat, marshy meadows which divided the mountains from the coast, to root around in the ditches and small ponds for frogspawn which they would fish carefully out of their natural element and place in large, water-filled jars. They stood the jars in the middle of the kitchen table and, each day as they ate, the wonder of metamorphosis took place before their eyes. Tiny blobs of jelly gradually formed into big-headed, narrow-tailed tadpoles and these, in their turn, grew little legs, shed their baby softness, dropped their tails and lo! they were frogs.

And here it was at the end of February 1946 Amy Pratt could look her in the eye and assure her that she had never seen a live frog.

'I'll get you some spawn,' Nell had promised, recklessly considering that she was not familiar with the countryside around Tunbridge Wells. For all she knew, frogs might never spawn around here. But it was all right. She walked a long way, it was true, but at last she came to fenny, boggy land surrounded by small copses and ponds and, despite the fact that it was very cold, she forced her way through the tall, frost-whitened reeds and filled the bucket she had brought, first with pond-water, then with weed and, lastly, with a few blobs of frogspawn.

Nell was in Tunbridge Wells with her new fair – Marushka's – which over-wintered here and toured Kent and Sussex during the spring and summer. She had not intended to work the fairs again; after working on the land for so long she wanted to try for a job which paid reasonably well and allowed her to settle in one spot. A fair, she thought, would be a retrograde step; she needed more interesting work to take her mind off Dan. But getting a job was not easy. She had been right when she told Fleur that all the good jobs would go to the soldiers, sailors and airmen who were being demobbed. Girls were not even being considered for agricultural work, not with the men streaming back home, so despite her best efforts Nell was hard-pressed to find a job she liked and could do well.

At last she got work in a grocer's shop, and found that she spent most of the day counting coupons and points. It was incredibly boring, so she tried a bicycle repair place, but that was worse. Men did the repairs; all she had to do was write down what was wrong with the bikes and see that the work was done in the order the bicycles had been left. After that she moved to London, where she sold tickets in a theatre, but the money was bad and lodgings expensive. Then she moved down to Slough and worked in a factory which made towels for export, but she hated factory work, loathed being cooped up all day.

She tried being a groom at a big stables. That was all right until the head lad decided he liked her and assumed she also liked him; when he cornered her in the tack-room she punched him so hard that she broke his nose. She guessed he would have it in for her in future and walked out at the end of the week. Nell had a half-hearted look at other flattie employment, but there was a greyness and an exhaustion about ordinary people in the streets which made her long for the racy, take-as-it-comes life on the gaff. She found she was missing fair folk, the comradeship, the constant movement around the countryside.

She had received a letter from Snip who had been involved in a grisly accident and still wasn't home, so she wasn't likely to bump into him on a tober somewhere, and her pain and misery over Dan had retreated to no more than a dull ache in the back of her mind. Time was beginning its healing process; she had loved and lost, now she must take up life in earnest once more. Then, when she was staying with Cissie and Fleur over Christmas, she saw an advert in the *Fairground Mercury* for a conjuror's assistant: MUST BE DARK-HAIRED, PRETTY, COOL-HEADED AND WILLING TO HOLD STILL. Tickled by the turn of phrase, Nell went along to be interviewed.

The conjuror, who called himself Giovanni, though his real name was Ted Smith, was a dapper, dark-haired little man with a magnificent moustache, the ends of which were waxed to needle-like sharpness. His hair was receding, his eyes protruded slightly, and at first sight he was not a commanding figure, but within a week of starting work Nell realised her new boss was a brilliant illusionist.

The trouble was, he was also a disappointed man. Ariadne, Ted's previous assistant, was tall, redhaired, beautiful . . . and had moved in with Sammy Scarface, who owned the Whale Scenic and was the nastiest, as well as the richest, showman on the gaff. Sammy had decreed that no wife of his was working for anyone else, so poor Ted was suffering all the pangs, not only of unrequited love, but of seeing the object of his desire apparently quite happy to be mistreated by another man. Which was why he had advertised for a dark girl to take Ariadne's place. He could not bear the thought of working with another redhead.

Because Marushka's fair over-wintered in Tunbridge Wells, Ted had advertised at Christmas, thinking that his new assistant would need the winter months to prepare himself for the act, and he was right. Nell had seldom seen a good illusionist – Gullivers had not run to such a thing – and had to be taught all the movements, facial expressions and so on before she could appear before an audience.

'You're a quick study though,' Ted had said the previous day. 'You aren't Ariadne, but the flatties will like you; there's something about you . . .'

'You mean I saw in half beautifully?' Nell had asked, twinkling at him. But Ted, it appeared, was being serious.

'Anyone can be sawn in half, Nell,' he said, 'but not everyone can make sure the flatties are watching her face all the while and not checking up on me.'

So the learning period had gone well and Nell, now the owner of her own spangly cloak and a shimmery bathing-suit with flesh-coloured tights, felt confident that she would not let Giovanni down when they took to the road.

Walking home to her lodgings on Mount Sion at dusk, with her jar of frogspawn tucked into the crook of her arm, Nell was wondering whether she would stay with Ted and Marushka's or if this was just another staging post in her life, when she saw Ariadne coming across the common. She waved and Ariadne waved back and gestured.

'Nell,' she shouted, 'telegram!'

Nell felt her heart break into a terrified gallop. A telegram! She had never received such a thing in her life, but had heard of them and knew they always brought bad news. Thoughts whizzed through her head; Philips must have crushed Hester, or Snip's injuries were worse than he had implied. Something awful was about to hit her.

'What is it?' she panted, still clutching the frogspawn to her chest. 'Is someone hurt? What's happened?'

'Dunno. Didn't open it, but Ted said to come and find you,' Ariadne said. 'Here, take it.' She thrust the small yellow envelope at Nell, then grabbed the jar of frogspawn just in time as Nell released it. 'Steady, luv – telegram's ain't allus bad news.'

But she was wrong. Nell opened the envelope with shaking fingers and spread out the sheet; even in the dusk she could read it clearly enough: NELL JACKS KILLED STOP CAN YOU COME QUESTION MARK YOUR LOVING HESTER

'Nell, are you all right?' Ariadne's face swam for a moment as Nell struggled to adjust to the words on the sheet of paper. 'You look awful – it's bad news, then?'

'Yes, I'll have to go right away. My – my step-father's been killed. Can you explain to Ted for me? Tell him I'll be back as soon as I can get away.'

'Right. I'll go back to the tober, you go to your lodgings. What about this stuff? Is it jam?' Ariadne flourished the jar.

'No, it's frogspawn; give it here, I'll take it back to Amy, drop it off as I go. And thanks for bringing the telegram, Ariadne. Tell Ted I'm sorry.'

'Your mam's goin' to need you, Nell,' Ariadne called as Nell began to trot towards Mount Sion once again. 'You won't be back for a week or two, I wouldn't be surprised, p'haps not ever.'

'Yes, I could be a while,' Nell shouted over her shoulder. She shot a backward glance at Ariadne and was surprised to find the other girl following her. 'Can you stand in for me if necessary? Will Sam let you?'

'He'll have to; the show's gotta go on,' Ariadne said grandly. 'TTFN, Nell, and good luck.'

Nell arrived in King's Lynn in the early hours, having caught a milk train from London. She was stiff and cold after the long, slow journey but she warmed herself by walking briskly from the station to the gaff and knocked on the door of Ugly Jack's trailer feeling worn out but at least human.

The lamp was burning so she guessed Hester had not gone to bed. Indeed, her mother answered the door so quickly that Nell suspected she had been waiting for her daughter's arrival, probably ever since the telegram had been sent.

With the lamplight behind her, Hester was just a dark silhouette, but the light was shining into Nell's face and Hester gave a strangled sob and grabbed her daughter convulsively.

'Nell, oh dearest Nell, I knew you'd come! Such a terrible thing . . . Jack was always careful, it was the ice . . . the tractor driver didn't see him until it was too late, he put his brakes on but the tractor slid, the brakes didn't grip or something. Jack tried to get out of the way and he slid too. The doctor says he didn't know a thing, he was dead at once, he didn't suffer.'

'Thank God,' Nell said fervently. 'Mum, I'm so terribly sorry. Jack was one of the best.'

'He was the best,' Hester said. She slumped into one of the easy chairs beside the fire. 'He put up with Phillips – he never liked snakes, you know – and saw my tent was always set up in good time. We never went short, me and Phillips, not even when things were at their worst. And, oh, Nell, I repaid him poorly!'

'You never did, you were all he cared about, the only thing that really mattered to him,' Nell said stoutly. 'He loved you ever so much, Mum, you only had to look at him to see that.' She looked hard at her mother's tear-stained face in the lamplight. 'Mum, when did you eat last?'

'I don't know . . . yesterday? We had breakfast, Jack had two eggs, I managed to get some from a farm up the road, I walked a couple of miles and sold the farmer's wife a bag of honey-toffee . . . oh Nell, Nell, I've been a wicked, selfish person all my life and now I'm repaid! How can I go on living with what I've done?'

'You've never done anything bad in your whole life, not on purpose,' Nell said, falling to her knees by the chair and taking her mother's shaking hands in her own. 'You went without often so that I should nave what a child needs, and I bet you never had an egg when Jack only had bread. You aren't selfish, you're the most unselfish person I know, and Jack loved you with all his heart. Now I'm going to put the kettle on and we'll have a nice cup of tea and you can tell me why you're saying such wild, foolish things.'

Hester would have spoken, but Nell shook her head reprovingly. 'No. Eat and drink first, then we'll talk. I mean it, Mum. You're in no state to explain anything right now.'

Hester heaved a great sigh and sank back in her chair. 'All right,' she said humbly. 'I'll eat and drink and then I'll tell you what I've done and you'll probably never want to speak to me again. I hate myself, I hate Hester bloody Coburn!'

Nell, slicing bread, stopped to glance at her mother in the flickering light of the oil lamp. Hester Coburn: what could that mean? Hester had called herself Makerfield for years now, ever since they had left Pengarth. What had made her, at this moment of pain and stress, revert to her old, despised name?

But Hester was gazing at the dying fire while slow tears coursed down her cheeks. She took no notice of Nell, who returned to her task then set in her mother's lap a wooden tray with a plate of bread and honey and a mug of hot sweet tea.

'There you are, Mum,' Nell said, 'eat that and drink your tea and then explain.'

Hester went on staring at the embers of the fire but her hand picked up the bread and honey and she began to eat, seeming not to notice when a thin trail of honey ran down her chin. Then, still without looking away from the fire, she drank the tea.

Nell made up the fire, poured herself a cup of tea and cut some more bread. Then she sat down opposite Hester with a slice of bread and butter in one hand. 'All gone? Good. Now why are you blaming yourself for what cannot possibly be your fault?'

'The accident, you mean? I'm not blaming anyone for that. It's how I've treated dear Jack all these years . . . never marrying him though I knew what a lot it would mean to him, never . . . oh, Nell love, never telling him how much I loved him, and I do love him, I do!'

'I expect lots of people never tell someone else how much they love them,' Nell said uncertainly. 'I expect he knew anyway, Mum. Deeds speak louder than words, and though you didn't marry you've lived together for a long time, and always happily.'

She smiled at her mother, but Hester was shaking her head mournfully, fresh tears glistening on her cheeks. 'No, you don't understand! I never, in all that time, let the words "*I love you*" pass my lips, not once!'

'Well, I'm sure dear Jack knew. Mum, you wouldn't have lived with him if you hadn't loved him.'

'But I didn't – live with him, I mean, not in the way you think.'

Nell had been about to take a drink of her tea; she lowered her cup, staring at her mother over the top of it, biting her lip.

'You . . . you didn't live with him? You mean you didn't . . .'

'We never slept in the same bed or made love,' Hester said baldly. 'We shared the trailer and we cuddled sometimes, but Jack said he understood. All that business . . . it always meant trouble you see, love, and I couldn't face up to it, not again. Every now and then he'd ask, mind, very wistful, whether I felt I could . . . but I always said no, it was too soon.'

'Too soon? When you'd shared the living wagon for a dozen years? Oh, Mum, that was . . .'

'I told you you'd despise me, not want to have anything to do with me,' Hester said thickly, through her tears. 'D'you not think I despise myself? If only I could go back in time I'd give him everything he wanted, everything. But it's too late. He's gone and he's never heard the words "I love you" on my lips nor lain with me.'

Nell sipped her tea in silence, then stood the cup back on its saucer with a clatter.

'All right, Mum, you never actually said you loved him and you never slept with him. But he didn't strike me as a deprived or unhappy man, he seemed deeply content and very much in love. He *knew* you loved him, even if you'd not got round to saying it, and he knew you'd make love to him one day, when you felt the time was ripe. So don't try to take on a guilt which would give Ugly Jack pain if he knew about it. Just be sorry he's gone from you and glad he didn't suffer. As for me, I know what you've done for my sake, how you've suffered. I was silly and babyish when you told me . . .' her voice faltered, then strengthened, '. . . about Dan and me being related, but I'm sorry for it, now. Dan wants to be friends and that will suit me, and one day I'll – I'll meet a man who is right for me and we'll marry and I just hope we'll be as happy as you and Jack were.'

'Darling Nell,' Hester said. Her voice was slurred with exhaustion and the outpouring of emotion. 'I know you're right and I'll do as you say. If you've finished your tea, we'd best go to bed. Tomorro᷈ I've got to arrange the funeral.'

Fourteen

Two days after the funeral Hester called Nell in from the gaff, where she was talking to the jukels as she fed them scraps in their big, stoneware feeding trough. Nell, returning to the trailer, was surprised to see her mother dressed in a smart black coat and high-heeled shoes, with a bright scarf tucked round her neck and a black hat with a tiny veil perched over one eye.

'What do you want, Mum? Are you going out? You look tremendously smart, a real swell.'

'I'm going away,' Hester said. 'I'll be away for a while. Will you keep an eye on things while I'm gone?'

'Yes, of course, but where are you going? And why? I mean Ted's been very good but he'll want me to go back to Marushka's as soon as I decently can so that we can practise the act.'

'I – I don't know how long I'll be gone, but I'll write as soon as I know what's happening,' Hester said slowly. 'I wouldn't ask you to hold the fort, but I can't carry Phillips about with me any more, he's too heavy, and as you know he's valuable and can't be left.'

'Right,' Nell said reluctantly. 'I'll stay until I hear.'

'Thank you, darling.' Hester had been standing by the trailer door; now she opened it and stepped outside. 'I'll keep in touch.'

'Aren't you going to tell me where I can contact you?' Nell said, rather alarmed. Her mother's initial self-blame and bitterness seemed to have evaporated and Nell had been congratulating herself that she would soon be able to return to Marushka's, but this was an entirely unexpected development. 'You can't just walk out on me!'

She was half-laughing, but her mother returned to the trailer at once, her face serious.

'You're right, darling, you should know where I can be found. I'm going back to Pengarth.'

'To *Pengarth*?' Nell's voice rose to something perilously akind to a squeak. 'After all these years? Why on earth . . . ?'

Hester came back into the trailer and sat on the edge of one of the chairs. After a moment's hesitation, Nell sat, equally uneasily, on the other.

'Why? I'm – I'm not sure. I think it's because I know now how deeply I wronged Ugly Jack by refusing to let him show his love for me. And I got to thinking that I might have wronged Matthew too. He was a sick man when he threatened me, perhaps not even in his right mind. And I'm not afraid to go back now, not any more. What could they do to me, after all? If Matthew wanted to kill me once he won't want to do it now, too much time has passed, and Mr Geraint can scarcely take you away from me – you went of your own accord when you joined the Land Army. So you see, I feel I owe it to Matthew to face up to things. He might be wanting a divorce, he might want to say he was sorry . . . Anyway, I'm going back.'

'Have you ever thought that Matthew might have left, too? And Mr Geraint?' Nell asked softly. 'Time hasn't stood still for any of us, Mum.'

'I've thought. They could both be dead come to that. Mr Geraint was fifty-five when we left so he's sixty-seven now. Even Matthew will be in his fifties. But I must *know*, Nell. I must try to put things right.'

'And you don't want me with you?'

'I do, believe me I do. But first I couldn't let you walk into . . . into whatever awaits me, and second, if I leave the trailer and Phillips and the jukels, what do you think will be left when I come back? Folk have their work cut out keeping body and soul together for themselves, they don't have time for other people's responsibilities.' She stood up, yawned, patted her mouth with the back of her hand. 'Oh, I'm so tired, I've been going over it all in my head for nights and nights, trying to think what best to do, but in the end I decided. My train leaves in less than an hour, so if you've done cross-questioning me I'll be on my way.'

She was smiling now, her cheeks faintly pink, her eyes shining. She's quite looking forward to it, Nell realised with some surprise. She's considering it a challenge – and a meeting of old friends. How very strange, when you think how she's dreaded even a mention of Pengarth over the years, yet all the time, underneath, she wanted . . . what? Matthew? Mr Geraint? Pengarth itself, the cottage, the castle? I don't suppose she knows herself, Nell concluded, standing up as well. But at last she's got the courage to look her past in the face, at last she's going to find out.

'I've done my questioning for now,' Nell said. She moved forward impulsively and kissed her mother's cheek, clutched her hand. 'I wish I could go with you, but I'll stay here. You will write?'

'I promise.' Hester patted Nell's cheek, then gently disengaged her fingers. 'Take good care of yourself.'

Nell stood on the trailer's top step and watched her mother out of sight, saw her stepping neatly and swiftly across the ice and mud until she reached the road and disappeared around a corner. Only then did she return to the fireside, feeling strangely alone, strangely flat.

My mother's going to have an adventure, and all I'm going to have is another cup of tea, she told herself, tilting the pot. Oh well, I'd best write to Ted and explain. Fortunately his act isn't on for another six weeks. Surely things will have returned to normal by then?

Hester walked up the once-familiar road, under the trees leaning over the tall, grey stone wall. She walked slowly, remembering.

Here she had come as a bride, bowling along in the pony-cart, flushed and excited at the thought of seeing her new home, marvelling at the size of the estate behind the wall which seemed to go for miles, glancing at Matthew's profile every now and then, thinking him wonderfully handsome, wonderfully kind.

She had come this way when she was expecting Nell, too. Proud, walking with her back very straight and her stomach as stuck out as she could make it. She was proud because this baby was her very own creation, never mind the part Matthew had played. The child would be her contribution to their married life, the only mark she had managed to make despite all her hopes.

Hester had longed for her own little home, but the lodge was so dark and so full of Coburn possessions that at first she hadn't been able to buy so much as a tea-tray to make her mark on the place. What was more, orphans don't have photographs of their ancestors but the Coburns must have taken pictures of every event in their family from the time photography was invented. She remembered the dismay with which she had greeted the main bedroom with its walls almost papered with photographs of ancient Coburns in lace collars and tall hats – but the balance would be redressed when she had her own little baby. Dreamily, she imagined the photographs they would have taken, of herself in a big picture hat and a muslin dress, her hair flowing freely over her shoulders, the baby sitting on her knee smiling up into her face while Matthew stood behind them, a fond but pro- prietorial hand on her shoulder. Then pictures of the baby grown to be a toddler, swinging on a swing in the orchard, and perhaps another baby, all lace and curls . . .

She didn't remember much about Nell's birth save that the doctor told Matthew his young wife was a marvellous girl, brave as a lion.

'Plenty of grunts and effort but not even one small scream,' he said as he emerged from the bedroom and handed the proud father his red-faced little daughter. 'Go and give her a kiss, man – that's a wife to be proud of!' She even remembered the kiss, the feel of Matthew's soft lips on her forehead, the awed reverence as he looked at her and then at the child.

She had not deserved all the praise of course, because she had longed to scream her head off, particularly at the moment of birth when she honestly thought she was splitting in two. But she knew better than to scream and make a fuss: this was her baby, the child she had longed for, what a greeting it would have been for little Helen if the first sound she heard were her mother's shrieks of pain!

Then there had been the day she had taken Helen – odd how easily the name she had not used for a dozen years came into her mind when she thought of the past – into Rhyl for a check-up at the hospital. They said she was wonderfully fit and so was Hester, and she had got on the bus in the rain, and got off it in the rain, and walked the mile and a half back from the village with the baby under her coat, beneath this very wall. Matt had picked her up and, later, they had made love again and it had been all right, very much all right, and she had been the happiest, luckiest girl in the whole of Flintshire, in the whole of Wales . . . the whole world!

So when, precisely, had the serpent entered her Eden? Where had it gone wrong? Then the road curved, following the curve of the wall, and the lodge was before her.

It looked smaller. Odd, that. And a great deal grimmer. Dirtier, too. Matthew had whitewashed it when Nell had started school and though Mr Geraint had grumbled and complained, it had looked much nicer, or she and Matthew thought so anyway. But now it was grey with green streaks again and the little windows were dull and cracked, the curtains falling down behind the glass.

It's empty, Hester thought, and for the first time, doubt and dismay clouded her mind. He's gone; perhaps they've both gone, and I've come here on a fool's errand. But she was here, so it was no use turning back without making certain. Resolutely, she walked between the wrought-iron gates and up to the lodge. She knocked timorously on the front door.

No one answered. After a few moments she abandoned the front door and went around to the little yard at the back. Her linen line, green with age and neglect, still swung too low, she had to duck to avoid it. The pole that Matthew had made her was there too, propped up against the coal house, but it had split at the fork and was now a travesty of its former self. No one has hung washing out here for some time, Hester told herself, and found that she was shivering.

What had she done when she left Matthew twelve years ago?

He had threatened her and she had been a silly little girl, afraid, confused, but oh God, what had she done? She approached the back door and, without really thinking, put her hand on the latch. It swung open easily, on well-oiled hinges, and there was the kitchen. Just the same only not so clean and spruce. I did keep things nicely, considering I'd never known a real home, Hester thought, surprised at how she remembered working in this room. Scrubbing the quarry-tiled floor, doing the washing in the low stone sink, cooking on the big central table, making bread, setting it to prove, putting the balls of dough into the old-fashioned oven and then, when the sweet scent told her the time was right, bringing the golden-brown loaves out to cool on a tray in the yard outside.

She looked slowly round the room, remembering. Before they had left, the kitchen had begun to feel like home, like her own place at last. She'd bought a fat yellow jug for the dresser and kept it filled with flowers when there were flowers to pick. The jug was still there, but empty now. And there were her books . . . yes, a cookery book by Mrs Beeton, some old novels, a play, half a set of Dickens which Mr Geraint had brought her back from market . . .

A chill struck her and she looked around, thinking the back door must have blown ajar, but it hadn't, it was just memories again. It had been Mr Geraint who had killed the little, struggling plant of love and trust which she and Matthew had been growing. Mr Geraint with his casual lust which hadn't included the slightest interest in her mind or personality – and me too young and silly to realise, too in awe of a man so much my senior. Too eager, she remembered sadly, for the physical pleasures I had known in his arms to question the rightness of it.

Once he had got her up at the castle, she had been too busy to work on her relationship with Matthew. Too tired when she reached home after a hard day's work to do more than the minimum here. She had been content to let the delicate plant shrivel, she had taken Matthew for granted. Fool that she had been, she had lived for the touch of Mr Geraint's hand on hers, for the glance which said *Come up to my room*, for the promise, always unfulfilled, that some day, at some time, something wonderful would happen between them. Then the climax, the crunch. Mr Geraint claiming Helen; Matthew accusing her of adultery; the pair of them chasing her away from everything she knew and held dear. If I'd been older, wiser, Hester mourned now, gazing around at the pleasant, untidy kitchen, I'd have been able to handle it. I'd have told Matt to pull himself together, told Mr Geraint to do his worst, because when it came to the crunch how could he have taken Nell? Matt wouldn't have let him, if I'd said 'your dear Mr Geraint is a liar, he did seduce me when I was only a child but all the rest is wishful thinking,' Matthew would have believed me, would have scorned Mr Geraint, kept me close to him, defended me.

The only thing wrong with that little scenario, Hester reminded herself now, standing in the kitchen and looking round her, was that it was basically untrue, a downright wicked lie. Because although Mr Geraint had seduced her, she'd been unfaithful to Matthew without any particular qualms for five years, ever since Nell's second birthday. And she had known as soon as she'd seen that family portrait in the Long Gallery that Mr Geraint had a point: Nell was remarkably like his ancestress.

Still. Nell was a big girl now, she would be twenty in a couple of months. Unbelievable, that I'm the mother of a young woman of twenty, Hester told herself now, looking instinctively in the little round mirror beside the back door to check that she hadn't gone grey overnight. She had not. A lively, dark-haired woman looked back at her, a woman in her mid-thirties who carried her years lightly, whose skin was as clear as a young girl's and whose figure, Hester knew without looking, had benefited from being kept in trim by wrestling with Phillips, doing the hard physical work necessary to show off the abilities of a very large python.

However, it was no use being complacent, not if Matthew had left. She went through into the bedroom, feeling like a spy in a friend's camp but determined to find out for sure who lived in the lodge now and, if necessary, where Matthew had gone. The bedroom was almost the same, almost but not quite. Hester stared around her at the chest of drawers, the washstand, the bit of curtaining which, in the old days, had hidden her small supply of dresses and skirts. What was different? Something was, there was something . . . she saw it suddenly. The curling pictures of long-dead Coburn relatives had been removed. There was only one photograph left and she knew what it would be before she crossed the room to look hard at the faded sepia print.

It was the only photograph they had ever had taken and it showed her, Matthew and Helen on the baby's third birthday. Nell sat on her mother's knee, small and serious, grasping a rag doll the photographer had given her. Hester was looking straight at the camera, smiling and proud, and Matthew stood behind them, in his stiff best suit, with one hand on her shoulder and his gaze, like hers, fixed on the camera lens. A small, embarrassed smile hovered round his mouth and for the first time it struck Hester that Matthew reminded her of someone. Who? He wasn't at all like Ugly Jack; her heart squeezed painfully as she remembered that scarred, broken-nosed, much-loved face. No, Matt was nothing like Jack; she looked critically at the photograph of the man who had been only a couple of years older than she was now when it was taken, and saw that he was very handsome. He had a broad forehead, a straight, shortish nose, very dark silky hair that overhung his tanned brow and dark eyes which met hers, even in the photograph, straight on.

Gently, Hester touched the photograph with her fingers. I'm sorry for what I did to you, the touch said. I've come back to make what reparation I can, and at least I now know two things for sure. One is that you still live here, in this rather grim little cottage, and the other is that you haven't married because no woman, no matter how careless, would let the place get into the state I've seen today.

Having done what she set out to do Hester returned to the kitchen. She glanced at the unlit range, then at the table, then at the clock. Matthew would no doubt be having his midday meal at the castle. There could be no harm in lighting the range, making herself a pot of tea . . .

There was food in the pantry, but not very much. She found tea, a twist of sugar, some flour and lard. A further search produced a tin of stewing steak, some dried-up carrots, a few whiskery potatoes and an enormous leathery swede. A quick visit to the vegetable garden at the back yielded several heavy heads of dark green spring cabbage which she harvested triumphantly. There was a heel of bacon fat in the meat-safe; that stewed with the cabbage would be the makings of a meal.

Having lit the fire and made sure it was going well, Hester crossed the yard and climbed into the apple loft. A few wrinkled, rosy-cheeked fruit still nestled in their straw beds, so she put them in the pockets of her black coat. The kettle was boiling so she made tea and had to drink it black since Matthew either didn't bother with milk or had taken the day's supply to the castle with him, but it put new life into her, refreshed her after her long journey.

When the tea was drunk she went into the bedroom and pulled back the curtain and there was her faded blue cotton dress, her checked skirt, and the item she was searching for, the big, white, all-enveloping wrap-around apron she had always worn for cooking. She took it down and put it on, trying not to let her lip tremble as she did so. It smelt freshly laundered; she guessed that every now and then Matthew must take her clothes out and put them through the wash. He had always been handy; she could imagine him washing her things in the low stone sink, whistling softly between his teeth as he did so, thinking about her. Perhaps even missing her. Then hanging them on the dreadful green linen line, watching for rain, hurrying to bring them in, ironing them with the nice new iron she'd bought just before she left, replacing them behind the curtain in their bedroom . . .

You stupid thing, Hester scolded herself, brushing tears off her lashes and hurrying over to the pantry, you're nothing but a sentimental fool; if he washed your clothes it was to stop them going mouldy and smelling the house out, not in the hope that you'd come back. Now get on with the job in hand and stop being so daft. Obeying her own instructions wasn't difficult once she got started, because she had always enjoyed cooking. She made soup with the spring cabbage and bacon fat, stewing it slowly on top of the oven; while that cooked she made a suet crust and lined a pudding bowl, then tipped in the tin of stewing steak and a finely chopped onion. She wrapped the pudding in a cloth and put a pan of water beside the soup, then turned her attention to concocting a dessert.

An apple pie was soon made. Once it was cooking she peeled the potatoes and carrots and stood them on the back of the fire to simmer. She searched again for milk in the outhouses, under the sink – a custard would have gone down well with the apple pie – but could find none. She thought of dried milk and, sure enough, there was half a tin on the back of a shelf, so custard was a possibility.

Her preparations over, she peeped into the front room. It hadn't changed at all; heavy, over-stuffed furniture, dark oil paintings, too many reminders of other people, other times. China shepherdesses and goose girls, china ladies in crinoline dresses, their skirts full of primroses or violets, china dogs with bows under their chins and cats with baskets full of kittens. And then there were the Presents; Presents from Gt Yarmouth, from Blackpool, from Rhyl, from Colwyn Bay – they crowded every surface not packed with shepherdesses. How I hated cleaning them, how I resented every tiny hand, every dainty, flower-encrusted apron, Hester remembered, awed at her own youthful disgust with these pretty, powerless things. What a lot of energy I wasted, just wishing them elsewhere, when I might just as well have enjoyed their beauty, their sheer uselessness.

Matthew had kept the front room fairly clean, fairly tidy. The ornaments weren't washed as regularly as they should have been – many a tiny hand was grimy, many a petal blackened above or below – but he had plumped the cushions, dusted the mantel, arranged the religious books on the shelves by the fireplace. The windows were dirty though. The curtains hung, heavy with neglect, pulled off their rings here, unravelling there. He never could mend, Hester remembered. But he's done his best, poor Matthew, to keep things decent – I wonder what Mr Geraint has done, up at the castle?

She returned to the kitchen, checked that the food would not be ready for some time, then took off her apron, donned her coat and went out of the house. She began to walk up the drive towards the castle but, oddly enough, the nearer she got the more nervous she became. There it was, against its cliff, brooding, magnificent, seeming to scowl at her as she approached. She could just about make out the tangle of the wild garden, tamed by winter but still there, when she decided that enough was enough; she would go no further. She would return to the lodge and keep an eye on the dinner. She retraced her steps and as soon as the lodge was in view and the castle behind her, her nervousness vanished and she rebuked herself once more for silliness.

No one can hurt me, she thought, stepped out briskly nevertheless, but Geraint is a powerful man; he might still try to do me harm. He might not want me anywhere near him, not after all that happened. She stopped just short of the lodge. The sun came out from behind the clouds and shone, pale but bright, upon the cottage with the thread of smoke emerging from the chimney stack. It looked pleasant from here, homely. It looked, Hester thought wistfully, quite a nice place in which to live out one's days. Then she shook herself and set off for the back door at a quick pace. She would take a look at the apple pie, check the water level in the pudding saucepan and then make herself another cup of tea and have a sit-down while she drank it. Matthew was unlikely to return until evening, but you never knew . . .

Matthew came slowly out of the barn where he had stabled the pony and went towards the cart-shed. Best clean down the wheels before he snugged the little vehicle down, and perhaps he ought to clean out the bottom-boards, too. Pigs were dirty travellers even in deep litter and no one, himself least of all, would be pleased if pig-dung dried on the inside of the cart.

He was walking towards the shippon when he happened to glance down the drive and stopped short, staring open-mouthed. For a moment he had thought smoke was coming out of the lodge chimney, but it must have been his imagination; he remembered not bothering to light the fire this morning, cold though it was. No point, he had thought, since he was going down to the market in St Asaph and would not be back in time for his midday dinner. He had intended to eat at the Plough, believing that he would still be waiting for the beasts he wanted at dinnertime. He had not known that the best young pigs would be in the first lot sold or that nothing else would appeal to him.

He turned towards the shippon and drew the cart towards the pump in the middle of the yard just as Dewi rounded the corner pushing a barrow.

'What, back already are you, Matt?' the elderly man asked. 'No pigs good enough this mornin', then?'

'Bought 'em,' Matthew said briefly. 'They'm in the sties. Ten, a dozen nice 'uns. Take a look.'

'I will. Best give you an 'and wi' cleanin' that cart first, though, eh? 'Twon't tek the pair of us more'n ten minute at the most.'

'Where's Willi?' Matthew asked suddenly as they sloshed buckets of water from the pump into the flat-bottomed cart. 'Thought I saw smoke comin' from the lodge chimney just now, but I didn't put a light to the fire this mornin', thinkin' I'd be at market for me dinner.'

'Willi's cuttin' back the roses, young Ted an' Bertie are hedgin' and ditchin' out on Cuckoo pen and the lads are fetchin' a trailer o' gravel from the quarry for the paths, like you said,' Dewi said placidly. 'And there *is* smoke comin' from your chimney, man. I seed it when I barrowed the muck past the gate'ouse, just now.'

'Oh aye? Well, when the cart's finished I'll get down, take a look,' Matthew said. 'I never lock the back door; perhaps someone saw me come back early and put a match to it for me.'

'Probably Mrs Alice,' Dewi said, shooting a cautious look at the other man. 'Likes you, Mrs Alice do. Or she could've sent one o' the girls down there to give an 'and, like.'

Matthew snorted. 'My foot! She's too busy indoors to bother much wi' me and I can't see her sendin' anyone else.'

'Put my nose round the door I could, as I go 'ome for my dinner,' Dewi volunteered. 'Goin' right by I am . . . havin' dinner wi' Willi's old 'oman today we are. How'd that suit?'

'Mebbe,' Matthew said. 'One more bucketful will do it. Pass the yard brush, will you?'

Hester set the table. She put out a fine white cloth which she had only used half a dozen times in her married life. She found the frail silver and bone cutlery which had been a present to some long-dead Coburn woman from an employer, and in the garden under the great grey wall, just where she had expected, she found a cluster of early snowdrops.

There had been a little green glass vase which she had particularly liked for snowdrops; she searched the cupboards and found it, whole and unchipped but remarkably dirty. Matthew's housekeeping had clearly not extended to unused china and glass. She washed it with soap and water until it sparkled, then put the snowdrops in it and set it on the middle of the cloth-covered table. There was a wonderful smell from the meat pudding, so she popped plates in the oven to warm and took off her cooking apron.

When the back door opened, she looked up – and for the first time the enormity of what she had done struck her like a blow in the face. She was ashamed, terrified, shocked, all at the same time, and all she could think of was that she mustn't be found here, not only trespassing but virtually taking over the home of the man she had abandoned, left to his own devices for more than twelve years.

She dropped to her knees, below the level of the table and then, when the door neither opened wider nor shut, she peeped around the edge, keeping all but an eye hidden.

A man stood there. She could tell that he was staring, dumbstruck, at the table, sniffing the good smell of food, wondering what on earth had happened. She could not see who he was though, because he was hidden by the door . . . then he came forward and she saw him.

Matthew. Older, greyer, but still indubitably her husband. And he didn't look pleased; he just looked angry.

All her old doubts and fears came rushing back; he had said he would kill her if he ever set eyes on her again and here she was, mucking about, hiding behind his table, cooking his food, puzzling him and making him angry. You're not only a fool, Hester, you're a coward, she told herself . . . and stood up.

They stared at each other, standing like stone, eyes fixed, breath held. It could not have been more than ten seconds before he moved, but it felt like a lifetime to Hester. Then he said, 'Hes! It *is* you, isn't it?' and there was such pleasure, mingled with bewilderment, in his voice that Hester took a couple of steps towards him and burst into tears.

It was probably the best thing she could have done; Matthew had always been wonderful when she had been upset. In a trice she was cradled in his arms, she could feel his breath on her hair, the warm strength of him against her body. Thus held, she knew without a shadow of doubt that he still loved her, that his love had never wavered.

'My darling girl, is it really you or is this some kind of dream? I never meant it, you know, I'd never have hurt you or the baby. You should have known it, should have trusted me! I'd been concussed, it does strange things to a man. Oh Hes, I can't believe it, I can't believe it!'

Hester clung to him and sobbed into his rough grey shirt and thought of how she had treated him, how she had behaved to Ugly Jack, and hugged him hard, speaking through her sobs. 'Matt, I'm so sorry, I was a fool, but I've come to my senses at last. Nell's a big girl now, she's well, she's longing to see you. Can you forgive me for running off like that?'

'Course I can,' he said at once, stroking the side of her wet face. 'Course I forgive you, Hes my love. If only you'd seen my advertisements, come to me then . . . but no use cryin' over spilt milk. Are you back for good? You wouldn't leave me again, Hes? I don't think I could stand it again.'

Hester thought, briefly and even a little regretfully, of the trailer that was now hers, of Phillips and her friends, of the life she had enjoyed so much with Ugly Jack by her side. Then she tried to imagine what life must have been like for Matthew, alone for twelve years in this cottage, wanting her, wanting the child he had thought was his own little girl, unable to find them, always searching.

'I'm back for good,' she said, cuddling closer. 'If you want me, I'm here for you. I'll never leave you again.'

*

385

They had a lot to talk about, and even the talk was comfortable, easy, Matthew refraining from all the questions which must have crowded his tongue.

'You've been away, but you're back. All I'll ask is, are you still free, Hes? Free to stay with me.'

'Yes. I was working, but Nell's seeing to that. What about you, Matt?'

He smiled. They were sitting on either side of the table, having finished eating.

'There's never been no one but you for me, Hes. If I hadn't thought you'd come back I dunno what I'd ha' done. But Mr Geraint always said it were a mistake, that you'd come to your senses, realise it were the blow on the head talkin' and not Matthew Coburn. He helped me a lot, Hes – the old man ain't all self, despite what I've thought in the past. So I hung on, even when it seemed he were wrong. And here you are . . . oh, my dearest girl!'

Hester looked down at her hands; they were trembling. She knew she would have to ask about Mr Geraint, but suppose something in her tone reminded Matthew of the words flung at him that day on the mountain? Because it was clear he had not remembered them, and equally clear that Mr Geraint could never have repeated them.

She looked across at him, and the question came to her again: who did he remind her of, who? Then she put it from her; it didn't matter, what mattered was reconstructing their lives and going forward, this time together, hand in hand.

'Matt, shouldn't you be getting back to work? I wouldn't want to make trouble for you, particularly since you say Mr Geraint's been good to you these past years.'

Matthew smiled. 'He ain't here at present, Hes. It's a long story – d'you want to hear it now, or later? Only I'm in charge up there; perhaps I ought to go back for twenty minutes or so, see things are going on right.'

'You go off then, while I wash up and clear,' Hester said. She was longing to hear what had happened in her absence, but there was no point in rushing things. Matthew had suffered enough through her, without adding to it. 'Don't rush, just do your usual work and then come back. What would you like for your tea, Matt?

A slow smile spread across Matthew's face. He got to his feet and Hester followed suit. 'You – you won't disappear? You'll wait for me? I could just go up and tell 'em how to go on, only there's a deal of work for me to do and I'd be happier gettin' it settled. Why don't you come up wi' me, meet 'em all?'

'Not today, Matt,' Hester said, standing on tiptoe to smooth the silky, greying hair from his brow. 'Don't *worry*, I shan't stir from this place. But there isn't much food in the house – I've brought my ration book, but I'm not registered here. I could walk into town and see if Evans the meat remembers me . . .'

'No,' Matthew said at once. 'Don't! I'll bring something back from the castle, they always seem to have grub in. We killed an extra pig last back-end so there's plenty o' bacon and I'll fetch a pan o' lard and mebbe some eggs. And I'll cadge a loaf off Mrs Alice. They'll be all agog that you're home, Hes.'

'Right,' Hester said, not asking about Mrs Alice though she longed to do so. She gave him a squeeze, kissed his cheek, then released him. 'See you later on, then.'

While Matthew was gone, Hester cleaned. How she cleaned! She found an old bar of carbolic soap, cracked and dried out, and soaked it into softness. Then she got every ornament out of the front room and washed them lovingly. She brushed, dusted, polished, took the curtains off their rods, cleaned the windows with vinegar and water, set the curtains in the tin bath to soak, then got out the crock of flour and began to peel and grate potatoes. She would make potato cakes with the rest of the lard, since Matthew had said he would bring more when he came in. And if he did get eggs he should have one of those cakes Ugly Jack had been so fond of, made with carrots instead of dried fruit but tasting grand, or so Jack always said.

Because she was so busy, the afternoon passed in a trice; she hadn't finished when the back door opened and Matthew, his arms full of food, stood there, grinning at her. 'So it weren't a dream,' he said, beginning to unload his burdens on to the kitchen table. 'I told 'em you was back, Hester . . . Willi's chin nigh hit the floor and Dewi couldn't get over sayin' how glad he were. Mrs Alice has sent you all sorts . . . I'll put 'em away in the pantry, shall I?'

'You do that while I finish the front room,' Hester said, bustling past him with a tray loaded with china ornaments. 'Then wash down and I'll start our tea.'

After tea, they settled again before the fire, only this time both in the one chair.

How did I forget all this, for all those years? Hester asked herself, with the front of the range open and the flames strong enough to light the room as well as warm it. How could I have doubted Matthew's goodness when I'd seen it every day for years and years?

'Well now, who's goin' to start?'

'You,' Hester said quickly. 'You were going to tell me where Mr Geraint was and what had happened.'

Matthew chuckled. 'Tis a good tale,' he admitted. 'After you left, love, the old man weren't himself, not for many a month. He did his best to find you, helped me wi' advertisements and the like, and then he said to leave it 'cos you'd come home, he was sure you would. But he got awful moody and difficult, we couldn't keep staff, the place began to fall off . . .'

'Oh, but he didn't care about us,' Hester protested. 'He was fond of Nell, I grant you, but I was just his cook-housekeeper.'

She waited, dreading Matthew might remember that Mr Geraint had claimed she was very much more than his housekeeper, that he had called her his mistress. Matthew had called her an adulteress, but he wasn't in his right mind at the time, he had said so. Whether he remembered later who had told him what was open to question, but she would have to know; she could not stay here if he was waiting for her confession all the while.

'You made that old ruin seem like a home, Hester. Without your care it went down'ill fast; and as you say, he were rare fond of our Nell.' Matthew's lazy smile had that edge of pride to it which Hester remembered from the faded photograph. 'Who wouldn't? Will she come back, Hes? Just to see us, mebbe?'

'She'll come back,' Hester promised. 'Look, Matt, I don't

want to tell you anything which will distress you, but – but Mr Geraint sometimes did try to –'

She was interrupted. He turned in the chair and kissed her mouth, astonishing her with the passion, kept in check but still self-evident, she could feel running through him. Then he drew back. He was breathing hard but the expression in his eyes was understanding. 'D'you think I didn't know that, sweetheart? He were always the same with any woman, why even Mrs Cled, little Mrs Clifton, but that didn't matter, so long as it were me you loved, see? I knew he wouldn't go too far, but it weren't in him to leave a pretty lass alone. So no word o' that, hey? That's best forgot.'

Hester heaved a great sigh. She was sure, now, that he knew there had been something between her and Mr Geraint, but he didn't know how much and didn't want to know either. She patted his knee, then clasped her hands in her lap, shocked by the stab of sexual excitement which had made her want to turn in his arms and admit to an equal desire to that she had sensed in him. We'll get all our explanations over first, she told herself, not finishing the sentence even in her mind.

'Right, we'll forget it then. So where's Mr Geraint now? And when will he be back?'

'Wait on, best have a round tale,' Matthew said, then paused to sort out his thoughts. 'The summer after you went, Mr Geraint was left a property, in Kent. I don't mind tellin' you, he was in a bad way. He'd taken to drinkin', he didn't keep himself clean . . . he missed the pair of you almost as badly as I did. So when he heard Uncle Leo had made him his heir, he decided to leave. He offered me to go with him or stay here, in charge, like.

'After he'd been there a year he got this gal, pretty little thing, but far too young for him, if you ask me . . . Dolly Frost her name was. It can't have been more'n a month before she were sharing his bed, insisting that he got someone in to help her or she'd go, and managing him better than you could possibly guess to look at her.'

'What did she look like?' Hester asked. She had felt a stab of something like envy and was intent on banishing it. 'Dark,

I suppose?'

Matthew shook his head. 'I've only clapped eyes on her the once, when he brought her up here. And she isn't dark, she's fair as a lily. Tall, slim, wi' a haughty little nose which she kept cocked in the air when she spoke to us, and big, light blue eyes. Hair the colour of clotted cream, white skin . . . oh, she were pretty, all right, we could all see it. But Mr Geraint, he's fair besotted. I reckon it hits you hardest when you're old, and Mr G ain't no chicken.'

'Don't say he's going to marry her!' Hester exclaimed, wide-eyed. 'I thought he was far too fond of his independence.'

'He hasn't yet, but she's got him under her thumb, that's for sure, and she won't let him play around,' Matthew said with a certain satisfaction. 'When he tried she went off. The old man followed her, pleaded wi' her, I guess, and got her back – under certain conditions.'

'What?' Hester asked eagerly. 'What sort of conditions, Matt?'

'She didn't go for marriage, so that shows she's got sense. She wants to stay in Kent, doesn't want to come back here – well, she took one look at us and Pengarth and you could tell she thought we were a rough old lot and the castle a heap. She wanted a bit of money put by, for later. He laughed when he told me, but it's my bet he paid it over meek as a lamb. He come up here and explained what had happened and put me in charge and ever since it's been a visit every couple o' years, wi' the old man lookin' older and tireder each time, just to see all's right here. *She* hasn't been here since,' he added. 'Not int'rested, particularly now she's got what she wants.'

'Gosh,' Hester said inadequately. 'What about this Mrs Alice, then?' She turned in her seat to look up at him. 'I was sure she was Mr Geraint's latest!'

Matthew looked self-conscious. A flush reddened his cheek-bones and his eyes tried to avoid hers. 'Oh, I got her in. The old man don't give a toss about the castle but he knew I'd not keep staff if I couldn't feed 'em, dinnertimes, and see to the harvest. I've got extra men, too. The land and outbuildings are in good heart, the stock's healthy, the crops are fine. With all of us pullin' together we've done a better job for Mr Geraint than he did for himself. You must come up and tek a look in a day or two, when you've settled down.'

'I will,' Hester said faintly. Her mind was almost unable to take in Matthew's story. Fancy a chilly blonde, called Dolly of all things, managing to wind Mr Geraint round her little finger to the extent of keeping him away from Pengarth! A thought occurred to her. 'Are there any kids, Matt? Mr Geraint did like children, as I recall.'

'No kids,' Matthew said. 'I don't reckon he can, Hes, if you understand me. Otherwise there'd have been half-a-dozen brats wi' his face on 'em be now.'

Hester swallowed. Let him go on believing that, she found herself praying. Let dear Matthew go on believing it!

'So now it's your turn, Hes. What were you doing while we were turnin' the Pengarth estate into a decent sort o' proposition?'

'Right from the start?' At Matthew's nod she nodded too. 'Fair enough. I'll keep it short, but we had it hard when we first left, Nell and I. Until I joined a travelling fair we had nothing to call our own.'

He stared at her, eyes rounding. 'A travelling *fair*?' His eyes swept her from top to toe, a slow, loving appraisal, which set her tingling. 'Well, you weren't the fat woman, that's for sure, so what did you do?'

'I wrestled with a snake. I was Hester the Snake Woman, and I had this huge snake, Phillips, who pretended to fight with me and I had to charm him so that he gradually calmed down. You know the sort of thing.'

'A snake called *Phillips*? Why Phillips, for Gawd's sake?'

'Matt, how practical you are,' Hester sighed. 'The man who first brought him to the fair was Reg Phillips and the last bit just stuck. But he wasn't billed as Phillips, he was Venom, the giant poisonous snake from the South American jungles . . . don't laugh!'

'Can't help it,' Matthew spluttered, wiping tears of mirth from his cheeks. 'Hester my love, how in heaven's name did you get mixed up wi' that little lot? You were always such a practical, sensible young woman.'

'Hunger, desperation – and the fair folk were very good to me,' Hester said soberly. 'I know it sounds funny, well, it shouldn't, but I suppose it must do since you laughed, but Phillips saved our bacon, mine and Nell's. He gave us a living and something to live for, because when we first left . . . but that's all far in the past. It was thanks to Phillips that we did so well. Why, in the end we even got our own trailer.'

'What's a trailer? And what sort of snake was he?' Matt asked, fascinated. 'I didn't know the poisonous sort were big enough to wrestle with.'

'He wasn't poisonous, not really, that was just for the flatties,' Hester said. 'Fair folk live in trailers, they call them living wagons. As for Phillips, he's a python and he must be ten feet long at least. He's really heavy now though, it's all I can do to handle him.'

'And you've left Nell with a creature like that? My little Nell?' Matthew's voice rose. 'Hester my love, have you done right?'

'Nell's taller than me and nearly as strong,' Hester said defensively. 'Besides, she isn't working Phillips, she's just taking care of him. And if you want me back, truly want me, then I suppose I'll have to retire the old feller and . . . bring him back here to live.'

Matthew blinked, then rallied. 'If that's what you want,' he said gamely. 'There's always the chicken-run, I suppose.'

Hester chuckled and leaned up to caress Matthew's thin brown cheek. 'It's all right, if Nell doesn't want to work him, I'll give him to a zoo, unless I can find someone else to take him. He's a gentle creature though, quite content with a place by the fire in winter and the warmth of the sun in summer. But he's valuable; I'm sure either Nell or one of the showmen will take him on and willing.'

'Good,' Matthew said, not troubling to hide his relief. 'Now I don't want to ask too many questions and I'm sure you don't want to answer them, but . . . Hes, you didn't remarry?'

'I didn't,' Hester promised him. 'I shared living accommodation but never a bed, I promise you, so you can rest easy on that score.'

Matt sighed and got heavily to his feet. He began to clear away the supper dishes, piling them beside the sink. Hester, taking her cue from him, emptied boiling water from the kettle into the stone sink and began to wash up.

'Nor me. Why didn't you take a man though, love? I remember you was warm-hearted and affectionate.'

'Hot-arsed, you mean,' Hester said grimly, and saw Matthew's eyebrows shoot up; clearly he wasn't used to plain speaking, not after living so long alone. 'Matt, I won't pretend I was ever an angel, but the way I saw it I was married to you and no one else and if I messed around it could only lead to pain and heartbreak. So I kept myself to myself.'

It wasn't exactly true, but it wasn't so far from the truth either, Hester thought defensively. She had never been unfaithful to Matt with anyone but the old man, and, from what Matthew had said, he had known full well the risk he was running, letting her work up at the castle. Besides, it was so long ago, and Mr Geraint was practically a married man now. Did marriage wipe out infidelity? She hoped so.

'That's good,' Matthew said now. He began to dry the dishes. 'What made you come back, love? If you can bear to talk about it, that is.'

'The man who helped me with my act and whose trailer I shared was killed. Nell had moved out years back and I was alone, and it struck me that you might ... might want me back. So here I am.'

Matthew finished the dishes and hung the towel by the range to dry. He turned and looked straight at Hester, his gaze candid.

'Time we thought about bed. Hester, my love, do you want to sleep in Nell's room for a while?'

It's now or never, Hester told herself. Do you really mean to do right by Matthew, or are you going to hold back, keep something in reserve? After all, it would be fair enough. She had not shared a room, let alone a bed, with this man for a dozen years, it would be like sleeping with a stranger. No one would blame her if she asked for a few days grace.

'No thanks, Matt; we'll start as we mean to go on,' she

said steadily. 'We've been wed on and off for nearly twenty years, it's no time to turn coy with one another. I've shared your meal and your board; later on, if you agree, we'll share your bed.'

She turned to smile at her husband. His face had flushed like a young girl's, but the eyes he turned on her were hot with longing.

'I agree,' he said huskily. 'Oh Hester, I've dreamed of this moment!'

Fifteen

When the letter arrived saying that Hester had moved back in with Matthew, and that everything was fine, Nell was, for a moment, dismayed.

She was stuck here, then. Oh, Hester wanted her to visit them, 'when we've settled down', as she put it, but when was that likely to be? The letter, even after a second and third reading, said so little.

We've agreed the past is best forgotten and we're going to take it from here, Hester wrote, having broken the news that she and Matthew were going to live together as man and wife once more. *Mr Geraint left years ago when he inherited property down south and Matthew is running everything and doing it very well, furthermore. He told me something I didn't know – that he now actually owns the lodge outright, so we'll always have a home here, no matter who inherits the castle. Do you want to work Phillips, darling? If so it would ease things in a way, but if not I'll talk to a zoo. He's got a bit big for a stranger to take on. And Matthew wants to see his grown-up girl very much, when you can arrange it.*

'I think Phillips is a bit big for me,' Nell told Jack's brother, Fred Gulliver, when she explained that her mother would not be returning to the fair, saying only that Hester had got herself a job as housekeeper somewhere in Wales. 'I ought to go over to Marushka's and explain to Ted what's happened. I'm sure he'll understand.'

'Don't do nothing hasty; take a day or two off and go and see what they say at Marushka's,' Fred advised.

'I think you're right, I should see how things stand before I make a move. But what about the trailer, Fred? I suppose you wouldn't move into it for the days I'm away? The fact is, with so many people homeless, I dare not leave it empty.'

'Sure,' Fred said easily. 'I wouldn't mind a few days out of mam's wagon; it's crowded in there.'

'And you'll give an eye to Phillips? He won't need feeding for a week, but then, if I'm held up and still not back, he'll want a rabbit or two. Can you do that?'

'Sure,' Fred repeated. 'Piece o' cake. You run along, there's a good gel. Sort things out. Look, you've paid your rent at the lodgings, 'aven't you? Well, take the old gal a little something, to sweeten your return, like. I'll get you some veg if it'll 'elp.'

Nell accepted the offer gratefully, though she had a nasty suspicion that free vegetables provided by Fred would probably hav: 'een lifted from some unsuspecting farmer's field. Ugly Jack had been the soul of honesty, but Fred was a different kettle of fish. She did not want to look a gift horse in the mouth though, and Fred was right: she would be welcomed back more warmly if she brought some food with her. So the following day Nell pushed the vegetables on top of the change of clothing which was all she had brought with her from Marushka's, said goodbye to the Gullivers, and left. Despite the fact that the country had been at peace for almost seven months, the railways were still chaotic and her journey took eleven hours. At last she found herself, bag in hand, stepping off the train at Tunbridge Wells station and setting out in the sparkling frosty dusk to walk first to her lodgings and then to the spot on the common where Marushka's were over-wintering.

Mrs Pratt smiled broadly when she opened the door and saw who was standing on the doorstep; Nell had always paid her rent promptly, but the landlady must have wondered whether she had lost her lodger for good when the days had gone by without a word.

'It's nice to see you, Miss Makerfield. And how is your poor, dear mother?'

'She's much better, thank you, Mrs Pratt. I've just popped in to leave my bag, then I'll go up to Marushka's. I'll be back for tea, though.' Nell rummaged in her bag and produced her ration book. 'Here you are. Oh, and I thought you might find these useful.'

She handed her landlady the bag of potatoes, some carrots and two large onions which Fred had pressed on her just before she left.

'Well now, it's good of you to think of us,' Mrs Pratt said. 'We'll have a nice shepherd's pie for our tea today. See you later, Miss Makerfield.'

'I shan't be late,' Nell said cheerfully. 'It was a bad journey though; I'm very tired.'

'Amy can't wait to show you the tadpoles,' Mrs Pratt called as Nell walked down the short path to the gate.

As she had walked through the streets and across the common, Nell had almost decided that she would bring the trailer up to Tunbridge Wells and throw in her lot with Marushka's. She was fond of Phillips but she was also a bit afraid of trying to work with him. He was good with Hester, but would he be as good with her? She had seldom handled him and though he had seemed complaisant enough when she did so, she did not have Hester's years of experience behind her. No, working with a python of that size was not for her. She would give him to a zoo or pass him to another showman, if she could find one who would treat him properly. Then she would throw herself wholeheartedly into the job of illusionist's assistant.

Walking back across the common an hour later, however, Nell's plans were in pieces.

She had arrived outside Giovanni's living wagon and knocked on the door, to have it opened by Ariadne.

'Hello, I'm back,' Nell announced. 'Where's Ted?'

'Inside. Nell, there's been a bit of . . .'

A figure appeared behind Ariadne and peered mournfully around her, trying to see Nell in the gathering dusk.

'Who is it, Arry? Who's there?'

'Oh, it's Nell; you'd best come in, love,' Ariadne said.

As she followed the other girl inside, Nell noticed that she was wearing ancient carpet slippers. Odd. Sammy Scarface was a jealous lover and had not encouraged Ariadne to speak to Ted, let alone to visit his trailer.

397

'Sit down, love. Have a cuppa,' Ariadne urged. 'How's your Mum?'

'She's all right, thanks.' Nell accepted the cup, round-eyed, but did not drink. 'What's going on? Have I missed something?'

Ariadne chuckled and held out a slender hand, upon the third finger of which sparkled a gold wedding ring.

'You sure have! Sam didn't like me working wi' Ted again, not one bit, and one night after the show he lay in wait for us, didn't he, love?'

Ted nodded vigorously. 'Aye, that he did. There was a nasty moment when I thought 'e was going to kill me. I was down on the ground wi' me arm bent up behind me and me face rubbed in the mud, I couldn't so much as draw breath . . . then Arry grabbed a plank an' brought it down on the back o' Sammy's 'ead . . .'

'And Sam sort of folded up, breathin' very heavy,' Ariadne finished triumphantly. 'I saw the error of me ways and me and Ted bought the ring. We got hitched two days ago so this time there's no mistake. This is for good.'

'Congratulations, I'm happy for you both,' Nell said sincerely, hastily revising her plans. 'Oddly enough, I came to tell you I'd have to quit, but you were going to tell me the same, anyway. So all's well that ends well, eh?'

Ted's face cleared. 'That's wonderful news,' he said enthusiastically. 'We've been wonderin' what we'd say to you . . . by 'eck, that's good news!'

So, in an atmosphere of great goodfellowship, Nell was told all about the fight, their future, their plans and prospects, and when she had to leave Ariadne insisted on walking back to her lodgings with her.

'You'll mebbe wonder what got into me,' she said shyly, as they walked. 'After I'd took up so – so strong with Sammy Scarface an' all. Well, the truth is, Hes, that it only took a couple o' weeks wi' Sam to mek me see I'd been a fool treatin' Ted the way I did. But then you come along, and Ted obviously took to you, said you were a natural, and I didn't feel I could back down, admit I'd made a mistake. Only then you left to go to your ma, and I started workin' wi' Ted again, and then there was the attack . . .' Ariadne heaved a blissful sigh, hugging herself reminiscently as the two girls walked across the common in the increasing dusk. 'I more or less proposed to him – *me*, Nell, what didn't want to marry anyone who wasn't six foot tall and a bit of a swaggerer! Only I guess Ted's special to me an' always will be.'

'Good for you, I'm glad,' Nell said. 'As for me, I'm going back to my old gaff because my mother's moved back in with my father and says I can have her trailer and her show and everything, so I'm going to be all right too.'

'And you'll find a man of your own,' Ariadne said eagerly. She plainly felt that marriage was the only true happiness for a female of the species. 'There's someone for you, Nell, just see if there ain't!'

Nell explained to Mrs Pratt what had happened, spent a night in her old room and said goodbye to her landlady and Amy the next morning. After another long and boring journey she set out once more to cross a dusky town, tired and irritable, but knowing that she would soon be sitting at her own fireside with a cup of tea made in her own pot.

Or that was what she thought, until she arrived at her mother's trailer. The first thing she noticed was a child, sitting on the steps of her trailer, eating an apple.

'Hello,' Nell said cheerfully, stooping to the child. 'Can you move, please? You're sitting on my step and I want to get past.'

The child stood up. She was a fat little creature of four or five with shaggy hair and an extremely dirty face. She wore a filthy cotton dress, a man's old cardigan and some large wellington boots. Nell had seen her and a couple like her playing around the gaff but could not immediately place her. The child, however, recognised Nell. 'Hello,' she said, giving Nell a hard stare before turning to the door behind her. 'Pa, she's back!'

The trailer door opened. Nell went to pass the child but stopped short. Fred's face was poked round the door in an odd fashion, as though he didn't want her to enter.

'Oh, it's you,' he said shortly. 'What 'appened? You said you'd be gone a few days, mebbe more.'

'Yes, I know, but when I got there I found they didn't need me at all. Ariadne, the girl I replaced, was back,' Nell explained. 'So if you don't mind, Fred, I'll come in now and take the weight off my feet. I'm worn out with all that travelling.'

'Ah,' Fred said heavily. 'Wait 'ere a mo.'

He shut the door. With a sigh, Nell sat down on the lowest step and prepared to wait, with what patience she could muster, until Fred let her into her home.

Two hours later she was sitting in Dr and Mrs Burroughes's kitchen in King's Lynn, telling her tale of woe.

'I asked Fred to stay in the wagon while I was away so that squatters didn't move in,' she said heavily. 'And now he tells me quite blandly that he would have agreed Hester had rights to Ugly Jack's trailer, but these didn't apply to me, and would I please scarper as soon as I liked. I tried to reason with him, I talked to Mr and Mrs Gulliver, but there was no shifting them. The trailer was the property of their dead son and since their dead son's woman moved out, it becomes theirs by right. I have no legal claim whatsoever.'

'I suppose they do have a point, my dear. After all, your mother and Jack were never married, were they, and that counts for something among fair folk. But it seems strange that they wouldn't offer you accommodation of any sort, really unfriendly. What about the snake?'

That was Dr Burroughes, having his tea at the kitchen table, eating his tiny piece of liver with considerable enjoyment, mashing his potatoes with his fork, spinning the meal out with sips of tea.

'They want the snake, too. They say I owe them Phillips, because my mother took from Jack and lived in his van and now the snake's theirs if they want him, which they do. I must admit he'd be an embarrassment to me, without a show-tent or a trailer or anything. And Mr Gulliver did remind me that he'd bought Phillips and all the paraphernalia off the Allinghams, years ago, when Mum wanted to move. As for not offering me accommodation, I do understand that; they have nothing to spare, and this isn't the time of year for a tent. What's more, what could I do? I don't want to work Phillips, to be honest. He's awfully big and tremendously strong.'

'Who *will* work Phillips, though?' Dr Burroughes asked mildly. 'It isn't something just anyone can do, I'd have thought.'

'No, I know that, but Fed's wife, Ivy, has been practising, I understand. She says Phillips likes her, which is probably true. I don't think snakes are very fussy who they like or don't like. She's a strapping girl, Ivy. Probably much more capable than me of controlling the old fellow. Even Mum had a job at times.'

'Well, I think it's downright disgraceful,' Mrs Burroughes said roundly. 'Have some more bread and jam, Nell. I'm sorry about the liver, but you know what rationing's like, if you don't know you're going to have a guest . . .'

'I'm just so grateful for you taking me in,' Nell said, taking another slice of bread and spreading it thinly with blackberry jam. 'Honestly, I shan't be here long. I'll make up my mind what to do first thing in the morning. Only when I realised it was dark and I had very little money and no chance of a bed, I panicked a bit.'

'Not at all, you acted just as you ought. Friends, my dear girl, are always happy to see one another. Now if you've finished eating you can go off to bed and we'll talk again in the morning.'

It took some deciding, but at last Nell made up her mind. She had no home of her own; so what? Neither did thousands of others. She had no job either and no particular prospects. But she had longed for years to see Pengarth again, and this looked like being a good opportunity, while Daniel was still in Aden and not about to return suddenly. He had said it would be a twelve-month tour and he hadn't gone until August, so he wouldn't be back for another five months.

She did not expect Daniel to return to Pengarth when he did come back, of course, but he might search for her. It was odd, how she longed to see him yet dreaded it. They could not marry, she dared not tell him the reason, so it was wiser that they stayed apart, but she knew that if the opportunity arose she would want to see him, if only from a distance.

She had discussed the problem with Mrs Burroughes, who had been both helpful and sympathetic. Their home was hers for as long as she wanted to stay, Mrs Burroughes said, but they understood that she might want to visit her parents. Nell had told them the whole story and they appreciated her invidious position with regard to Matthew but, as Dr Burroughes said, it wasn't so much the physical act of fathering a baby which mattered, it was love, and the upbringing of that baby.

'Matthew may or may not be your natural father, but for the first seven years of your life he treated you with deep and abiding love and gentleness,' he told her. 'A child's real father is the man who acts like one, not the rogue who enjoys a moment's physical intimacy with the mother and then goes off to live his own life. Matthew, my dear child, deserves you. Don't think beyond that.'

On the other hand, they agreed that to drop everything and go up to Pengarth, with the relationship between Hester and Matthew so new and perhaps delicate, would not be fair.

'Leave it a month or two,' Mrs Burroughes urged. 'Let them settle; there are plenty of little jobs here which are well within your means. They'll be wanting girls to pick daffodils any day now; go down to Cuthbert's place and say you'll work in the flower fields. He can always do with another pair of hands.'

'And go down to the gaff and tell Fred Gulliver you understand and bear no grudge,' Dr Burroughes advised. 'They were good to you and your mother for years; don't let a little thing like their need of Jack's living wagon estrange you.'

Nell was happy to take their advice, and Cuthbert said she could take her place in the flower field and willing. 'Girls work better wi' flowers than the fellers,' he said gruffly. 'You've got a bike, I daresay?'

Nell, who had borrowed Mrs Burroughes's old bone-shaker to reach the farm, nodded. 'Yes, I'm all right for getting here. What time do you want me tomorrow?'

He named an early hour and Nell agreed. The money was quite good, and she was sure the work would prove congenial since it was out of doors. Dr and Mrs Burroughes, with their usual easy hospitality, said she could stay with them as long as she liked.

'I'll take a couple of bob and not a penny more. Don't forget, you and your mother are friends,' Mrs Burroughes insisted, when Nell tried to pay half her new salary for her keep. 'After all, it's only until you decide you can go back to Wales and Hester. Now go down to Gullivers, there's a good girl, and make your peace with them. They'll be gone in a day or so and then it'll be too late.'

So, having worked hard at picking daffodils all week, on Saturday morning, before it was light, Nell took herself down to the gaff, where the chaps were already lining the stuff up for departure. She went straight to the Gullivers' big living wagon and made her peace with them all.

'Fred was right, your Jack would have wanted you to have the trailer,' she said, giving fat Mrs Gulliver a hug. 'I'm sorry if I stormed off in a bit of a huff but it was a shock; I couldn't think what I'd do for a minute.'

'Eh, we felt bad, lass,' Mrs Gulliver admitted. 'Tekin' Phillips off you an' all, but fambly comes first, your mam would feel the same. Now sit down a minute and tell us what you're a-doin', then, to keep body an' soul together? Workin' in one of them factories?'

'No, I'm flower picking,' Nell said promptly. 'And staying with Dr and Mrs Burroughes. And I'm happy, really I am.'

'Good. Now keep in touch, understand? Oh, by the way, a letter come for you a day or so back. Ivy, chuck us that letter.'

Ivy, a strapping wench with a high colour and black hair curly as a lamb's fleece, brought the letter over. 'Ere y'are, Nell,' she said shyly. 'I'm that sorry about Phillips an' all, but we get along fine, him an' me. I've allus been fond o' beasts, and he's a nice crittur. Any time you like to visit . . .'

'Thanks Ivy; I know you'll take good care of the old fellow,' Nell said gruffly. 'I'll come in and see you when you over-winter next year, if I'm still in Lynn, that is.'

'Have a cuppa whiles you're here,' Mrs Gulliver suggested. 'Read your letter in the warm. We shan't leave for another hour or two, plenty of time for a cuppa.'

But this Nell would not do, knowing that everyone was longing to get on the road. 'I've got to get back,' she said, standing up. 'I'll read my letter over breakfast. Good luck, everyone, see you next back-end.'

Walking back to the Burroughes's house, she glanced at the letter again. She did not recognise the writing, but then Snip had been unable to write for himself for a while. She looked again; it was very odd writing, it rambled and spiked and slid sideways. Perhaps it *was* Snip's hand, though almost unrecognisable. She was glad but couldn't help wondering how he would make out since the friend who had written to her, telling her about Snip's accident, had admitted that Snip's condition had been serious.

Still, he seemed to have addressed the letter himself, awful though the writing was. So different from Daniel's elegant, dashing hand . . .

'Ah, you're back, Nell,' Mrs Burroughes said rather unnecessarily as she slipped in through the back door. 'Sit down, it's only porridge, tea and some toast but it'll keep the wolf from the door until lunchtime. How did it go?'

'Very well, thanks,' Nell said. She slipped her coat off and hung it on the back of the door, then sat down and took the proffered cup of tea gratefully. 'The doctor was right, though, they were almost ready for the off. Still, we parted friends.'

'Good.' Mrs Burroughes put the porridge plate down in front of her, then ladled creamy porridge into it. 'I waited for you, but the doctor went hours ago. He's gone fishing with Alfie Brett. What a way to spend a day off, out there in that cold wind and up to his knees, like as not, in some stream! Still, it's relaxation, or so he says. Ah, you've got a letter, is it from your mother?'

'No-oo. Remember Snip Morris, Mrs B? Well, I don't know that you ever met, but I told you about him.'

'Oh yes, the submariner.' Mrs Burroughes leaned forward inquisitively to look at the envelope Nell had tossed down on the cloth. 'That's an English postmark.'

'Yes, I noticed. He must be home now, unless he got someone else to post it for him.'

'Well, open it, girl,' Mrs Burroughes said, twinkling. 'I'm curious, even if you aren't.'

'All right.' Nell finished her porridge, took a long drink of her tea, and tugged the envelope open. There was one page and that contained only a dozen or so lines. 'Yes, he's home. Staying with a mate, he says, in Southampton. Oh crumbs!'

'What?'

'Well, he's been very poorly, he says, and now he's obviously got into a muddle and forgotten that spring is move-on time for travellers, since he is assuming that I'm still in King's Lynn with the fair and won't be moving out for a week or so. He wants to come up to see me, or if there isn't time – which there certainly wouldn't be if I were still with the fair – he asks if I could go down to Southampton. He doesn't know where his father is and doesn't want to go back to their fair anyway. He's not sure what he does want to do, apparently. I suppose he wants me to make up his mind for him.'

'He's confused; a bit like you were,' Mrs Burroughes said placidly. 'Well, if the poor lad's had a bad time he needs a friend. Why don't you go?'

'And lose my job? Mrs B, you wouldn't want me to do that.'

'You're paid for what you do, you aren't what you might call regular,' Mrs Burroughes pointed out. 'Besides, if you go next weekend you could be down and back in no time. Go on, drop him a line and say you'll go. If you get it in the post in half an hour, it'll be with him by Monday morning. Poor lad, what a homecoming, eh? No job, no place to go . . . nip down there, dear, it would be a kindness.'

'It'll give him ideas if I go,' Nell said gloomily. 'He used to be sweet on me.'

'If you don't, you aren't the girl I thought you,' Mrs Burroughes said roundly. 'Now just you write and tell him you'll be there as soon as possible and I'll pop down and post it for you – I've a penny stamp in my purse.'

'You're bullying me,' Nell grumbled, reaching for the toast. 'I have a feeling in my bones that if I go I'll regret it.'

Mrs Burroughes slid another slice of toast from under the grill and turned the gas tap off.

'I wouldn't want to influence you, my dear,' she said, suddenly serious. 'If you don't want to go, it's all right by me.

No doubt the young man will find things aren't as bad as they seem.'

Spreading margarine thinly on her toast, Nell had a sudden vision of Snip. The square, ugly face which had always been cheerful, the rough hair, the pugnacious set of his mouth. Only now the mouth would be drooping, the eyes anxious. How could she even pretend that she would not go to his help? She might not be in love with him – well, she was *not* in love with him – but she certainly loved that skinny, neglected lad who had been so kind and so patient with a lost little girl all those years ago.

She smiled across at Mrs Burroughes. 'It's all right, Mrs B, I wouldn't let Snip down for the world, I was just having a good old grumble. I'll write immediately and buy my ticket on Monday.'

Snip awoke. His head was thumping and his mouth tasted indescribably nasty. He looked round him, at a whitewashed ceiling only a foot from his nose, at another bed almost as close, then listened. Bovver's heavy, ale-induced snores, the faraway hum of traffic and the drip, drip of water coming through the window. Drat! He had sneaked out of bed in the night and opened the window, unable to bear being shut in any longer, and look what had happened! He sat up, the better to look, and immediately, as well as acknowledging guiltily the huge rainwater puddle on the cracked lino, he felt the fusty closeness of the small attic room clutch at his throat like a strangling hand.

I've got to get out! The thought came simultaneously with his scramble from beneath the thin, patched blanket. He swung his legs out of bed and his right foot hit the puddle immediately, making him wince with the coldness of it. But then he was up and over to the window in a stride, pulling back the tatty little curtain, leaning out, breathing the freshness of the chilly, rain-washed air blowing across from the docks.

Phew! He leaned farther out, over the cloud-reflecting slates of the roof, and tried to steady his racing heart by counting his blessings. He was on dry land – well, three storeys above it – and safe from asphyxiation, drowning, enemy action. He was not in hospital, so no one was liable to come along to change his dressing – both his hands, the real and the imaginary, clenched into fists at the remembered pain – or give him an injection or tell him to prepare for an examination by a strange doctor and a number of students. He was in Bovver Bancroft's Mum's house, paying her an exorbitant sum each week to share his horrible little cupboard until he heard from Nell.

He didn't allow himself to think what he would do then, if she said 'Come up to such-and-such and I'll be waiting,' because he would have to hitch-hike. He didn't think he could face a train – not yet, not by himself at any rate. With a travelling companion it might be different, but he couldn't think about being shut up in a railway carriage without the fear beginning to build.

When had it come over him, this inability to bear small spaces? After five years in submarines you'd have thought that any tendency to claustrophobia would have come out or been well and truly slain. Instead, it had waited until he had left the Navy before making itself felt. In hospital he found he sweated with fear every time they drew the curtains around his bed. Then he couldn't lock the lavatory door, then he found he was happier not closing it. He had tried laughing at himself, testing himself by going into the linen cupboard and shutting the door, seeing how long he could stick it, but instead of getting longer and longer, the time he could bear to be shut away got shorter and shorter. He had spoken to one of the doctors who was seeing him about his stump – no point in pretending it was an arm since he'd got some sort of infection despite their care and a second amputation had been necessary, so now he didn't even have an elbow to bend – and the man had been dismissive of his fear.

'It's just the hospital,' he had said breezily. 'You'll find it goes off once you can get out, move around a bit. I feel like that myself after an eight-day spell on the wards.'

It had not gone, of course. It had got so bad that even walking into a shop had been an effort, and once or twice he had simply run out, desperate to get out of a building which seemed to be shrinking in on him.

But he fought it. He had to fight it or go under, admit he was mentally unstable. He had seen men go to pieces, both in

407

the sub and at the hospital, and it frightened him more than anything. To lose control of your mind: to shake and whimper like a frightened dog when thunder rolled or a child screamed; to jump when someone addressed you or cower in a corner, crying like a baby when anyone came near. He would rather die, far rather. But it had not come to that, not yet. He had been in Southampton for three weeks, practising using his left hand, trying to write legibly, before daring to contact Nell, but he had done it at last and he only had to think of her calm eyes, the touch of her hand, and his fears receded, became managable. If he was with Nell there would be two of them against the vast, terrifying world, someone else to understand, someone to help him, do that suddenly impossible task – pull himself together.

Mrs Bancroft had said that to him, not realising the impossibility. 'You oughter pull yourself together an' git a job,' she had advised him, not unkindly. 'Your money won't last for ever, young feller.'

It was that, really, which had made him put pen to paper and write to Nell. Time was passing, his dear love would be twenty in April, and she had not set eyes on him for over three years. Suppose she had met someone else? The mere thought was enough to give him the shakes. And Mrs Bancroft was right; his money would be gone if he didn't get a hold on himself. He hadn't saved all those years to spend it on board and lodging while he tried to come to terms with the loss, not only of his right hand and forearm but of his sturdy, fear-nothing approach to life.

So now he waited for her reply. It had occurred to him after the letter was in the post that the fair might have moved on, but even if it had she would get his letter eventually; the fair folk always left forwarding addresses. But of course it would take much longer, a fact which plunged him into deep depression as soon as the thought had occurred.

Still, it was Monday morning, raining steadily, and he'd not had a bad night's sleep. Not that he slept properly any more. He remembered, with nostalgia, nights before the war when he had just rolled into his sleeping bag and slept deeply and dreamlessly until something woke him – daylight, usually.

Even in the submarine – the shiver, the cold sweat on the spine whenever he so much as thought of HMS *Hesperides* – he had slept pretty well most of the time. But that didn't happen now, not any more. He slept lightly, jerkily, waking for a few moments every ten minutes or so, tossing and turning, the pain from his missing arm gnawing at him, the fear of the bedroom walls closing in stealing any small chance of peace.

In the other bed, Bovver turned on his back and gave an enormous grunt, then opened an affronted eye. It swivelled round, registered that his companion was no longer in his bed, and closed crossly.

'Whazza time?' Bovver asked in a slurred, morning-after voice. 'Snot time to get up, izzit?'

'Dunno,' Snip said. He collected his clothing and headed for the door. 'Go back to sleep, you dozy bugger, your mam will call you when it's time.'

'Strue,' Bovver mumbled into his pillow. 'Ah, Gawd, it's bloody Monday! Back to the bench!'

Snip laughed but left the room. The tall, narrow house didn't have a bathroom but if it was as early as he suspected he could wash at the kitchen sink and dress down there too. He wouldn't disturb anyone and could go straight out. He did a lot of walking now, exploring first the ruined, shattered streets of what had obviously been a beautiful city and then gradually going farther out into the country.

He creaked down the last few stairs and stole along the dark passageway which led to the kitchen. He opened the door and it was deserted, the curtains still drawn across. The kitchen overlooked the tiny backyard, so Snip pulled the curtains back, glancing without curiosity at the yard with its cracked and weedy paving. You couldn't blame the Bancrofts for the state of the place, they were all in work, but if Bovver had been interested he could have cut the weeds down or even swept the paving once in a while.

Still, it was none of his business, so Snip pumped himself some cold water and washed, still a hit-and-miss procedure with only one hand. When he felt he was clean enough, he dried himself on the roller towel and pulled on his shirt and trousers. He was standing by the back door about to open it and go out when the kitchen door opened.

'Bless the boy, you near on gave me an 'eart attack,' Mrs Bancroft said, coming briskly into the room. 'Where's you off to? What about your breakfast, then, eh? Too busy huntin' for that job to bother wi' food?'

Snip laughed dutifully. 'I didn't know what the time was,' he said apologetically. 'I thought I'd just have a stroll down to the docks, see what's going on.'

They were going to rebuild Southampton, that stood to reason, so Snip had been casing the joint for a couple of days now. He could do a labouring job, he thought, provided no one expected him to build tiny rooms and go into them. But so far all the builders he had approached seemed quite capable of resisting the lure of a one-armed labourer.

'It's seven-thirty, you softie – didn't you think to look at the wall clock in front of your nose? Is Benjamin awake yet?'

Snip glanced apologetically up at the clock over the stove. Why hadn't he looked at it? Was he really going soft in the head? He grinned uneasily at Mrs Bancroft. 'Too lazy to raise me eyes, I daresay,' he said. 'Bovver's gone back to sleep; want me to give him a shout?'

Bovver's given name was Benjamin, but Snip had never heard anyone but his mother use it.

'Would you, lad? I'd be grateful; them stairs do me knees in, to tell the truth. Say down in ten minutes flat or he won't get no grub.'

'That'll fetch him,' Snip said, grinning. He went back upstairs two at a time, feeling a certain pride in his achievement. He had been in hospital so long and in such a poor state of health that at first the stairs had been as much of an obstacle for him as for his landlady, but now . . . he thundered on their bedroom dor, then shot it open.

'Your mam says downstairs in two ticks or no breakfast, Bovver,' he said briskly. 'I'm off. See you!'

He slammed the door on Bovver's groan and descended the stairs again, then hurried along the passageway and into the kitchen. What a difference it made having Mrs Bancroft in it. She had opened the front of the fire and stoked it so that the flames were reflected on the ceiling and she was cooking something in the blackened frying pan, humming to herself. The clock ticked and a voice on the radio was assuring people that a bowl of hot vegetable soup and a couple of thick slices of bread were good for you and cheap.

'Greens make you Get Up and Go,' the speaker observed, clearly seeing no ambiguity in the remark, though Snip sniggered unkindly. And just where did that chap think people would get greens, anyway, in the spring of the year with another three months to go before the fields would begin to yield their bounty?

Mrs Bancroft snorted. 'Greens!' she said witheringly. 'One cabbage there was per ten customers in Bonners. I never got a look in. Mind, I told the old man that he could get hisself an allotment an' welcome, but they're scarce too. There's a waiting list to grow your own, I tell you, and who'll be at the head of the list? Them wi' big gardings awready, that's who.' She waddled over to the table and picked up a round of bread, then turned to Snip. 'Want a bit, fried? Best I can do this mornin'.'

'Grand,' Snip said, his mouth watering at the thought of fried bread. His obsessive, nagging urge to get out of the house was calming down, becoming a background noise now instead of a shriek in his ear. 'Bovver's on his way.'

Mrs Bancroft nodded placidly. The voice on the radio began to talk about food again, then it changed to religion, then to the housing shortage, then to foreign affairs and the Nuremberg trials. Snip sat at the table, scarcely fidgeting at all, eating his fried bread and drinking his tea, watching Mrs Bancroft as she moved around preparing the food.

He got an unexpected reward. Bovver came through, slouching, unwashed, hair all over the place. He paused by the table to chuck an envelope down in front of Snip.

'One for you,' he said. 'Feller just delivered it as I was comin' past. Gave me quite a turn, shootin' it through the letter-box like that.'

He continued on his way to the sink and rinsed his face and hands, then returned to take his place opposite Snip at the

411

table. 'Who's it from?' he asked inquisitively. 'Looks like a girl's handwritin'.'

'Yes, it's from Nell,' Snip said. But she couldn't have received his letter already, could she? Suppose she was writing to tell him she was marrying someone else? Suppose this was goodbye? He could not read his fate with the curious eyes of Bovver on him, so he drained his cup and stood up. 'Well, see you tonight, then.'

'Hang on, it's rainin' out there; why not read it in the dry?' Bovver said. 'Look, if you want to be alone . . .'

'It's all right,' Snip said quickly. He slit the envelope open and pulled out the single sheet it contained, telling himself he would just look at it with his eyes unfocused and pretend it was nothing much, just a letter. He had quite a job to unfold it one-handed, but managed it at last and then, without meaning to, began to read it under his breath.

Dear Snip, I'm working at present but have weekends free, so if it's all right I will be arriving in Southampton some time next Saturday. Perhaps you could arrange for me to stay at your lodgings just for the Saturday night? It will be good to talk over old times together. Much love, Nell.

'Well? Wha's she say?' Bovver's loud voice broke the silence, though the wireless's tinny crackle had continued to dispense information as he read. Snip felt a big grin spreading across his face. She was coming! No word of busy, or couldn't, or why don't you come here, just to say she was coming the very next weekend.

'She'll be here Saturday,' he said, trying to sound matter of fact and failing dismally. He sounded like a kid at Christmas and much he cared – he felt like it, too. 'She'll stay the weekend. Can she stay over please, Mrs Bancroft? She'll kip on the couch, anywhere.'

'Is that your young lady? She can have Clem's bed since he goes home, weekends,' Mrs Bancroft said at once. 'Only don't you say nothin' about it to 'im or there'd be trouble.'

Clem was the Bancrofts' regular lodger, a clerk in a shipping office. Mrs Bancroft revered him for his steady job and good salary, but he was engaged to a young lady who also worked

412

in his office and he usually spent weekends with her parents in the country. His room was nice – he had a little desk, a wash-stand, an easy chair and a gas-fire – so Snip thought exultantly that Nell would be very comfortable.

'I won't say a word,' he said at once. 'I'll just drop Nell a line, say I'll meet the train. I've got some paper and envelopes in my room somewhere.'

'I can't feed her, mind,' Mrs Bancroft said warningly. 'I'd like to oblige, Snip, but we just ain't got the grub. Still, you can take her to the British Restaurant and Sunday she'll be goin' home again, I suppose. If there's a train, that is.'

'I'll ask her to bring her ration book,' Snip said. 'We'll manage, Mrs Bancroft – and thanks ever so.'

He waited for every train the following Saturday, starting unbelievably early because he was scared of missing her. He put on his demob suit, polished his shoes, slicked his hair down with water and set off before breakfast, though he did allow Mrs Bancroft to give him a paper bag with sandwiches and a wrinkled apple in it.

He had been a bit afraid of the station, but it was all right when it came to the point because he walked around a lot and several times, when no trains were due, went out of the station and trudged the surrounding streets, filled with elation because she was coming, because very soon now his Nell would be here.

She didn't know much about his arm; he hadn't been able to write for a long time and had dictated cautious notes only, not wanting to say too much, scared of frightening her off. But the last letter he had written himself, every word, and despite having to take time over it – those ten lines had taken him days – he thought the writing had been reasonable. Considering it was written with his left hand.

He was growing clever as the days and the weeks passed; clever at doing things one-handed, at using his left hand for tasks once carried out by his right. He was beginning to see that he would conquer the loss of his arm and go through life scarcely noticing his lack, but he was less sanguine about the claustrophobic terror which haunted him. But with Nell beside him, he had high hopes of conquering that too.

At noon he ate the breakfast Mrs Bancroft had given him, munching sandwiches of margarine and a scraping of honey. He bought a cup of tea from a man selling them from a small barrow, and the next train steamed in and something, some inner instinct, told him to get over there, because she was near, he was sure of it. He ran, jogging unevenly along the platform, and there she was, looking abstracted, even worried, getting down off the train with an overnight bag in one hand and a paper carrier in the other. He shouted, lit up with excitement and the pure pleasure of setting eyes on her again. She was so damned beautiful!

She heard him, looked round, saw him; he had always loved her smile, the way it lit her face, warmed her eyes. He fairly flew across the short distance which separated them, took her in his arms, went to swing her into the air . . . He had forgotten his arm. He swung her and couldn't hold her. She fell and he fell with her, lurching against the stationary train, both of them embarrassed as hell, trying to get to their feet, to make a joke of it.

'Snip, that was you, not me – you should take more water with it!' She was laughing, patting his cheek as they struggled to their feet, she hadn't so much as glanced at the empty sleeve. He reached for her, hugged her close, one-armed. Bent his head to kiss her and felt the wetness of tears on his cheeks. He was crying like a baby at the happiest moment of his life so far – she would despise him, be embarrassed by him, want to escape!

She put her face up and kissed where the tears had run, hugging him convulsively. She did not stir from his arm, even when he began to stammer an explanation . . . sorry, not used to it yet, a matter of time . . .

'What's only a matter of time? You getting used to hugging women again?' she asked teasingly. 'I thought you did very well for . . . oh Snip, your arm, your poor arm!'

He had moved, to show her the empty sleeve. She was round-eyed, her lower lip trembling. She had obviously not had the remotest idea of the extent of his injury. Of course she could not have known because he had baulked at telling her, frightened it would make her decide not to bother with him after all. He had been wrong, he knew that now; Nell had a generous spirit, she would never desert a friend.

'Sorry I didn't tell you,' Snip muttered, turning her, still within the circle of his arm, so that they could walk out of the station still linked. 'It's not an easy thing to put into words, especially in a letter. Besides, I wanted you to come for me, not because you were s-s-s . . .'

His voice stuttered into silence. She was sorry for him, she couldn't hide it, the big dark blue eyes were brimming with unshed tears, her mouth drooped softly, all the joy gone from that expressive little face. But hadn't he been pretty damned sorry for himself, when it had first happened? Wasn't he still sorry for himself now, when all was said and done? He could scarcely blame her for pitying him . . . if only it wasn't just that, if only there were some other feeling for him in her heart.

'Oh darling Snip, of course I'm sorry for you! When I think of all the things we've done together, when I see you in my mind's eye on the fair, nipping on and off the dodgems, sneaking a ride on a gondola, always so strong and sure. But you'll be strong and sure again, I know you will!'

He started to speak and the words turned traitor on him; tears choked his voice because she was being kind, because he loved her so much and didn't have the words to tell her. He turned away from her, ashamed, but she pulled him back to face her, gently but firmly.

'Snip, don't worry, don't try to tell me about it. Let's go back to your lodgings and I'll leave my bag and then we can find a quiet spot where we can talk without being interrupted. Do you have plans? There must be some sort of rehabilitation for you, but I expect you've done all that. And just be thankful it's an arm and not a leg; you can still run and jump and do all sorts, I'm sure.'

They left the station and meandered through the streets, back to his lodgings. After a while they reached a tiny café, under an archway, so small that it had only four tables. Nell tugged at his arm. 'Couldn't we go in there, and talk in the warm? It looks quite clean and pleasant.'

He looked at the tiny café and his stomach contracted with alarm. It was tiny, womblike – worse, tomblike! He would never be able to stay there long enough to order coffee, let alone drink it. He looked down at her, formulating excuses, but his mind wasn't quick enough.

'All right, if you want,' he muttered. 'A quick coffee then.'

Nell drew him into the café, a firm hand on his wrist. Her heart had nearly broken when she had first seen him – so pale, so woebegone, so utterly unlike the Snip she had known so well. Every instinct told her that he'd had a terrible time and wasn't over it yet, told her, also, that he needed her. He can come back with me to Lynn if he doesn't want to get work down here, she thought, going over to the counter to order coffees and a couple of cheese rolls. He'll want to work the fairs again, of course, but that may take time. His father wouldn't want him in any event, and though the Gullivers always needed chaps they would be doubtful about Snip's ability to move heavy equipment with only one arm.

She stood by the counter watching the short, stumpy man behind it preparing the drinks. He had a huge pot full of hot milk and an even bigger one full of hot coffee; they simmered on a tiny stove and he mixed them together with great panache. A headwaiter at the Savoy couldn't have done it better, Nell thought, never having been to the Savoy in her life. Beside her, Snip was moving uneasily; she looked across at him, then stared. Sweat beaded his brow and his good hand was clenched into a fist. He was biting his lower lip; she could see how his teeth were digging into the soft flesh – was he in pain? Something was very wrong.

'Snip? Go and sit down, I'll bring the coffee over to a table. Go on, you look ghastly.'

He nodded and went. He chose the table nearest the door and she saw that his eyes had fixed themselves on the tiny, steamy panes of glass nearest him. They were the only customers – why had he chosen that table? It was colder over there, but

416

then it was more private, she supposed. She carried the coffee and cheese rolls over, slid into one of the slatted chairs and smiled reassuringly. She pushed a cheese roll into his hand, and watched it clench on the roll, clench and clench until the roll was hidden, squashed to almost nothing.

'Snip?' she said uncertainly. 'Is – is something the matter?'

He bent forward until his nose was a couple of inches from her face. 'I – can't – stay – here!'

The words were forced between stiff lips. Nell shook her head and took his hand in hers. Gently she uncurled his fingers and removed the soggy ruin of a roll.

'Darling Snip, what is it? Are you ill?'

'I – don't – know, Nell . . .' His hand, abandoning the cheese roll, clutched at her hand. 'It's too – sm-sm-sm . . .'

'Hush, sweetheart, hush.' She bent forward, stroking the hair from his forehead, feeling the sweat ice-cold on her palm. She moved her chair round, so that they were sitting side by side instead of opposite. 'Nell's here, Nell's with you, nothing will hurt you.'

He began to relax. It was strange to see the limbs which had been rigid as iron become flesh and blood once more. He let her take his hand and carry it to her mouth. She kissed it gently, one finger at a time, then each knuckle. He was crying again, tears raining down his cheeks, but at least that anguished rigidity had left him for the moment.

'You won't go, Nell? You *really* won't go? I don't know what's been happening to me, but I've been so bloody frightened! All sorts of things scare me now: I don't sleep, I can't bear closed doors; I'm nothing but a useless hulk if the truth were known.'

She rubbed against him as a cat might, looking up at him, her glance teasing, affectionate. 'What nonsense is this? My dear Snip, that door has been closed ever since we came in and you've managed to bear it. You've been ill and in hospital for a long time and horrid things have happened to you. It's natural and normal that you shouldn't be too keen on small spaces, if that's what you mean. It happens to lots of men.'

'It does?' He stared at her, the beginnings of a smile twitching his mouth. 'No one told me that. I thought I was the only bloke in the universe to go through the war in . . . to go through the war the way I did and then end up scared of . . . not liking . . .'

'I think it's called claustrophobia,' Nell said wisely. 'Want to leave? You can, of course, but I'm going to stay and drink my coffee and eat the cheese roll. Tell you what, if you stay you can have the nice one and I'll have the squashed one.'

'I'll – I'll try to stay.'

Companionably, side by side, they drank their coffee. Nell pressed against him, a hand resting on his knee. He would not let her eat the squashed roll; he ate it himself, in huge nervous bites, scarcely chewing at all, but he did eat it. And he stayed. Only when she rose did he get to his feet and then he followed her to the counter when she took their cups and plates back, thanked the man, turned back to the door.

They went out into the rainy afternoon. He put his arm around her waist, and they walked like competitors in a three-legged race, arms around each other, she trying to match her stride to his, laughing, getting tangled up with her overnight bag, telling him to stop fooling around and show her which turnings to take.

They reached a tall, thin house which Snip told her belonged to his landlady, Mrs Bancroft, and went around the back. Down a narrow alley, through a battered wooden door, across a small yard and in the back door. The front, Snip told her, was for the postman and visitors; he no longer counted as a visitor so she would not either.

Mrs Bancroft took her to her room; once there, with Snip in his own room changing out of his wet things, she faced the older woman.

'He's not well, is he?' she asked, rubbing her hair on the towel the landlady provided. 'He's changed a great deal.'

'He's a prince to what he was,' Mrs Bancroft said shortly. 'There's no bathroom but there's cold water in the jug there and I'll do you a cup of tea at eight tomorrer, wake you up. And don't you try to get up to no hanky-panky, no funny business,' she added flatly. 'Not under my roof, Miss. I wouldn't stand for it, young Morris would be out on 'is ear I tell you straight.'

Nell drew herself up to her full height and glared at the

woman. 'Snip Morris and I are old friends, we've never been lovers and we never intend to be,' she said furiously. 'How dare you insinuate that I'd misbehave with anyone, let alone an old friend, Mrs Bancroft!'

'Oh! Well, judgin' by the way Mr Morris looks at you and talks about you, he's of a very different persuasion,' Mrs Bancroft said sourly. 'However, I didn't mean to hurt your feelings, and I'm sorry. I'm sure you'll *both* behave just as you ought.'

Nell nodded and began to unpack her nightdress and lay out her toothbrush and a tiny piece of soap. The landlady departed, telling Nell a trifle stiffly that though she could not undertake to supply tea, there would be supper laid out in the kitchen between ten and eleven that night.

'Mr Morris said he'd take you out for tea this evenin' and tomorrer dinner,' she said. 'He knows the situation regarding food. But as I said, I'll do you both a supper, and breakfast tomorrer, of course.'

They went out for a meal and had fish and chips, tea and bread and butter and a small helping of trifle at a local café. They talked a great deal, but managed, Nell thought, to say very little.

Snip's obvious dependence dismayed her; how would he get through life if he couldn't face more than a few minutes in a small café? He seemed fine when she was with him, but when she got up from the table to go to the cloakroom she returned to find him white-faced and sweating, terror in every line of his rigid body.

Never having suffered from claustrophobia herself, she found it difficult to understand how he felt, but one glance was enough to convince her that he was undergoing a terrifying and cruel experience. And she could help, to some extent. So she sat very close to him, and touched him constantly, talked, laughed, told him stories about her life as a landgirl and then her experiences working in factories and shops. She made him laugh when she told him about Ariadne and poor Ted Smith and he was truly sorry to hear of Ugly Jack's death though Hester's story fascinated him, especially that she had a husband who was, of course, also Nell's proper father. Nell did not think it necessary to tell Snip the full story; indeed, she owed it both to her mother and to Matthew to do no such thing.

When she asked him, he told her a little about some foreign ports, notably Trincomalee, and even managed an amusing story or two about hospital, though the mention of the word made him clench his good hand. He told her about the other hand, the hand that wasn't there but hurt and ached and gnawed at him, and she kissed the side of his face and smoothed his hair and told him that none of it mattered, not now she was with him again, and watched him relax.

'I knew I'd be better with you,' he said on the landing outside her room, tilting her chin gently with one finger and looking into her eyes with more emotion in his own than she cared to interpret. 'It's like magic the way you make me feel I can cope with it all. Magic.'

'You'll cope,' Nell told him. 'It takes time, that's all. I'm incidental.'

'You're central,' Snip said. He grinned at her with some of his old humour. 'Oh, Nell, what'll I do?'

'Come back to Lynn with me if you don't want to stay here, and see if you can find a job,' Nell said promptly. 'You'll soon settle in. Goodnight, Snip, see you in the morning.'

'Goodnight, darling Nell. I wish . . .'

But she had turned away and was closing her door, not wanting to hear the words she knew would follow.

The noise started in the night; a moaning, followed by a terrified shout. Feet thudded down the stairs and Nell, only just awake, sat bolt upright in bed as the door burst open. Snip stood in the doorway, white and sweaty, panting hard.

'Snip, whatever . . . ?'

'I thought you'd left,' Snip said hoarsely. 'I woke up and heard you going quietly out of the gate so's not to wake me. I'm going to sleep outside your door, Nell, so you can't go off and leave me. I couldn't bear it if you went; I'd kill myself, I swear I would.'

'I won't go, Snip,' Nell said gently, but her heart sank. He couldn't come back to the Burroughes's house with her, it wouldn't be fair. And housing was impossible, he'd be lucky to get a shared room even in Lynn, which wasn't exactly the centre of the universe. She had to work, she couldn't be with him day and night.

'You might go,' Snip said wildly, sitting down on the landing and eyeing her with such distress and uncertainty that she could have wept. 'You might go, and then where would I be? But if you'll leave your door just the littlest bit open I'll be able to see you, all night. I won't have to worry then.'

'All right, all right. Come in and pull up one of the chairs close to the bed. If you can snooze in that, we'll hold hands and both get some sleep.'

He came in. On tiptoe, shyly. 'Nell, am I going mad? I'm so scared of going mad. I saw men go mad and it's not a nice thing, not nice at all.'

Nell was not yet twenty; her courage and resolution gave a distinct jerk and she was conscious of a desire to run away or lock her door and bury her head under the pillow. But then she reminded herself that this was Snip, her childhood hero and dear friend. He wasn't going mad, he was just ill and unhappy, and he needed her, for now at any rate.

'No, of course you aren't going mad,' she said robustly. 'Do you think I'd ask a madman to sit by my bed all night, and hold my hand? If I did such a stupid thing, it would be I who was mad.'

He looked at her doubtfully for a moment. Then he smiled, a broad, happy grin. 'You're right. I'm all right really, I know I am. Especially when I'm with you, dear Nell.'

421

Sixteen

Mrs Bancroft took the promised cup of tea to Nell next morning and found her guest already out, the bed stripped, the girl's small bag neatly packed. She then went up to the attic and found only her own son slumbering in his bed. The young couple returned for their breakfast, Snip looking better, Mrs Bancroft considered, than she had ever seen him look. He fairly bounced across the kitchen and gave her a hug.

'Mrs Bancroft, you're about to see the last of me,' he said exuberantly. 'Nell and me are going back to Lynn this afternoon. I'll get work up there, so we can be together.'

Snip Morris's money had been welcome but, truth to tell, Mrs Bancroft had worried about him, about his funny turns, the shouts in the night. She would not be sorry to see him leave, she decided.

'That's good news, Mr Morris,' she said. 'I'll be sorry to see you go, of course, and Benjamin will miss you, but it's for the best, I'm sure.'

She turned a considering gaze on Miss Makerfield, to find her looking white and strained and not nearly as delighted with the way things had panned out as Mr Morris plainly was. Ah well, Mrs Bancroft concluded, it's only natural. The boy's a big responsibility as things are at present, but he's got sense and he's young. He'll come through all right, given time.

What to do next had not been easy to settle, and when Snip brought up the subject of marriage it muddied the waters even further. At first, that was. Snip suggested marrying as they sat in the train travelling from Southampton to Waterloo, clutching her hand, beads of sweat forming on his brow and trickling down the sides of his face as he tried not to mind the enclosed space.

'I would've asked you right off, if I'd been meself, like, but it's different, now,' he mumbled into her ear. 'I've got nothing to offer, not like I did have. Oh, I've got me savings, but no job, no prospects . . . I thought I'd get work wi' engines when I got back to civvy street, but no one wants an engineer wi' only the one arm, and anyroad, I don't reckon I could work shut up. Not now, not any longer.'

'You'll be all right, honest you will,' Nell said in a desperate undertone. There was a woman in WRNS uniform sitting opposite who couldn't take her beady eyes off them. 'Give yourself time, dear Snip, don't try to rush anything.'

'I'm not,' Snip muttered. 'I daresay you wouldn't want half a feller, even if it was me, eh? Because I am only half a feller, what wi' only the one arm and my brain all shook up. I daresay you've got your eye on a normal bloke, eh?'

'You're as normal as you ever were, and that's normal enough for me,' Nell said, giving his hand a quick squeeze and smiling teasingly at him. 'When you reach Lynn and find yourself a proper job and start making new friends, you'll probably decide you don't want me, not the other way round!'

He took it wrong. He clutched her hand so tightly that she thought her fingers would snap like twigs and he turned in his seat to smile joyously at her, his eyes lit up like stars.

'Then you will marry me? Oh Nell, sweetheart, you don't know how happy that makes me! Ever since we were kids I'd told meself that when we were older we'd make a go of it. You mean everything to me, but you know that, don't you? I must've written it in a hundred letters, teased you about it, talked about after the war, when we could be together. But I was afraid, with me arm an' all . . . Some girls wouldn't be able to take it – I should've known you were different.'

Nell was silent for a moment. He had laid it all before her, his love, his dependence; how was she to tell him that she had not meant she would marry him? But why should she tell him, break his heart, she thought suddenly? Why was it impossible to marry Snip? It would not have seemed so impossible once.

She could never marry Dan, and he had not written back to her so perhaps he guessed that her letter had not just been a whim. If she were safely married to someone else by the time he came home, explanations would be unnecessary. She was very, very fond of Snip and unlikely to fall in love with yet another young man . . . she might just as well marry Snip, who needed her so badly. It was all very well to tell herself that Snip would meet someone else, but privately she doubted it. He was staunch and loyal was Snip Morris, his feeling for her had been a while growing, she did not think it would die easily.

But was she being fair to him? Could she marry one man while knowing she was in love with another?

She looked around the crowded carriage. It seemed that every other passenger was either watching her or listening to her words; she shrank from explanations in such a public spot. She leaned closer, lowering her voice to a quiet whisper.

'Darling Snip, this is neither the time nor the place. We'll discuss the details when we get home to Lynn.'

He leaned back in his seat; his hand found hers again and closed convulsively over her fingers. His smile was blissful.

'Home! Details! Oh Nell, Nell!'

The Burroughes were delightful, insisting that Snip should sleep on the couch in the living room so that the two of them could be under the same roof. Nell, mindful of what had happened at the boarding house in Southampton, pointed out to Snip that, should she wish to leave the house, she would have to pass the door he slept behind, but he just smiled and squeezed her hand. They were sitting side by side on that same couch, Nell waiting for Mrs Burroughes to make her a cup of cocoa, and Snip, it was easy to see, still in a daze of happiness, his worries forgotten, for the moment at any rate.

'Leave? Why should you? And why should I worry if you did go out early, anyway?' he pointed out with infuriating logic. 'We're going to get married, we love each other . . . I shall sleep like a log tonight.'

He may have done, but Nell, lying resentfully awake in her small bed, did not. Round and round in her head the disquieting thoughts buzzed: if I marry Snip I give up the hope of ever marrying Dan. I love Snip in a way, of course, but not in the way I used to love Dan ... but I can never marry Dan, the thought of it makes me squirm, so why not be sensible and give Snip what he wants? People fall in love after they're married – look at Mum and Ugly Jack. Well, they weren't married, but they did most definitely love each other. . . Oh dear, why can't I go to sleep and forget all about it for a while? But sleep continued to elude her and at six-thirty, when she heard Mrs Burroughes getting up and sneaking down the stairs to make the doctor his early morning cup of tea, she got out of bed and followed her old friend down to the kitchen.

Mrs Burroughes, in the act of putting the kettle on the gas stove, jumped as Nell opened the door, then sighed and relaxed. 'You naughty girl, I told you to lie in today! You won't be going back to work anyway; you and Snip have too much to arrange from what I gathered last night.' She smiled with real affection at her companion. 'Come for a nice quiet chat, dear?'

'I've come for some advice, I think,' Nell said, closing the kitchen door carefully behind her. 'Mrs Burroughes, I never did actually say I'd marry Snip, he just sort of read it into something I did say. And you know I'm not in love with him. He's changed and so have I, and you needn't tell me he needs me, because I know it, but is that a good enough reason for marrying someone?'

Mrs Burroughes picked up the teapot and stood it on the side of the stove to warm. Then she began to sort out cups and saucers.

'I wish I had a few nice biscuits,' she observed, taking her biscuit barrel off the dresser and peering into its depths as though she hoped the plain biscuits might have spawned fancy ones overnight. 'Still, the homemade ginger ones are quite nice – does Snip like ginger nuts?'

'He likes everything,' Nell said despondently. 'He had a tough childhood, his father used to hit him whenever he stayed still long enough and his stepmothers were always too busy raising their other children to worry about someone as self-reliant as

425

Snip. He fed himself half the time; he told me once that he lived on raw crops from the fields the year his real mother died.'

'Poor lad,' Mrs Burroughes murmured, tipping the biscuits on to a plate. 'Childhood's an important time; you were much loved, Nell. Your confidence goes deep because you've never been unappreciated. Perhaps in a way it's the price you pay for happiness – that other people, people like Snip, want to warm themselves at your flame.'

'He wouldn't have been like that once,' Nell said quickly. 'He'd have barged back into my life, tried to persuade me to marry him, and then, if I said no, he'd have barged right out again. Only now, it's different. He's different.'

'I don't agree,' Mrs Burroughes said calmly. 'He'd go now, Nell, if he thought you didn't love him. Perhaps he knows you better than you know yourself, love. Why say you would, or why let him think you would, if you meant you wouldn't?'

'He misunderstood,' Nell said reproachfully. 'Didn't you hear me, Mrs B?'

'Yes, I heard you, but it didn't make sense. You could have told him he was mistaken at once, quickly, before he had gone too far. He would have backed off you know. He's very sensitive to the fact that folk may judge him useless. I suppose you considered marrying him and decided it was the sensible thing to do, because you're fond of him.'

Nell got the jug of milk out of the scullery, and came back, chuckling and shaking her head. 'Oh, Mrs B, you know too much! Yes, I thought I might just as well marry Snip, because the chap I thought I loved . . . but I'm not sure, any more. Snip isn't himself, not yet. He depends on me so much, and . . . look, can I tell you the whole story?'

'Of course, dear. But first, pop this teatray up to my dear old Sam, would you? Mondays are always busy in surgery and visiting and I like him to wake comfortably and relax before he comes down for his breakfast.'

'Right; we'll talk when I get back,' Nell said.

It was a long story and Mrs Burroughes listened attentively; how Dan and Nell had met, their friendship, the long parting and the eventual reunion. Then to the painful moment when Hester had told her daughter that she and Dan were half-brother and sister.

When it was over she looked at Nell and smiled, but Nell could tell that she was neither shattered nor horrified by the news. 'It must have been a shock for you, I do see that,' she said cheerfully. 'But I find it difficult to believe that you could possibly be deeply in love with someone you'd only met a couple of times since you grew up. If you ask me, dear, you had a crush on a very handsome young man and that's about it.'

'I was in love with Dan when I was seven,' Nell pointed out crossly. 'I was, or I thought I was.'

'At seven, Nell dear, that was a crush, a pash, not love a such,' Mrs Burroughes said serenely, slicing bread and putting the slices, two at a time, under the hissing gas grill. 'Believe me, a child of seven isn't capable of deep emotional love, which is what a woman feels for a man and vice versa.'

'I'm not sure what you mean by deep emotional love; I don't see how anyone can feel love like that until they've been close for ages and ages,' Nell protested. 'But when Snip said he'd loved me from the first moment he saw me you seemed to think that was possible, and indeed I do think it's true, so why can't it be true for me, too?'

'Because Snip went on seeing you on an almost daily basis until he went into submarines, so his "crush", if you like, turned into the deep love he feels now. Whereas you knew Dan for a year, from the time you were around six until you were around seven, and then you didn't see him again for a very long time. You wrote to him, I grant you that, but he never wrote back, not so much as a word. Did he?'

'No-oo, but he couldn't, because he didn't have my address,' Nell said defensively. 'He wrote once we met up again though, and visited me on the farm, when I was in the Land Army.'

'How many times? And did he visit you before you joined up?'

'He didn't write much, and he didn't come and see me until I was at the farm,' Nell admitted. 'But men don't write as often as girls, do they? He said he would have come to see me more, only I was always moving about.'

'But Snip came. He didn't always know where the fair was, but he came, didn't he?'

'Ye-es, but it wasn't just to see me, the fair was his life, his whole existence. All his friends were fair folk, all his relatives . . .'

'His parents, you mean? Brothers, sisters?'

'Well, not his relatives, then, because Abel Morris moved his people on when the war started. But friends, yes.'

'But he had limited leave, and he had to search for you all; right?'

'Yes,' Nell said sulkily, seeing what her old friend was getting at and not liking it one little bit. 'But Dan would have come if . . .'

'If he'd cared enough, he would certainly have come. I don't mean this unkindly, I'm just trying to point out that Dan's love, at that point, was not equal to the love you believed you felt for him. You dreamed about Dan, of course, made up little scenarios where you met and fell into each other's arms, pinned photographs on the wall and talked about him to all your girlfriends?'

'Mrs Burroughes, you must have been just like me when you were my age. Yes, I dreamed, and I hardly got through a sentence without mentioning Dan's name. Girls do talk all the time about the men they love, don't they? Everyone at the farm did anyway.'

'Oh yes, that's true. But they need more than dreams, dear Nell, they need telephone calls, meetings. Yet you were quite content to worship from afar for the most part, weren't you?'

'In a way, but what has this got to do with me marrying Snip?'

'Well, if I honestly thought you were truly, deeply in love with Dan Clifton and he with you, I suppose I might have to think very hard indeed before advising you to marry Snip, even though marrying Dan is obviously out of the question. But I think you were in love with love, which is a very different thing, and quite possibly Dan was the same. You must take into account, as well, that love works both ways. Dan didn't seem to put himself out unduly for you, whereas Snip did, didn't he? I

428

expect he wrote weekly?'

'Daily,' Nell said, trying not to sound sulky. 'I didn't always get them, but he wrote reams.'

'And you've already gone to a lot of trouble for your old friend Snip, which seems to prove something. Nell, my dear, I was going to advise you, but I can't. This is one decision that only you can make.' She snatched a round of toast from under the grill and turned to scrape off the burnt crust. 'Dear me, look what you've made me do! What was I saying?'

'You were saying I'd have to make up my own mind,' Nell said gloomily, beginning to lay the table for breakfast. 'Which isn't much help, Mrs B.'

'No? But then I don't think you need help, do you, Nell? I think you've made up your mind already and nothing is going to change it. Come on, let me into the secret; what are you going to do?'

Nell laughed.

'I didn't know I'd made up my mind when we started talking, but you're right, I have. I'm going to marry Snip. What's more, I'm taking him home. Home to Pengarth, I mean. I daresay Mum and – and Dad will let him sleep on the couch, and then we can get a room somewhere. Snip's never been to North Wales and I have such a yearning to go back, to see Pengarth again!

The journey back to North Wales by train and bus was absolute hell for Snip, despite his giddying happiness at the start of the journey. Perhaps it was because he relaxed and was not on his guard, or perhaps it was because he had become aware that his happiness was not fully shared by his beloved. Whatever the cause, he was attacked not only by the dreaded claustrophobia but what he called, to himself, the black dog and the terrors.

The bad feelings began to manifest themselves on the train down to Liverpool Street Station. It was crowded and Snip had given his seat to an elderly lady within ten minutes of leaving King's Lynn. Standing by Nell, with her knees pressed gently against his calf, he was all right for about ten minutes, then he knew he would have to move.

The train was a slow one; it jerked to a halt at a small

station. Snip got off, and found he couldn't get on again. He was twitching like a dog, sweating like a pig, shaking like a tree in a gale. He stood on the platform, then tried to force himself to climb back into the carriage. He got in, among the smelly, damp-coated crowds in the corridor and just as the train began to move he jumped out.

He couldn't even stay on the platform but ran into the dusty road beyond, then came back red-faced and told the uninterested ticket clerk that he had got off the train to relieve himself and missed it.

Nell came for him by bus, having realised what had happened and abandoned the train at the next station. She said no word of reproach and would have booked them both into a boarding house for the night, so that he could recover himself, but he would not hear of it.

'I might not be any better tomorrow,' he growled miserably. 'We'll catch the next train. I'll try harder this time, be more sensible.' This time they both stood, for this train was just as crowded. All might have been well had Nell not needed to use the lavatory.

'Come with me,' she urged him, her eyes anxious. 'I don't mind, you come in with me.'

But there wasn't room, so she went inside and closed the door. The train was moving at a tremendous lick and her presence only a door away from him was like a magnet, so he stuck it out. He clung to the other side of the door and presently she emerged, took one look at his face and said gently that they would get down at the next stop, 'just for a breather'.

They walked from the next station, then caught a bus, then walked again. Snip was fine walking, fine so long as he could hold Nell's hand and stride out and feel the wind on his cheek, so they walked for at least part of every journey.

It took them five days to get to North Wales, 'dot and carry one', as Nell said gaily. They caught a train again at Chester, then walked from the coast, and with every mile they covered Snip could feel the black dog and the terrors receding as the beauty of the countryside, the space, the clean air, poured like balm into his war-torn mind.

'I've never seen mountains, not in this country,' he said in an awed voice as they trudged up from the coast. 'I never knew there was anything so beautiful, or so lush. Look at the grass, the trees . . . it's like a dream after trains and buses and that.'

'Perhaps we'll be able to get jobs here, and stay,' Nell said dreamily. 'I love it too, Snip. I'm so glad you do as well.'

'The air's soft; reckon I won't wheeze so bad here. I reckon I could get back to what I was, here – not the arm, I'll give you that – if we could stay. Nell, what's Hester going to be like wi' me? She didn't like me much when we were kids, she called me a gypsy brat more than once.'

'You're different now,' Nell assured him. 'Besides, she didn't mean to be nasty then, she was just jealous of anyone I liked. And I did rather harp on about you, you know. It was "Snip does this, Snip thinks that", until I would have driven a saint mad.'

'Is that so?' was all that Snip said, but that one short little sentence warmed his heart and gave him more hope than all her kindness since they had met in Southampton. Because he knew, of course, that she didn't love him as he loved her. He did not know why, had no idea what had happened to her or even if she loved someone else; he just knew that, fond though she was of him, she had some deep inner reservation about him. But he needed her so badly that he couldn't think of asking, perhaps opening up an avenue of escape for her which would leave him bereft.

Yet, because he loved her, he did it as they walked along a valley, with the mountains to their left and the flat meadows leading down to the sea on their right. 'Nell, you know how I feel about you, but if you want to wait a bit, give yourself time to know me as I am now, then I'll take it on board, learn to live with it. I'll manage.'

He heard his words and felt a shiver of apprehension run through him, curdling down his spine like icy water. If she agreed, pushed him back a bit, how would he bear it?

He did not have to; she turned to face him, pulling them both to a halt. She had always been beautiful, but with her words an aura of such splendour formed about her that he

431

could have bent his knee and bowed his head, dazzled by her. The pure, pale oval of her face, the eyes such a dark navy blue that they looked almost black, the wings of straight, shiny black hair which swung forward as she moved, the tender curve of her lips.

'Snip, we're getting married and we're not going to have any regrets or second thoughts if I can help it. Come on, step out, we can be home in twenty minutes and you can meet my . . . my father!'

Nell and Snip got married on Nell's twentieth birthday in the beautiful white church with its soaring spire where Hester and Matthew had exchanged their vows long before.

Outside the arched windows soft spring rain fell on the bed of daffodils which grew against the south wall, on the new grave mounds with their scattering of military crosses and on the older, local stones. It was very quiet and though Nell had worried that Snip might find the atmosphere claustrophobic, you only had to look at him to see that her fears were unfounded. The peace of the place had entered Snip, calming his fears and soothing him, and his dark eyes were steady on the vicar's face, his attention caught and held.

Nell was sorry that the sky was not blue because the church looked very beautiful when the spire pointed up into an azure sky, but she knew it did not really matter. What mattered was the vows they exchanged, standing at the top of the church before the vicar, her in her worn grey dress, Snip in his demob suit.

It was a quiet wedding, with only the four of them present; Snip, Nell, Hester and Matthew, plus the vicar of course. Nell didn't want any fuss and Snip agreed that a quiet wedding would be best. He would have concurred had she said she wanted to get married in Liverpool Cathedral or on a ship at sea. What mattered to Snip was marrying, not the means employed to reach that happy state. So the five of them stood in a small group close to the altar, kneeling, standing, bowing their heads, and Snip and Nell exchanged vows and rings. The vicar did his best to make it a memorable occasion, and Hester cried into her hanky and Matthew patted her arm.

When it was over they progressed down the aisle again and out into the thin spring rain. Matthew had bought an ancient Ford, and they all piled in and went into town, where they had booked a table at an inn for the wedding breakfast. It was a typical post-war menu but the landlady had done her best: the soup was vegetable, thick and good, the main course was roast lamb ('ask me no questions, but me sister's husband had to slaughter a beast when its leg got broke,') and the pudding was apples in a suet crust which, Snip said, he would have killed for.

Nell sat at the head of the table, her knee just touching Snip's, and thought how lucky she was. They all got on so well, the four of them. Hester had known Snip for years, of course, and if he was puzzled at her sudden change of heart – for Hester welcomed him into her home and her family as though his marrying her daughter had been her dearest wish – he said nothing about it. Nell, who realised that Hester was relieved to see her marrying anyone other than Dan, was nevertheless grateful for her approval. It made things very much easier, especially since the lodge was small and they were, perforce, on top of each other in the evenings, when Matthew was home from work.

Matthew liked Snip too, genuinely liked him. Snip had barely been with them a day before Matthew was taking him off to look at the sheds and barns, the beasts, the farming equipment.

'He's not a farmer, he won't know what Dad's on about,' Nell had said to Hester as the two of them worked in the kitchen. 'Still, Dad does like him, doesn't he, Mum?'

'He does,' Hester had said thankfully. 'He's proud of you both. He's a very generous man is Matthew. I never realised quite how generous until I came home after a dozen years away and found him still loving, still caring.'

'I know, I felt it as soon as I came through the door. But we can't stay here for ever, Snip and I. Tomorrow I must go into the village and down to Rhyl, see if we can get a room or something for when we're married. We'll move out after the wedding, Mum, you really don't have enough space for us now.'

'I know it,' Hester said ruefully. 'I suppose you couldn't find something in the village?' But they needed work, Nell reminded her mother, and there was nothing in the village for either of them.

When Snip came home, however, he was ablaze with excitement. 'That castle's amazin',' he said as he sat down opposite Nell. 'I've never seen anything like it – isn't it grand, Nell darling? I dunno how you ever bore to leave it, though Matthew says it's a real mess inside. Still, what a place, eh?'

'Snip would like to see around,' Matthew said as they began to eat. 'I wouldn't take him in, but you could, Nell love. I don't know the house that well, but you knew it at one time like the back of your hand.'

'Oh! but who lives there now? Surely whoever lives there wouldn't want us poking around?'

'No one lives there. We has our meal breaks in the kitchen, Mrs Alice works there, but we don't never go outside that one room and I don't believe Mrs Alice does either. It's a mess, but no harm in you takin' the lad around.'

So after they had eaten the two of them walked up the long drive, hand in hand, and stood outside the big courtyard, staring.

'It's like the sleepin' beauty's palace,' Snip muttered. 'I wouldn't be surprised at what we found in there, would you?'

'No-oo, but it was lovely, once,' Nell said longingly. 'Oh Snip, will it be horrid now? All a ruin, with damp and bugs and filth everywhere?'

Snip shrugged and tugged at her hand. 'Dunno, but let's look, sweetheart! You couldn't just walk away not knowing, could you?'

'I can remember it when it was beginning to be really lovely. I don't know that I could bear seeing it if the rain's got in and tramps have been sleeping rough there. Mum said they might have been.'

He pulled her into the curve of his arm, and kissed the side of her face. 'Silly little Nell, let's explore.'

They had to fight to get through the wild garden, though

it was nothing compared to how it would be later in the year, when the brambles and briars, the nettles and docks, put on their summer foliage. And once under the arch, it wasn't that bad. The paving was dirty and weedy but it was possible to cross it and to walk up the half-dozen steps to the big front door.

'It'll be locked,' Nell warned, and she was right, locked it was. But Snip turned over the big stone carved into the shape of a grinning face and there was the key, lying there as though Mr Geraint had put it there last night. He inserted it into the lock, and Nell turned and looked across the yard to the gatehouse room at the top of the flight of stone stairs. Suppose Mr Geraint was here still? Suppose he saw them breaking in and came down and . . .

'Come on, sweetheart.' Snip pulled her into the dim and shadowy hall. 'We'll start downstairs, shall we?'

They went through the castle room by room in the end, and it was nowhere near as bad as Nell had feared. In fact, it was quite reasonable, if you discounted a great deal of dust and almost as many webs, Nell said, as those encountered by the Prince fighting his way in to Sleeping Beauty.

'Why did that Geraint chap just abandon it?' Snip asked after a bit. 'Some of the rooms are magnificent and it must be hundreds of years old, I suppose. I like the round rooms, don't you?'

The rooms in the four towers were all round or hexagonal and Nell agreed a trifle doubtfully that they were picturesque.

'If no one's using it now,' Snip started as they stood in what had once been Mr Geraint's study, 'then I don't see why we shouldn't take over a couple of rooms. We'd be ever so careful, but it would be somewhere to live until . . . until there's more stuff available.'

'Live here? Oh but Snip, it's miles from anywhere, the drive is two miles long, you know, and we've got to earn a living, got to work. But I know what you mean and I don't suppose Mr Geraint would mind us making use of some of the space. Come on, let's go upstairs.'

She found she did not much want to revisit Dan's little room, but Snip gave her no choice. They went through all the rooms, one by one, until they reached the Long Gallery. There, they went inside and Nell stopped short, a hand flying to her throat.

It was exactly the same! To be sure the roses in the vases were long dead and the long windows, which had let in the scent of the summer garden all those years ago, were closed tight, but even so . . . sunshine slanted, golden, across the floor, touching the little tables, the chairs, the portraits and paintings on the walls. Even the chandeliers still hung from the high ceiling, though their diamond drops were defaced with webs, and dust, thick and soft as velvet, cloaked their once-gleaming facets. Snip walked the length of the room, calling out to her to come and see this, what did she think of that, but Nell stayed where she was and wave after wave of nostalgia and regret for times past poured over her.

It had all started here, in this very room! The portrait of Mr Geraint's grandmother, the likeness he saw, or said he saw, her mother's distress. She remembered that afternoon so well: the golden shine on the well-polished parquet flooring, the sweet scent of the roses, the excitement which radiated from Mr Geraint, his pride in what he had done to the room, how he had restored it.

'Nell? Do come and look at this old bag. Gawd, be glad she isn't your granny, old love! Isn't this a bloody wonderful room, though? Why don't you come down here, why are you standing there staring? Here, hang on, I'll come to you.'

He came down the long room at a lope, his eyes fixed anxiously on hers. 'Somethin' wrong, sweetheart? Don't you like it in here? What are you thinkin' to make you stare so?'

Nell smiled absently and her voice sank to a murmur barely above a whisper. 'Forty water-colourists! I wonder if they ever came? It's all set up for them. Oh Snip, do you realise what that means?'

'I don't know what you're talkin' about, love,' Snip said, understandably. 'Forty *what*?'

'Forty water-colourists. That's what you call people who paint pictures in water-colours instead of oils. Mr Geraint had arranged for the North Wales Water-colourists Association or some such thing to come here, pay him for the privilege, and paint. He was just starting, just beginning . . . Snip, it's given me an idea.'

In that long golden room, with the late afternoon sunshine slanting through the numerous windows, the two of them had stared at each other.

'You mean . . . us? You mean we might . . . but it ain't ours, Nell, we couldn't do that.'

'We could, Snip, indeed we could! Mr Geraint doesn't want the place to fall into disrepair, Dad said so, and this way he could get it made nice by us and he could pay our wages by letting us open it to, well, to forty water-colourists, just for a start.'

He picked her up in his good arm and swung her round. His face was alight with excitement, he looked like the old Snip, the tough, self-reliant one.

'We could stay here,' he breathed, and until he said it, Nell had not realised how he dreaded the return to the real world, to a tiny room, a stultifying job, to all the miseries of uncertainty and self-doubt which had haunted him since he lost his arm. 'We could stay here, live in this marvellous old place, and earn our living. Oh Nell, it's a dream, we'll wake up and find it won't work!'

They returned to the lodge and put the idea to Hester and Matthew. They agreed to say nothing, at first, about opening the place to the public, just suggesting that they might clean up a couple of rooms and live in them. Hester was doubtful but Matthew agreed at once.

'Mr Geraint wouldn't mind, he'd be real pleased,' he said roundly, when Hester voiced her objections. 'It makes sense, Hes, the whole country's short of housin', and here's a great old mass of decent rooms a-goin' beggin'. Better these youngsters do somethin' with them than those squatters the papers talk about move in.'

Once Hester had been talked round, she was as enthusiastic as the others. She and Matthew were eager to help because it meant that the young people would not have to move away, and in the choosing of which four rooms to use Hester proved invaluable.

'The study's small enough to heat easily,' she pointed out, when Nell asked why they could not use the white drawing-room. 'You need half a tree to keep the drawing-room fire lit – I should know, I remember how I used to grumble that it needed making up every hour or so. No, you stick to the study, you can get some of the furniture out of the white drawing-room and use that, and shove the desk in the gap.'

'Oh, all right,' Nell agreed. 'But why can't we use the library instead of one of the bedrooms?'

'If you have anyone to stay you'll need a spare bedroom. And if, one day, you have a family you'll need a second bedroom too,' Hester said. 'To tell the truth, I'm doubtful about the kitchen, it's such a big room and, besides, Mrs Alice and the farmhands use it. But for the time being it's the only room with cooking facilities and a proper deep sink, so it will have to do.'

Now, sitting in the private room at the inn and drinking the coffee which rounded off their wedding breakfast, Nell thought for the first time of what was to come: they would get up from the table and thank their hostess, make their way back to the Ford. And then they would drive back to the castle and she and Snip would go into the small courtyard and across it into the kitchen. They would sit by the fire in their living-room, which had once been Mr Geraint's study, and have a meal in the kitchen, a meal which Hester had prepared and cooked for them so that all they had to do was warm it through in the bake-oven. Then they would go up the long, curving staircase and into their bedroom. They would undress, wash, put on nightclothes, and climb into bed. Together.

A small shiver shook her. Snip was good to her, kind. He would never hurt or frighten her, but he would never thrill her either, never make her heart beat like a drum in her breast, never know just how to make her cling and shudder with the strength of her desire.

But that wasn't real emotional love, Mrs Burroughes had said so. That was just romantic first love, the sort that didn't last, the sort that faded away once it came face to face with real life.

Hester set her coffee cup on its saucer with a small clink. She caught Matthew's eye and they both stood up. Snip followed suit, holding out his hand to help Nell to her feet. I do love him, in a way, Nell told herself as they left the inn and returned to the old car. I am really very fond of him, I like him better than almost anyone else. But oh, how I wish I were head over heels in love with his beauty, his power over me, his giddying sensuality. It would make what is to come a whole lot easier.

They lay, politely separated by at least a foot of mattress, in the big bed where, Nell supposed, Mr Geraint had once sported with his various women, possibly including her mother. They had eaten their supper without tasting it, carried water up to the dressing-room which was separated from their bedroom by a small connecting door, taken it in turns to wash.

Snip was in bed first and he was lying on his back, staring at the ceiling as Nell entered the room. She saw that the candle made weird shadows as she crossed the floor in her beautiful white lace nightgown and climbed into bed beside him.

The nightgown had been a wedding present. Nell felt very silly wearing such a valuable thing and fully intended to take it off as soon as she could, not realising that this same thought was in Snip's head as he turned to watch her climb in beside him. The nightgown had been in the family, Matthew told them, for a very long while and was always given to the bride for her wedding night.

'It looks new,' Nell had exclaimed, and had seen the embarrassed grin exchanged by her husband and Matthew without understanding it at all. 'I'll give it back to you for the next bride, Dad. Did Mum wear it, incidentally?'

Matthew looked embarrassed. 'No, she didn't,' he mumbled. ' 'Tweren't here, then, 'twas down in Sussex. Mr Geraint sent it up wi' a note that we'd best have it now, since you were gettin' wed . . . well, that's what he said, anyroad.'

Then it must be true that Dan and I are both Mr Geraint's kids, Nell thought dismally. Matthew couldn't say so, of course, he had to pretend the nightgown was in his family, but that's the truth of the matter. Dan hasn't married, not yet, so I'm to have it.

The unwelcome thought hurt, but not much or for long. Her life was too full, too important, right now to waste time longing for what might have been.

'Warm enough?'

Snip's voice was husky, with a bit of a shake in it. Quickly, Nell turned in the bed and put both her arms round him, holding him close.

'I am quite warm, actually . . . Snip, would you mind if I took this nightgown off? I'm afraid of spoiling it and it's got to go back to Sussex for the next bride.'

Snip's voice shook even more. 'I – I was just goin' to suggest it,' he murmured. 'Oh, Nell!'

'I'll put on my ordinary cotton one, then,' Nell said, starting to sit up. Snip followed suit and blew the candle out as he leaned on his elbow. 'Oh Snip, whatever did you do that for? I'll never find my nightie in the dark, you fool!'

'I know. Here, let me.'

An arm looped around her waist and lifted her, then slid the nightgown to waist-level. She was lowered back into a sitting position and the hand eased the nightgown further up.

'Arms up, there we are.'

'Oh!' Nell said. 'Oh, but . . . Snip, where are your pyjamas?'

She glanced at the black silhouette of him which was all she could dimly see through the darkness, and became aware that he was grinning, though she could not see his expression very well.

'Never had none.'

'Oh . . . well, what do you usually wear in bed?'

'My skin.'

A tentative hand checked on the nearest bit of him, which happened to be his thigh. Her touch made him sigh and snatch his breath and his hand came out and smoothed its way around her waist. Nell's own breathing began to speed up. She moved uneasily.

'Umm, shall I just fetch my nightie? I can probably find

it if I . . .'

'No nightie. Has anyone ever told you, sweetheart, that your skin is like the finest silk?'

'No, I don't think so,' Nell whispered. 'Oh, Snip, don't you think . . .'

The hand smoothed up her back to her neck, up into her hairline, the fingers ·pushing into the hair, cradling her head. Somehow, Nell found she was lying on her back and that Snip was kissing her, leaning up on his elbow now and kissing her hard and excitingly, so that her arms wound around his neck quite of their own volition and her body, which had been astonished to find itself suddenly bare, began to sidle and purr against him like a cat against welcoming ankles.

He stopped kissing her for a moment and his lips moved warmly down across her neck, to chase wickedly across her body, rousing demons which Nell had never known she possessed. She groaned softly, then squeaked and grabbed at his head, seizing his ears, pulling him free of her.

'No don't, Snip, it isn't . . . you shouldn't . . .'

He raised his head. Her eyes were growing accustomed to the darkness and she saw for certain that he was smiling, though his breath was short and she sensed excitement and desire being curbed for her sake.

'Why not, sweetheart? Don't you like being kissed?'

'No, I . . .' Honesty reared a protesting head. 'Well yes, I do like it, but it's – well, it's –'

'It's nice,' Snip said. His hand reached out, gentling her, persuading her. 'It gets better.'

He leaned forward. Delicately and gently, his mouth touched hers. He kissed her until her strangely permissive body was purring again, then his lips began their now-familiar journey.

'Oh dear, Snip, I don't think . . . .'

He lifted his mouth from her glowing flesh. 'That's it, sweetheart, you've got it,' he said encouragingly. 'You shouldn't think, it's the last thing you should be doing. Just let me show you what we do next.'

They had been waiting for hours just to see her, to catch a

glimpse of a real fairytale Princess.

Mabs and Jenny were right in the front because they were determined to see her properly this time, not just like on the newsreels, when you caught a glimpse and then the camera swung round to her parents, or to the little one – not that Margaret Rose was that little now, not at sixteen. Neither Mabs nor Jenny was old enough to have been in the forces, but the Princess had; she'd driven generals, ambulances, things ordinary girls did, but she was no ordinary girl and they wanted very badly to see her at last.

'She'll be Queen one day,' Jenny's Dad had remarked that morning, while he and Jenny gobbled toast and jam – no butter – and then rushed for the bus. 'She'll know more about ordinary people than most Queens do, I'll say that for 'er.'

Jenny had agreed and announced her intention of being right at the front. But now there was a commotion at the back and a voice could be heard, high and excited.

'She's arrived! I just seen 'er, mekkin' 'er way down the print room!'

The news, hissed by Bet, one of the tea-ladies, reached Jenny's ears and she nudged Mabs joyfully. 'Did you 'ear that? Won't be long now!'

'I should 'ope it won't be long now! I'm so excited! I just 'ope I don't pee on the floor . . . we've been stuck 'ere a while already.'

'Mabel Arkwright, you are a shocker! Ello, someone's a-comin'.'

The double doors at the end of the long canteen were thrown back. All the tables and chairs had been removed the previous day and there was a roped-off walkway down the centre so that the Princess and her entourage could make their way through the room and out the other end, where the new wing of the factory was to be opened.

There was a buzz from the far end of the canteen and Jenny, straining sideways, saw them. A group of people, several of whom she recognised; managers, directors, their wives. And right in the middle, in a pale blue dress with an off-the-face hat and a smile, was the star of the show, the main attraction:

Princess Elizabeth Alexandra Mary, twenty years old. She was actually here, had begun to walk down the long room where the two girls stood, unbelievably excited by her presence in the same building as themselves.

The first thing that struck Jenny was that she was tiny, very much smaller than either Jenny or Mabs. I thought a Princess would be tall and slim and willowy, Jenny thought, with a small stab of disappointment. She's small and quite slim, but rounded too . . .

She was very young. Jenny sensed that the Princess was, in some ways, much younger than she, though Jenny was not quite nineteen. She saw that the Princess had wonderful skin and her hair was dark, soft, thick; it shone when she moved as though it had been polished. But she doesn't look – like I thought she would, Jenny told herself, irrationally disappointed. What had she expected? A crown? Something terribly glamorous? Then Princess Elizabeth smiled at something her companion was saying and Jenny recognised that this tiny, slender girl was a proper Princess, someone special, and she had been a fool not to realise it at first glance! She leaned over the rope, beaming as broadly as she knew how, cheering, clapping; Princess Elizabeth was someone special all right, but she was real too, that was what they forgot to tell you – a real person with a real smile and eyes which lit up when they met yours.

Beside her, Mabs was shouting, cheering. The Princess smiled straight at them both, friendship, understanding, all the things they had not even known they wanted to see in those dark blue eyes. Then she was moving on down the long room, half-hidden by the dignitaries who followed them.

Jenny turned to Mabs with a sigh. 'Ain't she perfect?' Jenny said faintly. 'Oh, I'm so glad I seen her. She's perfect, that's what she is.'

But Mabel was still shouting: 'Liz . . . Lizzie!' she bawled. 'Where's Philip, then? It's your birthday, ain't it, so you should be able to 'ave a bit of a treat, Princess or no Princess. So why din'cher bring Philip?'

'They were horrid, common girls to shout things like that at

443

Lilibet,' Margaret Rose said later that day, when her sister had gone to her room, leaving Margaret and Huntie to talk over what had happened. 'How do they *know* about Philip, anyway? I mean I thought no one was supposed to know about Lilibet and him.'

'I imagine the whole world knows,' Huntie said ruefully, fishing a stocking out of her pile of darning and slipping her wooden mushroom into its heel. 'Gracious, what a huge hole! I wonder if it's worth darning? But then I'll never get another pair, even when I save up the coupons, everything's so scarce.'

'How can the whole world know? Papa says there isn't anything to know, that they're just friends. *We* know differently, of course, but I don't see how other people can be so sure.'

'When Lilibet and Philip are together, dear, such happiness and affection radiates from them that it would be difficult not to guess their feelings. And though of course one relies on the discretion of one's friends and servants, such discretion can, and does, falter if the reward is great enough. Even friends will speak to newspaper reporters, or to someone outside one's own circle who has no scruples about passing such an interesting titbit on.'

'Oh, I see,' Margaret said doubtfully. 'But it's horrible for Lilibet, Huntie; she must wonder what people will say if papa decides they can't get engaged. I mean I'm sure she'll be Queen one day, and terribly important, but now she's just a daughter like me.'

'But a daughter of most loving parents, dear,' Huntie said gently. 'Your parents will do what's best for both you and Lilibet, I'm sure of it.'

'And in the meantime? Until they decide?'

'Until then poor Lilibet has to get used to having even her private life made public, I'm afraid,' Huntie said, plunging her needle into her stocking. 'It's hard, but she's a sensible girl. She'll come to terms with it.'

Margaret wandered across the schoolroom and knelt on the wide windowseat, staring through the window at the rapidly approaching April dusk.

'Poor Lilibet,' she said softly, more to herself than anyone else. 'Nothing of her own, ever. Not even her love affair.'

Seventeen

'She's so happy, Matt – as happy as I am, and that's saying something. Do you know, when she first brought Snip back here all I thought about was, well, all I thought was that she was jumping into the water without really looking, but now I think she did the right thing, even if her reasons weren't the usual ones.'

Hester and Matthew were sitting over breakfast on a bright sunny morning in early May, Matthew with a Sunday newspaper spread out before him, Hester energetically crunching toast. Matthew laid his paper down and grinned at her across the white cloth.

'They both did the right thing but for the wrong reason, same's you and me did,' he said contentedly. 'They've done marvels with the castle, an' all. How they did it, mind, when the snow come down and we were cut off – no electric, no food, no nothing – I can't say, except that they worked like a pair o' navvies, but it's rare grand, now. I keep wonderin' when the old man will come up and take a look, but he hasn't showed much interest, truth to tell. Got other fish to fry, I reckon. Now if our Nell was to have a babby . . .'

'She won't, not yet. She's only a baby herself, just twenty-one,' Hester reminded him. 'Besides, Snip still depends on her. Too much, I sometimes think. But if they make a go of it, and I believe they will, they deserve every ha'penny they get.'

'Yes, the place is beginnin' to look better'n when the old man did it up first. And as for the lad, he's twice the man he was,' Matthew said. 'I don't deny he leans on her but time was when he'd not have been able to come to market wi' me,

445

leavin' our Nell at home, and he does it now. He strolls round calm as you please, makes a bid or two, has a pint and a cheese barm, chats. Tis only if he feels shut in, like, or if he's havin' a bad day . . .'

'Which isn't often; I know, I know,' Hester said amicably. 'But you must admit he needs her, Matt. If she had to give half or more of her attention to a baby then I don't know quite how he'd face up to it. And I guess Nell thinks the same because I thought they'd have a family right off, but they've not done so.'

'Babies don't come for the askin',' Matthew pointed out. 'You'd ha' liked another, that I do know, but wantin' weren't enough. Does Nell ever tell you how she feels about kids?'

'I had a prolapse after Nell was born; that can stop you having another baby, Dr Burroughes told me. And with a daughter of twenty-one I'm not exactly keen to start again,' Hester reminded him. 'As for Nell, she doesn't want children until Snip's a lot more independent and their future's more assured. She's delighted with the way things are going right now, though. When they open the castle at weekends Snip will take parties round if she's busy, a thing he couldn't have done six or nine months ago. But he still has nightmares from time to time, and he won't wear his artificial arm. I wish he'd try, but he won't.'

'He says it hurts and why should he be hurt more'n he's been already, that's what I say. Hes, what's it like up there on a Saturday?' Matthew asked curiously. 'I know I ought to go up, take a look, but I feel awkward-like, with the people all starin' and wonderin' where you fit in. I work around the buildings, of course, but I haven't ever been inside the castle when the kids have got it open to the public, but that don't mean to say I'm not very curious.'

Hester shook her head chidingly, though she smiled as she did so.

'I'm not surprised you're curious, I was myself. I've not been in on a Sunday, because the locals are a bit po-faced about it and so I've held back, but at Easter, when they did teas and buns, I waited on and it was great fun. The folk are ever so friendly and when our Nell gets going about the ghost in the Long Gallery and the White Lady in the West Tower they drink in every word. There's more than a touch of the showman in that young lady – all those years of barking for me and Phillips, I daresay.'

'Then they're doin' all right?' Matthew asked, taking a drink of tea. 'It used to worry me that they'd get into a muddle wi' money, but they've both got their heads screwed on. Snip's a showman an' all, of course. I tend to forget that.'

'I think they're doing very well,' Hester confirmed. 'On Easter Monday there was a queue all day despite the frightful weather and they must have taken quite a lot of money. A shilling seems a large sum but people are paying it willingly enough, which Nell says may mean it's too little. And have you heard the latest? They've gone and traced Gullivers and asked if they could spare some joints and perhaps a couple of children's rides, so they can advertise a fair as an additional attraction during the summer. It means clearing the home paddock and levying some sort of charge on the fair, but I think it's likely to be a real money-spinner. There isn't a lot for kids at the moment, so a fair would be well patronised. I wish Gullivers would send Ivy and Phillips, but I don't suppose they will. He's a great attraction, old Phillips, so they'll want him down on the coast somewhere, to get the crowds in.'

'Why don't you catch a couple o' grass snakes and offer to do them a show yourself?' Matthew asked, grinning at her. 'Hester the Snake Woman and her Venomous Adders . . . See her wrestle them down, subdue their sinewy length . . .'

Hester laughed with him. 'Get on with you, I've gone soft, I doubt I could stand up in front of an audience without blushing all over. Besides, it's a knack, handling snakes, and I reckon I've lost it over the past couple of years. I won't remind you that grass snakes aren't adders, because poor old Phillips wasn't a cobra, either.'

'The flatties don't know that,' Matthew quoted. 'Except that country folk do tend to know grass snakes and adders be uncommon similar. Still, old gal, the kids do pretty well by themselves from what I've seen. So you think Nell has no regrets, eh?'

'I don't know that I'd go as far as that,' Hester said cautiously. 'Few regrets, anyway.'

'Few? Why not none?'

'Oh Matthew, you must have known she thought she was in love with someone else when she and Snip married!'

The words had slipped out before Hester had realised what she was about to say. She felt the colour rise in her cheeks and knocked her knife on to the floor, then bent to retrieve it, staying down for a moment until she had mastered her expression. After all this time, to say something like that in an unguarded moment! It just went to show you could never lower your guard if you had a secret.

Matthew, who had picked up his paper once more, put it down, his eyes rounding, his lips pursing into a silent whistle.

'I did not, then. If that was so, why did she marry Snip?'

'Because . . . because the other chap wasn't suitable, he was abroad, she didn't think . . . anyway, she was very fond of Snip and wanted to do what was right. And I'm sure she never gives the other fellow a thought now. She's really very happy.'

'Hmm.' Matthew picked up his paper but did not start to read. Instead, he continued to regard Hester steadily over the top. 'Unsuitable, you said? Was that why you took to Snip the way you did? I remember Nell said you'd not taken to Snip when they were kids. I just grunted, never said owt, but it made me wonder at the time. You never were a gal to blow hot an' cold, Hes.'

'I didn't like Snip when he was young,' Hester admitted, 'but I like him immensely, now. And when Nell turned up with him that day all I could think of was how the war had changed him. When I knew him before, he was aggressively sure of himself, rough as well as tough, not the sort of young man you'd want your daughter to marry. Afterwards he was a man not a boy and, well, we both liked him, didn't we?'

'Yes, but I never had any idea of the sort of man our Nell should marry,' Matthew said. 'This unsuitable feller – anyone I know?'

What on earth made him ask that, Hester thought uncomfortably. As though he could possibly have known the young man his daughter had doted on, except that in this case he did, of course. But she could scarcely tell him so because he would want to know why she considered Dan unsuitable, which would lead either to her telling lies which she did not want to tell, or to revealing a truth best left untold.

'Whatever makes you ask that, Matt?' Hester leaned across the table and tweaked the paper out of his grasp. 'If you aren't going to read the news . . .'

'Cheeky varmint!' He grabbed the paper back and it tore. 'Now look what you've done, you young spitfire! Come on, you've ruined me Sunday newspaper, now you can just come over here and give me a kiss to make up.'

'None of that,' Hester said, but Matthew leaned across the table, knocking over the marmalade pot, and reached for her. She pulled back, trying to right the marmalade pot, and he stood up and walked briskly round the table, grabbing her despite her squeaks and lifting her off her feet, crushing her against his chest and then kissing the top of her head.

'No horseplay, Matt! It's time I started doing the spuds for Sunday lunch. And tonight we've invited the kids down for a meal, so I'll have to do some fancy cooking, which takes . . .'

Her words were cut off by his mouth descending on hers. He kissed her hard and thoroughly, then held her back from him. He was breathing heavily, staring down at her with a look on his face she knew well. She reached up and stroked his cheek, then pressed herself against him.

'Now behave yourself, Matt, we're an old married couple, we can't play around like a couple of lovesick kids when we've all this work . . .'

He swung her off her feet and held her in his arms as one would hold a baby, smiling down at her.

'I'm a lovesick kid where you're concerned,' he said hoarsely. 'I can't touch your hand wi'out you set me afire. Besides, it's Sunday; a day of rest. I'll take you back to bed, we can rest properly there.'

'Rest! That's the last thing on your mind,' Hester said as he strode across the kitchen and into the bedroom, tossing her down on to their neatly made bed as though she weighed no more than a kitten. 'Just you stop it – any minute now folk will start streaming up into our garden, not realising it's private, and take a look through the window.'

Matthew, always a man of few words, walked across the room and tugged the curtains closed, then began to pull off his shirt and breeches. Hester lay on her back, watching him through half-closed lids. She marvelled at the way she loved him, marvelled more that she had ever allowed herself to believe ill of him, brought herself to leave him, but then she'd been a silly young girl, now she was a woman with a bit of sense and she knew pure gold when she saw it.

Presently, stripped, he stood close to the bed looking down at her. Hester smiled lazily up at him.

'Just what are you thinking, Hester Coburn, a-lying there all wicked and wanton on your bed on a Sunday morning?'

'Oh, I was just thinking how I love a man whose face and chest are burned to a rich chestnut brown, and whose – whose other parts are white as milk! Just wondering, Matt darling, how I ever came to leave you.'

He sat down on the bed and, leaning over, began to unfasten her blouse, then her skirt. Hester half sat up to help him, but he shook his head at her, his fingers quicker now on the fastenings.

'No, let me do it. I love to undress you.'

Hester sighed and trembled as the clothes came off and were tossed to the floor behind him. She told herself, as he took her in his arms at last, that it was a good ploy; it had caused him to forget totally about the unsuitable young man his daughter had wanted to marry. Of course it was wicked to entice her dear Matthew into bed on a Sunday morning when they should both have been in church – but it was the lesser of two evils. She did not want Matthew to remember Daniel and when they began to kiss, she forgot about Daniel Clifton too. It was Matthew who mattered, Matthew whose strong, suntanned body and big, sensitive hands were giving her such exquisite pleasure at this very moment. What did Daniel matter? His chance had come and gone, he would not trouble any of them again.

*

450

Anna was walking Beppo, the family fox terrier, along the bank of the River Yare, revelling in the hot sunshine and wondering what time it was. Earlier, she had bathed in the river, all by herself but for the dog, and though her tummy told her it was nearly teatime, she had no way of checking whether it spoke the truth or had been galvanised by the swim into early greed.

It was so lovely to feel the sun on her shoulders that she went on walking anyway, with Beppo racing ahead and barking like a mad thing every time he disturbed a pair of ducks or made a water rat desert the bank and plop into the cool brown river. The winter which had just gone, Anna reflected, had been one of the worst in living memory and it had seemed, only a matter of weeks earlier, that the freak conditions were going to last all year. Never had a summer come later or more reluctantly, but it had arrived at last and here she was, where she and Jamie had played so often as children, roasting in hot July sunshine and beginning to feel worried because she hadn't brought a hat and the back of her neck was painfully hot.

'Anna! Anna, darling!'

She turned at the sound of the voice and it was her mother, hurrying along the path behind her. Constance was wearing a lemon-coloured cotton dress with a large straw hat flopping over her brow and she held a newspaper in one hand. Anna stopped and turned to smile at her parent.

'Sorry, Mummy, have you been following us for long? I'm afraid I was in a brown study and Beppo never thinks of anything but the next water rat. What's up?'

Constance reached her and flapped the newspaper vaguely towards her. 'Well, it's teatime for a start and since JJ hasn't arrived home yet – he's gone sailing with a friend, but he's promised to be back for dinner tonight – I thought it might be fun if you and I had tea together and indulged in some real girl-talk. Jamie's cycled down to the coast with some girl or other and goodness knows what time they'll be back so it really will be just you and me. I really do need to talk to you.'

Inside herself, Anna groaned and flinched, but outwardly she just nodded placidly and fell into step beside her mother.

The trouble with being an adult was that everyone assumed you were now old enough to take on their troubles without being shocked or upset, but the truth, Anna thought miserably, was far otherwise. She had been so delighted with her father's apparent change of heart when he came home from the war. If only it had lasted, but within six months he had been up to his old tricks again and poor Constance, who had spent the war years looking incredibly young and pretty for her age, seemed suddenly to have given up the unequal battle. She used too much make-up, wore the wrong sort of clothes and behaved foolishly, batting her eyelashes at men twenty years younger than she was and resolutely pretending not to notice JJ's behaviour with an increasingly juvenile series of young women.

'And why the newspaper?' Anna asked, since Constance, having said what was on her mind, seemed indifferent, now, to silence. 'When I saw you waving it I thought they'd ended rationing or found gold down a coalmine or something!'

'Oh, this.' Constance waved the newspaper again. 'I thought you'd like to know that the suspense is over at last. Your Princess Elizabeth is engaged to Lieutenant Philip Mountbatten, RN. What about that, eh? Are you pleased for her?'

'Oh, that's wonderful, I'm awfully pleased,' Anna said as warmly as though the Princess herself were hiding behind the nearest stand of rushes, listening for her opinion. 'Isn't she lucky? Prince Philip's a dish, so tall and golden and aristocratic. I wonder when they'll get married? I'd wait until next June, I think, it's a lovely month for a wedding, but then she'll be twenty-two – so will I for that matter – and she might rather marry at twenty-one, as so many people do.'

'They'll probably marry quite soon; royal engagements are usually short,' Constance said. 'The Duke and Duchess of York had a three-month engagement, that was all. It's obvious why, of course.'

'Why?' Anna asked bluntly, and watched her mother's colour rise under the fair skin with some amusement. How odd that her mother could still blush over something like the reason for a brief royal engagement.

'Why? Well, because it wouldn't do for the future king

and queen to be seen hugging or anything like that in public
. . . and then if they overstepped the mark . . .' she saw Anna's
mouth twitch and shook her daughter's arm. 'You're a bad girl
to tease me when you know the answer perfectly well.'

'Sorry, Mummy, it was irresistible,' Anna said. 'Beppo, leave
that poor duck alone. Come along now or I'll put you on your
lead, I will really.'

Beppo, who could be deaf when he considered it necessary,
cast her a malevolent look but trotted back to her side. He hated
being put on his lead, especially so near the river. There was so
much to chase, so many exciting smells . . .

'Good boy,' Anna said, not fooled by his sudden meekness.
'Look, Mummy, you aren't going to nag me about George, are
you? Because if so, I'll have to tell you a thing or two which
you won't like.'

'I wasn't going to nag you at all,' Constance said indignantly.
'I was going to tell you that I'd had a word with your Auntie
Ella and she's coming to stay a bit earlier than she'd planned.
But let's wait until we get home, shall we?'

'All right, if you'd rather. Only I should have thought it
was quieter out here, with fewer people about. If you want
to say something confidential, that is.'

Anna spoke the words, but she didn't believe her mother
had confidentialities in mind. She thought that Constance was
going to tell her how foolish she had been to turn down George's
proposal, how if she didn't watch out she'd find herself left
on the shelf like Constance's friend Phoebe. Then Constance
would remind her that George was only the latest in a long
line of young men who had been encouraged right up to the
last minute and then slapped down and pushed away, to turn
– naturally – to other girls for consolation.

Constance looked sideways at her daughter, then turned
resolutely to the front once more. Anna saw that her mother
was pale despite the hot sunshine and the hat, flopping up and
down as she walked, cast an ugly freckled pattern of light and
shade over her well-powdered nose and cheeks. Abruptly, Anna
remembered when her mother's skin had been smooth and
golden, with a burnish of health on it, when her step had been

light, her limbs cool and smooth. It wasn't age, if she herself was twenty-one her mother was not long past forty, not nearly as old as she had begun to look.

'I'm leaving, darling. I'm going away.'

Anna shot her mother a puzzled glance.

'Do you mean you're going to stay with Auntie Ella? That will be nice, Mummy, though London in this heat isn't everyone's idea of fun. But I thought she was coming down here later in the month? Wasn't that what you just said? Or have her plans changed?'

Constance sighed and stopped walking. She turned to face Anna.

'I'm leaving JJ, darling. I've had enough.'

Anna couldn't take it in. What on earth could Constance mean? She was not a girl, she was a mature woman who had been married to JJ for twenty-two years. She couldn't mean she was leaving him, could she?

'You're leaving Daddy? But Mummy, for how long? Does he know? Why, for God's sake? He'll be awfully upset.'

Constance smiled; it was a tired smile but it occurred to Anna that it was the first genuine smile she had seen on her mother's lips for a long while.

'No, I haven't told JJ. I don't think he deserves warning, do you? The friend he's sailing with, darling, is little Josie Gaunt, that youngster Jamie's taken about a bit. Not an evacuee, not someone living under my roof and in my care, but our son's little bit of fluff. When I found out I suddenly decided I couldn't take any more, so I'm going. I rang Ella – she's told me time and again to be firmer with him – and said I'd had enough and Ella agreed to come down next weekend, to see if she could make him see reason. Only I'll be gone by then, of course.'

'But you'll come back won't you? You won't stay away? Daddy is awful, I know he is, but he does love you in his way. It's just that he's got a thing about young girls.'

Constance laughed harshly. 'He's got a *thing*, as you call it, about all women except the one he married twenty-two years ago. As for loving me, does he? *Does* he? I don't think your father knows the meaning of the word love, not between a man and a woman, anyway, and he knows nothing whatsoever about fidelity. For twenty-two years I've done everything in my power to please him, to make him happy, hoping he would turn to me in the end. Not only has he not turned to me, but he hasn't turned to anyone else either. Not for long. Never for long. Think of the women he's played around with over the last twenty-odd years! Now it's little girls of fifteen and sixteen! What's he trying to prove, for God's sake?'

The last words were said almost in a whisper, but Anna recognised them for the cry of agony they were.

'I don't know, I've never understood it,' she admitted, her own voice low. 'But what'll you do, Mummy? Where will you go? When I get a job I'll have to find somewhere to live . . . you can come to me, then. But right now I'm still slogging away at my degree, I can't help you much.'

'I've taken a job in town with an advertising agency,' Constance said, almost briskly. 'They needed someone who could speak French and I'll be writing copy and selling advertising in this country and in France. I can mug up anything I don't know, my new boss told me. I'm starting this coming Monday, but you mustn't tell JJ. He would come storming up to . . . to where I'm working or keep telephoning to persuade me to come home, and I can't stand that. I must see if I can exist on my own.'

As they talked they had climbed the long, dusty road which led back to the village and wended their way along the leafy lanes, arriving at last at Goldenstone. Before them the pond shone blue as the sky and the chestnut trees drooped over it, like beautiful women peering at their reflections. Anna felt as though someone had chopped the ground out from under her feet; no Mummy at Goldenstone, everyone knowing very soon what sort of a man Daddy was, Auntie Ella coming down to – to do what? The old order changeth, yielding place to new, and I don't like new things, Anna told herself almost tearfully. For ages I've wished Mummy would do something about Daddy, but not this, not this!

'Well, darling? Will you write to me when I send you an address? Come and visit me? I don't want to lose touch with you and Jamie, but if that's the price I must pay for my self-respect then I'll have to grin and bear it.'

'You won't lose me,' Anna said instantly. 'Nor Jamie, I'm sure. What does he say?'

'I've not told him yet. He may decide to come with me, darling, because he's still very dependent. But he won't finish school for another year and then he'll go straight into the forces to do his National Service, so I'd rather he stayed with Daddy, really. Jamie needs a stable home background, no one knows it better than I, but if he can't get on here, then I'll have him in . . . where I am. Daddy will just have to pay me an allowance for him.'

'You know where you're going, don't you, so why can't you tell me?' Anna said in what she hoped was a reasonable tone but suspected was more like a miserable whine. 'I won't tell, really I won't.'

'All right. I'm going to live in a tiny flat over a tobacconist's shop in Rampant Horse Street, and I'm working for Wilshire and Tillington, in London Street. You can write to me there or at Rampant Horse Street; I'll give you the full address before I leave this evening.'

'This evening! But you can't go as soon as that, you'll need to pack, to warn people . . . besides, Daddy might be back any minute.'

Constance shook her head. 'No, he'll be late. He always is when he's got a new girl.'

'What about packing? All your lovely things, your clothes . . .'

'I packed most of my stuff a week ago and sent it off, to await arrival. The rest is in my navy suitcase in my room, just waiting for me to pick it up. In fact, having told you now, I won't even have to stay for tea. I'll ring for a taxi as soon as we reach the house.'

Unable to risk speech, Anna just nodded. But when they entered Goldenstone she followed her mother up the stairs to her white-and-gold bedroom and sat on the bed as Constance tidied herself, put on her beautiful cream linen coat and rang for a taxi.

'Mummy, how do you feel?' Anna asked curiously as her mother cast one last, valedictory glance around the room. 'Sad? Frightened?'

'Relieved. At peace,' Constance said unexpectedly. 'I never thought I would, but I do.'

' "Sleep after toil, port after stormy seas, ease after war, death after life, does greatly please," ' Anna quoted softly. 'Oh Mummy, I never realised how it must be for you!'

'I think you did. I think that's why you haven't married, though goodness knows you've had enough opportunities. You've seen the darker side of marriage and that isn't something that encourages any intelligent woman to marry and risk a similar experience.'

'Yes, I'm afraid that's true,' Anna said, not bothering to deny it. 'Even the nicest of young men seems too great a risk. Even Dan – no, especially Dan.'

'Dan? Oh yes, I remember; charming young man. Too charming by half.' Constance cast a glance towards the window. 'Ah, here's my taxi.' She swooped across the room and kissed Anna's cheek in a flurry of perfume, face powder and fresh lipstick. 'Be good, darling, tell Jamie I'll be in touch. Daddy won't mind too much if the house runs smoothly. You will write? And visit me when I'm settled?'

'I will,' Anna promised, hugging her mother tightly. 'I've memorised your address and I won't tell anyone, except Jamie of course. But suppose Daddy's very, very upset and promises he'll never look at another woman . . .'

Constance, at the head of the stairs, turned and smiled lovingly at her daughter. Anna suddenly realised that her mother's face was glowing with happiness and looked shiningly innocent, like a child's.

'Darling, he says that every time – every time, without fail! Take good care of yourself and remember, I love you very much and I'm proud of you as well. I always knew you'd turn out to be someone special, and you have. Be a good girl, and take care of yourself.'

Carrying the navy-blue suitcase, leaning to one side with the weight of it, she went down the stairs and across the hall. Anna watched the slight, straightbacked figure climb into the taxi, say something to the driver and turn to wave, eyes suddenly large with unshed tears, mouth wobbling into strange shapes as the realisation hit her that this was it, the end of twenty-three years of uneasy marriage to JJ Radwell, the end of living at Goldenstone, mistress of so much that was beautiful and fine.

'Good luck, Mummy,' Anna shouted as the taxi driver revved his engine and roared round the corner and into the main drive. 'Be happy!'

She was still standing on the step waving, though the car had long since disappeared, when someone cleared their throat behind her. She turned and there stood Meg, a reproving look on her face and a tea-trolley in front of her.

'I don't know where your Mum's gone, Miss Anna, but she said tea was to be served on the terrace and there's me sittin' in the kitchen awaitin' for somebody to gi' me a call and all the time she's plannin' on a trip into the city or some such thing. What am I to do with all this?'

Anna looked at the trolley. On the top shelf were cups, saucers, plates and all the paraphernalia of tea-making. On the second shelf was a plate of cucumber sandwiches and another which looked like tomato. On the bottom shelf was a small slab of Meg's sticky gingerbread. It would all be mock, of course – margarine instead of butter, carrot instead of currants, dried milk instead of fresh – but it would be good, trust Meg for that. And there was far too much for Anna to tackle alone, though she could make some inroads.

'If you wouldn't mind taking it out to the terrace, Meg, I'll do my best with it,' she said reluctantly, for she found that she was no longer hungry and just wanted to be alone, to think. 'I expect Mr Jamie will be in later, and my father, of course. They can finish it up.'

Meg was looking past her as she spoke, now she put both hands to the trolley, eyes brightening, and began to wheel it back across the hall.

'Right, I'll take it to the terrace. And your Dad's back by the look of it, so doubtless he'll gi' you a hand with eatin' it up.'

458

JJ was climbing out of his car, stretching, yawning, then walking around to help his companion out of the passenger seat. For a second Anna thought that he must have met Constance, then she saw it was Josie Gaunt, looking shyly up at the house and at Anna, standing very close – too close – to JJ as though making it plain that she was here by his invitation, as his guest.

'Hello, darling! Jamie was busy, so I took little Jo here sailing with me. As we were driving into the village, we saw Mummy going out somewhere, so I thought it would be nice if Jo and I came home and had tea with you. All right if we join you?'

JJ turned to his young companion as they entered the hall, giving her a look which Anna immediately interpreted as 'I'd do anything for you, darling' – ugh! 'Where's tea being served?'

Anna gave JJ a long, cool look and he had the grace to go a little red. She had been dreading telling her father that his wife had left, but suddenly she began to look forward to it. How *dare* he bring his bit of fluff here, when his wife was out, how dare he put his daughter in such a difficult position!

'Oh, Daddy, hello Josie, do come in.' Anna waited until the maid and the tea-trolley had trundled on to the terrace and then she turned to her father, solicitously helping Josie out of her blue blazer, his large, clean hands touching her thin young arms with barely concealed desire. 'Tea's on the terrace, Meg's just taken it out.'

'And where's your mother gone off to in such a hurry? Not that it matters . . .'

'Don't worry about Mummy,' Anna said with syrupy sweetness. 'She heard about your latest friendship and she's decided to leave you, so she won't be having tea with you today or any other day. And I'll leave you to it, if you don't mind, I'm suddenly not at all hungry.'

She turned on her heel and ran up the stairs, looking back as she reached the galleried landing.

Josie was clutching JJ's arm; she looked sick, scared. JJ was staring up the stairs after Anna. He was white-faced, open-mouthed. He looked every one of his forty-six years.

Once the engagement was official everything seemed to happen

459

at once. Elizabeth, Miss Huntley reflected, was radiant. Always a pretty girl, she became beautiful, and because she had lost weight during the African tour she needed new clothes.

It was still make do and mend, of course, but everyone helped with coupons and advice, and the beautiful material bought by the royal family before the war came into its own at last. And the presents! Austerity Britain was staggering beneath the weight of war loans called in and enormous debts to be repaid while America, that brash and swaggering young colonial, said loud and long to anyone who would listen that the United Kingdom was finished, a has-been. But the British, fighting the unbelievably terrible weather which had afflicted them right up to the month of June, were too busy surviving to guard their backs against their recent ally. Instead, everyone worked as they never had before, production soared, every penny that came in went to pay loans – and then, when they needed it most, into their hard and boring lives came Romance. Their beautiful little Princess, who had suffered with them through the war, was to marry the young Greek Prince who had fought for Britain as a naval lieutenant and had recently become a citizen of Britain. The man who had brought him up, Louis Mountbatten, was already a favourite and now, with a great collective sigh, the British people took the young lovebirds and their eagerly awaited wedding to their hearts.

So what could they do to show their approval and delight? They could – and did – buy, make, beg or steal wedding presents. Some wonderful gifts came from abroad, but Huntie, and her Princess, valued the less valuable but more personal gifts most highly.

'Thinking of you on your great day – affectionately, Mabel Arkwright and Jennifer Bradley. Hope you like the scarf, we make them in the factory, only Jenny hand-painted the horse on to this one herself because we know you like them.'

'I'm a pensioner, I don't have much, but this grouse-claw was my gran's, I'd like you to have it and hope it brings you luck.'

'My brother Timmy made the egg-cup and I knitted the little hat you put on the egg. Sorry we couldn't send a egg, but we only have the dried sort. With lots of love, Sukie and Timmy Alcott'

'Sometimes I cry, because everyone's having such a hard time and I'm so exceedingly lucky,' the Princess told Huntie as they sat in her cosy little sitting-room in Buckingham Palace, unwrapping presents. 'Some of these girls are getting married themselves, but they won't have a nice home of their own, like we'll have, let alone two, a town one and a country one. Yet they save up and send me some little thing they would love to own themselves. Don't I just wish I could do something for them, in return!'

'You can – you do,' Huntie said. 'It's difficult to explain, dear, but they'll watch your wonderful white wedding and your handsome husband and you'll be putting romance and beauty into their lives, because they'll be right beside you in their imagination, enjoying every minute. In fact, your enjoyment is their reward, I suppose.'

'Vicarious pleasure isn't quite the same, unless you look at it as being like a cinema show. Yes, I suppose there's that.'

'Most certainly there is. Why, we'll all get pleasure from your happiness, Lilibet, every member of the staff, all your relatives, your friends. Perhaps it's a little like reflected glory, so don't think the folk who give you such nice presents are being entirely selfless. By accepting their gifts you give them a tiny stake in your special day.'

The Princess ripped the paper off another present, fielding the envelope which flew out at the same time with considerable dexterity.

'Goodness, that was lucky, it's fatal to let a note and a present get separated. Thank-you letters are hard enough without that! Oh Huntie, isn't that the prettiest thing? A Dresden china shepherdess with a little lamb in her apron! And a letter, of course.' She ripped the envelope open, then pulled out the single sheet and read the contents aloud.

'*Dear Princess Elizabeth, things are so difficult, I'm afraid we couldn't afford anything new, but this little lady has been in my family for a great many years, and we would like to think of her brightening your home as she once brightened ours. We have no kiddies of our own, but both Albert and I would like to wish you every happiness in*

461

your marriage to dear Lt Mountbatten. Our prayers and affection will be with you always.'

'Oh, Huntie, would you like this for your own home, when you move in later in the year? It's such a pretty ornament, but we've a great many already . . . I'd like you to have it.'

'That's sweet of you, Lilibet, and I'd be delighted to see the little lady on my mantelshelf,' Miss Huntley said at once. 'When you come and have tea with me you can make sure she's being dusted and looked after properly. I'll write the letter myself, though I shan't say that the shepherdess is on *my* mantel, of course.'

'Of course not. Though if anyone could see the number of presents they would guess that Philip and I couldn't possibly give house-room to them all. That reminds me, I must go down to our apartments today and see about the wallpaper for the study. Philip has excellent taste and I know he would like regency stripes, a deep red on cream, I think he said, but whether such paper is available or not is another matter.'

'I imagine that if such a paper exists anywhere in the world today you've only to say you're searching for it and it will turn up on your doorstep within the week,' Miss Huntley said, chuckling. 'Don't forget that you have to go for a fitting with Mr Hartnell in half an hour; it should be even more amusing than opening presents.'

'He does get excited,' the Princess admitted, smiling. 'Only another eight weeks, Huntie, and everyone will see his gown – including Philip. I think they'll like it, don't you?'

'How can I tell? The big secret doesn't include me, but if you like it then I'm sure I shall. And now let's open the odd-shaped one wrapped in yellow paper. I've been longing to do so; I wonder what on earth it can be?'

'It might be an octopus in an advanced state of rigor mortis,' the Princess said, chuckling. 'Or a short hat-stand with a great many pegs. Where are the scissors? We'll have to cut the string, it's got a whole ball wound round it I should think. Goodness, look at the time! This is positively the last present I open before I go to Mr Hartnell.'

*

462

'Well, if we could possibly manage it, I would like to go. I know November's a pretty miserable month and I know London will be absolutely crammed with people, but . . . oh Snip, but how will you get on if Mum and I take a couple of days off?'

'I'm going to come as well, didn't your mother tell you? Matthew says that the end of November is just about the deadest time for a farmer, so he's decided to come, and no one's likely to want to look around Pengarth at this time of year, so I don't see why I shouldn't come too.'

Snip and Nell were sitting companionably in front of the fire in their sitting-room, the erstwhile study, both energetically cleaning silver, with two cups of tea on a small table between them and a bowl of apples in case they got hungry later. Now, in the dancing firelight, Nell looked affectionately across at her husband. His skin was tanned, his eyes bright with health, his expression calm and self-assured. Examining him whilst he worked on the silver teapot he was gripping between his knees, Nell found that she could scarcely remember the pale, twitching young man she had brought back to Pengarth eighteen months before. He's a great deal better, she told herself now. And though I may not be giddily in love with him, the way I was with Dan, I most certainly do like him very much and want him close to me. It's odd, really, that I can be so fond of him yet not want to have children and sink into being just a wife and mother. I think if I did that I'd feel trapped, and I'd rather have the illusion of at least a degree of freedom. But Snip was looking up at her now, his expression expectant. Nell put down her own candlestick and smiled at him.

'If you came too that would be perfect. Mum never mentioned you or Matthew, she just said would I like to go up to London for the royal wedding, so I suppose she'd only just thought of it herself. She knew I wanted to go, because I can still remember the King's Coronation and what a wonderful day that was . . . you thought it was pretty good, didn't you? Awful little boy that you were, you climbed up the statue of Eros in Piccadilly Circus. What an exhibition you made of yourself – I wanted to climb up too, we waved and shrieked at you, Fleur and me, but our mothers dragged us away, tutting.'

'So I did. I didn't give a damn in those days,' Snip said proudly. He put the teapot down and picked up a tiny cream jug. 'If I promise not to climb Eros, or dance the polka on the Victoria Memorial or deface the lions in Trafalgar Square, will you let me come with you? Not that weddings are my cup of tea, exactly, but I don't like the thought of you goin' off by yourself and sleeping on the pavement and all. With four of us we'll make a party of it, but if you were with Hester and Matt the chances are you'd end up feeling left out.'

'If you promise to behave you *shall* come with us,' Nell said, leaning forward to pat his cheek. 'But what about the train? We can't possibly walk to London; it would take far too long.'

Snip polished vigorously for a moment, then stared into the fire. It was a wood fire because coal was rationed, and the flames were just creeping across the new logs, making the sap bubble and spit.

'I'll manage,' he said gruffly. 'I'm a heap better, love, you've said it yourself. I'm sure I'll manage.'

'And the crowds, and all the tall buildings? I'm not trying to make difficulties, Snip, but we must face facts before we tell Mum yes or no. Will you be all right in a big crowd?'

'There'll be the four of us; I'm sure I'll be all right,' Snip said stoutly. 'Anyway, it's a good time to put it to the test. Yes, buy me a rail ticket and we'll all go off to see your Princess Elizabeth marry her young feller.'

'My Princess? Why d'you say that?'

'Because ever since we were nippers you've cut out newspaper pictures and talked about her and reminded every Tom, Dick and Harry that the pair of you share a birthday,' Snip reminded her. 'When she's Queen you'll be unbearable, I shouldn't wonder. Now that will be an event – her coronation, I mean. Why, you'll probably get yourself put in the procession as a loyal subject and a birthday-sharer.'

Nell giggled, put her candlestick down in the hearth, and reached for her cooling tea. 'Then that's settled. I'll tell Mum to get Matthew to buy four return tickets and we'll start planning our day. Do you realise that this will be like a honeymoon for you and me? It's the first holiday we've had since we got married, anyway.'

Snip reached for his own tea, drank, then stood it down and leaned forward to hook his hand round the back of Nell's neck. A thumb rubbed affectionately under her ear. 'Every day since we've moved in here has been a holiday for me,' he observed. 'It's another life, Nell. I wouldn't change it for all the tea in China and I wouldn't swop places with anyone else either, not even with Lieutenant Philip Mountbatten.'

Nell touched his hand lightly: 'That's nice. I don't suppose I'd swop with the Princess either, though Philip is rather gorgeous. And now let's get this silver back into the dining-room so that we can go to bed. We'll have plenty to do in the morning, getting ready to go to London!'

Anna was extremely happy at the London School of Economics. She was reading economics and found her work hard but perfectly possible. She had expected to be years older than the other students, but this did not prove to be the case. Quite a lot were men who had fought in the war and were returning to the universities in droves to continue their studies, and even among the female students there were a good many of Anna's age, late starters for the same reason as their male colleagues.

The wedding was a topic of great interest to all of them, though it was a shame that it would take place in term time.

'But we'll be given a day off,' Billy Prince said, looking up from his ink-stained notebook at Anna, sitting opposite him in the small café where they were studying and drinking coffee just to be in the warm rather than roaming the chilly November streets. Anna was not supposed to take men up to her room and Billy was in the same boat, which meant that mutual studying had to be done in public places. 'We could go up West, and see the whole thing. Would you like that, Anna?'

Billy Prince was short and muscular, with tousled light brown hair and a pair of sensitive, honey-brown eyes. He had been a paratrooper during the war and one of the first ashore at the D-Day landings. Sometimes his whole face would jerk into a spasm. The hair hanging over his brow hid a bayonet scar three inches long, and the bayonet had done something to his face-muscles. It only happened now and then and since Billy never let it bother him, no one else did either.

The two of them had got on well from the moment they'd met, and not only because they had a subject in common. Billy was reading economics because he wanted, he said, to go into politics.

'Not immediately, but when I'm about thirty,' he'd said when Anna had asked why he had chosen their particular subject. 'I'll do something in industry first, probably, but you need a good grounding in economics to run the country.'

Anna, who was reading economics chiefly because she wanted to work abroad and had been told by the course tutor that a BSc in Economics with French as her second language would be helpful, admired Billy's zeal and foresight and took her problems to him. He was twenty-four, fiercely intelligent, ambitious and rather prickly, possibly because his mother was a hospital cleaner and his father a Billingsgate porter. Billy told everyone about his background as soon as he saw they might be friends; it was simpler, he told Anna, to get it over with, but despite this openness you still had to be careful what you said to him. Sometimes he took offence over a casual remark and that meant many of the students, particularly the younger ones, either avoided close contact with him or treated him with kid gloves.

Anna did neither of these things. She liked him very much, envied him his clear, analytical brain, enjoyed his company and always said just what she thought, soon realising that he valued her frankness more than empty compliments or constant agreement.

'You're an inverted snob, hoping someone will drop you because you're working class,' Anna accused early in their acquaintance, but Billy only grinned his lopsided grin which revealed his two broken front teeth, also a souvenir of Normandy, and shook his head.

'It isn't that at all. It's a kind of test. If they pass it, I know we'll get on okay and I don't have to worry about them. If they don't, then I shan't waste my time learning about them.'

'Your time! You're so damned clever that you've more spare time than the rest of us put together,' Anna told him. 'Billy me darlin', are you going to explain this to me like a kind little paratrooper? Because if you don't I'll fail my finals and then we'll never dance naked on the principal's lawn, as you said we would.'

It was Billy's boast that he didn't give a damn about anyone, and at some stage he had told Anna that if they both passed he would buy her a bottle of champagne, help her to drink it, and then assist her to dance the tango, in her birthday suit, outside the principal's windows. But right now, sitting in the steamy little café with a cup of acorn-tasting coffee, Anna's mind was on higher things than champagne or naked dancing. She was thinking how nice it would be to see Princess Elizabeth and Philip Mountbatten married. She had never told Billy about the shared birthday because it had never come up, but she did so now, ending, 'So you see I really would like to go to the wedding. And I could, because my Aunt Ella lives in Bloomsbury, so she'd put me up if I needed a bed. I'm sure she'd put you up as well, Billy, if you'd like to come with me.'

'That's kind, but if you want to see anything you'll have to nab a spot near the palace or the abbey and sleep on the pavement,' Billy said with relish. 'No use strolling down the road at half-past ten and expecting the crowds to part for you, like Moses and the Red Sea. It won't happen, honey-pie.'

'If you're with me you can push and shove and get me to the front,' Anna pointed out, sipping her coffee and wrinkling her nose with distaste. 'This stuff's bad enough hot, but cold it's disgusting. Can we run to another cup or shall we hie us to a library?'

Libraries were another place where they could study together on a rainy day when neither had a lecture.

Billy considered his own cup, almost down to the dregs. 'You're right, it's pretty foul,' he admitted. 'I'm skint, as usual, so we'd better find a library. This place is great in summer, but pretty grim in winter. Still, we can sit in a pub this evening if we choose a quiet one.'

He stood up and Anna followed suit, gathering her books and papers and shovelling them into the ancient canvas bag she carried around with her.

'Right, we'll do that. And shall we go up West for the wedding, Billy? I'm game if you are.'

'Yes, sure. It's probably the only way I'll get you to sleep with me, out on the pavement with a thousand other people in the same bed.'

Anna chuckled and headed for the door. 'Much you care! Look, if we go round to my aunt's place after the wedding, she'll give us a meal. How about that? I'd like you to meet her.'

'Let's play it by ear,' Billy said, seizing her hand and swinging it so vigorously that a passing cyclist swerved and swore at them. 'Sorry, sir, I didn't see you . . . I'm beginning to look forward to this royal wedding; it might easily be a lot of fun.'

It was not a bad day, weatherwise, which was a pleasant surprise, everyone having steeled themselves for rain or worse. Hester and Nell had been too excited to sleep much, though they had a blown-up air mattress between them and a blanket each, as well as their thickest jerseys and winter coats.

'We may not have slept, but you and Matthew snored like pigs,' Nell told Snip as she offered him hot coffee from the second of their flasks. 'Mum and I wouldn't have been able to sleep even if we'd not been too excited. Gosh, I'm stiff, but haven't we got a good place?'

They had. Quite near the abbey, so that they would see the Princess going in and the married woman emerging, with friendly people around them, all as keen to see the happy couple as were the Coburns and Morrises.

'I'd like a walk,' Snip said presently, but it was impossible, so he and Nell paraded up and down in front of the crowd to stretch their legs while Hester and Matthew guarded their small piece of pavement.

'You're bearing up fine,' Nell whispered as they walked.

'Even on the train you were fine and it was hellishly crowded, far worse than I thought it would be.'

'Thank you, Mrs Morris. The train was trying, I admit, but here I'm out of doors and with you – what more could I ask?'

'A seat? A place in the abbey? A proper cup of tea, not one from a flask filled more than twenty-four hours ago?'

Snip laughed and squeezed her shoulders. 'Let's buy some roasted chestnuts – there's a vendor farther up. At least it's a change from curling sandwiches!'

'They're coming . . . hear the murmur as they draw level with each section of the crowd? Well, I reckon he'll be pleased, he's been waiting for long enough! Oh, Billy, look! She's just one big smile and a little hand and something sparkly on dark hair. Oh, Billy, doesn't she look *happy*?'

The shouts from the crowd were deafening, but Nell put her head close to Snip's and breathed her words straight into his ear.

'The dress, Snip – she looks like a perfect lily, so small and straight. It's simple, perfect. I thought it would be all frills and lace, but it's far, far more beautiful than that – Norman Hartnell got it just right! She's smiling, smiling as if she'll never stop . . . how *happy* she looks.'

'She looked straight at us, at me,' Hester said to Matthew. 'Isn't she the most beautiful young girl? Purity personified . . . oh Matt, I'm so happy I could cry. I feel as if she and Nell and me . . . as if we're all a part of the same thing, somehow. Aren't I silly?'

Matthew's arm tightened around her waist. 'No, not silly. You're just feeling what every woman in this crowd feels this moment, I reckon. Every woman in the country, very likely. She's a nice kid, I reckon, just like our Nell.'

The ceremony was over; rings and vows had been exchanged, and Huntie, sitting in Poet's Corner to be near but not too near, mopped tears from her cheeks and smiled encouragingly at her pupil's slender, straight back.

469

It had been wonderful, absolutely wonderful, the most moving experience of her life ... and Lilibet had done so well and was so radiant as she turned to walk back down the aisle.

Outside, they waited. The patient men and women, the children, who had come to share this great day with their Princess. But none of them had been as patient as the Princess herself, sharing her life because that was her destiny, caring for the people who, one day, would be hers.

The King looked worn out. He had worked – and worried – too hard for years; now he was paying the price in ill-health and exhaustion. Miss Huntley found that she was praying for his life, praying that his life would be a long one, because he was a gentle, loving man who had done nothing but good for all of that life so far.

Elizabeth must have some time for herself, now, Miss Huntley told herself fiercely. She has cast off childish things, she and her husband are on their own. I pray it may be many, many years before her next great moment comes.

Eighteen

'Have some more marmalade, darling; you can't imagine me actually making marmalade, I don't suppose, but I assure you it was all my own work. I'm becoming tremendously domesticated – I'm still a member of the Women's Institute, though I have to drive out to the village for meetings, but ever since the war I've really appreciated what they've taught me and now I'm putting it into practice for myself.'

Anna and her mother, both still in their dressing gowns, were sitting over a leisurely breakfast in Constance's latest flat. It was on Ipswich Road in Norwich; a top-floor front in a large, red-brick block, and considering how difficult it was to find accommodation, Anna considered that Constance had surpassed herself in acquiring it, to say nothing of furnishing it with beautiful old pieces bought at country-house sales or from tiny junk shops tucked away in the older parts of the city.

Constance was looking good too. Sitting on the small, gilt chair on the other side of her walnut dining table, with her hair once more beautifully cut and delicately tinted, she had shed fifteen years, Anna considered, since she had left JJ. It was difficult to believe that the slim, elegant woman in the scarlet silk dressing gown writhing with black and gold dragons could be one and the same as the raddled, lack-lustre woman who had told her about JJ's continuing infidelities half-a-dozen years ago. Now, Constance looked nearer thirty-five than fifty, but what was even more important she looked happy and fulfilled.

'Anna, why are you staring? I suppose you think it's decadent to loll around in a dressing gown, but Saturday breakfast is my treat; on every other day of the week I'm in my office by nine, but on Saturdays I slouch and sip coffee and eat toast and don't even think about advertising, or my favourite customers or my key accounts. Isn't that an admission for you?'

Constance was an advertising executive for an up-and-coming local firm and enjoyed every moment of her busy life. But now Anna smiled at her mother and spread marmalade on a fresh round of toast.

'If you're decadent in a dressing gown, I am too,' Anna pointed out. 'If I stared it was because I think you're looking stunning, Mummy – that housecoat is so elegant you could entertain royalty in it and no one would raise an eyebrow. And don't fish for compliments, you know the marmalade is delicious, but it would be even nicer with more coffee. Any left in the pot?'

Constance chuckled. 'You're just like me, dear, good coffee's like a drug; we need it to get going in the mornings. Many thanks for bringing that big bag of beans from France, incidentally; what a clever present! Now tell me, how's life? Any fascinating Frenchmen courting my little girl?'

Anna, with a mouthful of toast, merely shook her head. She had been living in Paris and working for UNESCO for the past four years and had been out with several 'fascinating Frenchmen', but none of them had remained fascinating for long enough to interest Constance.

'No? Anna darling, you haven't let Daddy and me put you off marriage, have you? Because we had our good times . . . and anyway, all men aren't like JJ, but you know that, of course. You've had some lovely boyfriends, I liked all the ones I met.'

Anna swallowed her mouthful and took a deep breath.

'You don't still believe that marriage is the be-all and end-all of existence do you, Mummy? Because just look around you – look in the mirror, come to that! You're a happy and successful woman, and I see no man lurking around the flat.'

The sunshine streaming in through the window made the marmalade glow like another small sun and gilded Constance's hair to platinum, but it also made her blink so she leaned forward and drew the heavy brocade curtain half across the window, then leaned back once more and contemplated her daughter across the tablecloth.

'You're quite right, I'm far happier now than I was when JJ and I lived together. But you and Jamie are my *raison d'être*, Anna. Without you, my life would be pretty hollow.'

'That's a lovely thing to say, but you had to go through some horrid times before you reached your present haven, and I suspect I'm too selfish and not strong enough to put up with the bad side of marriage. So you could say I've opted out. As for children, babies are quite fun but having them's pretty grim, I'm told.'

'Oh, childbirth,' Constance said airily, patting her lips with her napkin and getting to her feet. 'A means to an end, dear. However, if you've not met a man whom you can't live *without*, then you're quite right not to marry. And now let's both get dressed and walk into the city. We can look around the shops, have a leisurely lunch in Garlands or in Prince's if you'd rather, and then this afternoon I thought we might go for a spin in the country and end up in Yarmouth for dinner.'

'Sounds lovely – only if you don't mind I'd rather have tea in Yarmouth than dinner,' Anna said, trying not to sound too guilt-ridden. 'The fact is, Mummy, I'm – I'm meeting an old friend this evening. I said Saturday would be all right because you'll want me round at Gran's for Sunday supper, and I know you've got a dinner party organised for Monday evening and a theatre visit on Tuesday.'

'An old friend? Male or female? Was it a dinner date, because if not, we could still go down to Yarmouth and have an early dinner. No, I suppose it would be too much of a rush . . . who did you say it was?'

'Oh, just an old friend,' Anna said, still smiling. 'Just someone who happens to be in Norfolk this weekend. And now I'm going to go and get dressed because I splashed out and bought the most gorgeous fine wool suit in the Champs Elysées and I can't wait for you to see it.'

'Ooh, lovely! Actually, I've got a little number which takes pounds off me as well as years . . . tell you what, we needn't have lunch in town, we can just have a coffee at Garlands –

everyone who's anyone has coffee in Garlands on a Saturday morning – and after that we can drive to Yarmouth and lunch at one of the big hotels over there, in our new finery. Would you like that, darling? Is it Mabel you're going to meet, by the by? No, of course not, she's living in Christchurch Road, you could meet her any time. Did you know she's just had another little girl? Three in six years! It's not Tina, is it?'

'No. I'm meeting Dan Clifton, actually,' Anna said, relenting in the face of her mother's blatant curiosity. 'But don't get your hopes up – if ever there was a man who was fun to be with but simply not the marrying kind, it's Dan. Still, he's a good friend. He writes regularly, rings me up if he's in France and comes and takes me out from time to time. And he's in Blofield this weekend, so I said I'd pop into the King's Head about seven o'clock and we'd have a drink together.'

'Dan Clifton? Good lord, I'd almost forgotten him, I didn't realise the two of you had kept in touch.' Constance opened the door and floated on to the landing, then paused outside her bedroom. Her long, blue-lidded eyes slanted thoughtfully towards her daughter, the expression in them a blend of hope and calculation which Anna remembered well from her youth. 'Dan's not married, old Mrs Lucas told me that much, though no doubt he's had a great many girlfriends. She dotes on the boy you know, says he's done awfully well for himself, all things considered. His mother married a foreigner, so old Mrs Lucas had to bring him up more or less single-handed. He certainly drives a very expensive car . . . what does he do?'

'He's something in the diplomatic service, I'm not quite sure what,' Anna said vaguely. 'His French is as good as mine, and his German's a good deal better. He even speaks Italian, though he says not as well, and some Spanish.'

'Oh, quite a linguist, then. And he visits you in Paris?' The blue eyes sparkled, the lips curved into an inquisitive half-smile.

'He visits me in Paris,' Anna confirmed, her own lips twitching. Constance was incorrigible, she would never change. Let an unmarried man and an unmarried woman enter the same conversation, let alone the same room, and Constance would be matchmaking. 'But we're old friends you see, Mummy, and old friends just like to meet, chat, share the gossip around . . .'

'He's rather handsome,' Constance murmured. 'Don't you think so, dear? Awfully handsome, really. I've always admired men with very dark hair and eyes and a sort of twinkle about them.'

Anna, about to enter the spare room, paused in the doorway.

'Yes, he's nice-looking, successful, and probably courted by every woman for miles around,' she said. 'So forget it, Mummy. Danny simply isn't my type.'

'No-oo. Because although your father's fair and Dan's dark, they do have something in common.' Constance sighed, then became suddenly brisk. 'Well, we'll never get lunch at all if we don't get a move on. I wonder if we ought to drive up and park on Orford Hill, in front of the Bell? Oh, see how we get on. Let's hurry!'

They walked into the city in the end. The sunshine was so warm, the breeze so mild, that neither wore a coat and they swung along arm in arm in their smart clothes, the yellow head and the brown one close together, looking, Anna suspected, more like sisters than mother and daughter.

It was a nice walk, and mainly downhill, which was even nicer. They passed the Norfolk & Norwich Hospital where Anna had visited her friend Betty when Betty's tonsils and adenoids had been removed. They plunged down St Stephens, glancing at the window displays but not going into any of the shops. Woolworth's and Peacocks looked tempting, and Gordon Thoday's, the silk merchants, was a shop which Constance rarely passed, but today, as she breathlessly remarked, if they wanted to get to Garlands while they were still serving coffee they could not afford to linger.

At the end of St Stephens they went along Red Lion Street and then crossed the road and dived down the steps into White Lion Street.

'Wilson's!' Anna said, jerking her mother's arm and drawing her attention to the shop on their right, from whose open doors came the strains of a popular melody. 'The hours Tina and I spent in there, choosing gramophone records – I listened to "There's a Tree in a Meadow" about twenty times in one of their little booths – but I couldn't afford to buy two, and I wanted Dinah Shore singing "Buttons and Bows" more, at the time. Gosh, that seems a long time ago!'

'And I went into Brahams and tried on every mink coat in the place when I was a flapper, only I never managed to get the money for even a teeny little mink stole out of your grandparents,' Constance said dreamily as they passed the top of the Royal Arcade. 'Now that was a long time ago – ah, happy days! Still, we do all right, you and I.'

Mother and daughter hurried along Castle Street and turned left into London Street, then crossed the busy road and went into Garlands. Anna felt herself begin to smile; this was the stuff of her early teenage years. It was delightful to remember the hours she and her friends had spent hanging around the perfumery, examining every garment on every rack in the big department store and wandering along the aisles luxuriating in the mere presence of such beautiful clothes. Even in the late Forties, with all the shortages, it had been a wonderful place to meet, and the big, brightly lit restaurant in the basement had been the natural gathering ground for young and fashionable Norwich people.

Now pleasantly relaxed, Anna sauntered beside Constance through the department store and down the stairs. It was rather nice to walk into a place and look around to see who you knew, she told herself, and indeed as soon as they entered the restaurant someone hailed them.

'Connie, old love, what a pleasant surprise! Why, if it isn't Anna, too! Do come over here and sit with us and I'll buy each of you the squishiest cake on the trolley!'

A glance was enough to tell Anna that it was her mother's cousin Ida and her daughter Linette. They were sitting at one of the large, round tables, drinking coffee. Another glance showed Anna that the place teemed with fashionable young men and women, but most of them were a good deal younger than she. Linette, to be sure, was her age, but her cousin was holding a cross-looking baby in one arm and trying to persuade a fat toddler to drink a glass of milk and stop demanding ice-cream. She was no longer the pink-faced, dreamy girl Anna had known but a determined young matron with permed hair, worry lines on her forehead and the beginnings of a double chin.

Everything's changed, Anna thought dolefully, greeting her relatives, smiling doubtfully at the children, then sitting down and choosing a cake from the display. This place belongs to a new generation, even Linette is out of it down here now. But of course it doesn't really matter to me because I'm only a visitor in the city; my home is in Paris. I'm far too intelligent and sophisticated to settle for a husband, a semi-detached house in suburbia and a couple of kids. I'm enjoying a varied social life, lots of exciting friends, an important career . . . why, I wouldn't change places with Linette for all the tea in China.

'Don' wan' yat milla-milla!' roared Linette's toddler. 'Wanna nicecweam!'

'Have a bit of my chocolate éclair,' Anna coaxed, and was told frostily, by Linette, that it was clear that she knew nothing, but *nothing* about bringing up the young. Thank God for it, Anna thought silently, whilst admitting aloud that she had had very little experience with small children. She sat back in her chair and watched her mother absently smooth a hand around the baby's plump, sticky little face, then take the child on her lap as she chatted to Ida; watched the toddler hurl the mug of milk to the floor so that Linette, red-faced, squirmed under the table trying to find it again. The waitress came over, smiling.

'Have he hulled that overboard?' she enquired affably. 'Here, my man, d'you fancy a chocolate finger, together?'

She gave him a chocolate finger and, instead of shouting that she knew nothing about children, Linette thanked her politely and apologised for the spilt milk. At the next table a slender girl with reddish-gold hair piled into a froth of curls on top of her head shrugged and smiled as she glanced towards the children. She was with a handsome boy of around her own age and she wore her clothes with an air: her long neck rose like a lily from the high collar of a crisp white blouse, her pale-grey flared skirt was almost ankle length and she wore dark red, high-heeled

shoes. She looked fashionable and modern and very, very young
... and suddenly Anna was glad that she was going to meet
Dan tonight, that she was reasserting her identity, confirming
her ability to attract a man, even if he was only interested in
her friendship.

And I'm only twenty-seven, she reminded herself hastily.
That's not so terribly old ... goodness, I've my whole life
ahead of me!

By half past six Anna was beginning to regret her promise
to meet Dan for a drink. She was fond of Dan; as she had
told Constance, they were good friends, but it was one thing to
meet him in Paris and quite another to share a drink at the pub
in the village, only a mile or so from Goldenstone. People would
talk, and Anna did not want them talking about her, especially
not to her father.

She had managed to remain on good terms with JJ by dint
of meeting him in the city from time to time and sharing a meal
but not actually visiting her old home. She would have loved to
go back, but not when it meant being entertained by the present
incumbent, a girl four years younger than herself.

'I'd never have remarried if there had been a chance of
Connie and me getting together again,' JJ had told his daughter
the last time they met. 'You can't blame me, darling – I got so
lonely, Goldenstone's such a huge barracks of a place for a man
by himself.'

'It doesn't matter; you and Mummy are both happy now,
and settled,' Anna had said gently. She did not believe he was
happy; it was common knowledge that his new wife could not
cope with the house and was wildly jealous if he so much as
looked at another woman. JJ, spoiled by Constance's feigned
blindness, could not get used to having his every peccadillo
brought out into the cruel light of day, criticised, talked about
and finally derided. He tried everything, he told Anna. Sulking,
punishment-by-absence, extravagant apologies and sheaves of
red roses. But nothing made the slightest difference. Felicity
got more and more bitter and spiteful, and each fresh discovery
was greeted with shouting, screaming and hysterics. In short,

she made scenes in a way Constance would never have done.

'You could try not looking at other women,' Anna had suggested over the dinner he was buying her in the Grill Room of the Castle Hotel. 'Have you ever considered that, Daddy?'

JJ looked at her over the top of his glasses; he favoured rimless ones, in the hope that no one would realise his sight was no longer perfect. Anna thought they made him look rather feminine but was too tactful to tell him so.

'But darling, of course I don't look at other women! It's all in the mind, I promise you. I've thought of getting Flicky to see a psychiatrist but when I suggested it she went absolutely wild . . . smashed three vases and a window pane, I was lucky it wasn't my head!'

'How did she do that?' Anna asked, genuinely interested. Felicity had seemed such a demure young creature at the wedding, with her bell of ash-blonde hair and her wide blue eyes. Anna could not imagine her raising her voice in anger, let alone a vase.

'Oh, when she's angry she just picks up the nearest object and throws it very hard at me, or sometimes at the wall,' JJ said, eating salmon in puff pastry with a good appetite. 'She's gone through most of the wedding presents and it's getting embarrassing ringing Mr Gedge up to replace the windows. It still isn't easy to get glass, so the study one is more or less permanently filled in with cardboard and sticky tape.'

'Oh, well,' Anna had murmured. 'I daresay she'll calm down a bit when you have a family, or doesn't she want children?'

'Children? We haven't discussed it.' JJ stared down at his salmon for a moment as though he had suddenly realised it contained ground glass. 'Oh no, we don't discuss having children. I don't really see Flicky as a mother, and I've got you and Jamie, you're quite enough for me.'

'I thought it might make her less excitable,' Anna had said. 'Like with dogs and things, you know. All that vase-throwing's a bit immature, wouldn't you say?'

'Oh, well,' JJ said, starting to eat his salmon once more. 'Temper apart, she's not a bad bargain, young Flicky. Can't cook, I'll grant you, but there are other things . . . she's most awfully good at them.'

He gave Anna a look which she immediately interpreted and decided to ignore. Boasting about his sugar-baby's sexual prowess to his daughter, Anna thought, helping herself to more green peas, simply showed that JJ was just as immature, in his way, as his new young wife.

But right now she was getting down off the Number 7 bus outside the King's Head. The pub was brightly lit and her watch showed her that she was about ten minutes late. She could have borrowed her mother's car, but that would have meant driving back to Norwich alone, and she knew Dan would offer to see her home. Anna was used to driving on the right, not the left, and had no desire to practise after dark and in a strange vehicle.

'You awright, my woman?' the bus conductor asked as she climbed down, leaning out on the step. 'Someone meetin' you? There in't another 7b now till tomorrer but if you give a knock to the cottage nearest the post office, old Buggy Fuller drive a taxi now. He'll git you back to Goldenstone.'

'I'm not going home, Sid, I'm meeting a friend in the pub,' Anna explained. Sid had been a conductor on the 7 and 7b for years; she remembered him from way back and was flattered that he had obviously remembered her too. 'Thanks for the offer, though.'

'That's awright, gal. Orf we go, then.'

He tinged the bell, the bus lurched into life and Anna began to cross the wide strip of gravel, heading for the bar. She was not likely to see either her father or Felicity in here, since if they went drinking locally she rather thought they would favour The Globe, farther down the road, but in any case she doubted whether Dan would want to stay long. It was simply somewhere they both knew, somewhere to meet. A village pub was scarcely the best place for a quiet talk, and she knew that Dan would have a good deal to say to her.

Anna hesitated for a moment outside the door. It was a windy April night with the stars very bright overhead and the scent of lilac from a nearby garden was on the boisterous breeze. Where would they go after a drink or two, she and Dan? As children they had traipsed over this countryside

480

on their bikes and on foot, investigating Braydeston Hills, the river, the lake at Pedham Dam, the railway cuttings and the broads themselves with the wild life which fascinated Anna still – the coypu, those enormous ratlike creatures which infested the waterways, splashing noisily into the water as dusk fell; the swallowtail butterflies fluttering above the reed-beds; the industrious water voles and the squabbling ducks and coots. Then as teenagers they had sailed on the Yare and competed in races on various broads, a group usually, seldom splitting into pairs. Since then, she and Dan had met in Paris, and what could be more romantic than Paris in the spring, except perhaps Paris in the autumn, with the leaves drifting down from the trees lining the Champs Elysées? That was why Dan had started to propose marriage every six or eight months, of course, because Paris was so romantic, such a marvellous city for lovers. But she, Anna, did not want a lover, certainly did not want a husband. Lovers let you down, husbands cast you off . . . it's better to have friends, Anna told herself defensively, standing outside the pub door and hearing, through it, the murmur of voices, the clunk of darts on the board, the landlord's wife calling for more help please, we're busy through here! Yes, it's better to enjoy your career, have lots of friends, and create a life which doesn't need a close relationship with someone else. That's safer, much safer, than even the best of lovers. Only . . . it was so cold somehow, such a chilly sort of life! Safe, yes, she acknowledged that it was safe. But cold, cold as charity. In her mind she saw the years stretching ahead like a long, grey road, with her walking down the middle of it, ignoring other people, needing only herself, wearing her solitude like a frosty nimbus about her person.

'Excuse . . . Good Lord, Anna, it's you! What on earth are you doing, hovering out here?'

Dan, warm and real, took both her hands in his and then, light as a moth, kissed her cheek. Without meaning to do so, Anna moved closer, to get into the aura of warmth and security which surrounded him.

'Oh, Dan, I was just going to go inside. I don't know why I was hovering, perhaps I was wondering who was in there that we knew.'

Dan nodded and put his arm around her shoulders, turning her away from the pub, with its promise of warmth and brightness, and back into the night. With him beside her the night, which had been simply dark, seemed to sparkle like a diamond.

'Yes, I know what you mean. All the people who knew us when we were kids. Where would you like to go, then? Have you eaten? We could go down to the coast, get ourselves a meal, or we could have fish and chips in newspaper, if you'd rather.'

The cold loneliness which she sensed in her inner self retreated, melted away, when Dan was near. He was so warm, so confident – he seemed to know just where he was going and he wanted to take her with him, to make her a part of his life. Why couldn't she give in, let him love her? But the risks, oh, the risks were too great, it was better to enjoy his company as a friend and not risk his realising that she was nothing special, that he could do better elsewhere. But now he was warm and close and very much her friend; his affection shone out of his eyes even in the faint light from the pub windows. Anna took his hand, smiling up at him, suddenly very happy. This meeting was just fun and friendship, she told herself. Enjoy it while you can.

'Oh, Dan, it's such a lovely evening . . . let's go down to the coast!'

He smiled back at her, eyes dancing, clearly infected by her mood.

'Right. Yarmouth's nearest, we'll go there.'

The drive was exhilarating. Dan had the hood down and all the scents of the night were carried on the wind as it blew across the flat marshy meadows, even the subtle scent from the pollarded willows which lined the road and the watery smell of the dykes which cross-crossed Acle marshes. Above their heads, huge stars glittered in the velvet black of the sky and the quiet, dark shapes of cattle grazing seemed to accompany their onward rush.

It was too early in the year for Yarmouth to be lit up for the season but they went down Regent Street and Anna hopped out and bought fish and chips, then they drove the full length of the street and turned on to the promenade, where Dan pulled the car to a halt.

'We're going to get greasy,' he said warningly. 'Shall we eat 'em in the car or on the beach? The beach is best.'

They clambered out of the car and down on to the cold white Yarmouth sand, unwashed by tides yet still smelling fresh, salty.

'I salted and vinegared them, but it'll only last about halfway down,' Anna said, digging out long strips of sea-fresh skate and cramming it into her mouth. Nothing had ever tasted so good, unless it was the crisp, golden batter or the beautiful greasy chips. 'We should have bought some pop to drink with it.'

'We'll go to a pub later,' Dan said thickly. 'I wonder why no one ever serves skate in Paris?'

'French fries aren't chips,' Anna said through a mouthful. 'Besides, they'd think battering fresh fish was a crime. I wonder why I don't agree?'

Dan laughed, rolled his paper into a ball and pushed it into his coat pocket. Then he peered hopefully into the newspaper on Anna's lap.

'You don't criticise English fried fish because we're in England and it's a mild night and the stars are much bigger and brighter over Yarmouth beach than they ever are over Paris. Got any chips going begging?'

'You pig! Well, you can have those few, but don't you touch my fish!'

When the food was eaten they took off shoes, stockings and socks and ran down to the sea, the slope of the beach too steep to allow more than the briefest of forays into the waves. Both Dan and Anna knew all about the North Sea shelf which meant you could walk in a foot or so then find yourself floundering in water up to your waist; one more incautious step could plunge you into ten or twelve feet of water. So they were careful, washing the grease off their hands and mouths, then retreating to stand on the hard, ridged sand as the waves crashed hungrily in, holding hands and staring out to sea while the wind tried to push them back up the beach and into the town.

'Shall we go back to the car, then? You must be getting chilly.' Dan's words were snatched from his mouth and hurled behind him by the strength of the wind, but Anna got the gist of what he said and nodded, clutching him tightly.

'All right,' she shouted. 'Race you!'

The wind was behind them as they slogged up the beach, vaulted on to the promenade and ran for the car. Dan reached it first and stood there, arms wide, and caught Anna as she reached him, clasping her to his chest. She stayed there for a moment, feeling the beat of his heart against her breast, then she sighed and pulled away.

'Oh Dan, wasn't that lovely? But we'd better get a move on. Mummy will worry if I'm too late.'

Dan ushered her into the car and climbed behind the wheel. Then he turned to her, just the flash of teeth and eyes visible through the dark.

'Anna, hasn't it been nice? You've enjoyed it as much as I have, I can tell. We're good together, we enjoy the same things, we've had similar experiences, we're in similar jobs. Anna, darling, do let's get married! I have to ask, but if you say "no" this time I won't bother you ever again. That's a promise, because if you don't want to marry me after tonight then I suppose you never will.'

Anna turned to him. He was not looking at her now, he was staring ahead of him, through the windscreen. He had put the hood up, so it was warm and private in the small sports car. His profile was achingly familiar and in a way she knew she loved him – but not enough, never enough.

'Oh Dan, I wish . . . but I'm just not the marrying kind! Please let's stay friends, it's terribly important to me. Please don't make it marriage or nothing.'

'I'm thirty years old and I want a home of my own and a family. A wife to kiss and cuddle, maybe kids . . . but somewhere of my own. If you're absolutely determined not to marry, darling Anna, then I – I suppose I'll have to look for someone else.'

'Don't try to pretend I'm your one love, Danny,' Anna said chidingly. It was meant to sound light, understanding, but it came out reproachful. 'There have always been girls, you know there have.'

He shook his head, a lock of hair flopped across his forehead. He still didn't look at her. 'No. There was a girl I thought a lot of, but it wasn't love or anything like that, it was just because we'd got on well as kids. And there were girls, of course, when I was at university, when I was in the RAF, even when I first started work with the Diplomatic Corps. A fellow has to go out with a few girls so he'll know when the right one comes along. And I knew at once, Anna. Since that first time after the war when we met up in Paris, I've not so much as dated another woman. It's just been you. And it'll always be you and no one else, if you'll marry me.'

It was odd, a part of her mind believed him totally, yet another part of her mind was sure he lied. There must have been girls, a great many girls . . . he was a man, wasn't he? Her mind whirled with confusing, conflicting thoughts. He was so attractive, there must have been other girls in the four years he had been taking her out. What was it Constance had said? *He's like your father . . .* something like that, anyway. He had fascinated Anna from the time they were children together; she could not believe that he had not fascinated others, very probably into bed. He knew all about the things Anna only guessed at with vague distaste, he was experienced, a man of the world.

But he had never tried his expertise on her. He kissed, cuddled, proposed marriage, but he had never tried to get her into bed. Which must mean, Anna supposed dully, that he simply did not find her sufficiently attractive. Yet he had asked her to marry him time after time, and she was sure – almost sure – that the desperation in his proposals rang true. He really did want to marry her, so why couldn't she just say 'Yes please, Dan', and make them both happy?

But it was no use, not really. He was fascinating and attractive, like JJ, and he would soon discover that she was neither and leave her, with a broken heart and an empty ache inside. Better anything than that, better even the ache she had now, each time he said goodbye and left her.

'And is that your answer, Anna? Are you saying that you won't marry me, now or ever, and I might as well forget the whole thing?'

'No, of course I'm not. Oh Dan, I'm so fond of you . . .'

She got no further. He leaned across the car and pulled her into his arms. He began to kiss her, but these were not the quiet, tender kisses she had associated with Dan. He kissed her hard, almost unkindly, yet instead of crying out or resenting this unbrotherly caress she almost purred, pressing closer to him, clinging, not even thinking about the rights and wrongs, pros and cons, simply enjoying everything, even the stubble on his chin which dug into her flesh as his mouth moved on hers. And presently he made the seats recline and heaved her on to his lap. She was so excited, so fired by him, she did not even pretend to herself that she did not want him. She found that her whole body tingling with desire, felt alive all over, in a way she had never felt in her life before. She clung to Dan and she told him she loved him and tears slid down her cheeks with the wonder of it. And she knew that he was going to make love to her, going to 'go all the way', as the girls in the office put it. Knew she wanted him, now, at any price.

Much later, she lay in his arms and the gentle kisses came again, travelling featherlight across her face, neck, breasts. She touched his cheek with her fingertips. Outside the car the night pressed close and the wind rocked their little cradle . . . *Rockabye baby, in a sports car, Daniel and Anna, how lucky you are.* She whispered the words beneath her breath and Dan chuckled and told her he loved her to distraction and didn't think he could have gone on living without her and Anna purred and rubbed her cheek against his and would not allow herself to think.

They drove home almost in silence, but when they reached the flat Dan said, 'Shall I come in? Or do you want to tell your mother you're getting married without me to mess it up?'

'I'll tell her myself,' Anna whispered. 'Oh Dan, we shouldn't have done what we did, should we?'

'No, we shouldn't have,' Dan agreed seriously. 'But I didn't seem able to make you see how I loved you – you don't doubt me now, do you, darling?'

'No. It's me I doubt.' Anna got quickly out of the car,

before he could kiss her again, then leaned in through the window. 'Goodnight, Dan. I'll give you a ring in the morning.'

He laughed and chucked her under the chin, leaning across the passenger seat. 'No; I'll give *you* a ring in the morning! Goodnight, sweetheart. Dream of me.'

She ran away, of course. What else could she do? Dan thought she was someone special, but she knew herself to be ordinary in the extreme and difficult to love. It had taken Constance years to learn to love her plain daughter; her father had stopped loving her as soon as she became a young woman instead of a child, and these were people of intelligence, people who knew her well.

Marriage was a lottery, people said. Well, she liked to choose her own path, not have it chosen by chance or luck. And she *knew* she wasn't in Dan's league, not really. Even the thought of seeing his loving look change hurt her like a sword in the soul. He would be better off without her, better off choosing someone else who wouldn't disappoint him.

She wrote him a short letter, then told her mother she had been recalled to Paris and left at once.

She did wonder, but he didn't follow her. She went back to her apartment and her friends at UNESCO, to her trips to the cinema and her letter-writing, her study to improve her German and her classes to learn Italian. She tried very hard not to think of Dan and often succeeded for several hours together.

She was deeply unhappy.

Dan Clifton, on the other hand, was not unhappy at all. It was true that when he rang Mrs Radwell's flat the next morning and was told that Anna had gone back to Paris unexpectedly, a pang of pure dismay had pierced him, but almost in the same breath he thought, yes, she would do that, run away. He acknowledged that Anna was distrustful of happiness, expected disappointment, disillusion. How strange it was that he, who had been brought up piecemeal by a mother who had never really wanted a child and a grandmother who resented the burden his presence put upon her, was a self-confident and well-adjusted person, whereas Anna, who'd had a stable, happy childhood in a beautiful home, was so insecure that she could not even acknowledge her own desirability.

The things parents can do to the children they love without any malice aforethought beggar description, Dan mused, walking across his grandmother's small, oak-panelled hallway and climbing the stairs two at a time. He knew all about JJ Radwell's infidelities, almost more about Constance Radwell's carrying-on. Unkind rumours in the village blamed Jamie's simpleness on an attempt by Constance to put an end to her pregnancy and every amateur psychologist – or was it psychiatrist? – for miles around put the blame for Anna's shyness and lack of self-confidence on parental attitudes.

'She's a lovely gel, but you won't ever get her to believe it,' Dan's grandmother had said only the previous day when he had told her he was taking Anna out that evening. 'Gels like Anna accept the value their parents put on them, more's the pity.'

So all he had to do, he told himself, opening his bedroom door and going across to his small wardrobe, was get himself packed and back to France, where he could take Anna in hand and make her see that love like theirs was not something to be lightly cast aside. He got his suitcase down from the top of the wardrobe and took his blazer off its coathanger. Then the telephone rang. Dan cocked his head; it rang three times, four times . . .

Cursing, he descended the stairs like a boulder rolling down a hill. His grandmother was out shopping; he remembered her saying she was going to catch the ten o'clock bus into the city. He snatched the telephone off its hook, full of hope. It would be Anna; she had rung to say she had changed her mind, was still in the city . . . wanted him as badly as he wanted her!

It was not Anna; it was the Foreign Office.

Half an hour later, when Mrs Lucas returned from her shopping trip, it was to find Dan packed and ready to go.

'Sorry, Gran,' he said, kissing her cheek and holding her close for a moment. 'I've just had a telephone call from my masters in

Whitehall. I've been seconded to London for six weeks or so – it's to do with the coronation in June, they need my languages, apparently. So I'll have to go off now and get my orders, arrange somewhere to sleep while I'm in London. But I'll see you again on Friday evening, because I'll be spending my weekends here, naturally.'

'You look quite pleased about it,' Mrs Lucas said, smiling up at him. 'What about the little Radwell girl, though? Going to be able to see her again before she leaves?'

Dan chuckled and shook a reproving finger under his grandmother's nose. 'Can't keep anything from you, can I? Actually, Anna's gone back to Paris, so I won't be able to see her for a couple of months. But sometimes things work out for the best, and this may be one of them. Take care of yourself, Gran; I'll give you a ring from London, get you up to date with my whereabouts as they say. See you on Friday evening!'

Mrs Lucas followed him out and watched him heave his case into the boot of the car and climb into the driver's seat.

'Don't forget to telephone, dear,' she called as he started the engine. 'I'll be waiting for your call.'

Driving along with the hood down and the roar of the wind in his ears, Dan considered the hand fate had dealt him. In one way it was a great shame that he could not return to Paris and Anna but, having thought about it, he believed it was probably for the best.

She would have time to decide whether she could be happy without him or whether she would take a chance. Knowing how he felt, he could not believe that she would throw away what they shared. As he drove he hit the horn softly with the heel of his hand, *parp parp de parp parp*, and he found himself singing Anna's little song of the previous evening.

Rockabye baby in a sports car, Daniel and Anna how lucky you are! He sang it over and over, accompanying himself on the horn, and he wondered how he would get through the next weeks. For four years he and Anna had seen one another a couple of times a month, sometimes more but rarely less. He could see her now in his mind's eye, the thick, golden-brown hair which refused to curl but was cut in the popular gamin style and showed to perfection the beautiful shape of her head. And the blue eyes with their long, slightly slanted lids, the delicately pointed chin, the body, slim yet rounded, which had fitted into his arms last night as though it had been designed for them. He thought about her efficiency at work, which went so strangely with a deep distrust of her ability to handle her personal life, and the sense of humour which could bubble up one moment and disappear the next, so that she was solemn, anxious not to offend.

Anna, Anna, Anna! I can't wait to see you in the flesh . . . but wait I must, he told himself, because every instinct shouts out that it's only Anna who can choose now. I've got to let her make this choice. But oh, God, don't let her choose wrong!

Nineteen

It was half-past nine on a fine spring morning and Nell, who had finished her household tasks betimes, was in the wild garden, weeding, tying back and generally tidying. The tourist season would soon be upon them and she wanted to get off to a good start; once people began to come down to the coast Pengarth would be busy from morning till night, except for June the second – Coronation Day for the new queen.

There would be no visitors at the castle then. On such an important day the public wouldn't be interested in going round Pengarth, in seeing the East Tower which was now known as the Haunted Tower, the Long Gallery, the owls and bats and kestrels which had made their homes in the roofless Great Hall. But the day following that, and all the days thereafter until they closed once more in September, the visitors would be coming up the drive again, on foot and on bicycles, in cars and buses, in the big motor coaches which could hold fifty people.

This year, for the first time, they intended to open the converted stabling to the left of the front door as a restaurant so they had moved Matthew's herd of pedigree Herefords into a new milking parlour which the men worked together to build. The milking parlour was nowhere near the house so the cows did not need to cross the courtyard, which, in its turn, meant that visitors need no longer be warned not to tread cow-dung into the front hall. The farming side of the business could now be kept separate from what Snip referred to as 'the show', though Matthew said this sounded a bit cheeky, somehow.

'It's a stately home, and don't you forget it,' he had kidded Snip. '*The Show* indeed – good thing Mr Geraint can't hear you!'

'Good thing he can't see all this,' Hester had said, as the four of them stood in the middle of the large, airy room, viewing the new restaurant with open delight. 'He'd be back here like a shot, interfering, taking the biggest share of the profit, trying to bend us all to his will.'

'He's not bothered,' Nell said. 'At first we wrote every time we did something new, and he never so much as replied. Odd, that. You'd think he would have shown some interest, wouldn't you? His new woman must be hot stuff, don't you think, Dad?'

Matthew grinned and looked self-conscious.

'He's probably had half-a-dozen since Dolly Frost,' he pointed out. 'And if they keep gettin' younger, the way they did, the latest is probably still in junior school.'

'She'll be wearing him out, that's why he don't reply to his letters,' Snip said with a grin. 'Like you wear me out, young Nell. Ah, us older men suffer for the delights of young and pretty wives; we're worn out before our time aren't we, Matthew?'

'It's a good way to go, though,' Matthew said, leering at Hester. 'Mind, you're slowin' down a bit now, aren't you, my love? Over forty you are – and you still don't look a day older than Nell here.'

'I feel nearer sixty when I've been sat in the box by the drive selling tickets from dawn to dusk,' Hester said. 'But I'm going to help to cook for the restaurant, aren't I, Nell? Some fancy stuff, but lots of good home cooking, my own bread, apple cake and meat pies. I'll enjoy that once in a while.'

'Don't forget we're only opening the restaurant at weekends, for a while,' Nell said hastily. 'I always thought selling tickets was a nice, easy little job personally. Nothing like the sheer slog of taking parties round.'

'Aye. And telling all them lies must be exhausting, too,' Matthew said genially. 'When I heard you the other day talking about the ghost in the Long Gallery and the forty water-colourists who'd all seen her and painted her into their pictures . . . well, I'm surprised your nose didn't grow six inches, young Nell.'

'It has,' Snip said, catching his wife's arm and swinging her round and pretending to scrutinise her small, smiling face. 'Yes, your nose is definitely longer, just like Pinocchio's. You'd better watch out, Nell, or we'll have our own freak show – see the woman with the longest nose in Great Britain . . .'

'Watch her wrestled a full-sized python to earth using only her large and sinewy conk,' Nell had replied, giggling. 'You're a born showman, Snip – that's why this place is so successful, because you don't tiptoe round talking about antiques and history, you know how important it is to interest people. But we'd better stop gloating and start working, or we'll never be ready when the season starts.'

So now, tidying the garden, Nell was looking forward to the official opening of the restaurant. They meant to have a bit of a party and combine it with her birthday and, although Hester would help, they had engaged a permanent cook, a Miss Lily Jones from the village, who had been in service with a family in London until homesickness had driven her back to Wales.

It was a pity, in a way, that the wild garden wouldn't be at its best for the opening. Nell, Hester and Snip had worked terribly hard to make it beautiful without losing the wildness, and in June it would be stunning, with roses, wild and cultivated, climbing up walls, rioting over pathways, clambering up rustic trellises and spilling on to the more formal beds which edged the garden. Still, it was nice in April too, though gentler, not quite so striking. There were thousands of primroses and violets, lots of the tiny, wild daffodils and a bed of lilies of the valley which could be smelt halfway up the drive when the wind was blowing in the right direction.

On her knees, Nell picked a bunch of the tiny blue violets, added some pale primroses, and sniffed her small bouquet luxuriously. The soft, subtle fragrances are best, she decided, feeling the rain-washed petals touch her cheek. Primroses smell of spring, of dew, of newly turned earth and moss – who could ask for a lovelier scent on their birthday? And the primroses would still be at their best a couple of days from now, when she would be twenty-seven.

'Nell? What on earth are you doing down there on your knees? Do get up and come into the kitchen. I've got something to show you.'

'Oh, Mum!' Nell scrambled to her feet, scattering spring

flowers, and bent to pick them up. 'I wanted these for the room over the gatehouse; it's a real attraction you know, with everything just as Mr Geraint left it when he went. Only I always put flowers on his desk and on the windowseat behind it, it just adds that final touch.'

'So you say. I don't think . . . but come into the kitchen, please. Matthew and I have had a letter. We think you ought to read it.'

Scooping the last violet from the ground, Nell turned obediently and followed her mother along the winding little path, under the arch, and into the kitchen courtyard. A couple of hens were picking at cracks between the paving stones and the back door was open. Through the doorway Nell could just see Snip, standing on a stepladder, trying to whitewash the last section of the stained ceiling. He turned as they entered the room.

'Hello, you're early, Hester! What's up?'

'Matt's had a letter from Mr Geraint. He's coming up to see us on Nell's birthday,' Hester said, not mincing words. 'I'm that shocked . . . I couldn't believe it at first when Matt read it out, then I just grabbed it and came straight up here. I can't think what the old devil is up to, but whatever it is it bodes ill for us all.'

'Oh come on, Mum, he was really kind to me when I was small,' Nell said uneasily. 'It's no use looking on the black side, and anyway, we've worked hard and had fun and made a lot of money, if he wants a share . . .'

'We wanted to pay rent,' Snip said crossly from his perch on the stepladder. 'Nell wrote ever such a friendly letter, saying how happy we were and suggesting we regularise things by paying rent. He never even wrote back to say he didn't want it. But you put the money away, didn't you, love? Only when we wanted to convert the stables and needed the money it seemed silly not to use it. So it isn't there now, and if he demands back rent . . .'

'He'll get it,' Nell said at once. 'We'd find it somehow. But Mum, what do you really think? What does Dad think? That the old man wants to take it away from us, give Pengarth to his latest Dolly Frost? Is that what you're afraid of?'

'I don't know,' Hester said miserably. 'I'm just afraid, love. The old man was always unpredictable – moody, difficult to pin down. I remember Matthew once saying that Mr Geraint would pick a quarrel because he was bored, being so much cleverer than the rest of us, and then he'd be sorry and try to make it up. I don't know what I'm afraid of, except . . . well, except that he'll change things.'

'You and Matt call him the old man, but how old is he really?' Snip asked. He finished the ceiling with exaggerated care, then descended his ladder and stood the bucket of whitewash down by the sink. 'He must be getting on, I suppose?'

'Pushing seventy,' Hester said after a moment's thought. 'Old devil, coming back to make us miserable after all these years!'

'You shouldn't prejudge him, Mum,' Nell said gently. 'Is he coming alone? Did he say?'

'No, he just says he's coming and will it be possible to book him a room at a decent hotel in town, and meet the train. That means he isn't driving and he is staying at least one night. Oh Nell love, I don't want to think badly of Mr Geraint, but this is so unexpected! It worries me more than I can say.'

Nell, who was dying to read the letter, put the flowers she had picked into a simple white vase and headed for the back door.

'I've got to take these up to the gatehouse room, Mum; do you want to come up with me, see how nice it is? You've never been, have you?'

'No, I didn't think . . . but I'll walk along with you now.' She followed her daughter across the yard, through the wild garden and under the big arch. Up the stone steps they went and into the gatehouse room. Nell put the flowers on the desk and looked round at her mother's face, but it told her nothing. Hester's eyes travelled over the big desk with the books scattered on it, several of them first editions of Geraint's works. They flickered over the manuscript he was working on when he left, a pile of scribbled notes. They took in the fact that the desk was polished, the furniture kept clean and fresh, the walls whitewashed, the pictures dusted. Then, very slowly, Hester lowered herself into one of the comfortable armchairs.

'The very first time I came in here I found you, hedged about by cushions, playing with a box of bricks whilst Mr Geraint watched over you,' Hester said slowly. 'Odd, it must have been a quarter of a century ago, but as I came through the door just now I glanced at the hearthrug, half-expecting to see my little girl there, smiling up at me.'

'Then he wasn't all bad, was he? I didn't think he could be,' Nell said. 'He could be kind, Dad says so.'

'Your Dad is the kindest person in the world, he rarely speaks ill of anyone. And he and Mr Geraint were boys together from what I can make out, because Matthew doesn't talk about his life in Sussex much. And yes, Geraint could be kind.' Her voice was low. Her eyes travelled the desk again, then flickered to the windowseat beyond. 'Nell, when you first came in here, did you find a – a red leather book? A sort of diary?'

'No, nothing like that, worse luck,' Nell said without having to think about it. 'I didn't know the old man kept a diary. It would have been worth a lot to us as an attraction. I wonder whether we could persuade him to sit in here and sign copies of his books for people?'

'Don't be silly,' Hester said wearily. 'I don't suppose he still writes books, and the ones he did write are probably all out of print.'

'They are not! Goodness, Mum, the man was your – your friend and you haven't followed his career at all, have you? He's done awfully well. First his books were just sort of adventure, but they got better, deeper . . . the year before last he won some prestigious literary prize. That was another reason why we thought he wasn't interested in taking a share of the money Pengarth was making, because he was very wealthy in his own right.'

'Another reason? What was the first reason, then?'

'Oh, that. Well, we thought that if he was my real father, perhaps he wanted me to profit from his home,' Nell said uncomfortably. 'I told Snip about Mr Geraint, Mum, because I had to explain about us leaving all those years ago. Besides, there's no harm in it; Snip can see how much you love Matthew, he must know, as I do now, that whatever happened between you and the old man it didn't include a wild love affair.'

'I think I was in love with him,' Hester said slowly. 'It's difficult to make you understand, but he was so – so glamorous, compared with Matthew! Matthew was quiet and never argued or contradicted or insisted on having his own way, he let Geraint ride roughshod over him. Somehow I didn't look beyond that to the kind and generous man inside.'

'I do understand, because Dan was a bit like Mr Geraint. Tremendously good looking, popular, sought after by women . . . it used to make me proud to walk down the street with him, which just goes to show that most women are fools for a handsome face! In fact I suppose I'd be proud of him as a brother if I could acknowledge him, which I can't.' Nell sighed. 'Oh Mum, we've woven some tangled webs in our time, you and I.'

'Yes, and the spider at the heart of them is Mr Geraint. Take care in front of him, sweetheart, that's all I ask. Don't be impulsive, think before you speak and perhaps we'll brush through it without too much bother. Matt's going to meet him at the station and bring him straight back to the lodge for coffee, then we'll come with him up to the castle. Can you give him lunch?'

'Yes, of course. It's the day we open the restaurant; can we give him lunch in there, do you think?'

'Why not?' Hester said, sighing and getting slowly to her feet. 'He's going to want to see everything. Matt will probably take him round the new milking parlour, the dairy, and so on. Though since Matt only draws a salary and Mr Geraint gets the profits, I don't suppose the changes on the farm matter at all; it's the castle I worry about.'

Nell's twenty-seventh birthday was just like any other day, to start with at any rate. She was baking scones in the kitchen and Snip was taking a party of tourists around the castle when Mr Geraint came carefully in through the back door, flanked by Matthew, with Hester hovering. He stood just inside the kitchen, staring across at Nell.

Nell stared back. She saw a tall, white-haired man with eyes so dark they seemed to burn out of his thin face. He had a high-bridged nose, a strongly cleft chin, and when he smiled at her his face lit up with mischief and wickedness and the little girl in her recognised him at once. Before she had thought she had flown across the kitchen into his welcoming embrace.

'Oh, Mr Geraint, I'd have known you anywhere! You haven't changed at all really, only your hair's gone white. But how rude I am – do sit down! Mum has given you coffee, I know, but we're going to give you lunch in the new restaurant . . . it's your restaurant really, but you've never written to us or said what you wanted, so we've just pressed on.'

'Little Nell, how you do prattle! You always were a child for chattering, I remember that very well.' He turned in his chair to wave a hand at Matthew and Hester. 'Thanks very much for bringing me up here. Perhaps you would call for me again in, say, half an hour, and we can all lunch in this new restaurant the girl speaks of? But I'd like to hear from Nell's own lips just what's been going on here.'

It was a dismissal, though charmingly put. Matthew turned at once, putting a hand on Hester's arm when she seemed inclined to linger.

'Right, Mr Geraint, we'll go about our business now,' he said cheerfully. 'We'll be back in forty minutes, Nell.'

Nell waited until the back door had closed behind her mother, then turned back to her guest. 'You aren't well.'

'No, I fear I'm not in rude health.'

'I'm sorry.' Nell hesitated, taking the seat opposite the old man. 'Is that why you've come, after all this time? Because you're not well and want to . . .'

The sheer tactlessness of what she had been about to say killed the words on her lips, but Mr Geraint did not seem to mind. He grinned and finished the sentence for her.

'. . . to settle my affairs before I die? Precisely, Nell. Precisely.'

'I see. Will this affect Snip and I very much, then? Are you going to take Pengarth away from us?'

He was watching her face, his eyes somehow wistful, almost hungry, as though he had wanted badly to see her and now that she was before him, was trying very hard to burn into his memory her looks, gestures, expressions.

'It's got to go to someone when I'm gone,' he observed mildly. 'Why should it go to you?'

She hesitated, looking across at him. 'I – I thought I was r-related to you,' she said at last, unable to stop her voice from shaking a little. 'My mother told me . . . when we left Pengarth and Matthew and the lodge she told me . . . you'd threatened her . . . you'd said . . .' her courage failed her. 'You'd said we were related,' she finished feebly.

His eyebrows were still dark, as were the thick, stubby lashes round his narrowed eyes. Now his brows rose. 'Did she believe it?'

'She said it was possible.'

'Ah. Possible, yes.' There was an even longer pause while he looked down at his hands, lying on his knees. They were thin and paper white, the veins standing out, blue and knotted. A sick man's hands, Nell thought suddenly. A man sick unto death. Perhaps she ought not to have said anything. She had not intended to speak of these matters but he was a man skilled in extracting information, turning a conversation the way he needed, she had been putty in his hands. 'Possible. Well, now. Highly desirable, perhaps, but not actually possible.'

'N-not . . . ?'

He raised his eyes to hers, then looked towards the back door.

'Your mother won't be long now,' he said conversationally. 'She would never willingly leave you and I to talk but she couldn't ignore Matthew, go against his wishes in such an obvious way. So she'll pretend to go back to the lodge and then make her way quietly back here. In about thirty seconds, if my reckoning is correct . . .'

They both heard the footsteps, then saw the back door open. Hester slipped inside. She looked from one to the other, pink cheeked; she was breathing hard, she must have been running.

'Well? What's he said to you, Nell darling?' She turned to face Mr Geraint. 'Why did you want to see her alone? Oh John,

499

you've made so much unhappiness, must you make more? We've been so content here, the four of us, if only it could just go on . . .'

'You told Nell that she and I were related; does that mean that you truly believed I was her father? Because it couldn't have been true, could it? I have no children. You must have known that she was Matthew's child. Surely Mrs Cled told you that I'd had no brats, though I wanted children? The pair of you were friendly enough, always chattering of this and that, surely she mentioned it?'

Hester's face flushed, the red mottling her neck. She shot an embarrassed look at Nell, then turned once more to face Mr Geraint.

'I don't know what you're talking about, all I know is that you told me blood tests would prove Nell was your little girl and that you intended to use legal means to have some control over her future. Naturally, I believed you, why should I not?'

'I'd have said *anything* to keep Nell by me – she was so full of life, so bright, affectionate. But I can't imagine why you believed me so unquestioningly, didn't think the remark might be bluff. You knew I'd had mistresses, it wasn't exactly a state secret, any more than it was a secret that I didn't seem able to father a child with any of them.'

Hester frowned, biting her lip, but now it was Nell who spoke.

'You mean you've never had a child of your own at all? Not even – not even Dan?'

'*Dan?* For God's sweet sake, Nell, he was my elder brother's boy. I didn't share my elder brother's interests, he was the shy, bookish one, but I'd never have done the dirty on him, we were fond of one another. In fact I didn't even meet the lovely Rosalie until Dan was three years old. What maggot got into your head to make you think that?'

Nell swung round and stared accusingly at her mother. Hester looked up at her, eyes bright, cheeks flying twin scarlet flags. 'I told her, and I thought it was true! Folk said in the village . . . both the children had black hair and blue eyes, pale skin, similarly shaped faces, and then there was the portrait in the Long Gallery . . . you said yourself that Nell took after the lady in the picture, so what was I to think?'

'That lady in the picture was Matthew's great-grandmother too! Matthew's father and mine were brothers, didn't you know that either, Hester? You were such a bright, curious creature I was sure you'd have all Matthew's secrets out of him before you'd lived at the lodge a month. The truth is my Uncle Frederick got a respectable girl pregnant, but she was only one of the tenant farmer's daughters, so no one expected him to marry her. But Isobel – that was her name, Isobel Stewart – had strict Methodist parents and they couldn't bear the shame of an unmarried daughter and her bastard child living under their roof, so grandfather married Isobel off to George Coburn and gave George a good job and a cottage on the estate. Which makes Matt my first cousin, though he's illegitimate.'

'Matt never breathed a word of any of this,' Hester said flatly. 'If he had, what a deal of unhappiness would have been saved!'

'Hester, will you let me finish?' Mr Geraint said testily. 'Since you obviously don't know the story, the least you can do is listen to me.'

'*I'll* listen,' Nell said softly. 'Go on, Mr Geraint.'

'Very well. I was born exactly ten years before Matthew, and despite the difference in our ages we became good friends. When I inherited Pengarth I told father I wanted the Coburns to take over the lodge – they were elderly by then and more or less retired – so that young Matthew could work for me as my farm manager. He knew a great deal about farming, did Matt, and I needed him badly, his loyalty and support as much as his knowledge perhaps.'

'And you both came here and started to turn Pengarth into a good estate and a reasonable home,' Nell put in. 'But then you lied to my mother and broke up Matthew's marriage and when you were bored with this place, you just left. It's a pretty disreputable story, Mr Geraint, no matter how you tell it.'

In the back of her mind her new knowledge throbbed like a fresh wound; Hester had deliberately told her she and Dan were brother and sister not because she believed it but because she did

501

not want them to marry. And I felt dirty whenever I thought about Dan after that, Nell remembered. We made love to each other at the farmhouse before I knew, and that was dirtied too, made a wicked act by my mother's words. Why did she do it? Why did she lie to me?

'I meant no harm, I just meant to bend Hester to my will,' Mr Geraint said reasonably, as though no one could possibly blame him once they understood his motive. 'I loved you, Nell, and longed for you to be my child. Perhaps I even fooled myself into thinking that I really had fathered you. And I was trying to do good, only I had to – to manipulate Hester a little because she wouldn't let me spend money on you, give you treats, take you out. She wanted you all to herself, she couldn't bring herself to share. I never thought for one moment that she'd run off and take you away from me and Pengarth.'

'She was my little girl,' Hester said, her voice thin, reedy. 'She was all I had . . . you never did understand, John, you never even tried. I was fond of Matthew, I was besotted by you, but I adored Nell. I would have done anything to keep her safe and by my side.'

'I think we've talked enough,' Nell put in. 'It must be time for lunch. Snip will be in any moment and Matthew will be back soon.' She turned to Mr Geraint. 'Well? Who's going to get Pengarth? Because if it's one of your fancy women then I'll burn the bloody place down sooner than see someone like that take over.'

Mr Geraint threw back his head and laughed until tears ran down his cheeks. Then he sobered. 'Don't worry, my fancy women wouldn't thank me for Pengarth. It'll go to someone who'll value it, rest assured. And now let's close the subject and have this lunch I was promised.'

Lunch was a silent meal and would have been worse had it not been for Snip. Mr Geraint decided to charm Snip and before the fascinated eyes of his ex-mistress and the girl he had already annoyed, he did just that.

He asked intelligent questions, listened with obvious interest to the answers, made sensible suggestions. He applauded most of the things they had done, but not all. He had not then seen round the castle itself but though he had never answered one of Nell's letters it seemed he had read every word and taken everything in.

'What happened to the idea of selling ice-creams and tickets at the lodge?' Mr Geraint asked at one point, after the meal was finished and the coffee cups were before them. 'That seemed sensible to me, and it would have enabled you to take money from those who only wanted to visit the fairground and weren't interested in a bit of culture.'

'Ah, we thought of that, sir,' Snip said, beaming, 'but there was a big snag – can you guess what it was?'

'Waste of manpower, having someone permanently in the lodge? I daresay you could have got over the fact that there's no electricity there for a refrigerator.'

'No, it was much simpler than that. Folk won't pay for what they can't see, that's what we reckoned. And from the lodge you can't really see the castle at all. If we can get them to come right up that long drive, they'll not turn back without paying their money and seeing the lot. So we scrapped the idea of using the lodge, or even of having the hut farther down the drive.'

'Then how does having the fair pay you?'

'They give us ten per cent of their takings, in theory, but in practice it's something for the kiddies rather than the adults. We didn't really want the big attractions, so Gullivers sent us a junior scenic, a couple of gallopers and a few joints. What's more, though some people might get cheated over the ten per cent, we've worked the fairs ourselves so we know more or less what they take and they hand it over all right. They wanted a concession for ices and candy floss, that sort of thing, but Nell said no, and though I was doubtful at the time I'm glad now. It wouldn't help the restaurant if folk could buy cheaper on the fairground.'

'You've worked the fairs? I knew nothing of this. Who's going to enlighten me?'

Hester, who had preserved a stony silence throughout, gave Nell a quick, forbidding glare. The Snake Woman and Venom

503

were to be kept a secret from Mr Geraint, then. But Snip, having glanced at the women, realised that the onus of the conversation was going to be on him. Matthew, eating steadily, occasionally casting affectionate glances at Mr Geraint, was a man of few words at the best of times. When food was put before him, he could be described at best as single-minded, at worst as taciturn.

Snip therefore smiled at Mr Geraint and launched into his explanation. 'Well, Nell and I first met when I was working the fairs with my father and it was only the war that stopped me working them for the rest of my life, I daresay. My Dad had a full scenic, dodgems and a junior scenic, or he did when I was living with him. After, I believe he branched out a bit. But any-way, take it from me that I know fairgrounds and that no one from Gullivers would cheat me.'

'But you said "we worked the fairs",' Mr Geraint remarked; there was the faintest note of querulousness in his voice and Nell, glancing quickly across at him, saw that the day had already tired him and felt a pang of compunction. It really wasn't all his fault, she told herself, clearing her throat. He told a lie but he had no idea what the consequences would be; we shouldn't blame him entirely. Besides, he is an old, ill man.

'I worked the fairs too, Mr Geraint,' she said rather shyly. 'I helped with a snake show for a time, then I was a conjuror's assistant for a little, and whilst I was with Gullivers I looked after the joints sometimes. Oh, joints are the side-shows, the penny-rolls and hoop-las and darts and things.'

Hester sat up straight and looked steadily at Mr Geraint. 'You're very tired,' she said. 'I don't think you're well enough to get dragged round the castle. Go back to your hotel now and Matt will pick you up at whatever time you say tomor-row morning. And although it's none of your business, when I left Pengarth I joined the fair, and Nell and I travelled with them for a dozen years. It wasn't an easy life, I came near to despair the first winter. So now you know as much as we do.'

He was staring at her with so much sadness in his expression that Nell jumped in once more, pity swamping her initial feeling that she and her mother had been used, had been mere pawns in his game.

'We had a dreadful time the first winter right enough,' she said, 'but after that we loved it, didn't we, Mum? We shared a trailer with a lady called Cissie and her daughter Fleur, ever so nice they were, and the trailer was warm and cosy and we had plenty of food. It wasn't bad, really it wasn't, Mr Geraint.'

He shook his head, still staring at Hester.

'My fault, all my fault,' he murmured. 'But did you ever wonder what you'd left behind, Hester? Two broken men, that's what you left. I started drinking, stopped caring about this place or any other place. Matt just existed, searching for you, longing for you. You and the child may have suffered, I've no doubt you did. If wishing could turn the clock back, I'd do it in a trice. But no matter how harsh your life was, I doubt you knew my mental anguish. Because I knew it was my fault.'

No one spoke. Nell could feel tears forming behind her eyes and blinked hard, determined not to let them fall. She looked down at the tablecloth as the tears inexorably rose, and heard her mother's chair scrape back.

'We none of us enjoyed what happened,' Hester said harshly. 'Come along, Mr Geraint, I'll give you my arm back to the car. Matt, can you bring the car round to the arch?'

'You could have cut the atmosphere with a knife,' Snip said, when he and Nell were strolling back to the castle kitchen. 'Anyone would have thought Hester really hated the old man. And you weren't very friendly at first, love, though you came round later.'

'I think Mum has good reason to hate him,' Nell said slowly. 'He did her a great wrong, Snip. But somehow, though I suppose you could say what he did affected me too, all I could see was an ill old man who had been good to me once. And though he was wicked to tell Mum I was his child when he knew I was Matthew's daughter, he did it to try to have some say in my life. In a way, he only wanted to help.'

'Well, if it hadn't been for him we wouldn't have met,' Snip observed as they crossed the courtyard and went into the kitchen. 'So I'm glad he lied. Then he admitted you weren't his child? He came right out with it?'

'That's right. He told Mum he's known for some time that he couldn't give anyone children. He had tests which proved he was sterile.'

'Hmm. I wonder why he never answered your letters, then? Never took money from us when he could have done? It obviously wasn't because he thought you were his kid!'

'He didn't want money when we wrote because he was already making a lot. And now I think it's his health; when you're as close as he is to death I don't think money interests you all that much,' Nell said shrewdly. 'And he *is* close to death, Snip. He knows it and it doesn't seem to worry him much.'

'So he came here to sort out his affairs. Does that mean to decide what to do with Pengarth when he's gone?'

'I suppose so. I don't know what he's decided, he didn't say. All he did say was that he wouldn't leave it to one of his fancy women, that it would go to someone who valued it.'

'Us,' Snip said unhesitatingly. 'Who else is there?'

'Not us. Don't get your hopes up, because Mr Geraint comes of a very big family and Mum was so nasty to him that I don't think he would want to help us, anyway. But there's Rosalie Clifton and her son Dan just for a start; if they came, I think we'd have to go.'

'Why?'

'We just would,' Nell said. 'But let's not talk about it, not yet. He'll be up here again tomorrow to look around. Perhaps he might give us a clue then.'

'Right. Ah, here comes Hester,' Snip said. He was standing at the sink, by the window which overlooked the courtyard. 'I expect you'll want to talk and I've got to polish the Long Gallery floor, so I'll go and do that and leave you to gossip. Bring us a cuppa at four, there's my girl.'

'I'll do that. And if Mum needs the kitchen for some of that fancy cooking she was talking about I'll come up and give you a hand. Don't forget the polish.'

'As if I would.'

Snip collected all the paraphernalia he would need for waxing the parquet flooring and departed, whistling, just as Hester came in through the back door. Nell raised her brows.

'Has Mr Geraint gone?'

'Yes. I went in the car with them and Matt saw him right up to his room. Matt's going to collect him at ten tomorrow morning. I said he could do the castle tour early, then have a good rest in the kitchen before taking a quick look at the outbuildings. That way, he might live to see Sussex again.'

Hester spoke without a flicker of feeling and Nell felt, for the first time, a slow burn of anger against her mother. She was being callous and hard to an old man who had done his best for Nell, albeit mistakenly. Suddenly she remembered that other lie, the one which had almost been forgotten in accusing Mr Geraint.

'Mum, now that we're alone I think you must tell me. Why did you lie to me about Dan? Make me think he was my brother? I'm not denying you truly thought Mr Geraint was my father, but you didn't really think he was Dan's, did you? So why say it? I think I've a right to know.'

'He looked rather like you, you both had similar colouring,' Hester said defensively. 'It's true I didn't think you and Dan were brother and sister, but I thought you were related and I was sure the boy would be wrong for you. You must have realised how like Mr Geraint he was, both to look at and in his ways! Selfish, beautiful, thoughtless, a privileged member of a privileged class, that was Dan Clifton, and if you ask me you had a very lucky escape. Anyway, it's all water under the bridge, isn't it? You're happy enough with Snip, you can't deny it.'

'A lucky escape? Who are you to decide my fate for me in such an arbitrary fashion?' Nell was so angry and hurt that her voice became perilously close to a shout. 'Snip and I are happy enough but that isn't the same as being deeply in love! Snip was second best and you knew it. When I said I'd marry him it was because I wouldn't have to explain to Dan that we were brother and sister! But Dan and I were very much in love and you tore us apart with no thought for what it would do to me. You talk about Mr Geraint wanting to have a say in what happened to me, but you wanted all of me, didn't you? When I was first friendly with Snip you were horrid to him too. It was only when you realised that I wasn't in love with him, never had been, that you withdrew all opposition to our being together. And Snip never had that . . . that *glow* which Dan had for me, he was just a nice fellow who needed me. If I'd known Dan and I were just some sort of cousins, I'd never have gone down to Southampton, let alone brought Snip back here!'

'Well, it's too late now,' Hester said, her voice catching on a sob. 'Whatever I did I did because I loved you and wanted the best for you, sweetheart. You were someone special, I didn't want you to be seduced by a practised charmer and then dumped, as I had been. Believe me, Dan wasn't the man for you just as Mr Geraint wasn't right for me. Look at the trouble Geraint caused, the pain and anguish, look how he tried to take you from me! Besides, Snip's a nice fellow and fits in well with us here. He's very like Matthew, steady and reliable, not the sort of chap to set the world on fire, but a strong shoulder to lean on when you're in trouble.'

'But I wanted to be set on fire! I wanted to bask in Dan's blaze – and Dan did blaze I can tell you! It's cruelly unfair to say that Dan's like Mr Geraint, because you've not seen him since he was about ten – and I have. He's a wonderful person and I almost hate you, Mum, for deliberately splitting us up. I almost hate Snip too, for trapping me, and it's all your fault, all of it, because you deliberately lied to me just so that I'd do what you wanted me to do.'

'It's too late,' Hester repeated tearfully. She sat down at the kitchen table and buried her face in her hands. 'You're a married woman with a home and responsibilities . . . what can I do except say how sorry I am? I never thought you loved Dan, I just thought you had a girlish crush on him. And darling, six years have changed you and they will have changed Dan too. He'll either be married, or one of those smart young men in a high-powered job, with no time for the likes of you and me. You've not seen him since the war ended, have you? People change, my dearest Nell, people change.'

Nell sat down too. She felt terribly tired, as if all she wanted was to sleep for a week. At the back of her mind, something Mrs Burroughes had once said echoed; something about Dan not caring for her the way she seemed to care for him. Something about her feelings for Dan being calf-love, having no roots in reality. But right now she was too shocked and miserable to want to remember, to examine her old friend's words. Hester had lied to her, Snip had trapped her into marriage, and she had lost Dan. Six years on, her memories of him were still sharp and clear, but what about the reality? Would that ever have matched up with the dream? Truthfulness, hovering still, told her that it probably would not, but she was still too angry and hurt to let Hester off the hook.

'Mum, you'd better go. We'll talk again when I've cooled down.'

'All right,' Hester said wearily, getting to her feet. 'Love's a funny thing, Nell. Mr Geraint loved us both and hurt us very badly. I love you desperately and only want the best for you, I didn't want you to be seduced, as I was, and then abandoned. But what I did hurt you, and that was the last thing I intended. So don't hurt Snip, dearest! Because his love is the best thing that's ever happened to you, even if you can't acknowledge it yet.'

Nell worked hard that afternoon. She baked, cleaned down the kitchen, polished the big hall, and then went and made a tray of tea and carried it up to Snip in the Long Gallery.

She walked carefully up the long, shiny corridor, approving of Snip's labours as she went. He had polished all along here and the dark boards looked like pools of water, clear and deep. When she reached it, she flung open the door of the Long Gallery and blinked in the flooding April sunlight. The sunshine fell on the golden glory of the parquet flooring, diamonded from the three great chandeliers which hung down the centre of the room, and illuminated the little tables and small gilt chairs.

The pile of cleaning equipment which he had used was tidily piled up near the door, but of Snip there was no sign.

He must have gone down to the WC, Nell told herself prosaically, but her heart gave a startled little flip when she saw, on the table nearest her, a sheet of white paper carefully held down by one of the empty flower vases. She walked over to it, taking her time, telling herself that it was something Snip had found, some bit of information, perhaps, which he wanted to remember.

But in her heart, suddenly, there was a yawning blackness, as though her heart knew very well what was written on the piece of paper. She picked it up. Read it.

Dear Nell, Listeners never hear good of theirselves; don't I know it! I'm dead sorry about that Dan fellow, I hope you know I didn't realise? I was shocked at what your Mum done, that wasn't right and I'm sure she's sorry. I don't want you to hate me though, not ever, so I'm leaving. Not for always or for good, nothing like that. Just so's we can both have a think. Not that I need to think. These have been the best years of my life so even if it is over, if we decide to call it a day, at least I'll have it in my head to look back at.

She had to read it through three times before it really sank in. He had gone! Well, he couldn't have gone far, that stood to reason. What must have happened was that he had come back for something he'd forgotten, started to open the door and heard the row. Only a saint would have gone away, not listened, once they realised what it was about, and Snip was no saint.

Nell sank into the nearest chair and stared at the note; she wondered what she should do. He said he wasn't leaving for good, just so that they could have a think. A think? But what on earth would she want to think about? She frowned, puzzling over it. Then her heart sank. He thought she meant all those awful things she had said, all the daft things, too, about Dan being a blaze of glamour and Snip being a mistake – things she had said to hurt Hester, to revenge herself for a lost dream, but not things she meant!

She scrambled to her feet, kicking the table as she did so and sending the tea-tray and its contents flying over the polished floor. If he believed things like that, he could do anything. She must find him at once, tell him it had all been wickedness and spite on her part, beg him to come back. She loved him, she knew that now; it had probably always been

Snip, but Dan and his good looks had got in the way, dizzied her silly young head as a moth is dizzied by light. Then Hester had added to it by making Dan forbidden fruit – her brother, indeed! She remembered, suddenly, all sorts of things she had not liked about Dan: the times he had got her into trouble when they were kids and failed to extricate her; when he had ignored her existence and gone his own way, and other times when she had been quite close enough for him to visit her had he cared to. Times when she had needed him and he had not come.

Why didn't I ever tell Dan about the fair? she wondered as she flew down the long, shallow flight of stairs. Because I knew he would despise it, think I was just a common kid after all. That was my hero, the man I thought I wanted to marry, someone I dared not trust with the truth about myself.

She had left the kitchen door open. She shot through the room and out the back door. Across the yard, under the arch, through the wild garden, and there was the drive . . . empty. No small figure with a suitcase trudged along it, no one on a bicycle, or in a car. He had a good start but she could catch him up if she was sensible. She would go to the lodge, tell Hester, find out if she'd seen Snip and then make for the telephone box at the end of the road. She ought to have telephoned from the castle for a taxi, but she had not thought of it in time.

She burst into the lodge. Hester was ironing and looked up. Her face was blotched and still damp with recent tears.

'Snip's gone,' Nell panted. 'Have you seen him?'

Hester was embarrassed by her tears. She kept her head down, surreptitiously wiped her cheeks, mumbled.

'No. He's probably with Matt.'

'No, he's left. Mum, he heard! He heard what we said in the kitchen, he left me a note. He's gone!'

Hester sat down suddenly. 'He heard? He's gone?'

'Yes! I'm going down to the box to phone for a taxi. He can't have got far, he'll go to Rhyl of course, catch a train, find Gullivers. What else could he do? I must find him, tell him it was all silly nonsense, that I didn't mean a word of it.'

'You didn't?'

'Oh, Mum, of *course* I didn't! I was hurt and upset and

511

very angry, but I didn't mean . . . Snip's someone so special that life without him wouldn't be life at all. Dan was just puppy-love, like you said, because he was so handsome. He wouldn't have been right for me, I know it now even if I didn't know it then. Look, tell Dad . . . I'll see you later. Oh, can you lend me some money?'

Hester lent her ten shillings and some pennies and Nell ran down to the road and dived into the telephone box. There was no sign of Snip on the road, but she hadn't expected it to be that easy. When the taxi arrived she jumped in and told him to take her to the railway station in Rhyl. When Snip was not there she tried the bus terminal, the taxi ranks, the surrounding countryside.

There was no sign of him. To all intents and purposes, Snip Morris had disappeared.

Twenty

It had not been an easy year for any of them. Ever since the news of King George VI's death had been broken to them in the early stages of their African tour, the Queen and her husband had been struggling to come to terms with what had happened to them. Their children were too young to understand or help; it was only Elizabeth and Philip who could face up to the fearful change in their lives and learn to live with it.

Peggy had watched and marvelled; they were so young, so totally unprepared, but so quick to grasp the nettle held out to them, so resolute. For the Princess to lose her adored and adoring papa had been bad enough, but to have to take on, at her age, all the responsibilities and cares of the monarchy was a task which would have been beyond many women twice her age.

'But she's been brought up knowing all about duty,' old Mrs Day says, when Peggy went around to her flat for a chat about the old days. Mrs Day had been retired for ten years, but her mind was as sharp as ever and her love and admiration for her nursling had never wavered. 'The King was always driven by conscience; she watched, and learned, and could not help but take it in. She'll be a wonderful Queen because she never thinks of herself, only of others.'

The terrible year had passed, it sometimes seemed to Peggy, on leaden feet. But the depth of sorrow, if it had not lessened, had eased. The move to Buckingham Palace had been put off for as long as possible, for the young couple had made Clarence House their own and it was a delightful and comfortable home. The palace, on the other hand, had never been either delightful or comfortable. But they can make it so, Peggy told herself. They've done wonders before, they can do it again. At least the shortages are not so severe now. At least it will only need a search to find regency striped wallpaper, not a miracle.

Imperceptibly, the planning of the coronation began to take precedence over other events. It had to be truly memorable, Elizabeth and Philip agreed; they wanted a slightly longer route than had previously been used so that more people might enjoy the spectacle. The Queen and her husband insisted that part of the ceremony be filmed so that those unable to be there might enjoy the scene inside the abbey also. They would both ride, side by side, to the abbey in the gold state coach, and Philip would be the first to render to the Queen his Act of Homage.

It was to be in June, when the weather might just possibly be fine: 'It's never fine for royal occasions though,' the Queen reminded everyone. 'It always rains − it's a good sign that it rains. But we must prepare for it, nevertheless.'

They prepared for everything. Rehearsals went well, but not too well, ancient peers of the realm were strategically placed so that someone could keep an eye on them, stop them nodding off at important moments and help them to their feet, to their seats, into the aisles. Elizabeth and Philip agreed to undertake a series of coronation visits, first to Scotland, Northern Ireland and Wales, then to the Commonwealth. They pored over Norman Hartnell's sketches for their coronation robes and perhaps Elizabeth remembered the argument at the previous coronation, when she had thought that Margaret, as the younger, should have a shorter train, and smiled a little at that long-ago disagreement.

The day before the great day dawned, people were assembling in their thousands. They took up their places on pavements, in squares, around London's great open spaces. They were cheerful, loquacious, undaunted by the wait which lay ahead.

It rained, of course.

Anna always knew she would attend the coronation. 'By hook or by crook', she had said to her friends. 'We were born on the same day, I've watched her grow up from a little girl like me to a young woman like me, I was outside the abbey cheering when she married, and now I'm going to be outside the abbey cheering as she's crowned Queen. She's *my* Princess, she always has been.'

Finding out that Dan was in England had nothing to do with it, of course. She had known that for a month, and had done nothing about it, because what could she do? He had proposed marriage, she had all but agreed to it, and then run away without a word. She had expected him to follow her and had braced herself to explain that she did not intend to marry anyone at all, but he had done no such thing. She had even gone around to the embassy in Paris and asked to speak to him, only to be told that he had been seconded to London until after the coronation.

Anna was friendly with most of the English girls working at UNESCO and with many of the other girls too. Her work was varied and interesting, though her social life, now that Dan was no longer in Paris, left a lot to be desired. She intended to take a couple of weeks' holiday in September, to go to Italy with Constance. The trip would increase her knowledge of the language and would, she hoped, strengthen the bond between her mother and herself. But she was grimly determined to see the Queen crowned, even if she did not set eyes on Dan.

'He'll be coming back after the coronation,' her friend Thérèse said comfortingly. 'Everyone says this is so. Already they miss your friend very much, in the embassy.'

Anna felt her heart give a bumpy, uneven bound and told Thérèse with unaccustomed sharpness that it was a matter of indifference to her where Dan Clifton worked. Thérèse slanted her long black eyes and shrugged, a shrug so typically Gallic that it made Anna laugh, and she felt constrained to tell Thérèse she was sorry for snapping her head off, and was told, with another of those humorous looks, that it was always so; girls in love always snapped at their *amies*. Anna shrugged too and muttered that she supposed she did miss him, Dan being such an old friend . . .

She had booked her holiday a long while before, so her boss was plaintive when she said she wanted four days in June as well. He said it would be very difficult, that she knew the rules of the department, that he would like to accommodate her . . . in the end he agreed because he must have guessed that she would hand in her notice if he persisted in refusing.

Anna had come to London by ferry and rail, popped in to see her aunt in the London flat to cadge the bits and pieces necessary for a night on the pavement, and set off again at four in the afternoon to find herself a suitable spot from which to watch. Elderly relatives, she had been informed by Aunt Ella, would get all the excitement they needed from listening to the commentary on the wireless and possibly watching part of the procession from a friend's flat.

So here she was at last, with an umbrella, two flasks of hot coffee, a paper bag full of sandwiches, her uncle's old naval binoculars, a rubber ground-sheet, a blow-up pillow and a tartan car rug. She and her possessions had got themselves a good little pitch among the crowds assembled outside the abbey and she had just been settling down for a long and lonely wait when two things happened. The first was that it began to rain; the second was that she spotted another girl, also by herself.

As the first drops began to spatter down the other girl looked up at the sky and moaned softly. 'Oh damn, I never should have come!'

As an introduction it wasn't much, but it was all Anna needed. She shoved her blanket and ground-sheet a couple of inches along the pavement, tugged at the other girl's sleeve, and said, 'Didn't you bring a ground-sheet? If you want, you can share mine; it's quite big, with plenty of room under it for us both.'

The other girl smiled gratefully. As far as Anna could judge, for her companion was still sitting down, she was small and rounded with black, shiny hair cut in a sort of Dutch bob, dark eyes and a sweet, three-cornered smile.

'Oh, that's awfully kind of you – I didn't really bring any-thing much because I left home in a great hurry. Well, I brought an umbrella, a rug and some food, but that's about it. Look, if we put both umbrellas up and sort of drape your ground-sheet over them . . .'

Kneeling up, laughing, struggling, the two of them made

516

themselves a neat little shelter with the two umbrellas, the ground-sheet and the dark girl's blanket.

'We can wrap my car rug around us as it gets colder,' Anna said, sitting well back in the shelter and watching the rain get into its stride. 'Someone farther up has got a gramophone, so we'll have a sing-song later, I expect. It's fun, isn't it? Did you go to the wedding?'

No need to say which wedding, that was taken as read.

'Yes, I certainly did. The Princess and I were born on the same day, you see, so I've . . .'

'You mean you were twenty-seven on the twenty-first of April? Well, if that isn't the oddest coincidence – me too!'

The two girls stared at each other, round-eyed.

'Gosh! Oh, my name's Nell Morris . . . Helen, really, but everyone calls me Nell.'

'I'm Anna Radwell. Nice to meet you, Nell. To tell you the truth, I felt the most enormous sense of relief when I realised you were alone too. I work abroad, you see, and it was touch and go whether I got away for the coronation or not, so I didn't have time to make plans with friends. It's not much fun to be alone in a huge crowd, so I was tickled pink when I saw you cursing the rain, obviously by yourself.'

'Nice to meet you too, Anna. I'm by myself because I've got a – a small business which ought not to be left, so my parents stayed at home to look after it for me. We live in the back of beyond, up in north Wales, in a very tiny village. It didn't occur to me to ask anyone else to come up to London with me; usually my – my husband and I do everything together, but he couldn't manage to get away this time.'

'I noticed the wedding ring,' Anna said. 'I'm still unattached and fancy free. I suppose you could say I was a career girl, at any rate I haven't married. Now, when shall we start on our sandwiches? I wonder if we ought to save them, because at the wedding people came round selling things to eat; it was only when the processions started that you would have gone hungry if you'd not provided your own.'

'There were hot chestnut sellers, because it was November, and everything else was rationed,' Nell said reminiscently. 'We

517

had some, Snip and I – they were delicious. I say, you weren't around here then, were you? We were almost on this very spot.'

'Really? Then we must have been within a few feet of each other,' Anna said at once. 'Isn't it the strangest thing? Were you at King George's coronation? We were only kids then, of course, and I wasn't allowed to sleep on the pavement or anything like that, but I stayed with my aunt and my cousins and afterwards we fought our way through the streets so we could see them come out on to the balcony. It was a wonderful experience, I'll never forget it.'

'I came up for it. Actually, my mother was working just outside London at the time and we came up in a family party, Jack, Mum, little Fleur and me. I remember Snip, who was always a little devil, climbing up Eros and waving to the coach with Queen Mary and the little Princesses in it, and they waved back. He was very cock-a-hoop over that next day, you can imagine.'

'The boy who climbed Eros? Gosh, my cousin Nancy and I saw him and were so envious, though Nancy, of course, said she could have done it easily if she'd thought of it. And you actually knew him – what fame!'

'Knew him? I married him,' Nell said. 'His name is Snip Morris and I'm Nell Morris. So now you're famous too.'

They began to laugh, giggling helplessly in their odd little shelter, warm side against warm side as they continued to gaze out at the steadily falling rain. But it wasn't the rain they were seeing, it was that other coronation sixteen years ago, when they had been so young, so carefree, so full of hope.

'So we've already discovered that we have at least one mutual acquaintance,' Anna said when their giggles had subsided. 'By the time morning comes, we'll probably know each other's life history. But I spy a chip van. If I uproot my brolly can you hold half our ceiling up while I rush over there and buy us sixpennorth? Hot food would be nice, don't you think?'

'Wizard,' Nell said approvingly. 'Take my brolly, it's bigger. Only give it a good shake before you shove it back in, we don't want it widdling over our legs.'

'How right you are.' Anna heaved carefully at Nell's umbrella and Nell held up the roof. 'Shan't be a mo – if he's selling fish as well, shall I get some of that, or would you rather just chips?'

'Chips will be fine. I'm not starving hungry, just peckish,' Nell said. 'Oh, don't forget the salt and vinegar on mine!'

It continued to rain; puddles formed. The valiant ground-sheet was found to be gathering a lake above their heads which had to be dealt with before it overflowed and soaked them both. Nell went out and guided the stream away from them while Anna, inside, pushed a careful palm against the fat, water-filled curve.

Nell, returning to their warm nest, was happier than she had been for weeks. She had been so desperately lonely, so totally miserable at the castle without Snip, so when her mother had suggested she go to the coronation anyway, her first instinct had been to refuse.

'I don't care about it any more,' she had said dully. 'It doesn't mean anything to me. Besides, there's no fun in going alone and you can't come; you've got too much on your plate right now.'

Hester was expecting a baby and no one was more surprised than she. But she was delighted too, though she kept telling anyone who would listen that forty-three was too old to become a mother for the second time, and sixty far too old to become a father.

'What does age matter?' Matthew had said, prodding her bump. 'Littl'un don't give a damn, you may be sure of that. I've got a quid on that it's a boy, too, so don't go lettin' me down, woman.'

But Nell knew he would be delighted with any child.

'Just because I'm expecting a baby, Nell, that doesn't mean you have to be around to coddle me; Matthew does a very good job of coddling,' Hester had said. 'Just you go, love. It'll take your mind off things. And remember Snip's note; he said he wasn't going for good and he meant it. He'll be back. We came back, didn't we?'

'Oh God, Mum, I can't wait twelve years,' Nell had cried. 'I want him now. I want to put my arms round him and give him a hard hug and tell him I love him. And I want us to have a baby, too . . . think how nice it would be for your little boy and my little boy to be chums!'

'It'll all be fine, he'll come home soon,' Hester said. 'He'll be with a fair somewhere, even if he wasn't with Gullivers. Come to think, he might have joined up with his father again, now that he's older and more capable. Why not put word around for the Morris family?'

'It's been two whole *months* – a lifetime,' Nell moaned. 'And it's all the fault of my stupid, spiteful tongue. Yes, I'll try the Morrises.'

She had, without success so far. So on the second of June, having spent most of the night in miserable wakefulness, she had got out of bed as day dawned, glanced out of the window, and decided to go to London. At least I'll be doing something, she told herself, getting together the things she thought she would need. At least I shan't be sitting here, missing Snip and cursing myself. On Coronation Day all the shops will be closed, all the old biddies will be gathered round their wireless sets, and I'll be unhappy and bored and unable to do a thing about it. So I'll go to London and see what's going on with my own eyes . . . see my dear little Princess become Queen.'

So she had come to London and now she was glad.

'I think the time has come for me to broach my first flask,' Anna said, as they settled themselves once more. 'Have you noticed that fat woman under the enormous fishing umbrella, right opposite us? I think she came to the wedding too. If it's the same one, she got uproariously drunk and kept offering people drinks – look, she keeps taking a swig out of that big bottle. She'll start singing presently.'

'I bet it's only cold tea,' Nell observed. 'I don't think she was drunk last time, either, I think she's a natural show-off. Would you rather open my flask first, though? What's in yours?'

'Coffee. What's in yours?'

'Coffee, but with a tot of brandy,' Nell said proudly. 'My Dad insisted on putting some in because he said it would be a wet night. He's a great believer in a tot of brandy against the cold, my Dad.'

'Wonderful! That's the sort of thing my father would have

thought of if he'd been around when I was packing my things. We'll save yours for a last tot before we try to snatch some sleep, then,' Anna said. 'I wonder how many of the people gathered here tonight were here last time? Quite a lot, I bet. You get sort of attached to a person like Princess Eliz . . . I mean the Queen, don't you? I remember when I was little I envied the Princesses their mother, she was so – so *motherly*, somehow, not like my own mother. My mother's very nice,' she added hastily, 'but she was too wrapped up in my father to be a very cuddly mother when I was young. Now, of course, it's different. She lives by herself in a really super flat and she's got a marvellous job and lots of friends. I really enjoy going to see her, now.'

'Is your father dead, then?' Nell asked. 'I'm sorry.'

'No, he's not dead, mother left him quite a few years ago. To tell you the truth he was not a good husband at all. He likes women, you see, and . . .'

The story intrigued Nell. She asked Anna where she lived and Anna told her about Goldenstone and Nell told her that their fair had been set up in Blofield, on the recreation ground alongside the Margaret Harker Hall, a few years before the war. 'I didn't know it at the time, but a friend of mine lived in Blofield,' she said, suddenly remembering. 'Dan Clifton – I don't suppose you know him?'

'None better. I went out with him for a while, he taught me to sail a boat,' Anna said, carefully tipping steaming coffee from her flask into Nell's cup. To her surprise her hand stayed steady and she didn't spill a drop. 'Fascinating he was, awfully good looking. I really fell for him when I was in my teens. How did you come to meet him, then?'

'It's a long story,' Nell said. 'Do you want to hear it?'

'Might as well. It'll pass the time and, besides, I'm rather intrigued. Dan and I both work in Paris now, so we see quite a lot of each other. To tell you the truth, he's asked me to marry him, but . . . oh, I don't know. I suspect he's the sort to chase after girls if he gets bored and I don't think I could ever learn to live with that. What did you think of him when you knew him? Did you know his parents? I met him when he'd been left with his grandmother, Mrs Lucas, and after they took him away from boarding school we caught the same bus into the city each morning during term time. He was headed for the Grammar school in the Cathedral Close and I went to the High School, on Newmarket Road, but we sat next to each other as far as Tombland. He must have been about twelve when we first met, I suppose.'

'I adored him when I was a kid,' Nell said frankly. 'Let me tell you the whole story though, and then you can tell me why you didn't snap him up when he offered.' She paused, looking thoughtfully before her, at the relentless rain. 'And I'll tell you why I didn't marry him, either,' she finished.

'So you didn't marry him because your mother said he was your brother, and I didn't marry him because I could see a certain resemblance to my father,' Anna said at midnight, when they had both told their stories and been temporarily silenced by the chimes of Big Ben, striking the hour. 'Poor old Dan! Nell, do you think he really is a bit of a bounder? Only from what you've said, his whole family are black sheep, at least where women are concerned.'

'No, I don't think Dan's like that, I think he's just very nice-looking,' Nell said after a moment's thought. 'Mr Geraint, who's his uncle, said that Dan's father was shy and bookish, not a bit like the rest of the family. When he came back into my life during the war he was kind and sensitive . . . I really did like him. But I only knew him briefly, you've known him for years.'

'Yes, I have,' Anna admitted. 'Well, I'm not going to marry anyone anyway, so it doesn't really matter whether Dan's a positive bluebeard! But you did marry; you said so. Is it nice, being married?'

'I did get married and I loved it. But two months ago he left me, indirectly because of Dan. That's another long story, but it would help me a lot to tell it to you, if you could bear it.'

'Tell on; by the time dawn breaks you and I will know more about each other than we know about our own parents,' Anna said cheerfully. 'Another tot of your delicious coffee would go down well, too. Hold still, I can reach the flask without moving. Now . . . tell on, Scheherazade!'

Dawn comes early in June, even when the sky overhead is grey and a fine, misty rain is falling. As the scene before them began to lighten, the two girls turned and smiled at each other.

'Well, what a night! It's been fascinating, and our talk has taught me quite a bit,' Anna said. 'I've been awfully silly to believe that I couldn't make a go of marriage because my parents made such a mess of it, for one thing. I mean, your parents managed to muck up and then they got together again and everything was fine. And you love being married to Snip, don't you, and you miss him quite horribly and want him back; isn't that right? Yet you drove him away because you were all mixed up over Dan Clifton.'

'I love Snip so much that I can't even imagine wanting to see Dan again,' Nell admitted. 'I don't give a tuppeny damn for anyone else, I just want my Snip back. If it takes me the rest of my life I'll find him though, and beg his forgiveness for the stupid things I said. Oh, Anna, don't fall in love, it's − it's so dreadfully painful when things go wrong!'

'I think it's better to fall in love and suffer, rather than never to fall in love,' Anna observed softly. 'I know very well that a part of me loves Dan very deeply indeed, but I was afraid of being hurt so I pushed him back. After tonight, I won't do that. If you want the glory of love you've got to take the pain as well. Isn't that right?'

'Yes, that's right,' Nell said, after a short pause. 'But that doesn't mean you have to enjoy the pain when it rakes at your heart and curdles your stomach. You put up with it because of the good times, and even suffering must have a purpose. It makes love more wonderful by contrast, I suppose.'

'I'll remember that. Nell, we mustn't lose touch, we must stay friends. After all, we were born on the same day! Will you come to my wedding, if Dan and I finally get together and I find the courage to tell him I've never loved anyone but him? You and Snip, I mean.'

Nell gave Anna her sweet, three-cornered smile.

'I accept; for both of us, naturally. And now shall we have some breakfast and take turns to stretch our legs? People are beginning to stir.'

It began at last. From a very early hour the peers and peeresses, the clergy, the heads of government and members of the civil service, all the hundred and one officials and those who were to watch or take minor part in the ceremony, began to make their way into the abbey. Minor royalty swept in, smiled, gave a small wave. Familiar faces, creased with anxiety or pale from unaccustomed early rising, passed through the crowd. Anna and Nell were among the most knowledgeable of royalty-fanciers, but if they failed to recognise a face someone near them unerringly remedied their lack.

Excitement mounted as the abbey slowly filled. The Lord Mayor of London's procession seemed a marvel, then it was eclipsed by the royals, by the representatives of foreign states, by Princess Margaret and the Queen Mother in the glass coach. The rain eased, then stopped. Anna and Nell took down their canopy and put on their coats, folded their blankets and sat on their possessions until the murmur of the crowd told them the great moment had arrived.

'Here she comes . . . here she comes!'

First the Household Cavalry, the Foot Guards, the Welsh and Irish Guards. Then the King's Troop, the Royal Horse Artillery – and the gold coach with that small figure in white, her face drained of colour, serious, remote, then waving to them, trying to smile.

Anna cried first, the tears running down her cheeks as the small figure was swallowed up by the vastness of the abbey.

'She's only our age – how can she bear it?' she asked her friend.

'She's got him to help her bear it,' Nell answered. Her eyes were brimming with tears. All that pomp and circumstance, all the trumpets and finery, the flags and bunting, the terrible responsibility and the weight of her people's trust and love, must surely crush that small, straight-backed figure in the heavy white gown encrusted with precious gems, going with such courage and dignity to meet her fate.

'Here somes the rest of the procession,' Anna said, having gained control of herself once more. She took Nell's hand, squeezing it tightly. 'Oh Nell, I wouldn't have missed this for the world!'

It was over. The loudspeakers had broadcast the trumpets, the choral singing, the deep voices of the clergy, the small, clear voice of the new Queen, as calm and matter of fact as though she were crowned every day and took it in her stride.

The girls held the ground-sheet over themselves, all their belongings packed away in their big shoulder bags, the flasks empty, the rugs rolled, the umbrellas furled. The rain stopped, started, stopped again. Queen Salote of Tonga swept past and was cheered because she kept the hood of her carriage down and just brushed the rain out of her face when it began to blur her vision.

'There's Winnie, three cheers for Winnie. Here come the children, three cheers for the littl'uns!'

Soldiers marched, trumpets blared, flags were unfurled and displayed bravely despite the wet. Anna laughed at dripping bearskins, Australians whose odd slouch hats funnelled the rain on to their shoulders. Nell jumped up and down and clapped when the Welsh Guards strode by, tall and elegant even in the downpour.

'They'll be on the balcony soon. Can we get to the palace?' Anna shouted as the crowd began to surge unevenly after the procession. 'Oh, it's been so wonderful, so unforgettable, I can't bear today to end!'

'We can try,' Nell shouted back. 'We must try. Hold on to me though, don't you dare let go!'

'Let's take a short cut, see if we can catch up with the tail of the procession,' Anna shouted at one point. 'See that road ahead? The one that's closed off? If we can climb over the barrier . . .' They climbed over it, ignoring a policeman who shouted and lunged after them. They tore along the wet and shining pavement, giggling like naughty schoolgirls, and wriggled through the barrier the other side. They emerged on another street, still lined with people, for the tail of the procession had yet to pass there.

'It's stopped raining,' Nell said, as they stood at last at the back of the crowd. 'Here, lend us your glasses, I think it's the Welsh Guards again. If I can just check . . .'

Anna handed her the precious glasses and Nell raised them to her eyes and swung them to look up the street. Yes, it was the Guards, marching with their chins up and their arms swinging, though they must be just about worn out. She was lowering the binoculars, starting to hand them to Anna, when something caught her attention. She swung the glasses up again.

He was there! She had no doubt about it, no doubt at all. Directly opposite them, perched halfway up a lamp-post, his wet hair slicked to his head and his good arm clinging to the lamp's cross-bar, was Snip.

Nell fought her way through the crowd, using fists, feet, anything which would get her to the front. And there he was, not looking towards her, looking up the road, to where the procession was approaching.

She ran out into the carriageway, not hearing the roar of horror from a hundred throats, not heeding Anna's sharp, appalled cry. She ran straight in front of the foremost horses, felt the sharp, buffeting blow of hoof and fetlock, felt the road swing up and slap her hard in the face . . . and felt nothing more. She didn't hear the dreadful, cracked shriek from the young man clinging to the lamp-post, or the scream of a terrified horse as its rider tried to rein it back, causing it to cannon into the animal behind. She knew nothing of the chaos which followed.

He must have snatched her right from beneath the horse's hooves, Anna thought as she sat in the ambulance, holding Nell's small possessions and her own and trying to see whether her friend was still breathing. But it was difficult, because the young man who had rescued her hung over the narrow bed, murmuring beneath his breath.

'You damned little fool, what did you do that for? Don't

you know you're the only thing on this earth that I care about? What good is my life to me if you aren't a part of it? Half killing yourself without a thought . . . oh Nell, my little sweetheart, don't die, don't die!'

'Is – is she very bad?' Anna asked timidly after a moment. 'There's blood in her hair and she looks so pale.'

The young man swung round. 'She's going to be all right,' he said fiercely. 'She's got to be all right. If only the bloody crowds would let us through! I dunno what's broken . . . heads do bleed, though. If this bloody ambulance stops once more I'll get out and carry her to the hospital, I swear I will. Ah, that's more like it.'

The vehicle had moved forward, jerked, and set off at a respectable speed at last.

'We must be through the crowds, or perhaps we've got a police escort,' Anna said. 'Don't worry, Snip – you are Snip, I take it? – we shan't be long now.'

Nell woke. She ached all over and her head was splitting; she tried to open her eyes and only one of them obeyed her; even when it was open she could see scarcely anything, only a dim light and the shape of someone's head.

But it was the right head, the head of the person she most longed to see. She tried to move her hand, to speak, but her hand was heavy as lead and her voice seemed to have disappeared into some far place. However, she must have made some noise, because the head, which had been in well-remembered profile to her, turned abruptly, came closer.

'Nell? Are you awake, darling?'

She wanted to nod, to speak, but nothing would come. But she could smile; she felt the smile spread across her face, wall-to-wall sunshine.

'Anna had to leave, she was due back in France two days or so ago. I promised to let her know the moment you came round. She left me an address and telephone number. Oh Nell, darling, you've had us so worried!'

He lifted her hand. She felt his fingers on hers, damp with excitement, the best, the nicest fingers in the world. She moved her head again and this time it responded. She tried to open her mouth to tell him she loved him, to ask him never to leave her, to explain . . . but only a croak came out.

'You want a drink,' Snip said lovingly. 'Here – lemon barley water. What a treat, eh, after days of a tube in your arm and nothing by mouth? Don't try to move, I'll spoon it in.' He spooned the lemon barley water into her eager mouth; she was very thirsty, dry as a desert. Then he ran his hand gently over her face; part of her face. There was a bandage or something over the rest of it. She made another of her incoherent noises, then the words were there, as though her mouth had been waiting for the lubrication of the barley water before it could make itself work.

'Snip, what's happened? Don't leave me!'

'As if I would! As for what happened, don't you remember? You ran in front of the horses, darling, and one of them trod on you. I fished you out and Anna and I brought you here in an ambulance.' He smiled at her lovingly, taking her hand and moving it gently up and down as he talked. 'You've had concussion, but you're much better now.'

She frowned. Ran in front of what horses?

'You still don't remember. You came up to see the Coronation, and . . .'

He went on talking, but there was no need. She remembered now, remembered perfectly! The girl Anna, their talk through the long night, the excitement and pageantry of the processions – and all the time, nagging away in the back of her mind, the urge to find Snip, to explain, to show him that she would be his wife now in every way, with no holding back, no secret dreams. The secret dreams had had no more substance than dust, no more importance than . . . than dreams. Snip was her reality, her lover, the person she wanted to spend the rest of her life with.

'. . . So you see you're quite famous,' Snip was saying. 'The Queen and Prince Philip sent you some flowers and a message before they went off to tour the country and there have been piles of letters and telegrams and good wishes. They put your picture in the papers, and Matthew and Hester came rushing down to see you were being treated right. They went again, darling, as soon as the doctors said you were out of danger, because they knew it would worry you to know they'd left Pengarth to its own devices.'

'Is – is Mum all right?'

'She's fine, absolutely fine. Now you sleep for a bit, darling. I'll still be here when you wake up, don't worry about that.'

She meant to say she wasn't tired, didn't need any more sleep. She wanted to ask what day it was, to find out how long she had lain here, see for herself the flowers sent by the Queen, ask a hundred thousand questions. Instead, she just closed her eyes for a moment and then it was such trouble to open them . . . she felt her lips curve into a smile of contentment, then gradually relax.

Anna had waited at the hospital until they were told that Mrs Morris would be all right, that she had come round, briefly, and was shocked and still concussed but would be fine. Then she left.

Her mind was in a turmoil. She had seen love in action at close quarters and she would never again believe that life could be as good without it. You must have been stark, staring mad, Anna Radwell, to let Dan go, she scolded herself, hurrying through the London streets and heading for Auntie Ella's flat. A man like that, so loving and giving, and you turn him down! Madness was the only answer, and even that was not good enough. Now all she could do was try to see Dan before it was too late.

The coronation was over, so she went straight to Liverpool Street Station and caught a train to Norwich Thorpe. Dan would not stay in London any longer than he need, she was sure of it. Arriving at Thorpe station, she caught a Number 90 bus to Ipswich Road, got off opposite the Norfolk & Norwich Hospital, and walked across to Sandringham Court and her mother's flat. It was six in the evening and a drizzly day, but Constance's welcome was warm and her understanding of the situation immediate.

'You left in a hurry last time because of Dan,' she said, giving her daughter a hug and leading her into the kitchen. 'My darling, I was a fool to say Dan was anything like your father. He came around next day and talked to me: he loves you very much, but he didn't intend to force himself on you. He's a delightful young man, and obviously sincere. If you love him then you must tell him so, only don't expect him to be surprised, because I believe he knows you as well as I do – and we both think you're someone special. Now how about a bite to eat? And some hot coffee to help you get over the journey. I've still got some of those marvellous French beans you brought me, all ready to grind.'

'Oh, Mummy,' Anna said, heaving a sigh and slumping into a chair, 'I've had such adventures, but all I want to do is to see Dan. Is he with his grandmother, do you know?'

'No idea; but I am on the telephone,' Constance said, smiling. There was a peaceful serenity in her smile these days, which Anna found herself basking in, as though it were hot sunshine. Mummy did know best, contrary to what Anna had believed for so many years; Mummy knew that Dan was the right man for her daughter. 'I'll give Mrs Lucas a ring and ask if Dan's with her, if you like.'

'Yes, if you . . . No! No, I'll go over there myself, first thing tomorrow morning.'

She had felt she was on the right track from the moment she got on the train, but now she was positive that Dan would have gone to Blofield and his grandmother. He wouldn't rush back to Paris because he knew that Anna would have moved heaven and earth to be at the coronation. He knows me, but that works both ways, she thought with a little smile. I know him: he'll stay in London and do his duty to the very best of his ability and then he'll go back to the place which is more home to him than anywhere else, his grandmother's Victorian villa on Garden road, with the long back garden, the chickens in the run under the damson trees, and the small, square front garden with its monkey-puzzle and its formal flower beds. Yes, Dan would be there, giving his grandmother a hand, telling her all about the coronation and waiting. Waiting for Anna? She smiled again; whether he knew it or not, she was on his trail and would not give up this time.

She went to bed as soon as she'd eaten scrambled eggs on

toast and drunk her coffee. She woke early, because Constance was moving around in the bathroom, getting ready for work. She was singing, something flippant about a girl who wore red feathers and a hooly-hooly skirt. She sounded happy. She is happy, Anna realised; she's a different person now she hasn't got to deal with Daddy.

Anna joined Constance for breakfast and they walked to the bus stop together. Constance got off on Castle Meadow and disappeared into Davey Place, but Anna stayed on the bus until Foundry Bridge hove into view, with the railway station beyond it. It was not practical to get a train, it meant walking up from Brundall, which was all uphill – but she got off her bus and ran all the way to the next stop, feeling sixteen again, with the June sunshine warm on the back of her head. Presently a Number 7 came into view and she boarded it.

'King's Head, please. Single.'

The conductor turned the little handle and a thin paper ticket came out, pink on white today. Anna paid, took her ticket and tucked it into her pocket. Why had she bought a single? She really should have bought a return, it was asking for disappointment . . . But her optimism refused to be damped; the smile which curled her mouth refused to disappear. She sat on the front seat and watched the familiar road unfurl, and smiled at the flat fields on either side, the old oaks and elms which grew on the verges and hung their great branches so low that now and again the rasp of their twigs on the bus roof made the passengers jump. Everything was good today, everything reflected her sunny mood.

At the King's Head she got down, crossed back over the street, and dived down Garden Road. She had not visited Mrs Lucas since she was a teenager but she felt no qualms now. She marched along the unmade road, so little used by traffic that horseradish plants flourished in the centre of the carriageway, turned into Mrs Lucas's gateway, went down the path, ignoring the front door, and around the side of the house. She was raising a hand to knock at the back door when something made her look down the long garden.

Dan was there, digging. In his shirtsleeves, with apparent

enthusiasm, he was digging what looked like a cabbage patch. He was concentrating on his work and had not seen her . . . She was halfway down the path, pushing between laden currant bushes, when he looked up. He dropped his spade, and straightened.

Anna did not know how she got there, but suddenly she was in his arms, gabbling a lot of nonsense, trying to explain . . . and Dan was just holding her, now and then kissing the side of her face. Then he was laughing, swinging her off her feet, calling her his darling, his best girl . . .

'Oh Dan, I'm so sorry, I behaved like a fool,' Anna said breathlessly. 'Please, let's get married very quickly, before I can be a fool again! These past two months have been the worst in my whole life.'

'And mine,' Dan said ruefully, resting his chin on the top of her head. 'I told myself you'd come back, that it was right to let you make up your own mind, but there were times when I nearly came over to France, threw you across my saddle, and galloped off into the sunset.'

Anna giggled. 'Oh Danny, do put me down, what's your grandmother going to think?'

'Doesn't matter; let them all think what they like,' Dan said, dropping small kisses across her forehead, cheek, chin. 'We'll go indoors and tell Gran, then we'll see the vicar. I've always rather fancied a June wedding!'

Snip sat on by the bed, holding Nell's hand, feasting his eyes on her. She had not meant any of the silly things she had said on that awful day when Mr Geraint had come to Pengarth. Perhaps he had known it even at the time, certainly he was sure of it quite soon afterwards, but dimly, in the back of his mind, he had realised that things could never be totally right between them until everything was out in the open, acknowledged. She had shown her love for him every day since their marriage, but she had never said outright that she loved him and wanted no one but him. His self-confidence had needed the reassurance of words as well as deeds, and it had not helped to know that she wouldn't have children because she felt a family would tie her, cut the slight connection which still existed between her and Dan while she was theoretically free.

But it was all right now. Even righter, in fact, than she knew. It had been a tremendous shock to him, after three days of crippling anxiety, to be told by a smiling doctor that she had come round briefly, had spoken rationally, and that she would not lose the baby after all, though they had been fearful . . .

'Baby? Do you mean Hester?'

The doctor was young and red-haired. He had light brows and lashes and an understanding smile. But now he looked totally bewildered, with the light brows almost touching his curly red poll.

'*Hester?* According to our records her name is Helen, not Hester. Have we made a mistake?'

'No, she's Helen all right. It's her mother who's Hester.'

The young doctor looked even more bewildered.

'Her *mother*? What's her mother got to do with it?'

'You said . . . a baby, you said,' Snip stammered. 'Hester's expecting a baby in September.'

'That's unusual,' the doctor said. He looked warily at Snip. 'Umm . . . do I take it, Mr Morris, that you were not aware that your wife, too, is pregnant?'

Snip could only stare, a tide of hot blood creeping up his neck and flooding his face. Nell, pregnant? There must be some mistake; he knew she had always been careful, she was determined not to have a family, she had said so often enough.

'Well, Mr Morris? I assure you your wife *is* expecting a baby. She's got a few months to go, but . . . does she know, do you suppose?'

'I don't suppose she does,' Snip muttered. That big, foolish grin which he could never hide when blissfully happy was beginning to break out; he could feel his cheeks cracking with the strain of suppressing it. 'She would have said something to someone . . . no, I don't suppose she knows.'

'And she's twenty-seven? Then it's high time she had a child,' the doctor said cheerfully. 'She's young enough to cope and old enough to enjoy it. So you'll have some good news for her when she comes round, Mr Morris.'

And now here he sat, holding her hand, looking down at her, trying to see a difference in the slight mound of her beneath the bedclothes. A baby! he had longed for children, but it was her right to decide if and when they should start a family.

He had not told Anna, or Hester, or Matthew. The only person who knew about the baby apart from himself and the medical staff was Mr Geraint. The old man had come laboriously into the small hospital waiting room just before visiting time one evening, and even to Snip's untutored eye, Mr Geraint had gone downhill since his visit to Pengarth less than two months ago.

'I read in the papers that the girl was here, so I came to tell the pair of you that you and she are to have the castle,' Geraint had said as soon as he set eyes on Snip. 'She's a good girl, always was. And you're right for her – saw at a glance. Besides, I thought afterwards, she *is* a relative. She's some sort of cousin, even though the bar sinister would stop Matthew from being publicly acknowledged. But I can leave Pengarth where I wish . . . most people think of it as a burden, not a gift . . . so it'll be yours quite soon now.'

'We're having a baby,' Snip had said, giving the only gift which was possible in return, and was rewarded. The old man's eyes lit up and his smile was gentle, incredulous.

'Little Nell, a mother herself,' he murmured. 'Well, well, I shan't see the child but it's good to know life goes on.' He paused, then looked shyly at Snip from under the thick, greying brows. 'Thought about a name for the nipper? Be nice to think there was something of me at Pengarth even when most of me's six foot under.'

'What if it's a girl?' Snip blurted, not pretending to misunderstand him. 'You can't call a girl Geraint!'

'Second name? Like a sort of linked surname, perhaps?'

Snip nodded and put out his hand. 'I'll see to it, sir,' he said gruffly. 'And thanks. For Pengarth and everything.'

'I've done little enough,' the old man said drily. 'Mine has been an enjoyable life, but a somewhat selfish one, I fear.'

'If it hadn't been for you I'd never have met Nell,' Snip pointed out. 'In fact, she might have married someone else if it hadn't been for a remark you made twenty years ago.'

534

Mr Geraint understood him. He grinned, and a mischievous look flashed across his face for a moment, stealing back the years, turning him into the handsome young man he once was.

'Even lies, uttered as a threat, can do good, you mean? Goodbye, young Morris. Give her . . . give her my love when she wakes up.' He turned to leave the room, then paused in the doorway. 'One thing – just between the two of us, eh?'

'Sure,' Snip said, nodding. 'I've always been good at secrets, especially other people's.'

'I never loved anyone the way I loved Hester Coburn,' Geraint said slowly, reminiscently. 'By God, she was a wild one . . . but the story would have had a different ending if I'd not lost touch with her after that first meeting in Rhyl, and found her again too late, married to Matthew.'

Nell woke for the second time to find herself alone, but with the warm feeling that someone – it must be Snip – had just left the room. She felt livelier now, altogether more like herself. She glanced down at the bed and there were her hands lying on top of the blue and white coverlet, pale but otherwise perfectly ordinary. She lifted one of them – this time it obeyed easily, naturally – and felt her face. A bandage was wound around her head. She poked her fingers beneath it; bristles? Oh glory, they must have shaved her hair; what a guy she would look when they took the bandages off!

She was still smiling as she looked about her. She was alone in a small room with a big window curtained in cream and gold chintz and a door with a glass panel. At the end of the bed was a chest of drawers with masses of flowers and cards arrayed on it and a padded bench with baskets of exotic-looking fruit. It struck her that this was a private room and she wondered guiltily what it had cost and where they had found the money. Or perhaps the staff thought she needed peace and quiet to recover and had put her in here at no extra cost, for her health's sake?

She glanced around again, but there were no answers to be read in the chintz-covered chairs, the small desk, the hospital dressing gown on the back of the door. She found she was hungry, and wished she could have some fruit, but it was out of reach. She also had wind, her tummy was gurgling, pulsating . . . she felt a flutter of movement which could only be wind – unless she had had internal injuries as well as concussion?

She was feeling her stomach with careful fingers when the door opened. Immediately her smile began, as though she knew it would be Snip who came cautiously into the room even before he was actually in view.

'Darling, you're awake! Feel better this morning?'

She blinked. This morning? But she had only been asleep a few minutes, surely, since they had talked before?

'Much. Only I'm a bit hungry. Am I allowed to have some of that fruit?'

He grinned and carried one of the baskets over to the bed, pretending to stagger beneath its weight. 'Trust you to sleep through breakfast, though I did my best to wake you! The food isn't bad here, all things considered. It was grapefruit segments, scrambled egg, toast and coffee. Here, have a grape.'

She took the bunch and detached a grape, then put the rest on the bedspread where it covered her stomach. She ate the grape and was about to reach for another when a most extraordinary phenomenon occurred. Seemingly of its own volition, the bunch of grapes slowly toppled off its perch as though pushed from beneath. Nell stared, round-eyed, then glanced up at Snip.

'Snip, did you see that? My tummy moved those grapes by itself! I've had wind before, but never like that!'

Snip sat down on the edge of the bed and put his arm around her. He kissed the side of her face gently, experimentally almost, then he began to speak.

'Nell darling, I've got two pieces of news for you. Both good, but very different. One will be quite a surprise to you, I think, and the other very comforting. Which do you want first?'

Saxton, Judith
Someone Special

DATE DUE

AUG 2 1995	504	
AUG 2 4 1995		
SEP 1995		
SEP 27 1995		
OCT 6 1995		